TAKING THE STAND

TAKING THE STAND

The Testimony of
Lieutenant Colonel Oliver L. North

With an Introduction by
DANIEL SCHORR

PUBLISHED BY POCKET BOOKS NEW YORK

The transcripts of the testimony of Lieutenant Colonel Oliver L. North before the Select Committee on Secret Military Assistance to Iran and the Nicaraguan Opposition were provided by Federal News Service, 620 National Press Building, Washington, D.C. 20045, (202) 347-1400. Federal News Service provides the public with verbatim transcripts of press briefings, policy statements and speeches from the Executive and Legislative branches of the U.S. government by satellite shortly after the event occurs.

Another *Original* publication of POCKET BOOKS

POCKET BOOKS, a division of Simon & Schuster, Inc.
1230 Avenue of the Americas, New York, N.Y. 10020

ISBN: 0-671-65938-3

First Pocket Books printing July 1987

10 9 8 7 6 5 4 3 2 1

POCKET and colophon are trademarks of
Simon & Schuster, Inc.

Printed in the U.S.A.

Introduction
By Daniel Schorr

[Mr. Schorr has covered Congressional inquiries dating back to the McCarthy investigation in 1953. He was, for a quarter-century, a foreign and national correspondent for CBS News. He won three Emmy awards for his coverage of the Watergate scandal. Mr. Schorr himself became a figure in that investigation when he turned up on the Nixon "enemies list" and the target of a Nixon-ordered FBI investigation that was cited in the Bill of Impeachment. More recently, for five years Mr. Schorr was senior correspondent of Ted Turner's Cable News Network. As commentator for Public Television and for National Public Radio, he has missed hardly an hour of the Iran-Contra investigation.]

The Senate Caucus Room, on the third floor of the Capitol's Office Building named for the late Senator Richard Russell, has become a visual symbol for Congressional trial by television. This cavernous high-ceilinged room, in the past three-and-a-half decades, has witnessed some of America's great dramas and traumas, played out for a sometimes bored, sometimes spellbound nation.

Politicians, acting as judges and prosecutors, often posture at the expense of their quarry in their well-staffed hunt for sensational misdeeds. Some of them cherish memories of predecessors (Estes Kefauver, Howard Baker, Frank Church) whose Caucus Room fame whetted their ambitions for national office.

But the Caucus Room is a tricky tribunal, the jury out of sight, spread across the country, making its judgments less on fact than feeling, its unpredictable verdicts sometimes rendered against the judge.

So it was, in 1954, that Senator Joseph R. McCarthy, probing for Communist influence in the U.S. Army, started the plunge from his pinnacle of power by smearing a young associate of Army Counsel Joseph N. Welch. With as much sorrow as outrage, Welch told McCarthy, while America watched, "Senator, I think I never really gauged your cruelty or your recklessness."

As the mighty can be suddenly humbled in trial by television, so can a star be born. In 1973, it was White House Counsel John Dean, who, having helped President Nixon fashion the Watergate cover-up, found himself designated as the "fall guy." He chose defection as the better side of valor and ended up before Senator Sam Ervin's Watergate committee, with limited immunity that did not save him from a subsequent prison sentence.

The lines from the Caucus Room ring nostalgically now like hit-tunes of the 1950s. There was Acting FBI Director Patrick Gray, who had followed instructions to "deep-six" incriminating documents, testifying, "I carried out my orders and I destroyed them." There was the sneering Nixon aide, John Ehrlichman, who testified that Gray had been left "twisting slowly, slowly in the wind." But the line that has survived for these fifteen years as the apotheosis of Watergate was Dean's as he testified of having told Nixon, "There is a cancer growing on the presidency."

Verdict by television can be a fickle thing. Before Senator Ervin's committee, Dean was treated by Democrats as a conspirator and by Republicans as a traitor. Yet in five days at the witness table, with his wife, Maureen, seated behind him, exactly in camera range, Dean became a media celebrity. I hesitate to say "hero," but can recall that, as the hearings went on to other witnesses, CBS received dozens of calls from viewers demanding, in the words of one, to "bring back that nice John Dean and his lovely wife."

But, whatever had happened before in that national arena called the Caucus Room, there was nothing that remotely rivaled the "Ollie North phenomenon"—the wave of popular approval and adulation that he generated by his testimony in July 1987.

The developments leading up to his appearance had

looked like a prolonged overture to his ruination. His only previous public appearance on Capitol Hill, seven months earlier, had been to plead the Fifth Amendment. Since then he had become projected as a furtive figure, ducking into cars, flashing mocking thumbs-up signs. President Reagan had long since stopped calling him "a national hero." While headlines told of his lawyer, Brendan Sullivan, stiffly bargaining on terms for Col. North's appearance, his own reputation sank under the weight of other testimony.

Even those who tried to speak well of him damaged him in the eyes of the Congressional committees and the public. Robert Owen, "the courier," told of bringing him travelers cheques, some of which he cashed for his own use. Glenn Robinette, the former CIA official who built a security fence around his home as a gift from Maj. Gen. Richard Secord, told how North had contrived to cover this up with invented documents. Secord himself, and his partner, Albert Hakim, told of earmarking large sums of money for North and his family. Assistant Secretary of State Elliott Abrams said that Secretary George Shultz had wanted North monitored as a "loose cannon." North's Marine comrade and former boss in the National Security Council, Lieut. Col. Robert C. McFarlane, suggested that North had behaved impetuously during the fateful May 1986 trip to Teheran and that efforts had been made thereafter to ease him out of the White House. His secretary, Fawn Hall, told about the shredding and doctoring of documents.

The testimony of friends was bad enough. But then, in final preparation for North's appearance, there was the testimony of Assistant Attorney General Charles J. Cooper, on June 25, that North had told barefaced lies to the lawyers sent over by Attorney General Edwin Meese, on presidential orders, to find out what had been going on. A false chronology had been concocted by Col. North, along with his boss, Rear Adm. John Poindexter, and his former boss, McFarlane.

Cooper, an arch-conservative from Alabama, said, under questioning, that he would not believe the testimony of North—whether or not under oath. Members of the Senate and House committees vied with each other in denouncing North. Rep. Bill McCollum, a conservative Republican from Florida, accused North of "treachery."

The Independence Day recess allowed eleven days for all that to sink in on the nation before Col. North finally appeared on July 7 to bear witness. The *Washington Post* headline that morning aptly summarized his plight, "Lacking Old Luster, North Returns to Testify. Disclosures of His 'Dark Side' Weaken Credibility of Affair's Most Intriguing Figure."

Then the miracle happened—a reputation was resurrected and a superstar was born.

Not inside the Caucus Room, where the view may be even more parochial than "inside the Beltway." At the press tables, reporters analyzed the opening skirmish for position by the House committee's counsel, John Nields, and North's aggressive lawyer, Brendan Sullivan. We noted North's self-confident, often eloquent, sometimes impassioned utterances. But, steeped in the background details, we also observed how he would slide away from the most probing questions, how he would fall back on generalizations about patriotic motives, obedience to authority, reverence for his commander-in-chief, devotion to family, the crushing pressures under which he had worked, the threat of assassination, and his dedication to saving contras in Nicaragua and hostages in Lebanon.

We noted an apparent strategy of disclaiming the role of mastermind by pointing to others responsible, exempting only President Reagan.

We noted, also, how often a renowned steel-trap memory went vague, or forgetful, or, in an effort to provide an instant answer, slipped into misstatement. So, for example, asked to explain the code-name "Joshua," North said, unhesitatingly, that it stood for an unnamed Israeli official. A puzzled committee counsel produced the key to the code, which listed "Joshua" as President Reagan. Without missing a beat, North said he had been mistaken. The error was unimportant, but the unblinking guess at a fact seemed revealing.

Yet, in the overcrowded Caucus Room, we were too close up to see what the nation saw—a handsome Marine with a distinguished war record who could articulate his convictions in soaring eloquence, an officer deserted by the superiors he had so ardently served, and now, facing possible prosecution, still standing up with pride and dignity against a cabal of persecutors and pettifogging politicians. It was a morality play of the the the sort America loves.

The good soldier North was not quite the North who emerged from the stack of documents that had escaped the shredder and the delete button on the computer backup system. This was a North who pressed his proposals for raising money for the contras and selling arms to Iran, who sometimes acted in anticipation or on the assumption of decisions, who operated on the advice of self-interested friends outside government. We saw evidence of deep friendships with an arms merchant like Richard V. Secord, an Israeli official like Amiram Nir and even a young Iranian official—the unnamed "Second Channel" to the Ayatollah's government in Teheran—whom North took for a tour of the Oval Office in September 1986.

None of this seemed to matter to "Ollie's" suddenly generated legions—the hundreds who demonstrated for him outside the Russell Building, the thousands who sent telegrams and money for his legal defense, and the millions who were simply wowed by the appealing image made incandescent by saturation day-after-day coverage on all the major networks.

This could not be dismissed as simply a "media event." It was a triumph of projected personality over complicated issues, reminiscent of the simple evocation of patriotism that has made President Reagan so successful a political figure. As the "Ollie" phenomenon fed back into the Caucus Room, the pile of telegrams mounting on the witness table next to him, the inquisitors became less inquisitional —even less inquisitive—and some committee members, like Rep. McCollum, who had denounced Col. North, sought to clamber their way aboard his bandwagon.

Daniel Inouye, chairman of the Senate committee, told me he was undismayed—that it would all look different in print than it looked on television. A reporter quipped, "Magnetic North is not the same as True North." But the Ollie phenomenon has had its effect, and will be long remembered.

Yet, even in this effort at instantaneous history, one must step back and broaden the focus on a man who has come to personify a period in American history. Col. North alluded to plans and purposes larger than the operations in which he played so central a role. There was "Project Democracy," which President Reagan had mentioned in his London speech in 1982 and which Col. North used as a kind of generic title for his ventures and "assets." There was the "Reagan Doctrine," which the President announced in his second inaugural address in 1985, but which North said had been promulgated earlier by CIA Director William J. Casey.

Reagan called for giving aid to everyone, from Afghanistan to Nicaragua, denoted as "freedom fighters." He spoke of "human freedom on the march . . . America its staunchest friend . . . We must not break faith with those who are risking their lives on every continent."

Implicit, but not stated, was the Reagan Doctrine/Project Democracy was intended to be a large-scale program of covert action—with Congressional support when available, by other means, when Congressional approval was not forthcoming, or even not sought.

President Reagan had read that President Lincoln, without Congressional authorization, raised volunteers to fight the Civil War and that he invoked his powers as commander-in-chief to free the slaves. So, when Congress banned aid to the Nicaraguan contras, the President, as quoted by Adm. Poindexter, said he wanted "to take action unilaterally."

Much of President Reagan's impetus for covert action came from Casey, his long-time friend and campaign chairman, who died in May 1987. If Reagan had dreams of spreading democracy in the Third World, Casey was the one who turned them into plans. Casey was the Reagan *alter ego,* the activist lieutenant to a passive President. Long before Reagan became the Chief Executive, he would listen by the hour while Casey regaled him with stories of derring-do from his OSS days in World War II.

It was primarily Casey who made the Reagan Doctrine operational, arranging for the arming of guerillas from Afghanistan to Angola, the mining of Nicaragua's harbors, the efforts to destabilize Libya's Muammar el-Qaddafi. The Administration's approach to Iran for release of hostages started with Casey's concern about William Buckley, the CIA's Beirut station chief, kidnapped and reportedly tortured to reveal secrets. It was Casey, in the end, who persuaded the President to say "yes" to arms for Iran when Secretary of State George P. Shultz and Secretary of Defense Caspar W. Weinberger counseled "no."

Impatient with the constraints of Congress and bureaucracy—including the CIA's bureaucracy—Casey reached out for an alternate mechanism to fulfill the President's wishes. He found it in the avidly willing Oliver North of the National Security Council staff. North has testified of his veneration for Casey and how much time they spent together—in each other's offices, traveling on airplanes and in cars, and at Casey's home. So the basic chain of command for the Reagan Doctrine ran around most of the CIA and around most of the NSC to Col. North's suite, Room 302 of the Executive Office Building, GHQ for Project Democracy.

Four-star generals and admirals in the Pentagon would sometimes bristle when the oak-leaf officer would say, "This is what the White House wants done." It was Casey's credentials that put stars on North's shoulder, as in his eyes, and made him "the world's most powerful lieutenant colonel."

It was at Casey's feet, North suggested in his testimony, that he had learned about covert operations. In the Marines, he had led troops, but had no experience in clandestine activities. From Casey he learned not only about uses of secret action in a twilight-zone war with the Communists around the world, but of their utility as a way of moving swiftly, without the cumbersome process of asking—or even telling—Congress and the American public.

North displayed how well he had been indoctrinated in the code of the covert warrior. "A covert operation is, in its nature, a lie," he testified. Lying to Congress, he maintained, is justified as necessary to avoid betraying hostages, operational personnel, or whatever. When documents are shredded, altered or even created, that is simply a part of "OPSEC," or "operational security," or, as Fawn Hall called it, "the protective mode."

Similarly, if officials, high and low—even Cabinet officers —are kept "out of the loop," that is because covert operations must be "compartmented." If memos go up to the President seeking authorization, but don't come back, that is because, in covert operations, the President's "plausible deniability" must be maintained. Accept the covert mystique, however alien it may seem to normal morality, and the rest follows.

The way North talked was the way the CIA's clandestine operations people used to talk before the agency was burned by Congressional investigations in the mid-1970s of assassination plots, illegal surveillance and drug experiments. Then the CIA grew up. It was, indeed, because the CIA had grown up that Casey found it difficult to get it to play his games.

His deputy, a career professional, John N. McMahon, resigned after protesting against the agency's involvement in the November 1985 Iranian arms shipment. For North, working on false Casey testimony to Congress about that arms shipment was—almost literally—child's play. Under the sun of President Reagan's smile, the White House covert warriors seemed to function in a fantasy world where no harm could come to their crusades for democracy abroad as long as they could be kept secret from the democracy at home.

So, although a lot of memoranda and computer "PROF notes" passed between Col. North and his superiors —McFarlane, later Poindexter—occasionally they must have had the uncomfortable sense that their gung-ho deputy was getting some of his real orders from elsewhere, and "elsewhere" would usually turn out to be Bill Casey.

McFarlane told me that only recently had Casey's role fully dawned on him. The former National Security Adviser said he believed Casey had known, as long as two years before his death, that he did not have much time left, and had decided to "do one or two things for which he would have to accept history's judgment." McFarlane added, "I think there's a real possibility that the last testament for Bill Casey was a very, very driven one that some of us may not have fully understood."

A driven man in the driver's seat, and Ollie North as assistant driver! It was Casey, North testified, who gave him a ledger to keep a record of secret payments, and Casey who told him to destroy that ledger and shred other documents when the Iran and contra operations were threatened with disclosure last October. It was Casey who, in the first place, had recommended engaging Gen. Secord as the commercial "cut-out" for contra re-supply despite the CIA's qualms about Secord's background and his inability to get security clearance.

Finally, as North testified, it was Casey whose brainchild it was to expand and institutionalize the Secord-Hakim "enterprise" into a Congress-proof commercial covert action facility, carrying out cloak and dagger operations around the world—the ultimate "privatization" of a government function.

An "off-the-shelf, self-sustaining, stand-alone entity," North called it. A "CIA outside the CIA," Senate Chief Counsel Arthur L. Liman called it. The revelation of this scheme helps to explain why Secord, Hakim and North were so evasive about the disposition of the estimated $8 million in proceeds from Iranian arms sales, foreign government and American private contributions still held in Swiss and other banks. And why, before being fired on November 25, North planned to transfer to Casey's staff as "Special Assistant."

There is something awesome about the sheer audacity of the scheme. Secord has testified that he didn't think the CIA was well run and that he believed he could run it better —not that he wanted to—without the need for official security clearance.

It is not clear whether he would have retained the network used in the contra and Iranian operations, which includes some former military and intelligence officials with a shadowy past. Several of them were previously linked to Edwin Wilson, a renegade ex-CIA officer serving a 52-year prison term for, among other things, selling munitions and paramilitary expertise to the Qaddafi regime.

Among the former Wilson associates who turned up in the Secord "enterprise" were Theodore Shackley and Thomas Clines, who were forced out of the CIA during the Carter administration. (It was discovering Clines' presence in the contra supply operation that led anti-Communist zealot Max Rodriguez, another former CIA officer—so he testified—to turn against the operation.) Wilson, whose offer to testify in the Congressional investigation was rejected, said, "If I wasn't in jail I'd have headed up this operation." Gen. Secord acknowledges knowing Wilson, but denies having worked with him.

North, in ways he may perhaps not fully understand, stood at a dramatic intersection of three subsurface networks whose cumulative effect has profoundly affected the conduct of American foreign policy. They are:

1. The cadre of military and intelligence veterans of failed anti-Communist ventures, from Cuba's Bay of Pigs to Vietnam. They rallied around the banner of the Reagan Doctrine out of mixed motives of patriotism and profit.

2. The partly overlapping web of international arms merchants, knowledgeable about the logistics of secret arms deliveries, caterers to Third World wars and dictators, and skilled in the manipulation of governments—most recently, our own.

3. Finally, and overlapping both of these, the corps of Reaganite "true believers," committed to dismantlement and privatization of governmental functions, frustrated with Congressional and bureaucratic obstruction, and open to extra-constitutional schemes to further their ideological objectives.

Hero, villain, scapegoat, fall guy—history will find its own epithet for Ollie North. He himself has both exaggerated and diminished his importance as a figure of his time, destined by circumstance to play a role in an effort to create a secret government within a government. Whatever the ultimate verdict on North, the week that shook the Caucus Room will ensure that he is not soon forgotten.

Tuesday · July 7, 1987

Morning Session—9:00 A.M.

CHAIRMAN INOUYE: The hearing will please come to order. Please—

REP. MCCOLLUM: May I direct an inquiry to the chairman. We, at this time, are engaged in a long process we've been involved with for some many weeks now. A number of the standing committees of the House, it has come to my attention, are in the process of beginning their own investigations in matters which overlap with jurisdiction of this Committee.

One of these committees which I serve on, which may issue subpoenas relative to this matter as early as this afternoon. I am very concerned about it and I'd like to ask Chairman Hamilton a parliamentary inquiry relative to that, if I could. Does the resolution of the House establishing this Select Committee, H. Res. 12, require the Select Committee to provide specific authorization to a standing committee of the House, or the subcommittees thereof, before such standing committee may conduct an inquiry regarding a matter within the jurisdiction of the Select Committee, such jurisdiction being set forth in Section I of H. Res. 12?

CHAIRMAN HAMILTON: I believe the answer to the gentleman's question is no. As you know, you're touching upon a matter which is not entirely within the control of the Select Committee. The leadership of the House obviously has some input in the response to your question, but it's my understanding that, as I understand your question, and I did not have an opportunity to consult with the gentleman

1

before we began, but as I understood the question, the answer would be no.

REP. DEWINE: Mr. Chairman, may I just respond just a moment to clarify this completely? The language of H. Res. 12 that bothers me seems very clear on the subject. It says the select committee may submit to standing committees, through majority vote of the select committee, specific matters within their jurisdiction. That's in Section 9 of the resolution. And further it says the records of the select committee may be provided to the standing committees, pursuant to such requested inquiries. In fact, H. Res. 12 states that all members may have access to the select committee records, unless the select committee, through a majority vote, directs that particular information shall not be made available, which is Section 10.

And it seems to me, at least, as one member, that it's quite obvious that the select committee may not allow such things to occur, unless we take a vote if it's in our jurisdiction. And right now, with the issuance, potentially, of subpoenas going in areas where we're investigating, it would seem to me to require a vote of this committee. And I just realized I hadn't had a chance to bring it up because of the weekend, the holiday weekend, with the chairman. But I would really request that the chairman take this advisement, if there's any doubt at all, because I think it's a very grave matter, if we're going to start pruning matters off from this committee's jurisdiction.

CHAIRMAN HAMILTON: I can appreciate the concern of the gentleman, and I'll be glad to work with him and consult with him, as we move through the process. I think we should proceed with the morning's hearing, at this point.

REP. DEWINE: Thank you, Mr. Chairman.

CHAIRMAN INOUYE: Before proceeding with the hearing, the Chair wishes to make the following announcement. Pursuant to the rules of the House and Senate select committees, and unless otherwise overruled by either one of these, the member of the panel presiding has and will continue to preside, act, and make rulings on behalf of both committees.

(Whereupon, Lt. Col. Oliver North was sworn.)

CHAIRMAN INOUYE: [audio interruption] The Committee received a letter from the counsel to Lt. Col. Oliver L.

2

North, and I wish to read this letter. It is addressed to the Chair and to Mr. Liman.

"Dear Chairman Inouye, Lt. Col. North would like to give an opening statement in the event he testifies tomorrow morning. We request Rule 5.3 be waived, and that as an immunized witness, he be permitted to make the statement. In view of the extraordinary vilification and the many comments by committee members regarding Lt. Colonel North's conduct and his credibility, fairness warrants a waive of the rule. We have not been able to review the massive quantities of documents which you provided to us under severe restrictions over the course of the last six days.

"Moreover, we were advised this afternoon that seven hours of tape recordings were located today as a result of our persistent requests. We simply do not have the time to review that information and large quantities of other material prior to the scheduled start of testimony on July 7th, 1987 at 9:00 A.M.

"As you know, there are many documents and slides which we have requested, but which have not been forthcoming. These factors have severely hampered Lt. Col. North's preparation for interrogation by numerous counsel and 26 members of the Committee. We appreciate your cooperation.

Respectfully yours,
Brendan V. Sullivan, Jr."

I think the record should show that the July 7th hearing date was at the request of Col. North and his counsel. I'm certain the record will also show that we had suggested a later date at about the middle of this month, but bowing to the wishes of the witness and his counsel, we did reluctantly agree to the July 7th opening.

Therefore, I would hope that counsel will keep in mind that if he is having troubles, it is not because of our doings. Secondly, as to the opening statement, I wish to read the pertinent parts of the rule, and I'm cetain that counsel and witness have studied the hearing rules very carefully, and I'm certain they know what they stand for.

5.3 says the following: "Any witness desiring to make an

introductory statement shall file 20 copies of the statement with the chairman or chief clerk 48 hours in advance of the appearance."

The opening statements were filed with this Committee 45 minutes ago. Unless the chairman determines that there is good cause for witness' failure to do so, a witness may be required to summarize a prepared statement if it exceeds ten minutes. Unless the Committee determines otherwise, a witness who appears before the Committee under a grant of immunity shall not be permitted to make a statement or testify except to respond directly to questions posed by committee members or committee staff.

We have been here sitting for several weeks, and we will continue to do so, to receive testimony and consider one thing above others, the rule of law. Here once again, the witness is asking us to bend the law and to suggest that he may be above the law. We will abide with his wishes, however, we will insist upon following the rule of law, and if the Colonel wishes to make the opening statement, he may do so Thursday morning, which is 48 hours from this date.

Mr. Nields, please proceed.

MR. BRENDAN SULLIVAN (NORTH'S COUNSEL): Mr. Chairman.

CHAIRMAN INOUYE: Yes, sir.

MR. SULLIVAN: Thank you, sir, for reading my—a letter that was delivered to you yesterday. In fairness, I think that the Committee should be aware of some very important facts. In order to prepare for Colonel North's testimony, we wrote a letter to this Committee, to you and to counsel, on March 19, 1987, many months ago. At that time, Mr. Chairman, we specifically requested that the Committee make records available to us, in order for Colonel North to testify fully and accurately before this Committee about his five years of service to the country. That letter specifically requested that we be provided with all of his documents.

Let me read the short letter, please, addressed to you, sir, and to Mr. Hamilton, care of your counsel—and to Mr. Culvahouse at the White House.

"Gentlemen, in the event Lieutenant Colonel North is called to testify about the subject matter under investigation by the Congress, it will be necessary for him to have prior access to the voluminous documentation and other materials, which we believe are in your custody and control. A witness cannot be expected to accurately recall all of the facts related to years of intensive works as a government official, without having access to those materials. We request that you provide us with all of the relevant material, well in advance, to facilitate complete and accurate testimony."

That letter was delivered to the Committee, and we heard nothing for months. The next significant event, Mr. Chairman, is that on June 30, 1987, just 7 days ago, we were provided with Colonel North's records under the most unusual of circumstances. They were delivered to us in five boxes. They were shuffled by date and subject matter so that one could not even begin to understand what those records said, much less read them all. And I say to you that this is the first time in my career I've ever had to appear with a client in circumstances in which I have not been able to read all the records. On June 30 when those records were delivered, we were so stunned by the volume of them and the lateness of their arrival that we actually tried to humor ourselves a little bit by piling the documents end on end and taking a photograph of them so we could demonstrate how serious our problem was. The documents piled together exceed the height of Colonel North and cannot possibly be read, studied in a week.

Sir, I assure you, and I think you know, that we have worked very hard with you, and with counsel, to facilitate the important work of this Committee while giving proper deference to the rights of one citizen. I don't come up here to the Congress. My life is spent a few blocks away in the courthouse, where we, as defense lawyers, focus on individual rights. We are not asking that the law be bended. We are not suggesting that Colonel North is above the law. We are simply requesting that you understand the needs of this particular citizen.

This is the most extraordinary proceeding I think, Mr. Chairman, in our 200 years. As a defense lawyer, I have never been in a position where a client is forced to testify about all matters which are the subject of a pending indictment. We believe he has an absolute right not to testify under the 5th Amendment. The Committee has worked hand in glove with the independent counsel in order to facilitate two things: one, so you can get your factual account, and secondly, to defeat the benefits of the immunity statute.

CHAIRMAN INOUYE: May I request that counsel cut his statement a bit shorter.

MR. SULLIVAN: Yes, sir.

CHAIRMAN INOUYE: Under our rules it is your responsibility to advise your witness, your client, not to advise the Committee.

MR. SULLIVAN: Yes, sir. I appreciate that, and I will conclude. Let me just say that the thing bothers counsel the most, and no doubt you all understand that my duty is to focus on the rights of Colonel North. The thing that bothers me the most is to have listened over the last many weeks when snippets of evidence has been introduced in the hearings, when false conclusions have been drawn, when members of this Committee have said on national television that Colonel North is guilty, when members of this Committee ridicule his assertion of his constitutional rights, when members of the Committee suggest that when he appears, Mr. Chairman, he will not tell the truth—that is what some members have said—and in the most astounding circumstance, even one member asks a witness—

CHAIRMAN INOUYE: May I, once again—

MR. SULLIVAN: —whether he would be believed if he took the stand.

CHAIRMAN INOUYE: May I advise the counsel that the witness will have ample opportunity to speak his mind, sir.

MR. SULLIVAN: Yes, sir. I understand. I just ask for reconsideration, Mr. Chairman. It is very important for the rights of this individual that he be allowed—

CHAIRMAN INOUYE: We will make certain, sir, that every right that the witness has under the Constitution of the United States will be reserved for him. May I also comment on what you just said, sir? In your March letter you indicated that in the event your client should decide to become a witness—those are important words. We had no idea and the nation had no idea whether Colonel North was going to testify before this Committee. And in fact a week

6

ago it was your proposal that we exchange documents simultaneously five days before this date, and we acceded to your wishes, sir.

MR. SULLIVAN: Mr. Chairman—

CHAIRMAN INOUYE: I'm sure you recall that—

MR. SULLIVAN: Mr. Chairman—

CHAIRMAN INOUYE: And secondly—if I may remind you again, sir this date, July 7th, was at your recommendation. We strongly suggested to you that it would be in the best interest of your client and also in the best interest of the proceedings to begin the interrogation at a later date. We also strongly suggested that it would be in the best interest of your client and the best interest of these proceedings if we have the opportunity to meet with your client for interrogation, deposition and interviews before this public hearing. But it was your suggestion that we should limit these executive meetings and we should begin on this date. Therefore, Mr. Nields, please proceed.

MR. SULLIVAN: Mr. Chairman, just one more thought if I may, sir. The reference in the letter—

(Chairman Inouye bangs the gavel.)

CHAIRMAN INOUYE: Mr. Nields?

MR. SULLIVAN: Mr. Chairman, could I make one more objection to the proceedings just for the record, please?

CHAIRMAN INOUYE: You will say it, sir.

MR. SULLIVAN: Pardon me?

CHAIRMAN INOUYE: Please state it.

MR. SULLIVAN: Yes sir. It is my request that the Committee withdraw the subpoenas to Colonel North in view of the fact that we believe that the immunity statutes as applied in this circumstance is unconstitutional. In view of the many statements made by various members of the Committee already indicating that Colonel North is guilty of some crime, we believe that his rights are adversely affected, and we request that you put Congressional prerogatives secondary to the rights of this particular citizen. Thank you.

CHAIRMAN INOUYE: Your objection has been noted and overruled. Mr. Nields.

MR. SULLIVAN: Could I ask one more question, please sir, and I'll be brief. I apologize. It's just one more. Since the Committee refuses to permit Colonel North to give an opening statement—

CHAIRMAN INOUYE: We have not refused. He may do so Thursday morning.

MR. SULLIVAN: I understand. Would it be—

CHAIRMAN INOUYE: Pursuant to our rules, he may do so Thursday morning.

MR. SULLIVAN: Right. Would you consider, sir, permitting him to give his opening statement during the lunch break today, utilizing this room after the Committee adjourns?

CHAIRMAN INOUYE: You may not, sir. Mr. Nields.

MR. NIELDS: Colonel North, were you involved in the use of the proceeds of sales of weapons to Iran for the purpose of assisting the Contras in Nicaragua?

LT. COL. NORTH: On advice of counsel, I respectfully decline to answer the question based on my Constitutional Fifth Amendment rights.

CHAIRMAN INOUYE: Colonel North, you're appearing here today pursuant to subpoenas issued on behalf of the Senate and House Select Committees. I hereby communicate to you orders issued by the United States District Court for the District of Columbia at the request of the Committees providing that you may not refuse to provide any evidence to these Committees on the basis of your privilege against self-incrimination and providing further that no evidence or other information obtained under the oath or any information directly or indirectly derived from such evidence may be used against you in any criminal proceeding. I, therefore, pursuant to such orders, direct you to answer the questions put to you.

MR. HAMILTON: Colonel North, I communicate a similar order obtained by the House Select Committee which is also at the witness table, and I too direct you to answer the questions put to you.

MR. SULLIVAN: We understand that Colonel North is here pursuant to compulsion of subpoenas issued by both the House and the Senate, is that correct, sir?

CHAIRMAN INOUYE: You are correct, sir. Mr. Nields, proceed.

MR. NIELDS: Colonel North, you were involved in two operations of great significance to the people of this country, is that correct?

LT. COL. NORTH: At least two, yes sir.

MR. NIELDS: And one of them involved the support of the Contras during the time the Boland Amendment was in effect, and another one involved the sale of arms to Iran, is that correct?

LT. COL. NORTH: Yes, it also involved support for the Democratic outcome in the Nicaragua vote before and after the Boland Amendment was in effect.

MR. NIELDS: And these operations—they were covert operations?

LT. COL. NORTH: Yes, they were.

MR. NIELDS: And covert operations are designed to be secrets from our enemies?

LT. COL. NORTH: That is correct.

MR. NIELDS: But these operations were designed to be secrets from the American people?

LT. COL. NORTH: Mr. Nields, I'm at a loss as to how we could announce it to the American people and not have the Soviets know about it. And I'm not trying to be flippant, but I just don't see how you could possibly do it.

MR. NIELDS: Well, in fact, Col. North, you believed that the Soviets were aware of our sale of arms to Iran, weren't you?

LT. COL. NORTH: We came to a point in time when we were concerned about that.

MR. NIELDS: But it was designed to be kept a secret from the American people?

LT. COL. NORTH: I think what is important, Mr. Nields, is that we somehow arrive at some kind of an understanding right here and now as to what a covert operation is. If we could [find] a way to insulate with a bubble over these hearings that are being broadcast in Moscow, and talk about covert operations to the American people without it getting into the hands of our adversaries, I'm sure we would do that. But we haven't found the way to do it.

MR. NIELDS: But you put it somewhat differently to the Iranians with whom you were negotiating on the 8th and 9th of October in Frankfurt, Germany, didn't you? You said to them that Secretary of Defense Weinberger in our last session with the President said, "I don't think we should send one more screw"—talking about the Hawk parts

—"until we have our Americans back from Beirut, because when the American people find out that this has happened, they'll impeach you"—referring to the President.

MR. SULLIVAN: Objection. Apparently counsel is reading from a transcript of a tape recording, Mr. Chairman, which Col. North may have caused to be made. We have not been provided with a copy of that material, and I think it's inappropriate for questions to be asked of the Colonel when counsel has a copy of the tape, but we do not have it. Thank you, sir.

MR. NIELDS: Col. North does has a copy of it. It was sent to him—

CHAIRMAN INOUYE: The objection is overruled.

MR. NIELDS: It was sent to him over the weekend, and it's in a notebook in front of counsel—

MR. SULLIVAN: Well, fine. Thank you, Mr. Nields.

MR. NIELDS: — entitled "Second Channel."

MR. SULLIVAN: As I walked in the door at five minutes after, I was handed all these notebooks which I'm now looking at for the first time.

Do you want to direct my attention to where it is, sir—which book and what page?

MR. NIELDS: The notebook titled "Second Channel Transcripts," at Tab 5. I believe it's the top notebook that you put your papers on top of.

MR. SULLIVAN: Tab 5, sir?

MR. NIELDS: Tab 5.

MR. SULLIVAN: And, what page sir?

MR. NIELDS: It's right at Tab 5, on that page.

MR. SULLIVAN: Well, would you give us a moment to read it, sir?

MR. NIELDS: Yes.

MR. SULLIVAN: Could you help us out, Mr. Nields? Do I begin the reading right on Tab 5, or the page behind it?

MR. NIELDS: Right on Tab 5, and my question is simple. Did you tell the Iranians with whom you were negotiating on October 8th and 9th that the Secretary of Defense had told the President at his most recent meeting, when the American people find out that this has happened, they'll impeach him? That's the entire question. Did you say that to the Iranians?

LT. COL. NORTH: Does it say that on this page, sir?

MR. NIELDS: Yes, at the very top.

LT. COL. NORTH: Mr. Nields, this is apparently one of the transcripts of tape recordings that I caused to be made of my discussions with the Iranians. I would like to note that for every conversation, whenever it was possible, I asked for the assistance of our intelligence services to trans—to tape record and transcribe every single session, so that when I returned there would be no doubt as to what I said. I am the one who created these tapes, plus the seven hours of tape recordings that your committee found yesterday, because I knew where they were, and I kept trying to alert you to them, and I am the one who created those tapes so there would never be any doubt in the minds of my superiors as to what I had said, or why I had said it. That is a bald-faced lie, told to the Iranians, and I will tell you right now, I'd have offered the Iranians a free trip to Disneyland if we could have gotten Americans home for it.

MR. NIELDS: Question was: Did you say it?

LT. COL. NORTH: I absolutely said it. I said a lot of other things to the Iranians, to get—

MR. NIELDS: And, when the Hasenfus plane went down in Nicaragua, the United States government told the American people that the United States government had no connection whatsoever with that airplane. Is that also true?

LT. COL. NORTH: I, I, when I—when the Hasenfus airplane went down, I was in the air headed for Europe, so I do not know what the initial statements were, and I couldn't comment on them.

MR. SULLIVAN: But who in the government, and when, sir? Are you asking him generally did someone in the government make the statement? I think we've made—

MR. NIELDS: We've had testimony that Elliott Abrams—

CHAIRMAN HAMILTON: (Off-mike.)

MR. SULLIVAN: Yes, sir. I think that we'd perhaps make more progress if he asked what the Colonel did, what he said, what he heard, with respect to his actions. A statement indicating that what someone in the American [government] had said seems to me to be a little far afield, sir. That's my only comment. Thank you.

CHAIRMAN INOUYE: Mr. Nields, proceed.

MR. NIELDS: That was not true, was it, Colonel North?

LT. COL. NORTH: Which was not true, Mr. Nields?

11

MR. NIELDS: It was not true that the United States government had no connection with Mr. Hasenfus, the airplane that went down in Nicaragua.

LT. COL. NORTH: No, it was not true. I had an indirect connection with that flight.

MR. NIELDS: Now in certain communist countries—

LT. COL. NORTH: And many others, I would point out.

MR. NIELDS: —in certain communist countries, the government's activities are kept secret from the people. But that's not the way we do things in America, is it?

LT. COL. NORTH: Counsel, I would like to go back to what I said just a few moments ago. I think it is very important for the American people to understand that this is a dangerous world; that we live at risk and that this nation is at risk in a dangerous world. And that they ought not to be lead to believe, as a consequence of these hearings, that this nation cannot or should not conduct covert operations. By their very nature covert operations or special activities are a lie. There is great deceit, deception practiced in the conduct of covert operation. They are at essence a lie. We make every effort to deceive the enemy as to our intent, our conduct and to deny the association of the United States with those activities. The Intelligence committees hold hearings on all kinds of these activities conducted by our intelligence service. The American people ought not to be lead to believe by the way you're asking that question that we intentionally deceived the American people, or had that intent to begin with. The effort to conduct these covert operations was made in such a way that our adversaries would not have knowledge of them, or that we could deny American association with it, or the association of this government with those activities. And that is not wrong.

MR. NIELDS: The American people were told by this government that our government had nothing to do with the Hasenfus airplane, and that was false. And it is a principal purpose of these hearings to replace secrecy and deception with disclosure and truth. And that's one of the reasons we have called you here, sir. And one question the American people would like to know the answer to is what did the President know about the diversion of the proceeds of Iranian arms sales to the contras. Can you tell us what you know about that, sir?

12

LT. COL. NORTH: You just took a long leap from Mr. Hasenfus' airplane. As I told this Committee several days ago, and if you'll indulge me, Counsel, in a brief summary of what I said, I never personally discussed the use of the residuals or profits from the sale of US weapons to Iran for the purpose of supporting the Nicaraguan resistance with the President. I never raised it with him and he never raised it with me during my entire tenure at the National Security Council staff. Throughout the conduct of my entire tenure at the National Security Council, I assumed that the President was aware of what I was doing and had, through my superiors, approved it.

I sought approval of my superiors for every one of my actions and it is well-documented. I assumed when I had approval to proceed from either Judge Clarke, Bud McFarlane or Admiral Poindexter, that they had indeed solicited and obtained the approval of the President.

To my recollection, Admiral Poindexter never told me that he met with the President on the issue of using residuals from the Iranian sales to support the Nicaraguan resistance or that he discussed the residuals or profits for use by the contras with the President or that he got the President's specific approval. Nor did he tell me that the President had approved such a transaction. But again, I wish to reiterate that throughout, I believed that the President had indeed authorized such activity.

No other person with whom I was in contact with during my tenure at the White House told me that he or she ever discussed the issue of the residuals or profits with the President. In late November, two other things occurred which relate to this issue. On or about Friday, November 21st, I asked Admiral Poindexter directly, "Does the President know?" He told me he did not. And on November 25th, the day I was reassigned back to the United States Marine Corps for service, the President of the United States called me. In the course of that call, the President said to me words to the effect that, "I just didn't know."

Those are the facts, as I know them, Mr. Nields. I was glad that when you introduced this, you said that you wanted to hear the truth. I came here to tell you the truth —the good, the bad, and the ugly. I am here to tell it all, pleasant and unpleasant, and I am here to accept responsibility for that which I did. I will not accept responsibility for that which I did not do.

CHAIRMAN INOUYE: Before proceeding, may I make an inquiry of the witness? Was that response from a written text?

LT. COL. NORTH: Those are from notes that I made in preparation for this session, sir.

CHAIRMAN INOUYE: It is not a verbatim written text?

LT. COL. NORTH: No, sir, it is not.

CHAIRMAN INOUYE: Mr. Nields?

MR. NIELDS: Colonel North, you left something out, didn't you?

MR. SULLIVAN: What is it, Counsel?

MR. NIELDS: You testified that you assumed that the President had authorized the diversion. Lieutenant colonels in the Marine Corps do not divert millions of dollars from arms sales to Iran for the benefit of the contras based on assumptions, do they? You had a basis for your assumption.

LT. COL. NORTH: I had the approval of my superiors. As I did for all the other things that I did, Mr. Nields.

MR. NIELDS: You had something else, didn't you, sir? You had a specific reason for believing that the President had approved. You wrote memoranda, did you not, seeking the President's approval for the diversion?

LT. COL. NORTH: I did.

MR. NIELDS: And indeed, you wrote more than one of them.

LT. COL. NORTH: I did.

MR. NIELDS: How many did you write?

LT. COL. NORTH: Again, I will estimate that there may have been as many as five.

MR. NIELDS: Now we have—

LT. COL. NORTH: Again, I'm trying to recall without access to those particular documents. You may have six, and I'm not trying to dissemble at all with you.

MR. NIELDS: And these five were written, I take it, on each occasion where there was a proposed sale of arms to the Iranians that you felt had reached sufficiently final form to seek the President's approval?

LT. COL. NORTH: Yes.

MR. NIELDS: And the first one was in February or January of 1986, is that correct?

LT. COL. NORTH: As I recall, it was.

MR. NIELDS: Now Exhibit 1—in the notebook, I believe, to Mr. Sullivan's left . . .

MR. SULLIVAN: Which book, sir? Book 1? Exhibit 1?

MR. NIELDS: Book 1, Exhibit 1.

(Pause while they look through papers)

MR. NIELDS: That is a draft, is it not, of the kind of document you were just referring to?

LT. COL. NORTH: (Witness peruses exhibit.) Yes.

MR. NIELDS: And, on page 5, at the end of that draft, there is a line heading "recommendation," and the recommendation is that the President approve the structure depicted above under "current situation" and the terms of reference at Tab A. And it has a line for "approved" and a place to check, and a line for "disapproved" and a place to check, is that correct?

LT. COL. NORTH: That's correct.

MR. NIELDS: And that's the kind of memorandum, again, that you just testified about?

LT. COL. NORTH: Yes, it is.

MR. NIELDS: This is a draft. But I think you just testified that on five different occasions, you put one of these drafts in final form?

LT. COL. NORTH: It is my recollection that each we prepared to conduct one of those transactions—and not all of them went through to fruition. There were only three that actually transpired during the time that I was supervising this activity. But it's my recollection that there were probably five times, total—that we actually got to a point where we thought, one, that the sale would take place; and number two, that we would have the hostages released and a dialogue with the Iranians, as a consequence.

MR. NIELDS: And you sent those memoranda up the line?

LT. COL. NORTH: It is my recollection that I sent each one of those up the line, and that on the three where I had approval to proceed, I thought that I had received authority from the President. I want to make it very clear that no memorandum ever came back to me with the President's initials on it, or the President's name on it, or a note from the President on it—none of these memoranda. I do have, as you know, in the files that you now have of mine, many, many memoranda have the President's initials on it. But none of these had the President's initials on it.

MR. NIELDS: Well, we'll get back to that in a minute, Col. North. My question right now is, you sent these memoranda up to the National Security Adviser, is that correct?

LT. COL. NORTH: That is correct.

MR. NIELDS: For him to obtain the President's approval?

LT. COL. NORTH: Yes.

MR. NIELDS: Frequently, you would send memoranda to the National Security Adviser seeking his approval for something, is that correct?

LT. COL. NORTH: Judging by the pile of paper you just sent me, I obviously sent too many. But, yes, I did send memoranda to my boss.

MR. NIELDS: Seeking his approval?

LT. COL. NORTH: Yes, sir.

MR. NIELDS: With a line under the heading "recommendation" in which you sought his approval?

LT. COL. NORTH: Yes.

MR. NIELDS: And, sometimes you sent memoranda up the line with a recommendation that he brief the President on something?

LT. COL. NORTH: As I recall, yes.

MR. NIELDS: And, occasionally you sent up a memorandum recommending that he obtain the President's approval?

LT. COL. NORTH: That's correct.

MR. NIELDS: And, that's what you did in this case?

LT. COL. NORTH: Apparently so. Those were the words that I had typed on a piece of paper.

MR. NIELDS: Because you specifically wanted before proceeding on a matter of this degree of importance to have the President's approval?

LT. COL. NORTH: Yes.

MR. NIELDS: Now, at any time did Admiral Poindexter tell you, "Don't send any more memos like this"?

LT. COL. NORTH: I don't recall such an instruction, and if I had been given it I would have followed it. There were times when we in both the case of Admiral Poindexter and

Mr. McFarlane decided no more memoranda on certain subjects and they'd be handled with verbal briefings.

MR. NIELDS: But, that was not the case with respect to these memoranda seeking approval of the diversions?

LT. COL. NORTH: Well, you, you insist on referring to it as "diversion". I,—my use of Webster does—leads me to believe that those were "residuals" and not diverted—the only thing we did was divert money out of Mr. Ghorbanifar's pocket and put it to a better use, but—

MR. NIELDS: I'm not asking you about words, now, Colonel. If I'm asking you whether you didn't continue to send memoranda seeking approval of diversions or residuals, whatever the word, for the benefit of the contras, up to the President for approval?

LT. COL. NORTH: I did not send them to the President, Mr. Nields. This memorandum went to the National Security Adviser, seeking that he obtain the President's approval. There is a big difference. This is not a memorandum to the President.

MR. NIELDS: And, my question to you is: Isn't it true that you continued to send them up to the national security adviser seeking the President's approval?

LT. COL. NORTH: It is my recollection that I did, yes, sir.

MR. NIELDS: And, Admiral Poindexter never told you, "Stop sending those memoranda"?

LT. COL. NORTH: I do not recall the Admiral saying that. It is entirely possible, Mr. Nields, that that did happen.

MR. NIELDS: Well, if it had happened, then you would have stopped sending them. Isn't that true?

LT. COL. NORTH: Yes.

MR. NIELDS: But, you didn't stop sending them. You just testified you sent them on five different occasions.

LT. COL. NORTH: I testified that to my recollection, there were about five times when we thought we had an arrangement that would result in the release of American hostages and the opening of a dialogue with Iran, and that we thought the deal was sufficiently framed that we could proceed with it. And, that I thought—because I don't have those records before me—that I had sent memoranda forward, as I always did, seeking approval. That's what I think, and that's what I recall. I'm not testifying to solid, on such and such a date, I did such and such a thing.

MR. NIELDS: And, was there ever a time when Admiral Poindexter said, "Don't send them up for the President's approval. Just sent them up for my approval"?

LT. COL. NORTH: Again, I don't recall such a conversation.

MR. NIELDS: Well, in fact, isn't it true that it was Admiral Poindexter that wanted you to send these memoranda up for the President to approve?

LT. COL. NORTH: I don't recall Admiral Poindexter instructing me to do that, either.

MR. NIELDS: Well, would you turn to Exhibit Two? (pause) Do you have that in front of you?

LT. COL. NORTH: I have a—what appears to be a PROFs note from Admiral Poindexter.

MR. NIELDS: And below that, is—there's a PROF note from Oliver North.

LT. COL. NORTH: Yes.

MR. NIELDS: And that's to Mr. McFarlane?

LT. COL. NORTH: I don't know how I can tell that, from what I'm looking at.

MR. NIELDS: Well, if you look right up above the reply denote of 4/7/86, it says, "To RCM."

LT. COL. NORTH: Right.

MR. NIELDS: And it's dated the 7th of April, 1986.

LT. COL. NORTH: Right.

MR. NIELDS: And that's three days after the date of the terms of reference on Exhibit One. You can check if you wish, or you can take my word for it. It's dated April 4th.

LT. COL. NORTH: Will you take my word? (pause)

MR. SULLIVAN: What is your question?

MR. NIELDS: I haven't asked a question yet. I'm simply —well, the question is, isn't this three days after the date on the term of reference on Exhibit One?

LT. COL. NORTH: Apparently it is.

MR. NIELDS: And this PROF message makes reference to Mr. Ghorbanifar in the first line?

LT. COL. NORTH: Yes, it does.

MR. NIELDS: And it makes reference to the $15 million in line three?

LT. COL. NORTH: That's correct.

MR. NIELDS: And then, in line six, it reads, "Per request of JMP, have prepared a paper for our boss, which lays out arrangements."

18

LT. COL. NORTH: That is what it says.

MR. NIELDS: And my question to you, sir, is, doesn't that mean, that you are telling Mr. McFarlane, that Admiral Poindexter, that's JMP, isn't it?

LT. COL. NORTH: Yes, it is.

MR. NIELDS: Had asked that you prepare a paper for the President?

LT. COL. NORTH: That's correct.

MR. NIELDS: That's our boss, isn't it?

LT. COL. NORTH: He is, indeed.

MR. NIELDS: And "laying out the arrangements," and that refers, does it not, to the description of the transaction, which is in Exhibit number one?

LT. COL. NORTH: That's correct.

MR. NIELDS: So far from telling you to stop sending memoranda up for the President's approval, Admiral Poindexter was specifically asking you to send memoranda up for the President's approval?

LT. COL. NORTH: Well, again, in this particular case, that's true, Mr. Nields, and I don't believe that I have said that Admiral Poindexter told me to stop. Did I?

MR. NIELDS: Did—where are these memoranda?

LT. COL. NORTH: Which memoranda?

MR. NIELDS: The memoranda that you sent up to Admiral Poindexter seeking the President's approval.

LT. COL. NORTH: Well, they're probably these books to my left that I haven't looked through yet and I'm going—if I try to guess, I'm going to be wrong. But I think I shredded most of that. Did I get 'em all? I'm not trying to be flippant but I'm just—(scattered laughter).

MR. NIELDS: Well, that was going to be my very next question, Colonel North, "Isn't it true that you shredded them?"

LT. COL. NORTH: I believe I did.

MR. NIELDS: And that would include the copies with the President—with a check mark where the line says, "approved"?

LT. COL. NORTH: That would have included all copies of—I tried, as I was departing the NSC, a process which began as early as October, to destroy all references to these covert operations. I willingly admit that.

(Pause.)

19

LT. COL. NORTH: Counsel, would you repeat that question again, please?

MR. NIELDS: My question was, "I take it that includes the memoranda with the check mark opposite the line 'approved'?"

LT. COL. NORTH: Again, I do not testify here nor do I believe I did so earlier, that I recall any specific check marks or initials. Admiral Poindexter's habit was to initial the approve/disapprove box. Occasionally, I suppose there would have been a check mark, but I do not recall a specific document coming back with a "JP" or a check mark or a "RCM" on this particular issue. Nor did, again, I want to repeat, nor did I ever see any with the President's initials on it.

MR. NIELDS: Well—

LT. COL. NORTH: And that's not entirely unusual, Mr. Nields. On a number of other activities, I would simply be told over the telephone, "Proceed," or in some cases, I would send up messages either in the PROF system or written, "Unless otherwise directed, I will proceed as follows."

MR. NIELDS: Well, that's the whole reason for shredding documents, isn't it, Colonel North, so that you can later say, you don't remember whether you had them and you don't remember what's in them?

LT. COL. NORTH: No, Mr. Nields, the reason for shredding documents and the reason the government of the United States gave me a shredder—I mean, I didn't buy it myself —was to destroy documents that were no longer relevant, that did not apply or that should not be divulged. And again, I want to go back to the whole intent of the covert operation. Part of a covert operation is to offer plausible deniability of the association of the government of the United States with the activity. Part of it is to deceive our adversaries. Part of it is to ensure that those people who are at great peril carrying out those activities are not further endangered. All of those are good and sufficient reasons to destroy documents. And that's why the government buys shredders by the tens and dozens and gives them to people running covert operations—not so that they can have convenient memories. I came here to tell you the truth, to tell you and this Committee and the American people the truth. And I'm trying to do that, Mr. Nields, and I don't like the insinuation that I'm up here having a convenient memory lapse, like perhaps some others have had.

MR. NIELDS: Col. North, you shredded these documents on the 21st of November, 1986, isn't that true?

LT. COL. NORTH: Try me again on the date?

MR. NIELDS: Friday, the 21st of November, 1986.

LT. COL. NORTH: I started shredding documents as early as my return from Europe in October. I have absolutely no recollection when those documents were shredded, none whatsoever.

MR. NIELDS: There's been testimony before the Committee that you engaged in shredding of documents on November the 21st, 1986. Do you deny that?

LT. COL. NORTH: I do not deny that I engaged in shredding on November 21st. I will also tell this Committee that I engaged in shredding almost every day that I had a shredder, and that I put things in burn-bags when I didn't. So every single day that I was at the National Security Council staff, some documents were destroyed. And I don't want you to have the impression that those documents that I referred to seeking approval disappeared on the 21st, because I can't say that. In fact, I'm quite sure, by virtue of the conversations I remember about the 21st that those documents were already gone. They were gone by virtue of the fact that we saw these operations unraveling as early as the mid part of October with the loss of the Hasenfus airplane and the discussion that the Director of Central Intelligence had had with a private citizen about what he knew of a contra diversion, as you put it. And at that point, I began to, one, recognize I would be leaving the NSC—because that was a purpose for my departure, to offer the scapegoat, if you will; and, second of all, recognizing what was coming down, I didn't want some new person walking in there, opening files that would possibly expose people at risk.

So I do not want you to leave with the idea that those documents were shredded just on the 21st. They might have been shredded on the 19th, or the 11th of November when I came back from a series of trips to Europe.

MR. NIELDS: Col. North, let me ask you this. There had

21

been some newspaper publicity about the Iranian initiative, starting in early November. Isn't that true?

LT. COL. NORTH: I don't recall specifically, Counsel.

MR. NIELDS: You do recall that there was some publicity, don't you?

LT. COL. NORTH: Oh, absolutely. But you're trying to fix me with a date. The very first revelations that we had concern about, as I recall, came about as a consequence —and I'm sure you have it in one of the transcripts that I haven't yet had a chance to review—is when the second channel in Europe at a meeting told us that pamphlets had been distributed in Iran exposing the McFarlane trip in May of that year. And as I recall, we came back, had a discussion with the Director of Central Intelligence. This further confirmed his assessment that this thing was going to unravel very quickly. That was before the as-Shari'a publication in Beirut in the first days of November.

MR. NIELDS: That's what I'm asking about. The first days of November, there was publicity, was there not, from Lebanon?

LT. COL. NORTH: Yes.

MR. NIELDS: And following that, the President and this administration was hounded by publicity having to do with Iran.

LT. COL. NORTH: That's correct.

MR. NIELDS: And the President made two statements to the nation on the subject of Iran?

LT. COL. NORTH: I recall a statement, and I do not recall the substance or the specific words, but I do recall the President making a brief statement when Mr. Jacobsen was brought to the White House, and I recall a statement on or about I think the 13th of November. And then, of course, the question was raised at a press conference on the 19th. Those are the ones I recall specifically.

MR. NIELDS: And following the press conference on the 19th, you had a discussion with Mr. McFarlane, did you not?

LT. COL. NORTH: I'm—I'm—

MR. NIELDS: Let me refresh you. You had a discussion with Mr. McFarlane on the subject of diversion.

LT. COL. NORTH: Well I had a number of discussions with

Mr. McFarlane throughout my tenure at the NSC, and even after he departed. I'm not sure what the point of your question is.

MR. NIELDS: The point of my question is, isn't it true that you had a discussion with Mr. McFarlane in which he said, "You still have one problem left," or words to that effect, "which is the use of the monies from the Iranian arms sales for the benefit of the contras."

LT. COL. NORTH: I may have, Counsel. I don't recall the specific discussion.

MR. NIELDS: And I take it you would agree you at least shredded some documents on the 21st of November.

LT. COL. NORTH: Oh, absolutely.

MR. NIELDS: And at that time, can you think of any document which would have been more damaging to the President than one of these documents seeking his approval for the diversion with a checkmark next to the box "approved"?

MR. SULLIVAN: Objection. Mr. Chairman, the question assumes that such a document existed. And the testimony so far has been that the Colonel does not recall—certainly never saw documents with the President's initials on it, and doesn't recall getting any documents even with Poindexter's initials or checkmark.

CHAIRMAN INOUYE: The objection is overruled—[inaudible, network voice-over]

LT. COL. NORTH: Would you repeat the question, Counsel?

MR. NIELDS: Can you think of any document which would have been more damaging to the President than a document which had his checkmark or had a checkmark opposite the "approved" box, which was one of these diversion memos?

(Counsel conferring with Lt. Col. North.)

LT. COL. NORTH: I'm hardput to answer your question, counsel, because as you know, there's probably an equally sized stack of documents on other subjects that I worked on, that if they were released, having the President's signature on it, lives would be lost, the national security interests of the United States would be severely jeopardized. I don't understand your concept to "damage to the President". Political damage? Domestic political concerns? International repercussions? What do you mean by damage to the President?

MR. NIELDS: Were you considering the issue of damage to the President when you were destroying documents from your files?

LT. COL. NORTH: I was considering the issue of damage to the President when I was preparing documents. You know, it's not a matter—

MR. NIELDS: What do you mean by "damage to the President"?

LT. COL. NORTH: Well, when I—damage to the President can come in several forms. Domestic political repercussions, international ramifications where other countries won't even talk to us again, like, perhaps the consequence of these hearings, or cooperate with us. I can see the risks that it would put on other people. The lives of the hostages, the damage potentially to international agreements, and quite apart from any other kinds of damage physically.

MR. NIELDS: Let's talk about political damage. Were you concerned about political damage?

LT. COL. NORTH: Of course. I think one of the responsibilities of a National Security Council staff officer is to be aware that that staff has to be concerned about the domestic political ramifications as well as the international relationships that are affected.

MR. NIELDS: And, the President was then suffering domestic political damage, was he not, as a result of the publicity surrounding the Iranian arms mission?

LT. COL. NORTH: Well, I—you'll have to leave that assessment to the political pundits. My concern—

MR. NIELDS: No, I'm asking you.

LT. COL. NORTH: You're asking what?

MR. SULLIVAN: Why don't you let him—excuse me, Mr. Chairman, I think it's only fair that counsel let the witness finish his answer rather than interjecting another question.

CHAIRMAN INOUYE: Proceed.

MR. NIELDS: I'm asking you, sir.

LT. COL. NORTH: Forgive me, Counsel. What were you asking me?

MR. NIELDS: I'm asking you, whether in your judgment the President was suffering domestic political damage as a result of the publicity surrounding the Iranian arms initiative?

LT. COL. NORTH: Yes.

MR. NIELDS: And, you were concerned about that?

LT. COL. NORTH: Always.

MR. NIELDS: And, can you think of any document, the disclosure of which would have caused him more domestic political damage than a document reflecting his approval of the diversion?

LT. COL. NORTH: The answer to your question is yes. I can think of a lot of documents that would cause domestic political damage—

MR. NIELDS: In your files?

LT. COL. NORTH: Not necessarily in my files—

MR. NIELDS: Well let's talk about the ones that were in your files that you were concerned about shredding. And my question to you is: Can you think of any document in your files that you were thinking about shredding, which would have caused him more domestic political damage than one of these diversion memos reflecting his approval?

LT. COL. NORTH: (Pause while conferring with counsel.) Can I give you more than a one-word answer?

MR. NIELDS: Why don't you try one word and then explain.

LT. COL. NORTH: All right, Mr. Nields. Yes. The answer is yes, I can think of many documents that could be damaging to the President. I want you to understand—

MR. NIELDS: That wasn't the question—

MR. SULLIVAN: It was the question.

MR. NIELDS: No it was not. The question was: Can you think of any documents which would have been more damaging?

LT. COL. NORTH: I suppose so, and I suppose those had already been destroyed. And I want to go back once again to what I tried to say at the very beginning. I happen to believe that this nation needs to be able to conduct deniable covert operations. I believe that this President, like all presidents, needs to have an ability to disassociate himself from those activities and that the US role should remain hidden or deniable, and not be revealed. And that is, after all, the essence of those operations.

The reason I destroyed documents—

MR. NIELDS: That was not the question, sir.

LT. COL. NORTH: I want to answer that.

MR. NIELDS: That is not the question on the table—

LT. COL. NORTH: But that's important, Counsel.

MR. NIELDS: The question on the table is different. Are there any documents, or were there, in your files, that you were thinking about shredding on November the 21st that would have been any more damaging politically than one of these diversion memos reflecting Presidential approval?

LT. COL. NORTH: The way you've—

MR. NIELDS: That is the question.

LT. COL. NORTH: The way you have asked the question I can tell you absolutely not because I don't think the documents existed on November 21st. By—

MR. NIELDS: Well that is my next question. Are you here telling the Committee that you don't remember whether on November 21st there was a document in your files reflecting Presidential approval of the diversion?

LT. COL. NORTH: As a matter of fact, I'll tell you specifically that I thought they were all gone, because by the time I was told that some point early on November 21st that there would an inquiry conducted by Mr. Meese, I assured Admiral Poindexter—incorrectly it seems—that all of those documents no longer existed. And so that is early on November 21st because I believe the decision to make an inquiry, to have the Attorney General or Mr. Meese in his role as friend to the President conduct a fact-finding excursion on what happened in September and November in 1985. I assured the Admiral, "Don't worry, it's all taken care of."

MR. NIELDS: You had already shredded them?

LT. COL. NORTH: I thought. That's right. So the answer to your question about November 21st is no sir. There were no documents.

MR. NIELDS: When did you shred them, sir?

LT. COL. NORTH: My answer, Mr. Nields, is that I started shredding documents in earnest after a discussion with Director Casey in early October when he told me that Mr. Furmark had come to him and talked to him about the use of Iran arms sales money to support the resistance. That followed shortly—was preceded shortly—by the crash or shoot down of the aircraft Mr. Hasenfus was on. And Director Casey and I had a lengthy discussion about the fact that this whole thing was coming unraveled and that things ought to be "cleaned up" and I started cleaning things up.

MR. NIELDS: And when you cleaned them up, did you or did you not shred documents that reflected the President's approval of the diversion?

MR. SULLIVAN: Objection. How many times do we have to have the question asked, Mr. Chairman. The witness has done it—answered that question, I think, about ten times this morning, and I request, respectfully, that we move on to a new subject.

CHAIRMAN INOUYE: I must overrule this because I have some difficulty in trying to get a clear answer myself. And I'm certain counsel is having that difficulty. Please proceed.

MR. SULLIVAN: What is your question, Counsel?

MR. NIELDS: Have you forgotten the question?

MR. SULLIVAN: Well, I have and I have to make objection. So you ask it again and I'll—

MR. NIELDS: You did and it was overruled, and the question stands. I'd like the witness to answer it, if he remembers it.

MR. SULLIVAN: Could we—he obviously doesn't remember it. He just asked you to repeat it. May we have—

MR. NIELDS: You did. You did. He did not. Sir, do you remember the question?

LT. COL. NORTH: My memory has been shredded. If you would be so kind as to repeat the question.

MR. NIELDS: You've testified that you shredded documents shortly after you heard from Director Casey that Furmark had said monies had been used from the Iranian arms sales for the benefit of the contras.

LT. COL. NORTH: That is correct.

MR. NIELDS: My question to you is—did you or did you not shred documents that reflected Presidential approval of the diversion?

LT. COL. NORTH: I have absolutely no recollection of destroying any document which gave me an indication that the President had seen the document or that the President had specifically approved. I assumed that the three transactions which I supervised or managed or coordinated—

whatever word you're comfortable with, and I can accept all three—were approved by the President. I never recall seeing a single document which gave me a clear indication that the President had specifically approved that action.

MR. NIELDS: I want to make sure we understand each other, sir. I'm talking about a document such as the type you've testified about, with a checkmark where it says "approved."

LT. COL. NORTH: I do not recall seeing a document with a checkmark "approved."

MR. NIELDS: Just so we're absolutely clear, are you telling the committee that, when you started shredding documents related to diversion, that you cannot recall whether any of those documents reflected Presidential approval?

MR. SULLIVAN: Now, Mr. Chairman, I'm not sure how many times we're at now, but isn't there some limit—in fairness, isn't there some limit in the number of similar questions that I can be asked? I believe the Colonel has answered that question as many as ten times this morning. I request that the record speak for itself, and that we move on. Please, sir.

CHAIRMAN INOUYE: Please continue.

MR. NIELDS: There's a question pending, sir.

LT. COL. NORTH: Would you be so kind, counsel, [as] to repeat the question?

MR. NIELDS: Yes, I will. Are you telling this committee that, when you went to shred documents relating to diversion, you don't remember whether any of them reflected the President's approval by a checkmark in the "approved" box?

LT. COL. NORTH: That is correct.

MR. NIELDS: You were interviewed by the Attorney General on the 23rd of November, is that correct?

Before I get to that, let me see if I can't summarize. You've testified that you've sent five documents, approximately, up the line, seeking Presidential approval of the diversion, of a diversion.

Would you prefer I used a different word? Would that help a little bit here?

28

LT. COL. NORTH: That would help. If I may re-characterize what those memos did? As you can see from what has been referred to as Exhibit—

MR. NIELDS: I don't think there is a question pending to which you are responding, sir.

MR. SULLIVAN: I think there is.

LT. COL. NORTH: But, I want to clarify the question for you, Mr. Nields.

MR. SULLIVAN: Excuse me, Mr. Chairman.

LT. COL. NORTH: I want to clarify the question first.

MR. SULLIVAN: Please, Mr. Chairman. When a witness is struggling to appear before a group like this, and anticipates being questioned by 30 skilled questioners, I think you have to give him some leeway in his responses. He's trying to explain. He's struggling to try to understand the questions and to explain the answers, and I don't think he should be cut off by counsel. Please, sir.

CHAIRMAN INOUYE: Proceed.

MR. NIELDS: You've testified about five documents, approximately, that you sent up the line.

LT. COL. NORTH: As I recall, that's correct.

MR. NIELDS: Seeking Presidential approval?

LT. COL. NORTH: Yes, but—and, the "but" is that it didn't seek specific approval for use of the residuals to support the Nicaraguan resistance. As you can see from the document that I believe you called "Exhibit"—forgive me, but I think it's Exhibit 1. That document lays out much more than an explanation of how the residuals would be used to support the resistance. In fact, that transaction never occurred. What I'm saying to you is those documents outlined the entire activity at that point as best I can define it. It would specify the expectation of a further meeting with senior US officials and senior Iranian officials. The hopes we had for ending the Iran-Iraq War and a very very brief mention in a 5-page document about the use of residual funds from that transaction to support the resistance.

MR. NIELDS: Twelve million dollars worth on that memo?

LT. COL. NORTH: Well, again, that transaction never occurred.

29

MR. NIELDS: And, those references to diversion were included in the memoranda that you sent up the line?

LT. COL. NORTH: As I recall the memoranda that I sent forward asking for approval to conduct one of those transactions specified that kind of information. That is correct.

MR. NIELDS: And, your recollection is that you received the approval.

LT. COL. NORTH: My recollection is that I—that the three transactions that I supervised, coordinated, managed were all approved by Admiral Poindexter. I assumed that Admiral Poindexter had solicited and obtained the consent of the President.

MR. NIELDS: And, you shredded documents thereafter relating to this subject matter, and I think you're telling us that you do not remember whether the documents that you shredded included one with a checkmark on it?

LT. COL. NORTH: That is correct.

MR. NIELDS: I think I was asking you, you had a meeting with the Attorney General on the 23rd of November?

LT. COL. NORTH: That's correct.

MR. NIELDS: And, you were aware, were you not, sometime during the day on Friday, November 21st, that the Attorney General's people were going to come in and look at documents over the weekend?

LT. COL. NORTH: That is correct.

MR. NIELDS: And, you shredded documents before they got there?

LT. COL. NORTH: I would prefer to say that I shredded documents that day like I did on all other days, but perhaps with increased intensity, that is correct.

MR. NIELDS: So that the people you were keeping these documents from, the ones that you shredded, were representatives of the Attorney General of the United States?

LT. COL. NORTH: They worked for him.

MR. NIELDS: And it was those people from whom you were keeping these documents.

LT. COL. NORTH: No, because as I have already testified, Counsel, I believed when I was apprised by Admiral Poindexter that the Attorney General, in his role as Mr. Meese, not that the Attorney General was going to come by and do a full-fledged investigation—the word "investigation" wasn't used—that Mr. Meese had been asked to do a fact-finding inquiry and would be sending people over to review documents, I assured Admiral Poindexter —incorrectly, it turns out—that all of the documents that pertained to the residual funds being used to support the Nicaraguan resistance had already been destroyed. I then went back to my office and I lined up on my desk—or on my table in my office, about the size of this table—a whole set of binders, all by subject and by date, unlike the documents that I have now received here for testimony. And each one of those were laid out on the table. I had already gone through those days before, removing documents like this and others—

MR. NIELDS: "This" is referring—

LT. COL. NORTH: —from those files.

MR. NIELDS: Excuse me. "This" is referring to Exhibit 1?

LT. COL. NORTH: That's correct. And I laid them out on the table. Later on in the day—I was going through my safe—I knew as early as mid-October that my tenure at the NSC was coming to a close. I had had lengthy discussions about this with Director Casey. I had talked to Admiral Poindexter about it. I believe I had even talked to Mr. McFarlane about it. And I stood there beside my safe, and I was pulling out things out of the safe and looking at them, and occasionally I'd drop one in the shredder which was right next to my safe. As I recall, my secretary then walked over to me and said, "Why are you doing this? You know, you could be doing work on the chronology or doing work on something else. Let me help."—or words to that effect. She then asked me, "What about the phone—phone call logs and things that are yours personally?" And I said, "They probably ought to go." And it is my recollection that most of this stack of foot and a half, or however it's been described in earlier testimony, consisted of phone logs, things that I had been told during my tenure at the NSC staff were mine and mine alone, plus the PROFs notes that I considered to be mine and mine alone, deeply personal communications between me and my colleauges, and in some cases, my superiors, and I asked her to put those in the shredder because those I considered to be mine. Not that they specifically related to this activity, but simply that they were not going to go anywhere and they ought to go in the shredder. And so, what has been created is this sensational, you know, horrible, final, last-minute, last-ditch shredding. And it wasn't that at all.

MR. NIELDS: You'd already done that shredding?

LT. COL. NORTH: I had—I thought I had gotten it all. That's correct, Mr. Nields.

MR. NIELDS: And the fact that you shredded a whole stack of documents in the afternoon of Friday, November 21st, right after you had heard the Attorney General's people were coming to look at documents in the morning is a pure coincidence? It had nothnig to do with the fact that the Attorney General's people were coming in over the weekend to look at documents? Is that your testimony?

LT. COL. NORTH: The documents that they were going to look at were already laid out on the table in my office, and I am sure that there are colleagues of mine who worked in that office who can testify to that effect.

MR. NIELDS: Is it your testimony that the documents that you shredded right after you found out that the Attorney General's people were coming in over the weekend to look at documents had nothing to do with the fact that his people were coming in to look at documents?

LT. COL. NORTH: No, I'm not saying that.

MR. NIELDS: So you shredded some documents because the Attorney General's people were coming in over the weekend?

LT. COL. NORTH: I do not preclude that as part of what was shredded. I do not preclude that as being a possibility —not at all.

MR. NIELDS: And you were interviewed by the Attorney General on the 23rd, which was a Sunday?

LT. COL. NORTH: And, as I recall, three of his colleagues.

MR. NIELDS: And during that interview, you were shown a copy of Exhibit 1?

LT. COL. NORTH: That's correct.

MR. NIELDS: And you expressed some surprise?

LT. COL. NORTH: I was surprised it was still around, that's correct.

MR. NIELDS: And you were asked, were you not, by the Attorney General, whether there were any other things like that—any other problem documents?

32

LT. COL. NORTH: I don't recall that specific question, but I don't deny that he asked that.

MR. NIELDS: Why don't you turn to page 18 of Exhibit 14? Do you have that in front of you, Colonel North?

LT. COL. NORTH: I do.

MR. NIELDS: That is a set of notes taken by Mr. Richardson during his interview for the Attorney General's interview with you on November the 23rd. And on page 18—you may check this if you wish, but there appear to be some preceding questions and answers relating to the diversion document—there's a question, "What else like Nicaraguan angle?" The notes indicate that question and an answer, "Nothing." And then if you turn the page to page 19, it states, "If this doesn't come out, only other is November Hawks deal." You see that?

LT. COL. NORTH: I see it.

MR. NIELDS: Did you suggest to the Attorney General that maybe the diversion memorandum and the fact that there was a diversion need not ever come out?

LT. COL. NORTH: Again, I don't recall that specific conversation at all, but I'm not saying it didn't happen.

MR. NIELDS: You don't deny it?

LT. COL. NORTH: No.

MR. NIELDS: You don't deny suggesting to the Attorney General of the United States that he just figure out a way of keeping this diversion document secret?

LT. COL. NORTH: I don't deny that I said it. I'm not saying I remember it either.

MR. NIELDS: And then you said, "The only other is November Hawks deal."

MR. SULLIVAN: Objection. You're reading from someone else's notes. They're not Colonel North's notes. I don't know whether they're accurate. I don't know whether they were rewritten for the occasion here today, and it's not appropriate to question a witness about someone else's notes. Mr. Chairman, it is appropriate to ask what he said at the meeting, but not with respect to someone else's notes as if it gives authority to what is transcribed in the notes. Thank you, sir.

CHAIRMAN INOUYE: For the purposes of a Congressional inquiry, the question is proper. Objection is overruled.

MR. NIELDS: Colonel North, did you say to the Attorney

33

General the only other possible problem or words to that effect is the November Hawks deal?

LT. COL. NORTH: I do not recall making that comment.

MR. NIELDS: Was there a problem with the November Hawks deal?

LT. COL. NORTH: There was an enormous problem with the November Hawks deal.

MR. NIELDS: And one of the problems, I take it, was that you had participated, had you not, in putting forward a false story with respect to it?

LT. COL. NORTH: That was one of the problems, yes. But I wasn't so concerned about my own role in doing that. I was concerned about the fact that there was considerable confusion about the 1985 shipments.

MR. NIELDS: Well, there was a little bit more of a problem than confusion, was there not?

LT. COL. NORTH: I don't know what you're—

MR. NIELDS: Well, let me put to you this way. I take it that we're on common ground that the President signed a finding in January of 1986, authorizing the sale of arms to Iran?

LT. COL. NORTH: It is my recollection he signed two of them, on or about January—one in early January, and then a follow-on was a minor modification later in January.

MR. NIELDS: Prior to the time the President had signed any such finding, the Israelis,—and the Committee has heard plenty of evidence of this—the Israelis had shipped, with our knowledge and approval, some 500 TOWs to Iran in August and September of 1985, and Benjamin Weir was released. Then in November of 1986, the Israelis shipped 18 Hawk missiles to Iran, also with our knowledge and approval, and indeed, in the case of the 18 Hawks, this country participated; indeed, we did the transportation.

Now, my first question is, were you aware at the time of the September Hawks tran—excuse me, September TOW transactions?

LT. COL. NORTH: I have not yet had a chance to try to reconstruct all of what I knew and when I knew it about September. It is my recollection now that I was aware that some kind of a transaction was going to take place, that I had been briefed on this by representatives of the Israeli

34

government, in general terms, that we alerted to—if I may, just one minute. (Witness turns to confer with counsel.)

I then asked the Director of Central Intelligence and another intelligence agency for increased collection of sensitive intelligence. Mr. Chairman, I defer to the committee on going much further than that on those aspects of how we collected information. Do you wish me to proceed further than that?

CHAIRMAN INOUYE: The witness is correct. We will take these matters, if necessary, in executive session.

LT. COL. NORTH: All right, sir.

CHAIRMAN INOUYE: So, please do not respond to that aspect.

LT. COL. NORTH: Very well. As a consequence of that sensitive intelligence, I was aware that there was, indeed, a transaction occurring, although I did not know, I don't believe, the specific details of it until somewhat later. I did make arrangements in September to position certain of our assets to receive Reverend Wier. And indeed, I went to meet with him carrying a letter from the President. So he did have specific foreknowledge that he would be released.

MR. NIELDS: You were well aware, however, at the time of the shipment of 18 Hawks in November?

LT. COL. NORTH: I was intimately aware at the point in time when it all began to happen. I was apprised of it—if you want me to go on with this.

MR. NIELDS: No, that's fine, that's enough. And the Committee has heard evidence recently, a couple of weeks ago, from representatives of the Department of Justice, the Department of Defense and CIA, supporting the conclusion that the shipments by the Israelis, prior to the time there was an intelligence finding, and our consent and participation in those shipments were a violation of law.

I have a feeling the Committee is about to recess for 10 minutes. And when we get back, I'm going to ask you some questions about the statements that were put together by you and others relating to those transactions.

LT. COL. NORTH: That's a cliffhanger of an ending.

CHAIRMAN INOUYE: The hearing will stand in recess for 10 minutes.

(Recess)

[The hearing resumed.]

CHAIRMAN INOUYE: Mr. Nields, please proceed.

MR. NIELDS: Thank you, Mr. Chairman. Col. North, in regard to the Hawk transaction, I want to ask you one or two more questions on the subject of diversion. Did you tell Gen. Secord that you and the President had joked about the fact that the Ayatollah was providing funds to the contras?

LT. COL. NORTH: I do not recall specifically telling Gen. Secord that joke, or story, but I did not joke with the President, if I may amplify on that. As I recall, there was a meeting in mid to late summer of 1986 in which the discussion focused on the fact that the Congress, both houses, had voted $100 million to aid the Nicaraguan resistance, and that the $100 million appropriations and authorizations had to be conferenced to be sent forward to the President. And, for whatever reason, the Congress was unwilling to send a coordinated bill forward for the President's signature. And, if my recollection is correct, the principle discussion focused on that issue as to what could be done to help or encourage the Congress to, indeed, send forward what both Houses had already voted to approve.

At the conclusion of that meeting, on leaving, at the door, as I recall, I said to the back of Adm. Poindexter, "It looks like the Ayatollah is going to have help the Nicaraguan freedom fighters a little longer," or words to that effect. It was an aside. I do not believe that the President could have heard it. And I exaggerated that to Gen. Secord. And I did so because Gen. Secord was, in my estimation, exhausted. He had been recruited by me to assist this country in carrying out what initially was one, and then a multiple of covert operations. I had brought him into these, and as a consequence, he was literally exhausted, and it was an enticement. It was an exaggeration on my part that I had told the President that little joke, and I had not.

MR. NIELDS: Now, first you said that you don't recall whether you said that to Mr. Se—General Secord—and then you said that you exaggerated to Mr.—General Secord —that you had joked with the President. Which is it?

LT. COL. NORTH: If—I guess maybe the way I should have characterized to counsel is that if I told it to General Secord that way, it was done as an enticement.

36

MR. NIELDS: So, you're not denying that you said that to General Secord?

LT. COL. NORTH: Absolutely not.

MR. NIELDS: So, what you're telling us is that you falsely told General Secord that you had had such a discussion with the President?

LT. COL. NORTH: Yes.

MR. NIELDS: I'd like to return to the Hawk transaction. Sometime in mid-November of 1986, were you asked to prepare summaries of the United States government's involvement in arms sales to Iran?

LT. COL. NORTH: My recollection, Mr. Nields, is that I was asked shortly after the revelations in al-Shari'a, and then the subsequent pick-up by that by the American media to prepare a chronology of the facts, and my recollection is that the very first of those was prepared during a rather frantic period of time, during the first week or so of November, and that my first effort at that was probably about the 7th of November, and it was simply an effort to factually recount what had happened.

I think there are two things, if I may just explain something to you, that explains some of the bewilderment that you may see, not only in me, but perhaps other witnesses who worked at the NSC. We all sincerely believe that when we sent a PROFs message to another party, and punched the button "Delete" that it was gone forever. Wow, were we wrong, and you have before you now recollections of facts, or collections of facts, as they were communicated back and forth to one another, for example, in November of 1985 or December of 1985, that we did not have at our disposal in November of 1986.

MR. NIELDS: Now, you're saying that when you pushed the "delete" button on a PROF message, you thought it was gone from the system forever?

LT. COL. NORTH: That's correct. We—

MR. NIELDS: Are you also saying that if it was gone from the system, that you could pretend it never happened?

LT. COL. NORTH: That's not what I said, counsel. What I was trying to explain to you is, perhaps, one of the reasons why some people seemed to be confused about events a year earlier, okay? When they didn't have much of what transpired in terms of authorities and descriptions and facts in 1985, they didn't have in their files anymore. Those weren't received—

MR. NIELDS: But when you pushed—

LT. COL. NORTH: —until after the Tower Commission found a way to pull them all back up.

MR. NIELDS: When you pushed the "delete" button on the PROF system, it didn't erase your memory, did it, sir?

LT. COL. NORTH: No.

MR. NIELDS: And you recall, do you not, being intimately involved in the shipment of 18 Hawks to Iran?

LT. COL. NORTH: I was—

MR. NIELDS: In November of 1985.

LT. COL. NORTH: I was, indeed, intimately involved in the shipment of Hawks to Iran in 1985.

MR. NIELDS: And that wasn't erased from your memory when you erased—pushed the "delete" button on the PROF message?

LT. COL. NORTH: Not at all.

MR. NIELDS: And during the month of November, you prepared a number of these chronologies?

LT. COL. NORTH: During the month of November, 1986—

MR. NIELDS: 1986.

LT. COL. NORTH: That's correct.

MR. NIELDS: And the Committees—(pause)—The Committees have a number of these chronologies which we were given—which have been obtained from your office at the White House. The most recent, the final version, was done on November 20th, and is Exhibit 23, in your second book of exhibits.

LT. COL. NORTH: While counsel gets that out, I would take issue with one word that you just said, Counsel, and that is "final version". I don't believe that prior to my departure, a final version was ever done or completed.

MR. NIELDS: It's marked "historical chronology."

LT. COL. NORTH: I agree, but I think that there was several other versions that said that, too. If you notice—

MR. NIELDS: We have been provided none that say "historical chronology" other than this one.

LT. COL. NORTH: Well if I may, counsel. In the upper right

38

hand corner, you see a date, 11/20/86, and then 2000—that is, 8:00 P.M. in the evening—and that means that there was at least one earlier version, and that this was a draft being prepared that would be updated further. And the reason why we put the date and the time is that they were changing so fast that I had to know which version someone else had commented upon in order to put their version of the facts into the chronology. So I—

MR. NIELDS: But you would—you would agree that at the time Exhibit 23 was prepared, you had been working on these chronologies for approximately 13 days?

LT. COL. NORTH: I would agree.

MR. NIELDS: And you had been doing those in your office, your suite of offices in Room 302 of the Old Executive Office Building?

LT. COL. NORTH: Don't make it sound like more than it was. I'm glad you said Room 302. It was not in the basement—the only third floor basement in Washington.

MR. NIELDS: I don't think you've answered the question.

LT. COL. NORTH: It was in my suite of offices, counsel.

MR. NIELDS: And you help of other people in preparing these chronologies?

LT. COL. NORTH: I had the help of many people—

MR. NIELDS: Including—

LT. COL. NORTH: —in these chronologies.

MR. NIELDS: —people from the CIA?

LT. COL. NORTH: Including people from the CIA, and people—former administration officials—

MR. NIELDS: Mr. McFarlane.

LT. COL. NORTH: Mr. McFarlane.

MR. NIELDS: Yourself.

LT. COL. NORTH: Myself.

MR. NIELDS: And were drafts of these sent to Admiral Poindexter?

LT. COL. NORTH: I honestly can't tell you whether this specific draft, the drafts—various drafts of these chronologies were sent to Admiral Poindexter, and I believe to others within the administration. And I can't absolutely testify to that, but I will tell you that I got back to my office versions of these chronologies, and this is but one of many, that had the writing of other people that I did not recognize on those margins, and cross-ins and line-outs—I did not recognize the handwriting; I did know that it was not Admiral Poindexter's.

MR. NIELDS: I'd like you to turn to page 6 of Exhibit 23. And I'd like to refer you to a paragraph in the middle of the page that begins "In mid-November", and I will read it.

(Reading from Exhibit) "In mid-November the Israelis, through a senior official in the foreign minister's office, Kimche, indicated that the government of Israel was convinced that they were nearing a breakthrough with Iran on a high-level dialogue. The Israelis contacted a US official, North, and asked for the name of a European-based airline which could discreetly transit to Iran for the purpose of delivering passengers and cargo. He specifically noted that neither a US carrier nor an Israeli-affiliated carrier could be used." And I want you to focus on this next sentence, "We were assured at the time that the Israelis were going to try 'oil drilling parts' as an incentive since we had expressed so much displeasure over the earlier TOW shipment. The name of the proprietary was passed to the Israeli who subsequently had the aircraft chartered through normal commercial contract for a flight from Tel Aviv to Tabriz, Iran on November 25th 1985. The Israelis were unwitting of the CIA's involvement in the airline and the airline was paid at the normal commercial carrier rate, approximately $127,700. The airline personnel were also unwitting of the cargo they carried."

And then in the next paragraph it says: "In January we learned that the Israelis, responding to urgent entreaties from the Iranians, has used the proprietary aircraft to transport 18 Hawk missiles to Iran in an effort to improve the static air defenses around Tehran."

The statement: "We were assured at the time that the Israelis were going to 'try oil drilling parts' as an incentive," is false, isn't it?

LT. COL. NORTH: There is much of what is in that paragraph that is false, and it was false because we were at that point in time making an effort to disassociate ourselves with the earlier Israeli shipments.

MR. NIELDS: For what reason?

40

LT. COL. NORTH: Well, I can answer part of that because I'm not sure that even today I know all of the reasons. My understanding was that because we had so many times told—well, let me back up just a second—there is no doubt that the Iranians were absolutely furious about the November Hawks shipment. These Iranians had apparently been promised something that would do considerably more than what a Hawk missile could do, and that promise apparently had been made by the Israelis through Mr. Ghorbanifar to the Iranians. They were indeed beside themselves. They accused the shipper of cheating, etc., etc. We, in our discussions with the Iranians starting in February of 1986, disassociated ourselves from that shipment. By 1986 in November, my concern and my principal concern was that if we associated ourselves now at this point with the September and principally October shipments—excuse me, November shipment of Hawks that we would jeopardize the hostages and potentially jeopardize the second channel, both of whom could be placed at great risk by that revelation. There may also have been other motivations. There is no doubt that that paragraph has several inconsistencies with the truth. I was deeply involved in that shipment because I got a phone call from Mr. McFarlane in Europe that you now have a copy of the contemporaneous notes that I made at the time. Actually, the first call I got was from an Israeli official, and it wasn't Mr. Kimche. It was from an Israeli official who was visiting the United States in New York who apprised me that he had just talked to Mr. McFarlane and Mr. McFarlane had told him that he should call me, and that I would "fix it." I think it was while I was still on the phone with this Israeli official calling me from New York that I got a call from Mr. McFarlane who told me I would be called shortly by an Israeli official. Mr. McFarlane was at the time, I believe, at the Summit in Geneva. I told him I was already on the phone with the official—

MR. NIELDS: Colonel North, I am going to ask you in a while to tell us the story of this transaction. But, just for the moment, my question was more limited. I think you've answered it, and I will put another one to you. I think you may have answered this, too.

You knew that the statements in this paragraph were false?

LT. COL. NORTH: Oh, absolutely, yes.

MR. NIELDS: And Mr. McFarlane knew that they were false?

LT. COL. NORTH: Yes.

MR. NIELDS: And Mister—

LT. COL. NORTH: Let me—I'm not here to impugn anyone else's testimony. I'm here to tell you the facts, as I know them. I don't know what Mr. McFarlane knew. I will tell you that Mr. McFarlane and I had a number of conversations about this transation in November of 1985, and that I recorded, in my notebooks, records of that. I communicated with both Mr. McFarlane and Adm. Poindexter about this transaction. I got authority to use the CIA proprietary—

MR. NIELDS: At the time, you're talking about?

LT. COL. NORTH: Yes.

MR. NIELDS: In 1985?

LT. COL. NORTH: In 1985, that's correct. You're asking me if Mr. McFarlane knew in 1986 if that was true or false? Don't ask me to tell you what Mr. McFarlane knew about it.

MR. NIELDS: Well, let me ask you this question, then. Who decided to put these false statements in this chronology?

LT. COL. NORTH: Counsel, I don't know who made that decision.

MR. NIELDS: Did you?

LT. COL. NORTH: Well, I certainly—

MR. NIELDS: On whose authority did you type in false statements in this chronology?

LT. COL. NORTH: I would like to point out to you, counsel—and I believe you may well have a copy of it because it probably didn't go into the shredder. There was an initial chronology prepared on or about the 7th. As you have noted from my travel schedule, I spent the 1st through the 10th of November coming and going out of the United States. And I was home for a brief period. I believe it was the 7th of November, I began the chronology. That chronology reflected exactly what was taking place. Subsequent to that—and I cannot give you the exact day or time—

MR. NIELDS: I'll help you on that in a minute, sir.

LT. COL. NORTH: I was provided with additional input

that was radically different from the truth. I assisted in furthering that version.

MR. NIELDS: Who gave you that input?

LT. COL. NORTH: It was my recollection it was provided by Mr. McFarlane.

MR. NIELDS: Did you say to Mister—are you telling us, you telling the committee that he told you a different version of the facts? Or, are you telling us that he told you to write down a different version of the facts?

LT. COL. NORTH: I was provided with a different version of the facts. They were, I believe, transmitted to me in a note, a PROF note or an actual written memorandum that is basically what's here, that is inconsistent with what I knew to be the truth.

MR. NIELDS: Did you say to Mr. McFarlane, "That's not the truth?"

LT. COL. NORTH: I don't have a specific recollection of that conversation. I do know that at one point, in trying to determine who was where and when, I had in my office General Secord. When General Secord saw that version —and I, again I may not be recalling it correctly, but I think Mr. McFarlane may well have been there at that point — General Secord said, "That's not true. I'm not going to help anymore in this. I'm leaving." And, he got up and left. And, I continued to work on this version because I believe that that's what needed to be put out, because that's what Mr. McFarlane had given me.

MR. NIELDS: Are you saying that you decided it was appropriate to put out a false version of the facts, or are you saying that you decided it was appropriate to follow Mr. McFarlane's instructions?

LT. COL. NORTH: I am saying that I decided that I would continue to participate in preparing a version of the chronology, not necessarily what would be the final historical internal version, but a version of the chronology that was inaccurate. I did participate in that activity, wittingly and knowingly.

MR. NIELDS: My question, sir: Did you raise with Mr. McFarlane or any other person the fact that this version of the chronology was false?

LT. COL. NORTH: Well, I believe I did. Again, I do not recall the specific discussion, but I came to be believe—or came to be convinced that there were good and sufficient reasons why that version had to go the way it was.

MR. NIELDS: So, Mr. McFarlane persuaded you that, notwithstanding the fact that it was false, it was the wise course to put this story out?

LT. COL. NORTH: Well, and again, I don't think it was just Mr. McFarlane. I mean, as the days went by between the—

MR. NIELDS: Answer with respect to Mr. McFarlane. I'm going to ask you about other people in a minute.

LT. COL. NORTH: Well, he convinced me to go ahead and put it into the chronology this way, yes. I mean, I did. After all, it was prepared on my machine and typed in my office.

MR. NIELDS: I don't want there to be any unclarity in the record on this point, Col. North, because it's an important one. I think you've answered it, but I want to make sure. Did you bring to Mr. McFarlane's attention prior to being persuaded that diversion he asked you to put out was false?

LT. COL. NORTH: Again, Mr. Nields, I do not have a specific recollection of that, "Hey look, boss, this thing isn't tracking with reality." I believe I did. I don't recall the specific discussion. I came to believe that there were good reasons for that. Now, I want—I wanna make one more point—

MR. NIELDS: And, these reasons—

LT. COL. NORTH: Counsel, let me finish this please.

He lived through this thing, just like I did. Okay?

I knew, I think, what he knew. Admiral Poindexter knew. There was, at the time, a record. We didn't have the specific PROFs notes there before us. I don't even think I had within my office, at that point in time, my notebooks that reflected that. But I knew enough about what—I could remember enough about what had transpired back then to know that this version was wrong and that he knew that it was wrong and that others, to include Mr. McFarlane, knew that that version was wrong. And I came to believe that there were good and sufficient reasons.

My reason, as I have said to you, my reason was principally the concern for the safety of the hostages and the Iranian second channel. I believed that if the proper version, showing US complicity and US support and US activity in the November '85 Hawk shipment came to be known to the

Iranians, that the American hostages could be killed and that the second channel could go the same way. I was also concerned that there may well have been, in that transaction, such a clear indication that the original decision had been based solely on arms for hostages, that it could, in turn, be an enormous international embarrassment for the administration and the President, and could well work a domestic disaster, as we now see before us.

So those were my—in order of priority, those were my concerns. I do not know what motivated others to start creating a chronology that was radically different from the facts. I give you my reasons. I did not hear from them their reasons.

MR. NIELDS: Was it Mr. McFarlane who made the decision to put the chronologies out in this form, or was it some other person?

LT. COL. NORTH: Well, Mr. McFarlane at that point in time was no longer a member of the administration.

MR. NIELDS: That was going to be my next question.

LT. COL. NORTH: And so I must defer to others who—I certainly was not the decision maker. I have sat here and admitted to you that I participated in that process.

MR. NIELDS: But you didn't make the decision?

LT. COL. NORTH: I didn't make a lot of the decisions I'm accused of making, Mr. Nields.

MR. NIELDS: Just talking about this one, for now—

LT. COL. NORTH: Or this one—

MR. NIELDS: —we'll get to others later.

LT. COL. NORTH: Or this one.

MR. NIELDS: And McFarlane wasn't in the government.

LT. COL. NORTH: That's correct.

MR. NIELDS: So although he had a point of view as to what ought to be said, he wasn't the person who got to make the decision. Is that a fair statement?

LT. COL. NORTH: I guess, yes.

MR. NIELDS: Who did?

LT. COL. NORTH: Well, I don't—I—again, I don't know who the ultimate decision maker was. I don't know who found this ultimate version on their desk, or this, perhaps final version, as you put it, because it's the last one I had a chance to prepare. But there is no doubt that Admiral

Poindexter was witting of this, and in my understanding, in my recollection of the facts of 1985, there were other people who knew that this was incorrect. Director Casey knew that this version was incorrect. If I remember the events in 1985 correctly, there was a whole cadence of people who met in November of 1985 and December of 1985 to include the secretaries of State and Defense, the Attorney General and others who participated in those activities. I didn't consider myself to be the lone wolf out here creating paper that nobody else knew about.

MR. NIELDS: Was the Attorney General aware in November of 1985 that 18 Hawk missiles had been shipped to Iran?

LT. COL. NORTH: I did not specifically address it to the Attorney General in November of 1985. I do remember discussions which included the Attorney General subsequent to this event. I believe there was one that Mr. McFarlane referred me to in December that I believe may well have addressed this issue because when he joined me in London we talked about how to fix the problems that had been created by the September and November shipments. One of the issues that had already come up by then was a draft finding prepared in concert with Mr. Sporkin who was at the time the General Counsel of the Central Intelligence Agency. I was led to believe or at least came to believe in 1985 that Mr. Sporkin had gotten the acquiescence or support—either he or Director Casey—of the Attorney General in that November finding. The November finding specifically referred to prior actions.

MR. NIELDS: Ratified them?

LT. COL. NORTH: Ratified prior actions.

MR. NIELDS: Was that finding ever signed?

LT. COL. NORTH: It is my understanding that the finding was signed.

MR. NIELDS: And what is the basis for your understanding?

LT. COL. NORTH: I believe, although I do not recall specifically, but I believe I saw a signed copy of that finding.

MR. NIELDS: Where?

LT. COL. NORTH: In Admiral Poindexter's office.

MR. NIELDS: Did you have a copy of it in your office?

LT. COL. NORTH: I did not. I had a draft copy.

MR. NIELDS: When did you see the signed finding?

LT. COL. NORTH: I think I may have seen a signed copy of it in early December.

MR. NIELDS: Of what year?

LT. COL. NORTH: 1986. Sorry—5.

MR. NIELDS: That finding referred only to arms and hostages, isn't that true? It didn't refer to any broader purposes?

LT. COL. NORTH: Exactly, and that, as I indicated a few moments ago, I perceived to be a serious deficiency in that finding.

MR. NIELDS: And a serious problem, therefore, with exposure of the Hawks shipment?

LT. COL. NORTH: Well, exactly. I mean, the exposure of the Hawks shipment, again, my priorities—safety of the hostages, safety of the second channel, the international repercussions of a—what clearly in that initial finding sent to the National Security Adviser by Director Casey was nothing more than an arms-for-hostage swap. And I would point out that Mr. Sporkin worked diligently over the course of the next few days and weeks to prepare a finding which addressed what I thought were the broader issues, and what I clearly believed Mr. McFarlane believed to be the broader issues, and certainly Adm. Poindexter in support of the broader issues.

MR. NIELDS: I want to return—we'll come to these subjects in a minute, Col. North. But I'd like to return to the chronologies and to the question of who it was in the Administration that decided that the false version of the facts should be put forward. Did Adm. Poindexter make that decision?

LT. COL. NORTH: I don't know. I did not ask Adm. Poindexter if he had this decision up the line.

MR. NIELDS: Do you know it went at least as far as Adm. Poindexter?

LT. COL. NORTH: Oh, yes. I know that he had versions —not necessarily this one, but he had versions of this chronology which reflected that kind of language. That's correct—that I had given him.

MR. NIELDS: And did he ask you to put that language in?

47

LT. COL. NORTH: No. As I indicated earlier, I had gotten that language from Mr. McFarlane.

MR. NIELDS: So you got the language from McFarlane. He persuaded you it was appropriate to put it in. You put it in.

LT. COL. NORTH: Who is "he?"

MR. NIELDS: McFarlane.

LT. COL. NORTH: Yes.

MR. NIELDS: You put it in, and you sent copies of the chronology with that false version in it to Adm. Poindexter.

LT. COL. NORTH: And others. I want to point out that I got back—as I was preparing—and there were many, many versions—I got back in my office handwritten notes in the marginalia, or marginalia on each of the documents—many of the documents, notes from various people that were not recognizable to me, making editorial changes, if you will.

MR. NIELDS: Did you discuss the wisdom of putting out a false version of the facts with Adm. Poindexter?

LT. COL. NORTH: I may have. I don't recall a specific discussion. Again, he and I knew what had transpired back in November of '85. He and I knew that this version of the document was wrong, intentionally misleading, showing a separation between the United States and Israel on the activity.

MR. NIELDS: Well, let me put it to you this way, Col. North. You have indicated that there were reasons that were given to you and that you had in your own mind why it was a good idea to put forward this false version. There were some reasons—

LT. COL. NORTH: I don't believe I said people gave me reasons. I think what I told you were my reasons, as I understood them. Whether I collected that up with the wisdom of other people, I don't recall.

MR. NIELDS: Well, you also said you were persuaded by Mr. McFarlane?

LT. COL. NORTH: Yes.

MR. NIELDS: And I take it when he persuaded you, he gave you some reasons.

LT. COL. NORTH: Again, I told you that I don't recall that specific discussion. I suppose there was one. I didn't willingly, you know, just willy-nilly do this kind of thing.

48

MR. NIELDS: In any event, my question to you, sir, is: There were reasons on the other side, were there not?

LT. COL. NORTH: Would you—would you give me—I, I don't understand your questions about "reasons on the other side".

MR. NIELDS: There were reasons—well, I'll give them to you, and see if you agree. First of all, you put some value, don't you, in the truth?

LT. COL. NORTH: I've put great value in the truth. I came here to tell it.

MR. NIELDS: So, that was—that would be a reason not to put forward this version of the facts?

LT. COL. NORTH: The truth would be a reason not to put forward that version of the facts, but as I indicated to you a moment ago, I put great value on the lives of the American hostages. I worked hard to bring back as many as we could. I put great value in the possibility that we could—

MR. NIELDS: We'll get back to that—

LT. COL. NORTH: —have ended the Iran-Iraq War—

MR. SULLIVAN: Let him finish, Counsel.

LT. COL. NORTH: — and that we had established for the first time a direct contact with people inside Iran who might be able to assist us in the strategic reopening, and who were at great risk if they were exposed. And, so, yes, I put great value in the truth, and as I said, I came here to tell it. But, I also put great value on human life, and I put great value on that second, second channel, who was at risk.

MR. NIELDS: By putting out this false version of the facts, you were committing, were you not, the entire administration to telling a false story?

LT. COL. NORTH: Well, let, let—I'm not trying to pass the buck here. Okay? I did a lot of things, and I want to stand up and say that I'm proud of them. I don't want you to think, Counsel, that I went about this all on my own. I realized, there's a lot of folks around that think there's a loose cannon on the gundeck of state at the NSC. That wasn't what I heard while I worked there. I've only heard it since I left. People used to walk up to me and tell me what a great job I was doing, and the fact is there were many many people, to include the former assistant to the President for National Security Affairs, the current national security adviser, the Attorney General of the United States of America, the Director of Central Intelligence, all of whom knew that to be wrong.

MR. NIELDS: We understand that, Colonel, and I take it one of your functions was to give people above you in the hierarchy advice.

LT. COL. NORTH: That is correct.

MR. NIELDS: And, by putting out this story, you were committing among other people the President of the United States to telling a version of the facts which wasn't true?

(pause while North confers with his attorney)

LT. COL. NORTH: Counsel, I think I've been through the question as best I can. I'm not too sure who you want to blame for committing—who—if you want to blame me for committing others, that's fine.

MR. NIELDS: No one has suggested that, sir. My question to you is this: Isn't it true—and I'll put it that others above you, by putting out this version of the facts, were committing the President of the United States to a false story.

LT. COL. NORTH: Yes, that's true.

MR. NIELDS: Did you ever say to any of those people, "you can't do that without asking the President"?

LT. COL. NORTH: No, I did not.

MR. NIELDS: Did you ever say, "you can't do that, it's not true and you cannot commit the President of the United States to a lie"?

LT. COL. NORTH: I don't believe that I ever said that to anyone, no.

MR. NIELDS: Did anybody else in your presence say that?

LT. COL. NORTH: No.

MR. NIELDS: So none of these people—Director of Central Intelligence, two National Security Advisors, Attorney General—none of them ever made the argument, "it's not true, you can't say it"?

LT. COL. NORTH: No, and in fairness to them, I think that they had a darn good reason for not putting the straight story out, and their reasons might have been the same as mine, they may have been different. And you'd have to ask them. The fact is, I think there were good and sufficient reasons at that time.

MR. NIELDS: Did anybody ask the President?

LT. COL. NORTH: I did not.

MR. NIELDS: Do you know if anyone else did?

LT. COL. NORTH: I do not.

MR. NIELDS: Can there ever be good and sufficient reasons to put out a false story about the President's activities without asking him?

LT. COL. NORTH: Counsel, I don't know that the President ever used this version. I know that other people did, but I don't know that the President of the United States was ever given this version. I don't know that the President had ever—was—had this put before him, and said, "use this". And I don't know that he's ever said that.

MR. NIELDS: Well once other people put this version out, and you have indicated that others did—I take it Director Casey among them?

LT. COL. NORTH: Director Casey certainly put out a part of that. And as I said, not all of that middle paragraph you've just shown me is incorrect.

MR. NIELDS: But some of it is, and Director Casey used it in his testimony, did he not?

LT. COL. NORTH: I have not seen Director Casey's testimony. I'd have to see it to tell you whether he did or didn't.

MR. NIELDS: It's been provided to you. It's been made public.

LT. COL. NORTH: So has a mountain of paper, counsel, bigger than I am.

MR. NIELDS: You were present, I take it, at a meeting on the 20th of November in Admiral Poindexter's office.

LT. COL. NORTH: Let me try to recall.

MR. NIELDS: Thursday, early afternoon, the day before Director Casey was to testify before the House and Senate Intelligence Committee.

LT. COL. NORTH: Yes, I was.

MR. NIELDS: And the purpose of that meeting—I take it present at the meeting were, among other people, Director Casey, Admiral Poindexter, you, Mr. Cooper from the Attorney General's office, the Attorney General, Paul Thompson?

LT. COL. NORTH: I recall—quite honestly, I didn't recall Mr. Cooper being present, but I do recall that the others were present. I also believe that Director Casey had one of his staff present with him.

MR. NIELDS: Was it Mr. Gates?

LT. COL. NORTH: I don't think Mr. Gates was there for that meeting. I think maybe it was Mr. Cave. I hope I haven't just given away a name I shouldn't have said, but I—

MR. NIELDS: No, that name is public. It's been released in the Tower report.

LT. COL. NORTH: His name ought to be public, he's a great American.

MR. NIELDS: My question is: I take it the purpose of that meeting was to go over the testimony that Casey was to give the next day?

LT. COL. NORTH: Yes, among other things, yes. I mean, one of the things we were talking about I think in a more closed meeting before this broader meeting—it was before—was how we would proceed with next steps on the hostages and the second channel. And I think that's why Mr. Cave was there.

MR. NIELDS: And I take it that the subject of the November Hawk shipment and what he would testify about it was discussed?

LT. COL. NORTH: As I recall, that was the subject of discussion. I had worked, as I recall, on various issues with CIA officers. Director Casey had been away, and as I recall, had been brought back early from a trip, and I had been working with a number of his staff on various testimony preparations. And at the meeting on the 20th, I recall it a lot differently than perhaps some other people have, my principal objective in that session was to create some closure between a CIA version, which showed this to be a quote "NSC operation," and make it more visible as a US government operation.

The CIA version of their chronology had said, "This is the NSC this, the NSC that, the NSC etc.," and my effort was to try and make closure between their version and one that would say, "This was the US government that did A, B and C." Nonetheless, the portion that dealt with the November Hawk shipment was, in part, in error. Now I understand that there's a lot of heroes walking around that have claimed credit for exposing the fraud, etc. Let me just make note as to what I recall and on what I recorded at the time. And you have my notes. After we left that meeting, I do not recall, incidentally, a great debate over whether the

52

US government knew or whether the CIA knew what was aboard the airplane. I very clearly knew what was on that airplane. So did Director Casey know that I knew what was on that airplane. The issue as far as I was concerned was what did the CIA know? I had told the CIA after my discussions—this is going back to 1985—after my discussions with the Israeli, which occurred the night Mr. McFarlane called, I believe I flew up to New York and we can go through that whole 1985 chronology, if you wish —there were subsequent discussions with the Israelis. General Secord went over and we eventually got a CIA proprietary to fly Hawks from Israel to Iran.

I knew it and by then, the CIA knew that they were flying something for me. I never told, I don't believe, the CIA what was really on those airplanes, I don't believe. I knew. And so in working the chronology, it was important that the CIA be able to say that they did not know what was on the airplane at the time, and I don't believe they did. They certainly found out shortly thereafter, because of the same sensitive intelligence I referred to earlier. There was no doubt that shortly thereafter, everybody who had access to that very sensitive intelligence knew what was going on. There was a discussion as I recall, relatively brief, in Admiral Poindexter's office, which included Admiral Poindexter, Director Casey, myself, Mr. Thompson, I believe Mr. Cave, and the Attorney General; and if he says he was there, Mr. Cooper, I just don't remember. It may have been the first time I ever met the man.

I then went back to Director Casey's office over in the Old Executive Office Building, the one that was just down the hall from my basement, and in that room, Director Casey and I fixed that testimony and removed the offensive portions. We fixed it by omission. We left out—it wasn't made accurate, it wasn't made fulsome, it was fixed by omission.

I know that there's a lot of other heroes who have exposed all this, but I will tell you that it was done within minutes of finishing that meeting and it was done in his Old Executive Building office, right down the hall from my basement.

MR. NIELDS: When you say, "The testimony was fixed," I take it, and "fixed by omission," you are saying that you and Director Casey agreed that he would say that they were told

53

to pick up bulky cargo and that the crew on the airline was told it was oil-drilling equipment and Hawk missiles would never be mentioned?

LT. COL. NORTH: That's right. My recollection of that agreement, by the way, goes all the way back to a year earlier, in which the discussions I had with the Israeli officials, we agreed that the storyline would be that they were shipping oil drilling equipment. And so when I contacted the CIA in November of 1985 and asked them to provide the name of an air carrier that was discreet in Europe, I told them that it was oil drilling equipment. I lied to the CIA because that was the convention that we had worked out with the Israelis that no one else was to know.

MR. NIELDS: You've heard, I take it, you listened or are familiar with the testimony of Mr. Cooper.

LT. COL. NORTH: I don't recall watching—I'm reminded that I've seen a tape of some of it, yes.

MR. NIELDS: Well, I will tell you if your recollection needs refreshing that Mr. Cooper said that he was at the meeting in Admiral Poindexter's office on the 20th with Director Casey and others, and that you were arguing in favor of changing Director Casey's testimony. So that instead of saying the CIA didn't know they were Hawk missiles that the testimony would read "No one in the United States government knew that Hawk missiles were involved."

MR. SULLIVAN: Did the statement, counsel, that Mr. Cooper said was written in by Colonel North in the document?

MR. NIELDS: I'm about to ask him a question concerning the writing—

MR. SULLIVAN: Is this the same Mr. Cooper that said he would not believe Colonel North under oath?

CHAIRMAN INOUYE: I believe the question should be asked by the witness. Please advise your witness.

MR. SULLIVAN: Excuse me, Mr. Chairman, if there's a document that counsel's referring to, we'd like to have our attention directed to it, please.

MR. NIELDS: Exhibit 31. But before we get to the document, I'm asking you the question. Did you at that meeting argue in favor of changing the testimony so it would read, "No one in the US government knew"?

LT. COL. NORTH: My recollection—and I appreciate you

54

showing me this one page of this document. I think what's also important is, if you have it, the rest of that document is important too because it was a multi-paged document. My recollection of the meeting is that this was indeed a multi-paged document. It was part of the Director's preparation for his appearance before the House and Senate Intelligence committees. And I had worked with his staff for several days prior to that to develop that testimony because many of them didn't know what was going on in these activities. And my concern was that the documents reflect as much as often as possible that this was a US government activity. Much of the—this is a CIA prepared piece of paper, by the way— much of the CIA paper showed that this was a "NSC activity." And so I had urged in this meeting that "Look, you got to stop calling this an NSC activity." The NSC is not a government unto itself, despite of what some of you may believe. The NSC was an organ of the US government. Showed that this was a quote, "NSC activity." And so I had urged in this meeting, that "Look, you got to stop calling this a NSC activity. The NSC is not a government unto itself, in spite of what some of you may believe. The NSC was an organ of the US government, and would you please, therefore, get closure. Stop, let's take out "NSC" and "CIA" and put in "US government" everywhere we can in the document. That is my recollection of what I was trying to do during that session.

Now there were many other people there. The important thing is that first of all, on this document, that's not my writing. Second of all, sitting in the room, are other people who have intimate knowledge of what had transpired in November of 1985. I'm not the only one in the room that knows what's going on. Perhaps Mr. Cooper didn't, but surely, with the possible exception of Mr. Thompson, everybody else did. So I'm not the only one sitting in the room having a construction problem here. And I do not recall emphasizing the US government aspect of it. And when we went back to Director Casey's office, my recollection is, we simply deleted the whole line and went back to the version that said, "The CIA was told that it was oil drilling equipment."

MR. NIELDS: Just to make sure the record is clear, are you saying that you don't remember whether you argued in

55

favor of saying "No one in the US government knew," or are you saying that you didn't?

LT. COL. NORTH: I'm saying I don't remember arguing for that particular proposal. I do remember arguing to put, everywhere we could, into the many pages of this testimony, the words, "US government," and to delete words like "the NSC" or "the CIA," and to put in as many places as possible an emphasis on a US government activity. And I—one of the reasons why I thought it was important is because going all the way back to November and December of 1985, I was in contact with officials in the Department of Defense trying to find out what does a Hawk cost or what—and eventually, what does a TOW cost, for replacement purposes, and things like that.

So I mean, there were many people in our government who knew what I was doing. Among them were the people in that room, with the possible exceptions of Cooper and Thompson. But surely everybody else in that room knew what had happened. We'd even gone to the Attorney General, in the period of time when Mr. Sporkin was the General Counsel, trying to get a ruling on a previous Attorney General's decision that it was legitimate to do these things, that it was legitimate to ship these kinds of arms under a finding.

MR. NIELDS: Would it be correct to say that you do not deny arguing in favor of writing "No one in the US government found out that the airline had hauled Hawk missiles"?

LT. COL. NORTH: I deny that—

MR. SULLIVAN (COUNSEL TO NORTH): I don't believe you've attached the page with that language on it. We only have one page here. Do you have a second page?

MR. NIELDS: It's on that page.

MR. SULLIVAN: Well, you've done pretty well in making it impossible to read.

MR. NIELDS: I'll read—

MR. SULLIVAN: Where is it?

MR. NIEDS: I'll read it to you. It's in the third to the bottom paragraph, middle of the paragraph. The words, "We in the CIA did not find" is crossed out. And above is written, "No one in the USG found out" or "found," that's what written in. And the rest of the sentence reads "out that

56

our airline had hauled Hawk missiles into Iran until mid-January, when we were told by the Iranians.

LT. COL. NORTH: I deny that that is my writing.

MR. NIELDS: No, that isn't my question. Do you deny that you argued in favor of that change?

LT. COL. NORTH: No. Again, but I don't recall—

MR. NIELDS: Do you know—

LT. COL. NORTH: —the emphasis of the meeting being on that change.

MR. NIELDS: Do you know who wrote the words, "No one in the USG found?"

LT. COL. NORTH: I haven't the slightest idea who's writing that is on any of that. That—I—my looking at the Xerox copies, you've got several different, at least, penmanship styles. I have no idea who's writing it is. I know it's not mine.

MR. NIELDS: I'd like to go back to the reason for putting out a false version of facts in the NSC chronologies concerning the Hawk shipment. Was the reason the fact that the pre-finding shipments by the Israelis were in violation of law?

LT. COL. NORTH: Well, let me just preamble that by virtue of saying I don't believe anything I did while I was at the NSC was a violation of law. Nor do I believe that anything we did while I was at the NSC was a violation of law. I didn't believe it then; I don't believe it now. If I'd believed it then, I wouldn't have done. That's a preamble. Now you're asking me if some people reasoned, perhaps, that there was some kind of flaw in the original November finding. And I don't know that. I know that we worked very hard—Mr. Sporkin and I, and eventually with the Director himself. And I believe that there was dialogue with the Attorney General at about that point in time, before and during the November finding was sent over and signed. I believe that everybody thought at the time it was legitimate.

MR. NIELDS: That isn't my question. I'm not asking about what people thought at the time. I'm asking whether the reason for putting out a false version of facts in 1986 was because people believed then that the transactions had been illegal.

LT. COL. NORTH: That reason was never addressed to me at the time—

MR. NIELDS: Okay.

LT. COL. NORTH: — by anyone, nor did I consider that to be such.

MR. NIELDS: I would like to explore that. I think the first thing to do is to refer you to Exhibit 18. That is a chronology that bears the date and time, November 17, 1986, two thousand—which I take is 8 P.M.

LT. COL. NORTH: Twenty hundred.

MR. NIELDS: I'm sorry, twenty hundred.

LT. COL. NORTH: Military time.

MR. NIELDS: I'd like you to turn first to page 4. In the middle of the page, there's a paragraph that reads as follows. "On August 22nd, 1985, the U.S., through the U.S. citizen intermediary, acquiesced in an Israeli delivery of military supplies, 508 TOWs to Teheran."

Down further in the same paragraph, it states, "U.S. acquiesence in this Israeli operation wsa based on a decision at the highest level."

Now Mr. McFarlane, who I gather was personally familiar with those events at the time, has told this committee that that paragraph is accurate, as it is written there, and that acquiescence at the highest level reflects the fact that the President had authorized the Israeli shipment?

Then, I'd like you to turn the page, to page 5.

LT. COL. NORTH: What was the question? Did I just agree to something?

MR. NIELDS: No, you haven't agreed to anything. If you want to disagree, you may, but the reasons I didn't ask you a question is that I believe, based on your prior testimony, that you had no first-hand knowledge of that approval and acquiescence.

LT. COL. NORTH: I want to clarify that record, if I left the impression—

MR. NIELDS: Go ahead.

LT. COL. NORTH: I had, by that point in time, already asked for the increased intelligence collection that would allow us to monitor this transaction. So, there is a part of that that's not accurate. I'm telling you now. Maybe you didn't know.

MR. NIELDS: Which part is not accurate?

LT. COL. NORTH: Well, the part which says, "Though we

were not aware of the shipment at the time it was made, we were certainly aware within hours."

Let me clar—without saying "hours" —we were certainly aware within days.

MR. NIELDS: But, in any event, there was acquiescence at the highest level, so far as you know?

LT. COL. NORTH: As far as I knew, it was correct.

MR. NIELDS: And, on the next page, first full paragraph, covers the November Hawk transaction. "In late November 1985, the Israelis responding to urgent entreaties from the Iranians provided 18 basic Hawk missiles to Iran in order to improve the static defenses around Tehran. The Israeli delivery of Hawk missiles raised US concerns that we could well be jeopar—creating misunderstandings in Tehran, and thereby jeopardizing our objective of arranging a direct meeting with high-level Iranian officials. These missiles were subsequently returned to Israel in February 1986, with US assistance."

At least as far as that paragraph goes, there's nothing wrong with it, is there?

LT. COL. NORTH: No. It is accurate as far as it goes.

MR. NIELDS: And, I think we've already established that the version three days later, November 20th, contains an inaccurate description of the same transaction?

LT. COL. NORTH: That is correct.

MR. NIELDS: Now, the next thing I'd like you to turn to is Exhibit #36. (Long pause)

Do you have Exhibit 36 in your book?

LT. COL. NORTH: I have an Exhibit 36, which is an extract from my notebook, dated 18 November '86. At the top of the page it says "1030 Keele".

MR. NIELDS: This is—unfortunately, this Exhibit is not yet in all of the other books, so I will ask you questions in some detail about it. I take it this is a page out of your spiral notebooks?

LT. COL. NORTH: It certainly is.

MR. NIELDS: Which you recently provided to the committee?

LT. COL. NORTH: I did.

MR. NIELDS: And it is a note reflecting an event on the 18th of November 1986?

59

LT. COL. NORTH: That's correct.

MR. NIELDS: And these are your handwritten notes?

LT. COL. NORTH: That is my writing.

MR. NIELDS: And the conversation took place at 10:30 in the morning?

LT. COL. NORTH: Apparently so, I—see if I can recall being there. Yes.

MR. NIELDS: And it's with Mr. Keele?

LT. COL. NORTH: That's correct.

MR. NIELDS: And who was he?

LT. COL. NORTH: He was the Deputy Assistant for National Security Affairs, the principal deputy to Admiral Poindexter.

MR. NIELDS: Is he one of the people who was given these draft chronologies?

LT. COL. NORTH: I'm sure he was. I do not recall saying, "Here, Al, here's a copy of the chronology." I would also like to point out that Mr. Keele was not in—or Dr. Keele was not in the NSC staff in 1985 when these events took place, and to my knowledge, was unwitting of—I want to get this—somebody ought to walk out of this thing alive, you know. Dr. Keele was, to my knowledge, totally unwitting of the use of residuals to support the Iranian contras right up to the very end.

MR. NIELDS: And presumably also ignorant of the true facts relating to the November 1985 Hawk shipment?

LT. COL. NORTH: That's correct.

MR. NIELDS: But he is asking you some questions here, I take it, and you're writing them down?

LT. COL. NORTH: Yes.

MR. NIELDS: And one of the questions he asks you at the middle of the page, is: "Did this violate Arms Export Control Act?"

LT. COL. NORTH: I'm sorry, I—my copy is—I—almost illegible even—okay. Yes. By the way, what these are—this is a preparation session where I'm being tasked to prepare "Q's" and "A's" for the President's press conference the following night. And what we normally did in the NSC, for a press conference, we would, based on the media and questions that were being asked, or things that were being said, we would come up with questions and answers to what

60

we anticipated the President could be asked at the press conference.

MR. NIELDS: He's trying to throw tough questions at you so you can come up with good answers for him?

LT. COL. NORTH: Yes.

MR. NIELDS: And right below that, he says, "Did Israeli shipments on our behalf violate law?"

LT. COL. NORTH: Right. Anticipating that these could be questions that would be asked at the press conference.

MR. NIELDS: And he was bringing these questions to your attention?

LT. COL. NORTH: Exactly. I think there were a total of seventy, or 56, or something like that. I remember bringing it back to my staff who was not altogether pleased with the—

MR. NIELDS: But these were—

LT. COL. NORTH: — (inaudible) deadline.

MR. NIELDS: These were two of them that you took notes on, on the morning of the 18th of November?

LT. COL. NORTH: Exactly.

MR. NIELDS: Then I'd like you to turn to Exhibit 37. Do you have that in front of you?

LT. COL. NORTH: I do. I have a page labeled 18 or 19 November, '86.

MR. NIELDS: Mine says 18 November, 1986. And about a third of the way down the page, it says, "1730, called from JMP." And that, I take it, reflects a telephone call from Adm. Poindexter?

LT. COL. NORTH: Yes.

MR. NIELDS: And that's at about 5:30?

LT. COL. NORTH: Seventeen-thirty is 5:30, that's correct.

MR. NIELDS: And you're taking notes of your conversation with him?

LT. COL. NORTH: That's correct.

MR. NIELDS: Now the first line refers to "Kimche came to see Bud."

LT. COL. NORTH: Right.

MR. NIELDS: That's Mr. McFarlane. And a little bit further down it says, "Hospital in Bethesda meeting, July, RCM."

LT. COL. NORTH: Right.

61

MR. NIELDS: Do you know what that refers to?

LT. COL. NORTH: Again, I don't recall the specific conversation, except by looking at my notes, but I think that refers to the fact that Mr. McFarlane met with the President in July at Bethesda. The President was in the hospital in July.

MR. NIELDS: Nineteen eighty-five?

LT. COL. NORTH: After his cancer surgery, that's correct.

MR. NIELDS: So he's talking about the pre-finding period?

LT. COL. NORTH: Exactly, and the pre-Hawk shipment period, pre-TOW shipment period.

MR. NIELDS: And then two entries further down, it said, "Big issue then was legality."

LT. COL. NORTH: Right.

MR. NIELDS: And do you recall him bringing that fact to your attention on the 18th of November, 1986?

LT. COL. NORTH: Well, I obviously wrote it down, so I can't—I'm not trying to deny that that was question.

MR. NIELDS: Then I'd like you to turn to Exhibit 38.

LT. COL. NORTH: Are we drawing a conclusion here based on this, though, counsel? I mean—

MR. NIELDS: So far, I'm asking you questions and other people will draw conclusions, perhaps, depending on your answers.

LT. COL. NORTH: I'm sure.

MR. SULLIVAN: So far, we're just reading his notes.

MR. NIELDS: Do you have Exhibit 38 in front of you?

LT. COL. NORTH: Right.

MR. NIELDS: And, is that a note that you also took on the same day, November 18, 1986?

LT. COL. NORTH: It appears to be a note I took on the—at 18:00 on the 18th, a call from Mr. Armitage.

MR. NIELDS: From the Defense Department?

LT. COL. NORTH: Yes.

MR. NIELDS: And, it has opposite—it says, "18:00, call from Armitage" and it has "lawyers" underlined.

LT. COL. NORTH: Right.

MR. NIELDS: Do you know what—and, then underneath that, it says, "Israeli shipments in 1985—did we know about it, when did we promise to replenish the Israelis?" Do you know what those—I take it you're taking down what he's saying to you?

LT. COL. NORTH: Yes.

MR. NIELDS: And, it's once again we're discussing, or he's discussing these Israeli shipments?

LT. COL. NORTH: Exactly. I'm—which is now very much in the news all over the world.

MR. NIELDS: And, he says "lawyers". Do you know why he has written a reference to lawyers?

LT. COL. NORTH: My—and, again, I don't recall the specific phone call. I'll bet there were a bunch of them those days. My sense is he had probably said, "You know, our lawyers have just asked me about what the Israeli shipments in '85, and did we know about it, and when did we promise or how." I guess it's, "When did we promise to replenish the Israelis?" And, therein, he has indicated, I think, that he came into that rather late, and my recollection, if you want to go all the way back to 1985 when this problem began, is that I didn't know we had an enormous problem with replenishment until later I got involved in trying to get an airplane to move the Israeli Hawks.

MR. NIELDS: Is he raising a question, or did he raise a question with you during that conversation regarding the legality of the Israeli shipments in 1985?

LT. COL. NORTH: Yeah. I don't remember the conversation, Mr. Nields, but I think—I don't believe Rich Armitage was initially engaged. My original, if I recall properly what happened in '85, my original point of contact was General Collin Powell, who was going directly to his immediate superior, Secretary Weinberger. At some point along in this effort to find a way to replenish, Mr. Noel Koch became a point of contact, and then subsequent to that, Mr. Armitage became a point of contact.

So, he's probably trying to reconstruct what happened before he became a point of contact on replenishment. And, my answer to him is—and I don't remember what I said. I may have said, "I'll have to get back to you." Which I had to do a lot at that point in time. Things were busy. But, my recollection is that we had made a commitment, unbeknownst to me, and it was a confusing commitment. The Israelis expected to be able, initially the way they presented it, to have gratis given to them 508 TOWs in replenishment for what they had shipped in August and September. And the same thing applied to the November Hawks. I mean, my introduction to this was a discussion with a senior Israeli official in New York. And it was not until January of 1986 that we came upon a way to actually replenish the Israeli stocks. Mr. McFarlane described one answer that he had given to the Israelis. The Israelis described another answer that they heard about replenishment. And when Mr. McFarlane resigned in December, I was left holding the bag of how to replenish the Israeli TOWs. We eventually got the Hawks back, so we didn't have to replenish them. But there were clearly two different understandings as to what replenishment meant, going all the way back to 1985, and I think that's why Mr. Armitage is asking the question at this point.

MR. NIELDS: My question is a little bit shorter and simpler. Isn't Mr. Armitage or didn't Mr. Armitage pass on concerns that were raised by lawyers at the Defense Department?

LT. COL. NORTH: Again, my recollection of this conversation is the lawyers had come in to him and said, "Hey, Ollie, the lawyers are asking me about the Israeli shipments in 1985. Did we know about it, and when did we promise to replenish these guys?" And here we are in 1986.

MR. NIELDS: My question to you is isn't it the case that on the 18th—the day that you received three telephone calls inquiring about Arms Export Control Act, raising questions of legality—you started changing the chronologies in order to deal with that question, and I'm going to ask—

LT. COL. NORTH: No. No—

MR. NIELDS: you to turn to—

LT. COL. NORTH: No, the short answer is no. I think the chronologies had already started to be changed. I think my initial input from Mr. McFarlane predates this.

MR. NIELDS: Well, let's check that against the record. I'd like you to turn to Exhibit 19. Do you have that in front of you?

LT. COL. NORTH: I do.

MR. NIELDS: If you turn to page—excuse me, that is a version of the chronology on the 18th of November at 1:00 o'clock in the afternoon, is that correct?

LT. COL. NORTH: That's correct.

MR. NIELDS: And if you turn to page 4—

LT. COL. NORTH: I'm sorry—

MR. NIELDS: If you turn to page 4, third full paragraph,

last sentence of the paragraph, you will see that there is an explicit mention of the Arms Export Control Act for the first time—If you turn to page 4, third full paragraph, last sentence of the paragraph, you will see that there is an explicit mention of the Arms Export Control Act for the first time.

And it says, the total value of this shipment was less than $2 million, and therefore, below the threshhold for required reporting of a military equipment transfer under the Arms Export Control Act.

LT. COL. NORTH: Right.

MR. NIELDS: So whoever is drafting these chronologies is now taking account of the Arms Export Control Act requirements.

LT. COL. NORTH: Correct.

MR. NIELDS: But there are a couple of problems, I take it. One is that the Hawk transaction was well over $2 million, isn't that true?

LT. COL. NORTH: That's true, but it didn't happen quite the way it was intended to happen, the Hawks eventually ended up back in Israel.

MR. NIELDS: But over $2 million was paid to Israel, indeed, $18 million was paid to Israel.

LT. COL. NORTH: I'm sorry?

MR. NIELDS: Isn't that correct, $18 million was transferred from the Iranians to the Israelis, and then later returned. Isn't that true?

LT. COL. NORTH: I do not know if that's true or not.

MR. NIELDS: Well, we'll get to that later. I believe it's mentioned in your PROF message which was not deleted.

LT. COL. NORTH: Okay. A little delete button. I—

MR. NIELDS: Then I'd like you to—

LT. COL. NORTH: I'm not denying that, Mr. Nields. All I'm saying is that what you just told me about money being transferred didn't come to the United States, I don't believe.

MR. NIELDS: I didn't suggest that it did.

LT. COL. NORTH: Okay.

MR. NIELDS: I said it went to the Israelis.

LT. COL. NORTH: From the Iranians?

MR. NIELDS: Yes.

65

LT. COL. NORTH: Okay.

MR. NIELDS: Then I'd like you to turn to Exhibit number 20.

CHAIRMAN INOUYE: Mr. Nields, is this a good place to stand in recess?

MR. NIELDS: In one question it will be, Mr. Chairman.

CHAIRMAN INOUYE: Please proceed.

MR. NIELDS: Exhibit number 20 is a chronology also written on the 18th, and this one, at 7:30 P.M., I believe that's after all three of these telephone conversations raising legality, lawyers' questions. And I'll ask you to turn to page 12. You'll see at the bottom of the page some new language added into the chronology. It says: "During the course of this operation and before, the US was cognizant of only two shipments from Israel to Iran. Specifically, the Israelis acknowledge the August '85 shipment of 508 TOWs after it had taken place," the word "after" underscored? And, then at the end of that sentence, it says, "We subsequently agreed to replace these TOWs in May of 1986."

LT. COL. NORTH: Actually, we agreed to replace them earlier than that, but we weren't able to do so until May of '86.

MR. NIELDS: But, this document doesn't say so. It only mentions "activity post finding". Is that correct?

LT. COL. NORTH: Well, it was post-finding. I think the actual understanding I reached with the Israelis on replacing the TOWs was reached in January, late January in a meeting in Europe.

MR. NIELDS: And, then at the bottom of that page, it says, "The November '85 shipment of 8,"—which is, I take it, a mistake—

LT. COL. NORTH: Yes.

MR. NIELDS: —"Israeli Hawk missiles was not an authorized exception to policy." So, wouldn't it be fair to say, Col. North, that you are—or whoever is drafting these chronologies—on the 18th is trying to deal with the issues raised by the Arms Export Control Act that have been brought to your attention during the course of day?

LT. COL. NORTH: I'm sure that's the case.

MR. NIELDS: And, then it was two days later that the narrative version was changed completely so as to deny any

66

knowledge of the Hawk transaction, and to assert our belief that it was oil-drilling equipment?

LT. COL. NORTH: I believe that the Director's testimony was changed to reflect that the CIA was told—

MR. NIELDS: I'm referring you to the chronology now?

LT. COL. NORTH: Okay. Yes.

MR. NIELDS: Mr. Chairman, thank you.

CHAIRMAN INOUYE: The hearing will stand in recess until 2:00 P.M. this afternoon.

END OF MORNING SESSION

Afternoon Session—2:00 P.M.

SEN. INOUYE: The hearing will please come to order. Mr. Nields?

MR. NIELDS: Thank you, Mr. Chairman. Colonel North, this morning you were answering questions concerning what was said about transactions that occurred in 1985. This afternoon I'd like to ask you what actually did happen. And perhaps we could take first the August-September shipment of TOWs. And I think it might be most helpful if you simply would describe to the Committee what your understanding and role was in that transaction at the time it happened. Would you do so, please, sir?

LT. COL. NORTH: The August-September '85 shipments are the one I believe you're referring to?

MR. NIELDS: Correct.

LT. COL. NORTH: I'm working without refreshed recall. Let me do the best I can to remember back to that period of time. I had had several meetings with Mr. Ledeen which led to a meeting or two with two Israeli citizens, private citizens. And then a subsequent meeting, as I recall, with Mr. Ghobanifar. That in turn led to a meeting with Mr. Kimche. And I believe all of these took place prior to the September shipment. Mr. Kimche and Mr. McFarlane then had a meeting, as I recall. And I was aware, I think, by virtue of the sensitive intelligence at the time that the Israelis were indeed involved in the transaction. I did not know at the time the exact nature of that, I don't think. But I did know that as a consequence an American hostage or

67

two was expected to be released. I was instructed to take precautions for that eventuality. We did so. Reverend Weir was picked up in accord with what we expected to happen, delivered to a US vessel and then shortly thereafter brought to a US military installation here in the United States. I met him and brought with me a letter from the President asking his assistance as best he could give it and expressing the President's well wishes on his release from captivity.

I don't have a specific recall of many things happening in between, although I believe I had another meeting with Mr. Ghorbanifar. My next very specific recollection are the series of phone calls I described to you on or about the 17th of November.

MR. NIELDS: I'd like to stop and ask you some questions about the TOW transaction, if I may, first.

LT. COL. NORTH: Yes.

MR. NIELDS: Who were the two Israeli citizens?

LT. COL. NORTH: Mr. Schwimmer and Mr. Nimrodi.

MR. NIELDS: Were the meetings that you described that you described with Mr. Ledeen, Mr. Schwimmer, Mr. Nimrodi and Mr. Ghorbanifar, meetings in which arms were discussed?

LT. COL. NORTH: I believe they were, yes.

MR. NIELDS: And hostages?

LT. COL. NORTH: Oh, yes, but also discussed were the broader purposes for an opening with Iran, the opportunity to end Shia fundamentalist terrorism.

MR. NIELDS: What was your authority for participating in those meetings?

LT. COL. NORTH: Well, Mr. McFarlane's authority as an NSC staffer.

MR. NIELDS: So that Mr. McFarlane was aware of the fact that you were having these meetings and he had authorized them?

LT. COL. NORTH: Well, I did keep Mr. McFarlane apprised of those, yes, I did—normally through the PROF system, I think.

MR. NIELDS: Was it your understanding that Mr. McFarlane had already had similar meetings himself with either the two Israeli citizens, Mr. Ghorbanifar or Mr. Kimche?

LT. COL. NORTH: I came to the understanding, and I'm not sure exactly when it was that Mr. McFarlane and Mr. Kimche had met several times, and further that there had been by the time, I guess, October or November got around that there had actually been discussions of this with the President. I was not a party to any of those discussions with the President, but I was told at some point that the President had authorized these Israeli transactions to proceed during the summer in July.

MR. NIELDS: And, I think you may have said this, but when did you first become aware of the fact that the President had authorized these transactions?

LT. COL. NORTH: My first awareness of a specific Presidential transaction, or authorization for a transaction, as I recall, in the time period when we were engaged on the Hawk shipment, wherein I believe I have a—I made a recording, a note to the effect that Admiral Poindexter told me the President had authorized it to proceed.

MR. NIELDS: Were you ever told that the President had authorized a TOW shipment to proceed?

LT. COL. NORTH: I was at some point, yes.

MR. NIELDS: To the best of your recollection, when?

LT. COL. NORTH: Well, I know I was told that in '86 as I was preparing the chronologies. I was probably told that in '85, or I would have asked more questions than I did about it.

MR. NIELDS: Who told—

LT. COL. NORTH: I don't recall it specifically.

MR. NIELDS: Who told you in 1986 that the President had authorized a TOW shipment?

LT. COL. NORTH: Mr. McFarlane.

MR. NIELDS: And, assuming that you were told it earlier, do you recall anyone other than Mr. McFarlane telling you that earlier?

LT. COL. NORTH: No, I don't at all. But, I want to make a point about—at some point in December, while I was overseas, there were meetings held at the White House among a number of Cabinet officers in which, apparently, these issues were discussed, and subsequent to that, there was a finding done, giving retroactive ratification to what had already transpired, that the Cabinet officers were also aware of.

MR. NIELDS: To the best of your recollection, when did you first have meetings with either Mr. Ledeen, Mr. Nimrodi or Mr. Schwimmer on the subject of arms and hostages?

LT. COL. NORTH: I can't recall a specific date. I would put it in summer of 1985.

MR. NIELDS: What was the purpose of these meetings? Why was the United States or any officials of the United States involved?

LT. COL. NORTH: Well, I don't know, other than the fact that the proposal, as it was being advanced to me, was that this is in our interest to achieve a strategic breakthrough with Iran, to establish contacts with moderate or pragmatic elements within Iran, and I happen to believe that. I think it was in our interest. I think it still is in our interest, that if we have a means of establishing some kind of a strategic relationship with this country, that it serves our interest. And so as I recall, the discussion started out in a very philosophical vein, but quickly moved beyond that over the course of several weeks to discuss specific activities that would allow that breakthrough.

MR. NIELDS: What—

LT. COL. NORTH: I believe the very first person to raise it with me was Mr. Ledeen, and then I—I'm sure that I then raised it with Mr. McFarlane.

MR. NIELDS: What, if anything, was the United States government being asked to do or agree to?

LT. COL. NORTH: Well, as I understood the September —just as I now understand what I understood about September of '85 what we were simply asked to do, as I understood it, was to acquiesce in the Israelis providing certain munitions as an—and it was probably unspecified as to what they were until later on for the purposes of opening this dialogue—and, at the same time, getting beyond the obstacle of the hostages.

MR. NIELDS: Why, to your understanding, was it necessary to obtain US government acquiescence?

LT. COL. NORTH: Well, we had obviously strictures on what we can—can and cannot allow, what—they knew what the strictures were and what they could or could not do in accord with US regulations and the like, but my guess is, and I'm—I'm trying to put myself in someone else's

70

shoes, what they wanted to do was to get our acknowledgement, acquiescence, concurrence in providing these materials that they otherwise could not legally or correctly move. And I'm not sure that "legally" is the right word, but that's my understanding. I did not, at the time, understand that there was any problem with what I eventually came to call replenishment. I didn't—it was never addressed to me that way.

MR. NIELDS: Was that discussed with the Israeli citizens or Mr. Ledeen, the issue of replenishment?

LT. COL. NORTH: I have absolutely no recall of the replenishment issue until November when it was basically said, "Okay, now what are you going to do about giving us some more TOWs?"

MR. NIELDS: I take it one thing is clear, and that is that the—the TOWs, or the weapons that were being shipped, were Israeli weapons that were in Israeli stocks, not US weapons in US stocks.

LT. COL. NORTH: It is my understanding—it would—it would—it was my understanding at the time that there were five hundred TOWs, which had originally been provided by the United States to Israel, that were shipped in August and September. In fact, my original understanding was that they were all shipped in September, but eventually I learned that there were two shipments of 200-plus each and that the shipment wasn't really 500; it was 504, and then they learned it was 508.

MR. NIELDS: When to your understanding were these TOWs originally shipped by the United States to Israel?

LT. COL. NORTH: I have no idea. I—I was never told.

MR. NIELDS: I'd like to move on now to the period following the release of Mr. Weir following the TOW shipment. Did you have—following his release, was there any increased interest in the United States government for continuing with this type of venture?

LT. COL. NORTH: Well, apparently there was a good bit of it going on elsewhere, probably at a level above me because I did get a call from a senior Israeli official from New York in mid-November asking for my help in—in a problem that had developed.

MR. NIELDS: Would you simply pick up the story of the Hawk shipment, starting with that call that you received from the Israeli official, and tell us in your own words what you remember, and we know that this is a more complicated story than the TOW shipment. And you can rely on me to ask you some questions after you have told your narrative.

LT. COL. NORTH: All right, sir. It is my recollection that on November 17th, I received a phone call in the evening from an Israeli official who was in New York indicating a problem. I then, I think while I was still on the line with him, got a call from Mr. McFarlane. My contemporaneous note at the time indicates that the two calls were, if nothing else, sequential.

MR. NIELDS: I take it this was a call from Mr. Rabin?

LT. COL. NORTH: It was.

MR. NIELDS: And what was the problem?

LT. COL. NORTH: Well, he did—at that point, he didn't go into it in any detail, that there was a problem with a shipment, a movement on the project that I knew about. I then got a call from Mr. McFarlane from Europe, telling me that Mr. Rabin would call. I told him I had aleady talked to Mr. Rabin. He said, "Look, just, you know, you go take care of that problem." This was a trans-Atlantic open line telephone call as I remember it. And so my recollection is I flew up immediately to talk with Mr. Rabin. He then sent several of his Ministry of Defense representatives to talk with me. It was in that period of time that I became aware of what was really trying to be moved. Now I may have already known some of that from sensitive intelligence, but the full parameters of it were laid out for me by Mr. Rabin and his representatives.

As I recall, the Director of Central Intelligence was out of townm, and in my discussions which followed with the MOD representatives, they specified a replenishment problem. In addition to solving the immediate problem of getting the Hawks, the original number of which was to be 120, moved from Israel through a European country and then on to Iran, there was the problem of replenishing the TOWs which had been shipped in August-September.

As I recall, I made a number of telephone calls to the Department of Defense to my point of contact—I think it was at that point either Mr. Koch or General Powell —trying to ascertain the cost of a Hawk system, the cost of a

72

TOW system. There was a rather protracted period of time in which all of this was worked out. I also took, at that point in time, a decision—with the approval of Admiral Poindexter and Mr. McFarlane—and asked General Secord to fly to Europe to see what he could do to straighten out the mess. My recollection is General Secord was reluctant to do that. He was already busy with another covert operation which I'm sure you'll want to talk about, and he was up to his ears in alligators. He nonetheless went. Through a series of meetings he had with Israeli representatives in Europe, then in Israel and at some point in the next—between the 17th and the 24th, I believe, he asked me for the name of a proprietory or—actually what he asked me for is, "Does Langley know of any discreet airlines that can provide the services that the Israelis were going to provide themselves," and basically it was an air support problem that had been developed. The reason I asked General Secord to go is he had contacts in the European country that they were planning to move these things through because of the other covert operation. He had a lot of experience in the aviation business, fixing aviation problems, particularly covert ones, and he was an expert on Iran. And so he went, met with the Israelis, met with a number of officials in the European country. The long and the short of it was I got the name of a proprietary from the CIA. The proprietary was passed to General Secord, and he contracted with the proprietary to pick up the Hawks. The aircraft flew to Israel, then flew in a circuitous route to Iran and delivered the Hawks. I believe the actual delivery took place on or about the 24th or 25th of November. More?

MR. NIELDS: Yeah, I'll come back to some of these issues, but I take it there was originally contemplated to ship more than 18 Hawks.

LT. COL. NORTH: The original number, as I remember, the original number I was told was 80. And then I was told later on that it was 120, and I—120 sticks in my mind as being the number that was eventually determined—that was intended to be shipped. And I think that we had some confirmation that that was the arrangement through sensitive intelligence.

MR. NIELDS: And can you tell us the story of why only 18 were shipped?

73

LT. COL. NORTH: A bit of a horror story. The original plans had been worked out by the Israelis would have put, as I recall, either 40 or 80 on a 747 cargo jet and that would offload in the European country, then reload onto other aircraft. General Secord said, "That's not going to work. It's going to be too visible to people. Let's move the stuff out of Israel directly." He worked that out with the Israelis and Gen. Secord said, "That's not going to work. It's going to be too visible to people. Let's move the stuff out of Israel directly." He worked that out with the Israelis. And only eighteen could be put into the kind of aircraft that was provided, because apparently the configuration of the door —I'd defer to experts on loading airplanes for exactly what the problem was. But it was, I think, a loading problem more than anything else, that only allowed eighteen to be loaded at once.

MR. NIELDS: Well, that explains why only eighteen went at one time. But why weren't the rest of them shipped later?

LT. COL. NORTH: To coin a phrase, I think the Iranians went ballistic, when they saw what they got. And the reason they did so is, they had apparently been told by the Israelis that they were getting a system that would shoot down Soviet and Iraqi high-altitude aircraft. And the Hawk system is a not a high-altitude weapon system. It is a low-altitude, defensive weapons system. And, apparently, they felt that they had been misled. Now, having not been a party to whatever the Iranians were told, either by Mr. Ghorbanifar or Mr. Nimrodi or Mr. Schwimmer, Gen. Secord was obviously concerned that someone had misled the Iranians at the far end. And they were very upset. I mean, we could see that in sensitive intelligence.

They apparently disassembled one of the eighteen Hawks, noticed that it did not meet what they had—in fact, it was the same as what they already had in their inventory from the United States, and were very, very concerned. We became concerned at that point—or, at least, I did. Because of the commitments that had been for something other than what was delivered, that we were, indeed, instead of rescuing hostages, creating a situation in which they were being placed at increasing risk because of potential reprisals, or something like that.

And, at that point in time, a proposal was developed by which we would take these activities and exert more control over them, and management over them, and that you just couldn't have people making commitments for American lives in faraway places and creating a situation where those who were supposedly helping to influence their release would think we were being—just cheating on them, is the word that was used frequently in the sense of intelligence.

MR. NIELDS: I'd like to go back over some of the issues arising out of this Hawk transactions. The first one I'd like to address, Col. North, is the issue of money. I think the best place to begin is with an item out of your notebook —spiral notebook. And I believe you'll find it in Exhibit Book No. 3. There are some documents collectively marked Exhibit 69-A. And I would like you to turn—they're in date order—and I'd like you to turn to one which bears the date of 18 November, and there are a number of those, you have to look for one which at the top of the page says, "Israel Account Credit Suisse." Do you have that in front of you?

LT. COL. NORTH: I do.

MR. NIELDS: I'd like you to take a look at the middle of the page. It says, "Secord to call a city in a foreign country."

LT. COL. NORTH: Yes.

MR. NIELDS: Then underneath that it says, "Ben-Youssif, start by orders at $14 million or less."

LT. COL. NORTH: Right.

MR. NIELDS: While we're on that, Ben-Youssif is the person at the Israel purchasing office, I take it?

LT. COL. NORTH: He is.

MR. NIELDS: And the suggestion to buy at $14 million or less has to do with the reporting requirements under the Arms Export Control Act?

LT. COL. NORTH: That's correct.

MR. NIELDS: The idea being if it's under $14 million you don't have to report to Congress.

LT. COL. NORTH: Someone had told me that, that's right.

MR. NIELDS: And then under that it says, "Schwimmer move $1 million to Lake."

LT. COL. NORTH: Right.

MR. NIELDS: "Lake" is Lake Resources, is that correct?

LT. COL. NORTH: Yes.

MR. NIELDS: And what was Schwimmer to move a million dollars to Lake for?

LT. COL. NORTH: It is my recollection that the intention was to use that for the purpose of carrying out this whole activity.

MR. NIELDS: Well, what activity?

LT. COL. NORTH: The movement of the Hawks to Iran.

MR. NIELDS: From where?

LT. COL. NORTH: Israel. And, there may have been at that point in time, I may have made enough phone calls to figure out that we were going to try and move stuff from the United States to replenish. I think the replenishment problem had been identified for me at that point; that I clearly understood we had—I clearly understood that the Israelis perceived that we had made a commitment to replenish their supplies. It was made very clear to me that the numbers of weapons were an issue for them and that they needed replenishment in very short order. I did not know at that point in time exactly what commitment had been made. Mr. McFarlane was still out of the country. I was being told by the Israelis that they had national security implications as a consequence of this and that they expected a prompt and full replenishment.

MR. NIELDS: Now right underneath "Schwimmer move $1 million to Lake", the words: "Schwimmer to pick up Hawks in US." What is that a reference to?

LT. COL. NORTH: My—I guess, and I don't remember the point in time or who I was talking to, my guess is that that's where he's buying the replacement.

MR. NIELDS: I need to ask this again: why is a million dollars being put into the Lake Resources account?

LT. COL. NORTH: As I recall, the intention of that million dollars was to cover the cost of this whole transaction in terms of running airplanes, and warehouse space, and the appropriate charges for various people on the ground —those kinds of things. That was my understanding of it.

MR. NIELDS: Whose idea was it that a million dollars for that purpose would be put into the Lake Resources account?

LT. COL. NORTH: I don't recall. It was probably arrived at mutually among Gen. Secord, the Israelis and I [sic]. I'm not sure who actually originated the figure. I'm sure that the Lake Resources account was one that was known to me. And since he was the one that was going to be the charter agent, my sense is, it was kind of mutually arrived at. We were very concerned that they had demonstrated a certain ineptness in trying to pull this whole thing off.

MR. NIELDS: Gen. Secord has testified in front of this committtee that he left for the foreign country, the European country, on the 19th: that either that day or the 18th was the first time he was contacted; and that it was his job at that point in time to do nothing other than facilitate the obtaining of landing rights for Israeli aircraft in the foreign, European country. And that it wasn't until sometime after he arrived in the foreign country that he had any responsibilities at all having to do with transporting arms. Is your recollection different from his?

LT. COL. NORTH: Not necessarily. I'm just saying that I thought maybe I had contacted Gen. Secord as early as the 17th, after I'd be contacted by Mr. McFarlane and the Israelis. And my sense is that that's how this whole thing evolved—that there was a consideration to have us take over the management of this thing, that it was royally fouled up, and to fix it. And that that right there would be the funds necessary to make this transaction work.

MR. NIELDS: Are you referring now, when you say "this transaction" to the movement of Israeli Hawks from Israel to Iran? Or are you referring to the flying of Hawks from this country to Israel?

LT. COL. NORTH: I don't recall whether we'd actually gotten to the point where we were thinking of the second phase or not. But it was at least the first, if not both.

MR. NIELDS: Well, are you saying that as of the 18th, Mr. Secord was the one who was going to take care of transporting and paying for the cost of transporting Israeli arms?

LT. COL. NORTH: No. I think what we're talking about is trying to arrange a better way of doing it, and having him be the person to do that. If my notes are accurate and I made that notation of the 18th on the 18th, the ideas at least occurred to me as early as the 18th. And so, whether I actually communicated that to them, my recollection is that this all came out of a mutual understanding among the Israelis, Gen. Secord and myself, and probably Adm.

Poindexter and Mr. McFarlane—although Mr. McFarlane may well not have been aware of it specifically at this point because he was still overseas.

MR. NIELDS: How did you arrive at the figure of $1 million?

LT. COL. NORTH: I have no recollection of it at all, although we did see in the sensitive intelligence large quantities of money which were being moved to take this process forward. I confess not to be able to remember how the $1 million figure came up.

MR. NIELDS: Was the $1 million to cover both the transporting of arms from the US to Israel and from Israel to Iran or just one?

LT. COL. NORTH: Well, as I said just a moment ago, it was at least the latter and may well have, at this point in time, included both. I simply don't recall.

MR. NIELDS: Now our records reflect that $1 million was actually deposited into Lake Resources on the 20th of November, which is also earlier than Mr. Secord testified was the first time when he had any obligations whatever with respect to transporting merchandise. And I need to ask you this question. It's an important question. Was there any understanding or discussion that a million dollars would be deposited into the Lake Resources Account for the benefit of the contras?

LT. COL. NORTH: Not at that point, no. I don't—I do not recall a specific discussion of that until much later.

MR. NIELDS: And when was the conversation that you do recall?

LT. COL. NORTH: My sense is, it was some time in January, maybe even February, when the Israelis were asking, "What about the rest of the money that was originally put up for the November Hawk movement since we didn't do all that was going to be done, where is the rest of the money?" And I told him we'd used it for the purpose of the contras. And they acknowledged that.

MR. NIELDS: When you say acknowledged, you mean they acquiesced?

LT. COL. NORTH: No one ever came back and asked for it again.

MR. NIELDS: What was your authority for using that money for the contras?

LT. COL. NORTH: Well, I don't know that I actually had any, in specifics. By the end of January and early February, we had come to a conclusion that we were going to proceed to use funds generated by the sale of arms to Iran to support this initiative. And we came that—to that through a rather circuitous route. And if you'd like, I can lay that out for you. And it is important to the whole decision process on the use of residuals or profits.

MR. NIELDS: We will want to hear your testimony on that, I can assure you, but for the moment I'd like to stay with the $1 million. I take it the $1 million was used for the contras prior to mid-January of 1986.

LT. COL. NORTH: I don't know that—I—I don't know that it was actually done before—anything was actually bought for the resistance prior to any specific date. I don't know.

MR. NIELDS: But I take it that you do recall having a conversation with the Israelis sometime in January and telling them that the money had been used for the contras.

LT. COL. NORTH: Or was being used, words to that effect, yes.

MR. NIELDS: And I take it what you're saying now is that you had, with respect to that—the use of that million dollars for the contras, you had not sought or received any approval from people higher in the US government?

LT. COL. NORTH: I don't know that I did. I'm not saying I didn't. I think I may have apprised Admiral Poindexter at some point that I'd done that, but I did not—I do not have a specific recall of that at this point, no.

MR. NIELDS: But you are telling the Committee that you did not discuss with Mr. McFarlane or anyone else in the government, at the time the money was put into the Lake Resources account, that it was a contribution for the contras?

LT. COL. NORTH: No, in fact I specifically do not believe that the original intention of that money was. And if you're saying that you've got indication that on the 20th, the million dollars mentioned here is indeed deposited, I'm not going to debate that. I don't know when the money was actually put in or even if it was a million dollars. But I do know that we'd had a discussion with them about making that kind of a deposit. My recollection is, it was to be used to fund this transaction. It was a covert operation being funded through this mechanism.

MR. NIELDS: There is also an entry in your diaries on November the 24th—

CHAIRMAN INOUYE: Mr. Nields, before proceeding, I shall advise the panel that these documents have not been made available to the panel. They're still not declassified, so I hope you'll be very careful with them.

LT. COL. NORTH: Mr. Chairman, if I may, there is a name on that particular page that I believe we have an understanding will not be used. And I would ask please, sir, that before any of these documents are distributed outside the Committee, that that name be stricken from those documents.

CHAIRMAN INOUYE: At this—

LT. COL. NORTH: I'll give the name to you—

CHAIRMAN INOUYE: At this moment, there are only two documents available, one in your hands, and one in the hands of the counsel. After this questioning, these two will be collected and declassified and made public. And I can assure you that the name will not appear in public.

LT. COL. NORTH: Thank you, Mr. Chairman.

MR. NIELDS: There is a reference on a page of these notebooks, bearing the date of the 24th of November, you may turn to it if you wish, but I will tell you that it says, "Dick Copp spent 750K in"—the European country that you've been testifying about. It's dated November 24, at the top of the page.

LT. COL. NORTH: I see the entry, and that's certainly my handwriting.

MR. NIELDS: How did you get that information?

LT. COL. NORTH: Is the previous page that we're looking at part of the same—are they in sequence?

MR. NIELDS: I believe so.

LT. COL. NORTH: I guess I got that from someone who called me, and I—maybe it's him. I—was he in Portugal at that particular point in time, I guess is the question. And, I don't recall.

MR. NIELDS: What did he spend $750,000 on?

LT. COL. NORTH: I do not know. I mean, I cannot explain exactly what the entry means, other than the fact that he's got an entry that shows at 16:54, which is almost five o'clock in the afternoon on the 24th. I've got an entry that says that.

My sense is he was in the process of doing something with the money in support of this initiative, but I can't confirm that.

MR. NIELDS: Our—the Committee's records reflect no expenditures from the Lake Resources account other than one much smaller one for transportation costs, and my question to you is where did Mr. Secord get $750,000 to spend in the European country?

LT. COL. NORTH: Well, he, he had a great deal of money at various points in time in the Lake Resources account, and I'm not even sure that this $750,000 mentioned here is part of the same transaction. I mean, at the same point in time, we're talking about moving Hawks and assisting in what was originally an Israeli initiative with Iran. He has also been deeply engaged for a protracted period of time in the covert support of the Nicaraguan resistance, and so I don't find it inconsistent to have an entry there on that issue. He was, after all, in a country where we had moved significant supplies through that country in support of the Nicaraguan resistance.

I simply, Counsel, don't know exactly what that entry means at that point. What I am saying to you is that over a protracted period of time, he had indeed been spending large sums of money in that country for the purpose of supporting the Nicaraguan resistance, and that at some point in this period of time, I told him he ought to go ahead and use some of that money to support the Nicaraguan resistance. I don't know that that is specifically the point in time or that that is specifically that money.

MR. NIELDS: Are you aware of any other source of money that General Secord had available to him to spend in the European coutry?

LT. COL. NORTH: Absolutely. I mean he had—

MR. NIELDS: I mean other than Lake Resources money?

LT. COL. NORTH: I am not aware of any—well—there were a number of accounts set up as a part of this covert operation, and so there was money in accounts other than Lake Resources, I believe. The one principle account to receive monies in support of the covert operations was the Lake Resources account, at least as far as I knew. And so, there may well have been other accounts called other things—I hope we get to that sometime—but there may well have been other accounts that were set up for the purposes of buying munitions, clothing and the like for the Nicaraguan resistance. So, yes I am aware that there were other accounts. I do not know all of them. In fact, I didn't know many of them until these hearings started.

MR. NIELDS: When you say there were other accounts, are you referring to accounts other than those under the control of Mr. Hakim?

LT. COL. NORTH: Well, at this point in time I'd not even heard of Mr. Hakim, I don't believe. But certainly I believe that General Secord had a number of accounts set up in Europe by which the Nicaraguan resistance was being supported, yes. Certainly by November of 1985. And that those accounts were going—and I knew that those accounts were in one fashion or another supporting this covert operation.

MR. NIELDS: I'd like you to turn to an exhibit marked Exhibit 48. Do you have that in front of you?

LT. COL. NORTH: I do, yes.

MR. NIELDS: I take it that's a PROF message from you to Admiral Poindexter dated the 4th of December, 1985.

LT. COL. NORTH: That's correct.

MR. NIELDS: On the third page—and it discusses both the 18 Hawks that had been shipped and a proposal to ship other types of weapons to Iran for hostages in the near future. And on the third page at the first indented paragraph, it states, "In response to Cobb's demands for funds to be deposited in advance to defray operational costs at what the Iranians were told were purchases on the arms market a total of $41 million has been deposited." What does that refer to?

LT. COL. NORTH: I don't know. I would guess that may refer to money deposited in the Israeli account. But I don't know. At this point in time I can't recall what that means.

MR. NIELDS: Down toward the bottom of the page, at the end of the last full paragraph on the page are the words "All dollars are now under our control." What did you mean by that?

LT. COL. NORTH: I don't know. Maybe if I read the whole thing I can make sense of it. I haven't seen this in at least a couple of years, and I think it might help.

(Pause while Mr. North looks at documents)

LT. COL. NORTH: (off-mike due to network voice-over)

—at that point in time. I can't tell for sure. All I can think of is that all the dollars were now under the control of perhaps the US and Israel. I'm not sure, but without sitting down and going through all of which transpired in that particular period of time and maybe what happened just before it, I cannot tell you more specifically than that.

MR. NIELDS: Do you recall that there was a time when some 41 million dollars was, in fact, paid into Israeli accounts?

LT. COL. NORTH: I—I know there were periods of time in which a lot of money—(audio feed suddenly drops)—based on what they told me and others told me and what we read in sensitive intelligence, and I must admit to you that there were a number of times when we had considerable questions, the analysts and I, looking at what these things meant in terms of how much money various people were making on the arrangement. I do not recall this specific one. I—I suggested early on, when we first had a dialogue on this, that it would be helpful to get the original sensitive intelligence, and as yet, we still don't have that. What exactly I am referring to there under "all dollars are now under our control" I just cannot recall. I don't believe it necessarily means that all 41 million dollars that we had seen perhaps in sensitive intelligence was in a US account. I don't believe that that ever hit a US covert account of any kind.

MR. NIELDS: Okay. I'd like to switch to the topic of what precisely it was that was being moved from Israel to Iran. I take it it was Hawk missiles.

LT. COL. NORTH: Yes.

MR. NIELDS: And what was the original quantity? Was there a time when the proposal was to ship six hundred Hawk missiles to Iran?

LT. COL. NORTH: I don't know what the original arrangement was, and I want to go—I'm not relying on sensitive intelligence because I can't remember it, but we saw a number of proposals being made in the time frame late September, early October, all the way through October and into November—a number of proposals having been advanced by the Israelis with the Iranians, and I—there were—I think the—the final number that I remember that we had some control over was a hundred and twenty, and that may even be high. It might have been as low as eighty. I don't recall us agreeing to something as high as that. I—but again, I may have my memory refreshed.

MR. NIELDS: Let's take the hundred and twenty. Were these Hawks that were already in Israeli stocks?

LT. COL. NORTH: It was my understanding—again, having been thrown into this on the night of November 17th—it was my understanding that everything at that point in time was coming from Israeli stocks.

MR. NIELDS: Was it your understanding that any of those stocks had very recently been supplied by the United States?

LT. COL. NORTH: I don't recall that that was ever discussed.

MR. NIELDS: Were you aware of any relatively contemporaneous shipments of Hawk missiles from the United States to Israel?

LT. COL. NORTH: I don't think so. I mean, you may refresh my memory again, but I do not know at this point in time that I knew that. No.

MR. NIELDS: I think you've testified that there were operational problems with this shipment, and I take it one of the operational problems was that there was difficulty in obtaining landing rights in the European country.

LT. COL. NORTH: Yes.

MR. NIELDS: And that was one of the reasons that—that Mr. Secord was sent to the European country?

LT. COL. NORTH: That's correct.

MR. NIELDS: And I take it that the problem of—of obtaining those landing rights turned into a diplomatic problem, among others.

LT. COL. NORTH: It did.

MR. NIELDS: And two things were done by you in order to help solve that. One of them was to contact Mr. McFarlane?

LT. COL. NORTH: That's right.

MR. NIELDS: And you asked him to make a call to the Foreign Minister of the European country?

LT. COL. NORTH: I don't know that it was necessarily the Foreign Minister. It might have been another official. But I did ask him to be in touch with an official of that foreign country, yes.

MR. NIELDS: And the other thing that you did was to involve officials at the CIA?

LT. COL. NORTH: I think we did use communications support from the CIA, that's correct.

MR. NIELDS: Well you, in fact, you contacted Mr. Claridge, didn't you?

LT. COL. NORTH: Yes, I did.

MR. NIELDS: And in fact, you went out to the CIA and spent virtually all the day Saturday there.

LT. COL. NORTH: What was that date?

MR. NIELDS: I believe it's the 23rd. You might want to check Exhibit 46.

(pause while they look at documents)

LT. COL. NORTH: That is correct.

MR. NIELDS: You spent most of the day on the 23rd at the CIA?

LT. COL. NORTH: Yes.

MR. NIELDS: And that was with Mr. Claridge?

LT. COL. NORTH: I'm sure that it was with Mr. Claridge —perhaps others—but he certainly did clear me in because his signature is right there.

MR. NIELDS: And indeed, you returned to the CIA the following day?

LT. COL. NORTH: On Sunday? I'll take your word for it. I did.

MR. NIELDS: And you are now looking at the second page of Exhibit 46, which I take it is another sign-in sheet at the CIA for Sunday.

LT. COL. NORTH: That's correct.

MR. NIELDS: And Mr. Claridge and you were in touch with the Embassy—the US Embassy in the European country?

LT. COL. NORTH: I don't recall specifically talking to the embassy, no. I know that there were discussions that were held, and I know that there were—there was message traffic exchanged. That's correct.

MR. NIELDS: Cable traffic?

LT. COL. NORTH: Yes.

MR. NIELDS: And the purpose of the cable traffic was to try to obtain from the officials in the European country the rights to land a plane carrying the missiles?

LT. COL. NORTH: That is correct.

MR. NIELDS: And they were then going to be taken off that

85

plane and loaded onto other planes to be transported on to Iran?

LT. COL. NORTH: Yes.

MR. NIELDS: And at some point, through Mr. McFarlane, you heard that the foreign country was going to permit the plane to land.

LT. COL. NORTH: As I recall, that's—that was, at one point, approved.

MR. NIELDS: But there was a problem because there was a condition, isn't that true? Isn't it true that the foreign country—

LT. COL. NORTH: There was a condition. I don't remember what it was right now.

MR. NIELDS: Isn't it true that the foreign country wanted us to acknowledge in writing—

LT. COL. NORTH: Yes.

MR. NIELDS: —what it was that was landing?

LT. COL. NORTH: That's right.

MR. NIELDS: The actual materiel.

LT. COL. NORTH: Yes.

MR. NIELDS: The Hawks.

LT. COL. NORTH: Right.

MR. NIELDS: And we weren't willing to do that.

LT. COL. NORTH: Not at all.

MR. NIELDS: Now did you discuss that with Mr. Claridge?

LT. COL. NORTH: I do not recall exactly what I discussed with Mr. Claridge. I know that there was a point in time where he certainly did become aware, and it may be through sensitive intelligence because the intelligence showed what was being moved. And I did at some point along there confirm to him that it was not oil drilling equipment, but that it was Hawks—as was very obvious to almost everybody out there at that point, because they were reading the same sensitive intelligence that I was. But I don't—when I say "that point" —I don't know exactly what point it is. But I did, at some point, confirm to him that that's what was taking place. And that—and it may have been after the fact, I'm not saying it was before the fact—and at that point Mr. McMahon was very upset with me.

MR. NIELDS: Now, at what point was Mr. McMahon very upset with you?

LT. COL. NORTH: As I recall, it was after the pilots returned from their mission or in which he saw a part of the sensitive intelligence, and I don't recall the specific timing, but it was at that point that we began to work on the finding with Mr. Sporkin, I think.

MR. NIELDS: Well, the record reflects that the finding was transmitted by Director Casey in a cover memo dated the 26th of November, that's Tuesday.

LT. COL. NORTH: Okay. So it would be in that time frame, I would guess.

MR. NIELDS: You're talking that day or earlier?

LT. COL. NORTH: Well, yes, as a matter of fact one of the things—I don't recall it specifically—but one of the things I may have done on that Sunday would have been to work on the finding, but I would guess the finding didn't actually begin until later on.

MR. NIELDS: The Committee's other information would indicate that the finding began on a Monday.

LT. COL. NORTH: Okay.

MR. NIELDS: But I'd like to take you back to the Friday/Saturday period of time when efforts were being made to obtain the landing rights in the European country and you ran into a snag because we were unwilling to identify the materiel in writing. I guess first I would like to ask you, "Was it your understanding that the materiel had not been identified orally?"

LT. COL. NORTH: To whom?

MR. NIELDS: To the foreign government officials?

LT. COL. NORTH: I'm not sure that I ever had a particular understanding as to what the foreign officials ever did know about that and I guess at some point, General Secord may have told me what he told them he knew because I had briefed him before he left, but I don't know what he or the US government people on scene actually told the foreign officials.

MR. NIELDS: Well, you can't land 120 or, let's say, 80 Hawk missiles in a jumbo jet, unload it, store it, and then put it back on three small planes at an airport, without people there knowing that you're transporting something other oil-drilling equipment, can you?

LT. COL. NORTH: Well, it depends on what they're packed

87

in, but I mean, what you've just hit on is one of the reasons why we were so concerned with this whole operation to begin with.

MR. NIELDS: Well, what I'm asking is—

LT. COL. NORTH: There were major problems operationally in this thing, right from the start, and what bothered me most of all, and I think I communicated that fairly clearly to my superiors, is, "Here. Fix it," and the thing is already on fire then and they throw the bag to you and you know what's in the bag. It's a serious problem.

MR. NIELDS: But my question to you is, when you suggested to Mr. McFarlane that he obtain approval from the foreign government official, are you telling it that it was your understanding that Mr. . . . Mr. McFarlane wasn't going to mention what he was asking approval for?

LT. COL. NORTH: I was going to leave that up to Mr. McFarlane's judgment. He knew what was on that airplane. I knew what was in the airplane. I am asking him to talk to the foreign official to get permission for him to get the airplane on the ground. I mean, I didn't—I don't think I made a recommendation one way or the other when I communicated with him.

MR. NIELDS: In any event, Mr. Claridge during this period of time is sending cables back and forth to the embassy in the foreign country on this same issue, and my question—

LT. COL. NORTH: I take it that he was. I'm not sure that I ever saw any of those cables, but I may have.

MR. NIELDS: Well, I don't want to go over them one by one, but there are a number of them which have been marked Exhibits, and they are #61, #62, #63, #64, #65, #66, #67, #68, and #69. You needn't read them because my question is going to be the same. My question is going to be, was Mr. Claridge aware at the time when he was responsible for sending cables back and forth on this issue, that the thing had run aground because we were unwilling to identify the cargo in writing?

LT. COL. NORTH: And, I cannot answer that question because I don't know.

MR. NIELDS: Do you—are you saying you don't know or you don't recall?

LT. COL. NORTH: Well, the way you asked your question

is, "Was Mr. Claridge aware," and I don't recall when Mr. Claridge became aware. I do recall confirming to him at some point that it was not oil-drilling equipment, that it was Hawks, and it was my understanding that at that point, he talked to either the director of operations or to the deputy director, who became angry, and I think there may be a contemporaneous note in my notebooks to that effect.

MR. NIELDS: In other words, you're saying that you told Mr. Claridge what the real cargo was prior to the time the deputy director got angry and insisted on a finding?

LT. COL. NORTH: I'm not saying that for sure. I'm saying that's the way it may well have happened. I do recall, although I do not recall the time and date, confirming to Mr. Claridge when asked, "The cargo is not oil-drilling equipment. The cargo is Hawks." I cannot tell you, Mr. Nields, here at this point, a good while after the fact when that point was.

MR. NIELDS: But, I take it you're saying it was very close in time to when a shipment actually was sent. And your best recollection is that it was prior to the time that the Deputy Director hit the roof, so to speak?

LT. COL. NORTH: Yes. I mean, my recollection is that's why he hit the roof.

MR. NIELDS: Now, I'm going to return to the question of what officials knew about this shipment in a moment. Before I do, I want to return to the question of why only 18 Hawks were sent, and there were no further shipments. Was it part of the agreement, as you understood it, that all of the hostages would be released before the plane carrying missiles arrived in Teheran?

LT. COL. NORTH: I don't recall exactly what the arrangement was. You know, having been through a number of these iterations with the Iranians themselves, with their intermediary, with the Israeli agent Ghorbanifar, with all of those actors, I would find it to be inconsistent with what happened for the following year in these transactions to believe that the Iranians had agreed to something like that. But having not been a party to that original agreement, it is much more likely that there was a phased step-by-step arrangement made, because that's the way it worked in every proposal and in every transaction that ever occurred after that.

MR. NIELDS: Exhibit 43 is a PROF message that you sent on the 20th of November to Mr. Poindexter. And on the second page, you describe this transaction. And in the middle of the first full paragraph, you say, "No aircraft will land in Tabriz until the AMCITs have been delivered to the embassy."

LT. COL. NORTH: Where was that again?

MR. NIELDS: It's in the middle of the first full paragraph. Take your time, if you want. My question is going to be, having read that, does that refresh your recollection in any way, that that was the understanding at the time?

LT. COL. NORTH: Well, that is clearly what someone had told me. And I don't know whether that was the Israelis or whether that was what I was reading out of sensitive intelligence, or whether that was relayed back to me by Gen. Secord. And it could have been all of the above. That was not something that I had negotiated. It was simply something I was reporting back up the line.

MR. NIELDS: Did that provide a reason not to continue with any further shipments of Hawks? I take it no hostages came out after the—before the plane landed?

LT. COL. NORTH: No. There was no one released in November.

MR. NIELDS: Did that provide a reason to stop shipments?

LT. COL. NORTH: Well, it may have. But what I'm saying —what I was told, okay, in the midst of this thing was, "The reason we're stopping is because the Iranians are so upset with the product that they have received." And the product that they had received, I was told—and there was apparently some confirmation to that in the sensitive intelligence, is that they'd been told they were going to get super Hawks or something, and what they got was plain old Hawks, and they were upset.

MR. NIELDS: I understand that, and we appreciate your testimony, and I'm going to continue to ask questions to see whether it jogs any other recollections. And I take it that the fact that the hostages didn't come out is not, to the best of your recollection, the reason why the shipment stopped?

LT. COL. NORTH: No. But again, I am not—I don't think I was fully aware of the arrangement that had been made at that time.

MR. NIELDS: Okay, now again referring to the November 20th PROF message, on paragraph further down, you discussed the subject of replenishment, and at the end of the paragraph you say, "I have further told them,"—that's the Israelis—"that we will make no effort to move on their purchase LOA request," and that's their purchase order, I take it, for replenishment Hawks—

LT. COL. NORTH: Yes.

MR. NIELDS: (Continues reading from Exhibit)—"until we have all five AMCITs safely delivered."

LT. COL. NORTH: Yes.

MR. NIELDS: Now, the AMCITs were not delivered.

LT. COL. NORTH: No.

MR. NIELDS: Therefore you had no obligation under this particular promise to replenish, and I'm asking, did the Israelis stop making shipments because they realized that they had no guarantee of replenishment?

LT. COL. NORTH: I don't know. I—again, I'm looking at this for the first time in a long time. Did I—my memory is jogged a little bit. One of the problems that we came up with, that somewhere in this time frame—was the fact that you couldn't do it that way. And I got a very quick education in what an LOA was and how it worked, and the AECA, and the need for findings, and all the rest of that over the course of that period of time between the 17th and the 26th, and it was a rather intense education.

MR. NIELDS: That was going to be my next question. Did we call a halt to this thing because people in the Department of Defense told you, or others at the NSC, that the transactions were illegal?

LT. COL. NORTH: No, I think the—what I was getting a sense for, Counsel, was the fact that, look we don't know what arrangements were made, what promises were made, but you can't do it this way. And I can remember a conversation with someone over there, and it may have been Mr. Cook or it may have been General Powell, say, "Look, Ollie, you can't go and you can't have them just go in and submit a new bill." I remember one point the Israelis were talking about making a cash transaction. Well, I didn't know it, but they—DOD quickly informed me that's not how it's done. And thus, we came back to the CIA route, and ultimately the finding, and having the stuff you purchased by the CIA from the DOD under the Economy Act. That's the routing of it, and it's not a sinister thing. It was simply ignorance on my part that assumed you could do it with an LOA.

MR. NIELDS: But, we've had tesimony from DOD officials before this committee, that not only was the replenishment a problem, but the transfer by the Israelis to the Iranians was itself a violation of the Arms Export Control Act, and our consent to it was similarly a violation. Now, was that brought to your attention at the time?

LT. COL. NORTH: No, but what was—in fact, I don't think anybody—well, you'll probably find something different, but I don't remember anybody saying, "Ollie, what was done is wrong." But, I do remember some, you know, at some point in here, saying, "Look, you had a Presidential decision back in July that authorized this thing. The way you North are trying to go about this, by making it a covert buy under a normal foreign assistance sale isn't right. The way to do it is to make a purchase under the Economy Act from the CIA, or the CIA buys it from the Pentagon and that's the way to do it."

What I'm saying, it wasn't a matter of someone trying to evade or avoid. It was a matter of getting this kid smart because I'd been given the job of replenishing, and so that's the way we went about doing it.

MR. NIELDS: Okay. Just to make sure my question is clear, and there are two of them.

LT. COL. NORTH: Yeah.

MR. NIELDS: One is, to your recollection, did—was this transaction halted in midstream because the Israelis got cold feet because they didn't think they were going to get replenishments?

LT. COL. NORTH: No. My recollection at this point in time is it was stopped solely because the product delivered was not what the buyer wanted. That's my recollection. And, that was the big problem, and it became a problem to get them back out of there.

MR. NIELDS: You've also testified that the deputy director at the CIA hit the roof, and insisted—

LT. COL. NORTH: Your word.

MR. NIELDS: —and insisted —you used some expression

like that—and that the CIA decided that a finding was required.

LT. COL. NORTH: That's correct.

MR. NIELDS: Did the delay in getting the finding signed provide a reason to halt shipments?

LT. COL. NORTH: No because I was led to believe, and I can't recall exactly how, but at that point in time that the President had made a finding, had made a decision back in July that authorized us to proceed. I was then in a meeting with Admiral Poindexter or on the telephone with Admiral Poindexter to confirm that this shipment should go forward, and I have a contemporaneous note that the President redecided at that point to let this go forward, and so the problem that you see here is one of North having been given—in addition to, "Get this stuff over there" —then finding out it wasn't the buyers product that he wanted, now has a replenishment problem for the original 508 that he didn't know he started with, and the whole thing is now stopped dead, cold. And, that's basically where we were by the early part of January. With 18 Hawks sitting over there, 508 Hawks owed to the Israelis, the whole project dead in the water, and people concerned.

MR. NIELDS: Did you become aware of some kind of—

LT. COL. NORTH: Correct the record, sir. It was 508 TOWs, not Hawks.

MR. NIELDS: Did you become aware at some point during this time that there was some kind of an investigation or a scandal or a problem in Israel that had to do with halting further shipments?

LT. COL. NORTH: Not that I recall now. Not that I recall that I knew then. But there was some discussion many many weeks later as to perhaps that had—and, when I say "weeks later", it may be months later—that that did have something to do with it. But, I did not even know about it at the time.

MR. NIELDS: When you say that the buyer was unhappy with the merchandise, did this have to do with the fact that the missiles were Hawks, or was it the kind of Hawk?

LT. COL. NORTH: Well, again, I'm not a Hawk expert, but General Secord explained it to me, and I think he actually explained it to Mr. McFarlane and Admiral Poindexter at one point, but apparently what the Israelis had told Ghorbanifar, and Ghorbanifar had told the Iranians, and I don't know who's to blame; I'm not trying to assess that. From what we saw in the sensitive intelligence, and what we were told by subsequent interviews with the Iranians themselves, who I sat down and talked with, is they were promised something that would shoot down airplanes at 60, 70,000 feet, in excess of that, specifically Soviet reconnaissance flights and Iraqi bombers at high altitude. Those were—I was told that's what they were looking for as a weapons system to deal with that. Clearly, the Hawk system, in any version was inadequate to that task, and they expected to get some product that was different from the one they received, and I am told that that is why they were unhappy, and why the program stopped at that point.

MR. NIELDS: Who, in the NSC, besides yourself, if anyone, was dealing with officials at the Department of Defense on the replenishment issue?

LT. COL. NORTH: The only other person I know for sure was dealing with DOD on that is Admiral Poindexter and, I guess, Mr. McFarlane, but I—I know that I had to go to Admiral Poindexter a couple of times and say, "Hey, look, I'm having a problem here with A, B, or C, and can you help?" And he would either call or write or whatever that was done, and then I'd get a call back and we'd get on with it.

MR. NIELDS: Was that the case with respect to this Hawk replenishment issue?

LT. COL. NORTH: Yeah, again, I—I'm having a hard time recalling exactly what was transpiring at the time. I know I was inquiring at the DOD probably about both the cost and the method for replenishing the Hawks, which had been shipped in September—a problem I hadn't even known about until November—and replenishing and replacing Hawks, which looked to me to be a very big problem, both in terms of dollars and in size and weight, visibility. The whole thing was just a nightmare.

MR. NIELDS: And who had authorized you to go to the Department of Defense and seek replenishment of the Hawks?

LT. COL. NORTH: Admiral Poindexter and Mr. McFarlane. I didn't—I did not go to the Pentagon, nor would they have answered me when I called if I didn't have authority. I'm sorry, were you talking about replenishment of Hawks or TOWs or both?

MR. NIELDS: Hawks.

LT. COL. NORTH: I would guess it—it was the same authority for both.

MR. NIELDS: Admiral Poindexter or Mr. McFarlane?

LT. COL. NORTH: Yes.

MR. NIELDS: Do you know whether either of them communicated directly with the Department of Defense officials on the issue of replenishment of Hawks?

LT. COL. NORTH: I do not, and I—and I do not know that they ever communicated direct—for sure that they communicated directly on the issue of TOWs, but I would like to point out that if a Marine lieutenant colonel called the Pentagon this afternoon and asked for 500 TOWs to be shipped overseas and he didn't have a little more backing than oak leaves on his collar, they'd come and collar him and take him away. So I—I mean, I had authority to do that, Counsel. I—I want to you understand that. I don't—I don't know exactly who called who, but I was talking to General Colin Powell, who is the aide to Secretary Weinberger. At various points, I talked to Mr. Koch. I eventually ended up talking to Mr. Armitage, and then when we finally got around to doing it the right way with through the Economy Act, in fact the only way it was ever done. I was talking with CIA logisticians and logisticians out at the Pentagon.

MR. NIELDS: So what you're saying is that somebody, either Admiral Poindexter or Mr. McFarlane, gave you the authority to go to DOD and seek replenishment?

LT. COL. NORTH: Yes.

MR. NIELDS: Do you recall reporting to one or both of them concerning your contacts with DOD on the subject of Hawks?

LT. COL. NORTH: I recall reporting to both of them voluminously about this whole problem.

MR. NIELDS: All right, you're getting into my—

LT. COL. NORTH: You've probably got the records and I don't, so—

MR. NIELDS: You're getting into the next area I want to take up, which is, who in the government was aware of the

Hawk transaction at the time that it occurred? And I take it you were aware?

LT. COL. NORTH: I was aware.

MR. NIELDS: Admiral Poindexter was aware?

LT. COL. NORTH: Yes, he was.

MR. NIELDS: Mr. McFarlane was aware?

LT. COL. NORTH: Correct.

MR. NIELDS: Now you've already given some testimony about Dewey Claridge, I'd like to ask you a few more questions about that. And I'd like you to turn to a page from your spiral notebooks, which again are Exhibits 69A, and this one is dated the 25th of November.

LT. COL. NORTH: Dated again, sir?

MR. NIELDS: The 25th of November, but I'm actually going to ask you to take a look at the last entry on the 24th of November first.

MR. SULLIVAN: We seem to go from 28 October to 1 December.

MR. NIELDS: I think—there are a number of pages that are—that have the wrong months on them, and I suspect that's what you're dealing with. I think 28th October is actually 28th November, so move backwards.

(Pause while looking for exhibit)

MR. SULLIVAN: What's the writing on it?

MR. NIELDS: On the 24th it's the last page that has the 24th as the date on it, and at the top it's "Dick Copp."

(Pause while looking for exhibit)

Do you have that in front of you?

LT. COL. NORTH: I have a 24 November, 16:54 Dick Copp.

MR. NIELDS: Okay, down in the middle of the page there's an entry, "18:52", you see that?

LT. COL. NORTH: I do.

MR. NIELDS: I take it that's 6:52 P.M.?

LT. COL. NORTH: Right.

MR. NIELDS: And in your handwriting it says, "Called to from Claridge."

LT. COL. NORTH: Yes.

MR. NIELDS: Dash—I take it this is a conversation with Claridge?

LT. COL. NORTH: Apparently so, yes. And it must have been on the telephone.

MR. NIELDS: And it says then, "no manifesto provided"—

LT. COL. NORTH: I think that's probably "manifests."

MR. NIELDS: Excuse me, manifests, "George says that they have hope of talking way out."

First of all, do you know what that refers to?

LT. COL. NORTH: If I knew—if I could remember who George was, that would help. I'm not trying to be flippant about that. I don't remember. There's a telephone number written below it for it for George, that's apparently a US number.

MR. NIELDS: Well, I think—

LT. COL. NORTH: My sense is that that's talking about—

MR. NIELDS: I think we won't mention his last name. But I think he's a CIA official. And I'm going to ask you whether the conversation doesn't have to do with the plane?

LT. COL. NORTH: Well, I would—I certainly sense that it has to do with the aircraft, and I would guess that the "no manifests provided" is a call from a person. In fact, if the George is in the air branch, that would indicate to me that he had called and said, you know, "This thing is still very screwed up. There's no manifests. Now what are you going to do?" And—

MR. NIELDS: So this is information that's coming from Mr. Claridge to you?

LT. COL. NORTH: Well, either that or I called—it says, if you'll note my note up above, "18:52, called to" and then "from Dewey Claridge." There may have been a series of phone calls back and forth, and I don't know which is which.

MR. NIELDS: Well regardless of who's calling whom, the information is flowing from the CIA to you?

LT. COL. NORTH: Apparently so. Yes.

MR. NIELDS: And they're saying that they have hope of talking their way out. I take it these are the people who are flying the plane carrying the Hawks?

LT. COL. NORTH: My guess is that's correct. Yes.

MR. NIELDS: And they've got to talk their way out.

LT. COL. NORTH: Talk their way out of wherever they're stuck, if that's what's happened.

MR. NIELDS: They're stuck at a landing point between Israel and Iran, I take it.

LT. COL. NORTH: I don't recall the event, but I'm —undoubtedly everything else having gone wrong with this, that went wrong, too. Yes.

MR. NIELDS: Well my question is, when you had this conversation with Mr. Claridge about no manifests and the people flying the plane are going to have to talk their way out of it, did Mr. Claridge know at that time what they were talking their way out of?

LT. COL. NORTH: They're talking—my guess is what that refers to is that they're going to talk their way out of the airfield. They're going to—you know, "we don't have a manifest. I'm sorry. We're carrying" —whatever it was they were saying at the time—"And we'll be leaving now." Kind of talk their way out of it.

MR. NIELDS: My question is, at that point in time, was Mr. Claridge yet aware of the nature of the cargo?

LT. COL. NORTH: By the 24th? I do not know.

MR. NIELDS: Turn the page, if you would. It says "25 November" at the top.

LT. COL. NORTH: Right.

MR. NIELDS: "7:20 A.M. call from Dewey" —do you have that in front of you?

LT. COL. NORTH: I do.

MR. NIELDS: This is a call from Claridge, I take it.

LT. COL. NORTH: Right.

MR. NIELDS: And you're taking notes of what he's saying to you?

LT. COL. NORTH: Yes.

MR. NIELDS: And are there—just answer this question yes or no, please. Are there words circled?

LT. COL. NORTH: There are.

MR. NIELDS: Okay. Don't mention the words that are circled.

LT. COL. NORTH: Understood.

MR. NIELDS: It says "aircraft," does it not?

LT. COL. NORTH: Right. Blank "have told us to us to use" blank, blank.

MR. NIELDS: And then it says, "Cargo must be listed as machine parts, spares for oil industry."

LT. COL. NORTH: Right.

MR. NIELDS: Now that's Mr. Claridge telling you.

LT. COL. NORTH: Again, I—by—I told you that I had

98

originally dissembled with the Agency. In my initial contacts with the Israelis, we agreed that we would call these machine parts for the oil fields, or whatever. That we specifically talked about, went —in my discussions with the Israelis way back on the 17th or 18th, that was the agreement we had come to. So I—you know, I had told people at the CIA that.

MR. NIELDS: My understanding—

LT. COL. NORTH: You're asking me if I have by now told Mr. Claridge the truth about what's on that cargo. And I cannot tell you, counsel, when it was that I apprised him of it.

MR. NIELDS: Or that he found out from some other source? My question is, why would—if Mr. Claridge is telling you—telling you—that the cargo must be listed as machine parts spares for oil industry, does that indicate that he was then aware of what the real cargo was?

LT. COL. NORTH: Not necessarily to me, because what that may indicate is that he has made arrangements with the people in the circles through his station chiefs for a clearance with a manifest that reads a certain way. And what he's telling me is to back through Copp—Gen. Secord—and make darn sure that the proprietary is instructed accordingly. I'm not sure what point—I'm trying to answer questions in a very straightforward manner. I don't know what question we're trying to answer here.

MR. NIELDS: You've answered it. I think you've said that you do not know, from looking at this note, one way or the other, whether Mr. Claridge was yet aware.

LT. COL. NORTH: That's correct. But I do want you to know that there came a point in time when I confirmed to him with integrity and honesty, yes, that's what's aboard there.

CHAIRMAN INOUYE: Do you think this would be a good time to take a recess?

MR. NIELDS: I have about five more minutes on this topic, Mr. Chairman, and I will abide by the Committee's wishes.

CHAIRMAN INOUYE: Please proceed.

MR. NIELDS: Again on the subject of who was aware of the shipment at the time it occurred, was the President aware of the shipment at the time it occurred?

CHAIRMAN INOUYE: I do not know. I was told that the President had approved it. I have a contemporaneous note to that effect.

MR. NIELDS: In one of your notebooks?

LT. COL. NORTH: Yes, sir.

MR. NIELDS: And was Mr. Casey aware of it at the time it occurred?

LT. COL. NORTH: I believe he was. If he was not aware of it at that instant, it was only because he was on a trip; and I don't recall whether he had returned by this point or not. But shortly thereafter, he was fully aware because he and I met several times on the issue, and it was he who sent forward the original finding which Mr. Sporkin prepared.

MR. NIELDS: So you met with him on this topic, i.e., the shipment of the 18 Hawks, shortly after the shipment occurred?

LT. COL. NORTH: I believe it was afterwards, yes, sir.

MR. NIELDS: But it might have been before?

LT. COL. NORTH: It may have been. I'd have to check to see when Mr Casey returned from his trip. I know that he was gone. He was not in the country, or at least not available when this whole thing began, on or about the 17th or 18th.

MR. NIELDS: You mentioned earlier the Attorney General. Was the Attorney General aware at the time that Hawks were being shipped?

LT. COL. NORTH: I was told—at least I understood. I don't know if I was told, but I understood that he was because it was through that effort that we ended getting on the right track for the finding. And that was—I think we went searching for some kind of previous Attorney General's determination or legal opinion on the use of a finding for these purposes. And it was my understanding, I think, then and it is now that these circumstances were explained to him. I thought that he had seen and approved the November finding, and he had provided an explanation for why this was a legitimate way to go about doing it. All this, at approximately the 25th or 26th, and all findings are reviewed by the Attorney General. And that finding, which eventually got signed by the President, I thought had been seen by the Attorney General, and I thought it was the Attorney General who had provided the earlier French

Smith determination on the legitimacy of this process. I also believed that it was the Attorney General who had —something to the effect—said, look, if the President made a mental finding back in July or June or whatever it was, that that can simpy be ratified by this later finding. And that's why those words were put into the finding that Mr. Sporkin and I worked on. But I did not talk to the Attorney General directly about it, nor did I talk to the President directly about it.

MR. NIELDS: Okay, I want to be clear about that. You did not have a conversation with the Attorney General on this subject at or about the time it occurred?

LT. COL. NORTH: I don't recall one, no.

MR. NIELDS: What is the basis for your belief that he approved the finding in November?

LT. COL. NORTH: Well, he—all other findings were brought to the Attorney General for his—uh—certification, I guess, for the legitimacy of it. I personally carried the January findings to him, and I believe that this finding went through that same kind of a process. But I can't confirm it.

MR. NIELDS: Do you believe that because someone told you it happened, or because it's normal procedure?

LT. COL. NORTH: I believe it's both, but I can't recall the specific conversation. What I am building for you is a description of various things that happened along the way that—that we ended up with a finding to begin with. That the way I had been going about trying to fix the problem was not going to work, and that we ended up going with the finding to fix the problem. And even then, we ended up having to go back and change it.

MR. NIELDS: Just so that the record is clear on this, it was your understanding that as a matter of procedure, the Attorney General signed off on all findings and you have a general recollection of hearing that he did it in this case, but not a specific one? Is that—

LT. COL. NORTH: I do not have a specific one in this case, no.

MR. NIELDS: Do you have a general recollection of being told that the Attorney General had signed off on this finding?

LT. COL. NORTH: Yes, I have a general recollection because

it was in that timeframe that I was apprised of Attorney General French Smith's earlier determination that this was the way to go about doing it.

MR. NIELDS: Now when you say "this," isn't it true that Attorney General French Smith's prior opinion related to using an intelligence finding as a way of transferring?

LT. COL. NORTH: Yes, that's what I'm talking about.

MR. NIELDS: And so what your—and your recollection is that that William French Smith opinion was discussed and known to you at or about the time of the November finding?

LT. COL. NORTH: Yes.

MR. NIELDS: Final question before we break. Do you know why the missiles were originally supposed to be flown to Tabriz and were in fact flown to Tehran?

LT. COL. NORTH: No.

MR. NIELDS: Thank you Mr. Chairman.

CHAIRMAN INOUYE: The hearing will stand in recess for 10 minutes.

(Recess)

MR. NIELDS: Col. North, I asked you before we broke about a number of particular individuals, whether they were aware of the Hawk shipments in November of 1985. Are there any other officials of the United States government who were aware of the Hawk shipments in November of 1985?

LT. COL. NORTH: I think I've given you the list that I believed—who have been aware.

MR. NIELDS: Were any officials at the Department of Defense aware that 18 Hawk missiles, or some number of Hawk missiles had actually been shipped by Israel to Iran?

LT. COL. NORTH: I—again, I believe that they may have —excuse me, I believe that they may well have been because I think I made several efforts to coordinate with them, the replenishment of Hawks—excuse me, of—yes, of the Hawks. I think I had a discussion, if I remember properly, with DOD officials about both Hawks and TOWs. And he wouldn't be asking him about Hawks, if they hadn't already been ordered up as a—a need for replenishing. But—I'm a little concerned I'm leaving the wrong impression because I—I honestly think that all of us who are engaged in this activity, were looking for the right way of doing things. That there was no intent to avoid—to in any way violate the

102

Arms Export Control Act. And that if there was confusion within the DOD over how I was going about it was because of my own ignorance in not knowing the right way to start. I want to come back to the finding issue, as why we arrived at, using the Economy Act procedures for that whole business. Much of the confusion that may exist out there may simply have been because when this kid was told to find a way to replenish things, I didn't know how to go about doing it. And, in fact, it wasn't until the latter part of January that a real methodology was proposed.

MR. NIELDS: I just want to make sure. My question is simply, who in the Department of Defense was told that there had actually been a shipment, if anybody?

LT. COL. NORTH: An unrefreshed, long time ago, memory would tell me that I probably talked about that delivery with Mr. Koch, possibly with General Powell, possibly with Mr. Armitage.

MR. NIELDS: How about Mr. Regan?

LT. COL. NORTH: I did not discuss this with Mr. Regan.

MR. NIELDS: The Vice President?

LT. COL. NORTH: Not with the Vice President.

MR. NIELDS: Anyone else you can think of?

LT. COL. NORTH: No.

MR. NIELDS: Col. North, I'm going to shift topics now, and ask you some questions about the support of the contras. And, I take it that prior to some time in the fall of 1984, CIA was principally responsible for our support of the contras, and sometime in October of 1984, Congress passed what has been referred to in these hearings and elsewhere as the Boland Amendment, which provided that no funds available to Department of Defense or the CIA or any other Department or Agency involved in intelligence activities may be spent in support of the contras' military or paramilitary effort. I haven't finished my question yet.

LT. COL. NORTH: I know. May I just address one question to you, sir? Are we going to come back to what eventually happens on replenishment, on Hawks, TOWs and other things? Because I think it's important. I mean, if we really want to get what I did and what I know others did in that process, I think it's important that we eventually come back to that.

MR. NIELDS: You can—you can rely on it.

103

LT. COL. NORTH: Thank you. Okay.

MR. NIELDS: But, I would like to turn for the moment to the subject of the contras, following the enactment of the Boland Amendment, and I think there has been some evidence here that, in explaining the meaning of the Amendment to the House of Representatives immediately prior to its enactment, Congressman Boland himself stated that this ended US support for the war in Nicaragua. I take it that that turned out not to be the case? That our support continued and indeed to a considerable degree, you managed it, following the enactment of the Boland Amendment? That's a question.

LT. COL. NORTH: What was the question?

MR. NIELDS: Is it correct to say that following the enactment of the Boland Amendment, our support for the war in Nicaragua did not end, and that you were the person in the United States government who managed it?

LT. COL. NORTH: Starting in the spring of 1984, well before the Boland proscription of no appropriated funds made available to the DOD or the CIA, etcetera, I was already engaged in supporting the Nicaraguan resistance and a democratic outcome in Nicaragua. I did so as a part of a covert operation that was carried out starting as early as the spring of '84 when we ran out of money, and people started to look in Nicaragua, in Honduras, in Guatemala, in El Salvador and Costa Rica for some sign of what the Americans were really going to do. And that help began much earlier than the most rigorous of the Boland proscriptions. And, yes, it was carried out covertly, and it was carried out in such a way as to ensure that the heads of state and the political leadership in Nicaragua—in Central America—recognized was going to meet the commitments of the President's foreign policy. And the President's foreign policy was that we are going to achieve a democratic outcome in Nicaragua, and that our support for the Nicaraguan freedom fighters was going to continue; and that I was given the job of holding them together in body and soul. And it slowly transitioned into a more difficult task as time went on, and as the CIA had to withdraw further and further from that support until finally we got to the point in October when I was the only person left talking to them.

MR. NIELDS: You're talking about now October of 1984?

LT. COL. NORTH: Yes, sir.

MR. NIELDS: Yes. That was my question. Following October of 1984, was the US government support for the war in Nicaragua managed by you? That was the only question.

LT. COL. NORTH: The US contact with the Nicaraguan resistance was me. And I turned to others to help carry out that activity.

MR. NIELDS: Did you manage it?

LT. COL. NORTH: I tried, in terms of coalescing the activities that went on, yes.

MR. NIELDS: You said you were given the job. Who gave it to you?

LT. COL. NORTH: Well, I guess it fell to me by default. McFarlane was the one who originally tasked me to go make contact with the resistance, assure them of our unflagging support. I made a trip in the spring of 1984 to that effect, and it basically just persisted thereafter.

MR. NIELDS: Well, maybe it would be most useful to get into specifics of the areas of your support. I take it one area of your support was to endeavor to raise money from sources other than the US Treasury?

LT. COL. NORTH: That's correct. Boland proscriptions did not allow us to do so. And so we sought a means of complying with those Boland proscriptions by going elsewhere for those monies.

MR. NIELDS: And you went to foreign countries?

LT. COL. NORTH: I did not physically go to those foreign countries.

MR. NIELDS: Representatives of—

LT. COL. NORTH: Representatives of foreign countries and I had discussions about those matters, yes.

MR. NIELDS: You asked them for money?

CHAIRMAN INOUYE: A vote is now in progress in the United States Senate, and, accordingly, members of the Senate will have to absent themselves. Please proceed.

MR. NIELDS: And yo asked them for money for the contras?

LT. COL. NORTH: I want to be a little more specific about that. I don't recall going hat in hand to anybody. I do recall sitting and talking about how grateful this country would be if the issue that they had discussed with others were indeed brought to fruition. For example, a representative of Country Three and I met, and we talked about an issue that had been raised with him beforehand by others outside the government, and I told him I thought that was a dandy idea. And I told him where he could send the money, and he did so.

MR. NIELDS: Before we get into the specifics, and I'm going to ask you more about Country Three in a minute, Mr. McFarlane has testified that he gave you instructions not to solicit money from foreign countries or private sources. Did he give you those instructions?

LT. COL. NORTH: I never carried out a single act, not one, Mr. Nields, in which I did not have authority from my superiors. I haven't in the 23 years that I have been in the uniformed Services of the United States of America ever violated an order; not one.

MR. NIELDS: But that wasn't the question. The question was—

LT. COL. NORTH: That is the answer to your question.

MR. NIELDS: No, the question was, did Mr. McFarlane give you such instructions?

LT. COL. NORTH: No, I never heard those instructions.

MR. NIELDS: And I take it that it was your understanding from what you've just said, that quite to the contrary, you were authorized to seek money from foreign countries?

LT. COL. NORTH: I was authorized to do everything that I did.

MR. NIELDS: Well, again, that isn't the question yet.

LT. COL. NORTH: I was authorized to have a meeting, in this particular case in specific, by Mr. McFarlane for the purpose of talking to the man about a suggestion that had been made to him by others, and to encourage that process along, and I did so. I had already provided to Mr. McFarlane a card with the address of an account, an off-shore account which would support the Nicaraguan resistance. And thank God somebody put money into that account and the Nicaraguan resistance didn't die, as perhaps others intended; certainly the Sandinistas, and Moscow and Cuba intended that, and they didn't die, they grew in strength and numbers and effectiveness as a consequence. And I think that is a good thing. And Mr. McFarlane was the person who asked me for the card on the account and with the account, and I gave it to him. And I don't know who he gave it to, but whoever he gave it to gave a lot of money. I don't know if Mr. McFarlane asked that person for the money or not. I did not go to the representative of Country Three and ask him for money. He suggested that he put money there and I told him where to send it. And thank God he did so, too!

MR. NIELDS: I take it you're saying not only did Mr. McFarlane not instruct you not to seek money from foreign countries, but that he was aware of each and every one of your actions to obtain money from foreign countries and approved of it?

(Pause while North consults with counsel.)

LT. COL. NORTH: I believe so, yes.

MR. NIELDS: And with respect specifically to Country Three, I take it that you originally had a meeting with General Singlaub in which he reported a discussion he had had with representatives of Country Three?

LT. COL. NORTH: That is correct.

MR. NIELDS: And, he told them that the discussion that he had with representatives of Country Three, which he told you about, had to do with money for the contras?

LT. COL. NORTH: As I recall, yes.

MR. NIELDS: And, I believe that the discussion you had with him was sometime in November of 1984? Is that consistent with your recollection?

LT. COL. NORTH: I have absolutely no recall when those conversations were, but I'm sure you have a contemporaneous record of mine that would reflect that.

MR. NIELDS: Yes. Exhibit #71. In book number four. (Long pause) Turn one more page.

LT. COL. NORTH: I have the document.

MR. NIELDS: Does that refresh your memory that it was sometime in November of 1984 that General Singlaub reported to you on his discussion with Country Three on the subject of funding the contras?

LT. COL. NORTH: I'm looking at the memo dated December 4th, 1984?

MR. NIELDS: Yes.

LT. COL. NORTH: This refers to the acquisition of surface to air missiles from another country.

MR. NIELDS: Well, that's why I asked you to turn to the next page.

LT. COL. NORTH: Okay.I see the entry.

MR. NIELDS: Okay, November of 1984?

LT. COL. NORTH: I'm missing the date, counsel.

MR. NIELDS: Well, at the very first part of the memo it says, "In accordance with prior understanding, I met on Wednesday, November 28th." And, that is an unrelated transaction.

LT. COL. NORTH: That happens to be the transaction that relates to the surface to air missiles?

MR. NIELDS: Yes. And, then if you turn to the next page, it says, "Later that afternoon, Major General Jack Singlaub visited to advise of two meetings held earlier in the day."

LT. COL. NORTH: Got it.

MR. NIELDS: So, my question is, did you have a discussion with General Singlaub in November of 1984 on the subject of his discussing money for the contras with Country Three?

LT. COL. NORTH: Later that afternoon, yes.

MR. NIELDS: Yes. And, then sometime a couple of months later, you, did you not, ask General Singlaub to go back to Country Three and seek two million dollars for the contras?

LT. COL. NORTH: I recall it a little differently. I think he said he was going to go back, and he suggested that he do that, but I'm not debating the actual sequence of who did what?

MR. NIELDS: Why don't you turn to Exhibit 72?

(Col. North and his attorney look through papers.)

MR. NIELDS: Second page.

LT. COL. NORTH: The second page on mine is blank unless you numbered this page.

MR. NIELDS: It's not—

LT. COL. NORTH: This is a cable to—

MR. NIELDS: Try the third page which is numbered 2, I believe.

LT. COL. NORTH: Got it.

MR. NIELDS: And you see at the top it said, "The FDN is

in urgent need of near-term financing, approximately $2 million—"

LT. COL. NORTH: Right.

MR. NIELDS: —"for the purpose of rifles, ammunition and boots for new volunteers." And then down lower it says, "Singlaub will be here to see me tomorrow. With your permission, I will ask him to approach," and then blanked out is country three, "embassy urging that they proceed with their offer."

LT. COL. NORTH: Yes, I would also like to point out that it says, "proceed with their offer." It does not say, "Proceed with what I asked for."

MR. NIELDS: But you asked General Singlaub, did you not, to go back and ask them to proceed with their offer?

LT. COL. NORTH: Yes, but again, I think what's important, Counsel, is the words, "their offer."

MR. NIELDS: Well, their offer didn't, in fact—

LT. COL. NORTH: I get the sense that somehow or another we've tried to create the impression that Oliver North picked up his hat and wandered around Washington and foreign capitals begging for money. I didn't do that. I didn't have to do it, because others were more willing to put up the money than the Congress because they saw well what was happening to us in Central America and the devastating consequences of a contra wipeout and an American walkaway and write-off to what was going to happen to this country and to democracy elsewhere in the world. I didn't have to wander around and beg. There were other countries in the world and other people in this country who were more willing to help the Nicaraguan resistance survive and cause democracy to prosper in Central America than this body here and that is an important factor in all of what you do, Counsel, what this committee is going to do.

It's got to be part of your assessment as to why is that other countries in the world were willing to step up and help in a desperate cause, when we were not willing to do so ourselves. That has got to be something that is debated, not just by pulling before this group and hammering at them and haranguing and reducing it to pettiness. It's got to be something that the American people come to understand how desperately important it was not just to us, not just to

Ollie North and not just to President Ronald Reagan. It was important to these other people who put forth that money and I didn't beg them. They offered and that's important, sir.

MR. NIELDS: And no money came in in March or April or May or June?

LT. COL. NORTH: I don't recall exactly when it came in.

MR. NIELDS: But none of it came in them and you had another meeting with Singlaub in June?

LT. COL. NORTH: If you are looking at something that indicates that, I would, I suppose—

MR. NIELDS: Well, take a look at Exhibit 73, which is a page from your spiral notebooks. 29th of June, 1985, middle of the page, "12:30, meeting with Singlaub." Do you see that, sir?

LT. COL. NORTH: I do.

MR. NIELDS: And then it says, "10 million—5 million from"—Country Three is blanked out, "call Sigur or North." And I take it he was telling you that he needed a signal from this government before Country Three was going to give any money.

LT. COL. NORTH: I don't recall specifically what that was about. I've admitted to you that I did meet with a representative of Country Three and confirmed that this country would be indeed grateful. I don't remember the specific—

MR. NIELDS: But you have also told us that there were these other countries that themselves, on their own, wanted to aid the contras, and I'm saying isn't it true that they didn't give any aid for several months and that Singlaub came back to you and said, "They're not going to give any money unless this government gives them a signal." And he met with you and asked you for that, and you said, "Have 'em call Sigur or North."

LT. COL. NORTH: Okay, yeah, that is exactly what transpired. I'm not saying that's exactly what transpired this day, but it did transpire.

MR. NIELDS: And then nothing happened for approximately a month, and you had another meeting with Singlaub, this time on the 30th of July.

(pause)

LT. COL. NORTH: Can you refresh me on that one?

MR. NIELDS: Yes, I can. Exhibit number 74. It's another

110

page from your spiral notebooks. Don't mention names that are circled. It says 30th of July, meeting with Singlaub, and then there's a name of an official from Country Three—

LT. COL. NORTH: Yes.

MR. NIELDS: —circled. And then it says, "Singlaub need $2 million the next two weeks."

LT. COL. NORTH: Yeah, I see what it says. I don't recall exactly what that means. I'm not sure that that actually relates to the contribution made by Country Three.

MR. NIELDS: And down below it, it says, "Please call Gaston or North."

LT. COL. NORTH: Mm-hmm .

MR. NIELDS: Same thing, isn't it?

LT. COL. NORTH: I guess so—

MR. NIELDS: They want some encouragement from the United States government. And you then actually instructed Mr. Sigur to go meet with officials of that country?

LT. COL. NORTH: First of all, I didn't instruct Dr. Sigur to do that. I probably asked him, and the word "ask" is indeed underlined in my notes.

MR. NIELDS: You "asked" him. Did you talk to Mr. McFarlane before you asked him to do that?

LT. COL. NORTH: Yes, I—

MR. NIELDS: And got his approval?

LT. COL. NORTH: You bet.

MR. NIELDS: And then you asked Gaston to go meet with the officials of Country Three.

LT. COL. NORTH: Yes.

MR. NIELDS: And then after Gaston had done that, you asked him to set up a meeting for you—

LT. COL. NORTH: Right.

MR. NIELDS: —and representatives of Country Three.

LT. COL. NORTH: Yes.

MR. NIELDS: And at that meeting, you told them that the country—this country—would be very grateful if they were to make the contribution.

LT. COL. NORTH: I did.

MR. NIELDS: And then, and only then, they actually made it.

LT. COL. NORTH: Yes.

MR. NIELDS: And Mr. Sigur has testified that your meeting with representatives of Country Three was in August.

111

That would be the month following this note. I take it that's consistent with your recollection?

LT. COL. NORTH: If you say—I did have a meeting—if you say it was in August, I'll believe you.

MR. NIELDS: And you then sent Mr. Owen with an account number so that the officials of Country Three would know where to send the money.

LT. COL. NORTH: I recall that happening.

MR. NIELDS: And that was the account which Mr. Secord had set up in Switzerland.

LT. COL. NORTH: I guess so, yeah. I don't remember exactly which account number I gave him.

MR. NIELDS: But it was one Secord's accounts?

LT. COL. NORTH: I believe it was.

MR. NIELDS: And those accounts had been set up at your suggestion.

LT. COL. NORTH: Absolutely. As part of a covert operation to support the Nicaraguan resistance.

MR. NIELDS: To receive monies to support the Nicaraguan resistance.

LT. COL. NORTH: Absolutely.

MR. NIELDS: And it wasn't under the control of the Nicaraguans?

LT. COL. NORTH: No.

MR. NIELDS: It was under the control of Secord, who was responding to your direction.

LT. COL. NORTH: I'm not sure that a major general's going to be happy with saying the words "responding to my direction." General Secord was, indeed, cooperating in every way that I asked him to, yes.

MR. NIELDS: Well, who—well, who was in charge? You were a government official; he was not. He's a major general; you're a lieutenant colonel. Are you telling this committe that because he had a higher rank when he was the government that he was the boss?

LT. COL. NORTH: Well, I—he was the boss of what? He was the boss of the organizations and the—the commercial enterprises that he set up to assist the Nicaraguan resistance and that I eventually asked him to expand out into other covert operations, and he did those things.

MR. NIELDS: So he did those at your request, did he not?

LT. COL. NORTH: That's correct, but it was—

112

MR. NIELDS: And it was—

LT. COL. NORTH: —direction, and I think that he would probably take umbrage with that.

MR. NIELDS: Well, I'm not asking you what—whether he would take umbrage. I'm asking you whether the United States Government retained control over this covert operation.

LT. COL. NORTH: I tried to, counsel. Tried to.

MR. NIELDS: And indeed all of the money that went into that bank account in Switzerland resulted from your efforts.

LT. COL. NORTH: I—I don't know that, no, because you say "that" bank account. I'm not sure about, to this day, exactly how much money went into "that" bank account or which bank account.

MR. NIELDS: Well, I can tell you that the committee's records reflect that the money that went into those bank accounts came from the proceeds of sales of arms to Iran, from Country Three, directly or indirectly from Spitz Channell's organizations, a little bit from the government of Israel, and one deposit from Joseph Coors. And my question to you: isn't it true that you were responsible for directing all of that money into those—into those accounts?

LT. COL. NORTH: My sense is that the ones that you have just identified—except that I don't know it's the government of Israel. I believe it was an Israeli private citizen. I would agree that I am the person that caused that money to go into those accounts.

MR. NIELDS: I'd like to turn now to Country 2. Do you have that country in mind?

LT. COL. NORTH: I do.

MR. NIELDS: Did you ever have any meetings with officials of Country 2 in which the subject of money for the contras arose?

LT. COL. NORTH: No.

MR. NIELDS: Did you ever ask Mr. Secord to have a meeting with the representative of Country 2 for the purpose of discussing contributions for the contras?

LT. COL. NORTH: I don't recall whether I asked him or he suggested. But, nonetheless, such a meeting did, indeed, occur.

MR. NIELDS: And did you have authority—

LT. COL. NORTH: At least, I am told that such a meeting

113

did occur. I was not present at the meeting, but I did talk to him before about it, and I believe I talked to him after about it. At least, it was reported to me that way.

MR. NIELDS: And was that meeting known to Mr. McFarlane?

LT. COL. NORTH: yes.

MR. NIELDS: And were you authorized in advance to either ask or consent [to] Mr. Secord making that request?

LT. COL. NORTH: I'm sure that I was, yes.

MR. NIELDS: And, to your knowledge, had Mr. McFarlane had similar meetings with representatives of Country 2?

LT. COL. NORTH: I do not know to this day whether he did or not.

MR. NIELDS: Well, did he tell you that he did?

LT. COL. NORTH: No, he did not.

MR. NIELDS: Did he tell you anything on that subject?

LT. COL. NORTH: You're asking me—let me get the bottom line on this thing. You're asking me, Do I know where the initial $25 million came from? To this day, I do not. I simply gave Mr. McFarlane a card. And on that card was an account number. And money shortly thereafter started to flow to that account.

MR. NIELDS: My question—

LT. COL. NORTH: And I don't know whether it was Country 2 or not. And that is also part of a covert operation. I didn't need to know that. In a compartmented, covert operation, my job was to get an account number for the Nicaraguan resistance to receive monies.

MR. NIELDS: Well, let me ask you this way. Did you—

LT. COL. NORTH: Please let me finish. And that's important, I think, to the American people understanding a covert operation. There are boxes within boxes to protect the operation. You know, one of the things that disturbs me about the way this is proceeding is that we constantly are coming back to the fact that the American people haven't been told everything. You're not going to make public all of this stuff when you get done with either, I hope. I mean there's Top Secret, code word documents that you've—that I've seen for the first time today in years, that I'm now having to look through. I pray to God you're not going to turn all these loose!

You know, even after the Russians got the secrets of our satellites from the spy, we didn't publish them in our periodicals, the Congressional committees didn't make them public for everybody to read. And there's nothing wrong with that. There's nothing wrong with the fact that Mr. McFarlane compartmented-off parts of the program for his knowledge, and that others in the program didn't know everything else that everyone else knew. There's nothing wrong with that in a covert operation, that's how they're conducted, and it's the right way to do it to protect lives and the people engaged in it, and lives are important.

MR. NIELDS: Did you tell Mr. Secord that Mr. McFarlane had already had a meeting with the official?

LT. COL. NORTH: No, because I didn't know. And I do not know, you know, for confirmed knowledge to this day, that Mr. McFarlane met with that official from Country Two. I do know that at some point further down the line Mr. McFarlane asked me to tell General Secord to back off his contacts with the person from Country Two, and he did so.

MR. NIELDS: And subsequently money came in?

LT. COL. NORTH: It did.

MR. NIELDS: Are you aware of anyone else, yourself, that had meetings with Country Two or representatives of Country Two on the subject of contributions for the contras?

LT. COL. NORTH: I have no personal knowledge that anybody other than General Secord—and I only know that because he told me—met with representatives of Country Two. And at the time, General Secord was not a part of the United States government.

MR. NIELDS: Are you aware of any approaches to Country Nine seeking support for the contras?

LT. COL. NORTH: I can recall that there was a discussion about that country between General Secord and I. I don't believe that anybody in the US government ever approached them.

MR. NIELDS: Did Mr. Secord?

LT. COL. NORTH: I know he approached them on the issue of terrorism. I don't recall whether or not he actually approached them on the issue of aid to the Nicaraguan resistance, no. I don't recall, I may—you may be able to refresh my memory, but I don't remember that.

MR. NIELDS: Well let's take a look at Exhibit number 78.

LT. COL. NORTH: I have a one-page piece of paper dated 8 August.

MR. NIELDS: 1985?

LT. COL. NORTH: 1985, I believe. It's hard to read.

MR. NIELDS: Headed "Call from Rich"?

LT. COL. NORTH: Yes.

MR. NIELDS: Who is Rich?

LT. COL. NORTH: Well Rich could be a number of people, but—

MR. NIELDS: Is it Richard Miller?

LT. COL. NORTH: Well, I don't know. I mean, I know Rich Armitage, Rich Miller, I know several other Richs. Do you have the pages the precede and succeed that?

MR. NIELDS: I can supply it to you if you wish, I do not believe it's going to shed any light.

LT. COL. NORTH: Well, again—

(Lt. Col. North confers with attorney.)

LT. COL. NORTH: Does this—after the "Rich", my copy is very difficult to read, counsel. Can—

MR. NIELDS: There are some—

LT. COL. NORTH: "Call from Rich" —

MR. NIELDS: There are some circled words there which should not be read.

LT. COL. NORTH: I understand that. But, what is right after "Rich"? It looks like a squiggle, or is it—

MR. NIELDS: "Ray".

LT. COL. NORTH: Ray? Okay.

I think that may well be, given the first circled name, that may well be Richard Miller, not Richard Secord.

MR. NIELDS: And, it refers down at the bottom—well, first of all, I take it Country Nine is—

LT. COL. NORTH: Circled.

MR. NIELDS: —mentioned.

LT. COL. NORTH: Right.

MR. NIELDS: —And there is a reference could be as much 4 to 5 million dollars.

LT. COL. NORTH: Right.

MR. NIELDS: Does that refer to a prospective contribution to the contras?

LT. COL. NORTH: I do not recall this conversation, but I do recall the circle is a codename for one of the people that was

116

in contact with us initially, of all things, on the hostage matter, and it turns out this guy is a "bad apple". At one point, Director Casey was concerned that this fellow might be a provocation. In any event, this man never produced anything. Talked a lot. Did nothing.

MR. NIELDS: Well, now, if you'll turn to Exhibit #79.

LT. COL. NORTH: Did I answer the question on who that "Rich" was? I do not believe—first of all, I never referred to General Secord as "Rich".

MR. NIELDS: You said you thought it was Richard Miller.

LT. COL. NORTH: Yes.

MR. NIELDS: And, if you'd turn to Exhibit #79,—do you have that in front of you? It's another page from your notebook, dated 24 September 1985, and down at the bottom it says, "Call from Dick." And, then there are some numbers, and below that, it says, "Meeting with Country Nine people tomorrow; 1C-7 ready now." What does that refer to?

LT. COL. NORTH: I don't know. It could be—again, I recall speaking specifically to General Secord about the issue of terrorism, and I don't know that he ever approached them for a contribution. It may well be that he did. I just don't remember, and you may be able to show me other notes in there where they were approached. I don't know that they ever made a contribution.

MR. NIELDS: Did you ever—

LT. COL. NORTH: I did not ever approach anyone.

MR. NIELDS: Did you ever meet with officials of any other country for the purpose of discussing contributions to the contras?

LT. COL. NORTH: Oh, sure. Not just financial contributions. I mean , I met with the senior military person from Country Four to get surface to air missiles, and I did that with the full knowledge of the FBI and the National Security Adviser. I mean, one of the things that kind of bothers me is this wasn't all done as some terrible nefarious thing, it was done as part of a covert operation. And I'd like to make a note about that one right there. I was very concerned about the meeting I had with Number Four, that someone not misunderstand why I was meeting with that person. And I asked for specific surveillance from the FBI on it, and they provided, as I understand it, that kind of protection. The Director of the FBI was aware of that meeting. This was not some deep, dark secret.

MR. NIELDS: Was that a meeting in which you were requesting a contribution of surface-to-air missiles? Or were you seeking to facilitate the transportation of surface-to-air missiles that had been purchased by somebody else?

LT. COL. NORTH: I was actually seeking to facilitate the transportation, but I was hoping I could turn it enough that they'd like to make the contribution. I will admit that.

MR. NIELDS: So you discussed the possibility of a contribution with representatives of Country Four?

LT. COL. NORTH: Well, when I say "contribution," I was speaking specifically of surface-to-air missiles, which at that point in time, the resistance was being devastated by the Soviet-supplied Cuban-flown HIND helicopters, and we were looking desperately for surface-to-air missiles that could be provided to the democratic resistance. And that man's country makes the kind that's—

MR. NIELDS: And did you ask them—

LT. COL. NORTH: —useful for that purpose.

(pause)

MR. NIELDS: Yes, did you ask representatives of Country Four at that time to contribute SA-7s?

LT. COL. NORTH: I don't believe I actually baldly asked them to contribute. I was—I had a—If I could just back up on that—that whole thing just for a second. That particular place was a good source for these weapons. We were concerned—I was concerned, I went to Admiral Poindexter and told him my concerns about the meeting. We knew that that was a good source for those weapons. I was concerned about the meeting because I did not want anyone in our intelligence services or others to misunderstand the purpose of the meeting. And so what I did, is I asked Admiral Poindexter—and I believe Mr. McFarlane, too—to please make sure that the Attorney General and the Director of the FBI was aware that the meeting was going to take place. And I believe that they did so—for obvious purposes. And I think that's, without saying more about—

MR. NIELDS: The question is just a very simple one. Did you ask for—

LT. COL. NORTH: Not—not in so many words—

MR. NIELDS: —Country Four to make a contribution of SA-7s?

LT. COL. NORTH: Not in so many words. We had a long philosophical discussion over lunch about Soviet hegemony, the kinds of things that I thought would be attractive and of concern to him. He shared my concerns, and I made him aware that there was a purchase under way, that these things were desperately needed. And he then facilitated that.

MR. NIELDS: Did he—

LT. COL. NORTH: But he didn't make a contribution.

MR. NIELDS: Did he ever—

LT. COL. NORTH: I don't think.

MR. NIELDS: He never made a contribution?

LT. COL. NORTH: Not that I'm aware of.

MR. NIELDS: Did you have any other meetings with representatives of Country 4 in which you sought a contribution?

LT. COL. NORTH: Not that I recall, no.

MR. NIELDS: Any other countries?

LT. COL. NORTH: At some point, I encouraged others, although I did not have the meeting to see if we could obtain radio equipment from Country 8, and—

MR. NIELDS: Who did you encourage to do that?

LT. COL. NORTH: I'm not entirely certain, but I think it was Gen. Singlaub.

MR. NIELDS: And on whose authority did you do that?

LT. COL. NORTH: Well, with my superiors.

MR. NIELDS: Mr. McFarlane?

LT. COL. NORTH: No, by then I think it was Mister— Adm. Poindexter.

MR. NIELDS: Did that prove successful?

LT. COL. NORTH: I don't recall. I don't think so.

MR. NIELDS: Any others?

LT. COL. NORTH: Well, Brunei, of course. Brunei had been under discussion for a long time.

MR. NIELDS: Any others?

LT. COL. NORTH: No. I think that's it. Now eventually —eventually—I talked to—this is very late in the whole process—to a senior person from Country 1 who then, indeed, provided some weapons.

119

MR. NIELDS: Physical weapons, free of charge?

LT. COL. NORTH: Yes.

MR. NIELDS: Now I've been asking you only about your own meetings and contacts. Did you ask any other person to approach any foreign country, other than the ones you've already testified about?

LT. COL. NORTH: Well, I, of course, asked Dr. Sigur to establish the meetings. And I believe at the time I probably told him why. The ones that I met would be Countries 3 and 4. I may have asked him to arrange a meeting with some representatives of Country 5. I don't recall specifically at this point, but I may have. And I'm not aware that others outside or elsewhere were doing it, other than the fact that I know that Mr. Abrams, Amb. Abrams, eventually made a contact wiht Brunei.

MR. NIELDS: Are you aware of any contacts made by other people in the US government, whether or not at your request or direction, to approach other countries for contributions to the contras?

LT. COL. NORTH: Not that I can recall specifically, other than I did talk to Adm. Moreau at length about a trip that was being made by a senior US official to Country 4, and I believe that contact was made while he was on that trip. And there's a country that's not on you list, so I don't know how to refer to it, but I did—I'm—I recall now that I did make contact with a senior official in another country on that matter and we can develop some convention for how we talk about it.

MR. NIELDS: We've simply been writing it on a sheet of paper, folding it over and handing it to the Chairman. And will you describe that contact?

CHAIRMAN INOUYE: Country 10.

LT. COL. NORTH: Country—I'm sorry?

MR. NIELDS: Country 10 . . . Would you describe that contact please, sir.

LT. COL. NORTH: I met with that senior official in a foreign country, not his, not ours, as part of a broader effort but it included assistance that he may be able to provide in the case of support for the Nicaraguan resistance. There was a broader context in that conversation, but that was certainly a part of it and no final arrangement was ever consummated because shortly thereafter, I was reassigned back to the Marine Corps.

MR. NIELDS: And were you seeking then a financial contribution, or a contribution of some kind of materiel?

LT. COL. NORTH: It was not so much financial, certainly is more a operational support. And I guess maybe—I don't want to sound like I'm assemblying it all because I went to the officials in Country 7 and other's of Country 7's neighbors, frequently, asking for operational support and getting it. Not financial, not materiel, necessarily, but assistance in operational support for him—everything from airplanes to places to park them, things like that. And so I—and I was—I was the person who did those.

MR. NIELDS: And on whose authority did you do those?

LT. COL. NORTH: My superiors.

MR. NIELDS: Is this just Admiral Poindexter, or Admiral Poindexter and Mr. McFarlane?

LT. COL. NORTH: Oh, no, I—again this all started way back in 1984. So it was started when Mr. McFarlane was there and it continued on through Admiral Poindexter's succession as National Security Advisor in 1986.

MR. NIELDS: Would you turn to Exhibit 80? That's a page from one of your notebooks, February 4—

LT. COL. NORTH: What year is that?

MR. NIELDS: I believe this is 1985. (Long pause) And I take it that—I take it that's a call from Claire George?

LT. COL. NORTH: I take it that it is, but there's more—I can't understand what this thing says with the—all the things blacked out. Did I black those out when I gave it to you?

MR. NIELDS: No, you did not. What's blacked out is the name of Country 5 and an official of Country 5.

LT. COL. NORTH: Okay.

MR. NIELDS: It refers to a contribution—a possible contribution of two million dollars, does it not?

LT. COL. NORTH: Right.

MR. NIELDS: Can you describe that conversation?

LT. COL. NORTH: Well, I don't—I can't recall specific —you say this is 1985, before 1985?

MR. NIELDS: I believe so. We're checking it right now.

LT. COL. NORTH: Okay. I don't recall it specifically. I do

recall in general that there was some conversation with Country Number 5. I don't believe that Country 5 ever made that contribution. I—I may well be wrong, but I think that we talked to them several times about operational support and encouraged them to provide or sell material to the resistance. I don't recall that that actually transpired.

MR. NIELDS: But this was something which was brought to your attention by a representative of the CIA?

LT. COL. NORTH: Sure. I mean, they knew what I was doing. I mean, they—they knew that I was the guy that was in contact with the resistance and was out trying to help them, in compliance with Boland I would point out.

MR. NIELDS: Now, my next question is you've indicated that the National Security Advisers for whom you worked authorized you to seek support from foreign countries, both financial and operational.

LT. COL. NORTH: Yes.

MR. NIELDS: Was your—were your activities in that respect known to others in the White House other than the National Security Advisers?

LT. COL. NORTH: Well, I want to go back to something I said at the very beginning of all of this, Mr. Nields. I assumed that those matters which required the attention and—and decision of the President of the United States did indeed get them. I assumed that. I never asked that. I never walked up to the President and said, "Oh, by the way, Mr. President, yesterday I met with so-and-so from Country 4." Nor did he ever say, "I'm glad you had a meeting with Country 4 and it went well."

MR. NIELDS: Do you know whether or not the President was aware of your activities seeking funds and operational support for the contras from third countries?

LT. COL. NORTH: I do not know.

MR. NIELDS: Were you—

LT. COL. NORTH: I assumed that he did.

MR. NIELDS: Were you ever—what was the basis of your assumption?

LT. COL. NORTH: Just that there was a lot going on and it was very obvious that the Nicaraguan resistance survived. I sent forward innumerable documents, some of which you've just shown us as exhibits, that demonstrated that I was keeping my superiors fully informed as to what was going on.

MR. NIELDS: Now, you indicate that we have shown you—that you made numerous documents and we have shown them to you. I don't believe we've shown you any that postdate August of 1985. Did there come a time when you stopped writing documents relating to your support for the contras?

LT. COL. NORTH: There came a time when I stopped sending up what we called "in system memoranda". I continued to communicate with my superiors, using the PROF system, and I continued to send forward non-log or out of system documents, yes.

MR. NIELDS: And, where are they?

LT. COL. NORTH: Well, the PROFs notes you've got, I guess.

MR. NIELDS: Where are the non-logged documents?

LT. COL. NORTH: I think they were shredded.

MR. NIELDS: And, the—

LT. COL. NORTH: Or burn bagged.

MR. NIELDS: And, the PROFs messages, you thought had been deleted.

LT. COL. NORTH: I had hoped that they had been, yes.

MR. NIELDS: And, I take it you stopped putting these memoranda in the system because of a problem that arose in connection with a Congressional inquiry?

LT. COL. NORTH: Actually, the problem arose as a consequence of media attention, which occurred in the summer of '85, and that was that my name surfaced in connection with, in some cases halfway accurate, in some cases wild and spurious allegations about my role in support for the Nicaraguan resistance.

MR. NIELDS: Well, we'll get back to this in more detail later, Col. North, but are you saying that your decision to stop putting these documents in the system had nothing to do with the fact that they were pulled out of the system by Mr. McFarlane for the purpose in response to a Congressional request for documents?

LT. COL. NORTH: No, I think we arrived at a point, and I don't recall whether it was his idea or my idea, in 1985 to stop putting these documents in the system. You're right.

I'm not saying that it was his idea. It might have been mine. But, anyway we decided not to.

MR. NIELDS: And, that arose out of the fact that Congress had asked to look at the documents, and the documents that were gathered for them all came out of the system.

LT. COL. NORTH: Exactly.

MR. NIELDS: And, you didn't want to show Congress the documents in the system?

LT. COL. NORTH: I didn't want to show Congress a single word on this whole thing.

MR. NIELDS: Who else in the government was aware of the fact that you and others at the NSC were approaching third coutries for the purpose of raising money for the contras?

LT. COL. NORTH: Well, the person most closely aware of it outside the NSC that I know of—I've talked to you about people that I was in contact with—was Director Casey, who I had many conversation regarding this, what we referred to as "off-line conversation," ones that weren't going to be recorded or transmitted, and Admiral Arthur J. Moreau, United States Navy, knew a great deal about it because he and I spoke a lot.

MR. NIELDS: Anyone else?

LT. COL. NORTH: Well, you're probably going to show me a document where I talked to somebody else, but that's about, you know, the limit of government officials that I talked to. Obviously, from what you can see here on the 4th of February, there were others who were aware within the United States government. There were other members in Congress who knew, you know, that I was the person in touch with the Nicaraguan resistance.

MR. NIELDS: Any other people in the CIA?

LT. COL. NORTH: Oh, I'm sure that Mr. Claridge knew. I mean he's the guy that had introduced me to the leadership of the Nicaraguan resistance way back in 1984. There were other people at CIA who I met with on a regular basis. I'm not saying that these people had intimate knowledge of my day-to-day activities, like my superiors did. But, certainly, they knew that I was the guy that was getting things done. That's why they called me up. That's why there's a note to the effect of "Hey, Ollie, You know. Here are these guys here from Country Whatever it is. They're talking about $2 million dollars. Why don't you go over and put the smile on 'em. Maybe they'll kick in."

MR. NIELDS: How about the Chief of the Central American Task Force?

LT. COL. NORTH: Oh, I'm sure that he had a detailed grasp of—well, I say a detailed grasp, I'm sure that he had an adequate sense of what I was doing.

MR. NIELDS: And, what is your basis for that belief?

LT. COL. NORTH: We used to have meetings with the restricted interagency group. We used to have secure conference calls, and on one occasion, I can recall, laying out for the group. In fact, I think it was after the hundred million dollars had been voted by both Houses, hadn't been sent forward to the President. I can recall a meeting in an office in the Pentagon where I went down, item by item by item, the things that I was doing, and asked them point blank whether or not I had to continue to do them to keep the resistance alive, because even though the money had been authorized, and both bills had been passed, we couldn't get it forwarded to the President, and we went down item by item by item on my checklist of what I was having directed out each month, or each quarter, or each week to support the resistance, and asked them point blank whether this should continue.

MR. NIELDS: Who was there?

LT. COL. NORTH: Well, I'd have to look at my contemporaneous notes of the time, but I think there is a note in one of the notebooks I gave you to that effect. Mr. Fires was there, Mr. Abrams was there, Mr. Armitage was there. I think Mr. Michael was there, I think General Moehring was there. But these—

MR. NIELDS: Would you go through them for us, please, item by item, what it was that you told this assembled group that you were doing?

LT. COL. NORTH: Well, what I'm saying to you is, I didn't say, you know, "Look, on a given day, I'm going to walk out and go talk to so and so about so much money." What I—what they knew is that I was the person who was causing these things to happen. There was no doubt in their mind. That's why when an airplane goes down in Honduras, they call me to get the bodies home and to pay the cost. That's why when somebody needs something done in the case of this contact right here you've pointed out as part of Exhibit Number 79, they called me. These people knew what I was doing. They knew that it was a covert operation being conducted by this government to support the Nicaraguan resistance. And—

MR. NIELDS: My question is, could you—you indicated that during this meeting at the Department of Defense, the Pentagon, you went down item by item. Would you go down for us item by item, what it was that you told—

LT. COL. NORTH: I don't have the list before me. But I gave copies of that to you. It's in the stuff that I gave to you, seven binders full.

MR. NIELDS: Did you discuss the resupply operation?

LT. COL. NORTH: I think so.

MR. NIELDS: Did you discuss efforts to obtain armaments?

LT. COL. NORTH: Probably, yeah. I mean, I'm talking about aid to the internal opposition—food, clothing, medical supplies, etcetera. I think it was all on that list. Tick, tick, tick, tick, tick.

MR. NIELDS: Including munitions?

LT. COL. NORTH: I'm not absolutely sure that it says munitions. It might have just said logistics, and it might have just said air support, and it might have just said certain things about the internal activities.

MR. NIELDS: But it—

LT. COL. NORTH: You've got it, and—along with the list of names of the people there—that were there at the meeting.

(Pause while North consults with his attorney)

MR. NIELDS: Is there anything else you can recall ticking off during this meeting?

LT. COL. NORTH: No, but you have the note and I'm sure you can find it. It's toward the end of my tenure. It's somewhere after June and July, when you—both Houses had passed it and before I got fired. And I—you got 100 and some odd folks to go through my notebooks, counsel.

MR. NIELDS: We'll find it.

LT. COL. NORTH: I'm sure you will.

MR. NIELDS: In addition to raising money from third countries, I take it you also raised some money from private individuals?

LT. COL. NORTH: I want to be very clear about that. Not

because of Boland, but because I understood that there were regulations against government officials soliciting, I do not recall ever asking a single, solitary American citizen for money. I want to make that very clear. You may have found someone who said that I did, but I sure don't remember it. And I tried very, very hard to live with that proscription, not because it was Boland, not because we perceived that the NSC was in any way obviated from doing what I was doing, but only because someone had told me that a U.S. government official should not, cannot, will not, whatever, solicit.

MR. NIELDS: Well, you asked Joseph Coors for $65,000—

LT. COL. NORTH: Wrong.

MR. NIELDS: —and a Maul airplane, didn't you?

LT. COL. NORTH: Not so. He offered the money, and I told him where to send it. And an airplane was bought with it, and it flies today in support of the Nicaraguan resistance, unless the Sandinistas have shot it down.

MR. NIELDS: Did you call him?

LT. COL. NORTH: No. He arrived in my office one afternoon.

MR. NIELDS: Would you describe that event?

LT. COL. NORTH: Well, again, I—you're probably going to pull out a note of mine that's got something on it. And if you can, refresh me. But, otherwise, I'll go unrefreshed. I had seen Mr. Coors a number of times, both before and since. It is my recollection that Mr. Coors arrived in my office one afternoon. I got a telephone call from Director Casey. Maybe I went down and met Mr. Coors in Mr. Casey's office, or maybe he walked into my office. I don't recall specifically. He offered to help—asked what he could do. I suggested various things—showed him an airplane that was desperately needed, a STOL airplane that would take off—short take-off and land. And he said, "Good, how much is it?," or words to that effect. I said, "There's the price list and the company." And Mr. Coors then made available that sum, and it was put in the account and an airplane was bought with it.

But I didn't ask him for that money. He offered it.

MR. NIELDS: We've had a lot of testimony from people who said that you made speeches to them about the contras, and then told them that you couldn't ask for money, but that Mr. Channell or somebody else could, and that they then were asked to make contributions, and that they did so. And we've also had some testimony from people who were told that if they made contributions in a certain amount, they would have a meeting with you or a meeting with the President. Did those things occur?

LT. COL. NORTH: I made a lot of speeches. I made a lot of speeches to people in favor of our policy in Central America. And I made speeches to those who were opposed to it. I even brought that same speech up here and gave it to Members of Congress. I gave it to various committees. I gave that speech to Americans who then went out and made contributions—not solicited by me.

MR. NIELDS: Well, for example, did you sit down with Ellen Garwood at the Hay-Adams Hotel and show her a list of munitions that the contras needed, together with Spitz Channell, giving an amount of money that needed to be contributed in order to purchase the weapons? And did she thereafter make the contribution?

LT. COL. NORTH: I do not recall the specific event that you are talking about, but I met a number of times with Lady Ellen Garwood. I met a number of times with a lot of different people. I'm not denying that I did those things. And if she said that I showed a munitions list, I showed a lot of munitions lists.

MR. NIELDS: You showed a lot of different people munitions lists?

LT. COL. NORTH: Sure.

MR. NIELDS: And told them how much—

LT. COL. NORTH: People would ask me, "What do these things cost?" And I'd take out a munitions list and I'd say, "Well there's what the cost of one of these things are—or many of those things are. That's what they cost."

MR. NIELDS: And did you let them know how much the contras needed money for munitions?

LT. COL. NORTH: I'd let them know how much the contras needed everything. The Nicaraguan freedom fighters were at a point where they were dying in the field under Soviet HIND helicopters—

MR. NIELDS: And did you do that together with Spitz Channell? Pardon?

MR. SULLIVAN: Let him finish, please.

LT. COL. NORTH: (to Mr. Nields) Pardon?

MR. SULLIVAN: I know you don't like the answer, but let him finish.

MR. NIELDS: I like the answer fine. It was not responsive.

MR. SULLIVAN: Well fine, then let him answer.

MR. NIELDS: He had finished answering the question.

MR. SULLIVAN: He had not finished answering, or I wouldn't have raised the subject.

CHAIRMAN INOUYE: Proceed.

LT. COL. NORTH: I don't know whose turn it is, Mr. Chairman.

MR. NIELDS: Did you sit down with these people together with Spitz Channell?

LT. COL. NORTH: Yes, on a number of occasions.

MR. NIELDS: And did—

LT. COL. NORTH: I sat down with Mr. Channell and others.

MR. NIELDS: And did you, after telling them what the contras needs were, did you tell them that Mr. Channell would be the one who would have to ask them for a contribution?

LT. COL. NORTH: I don't recall ever saying those words to anybody.

MR. NIELDS: Did you say—

LT. COL. NORTH: I want to make it very clear. I did tell people I could not and would not solicit, that I wasn't going to ask them for their money, and I do not recall ever being in the presence of Mr. Channell at any time when he asked someone for money—at any time. Nor do I ever recall Mr. Channell offering someone a visit to the Oval Office or the President of the United States of America for a price. I received several suggestions to that effect by several other people, and they were turned away. I never, ever heard that a certain contribution would result in a meeting with the President of the United States of America. I do not recall ever being at such a meeting.

MR. NIELDS: Did you arrange such meetings—

(Pause while North confers with counsel)

MR. NIELDS: Did you arrange such meetings with the President?

LT. COL. NORTH: I do not believe that I personally

129

arranged—I may have sent forward scheduled proposals and you would certainly have them because I would have had copies of them in my office. I don't remember more than one or two occasions where I actually asked for meetings that I set up. Now others at the White House did indeed set those up, and I was a party to that, knowing that these were contributors that had helped the resistance, or these are people who might contribute to the resistance. So those meetings did happen at the White House, yes.

MR. NIELDS: And some of them were with people who had actually made contributions?

LT. COL. NORTH: Oh, yes. Yes.

MR. NIELDS: And the contributions had been obtained in part through your efforts?

LT. COL. NORTH: People give me a lot of credit. I—if someone wants to say, "it was a speech by Ollie North that made me want to give money to help the Nicaraguan resistance," I appreciate that.

MR. NIELDS: Well, I'd like you to turn to Exhibit 10, it's in the first book.

(pause while North finds exhibit)

MR. NIELDS: It's a PROFs message from you to Admiral Poindexter, dated May 16, 1986?

LT. COL. NORTH: I believe it's from Admiral Poindexter to someone else. Either that or I'm looking at the wrong one.

MR. NIELDS: You're looking at the wrong one. I'm talking —it starts at the very bottom of the first page.

LT. COL. NORTH: Okay.

MR. NIELDS: Note from Oliver North.

LT. COL. NORTH: Right.

MR. NIELDS: I'd like you to take a look at the bottom of the second page where it says, "I have no idea what Don Regan does or does not know re my private US operation. But the President obviously knows why he has been meeting with several select people to thank them for their 'support for democracy' in Central America."

MR. SULLIVAN: Excuse me, Counsel.

MR. NIELDS: Pardon?

MR. SULLIVAN: Can you help us locate that, please?

MR. NIELDS: Yes, at the very bottom of the second page, second to the last line. I'll read it again.

LT. COL. NORTH: I got it.

130

MR. NIELDS: (Reads from Exhibit) "I have no idea what Don Regan does or does not know re my private US operation. But the President obviously knows why he has been meeting with several select people to thank them for their 'support for democracy' in Central America."

My first question is, what is quote "my private US operation"? What does that refer to?

LT. COL. NORTH: Well, I don't know. It must mean my activities, my discussions with people.

MR. NIELDS: Private contributors?

LT. COL. NORTH: Sure. I don't know exactly what I meant at that particular point in time.

MR. NIELDS: But you don't call it Spitz Channell's operation, you call it your operation.

LT. COL. NORTH: Okay.

MR. NIELDS: You don't need to respond to that. And when you refer to his meeting with several select people to thank them for their support for democracy, I take it those are people who have made contributions?

LT. COL. NORTH: I would guess so, yes.

MR. NIELDS: And I take it that when you gave speeches to these peoples, one of the purposes was to get them to make a contribution?

LT. COL. NORTH: One of the purposes of my talking to people was indeed to encourage that they do whatever they felt moved to do to support the cause of the democratic outcome in Nicaragua.

MR. NIELDS: Was the President aware of your US operation to raise funds for the contras from private contributors?

LT. COL. NORTH: Well I think that that PROF note right there indicates that I believed he was. But I didn't ever walk in and—by the way—say to him, "Mr. President, this is what I—" I know I've been accused of those kinds of things, but I didn't do that. And the fact is that I assumed, and I think that's a fairly clear indication, I'm sending my boss what I thought was going to be a very private note that would never see the light of day anywhere else, and I said to him what I felt, and I was asking him for guidance.

MR. NIELDS: And he certainly didn't tell you to stop?

COL. NORTH: Why would he? We were conducting a covert operation to support the Nicaraguan resistance, to

131

carry out the President of the United States' stated publicly, articulated foreign policy. Why should he tell me to stop? We weren't breaking any laws, we were simply trying to keep an operation covert.

MR. NIELDS: Thank you, Col. North. I have no further questions this afternoon, Mr. Chairman.

CHAIRMAN INOUYE: The hearings will stand in recess until 9 o'clock tomorrow morning.

END OF TODAY'S SESSION

132

Wednesday · July 8, 1987

Morning Session—9:00 A.M.

MR. NIELDS: Good morning, Col. North.

LT. COL. NORTH: Good morning, Counsel.

MR. NIELDS: Yesterday, you testified about a conversation which you had with the President of the United States on November the 25th, 1986. And, I believe you said that he told you, "I just didn't know."

LT. COL. NORTH: Or words to that effect, yes, sir.

MR. NIELDS: Now, following your conversation with the President, did you happen to run into Robert Earl, later that day?

LT. COL. NORTH: I'm sure that I did. I went back to my office later in the evening, and I, I'm sure that I did see him there.

MR. NIELDS: And, you mentioned, did you not, the conversation that you had with the President?

LT. COL. NORTH: Yes, I recall that Lt. Col. Earl was in the office and he had known that the President had called. I think probably because the original call in the effort to find the White House signal had called through to my office.

MR. NIELDS: My question is this, and I need to ask it of you, sir: Did you say to him in words or substance that the President had said to you, "It's important that I not know"?

LT. COL. NORTH: Counsel, I don't recall the conversation that way. I'm sure that what I said was basically what I told you yesterday, and that is that the President had told me, "I just didn't know." And, it may be that the President said it's important that "I" —Lt. Col. North—understand that he did not know, but I wouldn't have characterized it the way you have just indicated. I don't—I, I—I don't believe.

MR. NIELDS: Yesterday,—

MR. SULLIVAN: Excuse me—

CHAIRMAN INOUYE: I think it might help if you'd lift the mike a little higher.

MR. SULLIVAN: Thank you.

LT. COL. NORTH: Sir?

MR. NIELDS: Yesterday, I asked you some questions and you gave some answers about a one-page insert into a draft of Director Casey's testimony that he was going to give on the 21st of November.

LT. COL. NORTH: Yes.

MR. NIELDS: And, I asked you some questions about a meeting that you had had on the 20th of November in which his testimony was discussed and in which this one-page insert was discussed. Do you recall that?

LT. COL. NORTH: Yes, I do.

MR. NIELDS: And, I believe we brought your attention to a document which was marked Exhibit #31, which was that one-page insert, and it had a handwritten interlineation saying,—I'll read it verbatim—"No-one in the USG found—" and the sentence continues, "—out that our airline had hauled Hawk missiles into Iran." And, you pointed out that the interlineation was not in your handwriting.

LT. COL. NORTH: That is correct.

MR. NIELDS: Overnight, the committees have uncovered a second version of this one-page insert, which has now been marked, Exhibit #31A, and in the same place on the insert, the words, "we" and "CIA" are crossed out, and the words "no-one in the USG" is written in on this new document. Is that your handwriting?

LT. COL. NORTH: That is my handwriting.

MR. NIELDS: So, you wrote on the document, "no-one in the USG" and you wrote that in connection with the sentence that had to do with knowledge that the Hawks had been shipped.

LT. COL. NORTH: That is correct.

MR. NIELDS: Did you write those words in during the meeting, do you recall, or ?

LT. COL. NORTH: I—I don't recall. When I wrote them but—I—just to go back to yesterday's testimony. In my description of what that meeting was about I did not deny

134

that I was trying to change words. And I don't deny that I advocated that. My principal focus in describing the meeting to you was to say that that was not the principal purpose for the meeting and I willing admit that I inserted those words. I do not recall myself being an advocate for this being the only the subject discussed at the meeting. And I do not recall others at the meeting in any way objecting to those words. I do recall going back with Director Casey to his office in the Executive Office Building and deleting the offensive language.

MR. NIELDS: You're talking now, when you say the offensive language, is that the language that you wrote into this document?

LT. COL. NORTH: Well, I—I can't recall what the final version did, but the final version did indeed leave it clear that it was the CIA that did not have knowledge of the Hawk shipment.

MR. NIELDS: But, I'm asking you now about—you just referred to the offensive language. Is the offensive language the phrase, "No one in the USG?"

LT. COL. NORTH: Yes.

MR. NIELDS: And that's the language that you wrote into this document?

LT. COL. NORTH: That is my writing on this document.

MR. NIELDS: Was anyone else present in your meeting with Mr. Casey when you took that language out?

LT. COL. NORTH: I don't recall specifically, but it may well have been Mr. Cave. I—as I recall we went back directly to Director Casey's office from Admiral Poindexter's office and not only worked on this, but several other portions of his testimony in prepartion for his appearance the next day.

MR. NIELDS: Following the meeting on November 20th, the large meeting in Admiral Poindexter's office, did you receive any telephone calls from Admiral Poindexter or Paul Thompson, or anyone else, drawing your attention to the fact that the State Department was objecting to this version of the facts?

LT. COL. NORTH: No, the first recollection I have of anyone in the State Department objecting to that was in news media I think about the time I was being transferred, or shortly thereafter.

MR. NIELDS: Just—I want to make sure that I have asked

all the questions that are important to ask. Did you, later on that afternoon, tell someone either Commander Thompson or Admiral Poindexter that notwithstanding the fact that others claimed that the US government knew that you and Mr. McFarlane were sticking to your story?

LT. COL. NORTH: I don't recall that conversation, no.

MR. NIELDS: I asked you some questions yesterday about the Arms Export Control Act. Now I take it's true that you were aware long before November of 1986 that there was a problem under the Arms Export Control Act with the Israeli shipments.

LT. COL. NORTH: I think I became aware of a problem as early as November of '85, when we began to work on what I came to call the replenishment problem. I want to make it very clear, I didn't know there was a replenishment problem until I met directly with the Israeli officials on or about the 17th of November, that I can recall. I recall very vividly being told that they understood that there was a commitment for immediate replenishment. Mr. McFarlane was still in Europe, and I began to work on solving that problem, as well as solving the problem of trying to get beyond the Hawks issue.

MR. NIELDS: And I take it that the problem under the Arms Export Control Act was raised again in January of 1986?

LT. COL. NORTH: My recollection is that that was addressed that we could solve the problem by having a written finding which authorized these activities. And that's why I raised the issue yesterday of the discussions that resulted in the original November finding, and then the ultimate January 16th or 17th finding, whatever the—I don't recall the date on it. But I was led to believe that there had been a previous Attorney General determination—if that's the appropriate word—which specified that under a covert action finding, arms could be sold to another party and that the finding should address that issue of transfers to the CIA. What I'm saying is that we were looking, I thought, for a legitimate way by which these transactions could be either ratified, in the case of the previous ones, or carried out in the future. And thus, the finding was the document, if you will, that did that.

136

MR. NIELDS: So that it was an issue that was brought to your attention in January, as you were planning for the future, that there was a problem raised by the Arms Export Control Act, and it needed to be solved.

LT. COL. NORTH: I believe that that issue had already been addressed in November, and that's why I say I want to go back to the November finding. My understanding was that the finding that was prepared and sent to the White House by Director Casey solved that problem, essentially. So that in the course of the time between the 17th, when I was apprised of the need to replenish, and the 26th, my understanding was that we thought we'd solved it—(brief pause) —legally.

MR. NIELDS: I'd like to take it step by step. And I'd like you to refer to an exhibit marked Exhibit Number 57.

LT. COL. NORTH: Excuse me, which book, counsel?

MR. NIELDS: That should be book three. (Pause) Do you have that in front of you, sir?

LT. COL. NORTH: Yes.

MR. NIELDS: It's a PROFs message from you, and it's dated January 15, 1986. And just to orient you in time, that would be between the finding of January 6th, which was signed by the President, and the finding of January 17th, after the first one and before the second. And the Committee already has information and testimony that the January 6th finding contemplated sales by Israel and replenishments by the United States.

LT. COL. NORTH: The January—I believe the January 6th finding contemplates direct US sales, and I'm trying to recall from a finding that we wrote over that period of time.

MR. NIELDS: Before we leave that subject, we better turn to Exhibit Number 52. The Committee has heard testimony about this exhibit previously from Mr. Sporkin from the CIA. Exhibit Number 52 is a covert action finding for January the 6th with a cover memo. And the cover memo describes the operation contemplated by the finding. The bottom of the first page, it says, "Since the Israeli sales are technically a violation of our Arms Export Control Act embargo for Iran, a Presidential covert action finding is required in order for us to allow the Israeli sales to proceed and for our subsequent replenishment sales.

137

LT. COL. NORTH: Correct.

MR. NIELDS: So the earlier finding contemplated sales by the Israelis and replenishments by the United States.

LT. COL. NORTH: Correct.

MR. NIELDS: Okay. Now turning back to Exhibit Number 57. That's your PROF message of the 15th of January. I'd like you to turn to the second page. It deals with the proposed arms sales. You make reference to a speech by Secretary Weinberger on the first page, at Fort McNair, which you attended. And then at the top of the second of the PROF message, you state, "Casey believes that Cap will continue to create roadblocks until he is told by you that the President wants this to move now, and that Cap will have to make it work. Casey points out that we have now gone through three different methodologies in effort to satisfy Cap's concerns, and that, no matter what we do, there is always a new objection."

My question to you is this. "Cap" is Cap Weinberger, the Secretary of Defense. And his objections, I take it, were that the transaction, as contemplated, was illegal.

LT. COL. NORTH: Would you please restate the question?

MR. NIELDS: Yes. My question is, isn't it the case that the objections of the Secretary of Defense, which you refer to in this PROF message, were on legal grounds?

LT. COL. NORTH: I guess so. I'm trying to recall exactly what the various three methodologies we've gone through. But I suppose that they were were legal. And, again, I want to emphasize, we were looking for a legal way to do this.

MR. NIELDS: Now I would like you to turn to a page from your notebooks, which is dated the same date—January 15th. And it's Exhibit 69A. It's not going to be easy to find because the pages, as they were given to us, were out of date order. But it's a page—you should look for a page which just has the number 15 at the top, and it's toward the back, away two-thirds of the way through the exhibit, maybe three-quarters. There are a number of pages dated January 14, and then the following page just has a "15" at the top of it.

(The witness perused the exhibit.)

MR. NIELDS: Do you have the page with the "15" at the top?

LT. COL. NORTH: I do.

MR. NIELDS: Okay. Turn it one page over. Is there an entry "call to Ami?"

LT. COL. NORTH: Ami, yes.

MR. NIELDS: And that's Mr. Nir?

LT. COL. NORTH: It is.

MR. NIELDS: And he was your Israeli contact in connection with the arms transactions?

LT. COL. NORTH: By then, he was. In fact, the first of January he was.

MR. NIELDS: I take it you were making notes of a conversation you had with Mr. Nir?

LT. COL. NORTH: That is correct.

MR. NIELDS: And the first note is "Joshua has approved proceeding, as we had hoped." Who is Joshua?

LT. COL. NORTH: Joshua was an Israeli-originated code name for one of the Israeli officials.

MR. NIELDS: I'd like you to turn to the back of this Exhibit 69A, the very last page. Is that a code sheet?

LT. COL. NORTH: Yes.

MR. NIELDS: Relating to the Iranian transaction?

LT. COL. NORTH: It is.

MR. NIELDS: About three-quarters of the way down the page in the righthand column, you will see the word "Joshua." Do you see it?

LT. COL. NORTH: Yes, okay. I've got it. I was wrong. I'd forgotten the codes.

MR. NIELDS: Who is "Joshua?"

LT. COL. NORTH: The President.

MR. NIELDS: The second pargraph says, or the second line in your note is, "Joshua and Samuel have also agreed on Method 1." First I think I'd better ask you who Samuel is.

LT. COL. NORTH: Well, let me check so I don't make a mistake. (Witness consults exhibit.) Secretary Weinberger.

MR. NIELDS: And what is "Method 1?"

LT. COL. NORTH: Well, I don't recall. But it was probably the arrangement that we eventually consummated to replenish the Israeli TOWs and weapons through the CIA.

MR. NIELDS: Well, take a look again at your code sheet. In the middle of the way down the code sheet, it says, "Method 1, Method 2." And opposite "Method 1" it says, "Replenishment by sale," and "Method 2" is "replenishment by pre-positioning."

LT. COL. NORTH: That is—that does refresh my memory. The two alternatives that had been discussed—and I'm not sure how far we ought to go in public session on this, but one of their concerns, and I think a justifiable one, was that at this point in time we were back to discussing TOWs, and that there was a quantity of TOWs that was considerable, as you have seen in the memoranda I prepared, and they were concerned that if that many were shipped, and there was not either an immediate replenishment, either by sale, then Method 2 could possibly be acceptible to them, and Method 2 would have said, "We will preposition our stocks, our weapons there, so that in the event of a national security emergency for them, they could be immediately turned over."

That was one of the methods that we looked at of the many different alternatives for replenishing what the Israelis had already sent in September.

MR. NIELDS: So, prepositioning would be to have our weapons already in Israel before any Israeli shipments?

LT. COL. NORTH: Yes. And, as I recall, there was also a third method, that we would agree to replenish within a certain number of hours, as had been done, for example, in 1973, where we flew massive quantities of materiel in US military aircraft to Israel on very short notice.

MR. NIELDS: And, Method 1, I take it, was to have the Israelis ship first and the United States replenish later, and that's the method which you are communicating to Mr. Nir on the 15th that Joshua and Samuel have agreed to?

LT. COL. NORTH: No, the important point is—and I'm not too sure which sequence we get into as to whose weapons would actually go to Iran. The important point in this whole methodology in this discussion is that we were going to agree to sell to Israel the replacements for the stocks that they had already shipped, and if they shipped anymore in the future. Now, we eventually came to the point where we decided we didn't want them to ship directly because of other complications.

MR. NIELDS: We'll get to that in a minute.

LT. COL. NORTH: I understand.

MR. NIELDS: Let's stay with this conversation that you're having with Mr. Nir.

LT. COL. NORTH: I, I'm speaking specifically of the replenishment issue, which was brought to my attention in November, and that I worked to find a legitimate legal way to replace what they had already shipped, and that we would replace anything that they shipped in the future. The important thing to understand is that there appears to be, or appears to have been a considerable misunderstanding between the Israelis and Mr. McFarlane over what was agreed to as early as the summer of 1985. That generated an enormous amount of work on my part and the people in the Defense Department, as to how it was we were going to replace. They obviously felt that they had received a commitment for, perhaps, even simultaneous or very nearly simultaneous replenishment.

That was not what I was led by Mr. McFarlane to understand that he had committed to, but that is certainly what they had understood. And, so we began an intense period of activity, looking for ways in which either the DOD could sell directly through the foreign military sales, and we eventually found a way to do it legally, I think, through a finding. And, that's why yesterday, I said, "I believe that the November finding had been coordinated throughout the government, like other findings," not at a lower level, but certainly at a top level, as Director Casey advocated in his cover memo to Admiral Poindexter, or to Bud McFarlane. I don't remember who he addressed the November finding to.

It was clearly something that I thought we had solved at least the foundation problem, and we further amplified on that in the January finding.

MR. NIELDS: We're going to see whether it was solved in the earlier findings in a minute, Colonel, but I want to keep going with the conversaton with Mr. Nir.

LT. COL. NORTH: I understand, but let—

MR. NIELDS: And the next question I want to ask—

LT. COL. NORTH: Excuse me, Counsel. Let—

MR. SULLIVAN: Counsel, it might be obvious that the Colonel is trying to answer your question, and I think it's up to counsel, Mr. Chairman, to permit the witness to answer the question fully. Thank you, sir.

MR. NIELDS: I have not put a question to him. I am about to put—

MR. SULLIVAN: You're interrupting.

LT. COL. NORTH: I was trying—

MR. SULLIVAN: You're interrupting his answer.

CHAIRMAN INOUYE: (Bangs the gavel.) May I suggest to the counsel, as he knows what the rules provide for. Please address the chair.

MR. SULLIVAN: I thought I did, Mr. Chairman. I was, of course, didn't get any favorable rulings yesterday. I thought I'd take a straight shot at counsel. My point is, it's absolutely clear, the counsel interrupted the witness. That's why I felt compelled to bring it to your attention, and I think the witness feels he was interrupted, because for several moments he tried to say, "No, I want to say something else." So please, Mr. Chairman, direct your counsel to permit Col. North to answer the question the way he sees fit. Thank you, sir.

CHAIRMAN INOUYE: Please proceed.

MR. NIELDS: Col. North, your next note—

MR. SULLIVAN: Excuse me, counsel. He's going to finish his answer.

LT. COL. NORTH: Counsel, what I was trying to say is that—I'm trying to be very straightforward about this. I think that we all believed that by the time we had gone through the various iterations of trying to solve this replenishment problem, that we had solved that problem. I don't think that there was any chicanery, or efforts to hide that the fact that we worked very hard to find a legitimate legal way to do it.

There were certainly people who must have had concerns that we couldn't sell, from Pentagon stocks, directly to the Israelis, under the Arms Export Control Act prohibitions, etc. And that what we were looking for, and I thought that we found, and I am sure that the other people who worked on this, to include the General Counsel at CIA, and I thought that people at Justice who I eventually worked with directly had solved that problem. If what you're saying is that we all solved problems with the Arms Export Control Act, I'm not arguing with that. What I'm trying to say is that we were looking for a legal, legitimate way to do it, and I thought we'd found it.

And I'm asking not to make more of these conversations than there is there. There's not some hidden agenda, sir.

MR. SULLIVAN: Next question.

MR. NIELDS: Finished. (Laughter.)

MR. SULLIVAN: Finished.

MR. NIELDS: I take it, that was in answer to the question of whether you pursued Method One, which was replenishment.

LT. COL. NORTH: It was.

MR. NIELDS: Thank you.

LT. COL. NORTH: And, by sale.

MR. NIELDS: Now, the next entry on this note of a conversation with Mr. Nir is, "Resupply should be as routine as possible, to prevent disclosure on our side. May take longer than two months. However, if crisis arises, Joshua promises that we will deliver all acquired by Galaxy in less than 18 hours."

LT. COL. NORTH: Right.

MR. NIELDS: I take it you were communicating to Mr. Nir a decision that had then been made by the President concerning the circumstances under which we would replenish.

LT. COL. NORTH: Exactly.

MR. NIELDS: The next entry is, "Joshua also wants both your government and ours to stay with 'no comment' if operation is disclosed."

LT. COL. NORTH: That's what we committed to, on both sides.

MR. NIELDS: And again, you were communicating to Mr. Nir, instructions that you had received from the President.

LT. COL. NORTH: Well, I want to make it very clear. I did not receive those directly from the President of the United States.

MR. NIELDS: Who did you receive it from?

LT. COL. NORTH: Those instructions were received by me from Admiral Poindexter, who specifically told me that here's what had been decided, and here's how we're going to proceed, and communicate that to your Israeli point of contact. And I communicated it to him exactly as I had gotten it. And I don't see anything then—I did not see anything then, nor do I see anything today that is wrong with that kind of a commitment.

MR. NIELDS: The next entry is, "If these conditions are acceptable to the banana, then oranges are ready to proceed."What is "banana"?

LT. COL. NORTH: Turn back to the code sheet. (Pause) The

143

banana is Israel. (Pause) I can't find—oh, I got it. Oranges is the United States.

MR. NIELDS: However, in fact, when the finding was signed two days later, the transaction was structured differently.

LT. COL. NORTH: No, I—the transaction to replenish the Israelis didn't change, I don't believe.

MR. NIELDS: Well, I think I'd like you to turn to Exhibit 60. (Pause while looking through papers) Do you have that in front of you?

LT. COL. NORTH: Not yet, counsel.

(Looking through papers)

MR. NIELDS: You see that 60 is a covert action finding of the 17th of January, together with a cover memo relating to that finding?

LT. COL. NORTH: That's correct.

MR. NIELDS: At the bottom of the first page of the cover sheet, it states:

It says: "As described by the Prime Minister's Emissary, the only requirement the Israelis have is an assurance that they will be allowed to purchase US replenishments for the stocks that they sell to Iran." And above that is described an Israeli proposal of Israeli sales followed by US replenishments.

The next sentence reads: "We have researched the legal problems of Israelis selling US-manufactured arms to Iran. Because of the requirement in US law for recipients of US arms to notify the US government of transfers to third countries, I do not recommend that you agree with the specific details of the Israeli plan. However, there is another possibility. Sometime ago, Attorney General William French Smith determined that under appropriate finding you could authorize the CIA to sell arms to countries outside the provisions of the laws and reporting requirements for foreign military sales." And then it refers lower down in that page to direct sales by us to Iran, not involving Israel. So I take it it's fair to say that the plan changed?

LT. COL. NORTH: Yes.

MR. NIELDS: And that was because of concerns arising —legal concerns arising under the Arms Export Control Act?

144

LT. COL. NORTH: Exactly. And I—what I want to emphasize, counsel, is that between the 17th of November and the 17th of January we got smarter as we went along in terms of what the constraints might be and the proper and best way to carry this out.

MR. NIELDS: You discovered that the proper way to do it in the future and at the same time discovered that the way that it had been done in the past created legal problems under the Arms Export Control Act?

LT. COL. NORTH: To this day, counsel, I, who am not a lawyer and do not pretend to be, am not certain that there is any flaw in the way that it was done during the summer. Certainly by—summer of '85—certainly by January of '86, I and the people with whom I was working recognized that there was a better way. I do not admit here—and I was not necessarily a part of the earlier transactions as they were agreed to, but I don't believe that anybody set out to violate the law; I don't believe the Israelis did, I don't believe Mr. McFarlane did when the transactions which occurred in 1985 were arranged.

What I am saying to you is we were trying very hard to make sure that the Israeli TOWs which had been shipped in September got replenished. We were trying very hard to make sure that whatever we did in the future was proper. And what you have here is not a conspiracy, but an effort on the part of hardworking government employees to do it the right way for the broader purposes I tried to define yesterday; and that's all this is.

MR. NIELDS: In the middle of the first page of the finding, again after referring to the Israel plan, it says: "To achieve the strategic goal of a more moderate Iranian government the Israelis are prepared to unilaterally commence selling military materiel to Western-oriented Iranian factions." Of course, in fact, the Israelis weren't prepared to commence such sales, they were prepared to continue them—

MR. SULLIVAN: Where are you reading from?

LT. COL. NORTH: Counsel, I don't see this on the finding. Where are we?

MR. NIELDS: Middle of the first page of the cover sheet.

LT. COL. NORTH: I see.

MR. NIELDS: It's the second sentence of the second

paragraph and it reads: "To achieve the strategic goal of a more moderate Iranian government the Israelis are prepared to unilaterally commence selling military materiel to Western oriented Iranian factions."

LT. COL. NORTH: That is correct. In that—they were prepared, in fact they had already done so.

MR. NIELDS: But this memo doesn't say that they'd already done so, it says they're about to start doing so.

LT. COL. NORTH: Well, I—I guess they were prepared to commence, you know, any time we said we'll replenish. And that was the whole issue.

MR. NIELDS: But, there's no reference in this finding to the prior sales, is there?

LT. COL. NORTH: Well, this is not a finding. This is the cover memo to the President.

MR. NIELDS: There's no reference in the cover memo to prior sales, is there?

LT. COL. NORTH: I haven't read the whole thing. I—having written it a long time ago, I will read it again.

MR. NIELDS: Do you want him to read it, Counsel, or shall we agree that the document says what it says?

MR. SULLIVAN: If you are willing, I'm willing to agree that the document says what it says and makes no reference to prior sales.

LT. COL. NORTH: Okay. It does not reference to prior sales, that is correct.

MR. NIELDS: And it does say that the Israelis are prepared to unilaterally commence selling military materiel? That's on the first page. I'll simply state that. I'm reading it from the document. And, I take it again, I think you testified to this yesterday. A year later when the chronologies were prepared that did make reference to the Israeli sales, they said, in the case of the earlier sale that we did—the August-September sale, that the US didn't know in advance that it was going to occur. And with respect to the November shipment of Hawks, falsely said that the US government understood that it was oil drilling equipment. And that was on the 20th. I take it—

LT. COL. NORTH: Again, in reference—you're talking about testimony given, I do not and still have not read what Director Casey said to the Committees—

MR. NIELDS: Referring to the chronologies that you testified yesterday—

LT. COL. NORTH: That is correct—

MR. NIELDS: that you participated in preparing?

LT. COL. NORTH: That is correct.

MR. NIELDS: And, then, I take it, you were informed on the 21st of November, 1986, for the first time, that the Attorney General had come up with the idea that there could be a mental finding which would have justified the Israeli sales.

LT. COL. NORTH: I don—I do not know or recall, at least, when I was told about the mental finding aspect of it, or the verbal finding, whatever one wants to call—

MR. NIELDS: Why don't you turn to Exhibit 40, I believe that's in Book 2.

(The witness peruses the exhibit)

MR. NIELDS: I think you need to look at Exhibits 39 and 40. These are pages out of your spiral notebook, and they to us xeroxed in a somewhat confusing way. Exhibit 39 refers to a call from RCM with AG.

LT. COL. NORTH: Yes.

MR. NIELDS: I take it "RCM" is Mr. McFarlane?

LT. COL. NORTH: That is correct.

MR. NIELDS: And he's calling you from the Attorney General's office?

LT. COL. NORTH: That's what I wrote down, and I'm sure that's what I was told, or I wouldn't have written it

MR. NIELDS: And the Committee has heard other evidence that he had an interview that afternoon, the 21st, with the Attorney General, in which he told him that he first learned about the Hawk missile shipment in May of 1986. And he understood that they were oil-drilling equipment. I'm not asking you. I'm simply stating for the record that the Committee has heard testimony to that effect. Now the Attorney General is calling you from—excuse me. Mr. McFarlane is calling you from the Attorney General's office, and you take notes of your converation with him?

LT. COL. NORTH: That is correct, on little yellow stick-'em pieces of paper, which I see are fastened to the wrong page. I'm quite sure that those three pages of stick-'em were originally on this page right here.

MR. NIELDS: And on the third page of Exhibit No. 40, it states, "RR said of course, in July."

LT. COL. NORTH: One second, please.

MR. NIELDS: Do you see that?

LT. COL. NORTH: Yes, I do.

MR. NIELDS: Mr. McFarlane is telling you this?

LT. COL. NORTH: Yes. I assume that these are the notes that I made during his call to me on the 21st at 5:45 in the evening.

MR. NIELDS: And then it says, "Intent of pres is important." And then it says, "RR said he would support." And then it says, in quotes, "mental finding."

LT. COL. NORTH: Yes.

MR. NIELDS: Now, do you recall that Mr. McFarlane told you that the Attorney General said these Israeli shipments could be justified by a mental finding by the President?

LT. COL. NORTH: I do not recall this conversation. I willingly admit that I wrote those words down based on the phone call I had received from Mr. McFarlane.

MR. NIELDS: Well, whatever clarification may be served by it, I will turn to Exhibit Number 32, which is a PROF message from Mr. McFarlane to Mr. Poindexter, in which he refers to—it's also dated the same day. It's—was sent at 2101. I take it that's 9:01 P.M.

LT. COL. NORTH: Right.

MR. NIELDS: It refers to his meeting with the Attorney General in the first paragraph. And then it says, "But it appears that the matter of not notifying about the Israeli transfers can be covered if the President made a, quote, 'mental finding,' unquote, before the transfers took place." By that time, the false chronologies had already been drafted. And Mr. Casey had already testified.

I'd like to turn back again to Exhibit 60, which is the finding—the memorandum and the finding of January 17th. On the second page at the top, it states, "The objectives of the Israeli plan could be met if the CIA, using an authorized agent as necessary, purchased arms from the Department of Defense under the Economy Act and then transferred them to Iran directly after receiving appropriate payment from Iran."

LT. COL. NORTH: I'm missing where you are, Counsel.

MR. NIELDS: Top of the second page. I don't think you—

LT. COL. NORTH: I see it.

MR. NIELDS: I'm directing your attention to the phrase, "authorized agent."

LT. COL. NORTH: Yes.

MR. NIELDS: Who is the authorized agent?

LT. COL. NORTH: By that time, it was General Secord.

MR. NIELDS: So General Secord was acting in connection with the Iranian initiative as an agent of the United States government?

LT. COL. NORTH: I'm not sure that "agent of" is the correct—and I don't—I'm not trying to split legal hairs. The purpose was to have, as I understood it, what Director Casey wanted was a plausible deniability, separation, that the CIA would not be directly face to face with the Iranians or the Israelis. And what we basically did was to mirror what the Israelis had done the previous year.

The Israelis had set up a non-government agent, in the case of Mr. Schwimmer, Mr. Ledeen and Mr. Ghorbanifar, to carry out their transactions. And basically, what we were doing is replicating in mirror image their organization. We had weapons being sold by the Pentagon under the Economy Act to the CIA, and the CIA selling them to a third party or an agent, in the case of General Secord, who would then complete the transaction. So that there were, if you will, cutouts or compartments in the action.

MR. NIELDS: Well, let me pose the question to you this way: The evidence that the Committee has reflects that on the first two sales conducted pursuant to this finding, the United States—the—Mr. Secord's Swiss bank accounts received $25 million as the purchase price.

LT. COL. NORTH: Yes.

MR. NIELDS: And that—

LT. COL. NORTH: Again, I'm not saying yes—that I understand—you're talking about the first two sales in '86?

MR. NIELDS: First two sales in '86.

LT. COL. NORTH: February and—

MR. NIELDS: And from those bank accounts, $8 million was paid into bank accounts controlled by the CIA, leaving a difference of $17 million that remained in the Swiss bank accounts under Mr. Secord's control.

My question to you is who in the United States government chose to structure the transaction so that there would be $17 million left in Mr. Secord's bank accounts?

LT. COL. NORTH: Well I don't know that it was structured to leave $17 million in the account, to start with. It was structured so by the time we got to the February transaction, it was structured in such a way that General Secord would become the person who actually conducted the transactions, that the government of the United States would be paid exactly what it asked for whatever was shipped. And that was what we did with the 1000 TOWs in February, and that's what we did with the Hawk parts that were shipped in May. And eventually the Hawks—excuse me, the Hawk parts—and TOWs later in the Autumn. In each case, the decision was made to allow General Secord to be the broker, if you will, for that transaction, that it would be his accounts that would then transfer monies to the Israelis, to the various people who needed to be paid, to include the government of the United States. I initially thought the money was coming from the Israelis in the person of Mr. Ghorbanifar—who was widely regarded in our government, at least in the CIA people I talked to, as an Israeli agent—to Mr. Secord's account, to the CIA, and then to the Pentagon, to pay for the weapons—or the materiel, whatever it was that was being shipped.

That was done for a number of purposes. One, to accrue sufficient funds to pay for Israeli replenishments for what had been shipped in '85; second of all, to generate revenues to support the Nicaraguan resistance; and third, to cover the costs of these transactions; and ultimately, further the cause of the approach that we made with the second channel.

MR. NIELDS: Who made the decision to structure the transaction in such a way that there was $17 million left for these purposes that you've described?

LT. COL. NORTH: You keep coming back to $17 million. I—I've just told you that I got approval to structure the transaction for the purposes I just told you.

MR. NIELDS: Whose idea was it?

LT. COL. NORTH: If I—and I'm going to ask you for the latitude to make a more—a longer discourse than ten words. When Mr. Nir arrived in the United States in the end of December or early January of 1985, early '86, the principal concern that he had, as he expressed it to me, was to keep this initiative moving, to further the goals that we—that I clearly understood of an opening to a more moderate regime in Iran, to get beyond the obstacle of the hostages—in other words, to recover them safely, because they were both a—a—a legitimate political problem here in the United States—you couldn't deal with the Iranians without getting beyond that—and to carry out a hoped for, and I think successful while we did it, program of reducing Shia-sponsored terrorism. He also had as a—as a very obvious goal, insurance that the Israeli TOWs that had been shipped in September be replenished, and that the Hawks, which were sitting in Iran at the time, be returned to Israel.

I had, by this time, had absolutely come to the conclusion that there was no way to do it by having the Israelis walk into the Pentagon and buy 508 new TOWs without it becoming a public issue. They knew that, and I knew that. And so Mr. Nir is the first person to suggest that there be a residual, and that the residual be applied to the purpose of purchasing replenishments, and supporting other activities. Now, at that point in time in early January, he did not raise with me the specifics of supporting the Nicaraguan resistance. That proposal came out of a meeting in, as I recall, later in January, where I met with Mr. Nir and Mr. Ghorbanifar—I'm gonna say London, but it may have been Frankfurt or it may have been elsewhere—and in that meeting, I expressed our grave reservations as to how the structure, which at that point in time focused on several thousand TOWs, would result in what we wanted. And, what we wanted were laid out very clearly in the January findings, and what we wanted was a more moderate regime, ultimately, in Iran, the cessation of Iranian Shia fundamentalist terrorism, and the return of the American hostages, which I viewed as an obstacle, and we had to overcome as a first step.

I expressed our reservations that the arrangements that were being made by Mr. Ghorbanifar, and by then acting in our behalf as well as the Israelis, were not going to lead to what we wanted. What we wanted, as a part of that overall program, was to establish a higher level meeting, well above my pay grade. In fact, I suggested a number of people, and

151

I'm sure you've seen it in my messages to my superiors, a number of people who could meet with senior Iranian officials, in various ways in which that could happen.

In that January meeting, I told him that I was not confident that we were headed in the right direction, and I tape-recorded that meeting. Mr. Ghorbanifar, by then, was aware of my role in support for the Nicaraguan resistance. He had seen my name in the newspapers. He is a very well-read individual. I had been told by the Central Intelligence Agency, by Director Casey himself, and by others in the CIA that they believed Mr. Ghorbanifar to be an Israeli intelligence agent. Mr. Ghorbanifar took me into the bathroom, and Mr. Ghorbanifar suggested several incentives to make that February transaction work, and the attractive incentive for me was the one he made, that residuals could flow to support the Nicaraguan resistance. He made it point blank, and he made it by my understanding with the full knowledge and acquiescence and support, if not the original idea, of the Israeli intelligence services, if not the Israeli government. Now I must confess to you, Mr. Nields, and I think you have seen it in my messages to my superiors. I was not entirely comfortable with the arrangements that had been worked in the summer of 1985, and in the autumn-winter of 1985. I made it very clear.

I was, after all, the person who in the United States government had the responsibility for coordinating our counter-terrorist policy. I had written for the President's words, "We will not make concessions to terrorists."

For the very first time, in January, the whole idea of using US weapons or US-origin weapons or Israeli weapons that had been manufactured in the United States, was made more palatable. I must confess to you that I thought using the Ayatollah's money to support the Nicaraguan resistance was a right idea. And I must confess to you that I advocated that.

To this day, you have referred to it as a "diversion." My understanding of the word "diversion" is that what we did is we took something off the course that was originally intended. And what we did is we diverted money out of the pocket of Mr. Ghorbanifar. And in the enormous files of intelligence that I had received from our intelligence agencies, it was very clear that Mr. Ghorbanifar, and perhaps others, had made enormous profits on the September and November transactions. They didn't make them on the November transaction, because it was never completed. But they certainly had, in the August-September transaction.

And I saw that idea, of using the Ayatollah Khomeini's money to support the Nicaraguan freedom fighters as a good one. I still do. I don't think it was wrong. I think it was a neat idea. And I came back, and I advocated that, and we did it. We did it on three occasions. Those three occasions were February, May, and October. And in each one of those occasions, as a consequence of that whole process, we got three Americans back. And there was no terrorism while we were engaged in it, against Americans. For almost 18 months, there was no action against Americans, until it started to come unraveled.

I believe then, and I believe now, that we had a chance to achieve a strategic opening. And right up until the last minute that I left the NSC, I was in communication with the Israelis and others who were working on the second channel to achieve that end.

The fact is that whether it was Mr. Ghorbanifar himself who originated the idea, or Mr. Nir, or others within the Israeli government, it was a good idea. It was a good idea because we weren't using the taxpayers' money, we were using the Ayatollah's money. And it went, indeed, to support the Nicaraguan resistance.

MR. NIELDS: You say you were using the Ayatollah's money. And another time, you said you were using Mr. Ghorbanifar's money.

LT. COL. NORTH: Mr. Ghorbanifar was ultimately getting the money from the Ayatollah. I don't know that the Ayatollah signed the checks. I know it was Iranian money. We watched the transfers through intelligence.

MR. NIELDS: But the fact of the matter is, Mr. Ghorbanifar was willing to pay that money for those missiles, regardless of how the money was used by the United States government. Isn't that true?

LT. COL. NORTH: I'm not certain. I don't understand the question, counsel.

MR. NIELDS: Well, let me try it this way. You already

knew before that meeting with Mr. Ghorbanifar—well, first, maybe we'd better fix the date of the meeting. I take it the meeting followed the finding?

LT. COL. NORTH: I'd have to refresh my memory. But I think it did. I'm not positive.

MR. NIELDS: Well, prior to the time of the finding, Mr. Secord was not going to be the cut-out. The Israelis were.

LT. COL. NORTH: Well, at least someone else would be a third party. That's true.

MR. NIELDS: But, in any event, I take it, the best of your recollection is that this conversation occurred in January, after the finding?

LT. COL. NORTH: I don't want to commit myself fully to that until I look at my travel schedule, which you by now know was intensive. And I will be glad to do so, if you've got something that will refresh. But I think it was, yes. The first meeting with Mr. Nir I recall vividly was immediately after Christmas, and was either very late December of '85 or early January of '86.

MR. NIELDS: And you already knew then that Ghorbanifar was willing to pay $10,000 per TOW?

LT. COL. NORTH: No. What I knew then was Ghorbanifar was willing to get $10,000 per TOW. I, to this day, don't know—first of all, in the September transaction, we were never able to determine that I can recall whether or not Mr. Ghorbanifar ever paid a penny for the TOWs that were shipped from Israel. And what we did know is that Mr. Ghorbanifar was willing to receive at least $10,000. I was subsequently told that Mr. Ghorbanifar had actually gotten thirteen or thirteen-and-a-half thousand, $13,500, maybe $14,000 apiece from the Iranians. When we opened the second channel and did a transaction with the second channel, Mr. Nir was extraordinarily upset that we weren't charging the same "high price."

Now, in fairness to Mr. Nir, Mr. Nir very cleary wanted to support other activities, as he put it, through these transactions. There were a number of proposals made. Some of those are referenced in the files that I gave you. I believe that those are very, very sensitive documents. And, as I said yesterday, I would have believed tht executive privilege should have prevented those documents [from being] turned over, and certainly not disclosed to the world —because those operations can affect the lives of Americans. But those were proposals that Mr. Nir had, and that some of the residuals would be used to fund those operations. And I sought approval from my superiors for those operations. I discussed those operations directly with Director Casey, and there were various code names as you saw—TA-1, TH-1, et cetera—in my documents referred to, as Mr. Nir defined them.

Incidentally, just one last point, if you'll indulge me. I realize that people snicker when they refer to the code sheet. The reason we were using the code sheet was not some joke or some childish code from Captain Midnight. We were talking on open telephone lines. And I will tell you right now that, were it not for that code and the fact that we were able to talk over open telephone lines, we might not have been able to capture the terrorists who sea-jacked the Achille Lauro and killed Leon Klinghoffer.

MR. NIELDS: I think the only question has to do with price.

LT. COL. NORTH: I know it has to do with price.

MR. NIELDS: I think the only question has to do with price.

MR. SULLIVAN: Mr. Nields, Mr. Chairman, if the witness believes that something is related to the subject matter of the question he should be permitted to answer.

CHAIRMAN INOUYE: The question related to price and I hope that the witness will respond to the question.

LT. COL. NORTH: Mr. Chairman, I tried to respond to the question of price.

CHAIRMAN INOUYE: We have been—

LT. COL. NORTH: The way the question was asked, Mr. Chairman, was, who authorized $17 million etc. to go to that account? And I'm saying that what I was authorized to do was to allow that account to be used to further these transactions and the purposes to which the residuals generated by those transactions would be used, and I sought approval for that and I was granted approval for that.

CHAIRMAN INOUYE: And we permitted you over 10 minutes to make that explanation. The question now is price, please respond to that.

155

MR. SULLIVAN: Mr. Chairman, I object to that. Colonel North is attempting to do the very best he can. And I want to state to the Chairman, and I should put it on the record right now, that I believe that we're being subjected to a stall job. We met with you, Mr. Chairman—

CHAIRMAN INOUYE: Who is responsible for the stall, sir?

MR. SULLIVAN: Counsel. Let me, let me clarify one thing, sir, please. When you and I, and Senator Rudman, and Mr. Hamilton sat across the table and tried to arrive at a solution in which we balanced the interests of Colonel North and weighed his constitutional rights against the Committee's need to obtain the facts, we left that meeting and those negotiations relying upon the intention—not promise—the intention of the Committee to resolve its questioning of Colonel North within four days. A letter was sent to me by Counsel after that meeting saying that you intended to conclude these—the question by July 10th.

Over the last day and several hours, I must say that the rambling questions and the inability to finish the subject matter and proceed to another has caused me concern. When Colonel North wants to give an answer which seems to tell the story, he's cut off, and Mr. Nields keeps saying to him, "Well, we'll get back to that, we'll get back to that." I'd suggest that if you give Colonel the opportunity to tell the story, he can tell the story.

I was disheartened last night, Mr. Chairman, when I saw on the national news, two Senators make reference to the fact that these hearings were likely to go into next week. I don't know why they should go into next week. The intention of the Committee was that there be four days; that there be 30 questioners. I don't know what's happened, and I don't want to prejudge the Committee, as some members of the Committee have prejudged Colonel North, but I suspect, sir, that what's happening here is we're meandering through questions in a disjointed fashion so that when it comes Friday, you can say, Mr. Chairman, that it's necessary to continue on Monday, or perhaps Tuesday.

You know, as a trial lawyer I know a stall when I see one. There's never been a lawyer that tried a case that didn't know that stalling and putting a weekend in between a witness' testimony so you can disect his examination and ask further questions on Monday is not a good tactic. So I would request, Mr. Chairman, that if Colonel North is given the opportunity to answer the questions fully, as he believes —as he's trying to do, I would suggest that we'd make a great deal of progress and that the Committee would be able to fulfill its promise to us—its stated intentions that we finish this matter on Friday, and we're doing our best to do that.

And I might add, that we're willing, if the Committee is willing, to sit a longer day. For example yesterday, with a two hour lunch, and concluding at 5:00, those kinds of shortened schedules are likely to lead us into next week. So we earnestly request and respectfully request—and I hope the Committee hasn't changed its intention despite the statement of a couple of Senators last night—our goal here is to finish this by the close of business Friday, and I know Colonel North is trying his hardest to do that, and I'm trying to do so as well. Thank you, sir.

SENATOR GEORGE MITCHELL (D-ME): Mr. Chairman?

CHAIRMAN INOUYE: May the record show that it took four and a half minutes to explain the stall.

(Laughter)

Senator Mitchell.

MR. SULLIVAN: Mr. Chairman, I thought that if I did lay out, clearly and respectfully to you, what my concern was that perhaps it would facilitate speeding up instead of trying to drag this proceeding into next week, and submit Col. North to the incessant questioning of 30 people. Thank you, sir.

SEN. MITCHELL: Mr. Chairman, may I be recognized?

CHAIRMAN INOUYE: Yes, sir.

SEN. MITCHELL: Mr. Chairman, I was present at the meeting to which Mr. Sullivan referred, and I believe the record should show that at that meeting I stated to Mr. Sullivan that in my judgment his two requests, one that there be no prior private testimony, and second, that the testimony in public be limited to 30 hours, were inconsistent and incompatible, and that the inevitable effect of not having prior private testimony would be to make the public testimony much longer than would otherwise be the case. And, that in my view, if he insisted in pursuing his demand

157

for no prior private testimony, as he did, and as this Committee acceded to his demand, that inevitably Counsel would have to in public go over many areas that they would not have to do in private.

And, as you will recall, Mr. Chairman, and members of the Committee, it was at my insistence, anticipating that precisely this type of statement would be made at some point in the proceedings, but I insisted that the letter of intention include an explicit statement to the effect that this was not any binding commitment, and depending on the scope and nature of the testimony, and other facts and circumstances as they may arise, that the testimony might go beyond that.

Therefore, Mr. Chairman, I think the record should show that in my judgment, I believe the committee members should know this objection is wholly unfounded, without any merit, and I believe the Counsel should be permitted to question as he has, because he's not had the opportunity to question in private, and therefore he must cover these areas as thoroughly as he can.

MR. SULLIVAN: May I respond, Mr. Chairman?

CHAIRMAN INOUYE: I thank the senator from Maine, and may the record also show that as far as the Chair is concerned, Mr. Nields has been carrying on in a very orderly and professional manner.

MR. SULLIVAN: Mr.—may I respond briefly, Mr. Chairman, please?

CHAIRMAN INOUYE: Briefly, sir.

MR. SULLIVAN: Yes. This—Mr. Mitchell accurately describes the views that he presented at the meeting, and apparently those views were overruled, because I received a letter from Counsel, in paragraph 5, which says as follows: Quote, "The committees intend to complete Lt. Col. North's testimony by the close of the hearing on July 10th, 1987, and do not intend to recall Lt. Col. North for further testimony."

I'm leaving out some of the remaining words.

CHAIRMAN INOUYE: Read the whole paragraph in. (Laughter.)

MR. SULLIVAN: I'll be glad to. (Laughter.) I'll be glad to. (Laughter continues.) I'd like to make this a part of the

158

record. I left out the words becaue it's unrelated to this particular issue. I'll read it again. Quote: "The committees intend to complete Lt. Col. North's testimony by the close of the hearing on July 10th, 1987, and do not intend to recall Lt. Col. North for further testimony, unless (emphasizing) extraordinary developments create a compelling need therefor, and that any such recall"—not initial testimony, Mr. Mitchell—"recall would be limited to the matters that necessitated the recall."

My point is that in order to accommodate Lt. Col. North—

SEN. MITCHELL: Would you read the whole paragraph?

CHAIRMAN INOUYE: Read the whole paragraph.

MR. SULLIVAN: Yes, sir. Would you like to see it?

MR._____: Mr. Chairman—

MR. SULLIVAN: Let me make clear—this is—we were told—this is not a binding agreement. I don't want to mislead you. (Laughter.) This is the intention, the stated, a stated intention of Mr. Hamilton and Chairman Inouye. We are relying on the stated intention to go forward. I find it a little disheartening, last night, to see two senators say that they're going to go into next week. Now what happened yesterday, that all of a sudden the intention is not able to be complied with? It's just an intention. We're asking that the intention that we relied upon be kept.

CHAIRMAN INOUYE: I believe you've had enough time. May I just, for the record, so that the record will be clear, read the rest of this paragraph?

"Although it is not now the intention of the Committees, the scope and nature of Lt. Col. North's testimony could result in his testimony continuing beyond four days, and in his later recall. Matters on which the Committees are not waiving their power, and we understand that you are not waiving any rights."

MR. SULLIVAN: Mr. Chairman, I ask that the whole letter be put into the record as an exhibit.

CHAIRMAN INOUYE: It is so ordered. And your objection is overruled.

159

MR. SULLIVAN: Thank you, Mr. Chairman.

CHAIRMAN INOUYE: Mr. Nields, proceed.

MR. NIELDS: Col. North, my question is this. Mr. Ghorbanifar was willing to pay, I take it, a certain amount of money in order to acquire missiles from the United States.

LT. COL. NORTH: Yes.

MR. NIELDS: And that amount was $10,000 per TOW.

LT. COL. NORTH: I don't know that that was the peak price that he was willing to pay. Again, I think that—

MR. NIELDS: It was the price he did pay, wasn't it?

LT. COL. NORTH: I'd have to have my memory refreshed on exactly what he did pay. But I guess it's somewhere in that—

MR. NIELDS: One thousand TOWs, $10 million. I think the math comes up with $10,000 per TOW.

LT. COL. NORTH: Okay.

MR. NIELDS: And he was willing to pay that money, whether we used it to put into the United States Treasury, or whether we used it to support the contras. Isn't that true?

LT. COL. NORTH: Yes.

MR. NIELDS: He suggested that we might want to use it to support the contras, but that was up to us.

LT. COL. NORTH: Correct.

MR. NIELDS: So, it was "our" money that was going to the contras, not Mr. Ghorbanifar's.

LT. COL. NORTH: You've lost me, Counsel. I was with you right up 'til you said that. When you said "our money"—

MR. NIELDS: $10 million, Mr. Ghorbanifar was willing to pay to acquire US missiles. And he did pay it.

LT. COL. NORTH: Let me, let me—

MR. NIELDS: Am I correct so far?

LT. COL. NORTH: No. He was willing to pay, perhaps, even more. He actually charged, from what we were able to determine from intelligence, he actually charged considerably more—

MR. NIELDS: He was willing to pay $10 million, wasn't he?

LT. COL. NORTH: He did pay—

MR. NIELDS: And he did pay $10 million?

LT. COL. NORTH: Yes. But I want to make it clear that he was willing to pay that for those missiles whether he got them here, or he was able to get them from Israel, or wherever he could get them.

MR. NIELDS: That was what he was willing to pay, and did pay, for the missiles sold by the US government?

LT. COL. NORTH: If you say the first transaction was $10 million, I'll believe you.

MR. NIELDS: I do. And we could do with that money what we wished, as a government. Isn't that true?

LT. COL. NORTH: Yeah, look, I'm trying to be helpful. But the government of the United States was not out there dealing directly with Mr. Ghorbanifar.

MR. NIELDS: Well you just testified to a meeting you had in the bathroom—

MR. SULLIVAN: Mr. Chairman, please, sir.

(bang of gavel)

CHAIRMAN HAMILTON: Please address the chair.

MR. SULLIVAN: Mr. Chairman?

CHAIRMAN INOUYE: Yes, sir?

MR. SULLIVAN: Could counsel please permit the witness to finish his answer and not to interrupt him in mid-answer.

CHAIRMAN INOUYE: The counsel may decide the pace, sir. Mr. Nields—

MR. SULLIVAN: Mr. Chairman, I object. I believe you are making the rulings here. I make the objections, you make the rulings. Please don't permit him to make his own rulings.

CHAIRMAN INOUYE: The Chair is making the ruling, sir. Please proceed.

MR. NIELDS: Did you meet with Mr. Ghorbanifar directly, face to face?

LT. COL. NORTH: Yes, I met with Mr. Ghorbanifar face to face. And in those meetings, after the meeting in January, I then introduced General Secord—I believe he was using the pseudonym at the time that we had arranged for—and he became the person with whom Mr. Ghorbanifar negotiated prices, delivery schedules, arrangements. And Mr. Secord —General Secord then became the person who went back and paid the government of the United States through the CIA exactly what the government of the United States wanted for the commodities that it provided. You—you keep saying that it was "our money." General Secord was an outside entity who had been established as an outside entity

161

many, many months before—in order to support the Nicaraguan resistance, as I described yesterday—by authority that was given to me. And I am the person that recruited this poor man into this. The fact is, General Secord became the person who then was the outside party to be in direct contact.

So when I made the initial arrangements, I didn't establish the final price. I certainly didn't establish the price that the government of the United States wanted for the commodities that it was providing. That price was determined in dialogue between the Defense Department and the Central Intelligence Agency, through a system that is long and well established. When the government of the United States decided on its price, it communicated it to me, I told General Secord what the price was, and he further dealt with Mr. Ghorbanifar and the Israelis and others. He made arrangements to move them, he made the arrangements to deliver them.

MR. NIELDS: When you met face to face with Mr. Ghorbanifar in the bathroom, were you meeting with him as a representative of the United States government?

LT. COL. NORTH: I was.

MR. NIELDS: Now isn't it a fact that at that meeting, you already knew that Ghorbanifar was willing to pay $10,000 a TOW?

LT. COL. NORTH: By that meeting, as I said earlier, we knew from our intelligence that he was willing to pay at least $10 million, and that he received a sum above that from the Iranians—considerably above that.

MR. NIELDS: Who decided how that $10 million was going to be used—you, Mr. Secord, or someone else?

LT. COL. NORTH: I described for General Secord the purposes to which I thought that money ought to be applied. And throughout my long experience with General Secord —who, after all, had been referred to me by Director Casey who was the one that suggested him back in 1984 as the person to assist us outside the government to comply with the Boland proscriptions—I relied on General Secord to carry that transaction out. There were various points in time when we would discuss these activities. I certainly had to tell him what the government was going to charge for various commodities. But ultimately, the decision was his.

And yet, I wish to point out he always, to my knowledge, did what I asked.

MR. NIELDS: Are you testifying that the transaction was set up, structured in such a way that it was up to General Secord to decide how the residuals were going to be used?

LT. COL. NORTH: Well, I—I don't want to put it all on his back. There was always a concert of opinion that the purposes of the residuals were as follows: to sustain the Iranian operation; to support the Nicaraguan resistance; to continue other activities which the Israelis very clearly wanted and so did we; and, to pay for a replacement for the original Israeli TOWs shipped in 1985.

MR. NIELDS: And whose—

LT. COL. NORTH: And we, I think, used that money for that purpose.

MR. NIELDS: And whose decision was it, how those monies were to be used?

LT. COL. NORTH: Well, I got—I briefed my boss, I talked to Admiral Poindexter about it, I talked to Director Casey about it, and I communicated it back to General Secord, and said, "Here. Here's what we've got to do. You figure out how you're going to allocate the monies to accomplish those purposes. And to my knowledge, he did so.

MR. NIELDS: So you, and you testified to this yesterday, sought approval from the National Security Advisor and the President of the United States as to how this money was to be used, and you received it.

LT. COL. NORTH: I want to make it very clear, Mr. Nields. I did not say I sought it from the President. I assumed that I had it from the President—

MR. NIELDS: But you wrote—

LT. COL. NORTH: I was subsequently told that I didn't have it from the President.

MR. NIELDS: You wrote memoranda that you sent to the National Security Advisor recommending that he obtain approval of the President.

LT. COL. NORTH: That is correct.

MR. NIELDS: So you sought Presidential approval.

LT. COL. NORTH: Yes, but I—but something else that I tried to say yesterday, Mr. Nields, is, I sent forward memoranda that described what we hoped to accomplish. And in the one exhibit that you showed me that was left in my files, that was found by the Attorney General's representatives in my office and in my files, there is a very brief, two subparagraph mention, in a multi-page memo describing what we are about. That very brief reference is the only reference in that memo to what you have called "the diversion."

And what I'm saying to you is, the memoranda that I sent forward described the overall process that we were about. It described what we were trying to accomplish. And in very brief mention, it talked about what we hoped to achieve as part of that process.

MR. NIELDS: My question is, why, if it was up to Mr. Secord to decide what to do with the $10 million, did you seek the President's approval to use it for the contras?

LT. COL. NORTH: What I sought was, as I just tried to articulate, I sought the overall approval for the overall plan, a part of, and in fact a relatively small part of the overall plan for dealing with the Iranians, was the use of residuals from those transactions to help the Nicaraguan freedom fighters.

And it was, if you just look at the number of words dedicated to that aspect of it in the one memo that still exists, it is a very brief mention, not because it's trying to be buried, but because it was a very—relatively small part of it. It has been made an enormous political event, but I'm telling you it was a relatively small part of the overall objective. The overall objectives were what I just articulated.

We were striving, as the finding clearly indicates, and I wrote those words into the finding, those words had come from the earliest discussions I had with Mr. Ledeen and Mr. McFarlane in the summer of 1985, as to what we hoped to achieve as a consequence of these deliveries or transactions with the Iranians. That's what we were about.

MR. NIELDS: I don't want to belabor the point, but let me see if I can ask the question simply once, and see if you can answer this one way or the other. Whose decision was it whether the monies would be used for the contras or not—someone in the US government or General Secord?

LT. COL. NORTH: The decision was made that residuals from those transactions would be applied to support the Nicaraguan resistance with the authority that I got from my superiors, Admiral Poindexter, with the concurrence of William J. Casey, and I thought at the time, the President of the United States. I later learned that the President was unaware of that aspect of these transactions.

MR. NIELDS: And if the United States government had decided that the $10 million less expenses should all be paid into the United States Treasury, then that's what would have happened, isn't it?

MR. SULLIVAN: —the question—

LT. COL. NORTH: Please, Counsel—

MR. SULLIVAN: One time—(laughter)

LT. COL. NORTH: Pl—now, I—the United States government charged x-thousands of dollars for a commodity. If I were to buy a piece of land from the United States Park Service, for $10 thousand, and then a year later or a week later, go out and sell it for $20 thousand, would the government of the United States lay claim to my $10 thousand profit? I—I know I'm not supposed to ask the questions—but I just asked—

MR. NIELDS: That did not answer my question—

LT. COL. NORTH: But, that's what—

MR. NIELDS: Counsel said you'd already answered it—

MR. SULLIVAN: (Inaudible)

MR. NIELDS: I would like an answer.

CHAIRMAN INOUYE: —remind counsel, but he is well aware of the rules. Please address the Chair.

MR. SULLIVAN: Yes, sir—

CHAIRMAN INOUYE: And let's not stall the proceedings —(laughter)

MR. SULLIVAN: Mr. Chairman, if taking four minutes to explain my position can expedite the proceedings and remind the Chair of its intended—its intention to us to complete these hearings in four days, then I think it's four minutes well worth spent.

LT. COL. NORTH: Whose turn?

MR. NIELDS: The question was, if those higher-ups in the United States government from whom you sought approval decided that the $10 million should not—any part of it be sent to the contras, but should all come back to the United States Treasury, that's what would have happened, isn't it?

LT. COL. NORTH: Yes.

MR. NIELDS: So, it was our money that was going to the contras, wasn't it?

LT. COL. NORTH: I—I disagree with your conclusion, Counsel. I'm sorry, Mr. Chairman. I disagree with your conclusion. If my boss had told me, "Ollie, every penny that comes from this thing goes right back into the Treasury of the United States of America," that's exactly what I would have asked Gen. Secord to do. And I am confident that is exactly what he would have done. Okay? I was never asked to do that. I got approval to do what I did and I didn't do anything without approval. And I'm not trying to pass it all off on somebody else. I was a part of the decision-making process and that I strongly advocated positions as you have seen in my notes. As you have seen in the voluminous pile of documents. I was a part of a process, I took strong positions that I believed in, I tried to define the risks and the benefits and to lay before my superiors what I thought the advantages of doing it—pursuing a certain course of action. And I believed that they carried them out with—with the full authority that they had, and I still, to this day, Counsel, don't see anything wrong with taking the Ayatollah's money and sending it to support the Nicaraguan freedom fighters.

MR. NIELDS: Yes, Mr. Chairman.

CHAIRMAN INOUYE: Recess for 10 minutes. (Recess)

CHAIRMAN INOUYE: May we have order? Mr. Nields.

MR. NIELDS: Col. North, was it your arrangement, or any part of your arrangement or the government's arrangement with Gen. Secord that some part of the money received from the sale of arms to Iran was to go to Mr. Secord's personal benefit?

LT. COL. NORTH: The arrangement that I made with Gen. Secord starting in 1984 recognized that those who were supporting our effort were certainly deserving of just and fair and reasonable compensation. After all, I had—and it may be important to understand how he came to be engaged in this, because when, in 1984 we were approaching the proscriptions under Boland, Director Casey and I had had a number of discussions. I had made a number of trips and I had, obviously, by then become much more engaged in the support for the resistance. Director Casey is the one who

166

had suggested Gen. Secord to me as a person who had a background in covert operations, a man of integrity, a West Point graduate, a man who had experience in these kinds of matters, and was a man who—by Director Casey's definition—got things done, and who had been poorly treated. Those was his words.

I approached Gen. Secord in 1984 and asked that he become engaged in these activities. He was, at that point in time, out of the government and an American businessman. He thought for several days or weeks about the matter. I went back to him again. And, at some point in '84, he agreed to become actively engaged. He agreed to establish, and did, private commercial entities outside the United States that could help carry out these activities. It was always viewed by myself, by Mr. McFarlane, by Director Casey, that these were private commercial ventures —private commercial activities. And I always assumed —and I think I specifically said on a number of occasions —that certainly, because he was being taken from his other pursuits, that fair and just and reasonable compensation was deserved, as it was by the pilots who flew the airplanes and the mechanics that fixed them, et cetera.

CHAIRMAN INOUYE: May I interrupt? A vote is now in progress in the United States Senate. Mr. Sullivan, we will be leaving for a few minutes to vote. Please proceed.

MR. NIELDS: Just to make sure that we have the answer on the record, was it part of your understanding with Mr. Secord that the proceeds—some of the proceeds of the sale of arms to Iran would inure to his personal benefit?

LT. COL. NORTH: As fair, just and reasonable compensation, yes.

MR. NIELDS: And on whose authority did you enter into that arrangement?

MR. SULLIVAN: May I note, just for the record, that the rules require that one Senator be present in order that there be a quorum, I think—

SEN. JAMES MCCLURE (R-ID): Let the record show there's one here. (Laughter.)

MR. SULLIVAN: Thank you, sir. (Laughter.) I didn't see you hiding up there! (Laughter.) You got me on that one! One for the Senate. (Laughter.) It's just that when there are so few of us over here and so many over there it's hard to keep track, Senator.

MR. NIELDS: Do you have the question in mind?

LT. COL. NORTH: Forgive me, and please repeat it.

MR. NIELDS: On whose authority did you enter into an arrangement with General Secord that he would be able to take compensation out of the proceeds of arms sales to Iran?

LT. COL. NORTH: Well, I—again, I want to go back to what I said earlier. It was clearly indicated to Mr. McFarlane and Admiral Poindexter, and in fact, almost drawn up by Director Casey how these would be outside the US government. And that I told them right from the very beginning that those things that he did deserved fair and just compensation. And so I don't know that I specifically said that this transaction via some other transaction would or would not result in compensation being derived therefrom. So what I'm saying, it was simply a continuation on another mission by which he was entitled to that. I don't think I specifically addressed that issue to anyone because it was already known from his earlier activities in support of our foreign policy in those private activities from 1984 on.

MR. NIELDS: So, to your recollection you never discussed with Admiral Poindexter, for example, the fact that some of the proceeds of the sale of arms to Iran would inure to General Secord's personal benefit?

LT. COL. NORTH: No, but—and, Counsel, I'm not trying to be a nitpicker on this thing, but I'm saying that it was recognized that he had established a number of commercial enterprises or activities or companies outside the United States that needed to be supported, and that they would be set up as commercial activities and that he would be compensated right from the very beginning. I don't believe anybody focused on a specific activity that would or a specific activity that wouldn't achieve that benefit.

MR. NIELDS: How much, under your arrangement with General Secord, was he to take from the proceeds of the sale of arms to Iran?

LT. COL. NORTH: I don't recall that we ever discussed a specific amount of what reasonable compensation was. As I told you, I trusted that the General was, and as far as I am concerned today, still is an honorable man, and that when

168

he said, you know, "I'm being taken from my other activities," and I said, "Fair and just compensation is appropriate," I trusted that he would do so. And I don't—never recall discussing a specific amount or rate or percentage or anything like that.

MR. NIELDS: How did the government keep track of how much General Secord was taking for his own personal benefit?

LT. COL. NORTH: You keep saying it that way—and I relied on the reports I got from him.

MR. NIELDS: And what kind of reports did he give to you?

LT. COL. NORTH: I would periodically get a summary statement, as I know that there are some in my records, that indicated how much was left and where, and what purposes it was being spent for in broad, gross terms—but not in specific—I did not ask for an accounting sheet on a daily, weekly, monthly basis, or even an annual basis.

MR. NIELDS: Well, just using the rough sheets that you've got, how much money, according to your understanding, did Mr. Secord take from the sale of arms to Iran?

LT. COL. NORTH: I still don't know. I don't even know that he did.

MR. NIELDS: Do you know even in gross terms?

LT. COL. NORTH: No, sir.

MR. NIELDS: Was it your understanding, as of November of 1986, that there was $8 million, either in Swiss bank accounts or in investment accounts as CSF?

LT. COL. NORTH: No.

MR. NIELDS: Was it your understanding that most of that money had already been spent for the contras?

MR. NIELDS: It was my understanding throughout that money was being spent for the purposes I defined earlier. I think it's important we talk to that—that money be used to replace or replenish the Israeli TOWs, that money be used to support the Nicaraguan resistance, that money be used to support other activities. And I certainly tasked him with a number of those—and that money be used to keep alive the Iranian initiative. And that I relied on his judgment to see to it that the monies were appropriately allocated to those purposes. I would periodically call up on the phone, or call a meeting with him, and say, "Tomorrow, we need to have a ship at Point X." And he'd say, "That's a neat, unforeseen circumstance. Why didn't you tell me yesterday?" And I would say, "I didn't know about it yesterday." And he would go out and get a ship. That's what I referred to as another activity.

MR. NIELDS: How much money, according to your understanding, remained in these Swiss bank accounts under his control, as of November 1986?

LT. COL. NORTH: I did not know. In fact, at the very end of this thing and to this day, I still do not know how much money was under his control and where it was. I simply relied on the fact that I had a relationship of trust between myself and Gen. Secord, between Gen. Secord and Director Casey, obviously—that those activities were being carried out.

MR. NIELDS: In gross terms, if you can give it—as gross as need be in order to match your understanding at the time, how much money remained unspent under his control in November of '86?

LT. COL. NORTH: Again, I did not have a feel for that. In fact, I don't think I was aware of the final transaction's ultimate amount until after I—these hearings began, simply because I was transferred relatively quickly after those things happened and I spent, I think, almost the entirety of the first ten days in November in meetings or in transit thereto, back and forth around the world.

MR. NIELDS: I think you testified earlier that the thing that made this project truly appealing to you for the first time was when you learned in January from Ghorbanifar that the money could be used to support the contras.

LT. COL. NORTH: No, the way I put it was Mr. Ghorbanifar was trying to encourage us to proceed with the initiative. I had, in accord with my instructions, carried to that meeting very strong reservations on our part that what he was doing in this transaction, or the transaction which was first proposed in January, was going to lead to accomplishing our objectives. And so I went in there and I said, "Look, these things aren't going to work. It's not going to get us from where we are today to where we want to be tomorrow." And he started offering incentives to make it more palatable, and that's when he suggested, "Well look, we'll just use some of that money to support the Nicaraguan resistance. I have read about you, you have been in the papers" —in fact, by then I think I'd even been in *Izvestia* —"and I know what you really do in your spare time. You support the Nicaraguan resistance, don't you?" (I said), "Among other things." And he said, "Why don't you use some of this money for that purpose?" And as I described to you before we took recess, I thought it was a right good idea, and I came back and advocated it, and we did it.

MR. NIELDS: Even Ghorbanifar knew that you were supporting the contras.

LT. COL. NORTH: Yes, he did. *Izvestia* knew it, my name had been in the papers in Moscow, had been all over Danny Ortega's newscasts, Radio Havana was broadcasting it, it had been in every newspaper in the land.

MR. NIELDS: All our enemies knew it, and you wanted to conceal it from the United States Congress.

LT. COL. NORTH: We wanted to be able to deny a covert operation for the very purposes that I described to you yesterday, Counsel.

MR. NIELDS: The question is this: In the first Exhibit —you don't need to turn to it—you indicate that $12 million will be available for the contras from the Iranian arms sales. Our testimony that the Committee has taken has shown that some approximately $4 million from all of the sales were used for the contras. My question is this: Would it have surprised you in November of 1986 to learn that Gen. Secord had used $4 million—the proceeds of Iranian sales for the contras—and had $8 million remaining in the pot?

LT. COL. NORTH: I was surprised, and I—I want to note, I still don't understand that and I'm not willing at this point to accuse anybody, but I—I was surprised.

MR. NIELDS: I'd like you to turn to Exhibit 160, it's in Book 7. You have that in front of you?

LT. COL. NORTH: Yes.

MR. NIELDS: It's a short PROFs message from you to Admiral Poindexter. And it refers to a, I believe it's a transaction that you've already testified about with Country One?

LT. COL. NORTH: Yes.

MR. NIELDS: And then it says at the end of it, "As I told

you in the other note, I talked to Casey this morning about Secord." Excuse me, it's from Admiral Poindexter, to you, I—I beg your pardon.

LT. COL. NORTH: Yes.

MR. NIELDS: September of 1986. And in the end it says, "Keep the pressure on Bill to make things right for Secord." What was he talking about?

MR. SULLIVAN: To be accurate, I think we need a country list today, it wasn't provided to us.

LT. COL. NORTH: I think I recall which one is Country One. My recollection is that there was still a security clearance problem that existed that came about as a consequence of an earlier investigation of Gen. Secord during his tenure in the government. And Director Casey had mentioned that to me, in fact Director Casey is, I believe, the person, at least someone, and it may have been Director Casey who showed me a determination by Judge June Green of the US District Court, the US District Court which was a—whatever it's called, a legal opinion or a determination that he was an honorable man and his reputation should not have been impugned in a libel case or something, I'm not sure of the exact circumstances. Director Casey felt—at least as he described him to me, that Gen. Secord had been maligned, that he'd been wrongly dealt with. And, yet, when I would go to Director Casey or even when Gen. Secord, himself, talked with Director Casey, the bureaucracy was unwilling to do what was necessary to give him the appropriate security clearances and the like. There was also, by this point in time, a suggestion by Gen. Secord that he return to the government, and Director Casey, at least as far as he talked to me about it, was enthusiastic about that, and that it was seen by myself, and I guess by Admiral Poindexter. I assume that that's what it refers to, that that ought to be done, that there ought to be a clean-up, if you will, of the reputation problem that existed from his earlier and abbreviated tenure in the government.

MR. NIELDS: Just to make sure, to your understanding, does this reference, "making things right for Dick" in the PROF message from Admiral Poindexter, have anything to do with money?

LT. COL. NORTH: I don't think so.

MR. NIELDS: I'd like you to turn to Exhibit #161. It's the next exhibit, and the part I have referenced to begins at the very bottom of the first page, dated 9/17/86, and to get substance you have to turn to the second page.

LT. COL. NORTH: I don't have a second page, Counsel.

MR. NIELDS: Do you have Exhibit #161?

LT. COL. NORTH: I do. I have a one-page, top part is black, no second page.

MR. NIELDS: If you are hampered in answering my question because of the absence of the document, say so. And, we'll provide it later, and we'll return to it. There is a reference in a PROF message: "This is the one I tried to get Casey's people to pay for as a means of covering some of Dick's debts."

MR. SULLIVAN: Counsel, I think it's always better to have the document in front of us.

MR. NIELDS: We'll return to it. It's #161. We'll simply return to it.

MR. SULLIVAN: Very good.

MR. NIELDS: I'd like to turn now to Exhibit #164. Do you have that in front of you?

LT. COL. NORTH: I do.

MR. NIELDS: That's a PROF message of the same date, 17th of September, from you to Admiral Poindexter.

LT. COL. NORTH: I'm looking at one from Admiral Poindexter to me.

MR. NIELDS: Look at the one below it.

LT. COL. NORTH: Okay. All right. I see it.

MR. NIELDS: Do you see that one?

LT. COL. NORTH: Right.

MR. NIELDS: The first part of it deals with Iran, and down towards the bottom of the note, the middle of the bottom section of the note, there's a line that ends with the word "CIA," and it reads as follows: "CIA could not produce an aircraft on such short notice, so Dick has chartered the aircraft through one of Project Democracy's overseas companies. Why Dick can do something in five minutes that the CIA cannot do in two days is beyond me, but he does. How the hell he is ever going to pay for it, is also a matter of concern. But Dick is a good soldier and never even groused about it."

Was it your understanding at that time that Mr. Secord's accounts were out of money?

LT. COL. NORTH: Well let me—let me first of all try to figure out what we're talking about here.

MR. NIELDS: Okay. Take your time. (Pause)

LT. COL. NORTH: Okay. I believe that's the transportation of the second channel to the United States.

MR. NIELDS: My question is, was it your understanding that his Swiss accounts were out of money at that time?

LT. COL. NORTH: It was my understanding that there was a shortage of funds to be used for this activity at that time, or I would not have put that into the record.

MR. NIELDS: So that confirms that it—and explains why you've testified that you were surprised to learn that there was $8 million remaining?

LT. COL. NORTH: Well, I've taken your word that it's $8 million remaining. I don't know that. What I've also testified is that there were four purposes for the funds in what is referred to here as Project Democracy. And it was very clear that funds were to be allocated for different purposes, whether those were in separate boxes in the same bank, I don't know. What is important to understand is, I believed at several points that we were low on monies that could be used to support the Nicaraguan resistance, or at this point, that monies were low to support this particular activity.

MR. NIELDS: Iran?

LT. COL. NORTH: In this—

MR. NIELDS: Second channel?

LT. COL. NORTH: —particular case, this is Iran. But it's also important you understand that it was always the intention to make this a self-sustaining operation, and that there always be something there which you could reach out and grab when you needed it. As Diretor Casey said, you want something you can pull off the shelf and use on a moment's notice. And what I—and I'm not trying to excuse anybody in this thing, least of all myself.

The fact is, he, General Secord, may not have known that—or may not have perceived that he should take funds out of this pot and put them into another one, or that he had allocated certain funds for other purposes and didn't want to touch them. And I'm not—again, I'm saying that at the

174

point in time when I prepared that, which was on or about the 17th of—

MR. NIELDS: September.

LT. COL. NORTH: —September, that was the information I had at the time.

MR. NIELDS: And where did you get that information?

LT. COL. NORTH: Well, I would guess I got it from General Secord.

MR. NIELDS: Orally or in some—

LT. COL. NORTH: I don't—

MR. NIELDS: —form of a report?

LT. COL. NORTH: I've absolutely no recollection.

MR. NIELDS: But you—

LT. COL. NORTH: In fact, I didn't even remember the subject of this PROFs note 'til I read the whole thing.

MR. NIELDS: You would agree that $8 million would be adequate to charter an airplane?

LT. COL. NORTH: I would agree, Counsel.

MR. NIELDS: Let's turn to Exhibit 159.

CHAIRMAN INOUYE: May I announce that the—a vote is now in progress in the House of Representatives. Accordingly, members of the House may have to absent themselves. Please proceed.

MR. NIELDS: Do you have that in front of you?

LT. COL. NORTH: I do.

MR. NIELDS: That's a PROF note also from Admiral Poindexter. It's dated September 13, 1986, which I believe is the same date as the one where he says, "Keep the pressure on Bill to make things right for Dick." At the bottom of the page, it states, "Also went over the Secord matters. Bill agrees Secord is a patriot. He will check into our suspicions. I told him he could get more detail from you." What is the meaning of the reference "our suspicions?"

LT. COL. NORTH: I don't—I'm not absolutely certain about what that is, but I think it's probably what I referrred to earlier as—that there was a lot of internal friction within the bureaucracy about Gen. Secord, that there were people who just didn't like him, probably for the same reason that they don't like me. When you get things done in this bureaucracy, you step on toes. And he was certainly a man who got things done.

175

MR. NIELDS: The PROF message seems to refer not to other people's suspicions. It uses the word "our" suspicions. Was there a—

MR. NIELDS: I'm saying our suspicions about why this problem was being created for Gen. Secord—the bad-mouthing, as it were. And I think that's what it refers to, although I do not recall the specifics at this point.

MR. NIELDS: Adm. Poindexter says that Casey could get more detail from you.

LT. COL. NORTH: Well, I knew of people at his agency who kept bad-mouthing him. And I knew people in other agencies who said bad things about him and who were uncooperative.

MR. NIELDS: Maybe I'm not understanding. What were your suspicions?

LT. COL. NORTH: My suspicions were that, very often, we'd have problems, for example, when we were in the midst of one of these transactions—of even getting a fixed price on a commodity, or enough of the commodity moved around. And you'd inevitably hear, "Well, you just can't move things here, or you just can't move things there." You couldn't get an airplane out of these folks to move the second channel here to the United States for a secret meeting. And just the general lack of cooperation.

MR. NIELDS: From whom?

LT. COL. NORTH: From within the bureaucracy.

MR. NIELDS: Well, these are suspicions having to do with Gen. Secord, aren't they?

LT. COL. NORTH: No, I'm talking about the suspicions as to why the lack of cooperation is there. Yes, okay. I'm not certain at all that this refers to suspicions about Gen. Secord. I'm saying our suspicions as to why people aren't cooperating in getting various things done along the line. I think the way—perhaps it looks as though I was suspicious of Gen. Secord. That is not the intent, nor do I think it was Adm. Poindexter's. I mean, after all, the line above, Bill agrees Secord is a patriot. And that's, you know, what I was saying. This man is a patriot. He's given extraordinary time and energy to supporting our foreign policy, to carrying out this initiative. And we can't get people to cooperate on diddly.

MR. NIELDS: Did there ever come a time when you

entertained suspicions about the way in which money was being used by Gen. Secord?

LT. COL. NORTH: I know certainly that these hearings have generated questions and suspicions and things like that. I don't recall a specific time before that that that was a— that I perceived a problem with that, necessarily.

MR. NIELDS: Did you ever perceive a problem or hear about a problem having to do with the pricing of arms to the contras?

LT. COL. NORTH: For the contras? Well, I know we had a big problem pricing the May shipment, but that was to the Iranians.

MR. NIELDS: I'm ask—just to make it clear, I'm asking you about, did you ever hear adverse reports, or did you ever entertain suspicions that you weren't getting the straight facts from General Secord about the way he was handling the pricing of arms to the contras?

LT. COL. NORTH: No. I did hear a report from someone in Central America, that General Secord was overcharging on the arms that he delivered to the resistance, and I sought at that point in time a price list from him, and compared those prices to those that others had gotten. Some were higher. Some were lower. And, I believe at the time I talked to Adolfo Calero about it, who was at that point in time the principal recipient of the arms from General Secord. I don't recall any other—other than, you know, this—what you had was a very competitive environment down there. Once the US government withdrew in 1984 from directly supporting the resistance, you ended up with a lot of folks out there running a very cutthroat business.

There were two particular transactions or dealers that raised great concerns with Director Casey. One of them was a transaction of some $5 to $6 million dollars from a broker who he was concerned had also been involved in reverse technology transfer to the Eastern Bloc, and he told me to do everything possible to discourage further purchases. The other one was a so-called "warehouse operation" that was being run in a Central American country, that the Agency, and Director Casey, in particular, was very concerned about the source of their monies, and the fact that this enormous warehouse of several millions of dollars worth of ordnance had been stocked up in that Central American country, and the potential adverse consequences, and at one point, he apprised me that he was concerned that that Central American country might have diverted ESF monies, US economic support funds, to the military to purchase the arms that went in that warehouse. And, so he told me that there shouldn't be any further transactions with that broker until such time as he resolved, or they were able to resolve where those came from.

I then talked to Mr. Calero, and I talked to General Secord that they should avoid those transactions. My sense is that as a consequence of the advice I got from the Director to withdraw from dealing with those two dealers, that a lot of people started putting out very bad word about General Secord, and I think a lot of that was—was brought up here to Washington, I think it was made available to certain Members of Congress, and I think that's where a lot of the adverse publicity came from. And the fact is that I was told by Director Casey to—that there should be no further dealings with those two arms brokers, and to my knowledge, Gen. Secord ever dealt with them, ever—if he had up to that point, he certainly didn't do it again. But a lot of the very negative communications that came out about Gen. Secord, came out as a consequence of those two guys being cut out of the picture, as it were, in terms of supporting the resistance.

MR. NIELDS: Col. North, did you have any interest —personal interest I'm talking about, now—in any of the monies that flowed from the arms sales to Iran, or that were kept in Swiss accounts under Gen. Secord's control?

LT. COL. NORTH: Not one penny.

MR. NIELDS: There has been testimony, as I'm sure you're aware, that a death benefit account was set up by Mr. Hakim with the name Button, for the benefit of your family in the event of your death. Were you aware of any such account?

LT. COL. NORTH: No. Totally unaware of it. First I heard of it was through these hearings. I have never heard of it before and it was a shock. An absolute shock.

MR. NIELDS: There is a—a testamentary document which has been introduced in evidence, relating to a particular $2 million sub-account set up also by Mr. Hakim, which provides that in his death Gen. Secord can control the use of the funds and in the event of his death, you can control the use of the funds and it also contains a provision that if everybody dies, it will be distributed to their estates. Were you aware of such a document?

LT. COL. NORTH: No. I never heard of it until these hearings started. I still don't believe it. I was shocked and I have absolutely no idea where that all came from, what so ever. Never heard of it before.

MR. NIELDS: And you never heard of the idea, either, I take it?

LT. COL. NORTH: No. Ever. I—I do want to make one point clear. I did at one point express concern, after I would guess in February, March, April, somewhere, after I'd met Mr. Hakim, became aware what his role was in the financial network that had been established, I did at some point express concern to Gen. Secord, "Suppose both you guys go down on the same airplane, flitting back and forth to Europe or wherever you're going, what happens then?" And I was told, "Don't worry about it, arrangements will be made so that these operations can continue." But nobody ever told me that a single penny was set aside for my purposes, for my benefit, whatsoever. Ever. And I never heard of buttons or bellybuttons until these hearings began.

MR. NIELDS: I'd like to separate out, then, the two issues raised by this will or this testimentary document. You're indicating that the portion of it that provides for the monies being distributed to the estates of the individuals is a foreign notion to you.

MR. SULLIVAN: Excuse me, Mr. Chairman. Could we please have a copy of the document—

MR. NIELDS: It's Exhibit 169—

MR. SULLIVAN: —which the counsel's referring to?

MR. NIELDS: One-sixty-nine.

MR. SULLIVAN: Object to the term "will." Mr. Chairman, I believe the term has been used 50 times in these hearings, prior to today. This is not a will, and any lawyer in the room knows it's not a will. (Pause while Lt. Col. North studies the document.)

LT. COL. NORTH: It's the first time I've ever seen this document, ever.

MR. NIELDS: Understood. You've said that. I just want to separate out the issues. There's a part of the document that provides for distribution to individuals' estates in event of death. It's on the second page. And I take it your testimony is that that concept—not only have you not seen the document, but that concept is foreign to you. You never heard of anything like it?

LT. COL. NORTH: I never heard of it before. I don't know how much more clearly I can put it, Counsel. I never, ever heard that proposal before, that suggestion.

MR. NIELDS: There's a second part of the document that relates, simply, to control over the use of the funds; and that's on the first page of it, second paragraph. And I take it that, although you never saw the document, the concept that you would control disposition of the funds—I don't mean in your personal capacity, but in your governmental capacity, in the event of the death of Hakim and Secord—that's not foreign to you, is it?

LT. COL. NORTH: Well I—I never professed to have control over a—over a single penny of this. I elicited the cooperation of General Secord. To my knowledge, he cooperated in every case with the things that we asked him to do. But I never, once, saw those words; nor do I want to leave you with the impression that this was what I had in mind when I said to them, "What happens if both you guys drop dead?" I was more than willing to have anybody else they wanted, so that we could continue the activities. But I didn't necessarily wish to become the person who had to fly back and forth to Switzerland. I've never even been in a Swiss bank.

MR. NIELDS: There's been testimony that several thousand dollars was spent on a fence, security system that was put in at your residence, and that the monies to pay for it came from Gen. Secord. And my question to you is, were you aware—I take it there was a security system put in at your residence?

LT. COL. NORTH: There is a security system in at my residence. It has since this April been sufficiently supplemented that it is now extraordinary.

MR. NIELDS: And I take it—were you aware that that security system was paid for by Gen. Secord?

LT. COL. NORTH: I'm going to waffle an answer. I'm going to say yes-and-no. And if you'll indulge me, I will give you another one of my very straightforward, but rather lengthy, answers. The issue of the security system was first broached immediately after a threat on my life by Abu Nidal. Abu Nidal is, as I'm sure you and the intelligence committees know, the principal, foremost assassin in the world today. He is a brutal murderer.

When I was first alerted to that threat by the Federal Bureau of Investigation in late April, I was simply told that there was a threat that had been promulgated by Abu Bahar who is the press spokesman for the Fateh Revolutionary Council, which is the name of the Abu Nidal group. He targeted me for assassination. We then made an effort over the course of several days to have the story killed and not run in the US—not me, but the story, killed and not run on the US media. Nonetheless it ran, and I believe the date was the 28th of April. The initial assessment was that this was a response to the attack on Libya, which we had run a preemptive kind of terrorist raid on Libya on the 14th of April, [in] which I had a small role to play. CBS chose to run the film anyway. The FBI was then contacted again and told—asked—what protection can be offered. The FBI correctly said, "We don't offer protection." I then sought other types of protection.

I went to my superiors and said, "What can be done?" Contrary to what was said some days ago, this lieutenant-colonel was not offered at that time any protection by the government of the United States, Sen. Rudman. I asked for and I was told that the only thing that I could do is to immediately PCS—Permanent Change of Station. You and I, as Marines, know well what that means—jerked out of home and sent to Camp Lejune. In that I was preparing at the time to go to Teheran, and we didn't want to tell the whole world that, that was deemed not to be an appropriate thing to do. The next thing that we looked to try to do is to find a secure telephone to put in my home to justify the installation of a US security system. That, too, was impossible or not feasible or couldn't be done. The next thing I did was to ask for a list of who installs these things for the US government, maybe I can get a better price by calling them. I believe it was someone in the Secret Service gave me a list of three or four of these companies that do that kind of installation. I called two or three of them. It is now late April, early May, it's within days of this threat, and I called and I asked, can you come out and do a survey and give me an estimate. And in each case, I think it was two or three of them—and I was at that point relatively busy—I was told it would be several weeks before we can come out and do an estimate and a survey, and it will be several more weeks or months before we can complete the installation because, after all, summertime is our busy time.

At some point along in there, either General Secord raised with me or I raised with him this threat. And I told him I couldn't get US government protection, I couldn't find a contractor to come out and do it myself, and he said, "Don't worry about that. I've got a good friend" —or an "associate," I don't remember the words—"who's an expert. This guy has a company that does these things." And he shortly thereafter, I believe it was around the 5th of May, introduced me to Mr. Glenn Robinette. He was introduced to me as a man who, one, had been a former CIA—or perhaps, I understood at the time, FBI, I don't remember —technical expert, a man who owned a security company, and a man who could immediately go out and do a survey and an estimate. He did. Over the course of the next few days, he went out to my home, I called my wife— or told my wife, whatever—that he'd be out. He went through the situation and he came up with an estimate of $8500 "max"—as I recall it was $8000 to $8500 —and he could furthermore immediately install the system.

Now, I want you to know that I'd be more than willing —and if anybody else is watching overseas, and I'm sure they are—I'll be glad to meet Abu Nidal on equal terms anywhere in the world. Okay? There's an even deal for him. But I am not willing to have my wife and my four children meet Abu Nidal or his organization on his terms. And I want you to know what was going through my mind. I was about to leave for Teheran. I had already been told by Director Casey that I should be prepared to take my own life. I had already been told that the government of the United States, on an earlier proposal for a trip, might even disavow the fact that I had gone on the trip, on an earlier proposal, and we can come back to that at some time if you like. And so having been asked—having asked for some type of US government protection for my wife and children, and having been denied that—and perhaps for fully legitimate reasons. And if there is a law that prevents the protection of American government employees and their families from people like Abu Nidal, then gentlemen, please fix it, because this kid won't be around much longer, as I'm sure you know. But there will be others, if they take activist steps to address the problem of terrorism, who will be threatened. And I would like to just, if I may, just read to you a little bit about Mr. Abu Nidal, just so you know my mental state at the time. "Abu Nidal, the radical Palestinian guerilla leader linked to last Friday's attacks in Rome and Vienna,"—and that was the so-called "Christmas massacre"—"in which 19 people died and 200 were wounded, is the world's most wanted terrorist." That's the Christian Science Monitor. When you look at his whole career, Abu Nidal makes the infamous terrorist Carlos look like a Boy Scout.

Abu Nidal himself, quoted in Der Speigel, "Between America and us, there exists a war to the death. In the coming months and years, Americans will be thinking about us." "For sheer viciousness, Abu Nidal has few rivals in the underworld of terrorism." Newsweek.

Our own State Department, and we have copies of these that we can make available for insertion into the record, but the State Department's summary on Abu Nidal, not exactly an overstatement, notes that his followers, who number an estimated 500, have killed as many as 181 persons, and wounded more than 200 in two years. Abu Nidal does not deny these things.

We also have an exhibit that we can provide for you that shows what Abu Nidal did in the Christmas massacres. One of the people killed in the Christmas massacre, and I do not wish to overdramatize this, but the Abu Nidal terrorist in Rome who blasted the 11-year old American Natasha Simpson to her knees, deliberately zeroed in and fired an extra burst at her head, just in case. Gentlemen, I have an 11-year old daughter, not perhaps a whole lot different than Natasha Simpson, and so, when Mr. Robinette told me, on or about the 10th of May, that he could immediately install a security system, I said, "Please try to keep it to the $8,000 to $8,500. I am, after all, a Marine Lieutenant Colonel, and I live on my salary." And, he installed that system.

183

Now, let me go to your next question because I know it's coming and deserves an answer. I never got a bill, and it is, after all—

MR. NIELDS: Wait. Before you go to the next—

LT. COL. NORTH: It is, after all, the answer to your question. It is the answer to your question.

MR. NIELDS: I am—

LT. COL. NORTH: You asked me where it came from, and I'm trying to tell you.

MR. NIELDS: I am going to ask you that question, but—

LT. COL. NORTH: You've already asked me the question. You asked me whether or not the money came from General Secord.

MR. NIELDS: Correct.

LT. COL. NORTH: And, I'm getting there.

MR. NIELDS: All right. Okay.

LT. COL. NORTH: Okay? When that system was installed, it was practically—it was totally complete. It allowed, for example, that when my wife would trigger an alarm, an alarm would ring in the central station, and the Fairfax police would immediately be notified, and that arrangement was worked out with—this wasn't surreptitious. Fairfax police came out—you pays your taxes in Fairfax County, but you gets your money's worth—and by golly they came out, and they photographed the house, and they did the normal precautionary things to respond to the kind of terrorist alert that they had been briefed on by the FBI. And that's the best that they could do, and it was at that point, with that security system installed, it was adequate; that instantly, they would respond to one of those emergency alarms. And Mr. Robinette provided it.

Now, I then went on the trip to Teheran. I came back. I never got a bill. I didn't ask for a bill, and I never received one. I never asked, "Where's the bill?" until well after it was too late. And I'll cover that.

When I didn't get a bill, I basically understood what had happened. And I don't know exactly how it worked out, but I—I believe that an accomodation was worked between Mr. Robinette and Gen. Secord to make a gift out of that security system, that I did not pay for.

When I came to the end of my tenure at the NSC, it was, to say the least, a busy time. There were other things to be

184

done besides shredding documents when I left. There was a lot of work to be done. And one of the things that I did was to sit and contemplate the previous five and a half years of my work. And I am proud of that work. I believe that we accomplished a lot.

But there was one thing that just didn't look right. And that was that for the first time in my life, I had accepted something that I hadn't paid for. And even though I honestly believe that the government of the United States should have paid for it, should have put it in, I then picked up the phone and asked for a bill. I got a bill. In fact, I got two of them. I didn't ask that they be back-dated; but after all, Mr. Robinette is an old hand in the CIA. (Laughter.)

All right. The bills came with the old original dates, and I think there was another bill with a later date on it. And then, as I told you yesterday, I was going to tell you the truth—the good, the bad, and the ugly. This is the truth. I did probably the grossest misjudgment that I have made in my life. I then tried to paper over that whole thing, by sending two phony documents back to Mr. Robinette. It was not an exercise in good judgment.

I don't believe I have any particular monopoly on bad judgment. I think it was a gross error in judgment for this Committee to put my home address up on the screen for the whole world to see, when I've got 20 security agents guarding my wife, my children, and me right now.

I'd also like to point out that it's not quite as bad as it originally seemed. This year, and these things kind of come in Aprils, I guess, but this April, the FBI called again. This April the FBI called and told me that there was another threat on my life. The big difference was, this year I was back with a band of brothers that has a long reputation for taking care of its own. And the United States Marine Corps and the Naval Intelligence—Naval Investigative Service of Naval Intelligence, got together and immediately put security on me and my home, where my wife and children are protected.

I can't tell you how grateful I am for that. The security system that was installed by Mr. Robinette with Gen. Secord's money, or the Enterprise's money or Mr. Hakim's money, or I don't know whose money, was put in and supplemented, enormously, by the folks, some of which are sitting in this room right now. Some of whom are at my home, right now. Some of whom drive me around in an armored motorcade that makes it look like a European potentate. But the fact is, I am grateful for that assistance, beyond measure. Because when you think about what could happen, when somebody like that is out to kill you and doesn't care if he takes out your children with you, you run out of options in a big hurry. I ran out of options, I think the government of the United States should have stepped up to it, and didn't. Whether it's because of laws or regulations, I don't know.

I admit to making a serious, serious, judgment error in what I then did to paper it over and I'm willing to sit here and admit to that. But I'm also suggesting to you gentlemen, that if it was Gen. Secord who paid the bill, whatever it was, I thought it was $8 thousand, didn't learn until the hearing started, it was more. I also suggest to you that if it was Gen. Secord, first of all, "Thank you, Gen. Secord." And second, of all, you guys ought to write him a check because the government should have done it to begin with. Thank you, sir.

MR. NIELDS: Thank you, Col. North. I need to ask you one other question on this subject.

LT. COL. NORTH: I'll make my second answer shorter.

MR. NIELDS: The documents which I believe you had reference to that you wrote and back-dated, are Exhibits 172 and Exhibit 173.

LT. COL. NORTH: Yes.

MR. NIELDS: Before I get to the document. Who was it that you made the request for security to, and who turned you down?

LT. COL. NORTH: Well I—I went to—well first of all I asked the FBI what they could do about it. And the FBI told me and I have since checked and I was since told this, again this April, when they called about a threat this spring, that the FBI is not in the business of providing protection. And they indeed, are not. I'm not—I'm not necessarily, by the way, saying that I think they should have, because it is clearly not within their jurisdiction to do so. And it's up to you whether you change that jurisdiction, I suppose. But, I then asked if there was anything that could be done at the White House.

186

MR. NIELDS: And who was it, who was it that you asked at the White House?

LT. COL. NORTH: I asked Admiral Poindexter, and I was referred to Mr. McDaniel. I was then—it was then suggested that there's only two things that can be done. You can either get a secure phone— find a secure telephone and put it in your home and use that to justify the installation of a security system. Well, for whatever reason, no secure telephone could be found. And I'm not—that may well be the case. I don't know. I was also told that the other alternative was immediate PCS to Camp Lejune or another military installation, which did not seem entirely practical, given that I was getting ready to go to Teheran. Thus, there were no answers.

MR. NIELDS: That was Adm. Poindexter or Mr. McDaniel who told you that you could be transferred to Camp Lejune?

LT. COL. NORTH: I don't recall which one it was. I know that that issue came up and was dismissed.

MR. NIELDS: Okay. Turning now to Exhibits 172 and 173, I take it what you're saying is that they were both typed on the same day.

LT. COL. NORTH: No. Actually, I think they were typed on two different days, or maybe even three different days. But they're both phony documents. I mean, I've admitted to that. I'm here to tell you the truth, even when it hurts, okay? They're phony.

MR. NIELDS: The second one, Exhibit 173, there are three letters from the typewriter that don't type correctly. How was that arranged?

LT. COL. NORTH: It wasn't arranged. That's the way the wheel on the thing was when I typed it. And the wheel was defective. It was simply that way.

MR. NIELDS: Were the two letters typed on the same typewriter?

LT. COL. NORTH: No.

MR. NIELDS: Were they typed in the same place?

LT. COL. NORTH: No. Actually, one letter I think was typed on one typewriter that was similar to the other one, and I couldn't find a decent ball or the wheel thing that worked right, and that was the only one that was there. And I dummied up even the explanation on the bottom of it.

MR. NIELDS: When you say you dummied up the explanation—

LT. COL. NORTH: That's the way it was.

MR. NIELDS: So you didn't drop the ball?

LT. COL. NORTH: No. I mean, after all, thinking that you were—this was not typed at the White House. It was typed after I left. Incidentally, no one else knew about this besides me. I mean, this was my own little stupidity all on my own.

MR. NIELDS: And what was the purpose of writing an explanation at the bottom of Exhibit 173?

LT. COL. NORTH: Well, the only letter that you sent with a ball that doesn't work—it was a demonstrator model in a store that I typed it on. And you've got to provide some kind of an explanation as to why supposedly a White House typewriter doesn't write. So I explained it on the bottom by saying I dropped the ball—"the ball" being the explanation for the defective type.

MR. NIELDS: Why did you dummy up the explanation?

LT. COL. NORTH: Well, theoretically, I mean if—

MR. SULLIVAN: I object. Now, Mr. Chairman, Col. North has frankly admitted what he did here. I must believe that the United States Congress has better things to do than focus on two phony letters after the witness has admitted that they're phony. Could we please move on to another subject?

CHAIRMAN INOUYE: We will proceed in the fashion we wish to. Mr. Nields?

MR. NIELDS: The fact is, this letter was typed on a machine, but dated as though I were still at the White House. Right? 1 October '86, I was still at the White House. And the machine didn't work well, didn't write right. Somebody had screwed up the—the wheel on this demonstrator. And thus, I had to explain why a White House typewriter, where they usually work pretty well, didn't work well. And so I put that note at the bottom. It was simply an explanation for why the typewriter didn't work as I had hoped it to. It's not more sinister than it appears.

MR. NIELDS: There's been testimony about use of traveler's checks. I'd like to give you an opportunity to answer or explain that testimony. I take it you have it in mind.

LT. COL. NORTH: I do have it in mind, Counsel. I appreciate the opportunity. Again, you'll have to indulge me a bit. When I began the covert operation in 1986—excuse me, in 1984 in support of the resistance, we had enormous problems trying to solve near-time, real-time—what I call operational problems. The end result of that was that I talked to Director Casey about the difficulties. He—he had suggested establishing an operational account, and I did so. There were two sources of monies for that operational account. One was traveler's checks from Adolfo Calero, and the other one was cash, eventually from Gen. Secord.

My recollection is that the very first traveler's checks came either very late '84, or certainly early 1985, and that the sum total of traveler's checks was probably in excess of $100,000, or thereabouts. I also had cash, which I estimate today to be somewhere in the neighborhood of $50,000 to $75,000 in cash. So we're talking about an operational account that went from somewhere around $150,000 to $175,000. At various points in time, there would be considerable sums in it; and at various points in time, there would be none in it.

My recollection is that I got the traveler's checks in packages of less than $10,000. I understand that others have remembered elsewise, but that's how I remember it. Those funds were used to support the operations that we were conducting. They were used to support the covert operation in Nicaragua, and then eventually were used to support other activities as well. The fact that I had those funds available was known to Mr. McFarlane, to Admiral Poindexter, to Director Casey, and eventually, to Admiral Art Moreau over at the Pentagon.

It was also—came to be known to others, that—some of whom you've had testify here—the funds were used, initally, only to support the Nicaragua program. But eventually, it was broadened to include other activities as well. Let me give you some examples.

In the Nicaragua program, operational support was provided to a whole host of Nicaraguan resistance leaders, either directly by me from the fund, or through couriers that I used to carry it out. Other resistance activities inside Nicaragua were supported, of a less military nature in some cases. Europeans who helped us with both the public affairs aspect, and the acquisition of other arms, through a separate channel outside that you've already heard about from Gen. Secord, or Gen. Singlaub, were paid for out of this account. Money was mailed from this account to addresses in Caracas, San Jose, Tegucigalpa, and San Salvador, among other places, to support activities inside Managua. The Indian movement, the Atlantic Coast Indian movement, was supported from this account, and meetings with the Atlantic Coast Indians, both the Misurasata and the Miskito movement itself, were supported from this account. And eventually, the fund was used to support other activities, such as a DEA hostage recovery activity and the assistance of another European, who we have agreed not to talk about.

What's important that you realize is that meticulous records were kept on all of this. I kept a detailed account of every single penny that came into that account and that left account. All of the transactions were recorded on a ledger that Director Casey gave me for that purpose. Every time I got a travelers—group of travelers checks in, I would record them. And I would record them when they went out, even going so far as to record the travelers checks' numbers themselves.

The ledger for this operational account was given to me by Director Casey. And when he told me to do so, I destroyed it, because it had within it the details of every single person who had been supported by this fund, the addresses, their names, and placed them at extraordinary risk.

Every transaction that you showed on that chart that you had up on the wall or the screen, or wherever it was, hard to tell when you see it on a videotape, but when you had it up there, you showed a group of travelers checks with my name on it. Every single one of those travelers checks which bore my name were used by me to defray an actual operational expense as it happened. I'd cash a check, for example, at Miami Airport and hand the money to a resistance person who I met with there. Or I flew myself off to someplace; because we were trying to avoid the use of appropriated funds, we used this account to live within Boland and to hide the fact that NSC travel was being conducted.

Unlike the CIA, the NSC travel voucher system doesn't have a covert cover. We had one dickens of a time trying to protect my travel. And as you undoubtedly know, gentlemen, I made an enormous amount of travel. The schedule was brutal. Much of it was paid for out of that operational account.

There were times when that account was down to zero, no money in it. I didn't have any travelers checks, and I'd handed out all the cash, not to myself, but to others. Under those circumstances I would use my own money, Lieutanant Colonel Oliver North's paycheck money, his own money that he had earned, and I would use it for an operational expense. I would therefore make a notation in the ledger: spent $250 on going to Atlanta to meet with somebody. And the next time I got cash or travelers checks, I would use those checks to reimburse myself.

Every single penny on the checks that you saw that came to me was used to pay an operational expense on the scene or to reimburse myself. I never took a penny that didn't belong to me. Every single one of those checks—and I would also point out to you, Counsel, that you don't have them all, because by my own recognition and memory, there were checks used in 1986, and the ones that you depicted earlier were only 1985. And I used those travelers checks right up until shortly before I was fired, but only for the purposes that you saw.

And I realize that it—that this hearing is a difficult thing. Believe me, gentlemen, it isn't as difficult for you as it is for a guy that's got to come up here and tell the truth, and that's what I'm trying to do. And I want to make it very clear that when you put up things like "Parklane Hosiery" and you all snicker at it, and you know that I've got a beautiful secretary, and the good Lord gave her the gift of beauty, and the people snicker that Ollie North might have been doing a little hanky-panky with his secretary, Ollie North has been loyal to his wife since the day he married her. And the fact is I went to my best friend and I asked her, "Did I ever go to Parklane Hosiery?" And you know what she told me? "Of course you did, you old buffoon, you went there to buy leotards for our two little girls." And the reason I wrote the check to Parklane Hosiery, just like the checks at Giant, is

191

because I was owed my money for what I had spent in pursuing that covert operation.

You gentlemen may not agree that we should have been pursuing covert operations at the NSC, but we were. We had an operational account and we used the money for legitimate purposes within that covert operation. Does that answer your question, sir?

MR. NIELDS: Yes.

LT. COL. NORTH: Thank you.

MR. NIELDS: I have a couple of more on that subject. When was the ledger destroyed?

LT. COL. NORTH: My recollection is that the ledger—and I—I'm—anticipating your question, I have tried as best I can to reconstruct not only that, but when a lot of the more intensified destruction began. My sense is that it was probably destroyed along about the 4th or the 5th of November, and I say "probably" because the initial discussions I had with Director Casey about this operation coming unraveled began right after the Hasenfus shootdown, which was early October. I think it was the 4th or the 5th of October, and then the discussions that he had shortly thereafter with Mr. Furmark, who told him that, "Oh, by the way, a lot of people happen to know that Ollie North has been using money from the Iranian arms transactions to support the contras," or words to that effect.

I then went on in a very intensive period of travel, and I must tell you that we intensified our efforts considerably. Knowing that this operation was coming apart, we made an extraordinary effort to get the second channel going, to open it up, and to get as many Americans out as we possibly could before it all came down.

I believe that it was right after I returned from one of my early November trips. I had a meeting with Director Casey. Director Casey said, "Look. This revelation that's either occurring or about to occur is the end." At that point in time, he also told me, "You ought to go out and get a lawyer."

Now, from one of the guys who's one of the best lawyers in the world by my book—he used to remind me a lot not to say bad things about lawyers,—I've been reminded about that since—Director Casey told me to get a lawyer because there was probably going to be a civil suit against me by associates of Mr. Furmark to recover their money. And, so in that whole process, somewhere between what I would judge to be the 13th of October and the 4th of November, he told me specifically, "Get rid of things. Get rid of that book because that book has in it the names of everybody, the addresses of everybody. Just get rid of it, and clean things up." And, I did so.

MR. NIELDS: Where did the money come from?

LT. COL. NORTH: The two sources that I remember very vividly were Mr. Calero, by travelers checks, sometimes given by him to me directly or couriered to me, and then also cash from General Secord.

MR. NIELDS: Did you ever—you've indicated that on occasion you've advanced your own money and reimbursed yourself out of this fund. Were there occasions when it was the other way around?

LT. COL. NORTH: I don't understand.

MR. NIELDS: You borrowed from the fund—

LT. COL. NORTH: Never.

MR. NIELDS: —for personal purposes—

LT. COL. NORTH: Never.

MR. NIELDS: —and then reimbursed?

LT. COL. NORTH: Never.

MR. NIELDS: Did you ever permit Fawn Hall to do that?

LT. COL. NORTH: I did. I, as I recall, it was a very late, probably a Friday or Saturday night, and I had told her that she could take the weekend off, and she didn't have any money. And, she needed—she was driving to the beach or somewhere. And I, as I recall, gave her two or three checks, made the appropriate notation in the ledger, and told her that I had to have the money back as soon as she could cash a check, and she did. And I put the money back in the account. To my recollection, I ever advanced anybody anything out of the account. I never advanced myself out of that.

MR. NIELDS: There has been testimony about efforts to route money to you through your wife out of the Swiss bank accounts. I'd like to give you an opportunity to respond to those that—testimony on that subject, if you wish.

LT. COL. NORTH: I'd be glad to. Again, if you'll allow me

to go back in time a little bit, in February of 1986, we had the first direct meetings with the Iranians in five-plus years—between US government officials and the Iranians, other than the discussions that were going on in Europe over settlement of accounts. In those meetings, in the latter days of February, it was decided that there would be two trips to Teheran—that I would go on an advance trip with Gen. Secord, the purpose of which would be to establish an agenda for a higher-level trip to be taken by a senior US official. And that trip was planned to take place in April. My advance trip was to have taken place in March.

Because the US government had been unable to provide a translator for that session, Mr. Hakim came to that session and acted as translator. And that was, to my recollection, the very first time I had heard of Mr. Hakim. I think it is the first time I had actually met with Mr. Hakim, and I have no recall to the contrary. Mr. Hakim thought that this idea of an advance trip was lunacy. I mean, he put it in the strongest possible terms that this was not a good thing to do. The CIA officer who was with me at that meeting agreed with him. When the discussion transpired, it was actually pointed out that you could never be heard from on this trip again. The risks were known to Mr. Hakim very clearly because he is, after all, an Iranian. He fled the revolution that we now seek to get along with. The CIA officer thought that the trip was very high risk.

When I later talked to Director Casey—and this was within days of this whole event, Director Casey raised another issue, and that was, first of all, the trip—because it is so black, this advance trip is so hidden that we're going to use non-US government assets throughout, European or Middle Eastern airlines, no US air registration, air flights, you might never be heard from again. The government might disavow the entire thing. And, furthermore, I, Bill Casey, am not going to let you go unless you are prepared to deal with the issue of torture. We knew by then that Bill Buckley, a man who I knew, was probably dead, and that he had been tortured. We knew that he had given as much as a 400-page confession under torture that we were making every effort to recover. And Director Casey told me that he would not concur in my going on the advance trip unless I

194

took with me the means by which I could take my own life. I did not tell my wife and children that, and they may be hearing it for the first time right now.

In the course of that discussion, Mr. Hakim said to me, "If you don't come back, I will do something for your family." He did not say "we," that I recall, he said "I". Now by that point in time, I had come to know that Mr. Hakim was a wealthy man in his own right. I was grateful for the assistance that he had been providing in translating over several very difficult days of discussions with the Iranians. And several days thereafter, when he suggested that my wife meet with his lawyer in Philadelphia, I agreed that my wife should do so. The purpose, as I understood it, of that meeting was that my wife would be in touch with the person who would, if I didn't return, do something for my family.

My wife went to the meeting in Philadelphia several days thereafter. And you have notations in the notebooks that I surrendered to you about what happened. She went to the very brief meeting. There was no money mentioned, no account mentioned, no amount mentioned, no will mentioned, no arrangement. The meeting focused on how many children I had, their ages, and a general description of my family. A brief meeting in the offices, as I remember, of Touche Ross, a respectable firm in Philadelphia, with a lawyer. I then went, and, thank God, returned safely, from Iran. After that trip, there was one more call to my wife from the lawyer. On or about the first of June, almost immediately after my return from Teheran, the lawyer called again and asked for the name of an adult executor for our family, in the event, I suppose that neither my wife nor I were around. I told my wife, "Do not call him back. It is unnecessary." She never did. She never heard from him again, and she has never made contact with him again. No money was ever transferred to my possession, control, account, or that of my wife, or that of my children. I never ever heard about "belly buttons" until these hearings began. Does that answer your question, Counsel?

MR. NIELDS: Yes, and I take it that in answering the question, you've been telling us what happened at certain meetings that I take it were attended only by your wife, and I take it you are testifying to what you've been told by her?

195

LT. COL. NORTH: On advice of counsel, I have not revealed any of our confidential marital communications. I have given you a surmise, based on what I know the facts to be.

MR. SULLIVAN: In other words, Counsel, don't call his wife up here.

MR. NIELDS: No. That wasn't the question, at all. The question was simply what the source of the information was, and I take it, it's your wife?

LT. COL. NORTH: Counsel, I gave you a long story, and the sources are multiple for that story, but accurate.

MR. NIELDS: Well, other than your wife, what are the sources?

LT. COL. NORTH: Some of the information may be privileged or a work product of my attorney.

MR. SULLIVAN: In other words, we've done a little of our own investigation—Excuse me, Mr. Chairman—a little of our own investigation regarding these allegations, and have amassed some evidence and have concluded that they're absolutely baseless. From that information, Col. North has been able to draw certain conclusions, and if you have any proof to the contrary, why don't you present it?

MR. NIELDS: So, what he is testifying to is based on what he's been told by his wife and his attorneys?

MR. SULLIVAN: Not necessarily so. There are other factors as well.

MR. NIELDS: Okay, what else?

LT. COL. NORTH: I, I'm just telling you all that I know about the event. No money ever was received. (Pause) I obviously had a conversation with Mr. Hakim that initiated this entire business back in February or early March.

MR. NIELDS: Can you give the Committee any information that would shed light on why Mr. Zucker was meeting with a lawyer in Switzerland in October of 1986, seeking to find a way or routing a substantial sum of money to you through your wife?

LT. COL. NORTH: No. I can give you absolutely no insight to that.

MR. SULLIVAN: Objection to your question, "routing a substantial sum of money". There's no predicate to that.

LT. COL. NORTH: I cannot, Counsel, and I think it's

important for you to know that the very first time I heard these things was as a consequence of these hearings, and I was shocked. I never ever got a penny from those accounts. The only thing that it can be said that I ever received as a consequence of what I did in the course of these activities, or as a result of perhaps one of those accounts, is the security system which is at my home, and I still, to this day, don't know exactly who paid for it.

MR. NIELDS: Mr. Chairman, I have no further questions for the morning.

CHAIRMAN INOUYE: The joint panel will stand in recess until 2:00 p.m.

END OF MORNING SESSION

Afternoon Session—2:00 P.M.

CHAIRMAN INOUYE: Mr. Nields.

MR. NIELDS: Thank you, Mr. Chairman. Colonel North, you testified yesterday concerning approval that you received for the plan to use the proceeds of arms sales to Iran for the contras, and you testified about Admiral Poindexter and the President. Who else, if anyone, and I don't mean to imply anything in the question, but leaving those two people aside, who else in the government was aware of either the plan or the fact of using proceeds of arms sales to Iran for the contras?

LT. COL. NORTH: Well, if I may clarify what I testified to yesterday is my assumption the President knew, and then I subsequently testified that I was told he did not know. I know that Admiral Poindexter knew. I know that Mr. McFarlane knew at a point in time when he was no longer in the government, and Director Casey knew. Aside from that, I can't speak with certainty as to who else inside the government knew for sure, although there were certainly a number of people who, by the time November of '86 came along, certainly had great suspicions or belief that it was happening. But, the only ones that I know for sure who I confirmed it with were those three.

MR. NIELDS: Okay, if I may, I'd like to take them, and then ask you some questions about some others. When did

Mr. McFarlane, to your knowledge, first learn that the proceeds from the arms sales to Iran had been used for the contras?

LT. COL. NORTH: My recollection is that I first confirmed it with him during the May trip to Teheran, and it was probably on the return leg from that, either on board the aircraft or as we were changing planes, whatever week, we returned in an aircraft to Israel, and boarded another aircraft and flew back to the United States. So, it was somewhere in that timeframe that I can recall specifically telling him.

MR. NIELDS: Do you have any reason to believe he was aware of it earlier?

LT. COL. NORTH: He may have been. I have seen some of my own notes that would leave me to believe I had talked to him about it, but I don't recall the events. I do specifically recall, however, talking to him about it at the time of our return.

MR. NIELDS: When did Director Casey first learn of it?

LT. COL. NORTH: Actually, my recollection is Director Casey learned about it before the fact. Since I am confessing to things, I may have raised it with him before I raised it with Admiral Poindexter, probably when I returned from the February, er, from the January discussions.

MR. NIELDS: You're referring now to the discussion, the trip during which you had the discussion with Mr. Ghorbanifar in the bathroom?

LT. COL. NORTH: Yes. I don't recall raising the bathroom, specifically, with the Director. But I do recall talking with the Director. And I don't remember whether it was before or after I talked to Admiral Poindexter about it. But, I—I was not the only one who was enthusiastic about this idea. And I—Director Casey used several words to describe how he felt about it, all of which were effusive. He referred to it as "the ultimate irony," the ultimate covert operation kind of thing. And was very enthusiastic about it.

He also recognized that there were potential liabilities, and that there was risk involved. I believe that he was accurate, given what is now happened.

MR. NIELDS: What kinds of risks did he identify to you?

LT. COL. NORTH: This very political risk, that we see being

portrayed out here now; that it could, indeed, be dangerous —or, not dangerous so much as politically damaging.

MR. NIELDS: Do you have any reason to believe that Director Casey, given the "political risk," ever discussed the matter with the President?

LT. COL. NORTH: I have no reason to believe that he did, because he never addressed that to me. I never, as I indicated yesterday—no one ever told me that they had discussed it with the President.

MR. NIELDS: Did Director Casey ever tell you that he was planning to discuss it with the President?

LT. COL. NORTH: No. Nothing I recall.

MR. NIELDS: Did you have other discussions with Director Casey on the subject of use of these arms sales proceeds for the contras?

LT. COL. NORTH: Yes, we did. Director Casey, who is very clear in my records of communications with him, is a man for whom I had enormous respect. I respected him as a—a man of incredible experience; probably the most well-read man I have ever met and dealt with on a direct, face-to-face basis. I watched Director Casey, on trips when I'd travel with him, read an entire book in one plane flight.

In fact, on one occasion, he finished an entire book. As I recall, it was Paul Johnson's book, *Modern Times,* which is like this in paperback. And then I noticed he was working on the yellow legal pad as we were flying along. And I said, "What'd you do with the book?" He said, "I'm tired of reading. I've decided to write my own, and he'd finished Paul Johnson's book, which he then gave to me.

Director Casey and I talked at length on a variety of occasions about the use of those monies to support other operations besides the Nicaraguan operation. And you, no doubt, have seen record of my accounting of other activities that were planned beyond the Nicaraguan resistance. We always assumed—not just Director Casey and I, but all those of us who worked within the government on this problem of democracy in Central America—that there would come a time again, as, indeed, it did, where the Congress would make available the monies necessary to support the Nicaraguan freedom fighters. And, at various times, he and I talked about the fact that it might be necessary at some point in the future to have something, as he would put it, to pull off the shelf and to help support other activities like that. Now, none of those, aside from the ones that we talked about in terms of cooperation with Israel—the ones I referred to in my notes as "TA-1, 2 and 3" or "TH-1, 2 and 3" —I don't recall exactly which—

Aside from those operations, he was looking forward to the possibility of needing to support other activities beyond that. And that's why I'm not exactly certain as to what, perhaps, was intended beyond the use of those monies for support for Nicaraguan resistance, and the other purposes that I described to you earlier, in that I had, I think, communicated that to Director—to Gen. Secord. And he did prepare a layout which showed how other of those commercial entities could be used to support activities in other places besides Central America and besides the U.S.-Israeli operations, besides the hostage recovery operations. None of those plans were ever [brought] to fruition before all of this was terminated. But we did talk, he and I, about that. And I may have mentioned it at some point to Adm. Poindexter, although certainly not in the same detail that Director Casey and I talked about it. It is possible, although I don't recall it, that I may have talked to Mr. McFarlane about it.

MR. NIELDS: When you say "about it," "it" is the—

LT. COL. NORTH: The application—

MR. NIELDS: —use of funds for some other projects besides the contras?

LT. COL. NORTH: Yes. Well, I—I do—I am certain to Admiral Poindexter about the Israeli projects, the ones that are abbreviated with a "TA" or a "TH" in the records that I provided to the committee.

MR. NIELDS: Did you ever tell Director Casey that funds had actually been used to support the contras; that is, funds arising out of these Iran—Iranian arms sales?

LT. COL. NORTH: Oh—oh, yes.

MR. NIELDS: And I take it on more than one occasion?

LT. COL. NORTH: Yes.

MR. NIELDS: Was there anyone else in the CIA who was aware that funds from the Iranian arms sales were used to support the contras?

200

LT. COL. NORTH: I cannot say with certainty you—going back to November 21st again—did you on November 21st meet with the Attorney General, either alone or with others?

LT. COL. NORTH: Nineteen eighty—

MR. NIELDS: Six.

LT. COL. NORTH: On November 21st?

MR. NIELDS: Yes.

LT. COL. NORTH: It is possible that that issue came up in a discussion that I had on the 21st of November with Mr. McFarlane—obviously, also, with Adm. Poindexter, both of whom I met with that day.

MR. NIELDS: Did you meet with the Attorney General that day?

LT. COL. NORTH: I don't have any recollection of it, and I don't see any record of it in anything that I had tried to refresh my memory with.

MR. NIELDS: You seem to be looking at some pieces of paper. What are they?

LT. COL. NORTH: Stuff I gave you and stuff I assembled as work product with counsel since then. I mean, you've had that.

MR. SULLIVAN: Obviously, the witness anticipated you'd have a few questions, and he tried to review as many of his materials as possible, including the six feet of records which he provided.

LT. COL. NORTH: I have no recollection of a meeting with the Attorney General on the 21st.

MR. NIELDS: Do you have a recollection of telling Col. Earle on the 21st that you had asked the Attorney General how much time you had?

LT. COL. NORTH: No.

MR. NIELDS: Were there people in the CIA who were directly aware from you, or from working with you, that there was a difference between the amount of money that was paid into General Secord's accounts and the amount of money that was paid into the CIA accounts?

LT. COL. NORTH: Again, from—certainly from the intelligence, they would be aware of that. The intelligence we were collecting that I referred to yesterday and have since gotten guidance as to how to refer to it—but the—the intelligence that I referred to yesterday clearly indicated that there was a a difference between what the government of the United States was charging and what was actually being provided. So yes, it would be visible to those people that there was a difference.

MR. NIELDS: Was that discussed with people that you worked with directly at the CIA on this Iranian project?

LT. COL. NORTH: It may have been, Counsel, but I don't recall a specific session in which I sat down and said, "Okay guys, the Iranians are providing eight bucks for this and we're only giving the government five bucks, because that's all the government wanted." But I'm sure there were people who came to those conclusions. I don't—I do not recall confirming to them what the Delta—the difference, was being used for.

MR. NIELDS: Now you had an interview with Attorney General Meese on the 23rd of November 1986, at which the issue of the use of these proceeds for the contras was discussed.

LT. COL. NORTH: Yes.

MR. NIELDS: Do you have any reason to believe that the Attorney General was aware, prior to that time, that the proceeds from the Iranian arms sales were used to support the contras?

LT. COL. NORTH: No, I don't. I have no reason to believe that he was. But when he asked me, I told him.

MR. NIELDS: Now when he asked you, did you tell him that the difference was in accounts controlled by General Secord, or did you tell him that the difference went from the Israelis directly to contra accounts?

LT. COL. NORTH: I do not recall the specifics of that conversation. It was a—to put it mildly, a very long night before and a very difficult week prior to. And I have no real recollection of that interview, other than the fact that it did, indeed, happen on Sunday afternoon, and that when the Attorney General asked me, holding—one of the two of us holding the memo of April, which delineated as a part of that memo that residuals would be used for aiding the Nicaraguan resistance.

I do recall that the Attorney General asked me point blank, "Did this happen?" I told him that transaction did not happen. He then asked me if anything like that had ever happened, or words to that effect. And I told him it had.

MR. NIELDS: Did you listen to his press conference on the 25th of November?

LT. COL. NORTH: Yes, I did.

MR. NIELDS: Are you aware, or do you recall him saying in his press conference that the money had gone straight from an Israeli account into contra accounts and had not been handled by any US persons?

LT. COL. NORTH: I don't recall that specific part of it, but I do recall that there was something like that said, yes.

MR. NIELDS: And did you—did he get that from you?

LT. COL. NORTH: He may well have. And I'm not denying that at all. But I want to make something very clear, I did not have on that day as good a feel or as good an understanding of the actual financial transactions that I came to have in the days thereafter.

And, I mean, first of all it's important that you understand that we believed, at least I was lead to believe, that our intelligence services saw Mr. Ghorbanifar as an Israeli agent. Now he's an Iranian, at least that's where he was born and lived, but that he was viewed by, certainly Director Casey, and other members of the intelligence community as an agent of the Israeli intelligence services. And so my assumption was that if an Israeli agent was giving money to—an account in this case—an account which included the Nicaraguan resistance, that there would be an Israeli connection to that. I may well have been wrong, because in the subsequent days, in fact, later that day or perhaps the day afterwards, it was described to me differently, that no, the monies came directly from other places and went in there, and a whole host of other people to include Mr. Khashoggi and others were mentioned.

MR. NIELDS: But you—

LT. COL. NORTH: I did not know that at the time I was talking to the Attorney General.

MR. NIELDS: But you knew that the residue—the residuals, as you've called them, went into the custody of Mr. Secord and his Swiss bank accounts, didn't you? Not—

LT. COL. NORTH: I did know that they did go to the support of the Nicaraguan resistance and those other activities I have described at the time I talked to him, and that's what I tried to express.

MR. NIELDS: No, that wasn't quite my question. My

question was, you knew that the residuals had gone into accounts controlled by General Secord, not accounts controlled by the contras?

LT. COL. NORTH: That is correct.

MR. NIELDS: And do you recall the Attorney General saying that they had gone directly from Israeli accounts into accounts controlled by the contras?

LT. COL. NORTH: I do not recall that specific wording, but I don't dispute that he said it. I'm sure if it's on the transcript he did.

MR. NIELDS: My question is, did he get that from you?

LT. COL. NORTH: He may well have.

MR. NIELDS: But you knew at the time that that was not true?

LT. COL. NORTH: Well, I—

MR. SULLIVAN: He didn't say that he got it from him. It's the second time, this is now the third time.

MR. NIELDS: He said "he may have", and my question is, you knew that it wasn't true, whether he got it from you or not, it was not true.

LT. COL. NORTH: Well again, Mr. Nields, what I told the Attorney General that afternoon was the truth as I knew it. And that's what I always did, and that's what I'm doing now. The important thing is that I tried to reconstruct in an hour-and-a half, two hours, three hours, whatever I was in the Attorney General's office, for him answers to his questions that answered what he wanted to know.

(Long pause.)

LT. COL. NORTH: I'm sorry, I missed the question.

MR. NIELDS: I don't think there is one. But I will ask you—

LT. COL. NORTH: Well, I guess what I want to do is make sure that I am clear on it. I—what I do recall, and it was important enough for me to then call Admiral Poindexter and try to get ahold of Mr. McFarlane, who I think I eventually got through to, also—is that I do recall telling the Attorney General the truth about the fact that there had been funds diverted, if that's the word you want; or the residuals from the transaction, or from different transactions, transferred to the use of the contras.

I don't recall the specifics of what else I told them. I mean that was, for me, the deepest, darkest secret of the whole activity. And, I think I told the Attorney General that part, too, although I don't recall it specifically. As far as the specifics of the rest of what I told him about whose accounts, and things like that, I do not recall.

MR. NIELDS: Were there any other people in the NSC that were aware of the use of the proceeds from the Iranian arms sales for the contras?

LT. COL. NORTH: I don't know. I may have apprised my staff. I don't recall whether I actually told Ms. Hall, or—she certainly typed many memos on it. I think it's possible that I had talked to Lt. Col. Earle about it. I don't believe I talked to Commander Coy about it. And I don't believe that Ms. Brown knew about it. I don't believe that Mr. McDaniel, who was the deputy to Admiral Poindexter, knew; nor do I believe that Mr. Keel—or Dr. Keel, knew, until the very end.

MR. NIELDS: Commander Thompson?

LT. COL. NORTH: I don't know. I do not recall the discussion of Commander Thompson on that issue until the very end of my tenure.

MR. NIELDS: Do you recall discussing this subject with anyone else, other than the people that you've already mentioned today and yesterday?

LT. COL. NORTH: I don't recall it, no.

MR. NIELDS: Did you—going back to November 21st again—did you on November 21st meet with the Attorney General, either alone or with others?

LT. COL. NORTH: Nineteen eighty—

MR. NIELDS: Six.

LT. COL. NORTH: On November 21st?

MR. NIELDS: Yes.

LT. COL. NORTH: It is possible that that issue came up in a discussion that I had on the 21st of November with Mr. McFarlane—obviously, also, with Adm. Poindexter, both of whom I met with that day.

MR. NIELDS: Did you meet with the Attorney General that day?

LT. COL. NORTH: I don't have any recollection of it, and I don't see any record of it in anything that I had tried to refresh my memory with.

MR. NIELDS: You seem to be looking at some pieces of paper. What are they?

LT. COL. NORTH: Stuff I gave you and stuff I assembled as work product with counsel since then. I mean, you've had that.

MR. SULLIVAN: Obviously, the witness anticipated you'd have a few questions, and he tried to review as many of his materials as possible, including the six feet of records which he provided.

LT. COL. NORTH: I have no recollection of a meeting with the Attorney General on the 21st.

MR. NIELDS: Do you have a recollection of telling Col. Earle on the 21st that you had asked the Attorney General how much time you had?

LT. COL. NORTH: No.

MR. NIELDS: Do you recall telling Col. Earle that you had asked the Attorney General if you had 24 or 48 hours?

LT. COL. NORTH: No. I do not recall that at all—although there was another issue that was at stake here, an issue that we had—whether I actually communicated with the Attorney General or not on, I don't remember. But there was an investigation of an airline, and I know that we were trying to—we'd asked the Attorney General to delay an investigation on that airline because that airline had not only provided support to the Nicaraguan resistance, that was the matter that they were being investigated for and that airline had provided support to the transfer of US weapons from the United States to Israel, and then from Israel to Iran. And my concern was that in trying to answer the legitimate and—and I think straight forward answers that were being asked, or trying to answer the questions that were being asked about that airline's role in support for the resistance, that that investigation was going to uncover that airline support for the transfers to Iran. And our concern, at least my concern, I don't—I don't want to speak to everyone, but certainly my concern, certainly Director Casey's concern and I believe Admiral Poindexter's concern was that pursuing that investigation was going to disrupt ongoing efforts to achieve the release of another hostage as well as potentially compromise the second channel and cause people to die.

And so, what we were anxious to do was to postpone that investigation, not interfere with it from a criminal investigation perspective, but to insure that we had done all we could to, one, get people out of Iran, if they needed to get out; and two, to insure that any hostages we could get out were released. And that may be what I was referring to in terms of 24 to 48 hours. That was an ongoing action, almost up to the time I departed.

I do not recall talking to Col. Earl about 24 hours left in the NSC or anything like that. I—I don't think that—I had told Admiral Poindexter, several times as I think perhaps it started right after the Hasenfus aircraft was shot down and Captain Cooper and Buz Sawyer were killed, two brave men who were supporting the resistance, that I knew things were coming down and that I was prepared to leave at any point. And I know I talked to Admiral Poindexter on the 21st and told him that I though I had to leave right away. And I know that I'd said that several times before but we were then at the point where I thought that it was important to diffuse the controversy that I'd be relieved, that I'd be transferred. And, I say that because I had made it clear to Mr. McFarlane; I made it clear to Mr. Casey; and I made it very clear to Admiral Poindexter that I recognize that there would come a time when you may have to have a political —I emphasize the word "political"—fall guy, or scapegoat or whatever. I never in my wildest dreams or nightmares envisioned that we would end up with criminal charges. It was beyond my wildest comprehension, right up until the 25th.

MR. NIELDS: Did you—I take it you did meet on the 21st with Admiral Poindexter?

LT. COL. NORTH: Yes.

MR. NIELDS: And, did he advise you that representatives from the Attorney General's office were going to be coming in over the weekend to look at documents?

LT. COL. NORTH: Yes, he did.

MR. NIELDS: Did you ask him how much time you had?

LT. COL. NORTH: I may have. I don't recall saying that specifically. I think what he told me, if I remember properly, is that it would be in tomorrow, and that wasn't an issue of, you know, whether they'd be in at 8:00 or they'd be in at 10:00, that they were there in the morning. In fact, they were there before I got there in the morning, if I remember correctly. On the morning, Saturday morning the 22nd, and I had already laid out on my desk, not on my desk, but on the table in my office, all of the files that were pertinent to the Nicara—er, to the Iranian initiative—all the files that remained on the Iranian initiative.

MR. NIELDS: Okay. So, at the time of your conversation with Admiral Poindexter, you did not have 24 hours between the time of the conversation and the time the Attorney General's people were going to come in looking at documents?

LT. COL. NORTH: I am uncertain at this point as to what time of day I talked to the Admiral about that, but I was told—excuse me—at some point on Friday that they would be there the following day.

MR. NIELDS: Did you—did he purport, to the best of your recollection, to tell you anything that the Attorney General had said on that subject?

LT. COL. NORTH: No. My recollection is that the issue was a fact-finding inquiry. I think that's the way it was put regarding the September and November '85 shipments. I mean that's what I recall. I mean, there may have been more to that conversation, but that's what I recall.

MR. NIELDS: Did there come a time in November of 1986, or earlier, in which the Attorney General advised you that you should get yourself a lawyer?

LT. COL. NORTH: I—I don't recall him saying that to me. What I do recall is Director Casey telling me that, and I think maybe he said the Attorney General suggested it. And I'm not entirely certain of that, but I do remember Director Casey mentioning two specific reasons to get a lawyer. One was that he expected there to be a civil suit similar to the one that was already lodged in Florida against General Secord and others regarding the Nicaraguan resistance, and another one by associates of Mr. Furmark or others who were alleging that I was responsible, or that General Secord or both of us were responsible, for the fact that Mr. Ghorbanifar had not paid them.

There was another reason, and that was that the Congress had initiated a proposal—and I don't know what form that proposal took—but there was a proposal in '86 to convene an independent counsel to investigate, as I was told—I never recall seeing a piece of paper on this, I don't recall now seeing a piece of paper on it—but that there was a proposal from the Congress to the Attorney General to investigate me and my role in support for the Nicaraguan resistance. And that was through an independent counsel. And I think it was Director Casey that pointed that out to me. I don't recall the Attorney General recommending to me that I seek counsel. I do remember several occasions in which Director Casey urged that I seek counsel.

By the way, at no time did he ever say for criminal activity, and he specifically mentioned a civil suit. I mean, after all, he reminded me frequently that he was a lawyer, and by his definition and others, a good one.

MR. NIELDS: Did you, after you learned that the Attorney General's people were going to come in on Saturday, tell Mr. McFarlane that you were going to have a shredding party?

LT. COL. NORTH: No, I don't recall ever using the words "shredding party." I may have told Mr. McFarlane, as I know I told Admiral Poindexter, albeit erroneously, that I had destroyed the records pertaining to the use of Iranian funds to support the Nicaraguan resistance. I may have told him that point-blank. I don't—I don't recall the specific conversation. I also don't recall—I mean, it was just not my vernacular to use the words "shredding party." It's not the way I talk.

MR. NIELDS: Did you in words or substance tell Mr. McFarlane that you were planning to shred documents, on Friday, the 21st of November?

LT. COL. NORTH: Again, I think what I—if I—if I did refer to this with Mr. McFarlane, and I—I don't recall the conversation. But if I did, I probably would have said the same thing that I had already assured Admiral Poindexter earlier in the day, or perhaps at some point in the day, maybe it was later—that, "Don't worry about that, it's already taken care of. Those documents are gone." I was wrong. There was one left. And, I had believed at that point in time that they were all gone.

MR. NIELDS: I'm going to turn back to the subject that we were on yesterday afternoon, namely the contras. I think that you had testified yesterday about the efforts to raise monies for the contras after the Boland Amendment had come into effect. Did you also endeavor to procure arms for the contras?

LT. COL. NORTH: Yes.

MR. NIELDS: And did you receive, for example, lists of arms from Mr. Calero?

LT. COL. NORTH: Yes.

MR. NIELDS: And, I take it, you contacted Gen. Secord and asked him whether he would be willing to endeavor to purchase the arms and sell them to the contras?

LT. COL. NORTH: And others. I mean, I contacted a number of people, to include Gen. Singlaub and others.

MR. NIELDS: And I take it you made, in some instances, specific efforts to obtain particular kinds of arms, such as Blowpipe missiles, for example.

LT. COL. NORTH: Yes, I did.

MR. NIELDS: And I take it that—I think you've already testified to this—that you on one occasion interceded with Country Four?

LT. COL. NORTH: You'll have to allow me to—yes.

MR. NIELDS: —to facilitate a delivery of arms to the contras?

LT. COL. NORTH: That's correct.

MR. NIELDS: And I take it—

LT. COL. NORTH: Among others. I'm willing to—

MR. NIELDS: Among other countries with whom you interceded in a similar way, I take it, is what you're saying?

LT. COL. NORTH: Exactly.

MR. NIELDS: And indeed, I think that you've probably seen a document in which you endeavored to reward a Central American country that had provided end-user certificates.

LT. COL. NORTH: That's correct.

MR. NIELDS: And I take it that these—

LT. COL. NORTH: I didn't see the document, I wrote it. I'll stand up and take that.

MR. NIELDS: And, I take it you had had communications with officials of that country in advance of writing that document.

LT. COL. NORTH: That's correct.

MR. NIELDS: And you told them that you were going to try to get them some help as a way of rewarding them for the help they'd given to the contras?

LT. COL. NORTH: Let me—let me be very specific about that. I do not recall, ever, telling any country or representative of any country that if they did this, that we would do

210

that. What is very important, and I trid to articulate this yesterday, is that others, in other countries and other Americans, very clearly saw that help to the Nicaraguan resistance was in the best interest of those countries and was in the best interest of the United States of America. And those other countries, in almost every case, without even any prodding, stepped up and wanted to help. And so when I met with somebody, it didn't take a great deal of pushing.

What I'm saying to you, Counsel, is that there was a very clear recognition, particularly in Central America, that there was a disaster at hand, that they saw, in the words of one head of state, that they were in the mouth of the lion. And I have given you notes of my meetings with a number of heads of state.

Quite honestly, Counsel, I don't understand why I had to give you those notes. I would have thought, under normal circumstances, that they would have been accorded what we used to call executive privilege. Those were meetings I had with heads of state and representatives of other countries in the conduct of the foreign policy of the United States of America. And I honestly believe to this day, sir, that those ought not to be handed out and bandied about, that they were private communications, as I was authorized to make by a representative of our Executive branch in discussions with those people who represented their governments.

And when the head of state of that country said to me, "You must understand, Colonel, that we are in the mouth of the lion. And you Americans hold the lion's tail," that what he was talking about was the fact that they could be devoured by what was going on inside Nicaragua. They saw the Leninist, totalitarian regime in Managua as a disastrous threat to their own safety, the security of their people, and the opportunity for economic development. And I didn't have to push these people. All I had to do was nod and say we would be grateful. And indeed, I believe we should be. And so when I met with the representatives of any one of those countries on that list for that purpose, it didn't take prodding. All it took was saying we would be grateful. And indeed, I think we ought to be.

MR. NIELDS: I think the question was, I take it that you sought to reward this country for the help that it had given in getting arms to the contras.

211

LT. COL. NORTH: I sought, in the memorandum that I prepared, to acknowledge what they had done. I also sought to point out in that memorandum that that country, which we don't have listed as a number here, but that that particular country was suffering from a guerilla war sponsored by the Soviet Union and Cuba and Nicaragua, and that they were in desperate straits and they needed help. They needed economic help and they needed security assistance, and the memorandum that I attached also indicated that they had provided assistance to Nicaraguan resistance in the form of end-user certificates, but I never told the representatives of that country that if they gave us those, we would get something else to them. That's an important factor. I didn't make promises based on a quid pro quo.

MR. NIELDS: Well, I'd like you to turn, in that case, to Exhibit #145. It's in book six.

(The witness confers with his counsel.)

Do you have that in front of you?

LT. COL. NORTH: I do.

MR. NIELDS: And, that's a document memorandum from you to Mr. McFarlane?

LT. COL. NORTH: It is.

MR. NIELDS: And, it deals with this Central American country, and it's titled, "Aid to the Nicaraguan Resistance"?

LT. COL. NORTH: That's correct.

MR. NIELDS: And, it recommends that the national security adviser, Mr. McFarlane, send a letter to the Secretaries of State and Defense, among others?

LT. COL. NORTH: Yes, that's correct.

MR. NIELDS: And, the letter itself is a suggestion of providing some assistance to the Central American country?

LT. COL. NORTH: That is correct.

MR. NIELDS: And, in your memo, you say at the end of the memo, on page two, "Once we have approval for at least some of what they have asked for, we can ensure that the right people in that country understand that we are able to provide results from their cooperation on the resistance issue." Now, you wrote that. Was that your intention?

LT. COL. NORTH: That was one of my intentions. It was

very clear from the attached memo what the real problem is there too. And, the attached memo talks about in recent weeks there appears to have been an increase in guerilla attacks and subversion in that country.

MR. NIELDS: And, indeed, you indicate in the memo at page one that the real purpose of your memo is to find a way by which we can compensate the Central American country for the extraordinary assistance they are providing to the Nicaraguan freedom fighters. And, you also recommend that the letter that goes to the Secretaries of Defense and State, and this is on page two, not refer to the arrangements which have been made for supporting the resistance.

LT. COL. NORTH: That is correct, and I don't deny a single word that's in there.

MR. NIELDS: So?

LT. COL. NORTH: But, what I'm saying to you, and the point I was trying to make, is I did not tell the representatives of that country blanked out there, that if they did this, then we would do that. Never did I do that.

MR. NIELDS: But you wanted this done for the purpose expressed at the end of page two, which is so that you can ensure that the right people in the Central American country understand that we are able to provide results from their cooperation on the resistance issue.

LT. COL. NORTH: I do not deny that.

MR. NIELDS: But, you didn't want the Secretaries of Defense and State, who were being asked to provide these results to know why they were doing it?

LT. COL. NORTH: Let me be more specific than that. I did not want the memo that you see at Tab I, which is sent to the Honorable George P. Shultz, Caspar Weinberger, William Casey and General Vessey, which would be reviewed by hundreds of people en route to their offices, to have that reference in it. And, as I said yesterday, counsel, it was fairly well-known, certainly to those men, although they may all deny it, what I was doing. There came a time when the man at the top of that list, at the occasion of the retirement of Ambassador Robert Oakley, took me aside just weeks before I was summarily fired, put his arm around my shoulder and told me what a remarkable job I had done, keeping the Nicaraguan resistance alive.

There is no doubt that they knew what I was doing, and

213

yet I didn't think it was necessary that the hundreds of staffers, who would see that memo on the way to their front offices, had a clear recognition for what I was doing. I didn't seek the credit, and I didn't want the blame. I was simply willing to take the fall, if somebody needed a political scapegoat. That's what I was willing to do.

MR. NIELDS: I take it one of the other things which you did was to organize a resupply operation in Nicaragua, for Nicaragua?

LT. COL. NORTH: I helped do that.

MR. NIELDS: And you asked General Secord if he would be willing to run it himself, did you not?

LT. COL. NORTH: That is correct.

MR. NIELDS: And, you also asked Ambassador Tambs to help open a southern front.

LT. COL. NORTH: That is correct.

MR. NIELDS: And, you also asked him to help out on the resupply operation?

LT. COL. NORTH: I don't know that I asked him to specifically help on the resupply operation. I did ask for his help, and received it, in trying to obtain the use by virtue of a lease or a planned sale of real estate in that country for the purposes of building an airfield that would be used for supporting the Nicaraguan resistance—yes.

MR. NIELDS: And I take it that one of the purposes for the airstrip was as an emergency landing place for the resupply operation?

LT. COL. NORTH: And a place to supply small planes in and out of—yes.

MR. NIELDS: And just so we're clear, I take it the—a resupply operation involves the flying of goods including arms inside Nicaragua and dropping them to contras that were stationed there and needed to be resupplied?

LT. COL. NORTH: You said it.

MR. NIELDS: And I take it that you asked others to help out in obtaining the—this airstrip? There is a Mr. Haskell, who has been referred to in some of your documents as Mr. Olmstead, who I take it you knew and asked to help out in obtaining the property and developing it?

LT. COL. NORTH: I did. And I am pleased to note that he helped.

MR. NIELDS: And I take it that among other things, you interceded with third countries in an effort to obtain airplanes?

LT. COL. NORTH: Yes—and other things, as we already know.

MR. NIELDS: And I take it this resupply operation eventually got started and was operational sometime in 1986?

LT. COL. NORTH: I—I don't want to get pinned down to an exact date when it got going, but it did get going.

MR. NIELDS: And you obtained certain secure communication devices, KL-43s?

LT. COL. NORTH: Yes, I did.

MR. NIELDS: And distributed them to members of the resupply operation?

LT. COL. NORTH: And others, that's correct. American citizens.

MR. NIELDS: And I take it you utilized these and so did they to communicate with respect to the air resupply operation?

LT. COL. NORTH: And other matters. I would point out for the benefit of the Committee that Director Casey had on several occasions indicated to me how vulnerable our communications were to intercept from the Soviet signals intelligence site at Lourdes, Cuba, and that his suspicion was that our communications were being read altogether too frequently, and that I should seek some type of communications support which I did. The KL-43s were used for that purpose—and others.

MR. NIELDS: And you sent and received messages relating to the resupply operation on that KL-43?

LT. COL. NORTH: Many.

MR. NIELDS: And I take it that the messages that were sent to you were in many instances typed up by your secretary?

LT. COL. NORTH: Yes.

MR. NIELDS: And I take it they were among the documents which were shredded?

LT. COL. NORTH: Among the documents, yes. Apparently I didn't shred all of them, however.

MR. NIELDS: And among other things, you directed those who were operating the resupply operation down in Central

215

America with respect to when they should make drops, how they should make them, where they should make them, and so on?

LT. COL. NORTH: I—I doubt that "directed" is the right term. I'm not trying to back away from any of the things that I did, but it is hard to direct a war from a desk in Washington. And I wasn't trying to direct a war from a desk in Washington. I provided as much support for those activities as I was physically able. I went down frequently to coordinate with people in the region, and I would receive and try to coordinate those activities based on information that I received from a multiple of sources. And so "directing" I don't think is quite the right phrase to use.

MR. NIELDS: But you did, from time to time, given instructions about where items should be dropped—

LT. COL. NORTH: Oh, yes.

MR. NIELDS: —when they should drop, how they should be dropped.

LT. COL. NORTH: Well, again, I'm—they were going to be dropped by parachute, no matter what. But I would—I would have the communications in that would indicate that we needed a unit in a certain place, needed a certain number of items, and I would pick up the phone and the KL-43 and ask those guys to see if they could do that. Sometimes they could, sometimes they couldn't.

MR. NIELDS: Did they—

LT. COL. NORTH: (When you say?) directing, I don't think you—I don't think that I ever sent out, "I direct you to do the following at such and such a time."

MR. NIELDS: Why don't we just turn to Exhibit 88, I believe that's in Book 4.

(Pause while North looks through exhibits)

MR. NIELDS: Do you have that in front of you?

LT. COL. NORTH: I have Exhibit 88. Begins with a unit?

MR. NIELDS: Yes. And up at the top it says F. M. Goode

LT. COL. NORTH: Yes.

MR. NIELDS: I take it you are Goode?

LT. COL. NORTH: I was very good.

MR. NIELDS: And this is a message that was from you, I take it?

LT. COL. NORTH: It—it was.

216

MR. NIELDS: And it discusses, does it not, a proposed drop of weapons?

LT. COL. NORTH: Yes.

MR. NIELDS: D. in the first paragraph, it says "The unit to which we wanted to drop in the Southern quadron of Nicaragua is in desperate need of ordnance supply." And then you discuss various plans. In one sentence it reads, "Have therefore developed an alternative plan which," and the code name of the Chief of the Central American Task Force is blanked out—

LT. COL. NORTH: On my copy it is not, but I understand—

MR. NIELDS: "has been briefed on, and in which he concurs." Then down below, you say, "On any night between Wednesday, April 9th and Friday, April 11th, the supply should be dropped by the C23 in the vicinity of," and there are coordinates which are blanked out—

LT. COL. NORTH: Not on mine, but I know the place well.

MR. NIELDS: "The aircraft should penetrate Nicaragua across the Atlantic coast, south of," there's another word blanked out—

LT. COL. NORTH: Yes, not on mine, but I know it—

MR. NIELDS: "Call signs, frequency and zone marking, light diagram to be provided to Ralph at," and another place is blanked out—

LT. COL. NORTH: Not on mine—

MR. NIELDS: "by the new UNO, sir operator, we are taken care of. Hope we can make this happen the right way this time. If we are ever going to take the pressure off the Northern Front, we have got to get this drop in quickly." And then you say, "Please make sure that this is retransmitted via this channel to," there's a blank, Ralph, sat, and steel. "Owen already briefed and prepared to go with the L100 out of," another place is blanked out, "if this will help." Again, I take it, this message was sent by you and I take it this was not atypical of other messages that you sent dealing with the same kinds of issues.

LT. COL. NORTH: That is correct.

MR. NIELDS: By the way, this document was obtained from Mr. Secord and it is marked Top Secret. Now, is it normal for a purely private operation to have—have its documents classified?

217

LT. COL. NORTH: Private companies all over the United States of America, who do business with, or for the Government of the United States, have classified documents, probably at a much higher level than even that in terms of compartments—

MR. NIELDS: Are they—

LT. COL. NORTH: I would also point out that the KL-43 device, if I recall correctly, and I haven't used one in seven months, but I used it a lot when I had one, automatically put, I think, a code on the transmission. (Pause, confers with attorney). In any event, I see nothing unusual with that.

MR. NIELDS: And I take it that you would agree with the proposition that this resupply operation was doing business with or for the United States?

LT. COL. NORTH: They were certainly doing it to benefit the foreign policy of the United States of America. I will certainly agree with that.

MR. NIELDS: And was it in furtherance of a covert operation being run by the National Security Council?

LT. COL. NORTH: It was in furtherance of the foreign policy of the President of the United States to support the Nicaraguan freedom fighters.

MR. NIELDS: Was it—

LT. COL. NORTH: An activity that I was coordinating, that I wrote policy papers on, and on which I carefully kept my superiors apprised of what I was doing.

MR. NIELDS: And I take it among other things that you did was direct monies to various contra leaders and others persons in Central America?

LT. COL. NORTH: I did, as I testified this morning.

MR. NIELDS: And some of those were carried down by Mr. Owen ?

LT. COL. NORTH: Yes they were.

MR. NIELDS: And some of them were taken there by General Secord or people working under his direction?

LT. COL. NORTH: Yes, and others.

MR. NIELDS: And I take it that Mr. Owen did a number of things in furtherance of the support of the contras?

LT. COL. NORTH: Yes, he did, thank God.

MR. NIELDS: And indeed, you had a name for him, I take it it was "The Courier"?

218

LT. COL. NORTH: I don't recall giving him that name, but I do recall that his documents did come in marked "TC".

MR. NIELDS: And that stood for "The Courier"?

LT. COL. NORTH: Yes.

MR. NIELDS: And as you've already said, he would carry money down from your office to various contra leaders?

LT. COL. NORTH: Yes.

MR. NIELDS: And he scouted the airstrip?

LT. COL. NORTH: I guess he did, yes. I'm not too sure —yeah, I guess that was prior to Olmstead.

MR. NIELDS: And he would bring a list of weapons from the contras that they wanted?

LT. COL. NORTH: That's right, among other things.

MR. NIELDS: And he carried intelligence from you down to the contras for particular operations?

LT. COL. NORTH: That's correct.

MR. NIELDS: Indeed, I think he testified before this committee that he was, in his words, your "eyes and ears" in the contra movement?

LT. COL. NORTH: I don't recall his testimony, but I won't dispute the description.

MR. NIELDS: And I take it that you contacted—(Pause) I take it you contacted other people for the purpose of having them do, or talk to the contras about doing, special operations.

LT. COL. NORTH: I did, among other things, yes. And I keep saying "among other things" because I—I don't want you to leave this room and think that that's all we did. And what you described was a lot, and it kept us up for many long, sleepless days and night and away from home for many days at a time, and a lot of nights.

We also worked very hard to unify this resistance movement, and I would point out without taking undue credit or having undue credit given to those with whom we worked that this is the only anti-communist resistance movement that ever unified. We haven't succeeded in doing that in Afghanistan. We had—didn't succeed in doing that in Angola or Ethiopia, Guinea-Bissau, Mozambique, or other places where resistance movements have grown up to fight communism. It happened here. It happened here because, I think, there were so many people working so hard for a unified purpose, and that was a lot of what we did.

We also delivered food and clothing and medical supplies and provided prosthetic limbs for people with their—with their arms and hands blown off, and their legs, and tried to look after the families of those people who had been killed or badly wounded and were no longer productive wage-earners. And so there was a lot done. In a—in a word, Director Casey said it was full service covert operation, and I'm not too sure that's a bad description.

There was a lot of people who cared, and—and I say we cared because a lot of us, like Bob—Rob Owen and General Secord and Bill Haskell and myself came to know the young campesino who is fighting this war. These are young men and women who gave up everything they had and they fled a totalitarian communist regime, and they fled to another country because they could no longer live within the one that they'd been born in. And the took up arms.

I didn't create the Nicaraguan contra or the Nicaraguan freedom fighter, and the CIA didn't create it. The Sandinistas created it.

MR. NIELDS: But you said—

LT. COL. NORTH: And we all cared enough to do all of those things, not just the way you have left it—sending guns, sending guns, sending guns. It was all of that, counsel, as best we were able.

MR. NIELDS: And I take it one of the ways you got the leaders to unify was to send substantial amounts of cash down to them?

LT. COL. NORTH: People who are going to give up their lives and their livelihoods to join a resistance movement need to feed their families. And so, when it became necessary to help them eat and put a roof over the heads of their families to join a political and military opposition to the Communist regime in Managua, we sent money, yes.

MR. NIELDS: And, in one case, you sent a total of $225,000 to one leader.

LT. COL. NORTH: I give up. Who?

MR. NIELDS: We have been avoiding mentioning particular names, but there is a particular leader who was sent $225,000 over approximately a year-and-a-half period out of the Swiss bank accounts under Gen. Secord's control.

MR. SULLIVAN: May I suggest that, if you want accurate testimony here that you provide the Colonel with the name on a piece of paper, and let's see if he has a response to it. Thank you, sir.

LT. COL. NORTH: While you're looking for the piece of paper, the amount may be $225,000. It might well be higher. But I don't think the committee ought to be left with the impression that he was bribed or she was bribed into joining this movement. These are people who felt deeply —perhaps even more so than I—because it was their country. And I don't know that anybody was ever bribed to join the Nicaraguan resistance. No matter who the person is or how much he got, I think that they fought as best they were able and they used the monies that I provided for them to support the cause that they believed in.

In particular that man—who, after all, had been a part of the movement to throw out Somoza. And that's important for you to understand. This man joined up with what he had hoped to be a democratic opposition. And he had the revolution that he worked for stolen from him. And, yes, I sent money to that man. And I know, because I saw the product of it, that he helped form a southern front with that money. And if it helped him to live and to feed his family, good. And there's nothing wrong with that, Counsel, nothing.

MR. NIELDS: I'd like to ask you some questions now about who in the US government was aware of this full-service operation.

LT. COL. NORTH: I'm sorry?

MR. NIELDS: I'm going to ask you a few questions now about who in the US government was aware of this full-service operation.

Was Mr. Abrams at the State Department?

LT. COL. NORTH: Well, I certainly believed he was.

MR. NIELDS: Well, did you ever talk to him about it?

LT. COL. NORTH: Yes.

MR. NIELDS: Now what aspects of it did you discuss with him?

LT. COL. NORTH: Well, let me describe the situation. We're—you're in a meeting with the people who are in the business of formulating American policy and trying to coordinate what activities we can in the region. And the meeting goes, "We desperately have got to do something about X, Y, or Z, Ollie."

Now as I just indicated to you a few moments ago, when Secretary Shultz took me aside at Ambassador Bob Oakley's retirement, I knew what he meant. He didn't have to say, "You did a great job on the L-100 resupply on the night of the 9th of April." He knew, in sufficiently eloquent terms, what I had done.

And as I said to you, counsel, I didn't walk around bragging. I didn't walk around saying, "Hey, look at me. I sought to avoid that. I did not seek the credit, and I didn't want the blame. I'm willing to accept the blame for what I did. And I have told you a good bit of that here, and some of it has not been easy.

I honestly believe that there were many, many people within the executive branch who had a grasp, if not in specific detail, that in sufficient detail that they knew who to turn to when they wanted something done. And so when the airplane being flown by Captain Bill Cooper and copiloted by Buzz Sawyer, two of the braver people I've ever met on this planet, was shot down out of the skies over Nicaragua by a surface-to-air missile, I was the person who was called to raise the money to pay for the consular services to retrieve their bodies.

MR. NIELDS: Who called you?

LT. COL. NORTH: Mr. Abrams. Why would he—

MR. NIELDS: I'd like you to turn to Exhibit 94—

LT. COL. NORTH: —have turned to me if he didn't know I was doing it?

MR. NIELDS: Turn to Exhibit 94. (Pause) Do you have that in front of you?

LT. COL. NORTH: I do.

MR. NIELDS: And is that a note that you took on your spiral notepads of a conversation with Mr. Abrams on the 25th of April 1986?

LT. COL. NORTH: It appears to be.

MR. NIELDS: And is that of a meeting with Mr. Abrams?

LT. COL. NORTH: Well, it says, "Meeting with Elliott." And that's the only Elliott that I can recall.

MR. NIELDS: And that—

LT. COL. NORTH: I take that back. I do know other Elliots, but I'm sure that given the subject matter, that's what it pertains to.

MR. NIELDS: And one of the things that's written there

222

is—well, there are a number of items written under it. I take it those are matters that you discussed with Mr. Abrams at the meeting.

MR. NIELDS: I see the notation, Counsel. I do not recall that—what year is this? Must be '86, if it's—

MR. NIELDS: '86.

LT. COL. NORTH: —Ambassador Abrams. And it says—I don't even know what the first note means at this point, "Supplies for Southern Front." And there's a second item, "Airbase open in 'blank,'" item for 'blank,' and 100 Blowpipes" —BP's. That's not the gas station.

MR. NIELDS: Did you discuss those subjects with Mr. Abrams, at that meeting, to the best of your recollection?

LT. COL. NORTH: I do not have any recollection of that meeting, but I do not deny that I discussed those at various and times with Mr. Abrams and others.

MR. NIELDS: I take it there came a time when you gave Mr. Abrams the identity of a bank account in Switzerland.

LT. COL. NORTH: Yes.

MR. NIELDS: Which was the Lake Resources account.

LT. COL. NORTH: It was.

MR. NIELDS: And would you describe the circumstances under which you gave him that account?

LT. COL. NORTH: Well, I honestly—I—without being able to refresh my memory, all I remember is that at some point in time, I gave him a sheet of paper, or a card, or whatever, with a—the account number on it. And I knew, at the time, that he was going to—either he or someone from the Department of State was going to talk to a representative from—what country are we calling them? I guess they get to be called by their own name—a representative from Brunei. I cannot recall exactly when that was. It must have been sometime in 1986.

MR. NIELDS: Did you tell him anything about the account?

LT. COL. NORTH: I told him that it was an account in which he could determine what he wanted done with the monies in those—in that account; that it would be under US rather than foreign control.

MR. NIELDS: When you say "foreign," do you mean US as opposed to Nicaraguan?

LT. COL. NORTH: US as opposed to any other. In other

words, it wouldn't have to be in the—a US person would have control over the account; that it wouldn't be a foreigner, or some other banking company, or some other country, or whatever. That's what I recall.

MR. NIELDS: Did you tell him that it was preexisting account, one that you were already using for the contras?

LT. COL. NORTH: I don't recall whether I told him that or not.

MR. NIELDS: The only thing you recall about your conversation was that you told him it was a—an account under the control of a US person?

LT. COL. NORTH: Yeah. Unless you can refresh my memory better, that's all I remember.

MR. NIELDS: Any other people in the State Department who were aware of your full-service operation?

LT. COL. NORTH: I—I don't know specifically—I—you know, you asked me, "What did Ambassador Abrams know?" Okay. He knew enough to turn to me for those things. He knew enough to turn—that he and I could talk about these issues. And I don't see anything wrong with him knowing that. Unless I'm overly naive, it was appropriate for the Assistant Sectretary for Latin American Affairs to be aware of what was going on. These were matters that affected the policy down there. If the Nicaraguan resistance wasn't going to survive, he was going to have a first-class disaster on his hands.

MR. NIELDS: Let me sharpen my question. With whom else at the State Department, if anyone, did you discuss all or part of your full-service operation?

LT. COL. NORTH: Well, let's see. When—one other person I can recall specifically is Mr. John Miller, who at the time worked in the—I can't recall the initials of the office, but it was the Office of Public Diplomacy. And he was aware of it, at least part of it. I—I—

MR. NIELDS: Which part?

LT. COL. NORTH: The public diplomacy aspect of it in the effort to reach out and—and make contact with resistance leadership—leader—the resistance leadership in a unity effort. He was certainly aware of that.

MR. NIELDS: Any others at State Department?

LT. COL. NORTH: Not that I can recall of the top of my

head. You know, maybe we can flip to another page where I got someone else's name on it.

MR. NIELDS: How about the CIA? And let's proceed using titles.

LT. COL. NORTH: Well, I think that the—the level of knowledge that Mr. Abrams had was certainly shared among people who are engaged in the Central American task force. I mean, I want to go back once again to intelligence. And I—and I guess maybe I'd like to expand it out—I'm not trying to drag in a whole bunch of people in the "Ollie North Dragnet" here, but the National Intelligence Daily that is published every single day by the CIA, except I think Sunday, is provided to the intelligence committees up here, and—and there was ample indication frequently that there was resupply going on from 1984 through 1986. And so there were a lot of people who knew that something was happening. Now, I don't know if the intelligence that was being seen by the CIA actually had my name in it, aside from those issues that Director Casey brought up with me directly, but surely there were times when people pointed out to me that "Oh, by the way, is that ship leaving Country X headed for Country Y" and I'd say yes. And they knew enough to call me about that.

So Director Casey had specific and detailed knowledge because I briefed him frequently in detail. Below his level, I would guess the knowledge got thinner as—further down the—the ladder you went until you got to the Central American task force, and within the Central American task force there were people who had much more specific knowledge than in the intervening layers.

MR. NIELDS: And did—did you ever discuss with the chief of the Central American task force the specifics of your role in the contra resupply operation?

(Long pause)

LT. COL. NORTH: Yes.

MR. NIELDS: How frequently?

LT. COL. NORTH: As necessary.

MR. NIELDS: I take it more than once?

LT. COL. NORTH: Yes.

MR. NIELDS: Is it more like once a week?

LT. COL. NORTH: I don't know. I would guess that there

were occasions that were perhaps weekly. It wasn't necessary to do it weekly so much as it was just to get a feel for how things were moving.

MR. NIELDS: Now I'd like you to turn to a document which has been marked Exhibit 98A. (Pause.) Do you have that in front of you?

LT. COL. NORTH: I do.

MR. NIELDS: And I'd like you to turn to the second page of it, and I don't want you to read anything from it. My first question is whether that is the list of items that you referred to in your testimony yesterday?

LT. COL. NORTH: No. But that is certainly a list. The one I was referring to yesterday was at some later point with greater specificity, but it's the same type of thing.

MR. NIELDS: And this one does, I take it, record items discussed at a meeting with the Chief of the Central American Task Force.

LT. COL. NORTH: If you're talking about page 1, it's a telephone call apparently. Are we talking about the 6 August, 10:00 entry?

MR. NIELDS: No.

LT. COL. NORTH: I'm sorry.

MR. NIELDS: Ninety-eight A.

LT. COL. NORTH: Oh, excuse me. That's the list.

MR. NIELDS: And I take it that records subjects discussed at a meeting with, among other people, the Chief of the Central American Task Force?

LT. COL. NORTH: That is correct.

MR. NIELDS: And I take it on the second page there is a list of items that you discussed, including payments to various contra leaders and then "air ops" at the bottom?

LT. COL. NORTH: That's correct.

MR. NIELDS: And "air ops", what does that refer to?

LT. COL. NORTH: Aircraft resupply, parachuting supplies and flying them into Nicaragua to support the Nicarguan resistance.

MR. NIELDS: This is the resupply operation which was being run by General Secord?

LT. COL. NORTH: And by the resistance itself, yes.

MR. NIELDS: How about the Vice President? Was he aware of your role in the contra resupply operation?

LT. COL. NORTH: If he was, I didn't tell him.

226

MR. NIELDS: How about people in his office?

LT. COL. NORTH: Well I don't know what—the only other person I ever talked to in his office at any rate of frequency was Mr. Don Gregg, and I don't know what he knew. He had a lot more frequent—he had much more frequent contact with another person who was down there.

(pause)

MR. NIELDS: Would you turn to Exhibit 99? Do you have that in front of you?

LT. COL. NORTH: I do.

MR. NIELDS: It's dated 10/5/86, I take it that's immediately after the shootdown of the Hasenfus plane?

LT. COL. NORTH: I'd have to have my memory refreshed because I was overseas at the time, I think.

MR. NIELDS: It's October 5th, 1986.

LT. COL. NORTH: Well again, I think I was overseas at the time.

MR. NIELDS: There is a reference in Exhibit 99 which is on Office of the Vice President stationery.

LT. COL. NORTH: All right.

MR. NIELDS: (Reading from exhibit) "C-123 equals Ollie."

LT. COL. NORTH: I don't know what they called the C-123. It's—I've never seen this document before in my life, Mr. Nields.

MR. NIELDS: Did you ever discuss your resupply operation with Mr. Gregg or Mr. Watson in the office of the Vice President?

LT. COL. NORTH: I do not recall talking to Mr. Watson, I do recall talking to Mr. Gregg, I believe it was in terms of concern about Mr. Rodriguez. I don't recall going into any great detail with Mr. Gregg about it. I may—it just may have slipped my mind, obviously somebody knew something while I was traveling around in Europe.

MR. NIELDS: How about the Department of Defense, Southern Command? Were there people there who—with whom you discussed your role in the resupply operation?

LT. COL. NORTH: Well again, I don't think I made clear my role to people much below the level of Admiral Moreau, who had a detailed knowledge of it, until he departed for another assignment in Europe. I know that several of the people who worked for him on his staff had some knowledge

227

of what I was doing. There were occasionally people who I would see when I was traveling who were military officers, when I would travel to Central America, who were American military officers. The Ambassadors of those countries saw me (pause)—on occasion, I'm not saying they saw me every time or that I specifically sought them out on every trip, but they did see me.

MR. NIELDS: How about Gen. Gorman?

LT. COL. NORTH: I think Gen. Gorman had a general idea of what I was doing. Gen. Gorman had been the predecessor to Adm. Moreau at the Pentagon. I visited with him frequently. But I don't recall, with these people, sitting down and saying, "Oh, by the way, over the net 30 days, here's what Ollie North plans to do." What is more likely that I did is, I sat down and I said, "You know, over the course of the next six months, do these sound like good ideas for the Nicaraguan resistance? And what's your advice on how they should carry these things out?"

And so, what I'm saying to you is that, by inference, these people came to know what my role was in supporting the democratic opposition in Nicaragua, both military as well as political—and in trying to engender support from countries in the region, as well as in Europe.

MR. NIELDS: Would you turn to Exhibit 102?

(The witness perused the exhibit.)

MR. NIELDS: Do you have that in front of you?

LT. COL. NORTH: I do.

MR. NIELDS: And are those your notes of a conversation with Gen. Gorman on the 19th of February, 1985?

LT. COL. NORTH: They certainly appear to be, because that is my writing, or a copy of it.

MR. NIELDS: Now it says there, or you've written there, "Told him" —

LT. COL. NORTH: No. "FR told his priority should be FDN. Told him in delicate stage of transition from blank run op to blank run op with LRPs and PROWL." And I can't read beyond that because it's all scratched out.

MR. NIELDS: Well, you put in some blanks. You said "blank" in two places. There's nothing classified about either of those words. One of them is CIA—

LT. COL. NORTH: Well—

MR. NIELDS: —and the other is Southern Command.

"Delicate stage of transition from CIA run op to Southern Command run op."

LT. COL. NORTH: That's referring to the country in which FR was living, and I thought that that was a classified program. It has nothing to do with the Nicaraguan resistance. The only entry regarding the Nicaraguan resistance is the letters "FDN." And what Gen. Gorman was trying to do was to get FR away from those two items on the bottom, which were an approved activity—I thought they were classified—in support of military operations in that country. It's authorized. Appropriated money is being used for it. And what he was trying to do was get FR the heck away from those two activities. And I don't blame him for that because he saw a problem there, and I happen to agree with him. He's, after all, a four-star general. And what he was trying to do is to have me back him up, because that's what he was trying to accomplish.

MR. NIELDS: Was the President of the United States aware of your—the fact that you were running a resupply operation in Nicaragua?

LT. COL. NORTH: Again, I have absolutely no idea of what the President's knowledge [was] specifically about what I was doing. I made every effort to keep my superiors fully apprised as to what I was doing, and the effect that it was having in the region. And you have tons of documents taken from me, some of which I personally surrendered to you and you alone, and others that were taken from my files, that make that abundantly clear.

I don't know, to this day, what the President knew I, personally, was doing. I hope to God that people were keeping him apprised as to the effect of it. Because if we hadn't done it, there wouldn't have been a Nicaraguan resistance around when the Congress got around to putting up $100 million for it—sir.

MR. NIELDS: Did you obtain from Mr. Dutton a book of photographs?

LT. COL. NORTH: From who? Oh yes, I did.

MR. NIELDS: And did you tell him that you were —wanted that book of—and this was, I take it, a book of photographs of various aspects of the resupply operation?

LT. COL. NORTH: That's correct—

MR. NIELDS: Planes—

LT. COL. NORTH: And other things, too. I don't recall specifically what was in the book, then, but that is correct.

MR. NIELDS: And did you tell them that you wanted that book so that you would have something to show the President about the good work that they were doing?

LT. COL. NORTH: I'm not sure that I put it that way. I—you know, I—I want to get away from this "Ollie North wanted to get the credit" stuff, because I didn't. I think what I wanted to do was to—if I said something to that effect: "I think the President ought to see this." And I think I made an effort to send it up to the President through the National Security Advisor. And I don't know whether it ever got to the President or not.

But if the book is still around, somebody ought to send it to him. Because the President ought to be aware of what a handful of people did to keep the Nicaraguan resistance alive at a time when nobody in this Congress seemed to care. And it's important that the President know that good men gave inordinate amounts of time, and some gave their lives to support that activity. And some of them have been brutally treated by what has come about in these two parallel investigations—brutally treated.

MR. NIELDS: How did you go about making efforts —(pause)—how did you go about making efforts—

LT. COL. NORTH: I would like to correct something I just said, Mr. Chairman. And I apologize to those who did care, because there were many members of this—this body who cared a lot. And eventually a majority cared again, and chose to appropriate $100 million to support that resistance. And I apologize to those of you who have backed them all the way. And I pray to God you will not stop because what I have done or what I have failed to do, I desperately believe that if nothing else comes of these hearings, that you will have sufficient reason to vote, again, to appropriate monies to that cause. And I ask your apologies for overstating what I just did.

CHAIRMAN INOUYE: On that point, may we take a 10-minute recess.

(Short recess)

CHAIRMAN INOUYE: The hearing will please come to order. Mr. Nields.

MR. NIELDS: Thank you, Mr. Chairman. Col. North, what

230

was your legal authority for conducting a full-service covert operation to support the contras?

LT. COL. NORTH: The authority that I sought from my superiors in setting up the activity to begin with, and then the conduct of it.

MR. NIELDS: Well, you're aware that every covert activity abroad requires a finding by the President to support it, aren't you?

LT. COL. NORTH: I am aware that covert actions undertaken by the CIA do, indeed, require a finding. I am not aware, as you have just indicated, that, quote, "all covert actions require a finding."

MR. NIELDS: Well, there's an executive order that's been entered as an exhibit in these hearings that requires "all covert operations" to be supported by a finding, notified to Congress and it also requires—it's Executive Order 12333 —and it also requires a specific determination by the President before any agency other than the CIA may conduct a covert operation. Are you aware of any finding that supported your operation or any specific determination by the President that the NSC should conduct it?

LT. COL. NORTH: No.

MR. NIELDS: And, I should state for the record that at page 324 of the Tower Board Report, the following is stated: "The President told the Board on January 26th, 1987 that he did not know that the NSC staff was engaged in helping the contras."

Is the NSC itself authorized to conduct covert operations abroad?

LT. COL. NORTH: I haven't found nothing that in my experience as a National Security Council staff member that indicates that it is not.

MR. NIELDS: Well, then, I take it you were conducting an intelligence operation abroad, and I take it then, it would be your testimony that the NSC is an agency engaged in intelligence activities.

LT. COL. NORTH: I gues—I don't—

MR. NIELDS: The record should reflect that the answer was interrupted by counsel.

(Long pause as Lt. Col. North looks over notebook.)

LT. COL. NORTH: Counsel, would you please repeat the question?

MR. NIELDS: I take it that, during the time when you were supporting—conducting a full-service covert operation in support of the contras, the NSC was an agency involved in intelligence activities?

LT. COL. NORTH: I'm—I'm still uncertain as to how to answer your question. The—I was on the NSC staff coordinating the activities of a non—outside USG group of people. On occasion, I had contact with people inside the US government. I kept my superiors fully apprised as to what they were doing. Director Casey was intimately aware of the activities. On one occasion in the case of these—this —this broader operation supporting a subsidiary activity —for example, the DEA officers who assisted in a hostage recovery operation. We went specifically to the head of the DEA and, if I recall correctly, the Attorney General and sought his permission. And I—I—I did not see at that point in time, nor do I see now, the need for a finding, specifically that you'd have to have a written finding. I—I'm quite sure that, if we had seen that you needed a finding, we'd have done one.

MR. NIELDS: That would have required a determination by the President, is that correct?

LT. COL. NORTH: Well, I don't have before me the Executive Order or the—or the requirement for a finding, but I believe it—it would have, yes.

MR. NIELDS: Findings are signed by the President?

LT. COL. NORTH: Presidential findings are signed by the President.

MR. NIELDS: And there was no such finding covering your full-service covert operation that you've been testifying about for the last half of the afternoon?

LT. COL. NORTH: Well, I've only been testifying because you've been ans—asking me the questions, Mr. Nields, and—and I—what I'm saying is that I told you what we did and you've defined them as certain things. I'm not necessarily saying that that meant that we were doing this, that, or the other thing requiring some other written document. In fact, I'm not even certain that a presidential finding needs to be in—on paper.

MR. NIELDS: You're aware that there was a law of Congress—passed by Congress, a statute of the United States, in effect at that time which prohibited the use of funds available to any agency involved in intelligence activities to support militarily or paramilitarily the contras.

LT. COL. NORTH: I'm not sure that I understood the way the Boland amendent or Boland proscriptions of October 1984 read exactly the way you just said. But what I am certain is that we—Director Casey, other lawyers, looked at that and said that the NSC staff was not proscribed doing those activities.

MR. NIELDS: In fact, you had an opinion drafted by a lawyer for—within Congress in your files saying exactly the opposite, didn't you?

LT. COL. NORTH: I may have. I had a lot of files. I don't remember them all.

MR. NIELDS: Turn to Exhibit 106. It's in book number five. (Pause while North looks for Exhibit)

MR. NIELDS: Do you have that in front of you?

LT. COL. NORTH: I have Exhibit 105.

MR. NIELDS: Do you have that in front of you?

MR. SULLIVAN[?]: Five or six?

MR. NIELDS: 106. (Pause while North looks for exhibit)

MR. NIELDS: Do you have that in front of you?

LT. COL. NORTH: I have the exhibit in front of me.

MR. NIELDS: And the cover sheet is from Vince to Ollie.

LT. COL. NORTH: Yes.

MR. NIELDS: And it says, "On the chance Steve didn't give you a copy, attached is for your use." And the attached is a memorandum dated August 8th, 1985, on House of Representatives stationery, from a lawyer employed by the House of Representatives. And two-thirds of the way down the page, it says, "NSC is clearly a US entity involved in intelligence activities, subject to the Section 8066(a) prohibition." 8066(a) is the Boland amendment, which prohibits, and it's quoted right above, funds available to the CIA, the Department of Defense, or any other agency or entity of the United States involved in intelligence activities to be obligated or expended to provide military support for the contras. And I take it this document was in your files as of—on or about August 8th, 1985?

LT. COL. NORTH: Well, I will believe that you found—if you tell me this was found in my files, I'll believe you. I don't recall the document. I'm not saying I didn't receive it. I don't know when I received it. And I will tell you that I

233

had other people who suggested, in fact it was suggested regularly in our media that anything like this was contrary to law, but I will also tell you we also had opinions that said that we were fully legitimate. We had one of those from the Intelligence Oversight Board, I had the—you know, Director Casey and I who started talking about this in 1983, and then carried it on until I left the NSC, reminded me frequently that he was a lawyer, and others would remind me that he was a good one, and that it was clearly my understanding that what I was doing was legal.

MR. NIELDS: I want—the opinion that you made reference to, the one from the Intelligence Oversight Board, had the top cut off of it in your files so that you couldn't tell who wrote it. Can you explain why that occurred?

LT. COL. NORTH: No.

MR. NIELDS: I take it you were however, that in the summer of 1985 there were a number of press reports that raised questions about whether you were engaged in activities which violated this law, the Boland Amendment?

LT. COL. NORTH: Yes, and I think what it focused on is that somewhere along the line there was someone who made the assumption that we in the NSC were spending part of the NSC budget to support the Nicaraguan resistance, and we didn't. And my understanding of—and I have not read Boland—the Boland Amendments in some time, but my understanding then was that what we could not do is take and expend funds which had been made available to the CIA and the DOD etc. for the purposes of providing direct or indirect support for military and paramilitary operations in Nicaragua. Now that's a memory that's over seven months old, but I think that was what the intent was, certainly the way we pursued it. And we made every effort not to expend US government funds to support the Nicaraguan resistance. And thus, when Director Casey suggested setting up outside entities, and he gave me the name of General Secord as a person who could help do it, we did it as an effort to comply with the Boland prescriptions.

MR. NIELDS: And following these newspaper articles, there were various inquiries by committees of Congress?

LT. COL. NORTH: That is correct.

MR. NIELDS: And one of them was by the House Committee on Intelligence? (Pause.) That's a question, do you know the answer to it?

LT. COL. NORTH: I do not recall the specific inquiry to which you are referring, sir.

MR. NIELDS: Well, I will ask you to turn to Exhibit 114. (Pause.) It's a letter from Chairman Hamilton of the House Intelligence Committee referring to recent press accounts of alleged activities by National Security Council and it asks for a description of those activities. And if you will turn to Exhibit 118, my question is going to be, is that the reply that was sent back to Chairman Hamilton?

LT. COL. NORTH: I'm sorry, which one was the incoming Exhibit number?

MR. NIELDS: 114, and the reply is Exhibit 118.

LT. COL. NORTH: Alright

MR. NIELDS: Now, the incoming, as you put it was to Mr. McFarlane, and the reply is signed by Mr. McFarlane, but you were aware of that inquiry, were you not?

LT. COL. NORTH: I believe I was.

MR. NIELDS: And, indeed, you were consulted about drafting an answer to it?

LT. COL. NORTH: I'm sure that I was.

MR. NIELDS: And did—did you—you helped draft it?

LT. COL. NORTH: Yes.

MR. NIELDS: And the reply, again, answering questions about whether activities of the NSC staff violated the law, states in the middle of the first paragraph, and it's dated December 5, 1985, "like you, I take such charges very seriously." Did you also take those charges, seriously?

LT. COL. NORTH: Where are you reading, Counsel?

MR. NIELDS: Middle of the first paragraph.

LT. COL. NORTH: Can I just back up for one second? I acknowledge that that's what it says in that letter.

MR. NIELDS: My question is whether you, also, took those charges seriously?

LT. COL. NORTH: I take all charges seriously, particularly the ones that are pending, as counsel has indicated, by an independent counsel running an extraordinary, unbridled, enormous investigation and I am the only person on the entire planet, Earth, named in his appointment order. And I am up here trying to answer your questions at great jeopardy to that investigation, and I think that ought to be a consideration as you weigh whether or not I'm going to be up here next week again, Counsel.

MR. NIELDS: And the letter goes on, "and consequently have thoroughly examined the facts and all matters which in any remote fashion, could bear on these charges." And I take it, part of the examination that Mr. McFarlane did, was to talk with you?

LT. COL. NORTH: Yes.

MR. NIELDS: And then he states, "I can state with deep personal conviction, that at no time did I or any member of the National Security Council staff violate the letter or the spirit of the law." Then in the middle of the bottom paragraph on the first page, it states, "in the fall of last year with the enactment of the Boland Amendment, it was apparent that the freedom fighters were demoralized at the prospect of an end to US support for their cause."

Then the next sentence says, "While we acknowledged to them that we could no longer contribute directly or indirectly to the paramilitary prosecution of their resistance, we stated we could continue to seek Congressional support" and so on.

Did you acknowledge to the contras that you could no longer contribute directly or indirectly to the paramilitary or military prosecution of their resistance?

LT. COL. NORTH: I made it very clear that appropriated monies of the United States of America would be temporarily withheld, until the President could go back, as he said in public speeches time after time after time, and he did so, until the Congress appropriated the monies.

MR. NIELDS: And, in the last sentence of that paragraph, it states, "Our emphasis on a political, rather than a military solution to the situation was as close as we ever came to influencing the military aspect of their struggle."

Is that statement true, sir?

LT. COL. NORTH: Well, it is partially true. I'm not saying all of the rest of it's true. What I'm saying to you is that I continue to believe, as I did then, that there will ultimately have to be a political solution. Was is, after all, a political endeavour, and I do not believe that we're going to see a victory march down the streets of Managua. What I do believe that we can achieve is a democratic outcome in

Nicaragua, as part of a political process. It will require diplomacy. It also requires military pressure on the Sandinistas. It is the essence of guerilla war.

This country fought a guerilla war, one in which I had served, and we lost the war. We won all the battles, and lost the war.

MR. NIELDS: The part of it which is untrue is the part that says, "that this was as close as we ever came to influencing the military aspect of their struggle." Isn't that true, sir?

LT. COL. NORTH: With using appropriated funds, no, but I'm not going to knitpick this thing.

MR. NIELDS: That's a false statement, isn't it? You were conducting, as you've testified here most of the afternoon, a full-service covert operation to support the military efforts of the resistance.

LT. COL. NORTH: Yes, that is true.

MR. NIELDS: And, this statement that, "emphasizing a political rather than a military solution was as close as we ever came to influencing the military aspect of their struggle" is just false, isn't it?

LT. COL. NORTH: It's not entirely false, but it is false, and I admit that there are other parts of this thing that are false.

MR. NIELDS: Let's get to the next one, which is in the next paragraph. It says, "It is equally important to stress what we did not do. We did not solicit funds or other support for military or paramilitary activities either from Americans or third parties." That's just plain false, isn't it?

LT. COL. NORTH: Right.

MR. NIELDS: Then there was a meeting with members of Congress that followed that letter. Members of the Intelligence Committee.

LT. COL. NORTH: In 1985?

MR. NIELDS: Nineteen eighty-five. This was one, was it not, at which Mr. McFarlane did the talking?

LT. COL. NORTH: I must confess that I don't remember that meeting. I do remember one in 1986 with Chairman Hamilton's—

MR. NIELDS: We'll get to that in a minute, but I'm staying with 1985. Exhibit 120 is a cover letter relating to questions that were sent by the Committee following the meeting.

(The witness perused the document.)

LT. COL. NORTH: I have Exhibit 120.

237

MR. NIELDS: And it's a cover sheet from you to Mr. McFarlane, and it makes reference to responses—excuse me, a briefing before the Intelligence Committee on September 10, 1985.

LT. COL. NORTH: That's correct.

MR. NIELDS: Then if you go to Exhibit 121, that is a letter from Mr. McFarlane to the Intelligence Committee responding to the written questions that followed the briefing.

LT. COL. NORTH: That's correct.

MR. NIELDS: And you helped prepare those answers to those written questions, did you not?

LT. COL. NORTH: I'm sure that I did.

MR. NIELDS: And if you look at the first page towards the—the first page of the answers, the second page of the exhibit, there's a Question 3, and it says, "When the CIA had to withdraw from their day-to-day contact with the rebels, it has been alleged in *The New York Times* that Col. North tried to fill the void, partly through helping facilitate the supplying of logistics help. Did Col. North, in his capacity as a staff member of the National Security Council, use his influence to facilitate the movement of supplies, either raised privately in this country or otherwise, to the contras?"

And the answer reads as follows. "Lt. Col. North did not use his influence to facilitate the movement of supplies to the resistance." That's false too, isn't it?

LT. COL. NORTH: Yes.

MR. NIELDS: And then if you go to the fifth page of the exhibit, there's a Question No. 2, which is, "Gen. Singlaub has stated in *The Washington Post,* that he would often talk to Col. North and inform him what he was doing, and then state that, if it was a dumb idea, for North to send him a signal. Is that your impression of the relationship between Gen. Singlaub and Col. North?"

The answer is not a simple yes or not. The answer is, "There is no official or unofficial relationship with any member of the NSC staff regarding fundraising for the Nicaraguan democratic opposition. This includes the alleged relationship with Gen. Singlaub." That's false, too, isn't it?

LT. COL. NORTH: Well, I don't know what the definition of an official or an unofficial relationship. But I certainly saw

238

Gen. Singlaub a lot, related to support for the Nicaraguan resistance. I've, you know, testified to that.

MR. NIELDS: Indeed, you had seen him in that connection four times within the previous nine months that you've testified about already?

LT. COL. NORTH: I don't recall testifying about specific dates. But I willingly admit to you, as I did earlier today, that I met on a number of occasions with Gen. Singlaub, relating to support for the Nicaraguan resistance.

MR. NIELDS: And then going back to page 2, again, the second page of the exhibit, the first page of the question-and-answer. There's a Question 2 and Answer 2. The question refers to newspaper allegations, and the answer reads as follows: "The allegations that Lieutenant Colonel North offered the resistance tactical advice and direction is, as I indicated in my briefing, patently untrue." That wasn't true either, was it?

LT. COL. NORTH: I never sat down in the—in the battle-field and offered direct tactical advice, but I certainly did have a number of discussions with the resistance about military activities, yes, to include the broader strategy for a southern front and an—and an Atlantic front and an internal front.

MR. NIELDS: And at about this time, prompted by the same newspaper articles and congressional inquiries, counsel for the intelligence—President's Intelligence Oversight Board interviewed you and asked you if, in fact, you were engaged in fund-raising and military support for the contras.

LT. COL. NORTH: Are you talking about Mr. Cerrone?

MR. NIELDS: Cerrone. Brad Cerrone.

LT. COL. NORTH: I have absolutely no recall of that discussion. Mr. Cerrone's office, when I—until I moved my office to the suite in Room 302, was down the hall from Mr. Cerrone's office. We had many conversations. I do not recall the one which you refer to.

MR. NIELDS: Do you deny—he has testified that, in connection with his writing the opinion which you made reference to earlier, he conducted an investigation which included a review of documents and an interview with you. And he asked you about the newspaper reports that you were engaged in fund-raising and giving military advice to

239

the contras and that you denied that you were doing any such thing. Can you deny that you had that conversation?

LT. COL. NORTH: No, I just said I don't recall that specific conversation. He and I had many. We may well have had the one you just described, after all, we viewed this to be a covert operation and he had absolutely no need to know the details of what I was doing. By my understanding, the Intelligence Oversight Board does not have oversight authority over the National Security Council staff, I don't think. At least I didn't then.

MR. NIELDS: So what you're saying is, if you didn't feel that the Oversight Board had authority to investigate the staff, even if it was engaged in intelligence operations, that you felt free to lie to him.

(Long pause as North consults with his attorney.)

LT. COL. NORTH: Forgive me again. Would you please repeat the question, Counsel?

MR. NIELDS: The question was that, if you felt that the President's Intelligence Oversight Board did not have authority to investigate the NSC, even if it was engaged in intelligence activities, that you felt free to lie to him?

LT. COL. NORTH: Well, I—I don't want—I don't like the sound of that. I don't think I basically would have told him, you know, I probably would have said, "It's none of your business" or whatever. And in fact, I mean no disrespect to this body, none whatsoever, not to this Committee or to the Joint Committee, or to either House of Congress, but my approach and what I wanted to do in terms of answering these questions was to simply not answer them at all.

And I want to go back through what I said yesterday about a covert operation. We had the lives of people at stake, we had this nation's foreign policy at stake, we had the lives of the people involved in the resistance activity at stake, and we have, as in any other covert operation, a problem of deniability. I was to be the deniability; I was to go when the time came—political liability, he's gone.

The fact is that protecting the role of foreign governments who are assisting in that was important to them. I was sent down there and talking to heads of state and the leaders of foreign governments, and promised them, promised them absolute discretion, that we wouldn't reveal what support they were providing. And the reason we promised them that is because they were in great jeopardy of reprisals from the Sandinistas and reprisals from their own internal political dissent. So we promised them that we wouldn't talk about it. We also had—protecting the bases and the activities that they permitted on their terrority in support of the resistance. And they were concerned about that, and so we told them, "Don't worry, we won't divulge it." I was sent there and I told them that on instruction.

Now my answer toward protecting individuals and protecting the role of foreign governments and protecting the nature of the support to the Nicaraguan resistance—I mean after all, if we had announced in the newspapers, Counsel, that we were building an air field in a Central American country to support the Nicaraguan resistance and told the American people, and unfortunately, had we told the Congress, it would have become public and the Sandinistas would have known about it. What—

MR. NIELDS: Well, sir, you have already testified that Izvestia had written about it—

LT. COL. NORTH: Izvestia didn't write about—

MR. NIELDS: —Cuban newspapers had written about it, our newspapers were writing about it—

LT. COL. NORTH: But they weren't writing about it in specific detail—

MR. NIELDS: Are you saying the Sandinistas did not know about the resupply operation?

LT. COL. NORTH: I'm telling you Sandinistas didn't know what time of day and night that the airplanes were taking off.

MR. NIELDS: Did Congress inquire what time of day or night the airplanes were taking off?

LT. COL. NORTH: No, but that's what the general—the general—

MR. NIELDS: They asked whether you were engaged in supporting the contras—

LT. COL. NORTH: Yes.

MR. NIELDS: —during dependency of a law that prohibited it.

MR. SULLIVAN: Counsel, excuse me—

LT. COL. NORTH: That prohibited—

MR. SULLIVAN: Excuse me, Mr. Chairman, there were two

241

interrputions there, and I know that lawyers can sometimes get excited and fire rapid questions. But I'm asking that we be particularly sensitive to permitting the witness to finish the answers.

CHAIRMAN INOUYE: I believe we have been extremely sensitive to you and your client. I believe the record will show that we have not objected to unresponsive answers. Many questions that could have been easily answered by a simple yes or no have taken 15 minutes, and the Chair has not interrupted. We have permitted speeches to be made here.

MR. SULLIVAN: I know that, sir.

CHAIRMAN INOUYE: As you know, you're one of the best defense lawyers in town—

MR. SULLIVAN: Thanks.

CHAIRMAN INOUYE: —and in a court room, if the answer is not responsive, usually the court would stop you. So, Counsel, proceed.

MR. SULLIVAN: My experience is a little bit different, Mr. Chairman. Normally a witness is able to finish his answer.

CHAIRMAN INOUYE: We have permitted your client to answer completely. Has he been denied the opportunity to give a complete answer during these proceedings?

MR. SULLIVAN: Mr. Chairman, I'm not complaining about a lot of the questions. My duty is to object when I see a question posed which my client is not permitted to answer. There were two. And if you'd like to play the tape back, or read it back, it's quite clear that counsel jumped in before the answer was given. That's my only point. I'm not complaining about many of the questions. I'm only complaining periodically, when I believe there is a reasonable basis to bring the matter to your attention, and ask for a fair judgment. That's all.

CHAIRMAN INOUYE: That matter has been brought to my attention. Counsel proceed.

MR. NIELDS: I take it there came a time when another Committee of Congress made an inquiry in writing? Congressman Barnes, I take it, wrote a letter. And it is in your exhibit book as Exhibit 107. (Pause while Lt. Col. North searches for page.) Do you have that in front of you?

LT. COL. NORTH: Yes.

MR. NIELDS: And it also inquires about activities of

certain NSC staff members in providing advice and fundraising support to the Nicaraguan rebel leaders.

LT. COL. NORTH: That's right.

MR. NIELDS: And the reply is at Exhibit 109.

LT. COL. NORTH: Right.

MR. NIELDS: Do you have that in front of you?

LT. COL. NORTH: Right.

MR. NIELDS: And that, I take it, you also helped Mr. McFarlane draft.

LT. COL. NORTH: I probably did. I don't recall specifically. There were a number of these.

MR. NIELDS: And in the middle of the second paragraph, after citing to the Boland Amendment itself, it states: "There have not been, nor will there be, any expenditures of NSC funds which would have the effect of supporting, directly of indirectly, military or paramilitary operations in Nicaragua."

LT. COL. NORTH: Right.

MR. NIELDS: Do you see that?

LT. COL. NORTH: I don't see it, but I heard you—I got it.

MR. NIELDS: You have it?

LT. COL. NORTH: Yup.

MR. NIELDS: Now you were aware, I take it, that salaries were included in the Boland Amendment?

LT. COL. NORTH: Nope. Not mine.

MR. NIELDS: How about airplane trips?

LT. COL. NORTH: I made every effort, counsel, to avoid the use of appropriated funds. And as I said, that was why the decision was made in 1984, before this proscription ever became law, to set up outside entities, and to raise non-US government monies by which the Nicaraguan freedom fighters could be supported.

What I'm trying to say is that there was an effort to comply with Boland. It was a hard and difficult task. We tried very hard. And aside from those letters, there were many, many efforts to include the use of the operational account I described to you this morning, by which we tried very hard to live within the letter of the law.

That is not necessarily the answer you're looking for about these letters. Because these letters are clearly misleading.

MR. NIELDS: Well, let's take a look at page 2 of this letter,

243

where it states at the bottom of the partial paragraph on the top of the page: "Throughout, we have scrupulously abided by the spirit and letter of the law. None of us has solicited funds, facilitated contacts for prospective potential donors, or otherwise organized or coordinated the military or paramilitary efforts of the resistance." I take it that statement is misleading?

LT. COL. NORTH: Part of that is misleading, yes.

MR. NIELDS: Indeed—

LT. COL. NORTH: As I indicated this morning, I have never, to my recollection, solicited funds. But, I have just admitted to you that these are misleading responses. I would also, if you will indulge me in finishing what I started earlier, I would also point out to you, Counsel, that this is not my preferred response. My preferred response, and I tried it several times in this process, was not to tell the Congress. In no disrespect to this body, none whatsoever, but, in fact, exercising what I understood to be executive privilege, and I have a letter that I also drafted, that was drafted several different times in an attempt to answer this.

In fact, the one that I have that was never sent is addressed to Congressman Barnes, and if you don't mind, counsel will put it up so that you could all see it. And, in fact, this letter is my preferred answer. I was not entirely comfortable at all with this, but this letter lays out why I thought we had the right to deny that information, and why I think it was appropriate to do so, and why I am appalled that you now have the notebooks in which I kept records of my conversations with heads of state, and other foreign military and political leaders.

MR. NIELDS: Colonel North, the document which you have just put up in front of this committee as your preferred response—

LT. COL. NORTH: Yes.

MR. NIELDS: —states in its very first sentence, "This is in reply to your letter of October 29th—

LT. COL. NORTH: Yes.

MR. NIELDS: That was long after the letter which—

LT. COL. NORTH: Counsel.

MR. NIELDS: —is Exhibit 109, which is dated September the 12th, 1985.

LT. COL. NORTH: I agree. I am saying that the words below

referring to the J-treaties and executive privilege were used numerous times in an effort to have that be the answer to the Congress. This is simply one other effort on that document to have that answer sent to the Congress.

MR. NIELDS: Well—

LT. COL. NORTH: And, it wasn't sent.

MR. NIELDS: We have the letter dated October 29th, 1985, and it is Exhibit #111, and it is a letter requesting documents.

LT. COL. NORTH: Yes.

MR. NIELDS: The earlier letter requested answers.

LT. COL. NORTH: Yes.

MR. NIELDS: And, a letter was sent in reply that you've said you probably participated in that gave false answers.

LT. COL. NORTH: Yes.

MR. NIELDS: Then, Congress wasn't satisfied with the answers, and they sent the letter back dated October 29th seeking documents, and that is when the letter which you have put up here was drafted. To prevent Congress from getting any documents.

LT. COL. NORTH: Counsel, in each and every case, I advocated this philosophy in answering the Congress. There was no Executive privilege exercised, and instead, answers that were sent to the Congress that were clearly misleading. I'm not denying that, and I participated in that effort. I am admitting that to this body. What I am saying to you is that my preferred answer would have been no answer at all, and I believed then, and I believe now that the Executive was fully legitimate in giving no answer to those queries. And that others could be called forward to testify if they wished, but they shouldn't have been compelled to do so. And that is the essence of all that is in the bottom two paragraphs here.

MR. NIELDS: Let's get to the documents then. The documents that were requested were reviewed by you, were they not?

LT. COL. NORTH: I guess they were. I don't recall the specific event, but I assume that they were because I was asked to provide certain documents.

MR. NIELDS: And they were taken out of official NSC files?

LT. COL. NORTH: That is correct.

245

MR. NIELDS: And they were brought to the attention of Mr. McFarlane?

LT. COL. NORTH: Yes.

MR. NIELDS: And you and he sat down together and talked about them?

LT. COL. NORTH: I don't recall that we necessarily sat down and talked about it. I do know that he brought those to my attention, indicated that there were problems with them, and told me to fix them.

MR. NIELDS: There were six of them that there were particular problems with, is that correct?

LT. COL. NORTH: I don't recall the number.

MR. NIELDS: Well, do you recall the handwritten list that Mr. McFarlane made—

LT. COL. NORTH: I recall there was a handwritten list. I don't remember how many there were.

MR. NIELDS: It's Exhibit 112.

LT. COL. NORTH: Right.

MR. NIELDS: That's the handwritten list by document number of the problem documents.

LT. COL. NORTH: Right.

MR. NIELDS: Okay, now you just said that he asked you to "fix them"—what does that mean?

LT. COL. NORTH: Remove references to certain activities, certain undertakings on my behalf or his, and basically clean up the record.

MR. NIELDS: Did you?

LT. COL. NORTH: Tried to.

MR. NIELDS: Then?

LT. COL. NORTH: No, I don't believe I got around to it till just before I left.

MR. NIELDS: And indeed, I take it the references that you were therefore instructed to "fix up" were such things as references to your current donors?

LT. COL. NORTH: I'd have to look at each of those documents to refresh my memory, but I'm telling you those are documents that had problems with them, yes. It had reference to my activities—

MR. NIELDS: Activities—

LT. COL. NORTH: —and references to those things that I had done over the course of that period of time or things

246

that I reported on that had been done as a consequence of my activities.

MR. NIELDS: These were activities in support of military support and fundraising support for the contras?

LT. COL. NORTH: I will certainly admit to the former. I'm not sure about the latter, on fundraising. It may have been reference to that, too.

MR. NIELDS: Well, I will just state for the record—and we needn't look at them again, we have spent almost a full day with these documents, but they are Exhibits 141 through 153. That's in both original and altered form. And I will say that one of the things that is taken out of those documents are references to "our current donors." And I take it that refers to a particular foreign country—Country 2.

LT. COL. NORTH: Okay. Again, I told you yesteday that I still don't know who that particular donor was for sure.

MR. NIELDS: And I will note for the record that, even in the altered version of the documents, there are still some materials that have been blanked out because the executive regards them as classified.

LT. COL. NORTH: Okay.

MR. NIELDS: So you didn't just remove all sensitive materials. You removed the materials that demonstrated that you were conducting activities in support of the contras?

LT. COL. NORTH: All right.

MR. NIELDS: What was the reason for altering those documents right before you left?

LT. COL. NORTH: Well, he had asked me to do it some time before, and I simply hadn't gotten it done yet.

MR. NIELDS: While he was gone, what was the reason that he gave you for changing these documents?

LT. COL. NORTH: Well, those documents clearly indicated that there was a covert operation being conducted in support of the Nicaraguan resistance. And part of the whole thing with the covert operation is being able to protect those people with whom you are engaged, as we had committed to; and protect from political damage, as well as international repercussions, the government of the United States. And so, I very cleary understood why he wanted those documents cleaned up. And I sought to do so.

MR. NIELDS: Now I take it—I think you've already referred to another inquiry—Congressional inquiry, approximately a year after the firt one.

LT. COL. NORTH: Right.

MR. NIELDS: The summer of 1986. And I think you'll see at Exhibit 122 that there was a—before I get to that, Col. North, I want to stay with the documents for just a moment, you had a filing system, did you not, at the NSC?

LT. COL. NORTH: I myself or—

MR. NIELDS: The NSC had a filing system.

LT. COL. NORTH: The NSC staff has a document filing system, that's correct.

MR. NIELDS: And there are various categories in the system.

LT. COL. NORTH: In the systems, plural, yes—System 1, 2 and 4.

MR. NIELDS: And 4 is where the most highly classified documents are stored?

LT. COL. NORTH: Yes. And I take it you have a system like that so that if there are materials that should not be exposed to the public. there is a way of handling them to see that that doesn't happen.

LT. COL. NORTH: Say that again?

MR. NIELDS: I'm saying the whole reason you have documents classified as System Four documents is so that they will be handled and stored in such a way that they will not be inappropriately exposed to public view.

LT. COL. NORTH: True.

MR. NIELDS: So there was already in existence an official way of protecting information that ought not to be made public.

LT. COL. NORTH: Yes, but you have to remember that that system, just like any information in my safe, is very much what I would call successor dependent. And there is some uncertainty as to what your replacement might do with those things when he walks in the door. And so I have—I had absolutely no problem whatsoever with Mr. McFarlane telling me that documents need to be cleaned up.

In fact, we had earlier—perhaps subsequent to those documents being prepared, decided to take those kinds of documents out of the system altogether, so that they no longer were in the system. They were non-log, if you will. And they were hand-carried back and forth between my office and the West Wing. An effort was made, in other words, to keep them out of the system so that outside knowledge would not necessarily be derived from having the documents themselves.

MR. NIELDS: Well, these documents that were on Mr. McFarlane's list, after they were discussed by you with him in 1985, they were placed back into the system, were they not?

LT. COL. NORTH: I got them out of the system. I don't know where they sat in the interim, but I went to the system to retrieve them because I saw, toward the end of my tenure, that this list still had not been cleaned up. And so I went and then got the documents out of the system and started revising the documents.

I had created them, and I was now changing them, in consonance with what I believed he wanted on the documents to begin with. The documents, after all, demonstrated his knowledge and cognizance over what I was doing. And he didn't want that. He was cleaning up the historical record. He was trying to preserve the President from political damage, and I don't blame him for that.

MR. NIELDS: He was changing it to make it untrue.

LT. COL. NORTH: Yes. I think by omission more than commission, but I mean, we were certainly deleting in the redrafts of those documents, deleting portions of it which indicated the full depth of what I was doing and his knowledge of what I was doing.

MR. NIELDS: Just so that we understand. A few days before you actually left, and that would be a few days before August 25th, 1986—

LT. COL. NORTH: No—

MR. NIELDS: Excuse me. November—excuse me. November 25th, 1986.

LT. COL. NORTH: Correct.

MR. NIELDS: You obtained these documents, original documents, from NSC files.

LT. COL. NORTH: Correct.

MR. NIELDS: How did you obtain them?

LT. COL. NORTH: I went in and drew them out and—I

shouldn't say I did. I think I had my secretary go to the files clerk and withdraw the documents. And again, I'm not certain of that, but that's what I recall.

MR. NIELDS: Did you or she have authority to get these documents out of NSC files?

LT. COL. NORTH: Oh, sure. I mean, you can—the system is set up so that particularly an officer who creates a document, can go and retrieve his own documents. For the purposes of historical, you know, checking something, or whatever.

MR. NIELDS: Isn't it a fact that you had to get Mr. DeGrafenried's help to get these documents?

LT. COL. NORTH: I honestly don't recall that I did. I—my recollection of it, Counsel, is that I asked my secretary to go to his secretary and get the documents, but I—I may not be remembering correctly.

MR. NIELDS: So, you had to go to his secretary to get the documents.

LT. COL. NORTH: We—but they're kept in his office. I mean, his—the physical location of those documents, was his office space. And he was, after all—it was within his space that the custodian of that system resided. And he has stacks of files full of these things, of that systems documents.

MR. NIELDS: I take it that the handwritten list of the numbers on the documents had been kept by you for the almost year period from the time you first discussed these documents with Mr. McFarlane until the time you took them out in November of 1986.

LT. COL. NORTH: Yes, in fact I provided to the Committee, a copy of that list. I sent it back to you.

MR. NIELDS: Where had you kept it?

LT. COL. NORTH: I believe the original of it was probably underneath the blotter on my desk, I mean, I—my management style is perhaps due for criticism, but I think that's —it's probably on my desk, or underneath one of my computers, or something like that. I don't readily remember. I do remember, in the latter days of my tenure, at the NSC, coming across the list saying, "Oh boy, this isn't done." And going about doing what I'd been asked to do some period before.

MR. NIELDS: Go back again now to the summer of 1986,

Exhibit 122, is a resolution of inquiry. It relates to you and it seeks information about funding concerning the contras, military advice and asked specific questions about Robert Owen, General Singlaub, and a man named John Hull.

LT. COL. NORTH: Right.

MR. NIELDS: And there came a time, did there not, when you had an—an interview with members of the House Intelligence Committee—

LT. COL. NORTH: I did.

MR. NIELDS: —and staff?

LT. COL. NORTH: I don't remember if there was any staff or not. I defer to Chairman Hamilton; he convened his group in the White House Situation Room, and I met with him there.

MR. NIELDS: There's a memorandum which was done by staff, which is Exhibit 126. Do you have that in front of you?

LT. COL. NORTH: I do.

MR. NIELDS: And it's dated August 6, 1986. Is that at or about the time when you had this interview?

LT. COL. NORTH: I—again, I defer to the Committee and Chairman Hamilton. I had such a meeting. If that's when it was, I don't remember the date.

MR. NIELDS: And this was you personally talking to them?

LT. COL. NORTH: It was on instructions of the National Security Advisor. I was instructed to meet with Chairman Hamilton and, I believe, many of the members of the Committee.

MR. NIELDS: And they were interested in finding out the answers to the questions raised by the resolution of inquiry—

LT. COL. NORTH: Exactly.

MR. NIELDS: —your fund-raising activities—

LT. COL. NORTH: Precisely.

MR. NIELDS: —military support for the contras—

LT. COL. NORTH: That's right.

MR. NIELDS: —questions about Mr. Owen, General Singlaub, and John Hull?

(Long pause)

LT. COL. NORTH: Yes.

MR. NIELDS: The beginning of this memorandum that appears to be a description of what you said during that

251

meeting, it says "from Boland Amendment on North explains strictures to contras." Is that true? Did you explain the strictures to the contras?

LT. COL. NORTH: I explained to them that there was no US Government money until more was appropriated, yes.

MR. NIELDS: And it says "never violated stricture. Gave advice on Human Rights Civic Action Program."

LT. COL. NORTH: I did do that.

MR. NIELDS: But I take it you did considerably more, which you did not tell the committee about.

LT. COL. NORTH: I have admitted that here before you today, knowing full well what I told the committee then. I think—and I'm—I think we can abbreviate this in hopes that we can move on so that I can finish this week. I will tell you right now, counsel, and all the members here gathered that I misled the Congress. I mis—

MR. NIELDS: At that meeting?

LT. COL. NORTH: At that meeting.

MR. NIELDS: Face-to-face?

LT. COL. NORTH: Face-to-face.

MR. NIELDS: You made false statements to them about your activities in support of the contras?

LT. COL. NORTH: I did. Furthermore, I did so with a purpose, and I did so with the purpose of hopefully avoiding the very kind of thing that we have before us now and avoiding a shutoff of help to the Nicaraguan resistance and avoiding an elimination of the resistance facilities in three Central American countries—

MR. NIELDS: We—

LT. COL. NORTH: —where—wherein we had promised those heads of state. On my specific orders, I had—on specific orders to me, I had gone down there and assured them of our absolute and total discretion.

MR. NIELDS: We do—do live in a democracy, don't we?

LT. COL. NORTH: We do, sir. Thank God.

MR. NIELDS: In which it is the people, not one Marine Lieutenant Colonel, that get to decide the important policy decisions for the nation.

(Long silence)

LT. COL. NORTH: Yes. And, I—

MR. NIELDS: And, part of the democratic process—

LT. COL. NORTH: And, I would point out that part of that

answer is that this Marine Lieutenant Colonel was not making all of those decisions on his own. As I indicated in my testimony yesterday, Mr. Nields, I sought approval for everything that I did.

MR. NIELDS: But, you denied Congress the facts—

LT. COL. NORTH: I did.

MR. NIELDS: You denied the elected representatives of our people the facts upon which they needed—

LT. COL. NORTH: I did.

MR. NIELDS: —to make a very important decision for this nation.

LT. COL. NORTH: I did because of what I have just described to as our concerns, and I did it because we have had incredible leaks, from discussions with closed committees of the Congress. I, I, I was a part of, as people now know, the coordination for the mining of the harbors in Nicaragua. When that one leaked, there were American lives at stake, and it leaked from a member of one of the committees, who eventually admitted it. When there was a leak on the sensitive intelligence methods that we used to help capture the Achille Lauro terrorists, it almost wiped out that whole channel of communications.

I mean, those kinds of things are devastating. They are devastating to the national security of the United States, and I desperately hope that one of the things that can derive from all of this ordeal is that we can find a better way by which we can communicate those things properly with the Congress. I'm not admitting that what happened in this is proper. I'm not admitting, or claiming rather, that what I did and my role in it in communicating was proper.

MR. NIELDS: Were you instructed to do it?

LT. COL. NORTH: I was not specifically instructed, no.

MR. NIELDS: Were you generally instructed?

LT. COL. NORTH: Yes.

MR. NIELDS: By whom?

LT. COL. NORTH: My superiors. I prepared draft answers that they signed and sent. And, I would also point out—

MR. NIELDS: What superior?

LT. COL. NORTH: Well who—look who sign—I didn't sign those letters to the—to this body.

MR. NIELDS: I'm talking about the last—I'm talking about the oral meeting in August of 1986.

LT. COL. NORTH: I went down to that oral meeting with the same kind of understanding that I prepared those memos in 1985 and other communcations.

MR. NIELDS: Well, you had a different boss, and in fairness, you ought to tell us whether he instructed you to do it, understood you to do it, knew about it afterwards, or none of those?

LT. COL. NORTH: He did not specifically go down and say, "Ollie, lie to the committee." I told him what I had said afterwards, and he sent me a note saying, "Well done."

Now I would also like to point out one other thing. I deeply believe that the President of the United States is also an elected official of this land. And by the Constitution, as I understand it, he is the person charged with making and carrying out the foreign policy of this country. I believed, from the moment I was engaged in this activity in 1984, that this was in furtherance of the foreign policy established by the President. I still believe that.

MR. NIELDS: Even——

LT. COL. NORTH: I'm not saying that what I did here was right. And I have just placed myself, as you know, counsel, in great jeopardy.

MR. NIELDS: Even the President is elected by the people.

LT. COL. NORTH: I just said that.

MR. NIELDS: And the people have the right to vote him out of office, if they don't like his policies.

LT. COL. NORTH: That's true.

MR. NIELDS: And they can't exercise that function, if the policies of the President are hidden from them.

LT. COL. NORTH: Wait a second. Yesterday, we talked about the need for this nation, which is a country at risk in a dangerous world, having the need to conduct covert operations and secret diplomacy, carry out secret programs. I mean, we talked at some length about that. And that can certainly be the subject of great debate. And this great institution can pass laws that say no such activities can ever be conducted again. But that would be wrong, and you and I know that.

The fact is, this country does need to be able to conduct those kinds of activities. And the President ought not to be in a position, in my humble opinion, of having to go out and explain to the American people, on a biweekly basis or any other kind, that I, the President, am carrying out the following secret operations. It just can't be done. No nation in the world will ever help us again—and we desperately need that kind of help—if we are to survive, given our adversaries.

And what I'm saying to you, Mr. Nields, is the American people, I think, trust that the President will, indeed, be conducting these kinds of activities. They trust that he will do so with a good purpose and good intent.

I will also admit to you that I believe there has to be a way of consulting with the Congress. There must be. I would also point out to you, Mr. Nields, that, in June of 1986, not the Tower Commission—I gave a speech before the American Bar Association, on very short notice. I stood on the podium with Sen. Moynihan, and I advocated the formation of a small, discreet, joint intelligence committee, with a very professional, small staff, in which the Administration would feel comfortable confiding and planning and conducting and funding these kinds of activities. I still believe that that could be a good and thoughtful thing to do. There has to be that kind of proposal that allows the Administration to talk straightforwardly with the Congress.

MR. NIELDS: There came a time when one of the resupply operation's planes went down in Nicaragua.

LT. COL. NORTH: Yes.

MR. NIELDS: That was early October 1986.

LT. COL. NORTH: Yes.

MR. NIELDS: If you'll turn to Exhibit 133. (Pause.) Do you have that in front of you?

LT. COL. NORTH: Yes.

MR. NIELDS: It's a PROF message from Mr. Ken Astrawo. It relates to the plane that went down, and in the middle of the page, it discusses press guidance. Do you see that?

LT. COL. NORTH: Yes.

MR. NIELDS: And the statement is, "Press guidance was prepared which states, 'No USG involvement or connection, but that we are generally aware of such support, contracted by the contras.'" Were you aware at the time that this was the press guidance for the Hasenfus plane?

LT. COL. NORTH: I don't believe I was aware at that immediate moment, because, as I testified earlier, I believe I was overseas at that point. My recollection is that I was, but that is not inconsistent with what we had prepared as the press line, if such and such a—if such an eventuality occurred.

MR. NIELDS: And the next paragraph says, "UNO asked to assume responsibility for flight."

LT. COL. NORTH: Right.

MR. NIELDS: And then it says, "Elliott will follow up with Ollie to facilitate this."

LT. COL. NORTH: Yes.

MR. NIELDS: Was Mr. Abrams aware that UNO was not responsible for the flight?

LT. COL. NORTH: I think that the flight was certainly coordinated with people within UNO. UNO did indeed know about the flight. The flight happened to have been paid for by General Secord's operation. The airplane was paid for by his operation. The pilots were paid for by his operation. Those were not US government monies, but those were certainly his activities. And I was the US government connection.

MR. NIELDS: And was Elliot Abrams aware of the fact that you were the US government connection?

LT. COL. NORTH: You would have to ask Elliot Abrams exactly what he did know. He called me to take care of getting the bodies home.

MR. NIELDS: Did he ask you whether you or the NSC had any connection with the airplane?

LT. COL. NORTH: Counsel, he didn't have to ask me—

MR. NIELDS: Because—

LT. COL. NORTH: —any more than a congressman who called me up at one point and asked me to get an air drop to the Indians had to ask me. He knew. I didn't have to tell him. I didn't have to write a memo him. It was known. I would guess that that is probably why Chairman Hamilton convened his group in the Situation Room. I have no doubt about that, and—and what I want you to know is I still don't think that what we did was illegal.

MR. NIELDS: So you think that—

LT. COL. NORTH: I—please. It was not right. It does not leave me when—with a good taste in my mouth. I want you to know lying does not come easy to me. I want you to know that it doesn't come easy to anybody, but I think we all had to weigh in the balance the difference between lives and lies.

I had to do that on a number of occasions in both these operations, and it is not an easy thing to do.

MR. NIELDS: So you're telling us that some—you believe, some congressman knew of your connection. You said that Izvestiya knew of your connection. You said the Cubans knew of your connection—

LT. COL. NORTH: I—I—I didn't—

MR. NIELDS: —the Sandinistas—I haven't finished the question yet—the Sandinistas knew of your connection. But Exhibit 134 contains the adminstration's statement to the American people., It's a newspaper article about this flight, *The Washington Post,* top lefthand column, "Top Reagan Administration officials yesterday flatly denied any US government connection with the transport plane that the Sandinista government said it shot down in Nicaragua with three Americans and a man of Latin origin aboard."

And the next exhibit the Committees have already heard. It is Elliott Abrams' statements on Evans and Novak absolutely guaranteeing that there was no US government connection—and particularly no NSC connection.

Now the American people, I take it, in this country where we trust our government officials, believed those statements.

LT. COL. NORTH: Is that a question?

MR. NIELDS: Yes.

LT. COL. NORTH: Well, I don't know. I cannot speak for the American people. I've never pretended to speak for the American people. But I—(The witness consulted with counsel.)

MR. NIELDS: Col. North, I have only one more question.

LT. COL. NORTH: Wait, wait. I'm still trying to answer the last one. I got—I'm getting help here. I guess my problem is, counsel, that, while I well recognize that there may well be a lot of American people who want to know, I was trying to weigh—and I'm sure that others, like Mr. McFarlane and Adm. Poindexter and Director Casey and Elliott Abrams and the Chief of the Central American Task Force and others were trying to weigh in their souls what would happen to those, for example, whom I had sent money to or enticed into this activity or published pamphlets in Managua or ran radio broadcasts or blew things up or flew airplanes, if the American government stood up and announced it. And that is, after all, the essence of deniability.

And I was that deniable link, and I was supposed to be dropped like a hot rock when it all came down. And I was willing to serve in that capacity. I was not willing to become the victim of a criminal prosecution.

MR. NIELDS: I have only one more question, sir. You've given this committee several speeches on the subject of covert operations.

MR. SULLIVAN: I object to that. Mr. Chairman, the witness has responded as frankly and as truthfully as he possibly can. And I think that that is a pejorative term that mischaracterizes the extraordinary efforts of Col. North to be frank with this committee. And I'm tired, frankly, of going home at the end of the day and seeing members of this committee on the TV saying he's not being truthful. And that's another example of it.

I request, Mr. Chairman, that that kind of tactic not be utilized. Thank you, sir.

CHAIRMAN INOUYE: I would like to advise the counsel that he may characterize this as something else. But, as far as I'm concerned, it was a very lengthy statement. Some people consider lengthy statements to be speeches. Counsel, proceed.

MR. NIELDS: I'm perfectly happy to use the expression "lengthy statements." You've made several lengthy statements to the committee on the subject of covert operations.

MR. SULLIVAN: How about using "lengthy answer" —in order for him to get the truth before the committee?

CHAIRMAN INOUYE: Proceed.

MR. NIELDS: As a result of the fact that the operations you've been testifying about were conducted in the covert manner that you've been testifying about, as I understand your testimony, you and others put out a false version of facts relating to the 1985 Hawk shipment. You altered documents in official NSC files. You shredded documents shortly after you heard that representatives of the Attorney General of the United States were coming in to your office to review them. You wrote false and misleading letters to the Congress of the United States. The government lied to the American people about the connection of the Hasenfus plane. You received a personal financial benefit from opera-

258

ting funds of the covert organization without knowing where it came from. I'm referring—

LT. COL. NORTH: Sir—

MR. NIELDS: I'm referring to the security fence. 8 million dollars of operations funds was handled in a manner that you didn't know what had happened to it or whether it existed. My question to you is whether is an inevitable —these things are inevitable consequences of conducting covert operations or whether these are things that happened because of this—these two particular covert actions? (Pause) If you have an answer.

LT. COL. NORTH: Well, I have tried over the course of the last two days, Counsel, to answer every one of your questions accurately. I have tried to give you answers and—and explanations where needed for why I did what I did and the facts as they were known to me about what others did. I am not here to impune the testimony of others or to make excuses for anything that I did. I have accepted the responsibility for those things that I did, and some of that has not come easily.

I would also expect, as you keep raising the American people, that the tens of thousands of American people who have written to me and communicated with me since I was relieved of my duties at the NSC, and in particular over the course of the last two days, some of them seem to believe, and with very, very few exceptions—perhaps 50 out of 40,(000) or 50,000, perhaps 50—the remaining 50,000 or so who have communicated seem to believe that they think it was right that somebody would do something under those circumstances, and I tried to do it to the very best of my abilities. If they are found lacking, it is not for having tried not enough.

I sincerely believe that I did everything within the law. I made serious judgment errors, and I have admitted those. But I tried, and I don't regret having done it.

MR. NIELDS: I have no further questions, Mr. Chairman.

CHAIRMAN INOUYE: Thank you very much.

Colonel North, for the past two days, together with my colleagues on this panel, I've sat here very patiently listening to statements suggesting that members of Congress cannot be trusted with the secrets of this land. Although I have not discussed this in public before, but I did serve on the Intelligence Committee for 8 years, serving as chairman for the first two years. In fact, it was my assignment to organize the Intelligence Committee. During that period, according to the Federal [Bureau] of Investigation, the Central Intelligence Agency and the National Security Agency, there wasn't a single leak from that Senate Select Committee on Intelligence. I'm certain you're well aware that most of the leaks in this city come from the other side of Pennsylvania.

Secondly, I'm a recipient of the Distinguished Service Medal of Intelligence, the highest nonmilitary decoration that can be given to a nonmilitary person. And, last year just before Mr. Casey went to the hospital, he presented me with the Central Intelligence Agency agency medal.

Thirdly, a few days ago, General Alderman, Director of the National Security Agency, communicated with me to advise me that since the creation of these two select committees, they have not seen any leaks emanating from these two committees.

I don't know who you're talking about, but I can assure that these committees, the House and the Senate Select Committees, can be trusted.

The sessions of this day and yesterday have clearly demonstrated that if we had gone through the regular process that we have followed with all other witnesses, and that is going into executive session, taking depositions, we would not have had to have delays that we have experienced today, over classified information. Like you, I do not wish to see secrets of this land inadvertently and accidentally made public. Accordingly, at the conclusion of tomorrow afternoon's session at 5:00, the panel will enter into executive session to discuss matters of classification. The place will be announced tomorrow.

We will stand in recess until 9:00 o'clock tomorrow morning, at which time Mr. Van Cleve will conduct the investigation.

END OF AFTERNOON SESSION

260

Thursday · July 9, 1987

Morning Session—9:00 A.M.

CHAIRMAN INOUYE: The hearing will please come to order. This morning, the panel will resume the questioning of Lt. Col. North. May the record indicate that on 8:15 A.M., on July 7, 1987, the Select Committees of the House and Senate received a statement, the opening statement of Colonel North. This statement, pursuant to the rules, has been examined and determined there are no inadvertent disclosures of classified material, further, that we are satisfied that the statement does not exceed the bounds set forth by the court in the grant of immunity, and although the statement obviously exceeds ten minutes, we will not insist upon a summary of it. And if the Colonel wishes to present his opening statement at this time, he may do so in total.

LT. COL. NORTH: Thank you, Mr. Chairman.

CHAIRMAN INOUYE: Please proceed.

LT. COL. NORTH: As you all know by now, my name is Oliver North, Lieutenant Colonel, United States Marine Corps. My best friend is my wife Betsy, to whom I have been married for 19 years, and with whom I have had four wonderful children, aged 18, 16, 11 and 6.

I came to the National Security Council six years ago to work in the administration of a great president. As a staff member, I came to understand his goals and his desires. I admired his policies, his strength, and his ability to bring our country together. I observed the President to be a leader who cared deeply about people, and who believed that the interests of our country were advanced by recognizing that ours is a nation at risk and a dangerous world, and acting accordingly. He tried, and in my opinion succeeded, in advancing the cause of world peace by strengthening our country, by acting to restore and sustain democracy throughout the world, and by having the courage to take decisive action when needed.

I also believe that we must guard against a rather perverse side of American life, and that is the tendency to launch vicious attacks and criticism against our elected officials. President Reagan has made enormous contributions, and he deserves our respect and admiration.

The National Security Council is, in essence, the President's staff. It helps to formulate and coordinate national security policy. Some, perhaps on this Committee, believe that the NSC was devoid of experienced leadership. I believe that is wrong. While at the NSC, I worked most closely with three people: Mr. Robert C. McFarlane, Admiral John Poindexter, and CIA Director, William Casey. Bud McFarlane is a man who devoted nearly thirty years of his life to public service in a number of responsible positions. At the NSC, he worked long hours, made great contributions, and I admire him for those efforts. Admiral Poindexter is a distinguished naval officer who served in a number of important positions of responsibility. He, too, was a tireless worker with a similar record of public service, and I, too, admire him greatly. William Casey was a reknowned lawyer, a war veteran of heroic proportions, and a former chairman of the SEC. I understood that he was also a close personal friend and adviser to President Reagan.

There is a nearly a century of combined public service by these three men. As a member of the NSC staff, I knew that I held a position of responsibility. But I knew full well what my position was. I did not engage in fantasy that I was the President or Vice President or Cabinet member, or even Director of the National Security Council. I was simply a staff member with a demonstrated ability to get the job done. Over time, I was made responsible for managing a number of complex and sensitive covert operations that we have discussed here to date. I reported directly to Mr. McFarlane and to Admiral Poindexter. I coordinated directly with others, including Director Casey. My authority to act always flowed, I believe, from my superiors. My military training inculcated in me a strong belief in the chain of command. And so far as I can recall, I always acted on major matter with specific approval, after informing my superiors of the facts, as I knew them, the risks, and the potential benefits. I readily admit that I was action-oriented, that I took pride in the fact that I was counted upon as a man who got the job done. And I don't mean this by way of criticism, but there were occasions when my superiors, confronted with acocmplishing goals or difficult tasks, would simply say, "Fix it, Ollie," or, "Take care of it."

Since graduating from the Naval Academy in 1968, I have strived to be the best Marine officer that one can be. In combat, my goal was always to understand the objective, follow orders, accomplish the mission, and to keep alive the men who served under me. One of the good things that has come from the last seven months of worldwide notoriety has been the renewed contact that I've had with some of the finest people in the world—those with whom I served in Vietnam. Among the 50,000 or so messages of support that have arrived since I left the NSC are many from those who recount the horrors we lived through, and who now relate stories of their families and careers. After Vietnam, I worked with my fellow officers to train good Marines to be ready in case we were called upon elsewhere in the world, but at the same time to hope that we never were. I honestly believed that any soldier who has ever been to a war truly hopes he will never see one again.

My Marine Corps career was untracked in 1981, when I was detailed to the National Security Council. I was uneasy at the beginning, but I came to believe that it was important work, and as years passed and responsibilities grew, I got further from that which I loved, the Marine Corps and Marines.

During 1984, '85, and '86, there were periods of time when we worked two days in every one. My guess is that the average workday lasted at least 14 hours. To respond to various crises, the need for such was frequent, and we would often go without a night's sleep, hoping to recoup the next night or thereafter. If I had to estimate the number of meetings and discussions and phone calls over that five years, it would surely be in the tens of thousands. My only real regret is that I virtually abandoned my family for work during these years, and that work consisted of my first few

263

years on the staff, as the project officer for a highly classified and compartmented National Security project, which is not a part of this inquiry.

I worked hard on the political military strategy for restoring and sustaining democracy in Central America, and in particular, El Salvador. We sought to achieve the democratic outcome in Nicaragua that this administration still supports, which involved keeping the contras together in both body and soul. We made efforts to open a new relationship with Iran, and recover our hostages. We worked on the development of a concerted policy regarding terrorists and terrorism and a capability for dealing in a concerted manner with that threat.

We worked on various crises, such as TWA 847, the capture of Achille Lauro, the rescue of American students in Grenada and the restoration of democracy on that small island, and the US raid in Libya in response to their terrorist attacks. And, as some may be willing to admit, there were efforts made to work with the Congress on legislative programs.

There were many problems. I believed that we worked as hard as we could to solve them, and sometimes we succeeded, and sometimes we failed, but at least we tried, and I want to tell you that I, for one, will never regret having tried.

I believe that this is a strange process that you are putting me and others through. Apparently, the President has chosen not to assert his prerogatives, and you have been permitted to make the rules. You called before you the officials of the Executive Branch. You put them under oath for what must be collectively thousands of hours of testimony. You dissect that testimony to find inconsistencies and declare some to be truthful and others to be liars. You make the rulings as to what is proper and what is not proper. You put the testimony which you think is helpful to your goals up before the people and leave others out. It's sort of like a baseball game in which you are both the player and the umpire. It's a game in which you call the balls and strikes and where you determine who is out and who is safe. And in the end you determine the score and declare yourselves the winner.

From where I sit, it is not the fairest process. One thing is, I think, for certain—that you will not investigate yourselves in this matter. There is not much chance that you will conclude at the end of these hearings that the Boland Amendments and the frequent policy changes therefore were unwise or that your restrictions should not have been imposed on the Executive Branch. You are not likely to conclude that the Administration acted properly by trying to sustain the freedom fighters in Nicaragua when they were abandoned, and you are not likely to conclude by commending the President of the United States who tried valiantly to recover our citizens and achieve an opening that is strategically vital—Iran. I would not be frank with you if I did not admit that the last several months have been difficult for me and my family. It has been difficult to be on the front pages of every newspaper in the land day after day, to be the lead story on national television day after day, to be photographed thousands of times by bands of photographers who chase us around since November just because my name arose at the hearings. It is difficult to be caught in the middle of a constitutional struggle between the Executive and legislative branches over who will formulate and direct the foreign policy of this nation. It is difficult to be vilified by people in and out of this body, some who have proclaimed that I am guilty of criminal conduct even before they heard me. Others have said that I would not tell the truth when I came here to testify, and one member asked a person testifying before this body whether he would believe me under oath. I asked when I got here—if you don't believe me, why call me at all? It has been difficult to see questions raised about my character and morality, my honesty, because only partial evidence was provided. And, as I indicated yesterday, I think it was insensitive of this Committee to place before the cameras my home address at a time when my family and I are under 24-hour armed guard by over a dozen government agents of the Naval Investigative Service because of fear that terrorists will seek revenge for my official acts and carry out their announced intentions to kill me.

It is also difficult to comprehend that my work at the NSC—all of which was approved and carried out in the best interests of our country—has led to two massive parallel investigations staffed by over 200 people. It is mind-boggling to me that one of those investigations is criminal and that some here have attempted to criminalize policy differences between co-equal branches of government and the Executive's conduct of foreign affairs.

I believe it is inevitable that the Congress will in the end blame the Executive Branch, but I suggest to you that it is the Congress which must accept at least some of the blame in the Nicaraguan freedom fighters' matter. Plain and simple, the Congress is to blame because of the fickle, vacillating, unpredictable, on-again off-again policy toward the Nicaraguan Democratic Resistance—the so-called Contras. I do not believe that the support of the Nicaraguan freedom fighters can be treated as the passage of a budget. I suppose that if the budget doesn't get passed on time again this year, it will be inevitably another extension of another month or two.

But, the contras, the Nicaraguan freedom fighters are people—living, breathing, young men and women who have had to suffer a desperate struggle for liberty with sporatic and confusing support from the United States of America.

Armies need food and consistent help. They need a flow of money, of arms, clothing and medical supplies. The Congress of the United States allowed the executive to encourage them, to do battle, and then abandoned them. The Congress of the United States left soldiers in the field unsupported and vulnerable to their communist enemies. When the executive branch did everything possible within the law to prevent them from being wiped out by Moscow's surrogates in Havana and Managua, you then had this investigation to blame the problem on the executive branch. It does not make sense to me.

In my opinion, these hearings have caused serious damage to our national interests. Our adversaries laugh at us, and our friends recoil in horror. I suppose it would be one thing if the intelligence committees wanted to hear all of this in private and thereafter pass laws which in the view of Congress make for better policies or better functioning government. But, to hold them publicly for the whole world to see strikes me as very harmful. Not only does it embarrass our friends and allies with whom we have worked, many of whom have helped us in various programs, but it must also make them very wary of helping us again.

I believe that these hearings, perhaps unintentionally so, have revealed matters of great secrecy in the operation of our government. And sources and methods of intelligence activities have clearly been revealed to the detriment of our security.

As a result of rumor and speculation and innuendo, I have been accused of almost every crime imaginable. Wild rumors have abounded. Some media reports have suggested that I was guilty of espionage for the way I handled US intelligence. Some have said that I was guilty of treason, and suggested in front of my 11-year-old daughter, that I should be given the death penalty. Some said I stoled 10 million dollars. Some said I was second only in power to the President of the United States, and others that I condoned drug-trafficking to generate funds for the contras, or that I personally ordered assassinations, or that I was conducting my own foreign policy. It has even been suggested that I was the personal confidant of the President of the United States. These and many other stories are patently untrue.

I don't mind telling you that I'm angry that what some have attempted to do to me and my family. I believe that these committee hearings will show that you have struck some blows. But, I am going to walk from here with my head high and my shoulders straight because I am proud of what we accomplished. I am proud of the efforts that we made, and I am proud of the fight that we fought. I am proud of serving the administration of a great president. I am not ashamed of anything in my professional or personal conduct. As we go through this process I ask that you continue to please keep an open mind. Please be open minded, and able to admit that, perhaps, your preliminary conclusions about me were wrong. And please, also, do not mistake my attitude for lack of respect. I am in awe of this great institution just as I am in awe of the presidency. Both are equal branches of government with separate areas of responsibility under the constitution that I have taken an oath to support and defend, and I have done so, as many of you have. And although I do not agree with what you are doing, or the way that it is being done, I do understand your interest in obtaining the facts and I have taken an oath to tell the truth and helping you to do so. In closing, Mr. Chairman, and I thank you for this opportunity, I would just simply like to thank the tens of thousands of Americans who have communicated their support, encouragement and prayers for me and my family in this difficult time. Thank you, sir.

CHAIRMAN INOUYE: Thank you very much, Colonel North. I wish the record to show that the panel did not amend, delete or strike out any word, or words—or phrases from this opening statement. Furthermore, we did not put on testimony words which we thought were helpful to our goals and leave the rest out. I am certain you will agree with me, Colonel, that every word you wanted to present to the people of the United States was presented. Isn't that correct, sir?

LT. COL. NORTH: Yes, Mr. Chairman it was, and I was not referring to my testimony but that which preceded me, sir—about me.

CHAIRMAN INOUYE: And secondly, you have suggested that these hearings have disclosed matters of great secrecy in the operation of our governemnt and sources and methods of intelligence activities have clearly been revealed to the detriment of our national security. May I, once again, advise you that according to the director of the National Security Agency, General Odom, not a single bit of classified material has been leaked by activities of this joint panel. Questioning will be resumed by Mr. Van Cleve. Mr. Van Cleve?

MR. VAN CLEVE: Thank you, Mr. Chairman. Good morning Colonel North.

LT. COL. NORTH: Good morning, Counsel.

MR. VAN CLEVE: Colonel North in your opening statement, which you just gave, you testified that you graduated from the Naval Academy in 1968. Is that correct?

LT. COL. NORTH: Yes, I did.

MR. VAN CLEVE: And in 1969, did you serve on active combat duty in the Armed Forces of the United States in the Republic of Vietnam?

LT. COL. NORTH: Sixty-nine? Yes, correct.

MR. VAN CLEVE: And is it the case that, during your service there, you were awarded a series of military citations, including two Purple Hearts, the Bronze Star and the Silver Star?

LT. COL. NORTH: I was.

MR. VAN CLEVE: And the Silver Star was awarded for "conspicuous gallantry and intrepidity in battle," is that correct?

LT. COL. NORTH: I believe that's the way the citation reads.

MR. VAN CLEVE: Col. North, Robert McFarlane has suggested that your Vietnam experience affected your view of the contras in their situation in Nicaragua. Is Mr. McFarlane correct about that?

LT. COL. NORTH: Counsel, I don't believe that anyone who served in Vietnam, who saw what happened as a consequence of our efforts when, in my opinion, we won all the battles and then lost the war, could ever be unaffected by that, unless they were totally insensitive. I would also point out that we didn't lose the war in Vietnam. We lost the war right here in this city.

MR. VAN CLEVE: Can you tell the Committee, in your opinion, sir, what are the similarities between the war in Nicaragua and the war in Vietnam?

LT. COL. NORTH: Well, the similarities are only in terms of what I would call the geostrategic similarities in that we had invested, rightly or wrongly—and I believe correctly, American credibility in support of democracy in South Vietnam. And the abandoment of South Vietnam in the latter days of 1974 and culminating in the disaster that followed shortly thereafter, created just exactly what people said it would—the so-called domino effect, the collapse of Vietnam, the butchery of Cambodia, the communization of Laos, and a threat ot that part of the world. Aside from the devastation of tens of thousands of people, the deaths of hundreds of thousands—millions in Cambodia, the only other similarity comes when you invest that same kind of credibility of this nation in the support of a democratic outcome in Central America, and then begin to walk away from it.

It is my belief that what I saw in Vietnam, where I saw the army of South Vietnam and I saw the Vietnamese Marine, one of whom was my roommate as I was went through Basics School at Quantico, and who gave their lives for their country, the parallel is to see that in the campesinos, the young men and women of the Nicaraguan resistance—is extraordinarily profound.

269

Yesterday the Attorney General of the United States authorized 200,000 Nicaraguans to remain in this country as refugees from oppression. That is but a small fraction of the refugees who have already fled Nicaragua.

If historical precedent is an example, when a communist takeover occurs, between 10 and 25 percent of the population will flee that country and go to the next nearest democracy. And if that happens throughout Central America, from the Rio Grande to the Panama Canal you're talking about something in the vicinity of 10 million human beings. Already 10 percent of the population of Nicaragua has fled. And so when I said yesterday that the contra, the Nicaraguan democratic resistance, the young men and women who fight today in the fields of Nicaragua were not a product of Ollie North, or Director Casey, or even this government, they are a product—they were raised up as an Army of opposition by the Sandinistas themselves.

And what I see is a very distinct parallel in terms of the way the rest of the world sees our commitment, I believe that that's the way the President saw it, that what we have happening, not as a parallel experience to Vietnam where our commitment increases to the point where you have the commitment of American ground forces, but the fact is we have made a commitment to a democratic outcome in Central America and a majority of both Houses have consistently reported that that's what they want. There have been differences as to how that should be achieved, but once we made the commitment to support the democratic resistance, we should have made that commitment a consistent one. And as soon as we begin to back away, the rest of the world looked at us and wondered if we had lost heart. We cannot be seen, I believe, in the world today as walking away and leaving failure in our wake. We must be able to demonstrate, not only in Nicaragua, but in Afghanistan and Angola, and elsewhere where freedom fighters have been told "We will support you," we must be able to continue to do so. If we do not, we will be overwhelmed. Ultimately, we will be forced to commit American ground combat troops.

This nation cannot abide the communization of Central America. We cannot have Soviet bases on the mainland of this hemisphere. And what I worked very hard to achieve was an outcome of democracy in Central America without

270

the use of military force. There are certainly members of this body and perhaps the rest of the Congress who would feel that we should have used this, used military force, American military force. My effort, and I believe what the President has said on it, is that the worst outcome we could have would be the consolidation of a communist client state in Nicaragua and the spread of communism throughout the region. The second worst outcome would be to have to use American forces, Marines, like me, and the sons of, perhaps, many of the members of this committee, my son, and we ought not to have to do that. We will, if it comes to that, I am convinced. But, there is an alternative, and the alternative is backing the democratic resistance in Nicaragua, a consistent program of support for democracy in El Salvador, Guatemala, Honduras and Costa Rica.

MR. VAN CLEVE: All right, sir. I need to ask you the other side of the question. What, in your view, are the differences between the War in Vietnam and the War in Nicaragua?

LT. COL. NORTH: Ten thousand miles, to start with. You're talking about a war that is 400 and some odd miles from our borders. You're talking about the efforts of the Soviet Union, not on the other side of the Pacific Ocean, but right here in this hemisphere. Hours, I mean I have flown to Nicaragua in four and a half hours. You're—you're not talking about a day's trip, like it used to be to go to Vietnam. You're talking about something right next door. That's the major difference.

MR. VAN CLEVE: I think you've already said this, but I want the record to be clear on it. Would you agree that the United States finally withdrew from Vietnam because the war effort lost the support of the American people. Isn't that correct, Colonel North?

LT. COL. NORTH: It did.

MR. VAN CLEVE: Now, as you have said in prior testimony, in October 1984, Congress adopted an amendment that is commonly referred to as the Boland Amendment, one of a series of amendments, but it's generally agreed that the October 1984 amendment was the most restrictive form of that amendment, and I give you the date of the amendment to sort of help you place things in time because I want to ask you a series of questions about the Soviet military position and the Soviet investment in Nicaragua as of the time when

271

the United States decided to cut off funds to the resistance, and if you would please turn to Exhibit #212, which I believe your counsel in what we refer to colloquially as "the big books". These are not the subject matter books, but the large exhibit books, and it's my earnest hope that you have been provided with a copy of Exhibit #212.

CHAIRMAN INOUYE: At this point, I'l like to advise all of you that we will have a series of votes in the United States Senate, the first at 9:30, the second at 10:00 and the third at 10:30. This will account for the absence of members of the Senate during this period. Please proceed.

MR. VAN CLEVE: Thank you, Mr. Chairman. Colonel North, do you have a copy of Exhibit #212 in front of you?

LT. COL. NORTH: I do.

MR. VAN CLEVE: This exhibit, for the record, is an unclassified document. It's a Defense Intelligence Agency analysis, and the title is "Nicaragua: The Military Build-up, July 1979 to 11 January, 1985". In short, it covers the period roughly from the time you began your service on the National Security Council, slightly prior to that, to the period about the same time when Congress decided to cut off the funds to the resistance. Is that correct?

LT. COL. NORTH: That is correct.

MR. VAN CLEVE: If you would, Colonel North, I want to make sure that the Committee is properly interpreting this particular chart, so I'd like to ask you some questions about it, and make sure that I understand it correctly, and that the Committee has proper information.

I might say, by the way, just for your own reference, that this chart was used as a tab for a memorandum that you wrote at about this time, which appears in another exhibit, that—it will be used I think in later examination, and that's Exhibit 260. Just, again, for your reference and that of your counsel.

Now I take it what this chart shows, Colonel North, is the estimates made by the United States government of the investment by the Soviet Union in Nicaraguan military forces. Is that correct?

LT. COL. NORTH: That is correct.

MR. VAN CLEVE: And is it correct that the investment is shown, period by period, so that the chart demonstrates what the investment is estimated to have been, say, for example, between the first of January, 1981, and the first of January, 1982, for example?

LT. COL. NORTH: Yes.

MR. VAN CLEVE: And does the chart correctly show—if we turn to the column that says "millions of United States dollars per period" —that the investment appears to begin in the period just prior to the beginning of the Reagan administration, ending January 1st, 1981. And it's a small investment initially, isn't it—$6 million?

LT. COL. NORTH: That's correct.

MR. VAN CLEVE: And within one year, the investment grows to an additional $40 million, is that correct?

LT. COL. NORTH: That is correct. I would also—just if I may, Counsel—point out that our estimates about what was happening in Nicaragua as early as August of 1979 are—at least were—by the assessment of Director Casey, very poor. He viewed the earlier indications, prior to the administration, to be somewhat inaccurate, not because of any flaw particularly, but because the CIA was not collecting. And this is, after all, an attempt to go back post hoc and examine what actually occurred—perhaps, in some cases, several years earlier. Director Casey made several times, I believe before the two intelligence committees, notice that our estimates of what was occurring in Nicaragua shortly after the revolution took power in July of 1979, all the way through the early days of the Reagan administration, to be relatively poor. He's not saying that they're necessarily wrong, but we do not have a good grasp as to when that began. But it certainly began before the Reagan administration arrived in Washington.

MR. VAN CLEVE: All right. And does the chart further show that within one additional year, the level of investment—annual investment—had grown from $40 million to $90 million?

LT. COL. NORTH: Yes, it does.

MR. VAN CLEVE: Correct. And the force level by that point had grown to 41,000, is that correct?

LT. COL. NORTH: Yes.

MR. VAN CLEVE: And within an additional year, the investment had grown to $120 million, is that correct?

LT. COL. NORTH: That's right.

MR. VAN CLEVE: And within one additional year, and this

is by the first of January, 1985, the investment had grown to $250 million, is that correct?

LT. COL. NORTH: Yes.

MR. VAN CLEVE: Now I did some arithmetic, and my arithmetic is that that represents a total of $506 million through that period. Would you agree with that?

LT. COL. NORTH: I would.

MR. VAN CLEVE: Are you aware—

LT. COL. NORTH: And I believe that's a conservative estimate, and it is military hardware alone. It does not talk about other kinds of investments.

MR. VAN CLEVE: I understand. And I might add that the chart shows that, again, by that period, the force had grown to 62,000. Are you aware, Col. North, of any intelligence available to the United States government which would suggest that there is anything inaccurate about this publicly-available, unclassified Defense Agency data?

LT. COL. NORTH: I am sure that there are other indications, for example, that would show the force to be actually higher. My assessment of this—and I think it was consistent with what others were saying at the time—is that is a conservative estimate. For example, by 1985, there were probably more than 62,000 in the active force and in the reserves and the militia, given the limited capability for collection. There probably were, by that point in time, well over 62,000.

MR. VAN CLEVE: Now I take it that this would represent the largest military force anywhere in Central America, is that correct?

LT. COL. NORTH: It is not only the largest in Central America. It is the largest of all Central America combined.

MR. VAN CLEVE: And I take it, it also represents a force larger than that currently stationed by the United States in South Korea, is that correct?

LT. COL. NORTH: That is correct. What is also does not show, Counsel, is the number of Soviet, East German, North Korean, PLO, Libyan and Cuban advisors—all of whom were here early on.

MR. VAN CLEVE: To your knowledge, as of this time in early 1985, how would the level of support which the Soviets have provided in military assistance to Nicaragua compare to the level of support which the United States had given to the contras before the Boland Amendment cut-off?

LT. COL. NORTH: Well, it's about 50 to 1. I'm looking at a parallel. I don't have the exact figures before me, but it was considerably more by several orders of magnitude.

MR. VAN CLEVE: Now the Committee heard testimony in late May from Adolfo Calero. And Mr. Calero testified, if I recall his testimony correctly, that it was estimate that the Sandinistas had received about $2.5 billion from the Soviet Union in total assistance. Now this is probably both military and eocnomic assistance, plus what had come from the Eastern bloc and from other western countries. And he estimated that they had received more than 100,000 tons of materials—of lethal material —from the Soviet Union. And he further estimated that the contras had probably received about five percent, or perhaps as much, he said, as ten percent of that amount of material from their allies. Does that seem to you to be an accurate assessment of the relative levels of support?

LT. COL. NORTH: Yes, it does.

MR. VAN CLEVE: So, in terms of total assistance, if the Sandinistas have received what Mr. Calero is $2.5 billion, and what our own unclassified estimates show is about $3 billion in assistance. We have given the contras a small fraction of that level of support so far. Is that correct?

LT. COL. NORTH: A very small fraction.

MR. VAN CLEVE: And that was the situation, nearly at that level of investment, at the time of the Boland cut-off. Is that correct?

LT. COL. NORTH: Yes.

MR. VAN CLEVE: What effect would the Boland cut-off then have had on the contras, if they had been left completely unassisted by private individuals in the United States?

LT. COL. NORTH: Our assessment was that if there was not something done, beginning with the—first of all, cut-off of funds in '84, and then the proscriptions later on in the year, that within six to ten months the Nicaraguan resistance would cease to be; that they would be annihilated in the field, and that the refugee flow, which is already considerable, would probably treble. And that that would have a considerable effect on the neighboring democracies.

We knew at that point in time that the command and control center, logistic support, and basic guidance was all for the—for the Salvadoran communist guerrillas, known as the FMLN, derived directly from Managua. Their broadcast facilities, their command and control centers, were all in Managua. And we were very concerned that the considerable investment that we had made in assisting the Salvadorans in the restoration of democracy in that country; that the Honduran democracy, which was fledgling at the time, and beginning to grow; and that the democracy of long term, in Costa Rica, would be placed under great threat. Even more important, Counsel, is that those leaders in the region saw it the same way.

MR. VAN CLEVE: What, in your view, was the purpose of the massive Soviet investment in Nicaragua?

LT. COL. NORTH: Well, I think the Soviets have a neat way of doing it. I'm accused of dreaming up "neat" things. The Soviets, obviously, from what they have said, and every indication that we know of, are not willing to go to war over Nicaragua. And in fact, they neatly sidestepped the issue. And it's a very clever use of the dialectic. They don't come out and advocate until they're absolutely certain that the revolution is going to succeed, as it did in Cuba—they don't come out an advocate a 100 percent commitment. What they have done is they have provided a steady and consistent and increasing level of military and economic support to Nicaragua, in hopes that their revolution will succeed.

And of course, the quotes of the leadership of Nicaragua show them to be truly what they are. In fact, they aren't even Marxists. They are Leninists. They believe, deeply, in the "Vanguard of the Party." And these are the words that Vladimir Ilyich Lenin used in 1917, and in 1918, when he was taking charge of what was going on in the Soviet Union. These are the same words that Fidel Castro used. And yet, they are always consistent when they approach us here in this country, and people who think that they're agrarian reformers, or that they're simply labor organizers or democrats—they're very, very careful to stay away from those terms when they're talking with us. It's an extraordinary experience to see what's going on.

The Soviets desperately want to achieve the consolidation of a Soviet client state on the mainland of this hemisphere. It will be disastrous for our foreign policy. Ultimately, it will be disastrous for our ability to respond to NATO, to keep open trade routes through the Caribbean, and could well result, using Punta Joyte, the largest military airfield south of the Rio Grande, or the ports at El Bluff and Corinto for Soviet naval activities, something they have never had on this hemisphere since the last Russian colony in the West Coast of the United States in the 1800s.

MR. VAN CLEVE: So that—I believe you've answered the question, but so that it's clear, you're not telling us that the Soviets are a group of disinterested philanthropists who are hoping that some fellow ideological groups can succeed. They're making a military investment, aren't they, Colonel?

LT. COL. NORTH: They are making a major military investment, and an economic investment. The Soviets are outspending us in our own hemisphere about five to one, in dollars alone. They have more military advisers in this hemisphere than we do south of the Rio Grande.

MR. VAN CLEVE: Just very briefly, at some point the Soviet Union decided to allow the Nicaraguans, the Sandinistas to use the Hind-D helicopter, and in effect they were allowed to import a series of those helicopters. Roughly, when did that occur?

LT. COL. NORTH: I'm not sure the use of "allowed". The Soviets have every intention of bringing the Hind over there. The Soviets delivered the weapons system. Once we had indicated that we were failing in our effort to keep the resistance going, and made an effort to use it. Starting, I believe, in late 1984 or early '85, the first deliveries, they achieve significant operational experience with it in Afghanistan, knew it to be a very effective counter-insurgency weapon, were using it for that purpose in Afghanistan, had used it the same way in Angola, effectively flown by Cuban pilots. Soviet technicians delivered and assembled and test-flew the airplanes. Nicaraguan and Cuban pilots are flying them. It is the most devastating attack helicopter in the world today, and I am not trying to impune any of our defense contractors, but if we can get the model, we ought to build it.

MR. VAN CLEVE: I take it, it's clear from that then that the Soviets are willing to make available to the Sandinistas whatever type of military technology they need to win?

LT. COL. NORTH: To win—

MR. VAN CLEVE: They have, in fact, done so.

LT. COL. NORTH: I believe that the Soviets, and I think the intelligence committees and other committees have heard in open testimony that it is, at least was when I left the Adminstration in 1986 it was our assessment that the Soviets were willing to give them anything necessary to win, short of provoking an American military response. And, thus, the Soviets appear to be reluctant to give them MiG aircraft.

The Soviets have not done that. The MiG would be an extraordinary change in the balance of power in that part of the world. Today the only really effective deterrent to the Sandinista military machine in Central America is a now-effective field army in El Salvador and the air force in the Honduras. And were the Soviets to bring the MiG in, they have been told several times directly that that was a provocation that was beyond the bounds, and that we would respond—they were told that directly by officials well above my pay grade—and I think the Soviets have recognized that would be one step too far. They have walked to the edge, and they have backed their allies in Managua to the hilt. But they are not willing to provoke us into a military response.

MR. VAN CLEVE: I'd like you now, if you would, to turn to Exhibit 213. This is a document for identification for the record commonly referred to as the San Jose Declaration. It was prepared in early March 1985, and it's my understanding, Colonel North, that you were there when this document was written, is that correct?

LT. COL. NORTH: Counsel, I don't want to take anything from the leaders of the Nicaraguan Resistance. They are the drafters of this document. I was blessed to be with them and work on this and with them in the course of time that this was being prepared, and several other Americans assisted them. But this is their product, and I consider it an honor to have been invited to participate in assisting them. But it's their document.

MR. VAN CLEVE: The reason I ask whether you were present is that I'm going to ask you some questions about the political background of the document, and I thought that you would then be in a position to answer those questions. I take it the San Jose Declaration was a political unity document written by the contra leaders, is that correct?

LT. COL. NORTH: That is correct.

MR. VAN CLEVE: And it was written by people who were very uncomfortable with each other, is that correct?

LT. COL. NORTH: In any democracy, I think the great blessing of democracy is that there are always people who will be in contention, and one of the great things about this unity effort is there are people with differing views who are represented in this unity. I don't think it's so much that they were personally uncomfortable with one another. They all recognized that they were in unity on one issue, and that was in opposing the communists in Managua who had seized control of their country. And that brought them together, even though one might have one view of how the economy should work and another one ought to have another view of how big the military ought to be, they all wanted one outcome and that was democracy in their country. And so, they had differing views but I don't want to characterize it as that they were at each other's throats when I wasn't in the room.

MR. VAN CLEVE: So it's a pretty remarkable thing, isn't it? I had something a little more specific in mind, Colonel North. It's my understanding that some of the leaders who participated in drafting this document served in the Sandinista leadership and had actually participated in confiscating the property of some of the other contra leaders with whom they were sitting in the same room drafting this document, is that correct?

LT. COL. NORTH: That is correct.

MR. VAN CLEVE: So it's a pretty remarkable thing, isn't it, that they were able to sit down and draft a unity document together, isn't it?

LT. COL. NORTH: It is indeed.

MR. VAN CLEVE: And this document was intended as a peace offer to the Sandinista government. Is that correct?

LT. COL. NORTH: That is correct, and it was tendered as such.

MR. VAN CLEVE: And what the resistance leadership did

was to agree to a political program that they would tender to the Sandinistas as a peace offer. Is that correct?

LT. COL. NORTH: Exactly.

MR. VAN CLEVE: Let's take a look at this declaration and see what kind of an offer the contra leadership made to the Sandinista government. And this is in March 1985 now, about three and a half or four months, I guess, after the Boland Amendment was passed.

LT. COL. NORTH: That is correct.

MR. VAN CLEVE: If you look at the first page of the document down toward the bottom, I guess it would be the second full paragraph before the end of the first page, it starts, "In conclusion, the national crisis we face did not grow out of a confrontation between imperialism and the revolution as the Sandinista front pretends but out of the contradictions which emerged from the clash between democratic expectations of the Nicaraguan people and the imposition of a totalitarian system such as that which is being implanted in our country by the Sandinista front."

Now, what I want to ask you, Colonel North is, is that what the contra leadership honestly believed to be the case? Was that their view of what was happening in Nicaragua at that time?

LT. COL. NORTH: Absolutely.

MR. VAN CLEVE: Okay. Now, turning to the next page of the document, there is a section called, "Common Aspirations." And the document then lists a series of items that are part of the peace proposal that describe the political program of the contra leadership for the people of Nicaragua. And I note, if you'll look down toward the bottom of the page, the first element, A is—it says, "In order to carry out the foregoing, the following is required," and it starts, "to recognize the privacy of civilian society with respect to the state."

Now, that's basically the principal upon which this country is founded, isn't it?

LT. COL. NORTH: Yes, it is, individual liberty.

MR. VAN CLEVE: And the contra leadership believed that as well, and that's what they wanted for Nicaragua. Is that correct?

LT. COL. NORTH: That is indeed.

MR. VAN CLEVE: And the second principal, "Full respect

for human rights and the fundamental freedoms of expression, assembly, religion and education."

LT. COL. NORTH: All of which are denied in Managua today.

MR. VAN CLEVE: And that's what the contra leadership actually wanted for the people of Nicaragua, correct?

LT. COL. NORTH: It is.

MR. VAN CLEVE: I noticed that point G is, freedom to organize unions, and I take it that that's something that also is denied in Nicaragua today. Is that correct?

LT. COL. NORTH: Oh, you can be in an union in Nicaragua today—a state-controlled, state-operated, state-managed, state-directed union—unions.

MR. VAN CLEVE: But you can't be in a union that is like an American union, can you?

LT. COL. NORTH: Oh, no. But you can't in any communist society.

MR. VAN CLEVE: So, is it fair to say, Colonel North, that the San Jose declaration was an honest and complete statement of the political program of the contra leadership as it was presented to the Nicaraguan people at that time?

LT. COL. NORTH: Yes, and just like our own declaration of independence, and our own constitution which we celebrate the bicentennial year of this year. It was hammered out in compromise and with differing views by men who all sought a common purpose, and I think that's important. They have been mischaracterized in many cases by a very effective propaganda apparatus, the Soviets and the Cubans and the Nicaraguans, in some cases supported by Americans. An American public relation firm which works for the Sandinista government. And the fact is that this was hammered out in the same way as the founders of our own Constitution did, in a hot sweaty room with differing opinions, and it was something to be part of this, and I mean that. I get a little emotional about it perhaps, more so than perhaps some thought I should have, but when the President of the United States referred to the similarities between the Nicaraguan resistance and our own founding fathers, he meant that. He knew what this document represented, and it means a lot. And it was truly an effort to arrive at an amicable conclusion to a bloody war inside that country. And it was a war of liberation and it still is a war of liberation. And these men made those kinds of compromises just like the men who gathered in Philadelphia did 200 years ago. And that is, after all, the essence of democracy.

MR. VAN CLEVE: Would you turn to Exhibit 214, please? Now I need to ask you about this document, Colonel North, because it was published by the government of Nicaragua shortly after the San Jose Declaration. For the record, this is an opinion piece written by the Nicaraguan ambassador to the United States, Carlos Tunnermann Bernheim and was published in the Washington Post on March 30th 1985, and it's entitled, "We Will Never Negotiate with the Contras." And I need to ask you about the—some of the statements made in this editorial because they purport to be factual statements by the Ambassador, and I want to find out how accurate they are.

If you would look first at the first paragraph, the first numbered paragraph of this editorial, and after Bernheim says, when he's explaining why we will never negotiate with the contras, which apparently is the stated position of the Nicaraguan government, he says, number one: "The contras are led by officers of the hated Guardia Nationale, the main prop of the Somoza dictatorship that brutalized the Nicaraguan people for more than 40 years until our Sandinista revolution threw them out in July 1979."

Now is that an accurate statement or not, Colonel North?

LT. COL. NORTH: No, but I don't think we should expect accuracy in media from the folks in Managua. The—

MR. VAN CLEVE: I want to give them the benefit of the doubt, Colonel North, I just asked you whether or not you thought it was an accurate statement?

LT. COL. NORTH: No, I do not believe it to be accurate.

MR. VAN CLEVE: And would you say specifically why not?

LT. COL. NORTH: Well, because much of the leadership of the Nicaraguan resistance, even in the largest of the groups opposing the Sandinistas, are composed of former Sandinistas themselves. Two of the three principal members in the leadership of the United Nicaraguan Opposition which came from the San Jose Declaration—two of the three of them were former Sandinistas themselves. So the fact is that the leadership of the Nicaraguan resistance are comprised of real Nicaraguans, not members of the Somoza guard. There are indeed members of the former national

282

guard who are a part of the Nicaraguan resistance, and they are Nicaraguans too. I do not define those people as the brutal precursors of a return of Somocismo as the Sandinistas put it.

MR. VAN CLEVE: Turning to paragraph number two, and this is a particularly, I think, important statement by the Ambassador. He says, "The contras are terrorists whose attacks are directed primarily against our civilian population." Now, is that true or not, Colonel North, based on your experience?

LT. COL. NORTH: No, it is not. And major efforts were made certainly when I was involved and as I have admitted to the committee in discussing military activities with them. Their efforts were made when the CIA was engaged with them, and I'm sure that they are being made now. To focus on those kinds of targets which are principally military and principally those things that will avoid civilian casualties, and there's a very real reason for that. No guerilla army can ever survive if it alienates the civilian population. The Nicaraguan resistance grew from about 6,000 to over 16,000 during the period of time in which I was their principal point of contact. And the reason it grew is because it enamored—the Nicaraguan people of a solution to the problem of communism. In other words, the resistance couldn't and wouldn't have survived had it done the kinds of things that Ambassador Tunnermann has described here.

MR. VAN CLEVE: Turning to numbered paragraph three, and I think probably this is the last relatively specific allegation or statement by the Ambassador. The Ambassador says, "The contras are not an indigenous rebel group, but a collection of mercenaries recruited, paid, armed, and directed by the CIA, and they would cease to exist without US support." Is that correct or not?

LT. COL. NORTH: That is absolutely incorrect. The contras —the Nicaraguan democratic resistance—the freedom fighters—are indeed Nicaraguan. In fact, there are far fewer foreign, that is American or other Western democratic advisors, with the Nicaraguan resistance than there ever were with the Sandinistas themselves. The Sandinistas came to power with the direct support of Cuba and the Soviet Union. The Sandinistas could not have arrived in Managua without that support. They would not have arrived there without it. And they could not sustain themselves there without continuing it today.

MR. VAN CLEVE: I'd like now to turn to another line of questioning. Before I do, let me just very briefly summarize your testimony to this point and see if I have it accurately. You've testified that during the period from 1979 through the beginning of 1985, the Soviet military and economic investment in Nicaragua outstripped by a factor of at least five to one any investment made by the United States in supporting the contras. You've further testified as to the outlines of the political program of the contra leadership based on your personal knowledge and conversations with that leadership. And you've, finally, testified about the nature of the contra forces and their activities in trying to support their opposition to the Sandinista regime. Is that correct?

LT. COL. NORTH: Yes.

MR. VAN CLEVE: I'd like now to turn to the Boland Amendment itself, Colonel North, and obviously this is one of the key issues before the Committee. And you testified yesterday about it to a certain extent. And I know that you're not a lawyer. And you probably feel fortunate about that, and I think I could probably understand why.

LT. COL. NORTH: I have developed a fond rapport for lawyers, certain of them.

MR. VAN CLEVE: And I make that statement, Colonel North, because I want to preface my questions with a clear understanding that I am not going to ask you for your legal opinion. I'm going to ask you for your understanding about things at the time as they were.

Now yesterday, you testified that you believed that you and the people you had worked with in the government had made every effort to comply with the Boland Amendment. Is that correct?

LT. COL. NORTH: I believe we did.

MR. VAN CLEVE: And what I want to do is, I want to find out, as best I can, and again, at about the same period of time, say, early to mid-1985, exactly what it was you thought that you, personally, as a member of the NSC staff, were prohibited from doing by the Boland Amendment. Because I've reviewed your testimony yesterday, and it's not entirely clear to me. So you knew that there were restrictions being imposed on the government by the Boland Amendment, but what was your understanding of the restrictions that applied to your activity as a member of the NSC staff?

LT. COL. NORTH: My understanding was that, first of all, we were to work to comply with Boland, and that we were to work to keep alive the Nicaraguan resistance. Second, I did not view, nor did my superiors view, that the National Security Council staff was covered by Boland. There were people who were concerned about that, and we sought and obtained legal advice to the effect that it was not; not the least of those was Director Casey.

MR. VAN CLEVE: Did you ever get any kind of a written legal opinion from Director Casey on that point?

LT. COL. NORTH: I don't recall. I—we may have, I—and if I did, it would have been left in my files, I suppose.

MR. VAN CLEVE: Can you tell the Committee whether you ever obtained any other written legal advice on that specific question of the coverage of the Boland Amendment—

LT. COL. NORTH: There was a—

MR. VAN CLEVE: —for the NSC?

LT. COL. NORTH: There was a legal opinion provided by counsel to the Intelligence Oversight Board.

MR. VAN CLEVE: Any other opinions?

LT. COL. NORTH: I'd have—

MR. VAN CLEVE: Either way. Either taking the position that the NSC was covered or taking the position that it was not covered—

LT. COL. NORTH: Well certainly—

MR. VAN CLEVE: —that you can recall.

LT. COL. NORTH: Certainly we had many newspaper articles at the time that no US government support whatsoever of any kind, etcetera, could be provided. There were lots of so-called "legal scholars" who provided that kind of advice to the media. I had discussions with—I'm trying to remember, excuse me. I had discussions with Mr. John Norton Moore of the American Bar Association on a number of occasions. He—

MR. VAN CLEVE: About this subject?

LT. COL. NORTH: Yes. He clearly did not view this to be—first, he did not view Boland to be constitutional within the framework of the constitution. Second of all, he did not think it applied to the NSC, and there were several other lawyers who felt the same way. The bottom line of it is, we looked at that as saying that very clearly the CIA could not use its appropriated monies for this, and we couldn't use DOD monies for these purposes, but very clearly Boland did not proscribe the National Security Council from being the point of contact, the coordinator, whatever.

MR. VAN CLEVE: Yesterday, you were asked about Exhibit #109, Col. North, which is a letter from Robert McFarlane to Congressman Michael Barnes, dated September 12, 1985, and I hope that your counsel has the exhibit before him at the witness table.

LT. COL. NORTH: Which book?

MR. VAN CLEVE: I think probably in the large set of exhibit books.

MR. SULLIVAN: What number, Counsel?

MR. VAN CLEVE: One hundred and nine.

LT. COL. NORTH: Yes.

MR. VAN CLEVE: Now, would it be fair to say that Mr. McFarlane's letter appears at a minimum to accept the view that NSC expenditures must comply with the Boland Amendment?

LT. COL. NORTH: It appears to, yes. But I,—my understanding of that at the time was we were talking about talking a hunk of the NSC budget and going out to buy guns with it, and obviously we weren't going to do that.

MR. VAN CLEVE: Did you discuss that specific question of NSC coverage with Mr. McFarlane at the time the letter was being drafted?

LT. COL. NORTH: I honestly don't recall, and I admitted yesterday that this is a misleading, evasive and—

MR. VAN CLEVE: I'm sorry. That's not where I'm headed at present. I just wanted to know whether or not you and Mr. McFarlane had, in fact, discussed this question at the time?

LT. COL. NORTH: At the time of the letter, I don't believe we did, but almost well over a year before, when I became engaged as the point of contact, if you will, for the resistance—

MR. VAN CLEVE: Right.

LT. COL. NORTH: I mean, we had looked at where we were heading. We had already seen drafts of various pieces of legislation coming down, and looked at the fact that the NSC was not proscribed by those statutes, or resolutions.

MR. VAN CLEVE: Okay. Again, to your knowledge, Col. North, the Boland Amendment is not a criminal statute, is it?

LT. COL. NORTH: Certainly not.

MR. VAN CLEVE: And the reason I ask you that question is that it is not a statute. It's a statute that's intended to control the relations between the executive branch and Congress, where the spending of taxpayer funds is concerned. Is that right?

LT. COL. NORTH: Yeah, it's—I understood Boland to be an appropriations measure.

MR. VAN CLEVE: Right.

LT. COL. NORTH: In other words, here's monies, and here's what you can and cannot do with those monies.

MR. VAN CLEVE: Right. Now, you said in your opening statement words to the effect that the NSC itself is the direct personal arm of the President, in advising the President, coordinating, and thereby directing the execution of the foreign policy of the United States. Is that correct?

LT. COL. NORTH: That is correct.

MR. VAN CLEVE: So your actions with respect to the contras represented the direct implementation of the policy of the President on these sensitive foreign policy issues. Correct?

LT. COL. NORTH: Yes.

MR. VAN CLEVE: Now, if you were directly carrying out the foreign policy of the President in working with the contras, it would be necessary to show that Congress intended to interfere with the President's carrying out of his foreign policy, before it could be shown that you were violating the Boland Amendment, wouldn't it?

LT. COL. NORTH: Yes.

MR. VAN CLEVE: And it's clear, isn't it, that when Congress wants to control the President's conduct in a statute like this, especially in foreign policy, it usually says so explicitly?

LT. COL. NORTH: Yes.

MR. VAN CLEVE: In fact, since the NSC was created in 1947, no significant change in its operations has been made by Congress without explicit mention of the NSC, has it?

287

LT. COL. NORTH: That's correct.

MR. VAN CLEVE: And it's also clear, isn't it, that if Congress told the President he could not ask foreign countries or private individuals for financial or other official assistance for the contras, there would be serious doubt about whether Congress had exceeded its constitutional power. Correct?

LT. COL. NORTH: Well, if you're asking for my opinion, I think there is no doubt that if the Congress had passed such a measure, it would clearly, in my opinion, be unconstitutional.

MR. VAN CLEVE: And you're basing that at least in part with your conversation with John Norton Moore of the University of Virginia Law School. Is that correct?

LT. COL. NORTH: And others. Marines can read. I'm just telling you—

MR. VAN CLEVE: I understand.

LT. COL. NORTH: —that we went to some lengths to look at these things.

MR. VAN CLEVE: I understand. Now, the Boland Amendment wasn't intended to prevent the transfer of basic intelligence information to the contras, was it?

LT. COL. NORTH: No.

MR. VAN CLEVE: And this was, in fact, by far the principal form of assistance rendered to the contras by United States government officials at your request during this period, wasn't it? The transfer of basic intelligence information?

LT. COL. NORTH: Yes. And we're talking specifically of the two principal government officials, three perhaps, with whom I was in touch. That was, to my knowledge, the only real substance of what they did.

MR. VAN CLEVE: I understand. And as part of your job, you were expected to know in detail, exactly what the contras were doing, both politically and militarily, weren't you?

LT. COL. NORTH: I tried to, yes.

MR. VAN CLEVE: There's nothing in the Boland Amendment that was intended to prohibit that, is there?

LT. COL. NORTH: No.

MR. VAN CLEVE: The Boland Amendment can also be read to allow general strategic military advice, as opposed to advice on specific operations and tactics, can't it?

288

LT. COL. NORTH: Yes.

MR. VAN CLEVE: And the military advice that you gave was, in fact, limited to that type of general strategic advice, wasn't it?

LT. COL. NORTH: Yes. I want to clarify one thing, and I think I owe, at least Chairman Hamilton—because I did appear before your committee, and I did mislead your committee. But I want to reiterate, again, that I never did sit down in the battlefield, and sit and plan a specific tactical operation with them; that I did provide, as much as I was able, and as oft as I was able, the kind of broader strategic advice that I thought was appropriate to the circumstances.

On a number of occasions, I addressed issues that I thought were important to them, that they could not or should not attack certain types of targets, because it would, indeed, have the effect of alienating the population. And to my knowledge, they made efforts to abide by that kind of advice. It was certainly not given as direction, or specific "You must do this," but to simply say: "Here's what needs to be done. Here's how the training ought to be done." We even published a first draft of a code of conduct for the forces while they were down there, during the period of time that the Boland proscriptions obtained. And, although I did mislead your Committee when I appeared before it, I want to reiterate at least that part of it, that that was done in good faith, and the whole effort to open the southern front was done with that same kind of good faith effort to the resistance.

MR. VAN CLEVE: The Boland Amendment, as far you know, is not intended to control the conduct of private citizens, is it?

LT. COL. NORTH: There is nothing in the Boland—any of the Boland proscriptions, to my knowledge, that refers to them.

MR. VAN CLEVE: So it doesn't prevent private citizens from raising money or contributing money to the contras, does it?

LT. COL. NORTH: Nor do I believe it could.

MR. VAN CLEVE: Now do I understand correctly that you gave a number of speeches to people who were interested in the problem in Nicaragua, is that correct?

LT. COL. NORTH: Yes, and I would point out, Counsel, that

I not only gave that to proponents, I also gave that same speech to opponents.

MR. VAN CLEVE: And do I understand correctly that at least at one point you developed a slide show that went with that presentation?

LT. COL. NORTH: I did.

MR. VAN CLEVE: And, to your knowledge, does the slide show—let me step back here—the Committee wanted to find out what in substance you were telling these groups of people who were for or against the President's contra policy. One good way of doing that would be to look at that slide show, wouldn't it?

LT. COL. NORTH: I would welcome the opportunity to at least show the first of the two punches that I've been accused of delivering.

MR. VAN CLEVE: And to your knowledge, Colonel, where are those slides today?

LT. COL. NORTH: My knowledge is that they were left behind in my office and Lord only knows where they are now.

MR. VAN CLEVE: So, but for all you know, they may still be there?

LT. COL. NORTH: They could be.

MR. VAN CLEVE: And if the Committees wanted to obtain them, they would simply have to make a request for that?

LT. COL. NORTH: Counsel advises me that they are still there.

MR. VAN CLEVE: I see. And, again, so if the Committees wanted to obtain them, they're unclassified and we would simply have to ask for them?

LT. COL. NORTH: Yes, there are several slides in the presentation which were declassified reconnaisance aircraft photographs, some of which have already been published in various publications put out by the State and Defense Department.

MR. VAN CLEVE: But they're all unclassified?

LT. COL. NORTH: Yes.

CHAIRMAN INOUYE: May I interrupt at this point, so there will be no misunderstanding. When the Committee submitted the request for documents, we requested everything. We did not exclude anything. If those slides were in the possession of the Executive Branch, they had to give it to us. So I don't want the impression to be left that this panel excluded certain documents and accepted only those that we needed or wanted. And I'm certain that counsel is well aware of this.

LT. COL. NORTH: Mr. Chairman, may I just say for the record that of course I did not intend to suggest otherwise. I believe the slides may have been recently located, and it is obviously a matter of of inadvertence. I simply wanted to confirm for the record that the slides were in fact available.

CHAIRMAN INOUYE: Mr. Liman?

MR. LIMAN: Mr. Chairman, I do not believe that it was a matter of inadvertence. I think the record is clear, but because Colonel North chose to invoke his Fifth Amendment privilege, we did not have information either from Colonel North or his counsel until recently, and his counsel brought to our attention that these slides existed last week. And as a result of that information that he brought to our attention, we were able to locate them. But we and the NSC and the FBI and all the other agencies that have been going through documents have been doing it without the guidance of the author.

MR. SULLIVAN: Just so the record's straight here, Mr. Chairman, if I might. We understand that those slides have been available at the White House since Colonel North left there. And they've been sitting over there, and they're presently in the possession, I believe, of White House counsel staff. When it came time for Colonel North to be given the documents that the Committee had, we requested that he be given his slides.

The Committee stated that it did not have the slides. We made a half a dozed insistent requests to the Committee. We said, "They must exist, go and find them." And in fact, out of that process, they were found. They exist over there at the White House, and if you have made a request for everything at the White House and it has been pending for some months, then they were there and they weren't given. I suspect it was just inadvertence and no is to blame for the problem. And I certainly hope that the assertion of one's constitutional rights to remain silent cannot be grounds for fault, Mr. Liman.

CHAIRMAN INOUYE: Well, I just didn't want the record to show that we had excluded those slides and intentionally not requested that. If I may through this means, I am now officially requesting the White House to forthwith send those slides to the joint panel.

MR. SULLIVAN: I might add, Mr. Chairman, that we made the insistent request with respect to tape recordings, and, I think, as a result of our request to the Committee, the Committee has gone back to the White House and has bound tape recordings made by Colonel North during the course—

CHAIRMAN INOUYE: Mr. Sullivan, you are correct.

MR. SULLIVAN: Thank you, sir.

MR. VAN CLEVE: Mr. Chairman, may I procede?

CHAIRMAN INOUYE: Please do.

MR. VAN CLEVE: Thank you, Mr. Chairman. Colonel North you are familiar with the Neutrality Act, aren't you?

LT. COL. NORTH: I hope you are not going to ask me to quote it, but yes I know what it pertains to.

MR. VAN CLEVE: Basically—and I am paraphrasing, obviously, the Neutrality Act prohibits the organization of military expeditions from the United States against other countries with whom we are at peace. Correct?

LT. COL. NORTH: Correct.

MR. VAN CLEVE: And you and General Secord—let me ask you, is this your testimony: that you and General Secord scrupulously tried to comply with the Neutrality Act in setting up and running the contra resupply operation?

LT. COL. NORTH: Absolutely.

MR. VAN CLEVE: Did you ever request, direct, or otherwise participate in the shipment of arms from the United States to Central America as part of the covert contra resupply operation.

LT. COL. NORTH: Never.

MR. VAN CLEVE: I take it then, that any report in a publication such as the recent report in the Washingtonian magazine suggesting that there were, in fact, arms shipments from Dulles Airport under false manifest is, to your knowledge, untrue?

LT. COL. NORTH: I have not read the Washingtonian report. I don't read most of the news about myself. But I will tell you absolutely, categorically, there was never a single bullet, rifle, and piece of ordnance that I know of that was shipped from the United States of America as a part of the covert operation that I was coordinating or managing, or directing. I will tell you also, that when I was alerted by a—one of our people working on this project, that there was to be a shipment from a US airfield, not a military field, but a civilian field, I alerted the customs department and I alerted the FBI to it. We—we scrupulously avoided breaking any US law. We made every effort to comply, not only with Boland but with the Arms Export Control Act and what I thought were sanctions against solicitation. We made every effort to comply with the law.

MR. VAN CLEVE: Colonel North, I don't want to ask you to repeat your testimony of yesterday afternoon, but I believe that you did admit that the correspondence with Congress that you drafted together with Robert McFarlane in 1985 and 1986, was misleading.

LT. COL. NORTH: It was, indeed.

MR. VAN CLEVE: You've also admitted that you altered some of the documents in which you most clearly described your role and Mr. McFarlane's role in assisting the contras. Is that correct?

LT. COL. NORTH: I did.

MR. VAN CLEVE: I take it you intended to mislead the Congress?

LT. COL. NORTH: I did.

MR. VAN CLEVE: If you weren't violating the Boland Amendment why was it necessary?

LT. COL. NORTH: I want to—I want to first of all say that I am not justifying that either. I happen to have very high regard for Chairman Hamilton, and any of the things I have said about leaks from the Congress I did not mean to impugn Congressman Hamilton or Senator Inouye. What I was concerned about, and I think my superiors were concerned about, is the fact that we had lives at risk, we had a program at great risk. I do not believe that there ought to be circumstances in which people like myself have to make judgments over lives or lies. And as I advocated back in June a year ago, I think that we need to have some kind of process by which the Executive can, in and of itself, discreetly prepare to talk to discreet members of Congress about what should be done. We, after all, have to go to the Congress to get appropriated funds if we're to conduct covert operations as they are currently specified in the

National Security Act and Hughes-Ryan, and by Executive Order 12333. We have to come to the Congress to get those monies. What I am suggesting, gentlemen, is that the process has not worked. It has been indiscreet at both ends of Pennsylvania Avenue. And I am not justifying what I did, except to say to you that if I had divulged what I was doing, if Mr. McFarlane had divulged what I was doing, many, many lives were at stake.

MR. VAN CLEVE: I'd like to move on now to questions concerning the Iran initiative. And I'd like to begin by asking you some questions about terrorism, and the government's actions toward terrorism as background for your involvement in the Iran initiative itself.

Colonel North, can you define terrorism for us?

LT. COL. NORTH: We went through a great effort in the Vice President's Task Force to come up with a definition of terrorism. I have been described as a terrorist by people outside this country. It was written up that way in Izvestia, I believe.

Terrorism is, in itself, acts of violence or threats of violence perpetrated in such a way as to cause some kind of political outcome absent what one would consider to be an act of—a declaration of war. Most often those are acts of hostage-taking, or of brutality designed to influence the political process in a particular country. We see acts of terrorism, like the kidnapping of President Duarte's daughter designed to influence his policies toward the FNLM communist guerillas. You see acts of brutality in Europe at the Rome and Vienna airport perpetrated by Abu Nidal —the one who's threatened to kill me—designed to intimidate American tourists from traveling to Europe and even affect the economic situation and the willingness of Americans to feel that they can travel anywhere, as they should.

We have been blessed in this country that we have not seen the kind of terrorism that has been so rampant in the Middle East and in Europe. We have been blessed because, for whatever reason, even in the days of the late '60s and early '70s when there was great political dissension in this country, Americans, by their very nature, thank God, don't believe in those kinds of activities. And so even though there were groups of people who would like to have done more then they did, they were brought to justice and turned

294

in, most often, by plain old Americans who pick up the phone and call the police, or the FBI. We also have, I think, need to be concerned about the future and terrorism. We have, to this point, not had our schoolhouses captured by terrorists, as they have in the Netherlands, or trains stopped on the tracks or blown up or our powers stations disabled, like they are in El Salvador.

One of the trends that people ought to look at is the fact that there were more terrorist acts against Americans in this hemisphere in the last few years than there were in the Mideast. A dramatic change in trend, it is coming closer to home, and we need to be wary of that. We need to be concerned that if we don't find a way to address the terrorist threat at arms' distance, we'll be dealing with it when it's right in our face.

MR. VAN CLEVE: Would it be fair to say that terrorism uses means which we would usually define as criminal to achieve military or political ends? And, these means would include murder, kidnapping, theft and deception. Is that correct?

LT. COL. NORTH: Exactly.

MR. VAN CLEVE: What has been the general policy of the United States toward terrorism while you served on the NSC staff?

LT. COL. NORTH: Well, our general policy was to assist others in dealing with the problem, and to take active steps to neutralize terrorists where they were, to prevent the terrorist act, if you could, and to respond to a terrorist act, if it had already occurred.

MR. VAN CLEVE: Have United States government resources been increased or redirected to combat terrorism—

LT. COL. NORTH: Yes.

MR. VAN CLEVE: —during your tenure on the NSC? If so, how?

LT. COL. NORTH: Yes, there has been a significant increase in funding for first of all protective measures against terrorism, and second of all, to enable us to respond more effectively to a terrorist act, once it's started. And, basically, that's what you're left with when you get all done with it; if you can't convince those who sponsor terrorism to desist from their support, then you are left with either protecting yourself close in or in reaching out to prevent and deter the act or respond to it when it's happened. And, we have devoted considerably more resources to that end during the Reagan Administration than before, and with good reason, I believe.

MR. VAN CLEVE: Now, I want to ask you about two specific terrorist incidents, and I want to do that for the specific purpose of providing the committee with some background about developments prior to the beginning of the Iran initiative in roughly the middle of 1985. So, what I'd like to ask you to do is to briefly describe these circumstances for the committee, and then I'm going to have some very specific questions for you about some of these events.

Could you briefly describe for the committee, please, the TWA-847 hijacking, and take the committee through the hijacking, how it was handled by the government, and whatever cooperation our government sought from other governments during that hijacking?

LT. COL. NORTH: Well, I, um—Mr. Van Cleve, I want to do that in such a way that we don't injure sensitivities elsewhere, but very briefly when the TWA aircraft was hijacked, we immediately took steps to improve the security situation at the point where the aircraft was actually hijacked, that country's airports. We immediately took steps to see if we could in some way rescue the hostages. Perhaps, stop the aircraft at one of the points where it flitted back and forth across the Middle East. By the time the aircraft landed in Beirut, we had run basically out of options in between. We took a number of diplomatic initiatives with other countries, with the government of Lebanon and with those that we thought had influence over the captors. I would like to point out that the Shia fundamentalist terrorists who perpetrated that act are but a small portion of those kinds of people around the rest of the world. And I am not talking just about the Middle East, but I am talking about places like the Philippines and Indonesia and the Far East where Shia fundamentalists appear to have a certain allegiance, if not philosophically then politically, with the Iranian government. We took steps secretly, diplomatically, to see if there was something that could be done to achieve leverage with the captors, and it was a protracted ordeal. We did not get the cooperation that we had hoped for from

296

various Middle Eastern leaders. And ultimately, the solution was found in dealing with one of them, who acted to achieve the release of all but a handful. Right at the very end of it when there was only a small number of Americans still held separately, we intervened with another power—asked them to intervene with a senior Iranian official. They did so, and the hostages were all released. We were never able to gain direct access to the captors themselves. I think one of the things that's unfortunate is that we have somehow articulated a policy of no negotiations with terrorists. I never wrote a single directive for the President's signature, or a single memorandum for coordination within our government that had those words in it. We do not make concessions to terrorists. But we will talk to anybody, anywhere, anytime, anyplace, on any issue, and that is very important that it be articulated that way. And I don't think we should ever get ourselves in a position where we say, "We won't talk to you." There isn't a police force in this country—the FBI itself trains what they call hostage negotiators. We have experts at the Central Intelligence Agency, and one of them who I knew well flitted all over the globe everytime we had one of these circumstances occur in trying to establish a contact and a dialogue, and yes, a negotiation, without making concessions, and that's important. We should be willing to talk to anybody. We cannot have Americans blown off airplanes or blown up in airports just because somebody thinks we won't talk. We do have a policy of no concessions and we ought to, but we ought to be willing to talk.

MR. VAN CLEVE: You've confirmed part of the information that I had intended to try and illicit and I'm particularly interested in your comments with respect to the participation of the Iranian government. Is it fair to say that they were in fact significantly involved in resolving the TWA-847 hijacking?

LT. COL. NORTH: Yes.

MR. VAN CLEVE: It is also correct as has been reported that during that hijacking the United States and Israel reached a new level of—how would I guess I describe this?—cooperation in the mechanics of the hijacking? Is that a fair statement?

LT. COL. NORTH: Yes.

MR. VAN CLEVE: And is it fair to say that there was consideration given during that hijacking to joint either military or covert operations for the first time?

LT. COL. NORTH: Counsel, I'm uncertain as to how much further we should go on this issue—

MR. VAN CLEVE: Colonel North, I'm looking just for a yes or no answer.

LT. COL. NORTH: Yes.

MR. VAN CLEVE: Thank you. Now, that hijacking started on June 14th, 1985, and as the committee will know, that is approximately the same period of time during which the United States government and Israeli officials began to discuss the Iran initiative itself. Is that a fair statement?

LT. COL. NORTH: It is within that time frame.

MR. VAN CLEVE: The second operation that I wanted to ask you about in some detail, Colonel North, was the sea-jacking of the Achille Lauro which began, as I understand it, on the 7th of October, 1985, when shortly before nine o'clock in the morning, a group of Palestinians burst into the ship dining room, and began firing at the passengers in order to take over the ship. Is that correct?

LT. COL. NORTH: That is correct.

MR. VAN CLEVE: And could you take the narrative from there and just briefly describe the circumstances, again focussing on the diplomatic efforts that were made to deal with the situation and whatever steps our government took to resolve the matter?

LT. COL. NORTH: Well, again, without disclosing classified information, the terrorists shortly thereafter murdered Mr. Leon Klinghoffer, an American citizen. We became aware, through intelligence, that the ship was headed for a port. We importuned the government of that country not to let the ship.

VOICE: (off-mike) What about the cocaine dealing that the U.S. is paying for? Ask about the cocaine project. Ask about the main operation and (audio interruption). Why don't you ask how many non-combatants have been killed by the (inaudible) contras? Why don't you ask questions about drug deliveries? (Network audio interruption as demonstrators raise banner inscribed, "ASK ABOUT COCAINE, ASK ABOUT THE KILLING OF NON-COMBATANTS.")

CHAIRMAN INOUYE: We will stand in recess for ten minutes.

(The hearing recessed.)

CHAIRMAN INOUYE: The hearing will please come to order. I wish to advise the audience that this panel will not tolerate demonstrations. Before proceeding, I wish the records to be clear that the Committees do not believe that the White House or the National Security Council withheld any tapes or slides called for by our request. In fact, I understand that the White House did not have the tapes until a few days ago, and immediately provided access to us and Colonel North. Further, as soon as the counsel for the Colonel brought the slides to our attention, and we brought them to the attention of the National Security Council. The slides were later located by the White House, and we were called and notified of its location and access was immediately made. And in response to my request of this morning, the White House called and agreed to provide temporary custody of the slides to the Committee. Our staff will work out the details, and I wish to officially thank the National Security Council for its prompt response and cooperation. Furthermore, on May the 5th, 1987 at the opening session of these hearings, I said the following, and I believe this represents the official understanding of the members of the panel. Let it be clear that our concern in this inquiry is not with the merits of any particular policy, but with flawed policy making processes. Our hearings are neither pro-contra nor anti-contra. I would hope that in our questioning and in our responses we will keep that in mind. Mr. Van Cleve.

MR. VAN CLEVE: Thank you, Mr. Chairman. Colonel North, I believe that when the Committee recessed you had begun to describe the circumstances surrounding the seajacking of the Achille Laurel. Would you please proceed?

LT. COL. NORTH: As I recall, we had indications that the ship was to pull into a certain port. We, through a series of diplomatic overtures, importuned that country not to allow the ship to be received in the port, and it did not. It then proceeded on to Egypt. When the ship pulled into port, the initial indications were that the terrorists were allowed to immediately depart. We, however, had intelligence to the contrary and our special purpose forces in the region, initially headed home, were then returned to Cigonella as we found the aircraft with the terrorists aboard headed from Egypt to Libya. The aircraft was intercepted by the United States Navy, principally because we had some very, very real time intelligence. We knew the aircraft flight number, the path it was on, the tail number and practically everything that was in it. I would like to acknowledge that this could not have happened without Admiral Poindexter's very, very quick response; the assistance of Admiral Art Moreau, who at the time was the Special Assistant to the Chairman of the Joint Chiefs of Staff; or the very real courage of our special purpose unit that was on the ground just moments before the aircraft landed in Italy, and in particular, the leader of that group, Major General Steiner, who heroically, without firing a shot, apprehended the terrorists. They were turned over to Italian authorities, and all but one of them is jailed there now. The leader of the group, Abul Abbass, was allowed to leave the country; we made efforts to prevent that from happening, nonetheless, he did escape and we still seek him for the murder of an American citizen.

MR. VAN CLEVE: I have a couple of specific questions for you, Colonel North, about the manner in which the government responded to that seajacking. The first question is, did there come a time when the government relied on the assistance provided by another government in order to make sure that it could execute the tracking and force-down of the plane carrying the hijackers?

LT. COL. NORTH: Yes, it did. We could not have done this operation without the very, very real direct and immediate assistance of the government of Israel.

MR. VAN CLEVE: And is it also the case, Colonel North, that after the incident was essentially concluded, a member of the Senate Intelligence Committee inadvertently revealed to the press and to the public sensitive intelligence information in his possession?

LT. COL. NORTH: That is true.

MR. VAN CLEVE: And was that damaging to our security?

LT. COL. NORTH: It was.

MR. VAN CLEVE: Now I want to turn, Colonel North, to the Iran initiative itself, and I'd like to begin with some questions about the diversion of funds.

I'm advised that I'm still too close to the mike; I want to make sure that you can hear me, but I seem to have a problem with the TV technicians.

The—as described in Exhibit 1, the mechanism used for the creation of the diversion of funds to the contras, or the "residual", as you termed it, was that arms would be sold to Richard Secord, and then Richard Secord would sell them in turn to Iran, is that correct?

LT. COL. NORTH: That is correct.

MR. VAN CLEVE: Why was Richard Secord used as a middle man for these transactions?

LT. COL. NORTH: Well, we tried to establish a mirror image of what the Israelis had done in their earlier transactions, first of all. Second of all, we were trying to provide a plausible—plausibly deniable link directly back to the US government. And it was accepted that he could provide that kind of deniability. The effort was made, in other words, that the hand of the government of the United States was not showing in this action.

Are you talking about in the transaction itself—

MR. VAN CLEVE: Yes—

LT. COL. NORTH: —or are you talking about in the use of the residuals?

MR. VAN CLEVE: In the transaction itself.

LT. COL. NORTH: That is why he was put in that position.

MR. VAN CLEVE: Is it your testimony that no other individual could have fulfilled that role?

LT. COL. NORTH: Not at all. I mean, there's—if you wanted a plausibly deniable link, we could have used any number of people who were outside the US government. The fact is, he had been brought into this thing in November when I had basically sought him out for assistance in the Israeli Hawk transfer. And since he was already there, the decision was made to leave him in it, because he was now aware of something that was going on that was very, very sensitive. There's no point in broadening it further than we had to.

MR. VAN CLEVE: Now General Secord basically provided transportation services to the United States, is that correct?

LT. COL. NORTH: In which role that General Secord—

MR. VAN CLEVE: In his role as a middle man for the Iran arms transactions.

LT. COL. NORTH: Yes.

MR. VAN CLEVE: Wouldn't the commercially reasonable thing for the United States government to do have been to pay General Secord a fee for his transportation and leave it at that?

LT. COL. NORTH: I'm not—

MR. VAN CLEVE: Put it to you another way, Colonel North. Isn't that what the government would normally do when it wanted to move material from Point A to Point B, hire a mover, pay the mover's fee, and leave it at that?

LT. COL. NORTH: Well—

MR. VAN CLEVE: Why wasn't that done here?

LT. COL. NORTH: Well, this was a—this whole thing was being conducted with someone else's monies. There was no US government money involved in this activity. In fact, the US government made money in this transaction.

MR. VAN CLEVE: Okay. You testified yesterday that when you met, and I think this may have been for the first time, with Manucher Ghorbanifar in Europe, you expressed strong reservations to him about proceeding with the type of transaction that we've just described. And you told the Committee why you had those reservations. And you further told us that Ghorbanifar offered to make it worth your while to forget about those reservations, is that correct?

LT. COL. NORTH: That is correct. I want to correct one thing. I do not wish to leave that impression that was the first time I had met Mr. Ghorbanifar. I had met him on at least one other occasion when he was here in the United States.

MR. VAN CLEVE: Okay. I appreciate the correction. My question is, weren't you in a situation where you were trading off the achievement of the Iran arms initiative for the achievement of your goals for the support of the contras in accepting his offer to make it worth your while?

LT. COL. NORTH: I'm not sure I understand the question, counsel. When you say "trading off one for the other," my sense was that we were able to accomplish both. In other words, when the suggestion was made and I described it yesterday as what I consider to be a good idea, that we not only were going to achieve the strategic breakthrough with Iran—possibly end the Iran-Iraq War, get our hostages back—but we could also in that same instance find a way to support the Nicaraguan resistance. So I did not see it as one or the other—that we'd be able to do all of it.

MR. VAN CLEVE: What financial risks did Gen. Secord take in these transactions?

LT. COL. NORTH: Well, you'd have to ask Gen. Secord specifically, but there obviously was a risk that you could lose someone else's aircraft since we were using borrowed, uninsured airplanes. There was a requirement that we had to insure every aircraft that—what I call "self-insure," what Langley refers to as "self-insurance" —the expectation that the aircraft is lost, it belongs to someone else, it has to be paid for. That's just one example. There was obviously —death gratuities to pilots, who were Americans. Even though the aircraft belonged to other countries, the pilots were always American.

MR. VAN CLEVE: What would have happened if the weapons themselves had been lost in transit? Whose problem was that?

LT. COL. NORTH: Well, it was certainly, let us say, under the very worst of circumstances, the aircraft went down with everything aboard, and there were no survivors. It would have been the commercial entity which had actually done the charter work which was one of Gen. Secord's private commercial activities which would have had to defray all of those expenses.

MR. VAN CLEVE: Including the value of the weapons—i, that your testimony?

LT. COL. NORTH: Yes, because, furthermore, the weapons had already been paid for to the United States before we ever took possession. Or, before Gen. Secord ever took possession of a single part of TOW, the government was paid for those items.

MR. VAN CLEVE: What other financial, entrepreneurial risks did Gen. Secord bear in these transactions, if any?

LT. COL. NORTH: Well, when we say "these transactions," as I described yesterday, I initially involved Gen. Secord only in the Nicaraguan resistance. Then I asked him to further involve himself—

MR. VAN CLEVE: I can be more precise, Colonel. I'm happy to be more precise.

LT. COL. NORTH: Yes.

MR. VAN CLEVE: I mean, specifically the Iran arms sales

that occurred in February, May and October 1986, what other types of financial, entrepreneurial risks did Gen. Secord bear in those transactions, if any?

LT. COL. NORTH: Well, the companies that had been established, some of them had to be opened and closed or put back on the shelf. All of that cost money. We ended up buying a ship for the purpose of supporting this activity and several others. There were costs to be borne by, as I understand it—in dealing with the Iranians themselves. There were people who were accepting monies and asked for—I heard one of them ask specifically to Ghorbanifar that an account be established for him, an Iranian government official. And I know that those arrangements were being made for others.

MR. VAN CLEVE: Are we talking about substantial amounts of money?

LT. COL. NORTH: I do not know the amounts. I believe them to be substantial.

MR. VAN CLEVE: Any other risks that General Secord bore, financial, entrepreneurial risks in these transactions?

LT. COL. NORTH: Off the top of my head, I can't think of any right now.

MR. VAN CLEVE: In response to questions that Mr. Nields asked you yesterday, you described an extensive process of legal review that the United States govenment undertook between November 17th 1985 and January 17th 1986, in order to properly structure the Iran arms sales transactions. Is that correct?

LT. COL. NORTH: I'm not tracking completely, counsel. You're talking about between November—

MR. VAN CLEVE: 17th, '85, and January 17th, 1986. You described a process, and this is simply a predicate for the next question. You described a process in which there were extensive consultations between yourself, Department of Defense, the CIA, in an effort to make sure that the future sales, in fact, complied with the law.

LT. COL. NORTH: That is, indeed, correct.

MR. VAN CLEVE: Did it ever occur to you at the time that anyone might later suggest that since the weapons were United States weapons, the proceeds of the sales were United States funds?

LT. COL. NORTH: Never.

MR. VAN CLEVE: Never occurred to anyone involved in the planning of these transactions that that might be a problem?

LT. COL. NORTH: No, and, in fact, the specific indication that I had, counsel, was that the government of the United States would charge what it thought it was owed for those weapons, and somehow there may be a perception that I, somehow, influenced the price downward. That is not the case. Every effort was made to determine what the proper price should be, and when we discussed things this evening, we can talk about the status of some of those weapons, of what would have become of them otherwise, at least as I was told. And, it was not an issue of replacement value that was ever raised with me. That was never an issue. I was always told that here is the current cost, or current value of those weapons. That was passed to the Central Intelligence Agency, who in turn passed it to me. I passed it to General Secord, and that amount was transferred through whosoever account, whether it be Israeli, as I first thought it was, or Ghorbanifar, that it eventually to General Secord, and then to the CIA, and then to the Pentagon.

And so, no-one ever raised with me the suggestion that there was any more money due the US government.

MR. VAN CLEVE: Can you tell the committee whether or not you ever informed any of the people in the departments or agencies with whom you were dealing that, in fact, somebody would be collecting a whole lot more money for these weapons than the United States government was going to get?

LT. COL. NORTH: Well—

MR. VAN CLEVE: During that same period of time?

LT. COL. NORTH: Director Casey knew well, and I believe that anyone else who was in receipt of the intelligence at that point in time knew well. Admiral Poindexter knew well. I mean, they all knew that there were monies—the DOD charged $500 dollars for something that was eventually being sold to the Iranians for a thousand dollars, or whatever. Because there was a delta between the cost paid to the US government and the cost put into the fund which was eventually being used to support a whole range of covert operations.

MR. VAN CLEVE: Did anyone else other than the officials

305

of the Central Intelligence Agency have that same information, to your knowledge? Did the Department of Defense, for example, have that information?

LT. COL. NORTH: I do not know the distribution of that intelligence, and I am speaking specifically of the intelligence that you advised me on the other day. But there was a distribution outside just me and the CIA, I believe.

MR. VAN CLEVE: But my question was, did you ever tell an official of any other agency?

LT. COL. NORTH: No, I did not. I did not, that I recall.

MR. VAN CLEVE: And I take it, though, that your testimony is that the Central Intelligence Agency never suggested to you that there might be a question of ownership of any excess over what they were due?

LT. COL. NORTH: Never. I want to qualify that a little bit. Director Casey, in October of 1986, raised with me the thought that had been given to him by Mr. Furmark, that someone else was owed; and it was undetermined, at that point, who even owed that someone else. Several names were mentioned; among them Mr. Kashoggi, a man who I never met, contrary to press reports, I've never seen the man, nor do I think he has seen me. Nonetheless, it was suggested at that point in time that someone may have owed Mr. Kashoggi and others money. It was never suggested that money was owed to the government.

MR. VAN CLEVE: And to be specific about it, during the period November 17, 1985 to January 17, 1986, it is your testimony that subject was never brought up.

LT. COL. NORTH: That is correct. My recollection, at least.

MR. VAN CLEVE: I am going to try now, to ask you a series of relatively specific questions about the Iran initiative and I am going to try and do it pretty much in chronological order. The chronological order may not be entirely perfect, but I want to sort of walk you through some of these issues roughly in chronological order. As you, I think, have testified by now, the first channel relied on—for the Iran initiative—relied on the use of Manucher Gorbanifar as an intermediary. Is that correct?

LT. COL. NORTH: Mr. Van Cleve you are referring to—at the point in time I got involved in it, correct.

MR. VAN CLEVE: —and for some time thereafter.

LT. COL. NORTH: Yes.

MR. VAN CLEVE: Okay. Were you aware as of the middle or end of 1985 that Gorbanifar was a known liar who was the subject of a burn notice, or what is known in the trade as a burn notice, but what is actually a fabricator notice issued to the entire United States government by the Central Intelligence Agency?

LT. COL. NORTH: Yes, yes.

MR. VAN CLEVE: You did know that?

LT. COL. NORTH: We—and throughout, Mr. Van Cleve, I knew and so did the rest of us who were dealing with him, exactly what Mr. Gorbanifar was. I knew him to be a liar; I knew him to be a cheat, and I knew him to be a man making enormous sums of money. He was widely suspected to be, within the people I dealt with at the Central Intelligence Agency, an agent of the Israeli government or at least one of—if not more, of their security services.

That is important in understanding why we continue to deal with them. We knew what the man was, but it was difficult to get other people involved in these kinds of activities. I mean, one can't go to Mother Theresa and ask her to go to Tehran. And I am not being light about this but you have to deal with who you've got at the time. And the good fairy wasn't there.

And I know there's a lot of folks that think we shouldn't have dealt with this guy, but at the bottom we got two Americans out that way, and we started down a track that I think we could have succeeded on. As bad as he was, he at least got us started there.

MR. VAN CLEVE: I appreciate the answer. You got a little ahead of where I wanted to go. You also knew, did you, that Ghobanifar had failed the lie-detector test given to him by the CIA on all counts?

LT. COL. NORTH: Yes.

MR. VAN CLEVE: On all counts?

LT. COL. NORTH: Yes. On all counts to include his name, as I remember.

MR. VAN CLEVE: I understand. I guess my question is—you know, were you relying on the judgment of the Israelis in deciding to deal with Ghobanifar and those he represented?

LT. COL. NORTH: Yes.

MR. VAN CLEVE: Were you in that position because the

Israelis had intelligence sources and the United States did not?

LT. COL. NORTH: I think, perhaps we—

MR. VAN CLEVE: Without getting into detail here, is that the position our government was in at that point?

LT. COL. NORTH: Yes—

MR. VAN CLEVE: Relatively speaking?

LT. COL. NORTH: Yes.

MR. VAN CLEVE: Isn't it a fact that at least since the time of the Shah in late 1979, the US has had very poor quality human intelligence in Iran? Again, I'm looking for—

LT. COL. NORTH: Yes—

MR. VAN CLEVE: —what I think should be a yes or no answer. In retrospect, didn't this lack of intelligence adversely affect your ability to conduct this entire operation?

LT. COL. NORTH: Yes, and it was one of the principal objectives of the whole thing.

MR. VAN CLEVE: Colonel North, there has been testimony before the Committee that the interests of the United States and those of Israel in connection with Iran and specifically in connection with this initiative were not completely identical? Is that a correct statement?

LT. COL. NORTH: I do not believe that they were necessarily completely identical, but I think there was at least a congruence of objectives that was sufficient to justify us proceeding. There is no doubt that the ultimate Israeli objectives in the Iran/Iraq War may not be the same as ours. Our objective, at least as far as I was able to articulate it to my superiors, and as far as I understood my guidance in carrying out the dialogue that I pursued with the Iranians, was that we sought an end to that war. It may well be that the Israeli government would like to see the war go on, and I'm not saying that's necessarily what their policy is. There's certainly people in this country who felt that that was their objective. I believed that there was sufficient congruence between Israeli objectives and American objectives that made this project worthwhile, principally because we both saw the need to get to some faction within the Iranian government that would lead to a more moderate, more pro-Western government in Iran, if not immediately then over time. That is important for two reasons. If there is

308

absolute chaos in Iran when the Ayatollah Khomeini departs this veil of tears, then we have great expectations that the Soviets will take advantage of that situation. Second, Iranian-sponsored Fundamentalist Shiite terrorism is something that this world desperately needs to be concerned about. A few minutes before we had the interruption, I mentioned the fact that the Ayatollah's picture is not just up in Tehran or in the streets and back allies of Beirut. His picture is up in the Philippines and in Indonesia and in the Far East. This is a very serious long-term problem. And if we can get through a relationship with the Iranian government wherein Americans need not feel threatened —but not just Americans, but others as well—by Islamic fundamentalist terrorism, because we have a relationship with that theocracy that guides the country, then we will be far better off. And those were part of the broader strategic objectives in this whole initiative. And I believe that the Israelis and the Americans have a congruence of objective in that purpose.

MR. VAN CLEVE: Are there any other respects in which the interests of the United States and Israel differ with respect to the Iran initiative, other than what you've just testified to, to your knowledge?

LT. COL. NORTH: Well, clearly there were certainly people, and I don't pretend to be able to speak nor do I wish to speak for the Israeli government or their foreign policy, but there were clearly people in Israel who had objectives, for example, that were financial in dealing with the Iranians, and may well have had objectives in dealing with the neighboring governments that were not in consonance with us. Nonetheless, there was a basic, fundamental agreement between the United States and Israel on certain objectives.

MR. VAN CLEVE: How were these difference of interests taken into account by the United States government in conducting this operation?

LT. COL. NORTH: Well, I think I—to the extent that I was aware of them, I think I apprised my superiors of what those issues were. And on a number of occasions we sat down with representatives of the Israeli government—not just myself, but my superiors, both Admiral Poindexter and Bud McFarlane—and explained them to them. Said, "Look, you

309

may have this view, but we have that view, and if we can agree on something in the middle, we'll proceed." But it wasn't simply a matter that we ignored them.

MR. VAN CLEVE: But isn't your previous testimony pretty much to the effect that we were relying on the Israelis themselves as a principal source of our information about what was in fact going on?

LT. COL. NORTH: Yes, and that is one of the reasons why we sought so hard to establish direct contact with the Iranian government—US direct contact.

MR. VAN CLEVE: That was going to be my next question. I take it that a significant part of the reason for a move to a second channel was our concern about the accuracy of information we had in fact received from the first channel?

LT. COL. NORTH: Again, I happened to have developed over the course of the time that I was engaged in this, certainly from early January 1986 through the time I was reassigned, a very close relationship with a man that I have a great deal of respect for, and that is Mr. Amiram Nir, who, according to today's paper has been fired because of my testimony. If that is the case, I sadly regret it. He is a brave man who served his country well, and I believe tried to help us in carrying out our policies well. It was not that I had any distrust for Mr. Nir or the information that he gave me. Mr. Nir—if you can consider this, that the assessment of the Director of Central Intelligence was that the trip to Tehran was potentially a suicide mission, and an Israeli, not an American, but an Israeli government official had the intestinal fortitude to go on that trip, that, gentlemen, is to me, an indication of bravery. And I think the world of that young man. And if he has been fired because of my testimony, I regret it. There may have been differences of view between Mr. Nir and myself, and I articulated them to him and his superiors when I met with them. I articulated them to my own superiors. My own superiors met with him also, and his superiors. I think that there was a sufficient understanding that he knew we needed to have our own sources of intelligence, that couldn't be totally dependent upon Israel. And as close an ally as they have been—and we could not have done *Achille Lauro* without him, and the relationship that existed between he and I, and a number of other people—and I feel strongly about that. But were it not for the relationship that he and I had, there might have been even greater misunderstandings. Well, I don't think the government of Israel has any reluctance to understand that we needed to have our own sources inside Iran, too. And I don't think they object to that. I hope not.

MR. VAN CLEVE: I appreciate your testimony. And just so the record is clear, I take it that you are agreeing that part of the reason, a significant part of the reason for a move to a second channel, was our concern about our lack of intelligence information.

LT. COL. NORTH: Precisely. And I believe you'll find that in the records that I sent forward to my superiors.

MR. VAN CLEVE: I want to move a little bit in time from mid-1985 to that same period of time that we were talking about a few minutes ago. And that is, the period from November 1985 to January 1986. I have some questions about your prior testimony with respect to the participation of Attorney General Meese, in the planning that surrounded the January 17th, 1986 finding.

On Tuesday, you testified that you believed that Attorney General Meese became aware of the November 1985 Hawk shipment shortly after it occurred. Is that correct?

LT. COL. NORTH: No. I don't think that is correct.

MR. VAN CLEVE: Would you please—then I may have misunderstood. And I want the record to be very clear on this. When do you think that Attorney General Meese found out about the November 1985 Hawk shipment?

LT. COL. NORTH: It was my understanding, at the time, that Attorney General Meese became aware of the 1985 transactions at about the time we were preparing the first covert action finding.

MR. VAN CLEVE: Can you be as specific as possible, please?

LT. COL. NORTH: That finding was sent forward by Director Casey after being worked on by the general counsel at CIA, and myself, on or about the 26th of November, 1985. My understanding was that that finding was—either had been, or was then coordinated, with the Attorney General's office. And that we found a—one, clearance for a rationale of ratification; and that number two, we covered the issue of whether or not this was an appropriate way to handle the transaction. And the reason I—again, I—this may all be an assumption. Because I did not talk to the Attorney General about this issue, at that time.

MR. VAN CLEVE: From whom did you obtain your understanding about the Attorney General's participation in the preparation of that finding?

LT. COL. NORTH: Well—and it may all be heresay, but I—and it may just be imagination. But, every other finding that I worked on, and there were several, on this and other issues, I coordinated with the Attorney General. It was a routine thing to coordinate with the Attorney General. Number two, I was—I understood that the determination that we could indeed proceed in this direction, selling through a finding, selling arms through a finding had been obtained from the Attorney General, because he had it in his files from his predecessor, and number three, that the ratification kind of language had been approved by the Attorney General, and thus, I was not surprised, therefore, to see the finding signed later on.

MR. VAN CLEVE: So—

LT. COL. NORTH: What I'm saying is I do not have specific knowledge of what the Attorney General knew in November. I do have specific knowledge of what the Attorney General knew in January because I personally coordinated the second finding with he and Mr. Jenson.

MR. VAN CLEVE: Okay, before we get to the question of what the Attorney General knew in January, is it your testimony that you do not have any specific information at all about what the Attorney General in fact knew in November 1985, or between there and January about that November Hawk shipment?

LT. COL. NORTH: That is exactly correct, and that's what I thought I said when I testified the last time.

MR. VAN CLEVE: You may have, sir, and I simply wanted the record to be as clear as possible.

LT. COL. NORTH: Please make that very clear. I did not discuss this with the Attorney General until January.

MR. VAN CLEVE: Or, with anyone else who told you, I take it, that the Attorney General, in fact, knew about the November finding. Is that correct?

LT. COL. NORTH: Well, again, I—and, I'm not trying to pass the buck at all, Mr. Van Cleve. What I—I had come to an understanding that the finding which had two or three

312

critical elements in it, had indeed, because it was signed by the President, been cleared by the Attorney General. It was an established procedure. We had the former Attorney General's opinion that you could sell and the ratification language.

MR. VAN CLEVE: But, are you telling this Committee, sir, that some individual told you the Attorney General reviewed this finding, for example?

LT. COL. NORTH: No.

MR. VAN CLEVE: Okay. Now, I think I understand your testimony, sir.

LT. COL. NORTH: I'm not sure I understand that last answer, but I—I—no one specifically told me, "Ollie, the Attorney General of the United States has vetted off on this thing, and said it's approved." No one did.

MR. VAN CLEVE: In January, 1986, you say that you personally coordinated that finding with the Attorney General and Lowell Jenson, correct?:

LT. COL. NORTH: That is correct.

MR. VAN CLEVE: And, did you at that time tell the Attorney General about any of the prior arms shipments?

LT. COL. NORTH: Counsel, I have made an effort to try and remember exactly how that meeting went, and I have gone through the records I gave to you, and I do not find any reference to the fact that in the discussion with the Attorney General, that I specifically went over and said, "Oh, by the way, here's what happened in September. Here's what happened in November, and we're proceeding on from here with this new finding."

I do not recall that conversation. I do know that I met with he and I'm 99 percent sure it was Mr. Jenson who was also in the office, and we went over the 1986 finding. I may have gone back over to him when we made a minor modification to it after that although I don't seem to have an entry on that. I do not recall addressing the earlier shipments with him specifically.

MR. VAN CLEVE: Would there have been any reason, sir, for you to have discussed the previous shipments with him if what you were doing was seeking clearance for future shipments?

LT. COL. NORTH: Not specifically, but I do not recall myself being in a situation where I was trying to hide anything. So, it would not be inconsistent to discuss what had transpired and what was going to transpire, all under the provisions of covert action findings.

MR. VAN CLEVE: But, you don't recall any such discussion?

LT. COL. NORTH: I do not.

MR. VAN CLEVE: Colonel North, you say that you coordinated the other covert action findings with the Attorney General or his staff? Is that correct?

LT. COL. NORTH: When I say the other, I—I should—I can recall—

MR. VAN CLEVE: I didn't mean the other in the sense to be all inclusive. What I mean is there were other findings you worked on—

LT. COL. NORTH: Yes.

MR. VAN CLEVE: —and you've testified that you did coordinate them. Is that correct?

LT. COL. NORTH: Yes.

MR. VAN CLEVE: Are you aware of any requirement that that kind of coordination be done, or was that simply a matter of customary practice within the Administration?

LT. COL. NORTH: It was only required because my boss said, "Take that thing over and coordinate it with the Attorney General." I—

MR. VAN CLEVE: All right.

LT. COL. NORTH: There may be a written requirement that I'm not aware of.

MR. VAN CLEVE: Okay. If I recall your testimony correctly, you also testified that you believed the November 1985 finding was intended to cover the prior August/September Israeli shipment as well as the November Hawk shipment.

LT. COL. NORTH: Absolutely.

MR. VAN CLEVE: What is your basis for that testimony?

LT. COL. NORTH: Well, I mean—I was by then looking for a way to replenish the Israeli TOWs that had been shipped in September or August/September. I mean that was one of my principal "running around town trying to solve a problem" modes. And that was indeed the problem that —one of the problems I was trying to address. So that finding was designed to be able to one: Cover the fact that the CIA had indeed helped with the November shipment and was involved in—was going to have to be involved in getting them back—we knew that by then; and had indeed been—the government of the United States had been a party to the September shipment.

MR. VAN CLEVE: Now, Judge Sporkin was the principal drafter of that November finding, wasn't he?

LT. COL. NORTH: As I recall, yes.

MR. VAN CLEVE: Did you have a chance to review any of his testimony before the committee?

LT. COL. NORTH: I cannot say that I have, no.

MR. VAN CLEVE: I see. I believe—

LT. COL. NORTH: I have been provided with a summary of it, so—

MR. VAN CLEVE: I believe that it's accurate to say that Judge Sporkin testified that in drafting the November 1985 finding, he was not told about the prior August/September shipment of weapons. Are you aware of that, sir?

LT. COL. NORTH: I am not aware of that in his testimony, no.

MR. VAN CLEVE: Did you in dealing with Judge Sporkin on this finding ever tell him about the prior shipment?

LT. COL. NORTH: Would you repeat the question Counsel?

MR. VAN CLEVE: Let me break it up into parts so that it's as clear as possible. Did you ever discuss the November 1985 finding with Judge Sporkin at that time?

LT. COL. NORTH: Oh yes.

MR. VAN CLEVE: And did you ever tell Judge Sporkin that there had in fact been an August/September shipment of Israeli TOWs?

LT. COL. NORTH: I do not recall a specific discussion. But, I mean, it was widely known within the CIA. I mean, we were tracking that sensitive intelligence. I—I honestly don't recall, Mr. Van Cleve. I mean it—it didn't seem to me, at the time, that it's something that I was trying to hide from anybody. I was not engaged in it. And, one of the purposes that I thought we had that finding for was to go back and ratify that earlier action, and to get on with replenishing. I mean, that was one—what I understood one of the purposes of that draft finding to be.

MR. VAN CLEVE: And did you communicate your desire to have that purpose included in the finding, to Judge Sporkin?

LT. COL. NORTH: I honestly don't recall. But I clearly saw that the finding fulfilled that purpose. At least, that's how I read it. Again, I'm not trying to say that—if Judge Sporkin says I didn't talk to him about it, I'm not—I don't want to argue with that. I can't imagine that I would have tried to conceal it from him. And by then, certainly, the Director knew about it. Many other people at the CIA knew about it, because they were the ones who helped set up the intelligence collection on it.

MR. VAN CLEVE: I'd like to turn to the subject of weapons replenishment. One of the issues of concern to the Committee, Col. North, is how the arms sales transactions were actually carried out. In particular, your testimony on Monday indicated that there was substantial uncertainty about the terms on which the replenishment of the Israeli weapons was to occur. Is that correct?

LT. COL. NORTH: Yes. It was presented to me one way by the Israelis, and then when I went back to—not even knowing that this problem existed in November, managed to get Mr. McFarlane, who was in the process of getting ready to leave the NSC. His explanation was not consistent with what the Israelis told me they understood, from at least his commitment to them. To this day I don't know—I was not part of that dialogue. But it was very clear to me that the Israelis expected a replenishment. Initially, they expected that it would be free—at least, that's how it was communicated to me. And when I told them that that was out of the question, it was Mr. Nir who, I think, had the ingenious idea of using residuals to pay for it.

MR. VAN CLEVE: Is it a fact that, during the November 1985 to late January 1986 period, extensive consideration was given to upgrading Israeli weapons stocks by providing the Israelis with newer or better weapons than the ones they had shipped to Iran?

LT. COL. NORTH: There was some discussion of that. The bottom line of that—I mean, there were—and what you need to understand is, there was—there were proposals for everything in the world, not just from the Iranians, but from all kinds of people, many of which were impractical or unworkable or impossible. And what we had finally arrived at, is that we would try to—and I think we did—replenish the Israelis with weapons that were identical to the ones that they had shipped. And second of all, of the same era of manufacture, and I think there was a safety feature added to the new ones that we didn't even charge for. And maybe the ones that they'd shipped had the safety feature too, I don't recall. But the bottom line was, we agreed, the Israelis and us, that we would replenish them with items similar and as identical as possible to the ones that they had shipped.

MR. VAN CLEVE: So I take it your testimony is that, in fact, we never did replenish by providing the Israelis with newer or better weapons then the ones they had shipped, is that right?

LT. COL. NORTH: We did not. In fact, the first time we tried the replenishment, we ended up, even though I had asked for newer weapons then the ones that we were sending to the Iranians, they sent older weapons to the Israelis, for whatever reason. And we went back through—and we had to take them back out of the Israeli stocks and send them on, and finally got, I think it was in May or October, the proper dates to replace the Israeli weapons. And as a soldier, I understand that, and I understand why the Israeli Defense Ministry insisted on that, and I think it was proper that they do so.

MR. VAN CLEVE: All of the replenishments occurred during 1986, correct?

LT. COL. NORTH: Yes.

MR. VAN CLEVE: Was replenishment ever done in 1986 at concessionary prices? That is, at prices below which Israel would otherwise have had to pay for the same weapons?

LT. COL. NORTH: Not to my knowledge. And I say "not to my knowledge" because I'm not the one that priced the weapons. The Israelis could no longer buy from the United States that—if the Israelis, through the Foreign Military Sales Program, came to us to buy a TOW weapon today, they would end up buying a TOW II, or TOW II PIP, or whatever the most current version being produced by the US vendor was.

MR. VAN CLEVE: Right.

LT. COL. NORTH: They don't normally buy out of US stocks except under emergency authorities like we did in '73. And so, and I'm going to guess at numbers, the current model that they would get from the producer, the defense contractor, might be $10,000, but the product they got from the United States was at the price established by the United States. In other words, we were not charging a preferential price just because it was Israel. We charged the price for those weapons at that date based on what the DOD estimated the price to be, I believe. I was not in the Pentagon pricing it and I wasn't down in the arsenal we took them from.

MR. VAN CLEVE: But you never asked, I take it, that the Defense Department give the Israelis a better deal then they otherwise would have been given if they had purchased the same weapons?

LT. COL. NORTH: No.

MR. VAN CLEVE: Michael Ledeen served as a principal intermediary between the United States and the Israeli government with respect to Iran during 1985, is that correct?

LT. COL. NORTH: That is correct.

MR. VAN CLEVE: Can you tell this Committee why Mr. Ledeen was chosen for this role?

LT. COL. NORTH: I can not, because it was done, as I understand it, by Mr. McFarlane, and I would have to defer to Mr. McFarlane as to why. I would like to get something on the record, if I may, Mr. Chairman, and that is that there was an indication that I had accused Mr. Ledeen of making money on the transactions in 1985. I want it noted, and you have it in my records that that information was provided to me by two foreigners who had made that allegation. Now, I know many of the allegations made against me are untrue. I know them to be, and I hope you know at least some of the ones that have been made about me are untrue, and when I asked that question to Mr. McFarlane, I did not expect that it would come out in this committee hearing; I did not expect that it would be the subject of debate. Mr. Ledeen assured me when I asked him that question that he had not made money on it. I have no reason to believe that what the Iranians told me, or that one of the Israelis told me is necessarily true. I do not want it noted by the committee record that I have accused Mr. Ledeen of making money on the transaction. I do not know if he did. And, I do not know if he didn't. When he told me he didn't, I believed him.

MR. VAN CLEVE: Do you have any evidence that Mr. Ledeen was paid by the Israeli government?

LT. COL. NORTH: I have none.

MR. VAN CLEVE: I have some questions about the Teheran

318

trip, Colonel North. One of the unanswered questions for the committee is the nature of the agreement, the precise nature of the agreement between the United States and Iran, leading up to the May 1986 meetings in Teheran. My first question is, did the United States agree, to your knowledge, to bring a specified percentage or quantity of Hawk spare parts to Teheran, such as 50%?

LT. COL. NORTH: No. The governing factor in the trip to Teheran that I went on in May was what the aircraft would handle, and I'm not talking about the aircraft we were on. I'm talking about the aircraft that was going to come, once we were there. And, it was necessary by virtue of fuel load, weight and space that some of the stocks had to come with us, and that was made known to my superiors, and everybody on the aircraft knew that those supplies were aboard the aircraft because the pallette of supplies was directly behind the seats in the Israeli 707. You had to trip over it to go to the "head", and I recognized that some people may have said they didn't know they were on the airplane, but that wasn't dogfood. They were Hawk parts.

MR. VAN CLEVE: Did the Iranians, to your knowledge, ever agree that all of the hostages would be released prior to or on Mr. McFarlane's arrival in Teheran?

LT. COL. NORTH: It turns out that the Iranians did not. Manucher Ghorbanifar told us that they had agreed to that, and what had happened is we had gone too far down the line with Ghorbanifar. What was his—his process, if you will, was to tell the Iranians one thing and tell us another, then let the two sides sit down and duke it out. Well, as I said, we knew Ghorbanifar for what he was. We did not know of the letters that he had sent to Teheran committing us to certain things until after we got there.

When we exchanged letters face to face with the Iranians in Teheran, it was very obvious that he had lied to both sides. And we knew that he did this, but we didn't know that the lie was quite so blatant. We had expectations from him communicated to us directly and through the Israelis that that would be the outcome if things went well in Teheran. We did not know all of the expectations of the Iranians as to what it would take to make things go well. And thus, when we got there, both sides were surprised at the intransigence of the other side's opinions. And that is why I had

319

advocated—despite the risks, despite the deep concern of Director Casey that information about a very covert program would be revealed if I went on the trip and were tortured—despite all of that, I was a proponent of the advance party trip because I knew Ghorbanifar to be what he was. I knew he was a duplicitous sneak, and I thought that we could do better by General Secord and I going to Teheran. It was that trip—the advance trip—that resulted in Director Casey saying, "I'm not going to allow you to go because of the project that you are involved in unless you are prepared to deny that information under torture." And he was very concerned about that. Now, I think it was an error on our part not to have the advance trip. I'm not saying that the May trip would have necessarily gone better. I'm not blaming anybody for the fact we didn't bring any hostages out or end up with a strategic treaty with Iran. What I'm saying is I think it was an error not to have gone on that trip. I think that opinion is shared by some of the experts on Iran who participated to include Mr. Cave.

MR. VAN CLEVE: So, is it your testimony that Mr. McFarlane's understanding as to the conditions under which the hostages were to be released was based on assurances that you'd received from Ghorbanifar?

LT. COL. NORTH: And the Israelis, and I think they got theirs from him. I'm not blaming them. I'm just saying that's how we got them, yes.

MR. VAN CLEVE: The Committee has heard testimony that on one of the last nights during which the Delegation was in Teheran, while Mr. McFarlane was asleep, a decision was made to allow the second plane containing the remainder of the Hawks spare parts to leave Israel and begin its flight to Teheran. Is that correct?

LT. COL. NORTH: I don't know what the Committee's heard. But let me just tell you about that last night because I was there. Okay? It was the plan consistent throughout that that aircraft which was based at an Israeli Air Force base would have to launch by a certain time of day in order to get to Teheran. It was always the plan that the aircraft would be turned around at what we call the fail-safe or turnaround point wherein if it went beyond that it had to go all the way into Teheran because it would run out of fuel before it got back. It was always a part of the plan. It was in the op plan

320

that I wrote up for this entire thing, and it all proceeded accordingly. And thus at 6:00 o'clock in the morning when Mr. McFarlane got up, I told him, "In accord with the plan, the airplane is two hours from turnaround point." And we allowed the meeting to go on for a little bit longer to see if we were going to prosper, and then both of us reluctantly agreed to turn the plane around. I don't know—there were many other people who were there. There was a CIA communicator. The communications were being monitored in Tel Aviv and in Washington. Everybody knew what was going on with that airplane. It wasn't some secret Ollie North, in the middle of the night, flying off on his own hook. Ollie North didn't do that, and I don't know why the Committee was left to that impression. You'd have to ask others. But there were others who were there that know that this entire plan was already in the op plan, fully briefed, and that's just exactly the way it went. In a very calm and moderate and reasoned way, we decided that we would turn the airplane around, in accordance with the plan that we had all worked on.

MR. VAN CLEVE: Your testimony is that you'd been specifically authorized in advance to make that decision while Mr. McFarlane was asleep, is that correct?

LT. COL. NORTH: I didn't even have to make a decision. The plane launched in accord with the previously established schedule. I don't even recall that we even confirmed it, except that I got the call from the command center in Tel Aviv—"The airplane is up, it made it off the ground, it didn't crash with that fuel on board." It had to launch in the early morning or midnight hours because the heat and the air temperature and all the rest of that stuff that makes airplanes fly.

MR. VAN CLEVE: Col. North, in November 1986 or thereabouts, after the press began disclosures concerning the Iran matter, did there come a time when you received a phone call from a representative of a very high Israeli government official who expressed concern about the public position of the United States on disclosing the McFarlane trip to Teheran?

LT. COL. NORTH: I'm—my memory is not clear on that. Would you repeat the question, Counsel?

MR. VAN CLEVE: I'd be happy to. In November 1986, after

321

the press disclosures began concerning the Iran operation, did there come a time when you received a phone call from a representative of a very high Israeli government official who expressed concern about the public position of the United States on disclosing the fact of the McFarlane trip to Teheran?

LT. COL. NORTH: I believe I did, yes.

MR. VAN CLEVE: And what did that individual advise you should be the position of the President of the United States?

LT. COL. NORTH: Well, if my recollection serves me right, we agreed to stay with "no comments."

MR. VAN CLEVE: Isn't it a fact this individual advised you that the President should flatly deny that the McFarlane trip to Teheran ever occurred?

LT. COL. NORTH: Well, I'm going to have to—I'd have to go back and look at my contemporaneous notes. That sounds correct, but I don't want to—I honestly don't remember those days all that clearly without being able to refer to that, counsel. I mean, you may be looking at something that I—I don't recall—I'm trying to remember from the work product I've tried to assemble on those latter days. There were a number of calls, day and night, at that point in time. Our principle focus, I do remember vividly, was to keep the second channel alive and get as many hostages out as we could before it all came crashing down.

MR. VAN CLEVE: Would you like to take a moment and think about this specific question, to see whether or not you can recollect—

LT. COL. NORTH: As I recall, your question is, did a high-level Israeli official call and tell me that their advice was to deny the McFarlane trip?

MR. VAN CLEVE: That the President should flatly deny that the McFarlane trip ever occurred.

LT. COL. NORTH: Counsel, I will try to do more research over lunch, if you like. I do not recall specifically this particular matter. I do recall a number of—probably several a day phone calls at that point.

MR. VAN CLEVE: I understand. I think the Committee would appreciate it, if you would try and recall over lunch. And if you want to make an additional answer for the record later, we'd be happy to have it.

LT. COL. NORTH: Very well. Do you have anything that will help me? I mean, you've got all my stuff.

MR. VAN CLEVE: I do not have a specific document, Col. North. And, if I did, I certainly would have provided it to you and your counsel for your examination.

LT. COL. NORTH: Understood.

MR. VAN CLEVE: Colonel North, previously you testified that a decision was made in late November 1986, that the United States would disassociate itself from the 1985 arms shipments made by Israel in the chronologies prepared in 1986. Is that correct?

LT. COL. NORTH: That is correct.

MR. VAN CLEVE: Did you ever discuss with Mr. McFarlane or Admiral Poindexter the political effects of this decision to portray Israel as having acted on its own?

LT. COL. NORTH: I don't recall that particular aspect of it. I do know that it seemed to me that their was a reason to do so. And my reasons, as I have indicated earlier in the testimony, were—are already on the record.

MR. VAN CLEVE: That's correct. And my question was, thought, did you discuss the political ramifications of that decision with either Admiral Poindexter or Mr. McFarlane. I do not recall the conversation, Counsel, but I am sure that I did. I mean, it was one of those things that would have been very vivid to me. And I can't imaging I would have ignored it.

MR. VAN CLEVE: I understand. And was there any discussion of this decision with Israeli officials?

LT. COL. NORTH: No. The Israelis, to my recollection, were—and that's why I had a hard time with your earlier question. The Israelis were going to try to stick with no comment. And as you have seen in my contemporaneous notes, there were calls to that effect right off from the start. And it was one of the things that was written up in one of the initial notes I sent up when the whole activity started. And I think they sincerely hoped we'd be able to do that. I sincerely hoped we would be able to do that.

MR. VAN CLEVE: But did anyone call them up and say, "Listen we're thinking about leaving you out on a limb here. How do you feel about that?"

LT. COL. NORTH: I do not know whether those versions

were communicated with the Israelis or not. We did, at that point in time, have a secure communications means that was outside the normal diplomatic communications. And I was able to communicate with Mr. Nir, but I do not recall specifically addressing that with him.

MR. VAN CLEVE: The chronologies themselves did specifically acknowledge that the United States had, in fact, dealt with the government of Iran. Didn't they?

LT. COL. NORTH: Oh, absolutely.

MR. VAN CLEVE: Would you explain to the committee why you felt that a revelation of the 1985 transactions, which the Iranians themselves probably knew had US support, was likely to jeopardize the lives of the hostages and the second channel?

LT. COL. NORTH: Yes. Because we had gone to—the way it was presented to me, and what we were seeing in intelligence, was that they were very, very upset about what they perceived to be a double-cross in November with the Hawks. It is my understanding, and of course we have a hostage here to show for it, that they were pleased with what they got in the August/September transaction before I became operationally engaged in this. The November shipment was a disaster. It was very clear from the intelligence that we were seeing. And we made great efforts in every meeting with the Iranians both in the first and the second channel, to tell them very clearly, "That's not what happens when you deal with us." Well, in fact, we had been associated with that second delivery—the Hawk transaction in November. It was done with the assistance of the CIA's proprietary, General Secord, who jumped into it to make it work and me. And so, we—I—my concern was that there was—the duplicity to which we had worked with the Iranians, in denying any association with that second shipment would work to the detriment of the hostages, that the second channel, whom we had assured, brought here to the United States, as you know, taken through a tour of the White House, just like my family has been taken through a tour of the White House, coddled and coached, and encouraged, would indeed find themselves all dead somewhere. And, so my principal concern was the hostages and the second channel.

There may well have been other concerns about that

November shipment that I am not aware of. I did not then, nor do I now see a legal flaw in what we attempted to do. I do see that the protracted period of time, particularly the first finding which demonstrates it is solely arms for hostages, is a politically damaging position for the President. It is also internationally damaging for this administration and this country, and thus when it came time for us to be talking about that earlier transaction, there may have been people who were looking beyond my immediate concerns for the hostages and the second channel, and that relationship to the domestic and international political repercussions on beyond to look at some other legal flaw that I am unaware of.

For many different reasons, therefore, it may have been deemed prudent to change those chronologies. I have given you my reasons. I cannot explain the reasons for others.

MR. VAN CLEVE: Colonel North, I have the, what I regard is the personal and painful task of asking you the following questions: You've admitted before this committee that you lied to representatives of the Iranians in order to try and release the hostages. Is that correct?

LT. COL. NORTH: I lied everytime I met the Iranians.

MR. VAN CLEVE: And, you've admitted that you lied to General Secord with respect to conversations that you supposedly had with the President? Is that correct?

LT. COL. NORTH: In order to encourage him to stay with the project, yes.

MR. VAN CLEVE: And, you've admitted that you lied to the Congress. Is that correct?

LT. COL. NORTH: I have.

MR. VAN CLEVE: And, you admitted that you lied in creating false chronologies of these events. Is that correct?

LT. COL. NORTH: That is true.

MR. VAN CLEVE: And you've admitted that you created false documents that were intended to mislead investigators with respect to a gift that was made to you. Is that correct?

(Long pause)

LT. COL. NORTH: No.

MR. VAN CLEVE: I think I understand the reason for your hesitation. You certainly have admitted that the documents themselves were completely false. Is that correct?

LT. COL. NORTH: That is correct.

MR. VAN CLEVE: And, they were intended to create a record of an event that never occurred. Is that correct?

LT. COL. NORTH: That is correct.

MR. VAN CLEVE: Can you assure this committee that you are not here now lying to protect your Commander in Chief?

LT. COL. NORTH: I am not lying to protect anybody, counsel. I came here to tell the truth. I told you that I was going to tell it to you, the good, the bad, and the ugly. Some of it has been ugly for me. I don't know how many other witnesses have gone through the ordeal that I have before arriving here and seeing their names smeared all over the newspapers, and by some members of this committee, but I committed when I raised my right hand and took an oath as a midshipman that I would tell the truth, and I took an oath when I arrived here before this committee to tell the truth, and I have done so, painful though it may be for me and for others. I have told you the truth, counsel, as best I am able.

MR. VAN CLEVE: I have no further questions for this witness, Mr. Chairman.

CHAIRMAN INOUYE: Thank you very much. When we resume our hearings at 2:00, Mr. Arthur Liman will continue the questioning. We'll stand in recess until 2:00 P.M.

END OF MORNING SESSION

Afternoon Session—2:00 P.M.

CHAIRMAN INOUYE: The hearings will please come to order. Before proceeding, may I advise the guests that the chair will not tolerate any demonstrations. Mr. Liman.

ARTHUR LIMAN (SENATE CHIEF COUNSEL): May I proceed? Good afternoon, Colonel.

LT. COL. NORTH: Counsel.

MR. LIMAN: Colonel, is it fair to say that November 25, 1986, was one of the worst days in your life?

(Pause while North confers with counsel)

MR. LIMAN: I wasn't asking whether it was one of the worst days in Mr. Sullivan's life. (Laughter in room)

LT. COL. NORTH: I didn't meet him till the next day.

I will tell you honestly, counsel, that I have had many

worst days than that. Most of those were days when young Marines died, and there have been days since then that are worse in some respects. I would not recount the last three days that I have been here as being particularly pleasant. It was a difficult day.

MR. LIMAN: On the preceding day, you had offered your resignation to Admiral Poindexter?

LT. COL. NORTH: My recollection, counsel, is that I first tendered it on Friday before I met with the Attorney General. We had talked about it several times prior to that. And I retransmitted it, as I recollect, either Sunday or Monday.

MR. LIMAN: And you retransmitted it the preceding day in a PROF note that expressed your prayer that the President is not further damaged by what has transpired?

LT. COL. NORTH: I don't recall the exact words of the PROF note, or the actual transmission of the message. It was a deeply personal communication between myself and a man for whom I had and still have a great deal of respect, Admiral Poindexter.

MR. LIMAN: And then on the 25th, you learned from the press conference that you had been fired. Is that fair to say?

LT. COL. NORTH: I believe that the words that were used was that I had been dismissed.

MR. LIMAN: And, to use those words, if you'd prefer, you had been dismissed by a President whom you had served with dedication for some five years?

LT. COL. NORTH: Five and a half. Five and a half years.

MR. LIMAN: And, you learned at that press conference that you were the subject of a criminal investigation that was being initiated for an action, the diversion, which had been approved by your superior Admiral Poindexter, and had been described in some 5 memoranda that you sent to Admiral Poindexter for approval by the President. Is that fair to say?

LT. COL. NORTH: Well, I, I don't want to characterize anyone's reasons for doing—

MR. LIMAN: I didn't ask you—

LT. COL. NORTH: —they did.

MR. LIMAN: —but you learned that you are the subject of a criminal investigation in that press conference.

LT. COL. NORTH: That is correct.

MR. LIMAN: And, you learned that it was a criminal investigation relating to the diversion, or what we call the diversion, the use of the profits of the Iranian arms sale to support the contras. You learned that, correct?

LT. COL. NORTH: That is correct.

MR. LIMAN: And, that was action that you took that had been authorized. Correct?

LT. COL. NORTH: It is action that I took that I believed I had the full authority to take. That is correct.

MR. LIMAN: Well, it had actually been authorized by Admiral Poindexter. Is that not so?

LT. COL. NORTH: Yes.

MR. LIMAN: He had communicated his approval to you. Correct?

LT. COL. NORTH: Yes, he had.

MR. LIMAN: You seem to be hesitating. Is there any doubt in your mind?

MR. SULLIVAN: He's just looking for tricks, Mr. Liman.

MR. LIMAN: Well, I can assure you,—

MR. SULLIVAN: He testified—

MR. LIMAN: —I have none in my—

MR. SULLIVAN: He testified fully about these matters.

(Gavel bangs.)

MR. SULLIVAN: Mr. Chairman, excuse me, Mr. Chairman. He's testified fully about these matters. I thought we'd be on to some new important subject by now.

CHAIRMAN INOUYE: Please proceed.

MR. LIMAN: Was it approved by him?

LT. COL. NORTH: The actions that I took, all of them, to include the use of residual funds from the sale of arms to Iran to support the Nicaraguan resistance and other activities were approved. All of them.

MR. LIMAN: And, is it also so that for some months you had been telling friends like Mr. Owen that you were going to be the fallguy?

LT. COL. NORTH: I may well have, as I believe I have already testified. I may well have told Mr. Owen and perhaps others that if this whole thing came down to creating a political controversy, or embarrassment, and remember again that Mr. Owen did not know, I don't believe, anything about the Iranian initiative, that I would

328

be the person who would be dismissed or reassigned or fired or blamed or fingered or whatever one wants to use as a description. That I was willing to serve in that capacity. All of that assumed that this was not going to be a matter of criminal behavior, but rather one of deniability for the White House, for the Administration, or whatever, for political purposes. And when I say "political purposes" I'm speaking of not only domestic, but the international ramifications. That is one of the essences of plausible deniability in a covert operation.

MR. LIMAN: Are you saying, Colonel, that you were prepared to take the rap for political purposes, but not for criminal purposes?

LT. COL. NORTH: Precisely.

MR. LIMAN: Is that what I just heard? Precisely. And is it a fact that on November 21, after meeting with Admiral Poindexter, you told your colleague, Colonel Earl that you were going to be the scapegoat?

LT. COL. NORTH: I don't recall that specific conversation on the first, I don't believe, with Colonel Earl.

MR. LIMAN: Twenty-first, that's Friday.

LT. COL. NORTH: I may have. I don't deny that I said that to him.

MR. LIMAN: Did you use the term "scapegoat?"

LT. COL. NORTH: I don't recall, counsel, I may have.

MR. LIMAN: All right. Well, scapegoat means someone who is going to take the blame for others. For whom did you expect to take the blame?

MR. SULLIVAN: Objection. He said he didn't recall whether he used "scapegoat."

MR. LIMAN: Well, yesterday you said that when the time came, you were going to be dropped like a hot rock, that you were going to be the deniable link, and I think you also used terms like scapegoat. For whom were you going to be the scapegoat?

LT. COL. NORTH: For whoever necessary; for the administration, for the President, for however high up the chain that they needed someone to say, "That's the guy that did it, and he's gone. And now we've put that behind us and let's get on with other things."

MR. LIMAN: And did you tell Admiral Poindexter that you were prepared to play that role?

329

LT. COL. NORTH: I had told Admiral Poindexter that and I had told Mr. McFarlane that as early as 1984.

MR. LIMAN: Had you told Mr. Casey that?

LT. COL. NORTH: I think it may well have been his idea to begin with that there had to be somebody who was going to stand up and take the rap for this.

MR. LIMAN: And "this" means what, sir?

LT. COL. NORTH: Well, starting in 1984, for the political or international consequences of what we began to call the support for the Nicaraguan democratic resistance.

MR. LIMAN: And after that became involved, linked with the Iranian arms sale and the proceeds? You were the person who was going to take the rap for that, too?

LT. COL. NORTH: I saw no difference from one to the other.

MR. LIMAN: And you were prepared to do that?

LT. COL. NORTH: I have testified to that.

MR. LIMAN: Now, Admiral Poindexter, who is your superior and who had approved this, was not dismissed. Am I correct?

LT. COL. NORTH: Counsel, I don't recall the exact words that were used in that press conference.

MR. LIMAN: Do you remember that he was treated differently, Colonel?

LT. COL. NORTH: Admirals should be treated differently than Lieutenant Colonels.

MR. LIMAN: Well, do you remember that he was allowed to resign and be transfered with honor?

LT. COL. NORTH: I don't recall those words specifically, but it that what it was said in the press conference, I assume that's what it was.

MR. LIMAN: Do you recall at the press conference the Attorney General indicated that Admiral Poindexter's problem was that he had gotten some indication of the diversion and had looked the other way—words to that effect?

LT. COL. NORTH: I do not.

MR. LIMAN: Do you remember, sir, that as you listened to the press conference that the Attorney General said nothing about the fact that Admiral Poindexter said nothing about the fact that Admiral Poindexter had approved the diversion.

330

LT. COL. NORTH: Quite frankly, Counsel, I don't remember a great deal about that press conference.

MR. LIMAN: Well, I can, but I'll move on because I don't want to carry on that. On the 21st you did, in fact, discuss with Admiral Poindexter the problem of the diversion. Is that so? I'll tell you—you're looking at a book there. What is the book, sir?

LT. COL. NORTH: The book is made up of notes that I have made in trying to prepare with counsel for this hearing.

MR. LIMAN: And—

LT. COL. NORTH: It includes

MR. SULLIVAN: Don't tell him what it includes.

MR. LIMAN: Well, I think that if a witness is looking at something that I, as counsel, am entitled to see what he's refreshing his recollection on.

MR. SULLIVAN: I think you're wrong. That's a product of lawyers working with clients.

MR. LIMAN: And you think that a witness is entitled to read something and that we're not entitled to see what he is reading?

MR. SULLIVAN: He is entitled to use his notes and to preserve the attorney/client privilege. Everything in that book is a product of the attorney/client and work product privilege, Mr. Liman. And you know that.

MR. LIMAN: Are you able to recall your conversation with Admiral Poindexter on the 21st about the diversion without looking at that book?

MR. SULLIVAN: That's none of your business either. You just ask him the questions.

CHAIRMAN INOUYE: Please address the Chair.

MR. SULLIVAN: Mr. Chairman, let's get—let's get to the substance of these hearings and stop trying—get off his back!

CHAIRMAN INOUYE: We have a peer system here. You need not shout, sir.

MR. SULLIVAN: Just—Mr.—

CHAIRMAN INOUYE: Please proceed.

LT. COL. NORTH: Counsel I would—

MR. SULLIVAN: Don't answer the question. Next question, Mr. Chairman—it won't be answered!

MR. LIMAN: Lieutenant, do you recall testifying as recently as yesterday and the day before that on the 21st of

November you told Admiral Poindexter that you had gotten rid of all memos relating to the diversion.

MR. SULLIVAN: May we see the transcript that you're referring to. If you're trying to impeach him with yesterday's transcipt, I want the page and the line, please, Mr. Chairman. That's the only fair way to do it.

MR. LIMAN: Mr. Chairman, if he recalls, I'm entitled to have his answer.

CHAIRMAN INOUYE: Please answer.

LT. COL. NORTH: Counsel, first of all, I'm a lieutenant colonel. I have been a lieutenant colonel for a couple of years now. Second, the sole reason for me to consult, with anything, is for the purpose of trying to give you a more accurate answer. And I have been asked questions that covered five and a half years of work, many of the days in which were non-stop. I am trying to give you honest, straightforward, and factual and complete answers.

And now that you have refreshed what I said the other day, yes I do recall speaking to Admiral Poindexter on the morning, or at some point in the day on the 21st.

MR. LIMAN: Now, when you spoke to him on the 21st, would you tell us what occasioned the conversation about diversion?

LT. COL. NORTH: My recollection is that the issue came up that there would be an inquiry by the Attorney General's office, or by the Attorney General, on a fact-finding activity, to find out what had happened in '85 as a consequence of Israeli transfers to Iran. And during that discussion I assured Admiral Poindexter—erroneously, it turns out —that all references to the use of funds generated by US sales to the government of Iran, and using the residuals from those transfers for support of the Nicaraguan resistance, had been removed and destroyed.

MR. LIMAN: Are you finished?

LT. COL. NORTH: I think that answers your question.

MR. LIMAN: All right. Admiral, you say that you —Lieutenant Colonel—

MR. SULLIVAN: He'll accept a promomtion.

MR. LIMAN: You say that you assured him, in the course of that conversation, that the documents that referred to this no longer existed. Did he ask you whether the documents existed?

LT. COL. NORTH: I don't recall who raised the subject, whether it was the Admiral or I. But I do remember assuring him that they had all been destroyed.

MR. LIMAN: Did you discuss when you destroyed them?

LT. COL. NORTH: I don't recall. But I had been in the process of destroying things for some time, by that point.

MR. LIMAN: Did he ask you whether any other documents, besides those that referred to the diversion, had been destoyed?

LT. COL. NORTH: Not that I can recall right now.

MR. LIMAN: And so is it fair to say based on your recollection that the conversation that you had with him on the 21st about documents that no longer existed related to the diversion?

LT. COL. NORTH: I'm sorry. Is it fair to say what, Counsel?

MR. LIMAN: That the conversation related to the diversion only, in terms of what documents had been destroyed.

LT. COL. NORTH: I'm not certain of that. Again I want to reiterate that that may have been the conversation on Friday or maybe it was a preceding one. I can recall that we talked several times that day. He was very busy and so was I, but we had talked at one point on Friday about my departure —I believe that's when I first tendered my resignation in writing to him, and we may have talked about the Nicaraguan resistance and the fact that I probably destroyed documents pertaining thereto.

I honestly don't recall specifically.

MR. LIMAN: Colonel, if you look at whatever it is in front of you, will that refresh you?

MR. SULLIVAN: Well, Mr. Liman, when he wants to look at something, he'll look at it. Don't you suggest what he looks at. Get on with the questioning.

(Chairman Inouye bangs the gavel.)

CHAIRMAN INOUYE: Counsel, I'm certain you're aware of the rules as well as anyone of us. First of all, I would hope that you will address the chair and, secondly, we'd like to get the business on the road ourselves, and thirdly, our public address system, I believe, is working very well. You need not shout, sir.

Proceed.

LT. COL. NORTH: Would you please repeat the question?

MR. LIMAN: I said, does the document that you have in

333

front of you refresh your recollection as what else what discussed on this subject?

MR. SULLIVAN: Objection, Mr. Chairman.

CHAIRMAN INOUYE: On what basis, sir?

MR. SULLIVAN: Counsel should simply ask the question. If the witness wants to look at his notes, his whole book that he has here, he'll do so for the answer. If he doesn't, he won't do so. If he thinks it helps him, he will look. I think it should be fully understood by the Committee that Colonel North has been struggling here for 2½ days to tell the truth and the whole truth. He's also exercising great care in addition to telling the truth, because, Mr. Chairman, this body has created an independent counsel, which occupies an office down the street and he's like a separate "super-Justice Department" to those of us that work in the defense of citizens. He has 100 people, you have 125—he's got 100 people down there looking at Colonel North and everything that he did, just the way your staff is. He's got 26 bright lawyers, 35 FBI agents, 11 IRS agents, four customs agents, investigators, and they're all pouring over the testimony and so, sir—

CHAIRMAN INOUYE: What are the grounds of your objection, sir?

MR. SULLIVAN: My grounds are that he will look at his book when he wants to look at his book and it's improper for any questioner to say, "Look at your book and see if you can find an answer."

CHAIRMAN INOUYE: I think it is up to the Chair to decide whether it's proper or improper. I think the question was proper, sir. Please proceed.

MR. SULLIVAN: Would you like him—are you directing him to look at his book, Mr. Chairman? Would you like him to start at page one?

CHAIRMAN INOUYE: He may look at it or he need not look at it. It's up to him.

MR. SULLIVAN: Thank you, sir. I appreciate that, and that's the ruling I was looking for.

LT. COL. NORTH: Occasionally it does help, counsel. It does not help me in this specific case.

MR. LIMAN: Now, when you had been—

LT. COL. NORTH: If I may make one observation, counsel? I provided to the Committee, when compelled to do so under subpoena, the documents and records that I had in my possession. And many of those refer to these issues. I do not have them before me, but you have them in the exhibit books.

MR. LIMAN: Colonel, before—during the last six months or so, did you look over the steno books that you turned over to us?

MR. SULLIVAN: Objection, Mr. Chairman.

CHAIRMAN INOUYE: What is the basis of your objection?

MR. SULLIVAN: What a witness does to prepare himself to tell the truth is none of the business of the questioner.

CHAIRMAN INOUYE: It is the business of this Committee. Proceed, sir.

MR. SULLIVAN: Answer - ask the question again, please.

MR. LIMAN: Did you read your steno books in the last six months?

LT. COL. NORTH: I did review them with counsel.

MR. LIMAN: Did you find in those steno books any references to conversations that you had with Admiral Poindexter about the diversion?

LT. COL. NORTH: I do not recall. There were 20 some odd books that I delivered up here, counsel.

MR. LIMAN: Now, your counsel had referred to the fact that you provided some 20 books to us. The fact of the matter is that those 20 books did not include the six—five or six diversion memos that you had written during the course of 1986, is that correct?

LT. COL. NORTH: The memos themselves were contained in documents that were created in my office on a typewriter. There were no typewritten pages in the books that I gave you.

MR. LIMAN: And those memos were destroyed by you, or at least you tried to destroy them all. One survived, is that—

LT. COL. NORTH: I did—

MR. LIMAN: —fair to say?

LT. COL. NORTH: Yes.

MR. LIMAN: Now, when you were meeting with Admiral Poindexter on the 21st, you believed in good faith that you had gotten rid of all five memoranda that you referred to, is that so?

LT. COL. NORTH: That is correct, and I—just to amplify

on that—it is very likely that the two that were not approved or that did not proceed, as I have indicated in earlier testimony, could well have been destroyed right at that time.

And so what I'm saying is that the very most that may have been left in the waning days of my tenure might well have been just the three, and that's why, when the question was asked yesterday or the day before about how many memos I actually destroyed in those closing days, I couldn't tell you because I honestly don't remember.

MR. LIMAN: There were five memos and—and what you're saying now is two may have been destroyed at the time that those transactions didn't occur, and the other three would have been destroyed later?

LT. COL. NORTH: No, what I'm saying is—I want to make it very clear—the one memo that you do have was a transaction that did not go through. As was my habit, if we had done something that—or prepared a memo on something that was not done, I would very often destroy that memo at that point in time when the decision was made not to proceed. Obviously, there was a memo still remaining in the files that pertained to a transaction which did not occur, or referred to an April plan that was never executed or implemented.

MR. LIMAN: And then there were three other transactions that did go through—

LT. COL. NORTH: That's correct.

MR. LIMAN: —for which there are no memoranda extant now that you're aware of, correct?

LT. COL. NORTH: That is correct.

MR. LIMAN: And those are ones that have been destroyed, correct?

LT. COL. NORTH: Yes.

MR. LIMAN: And so at the time that you gave Admiral Poindexter this assurance, you believed in good faith that no record existed of the diversion that you had written, is that correct?

LT. COL. NORTH: When I talked to the Admiral on the 21st, I assured him that all references to the sale of arms as it related to the Nicaraguan resistance had been destroyed, and I was wrong.

MR. LIMAN: And at that point, you were in a position in

which you did not have a single document that indicated that your actions had been authorized by your superiors. That's the way you believed—you thought—correct?

LT. COL. NORTH: Well, yes, and I also believed that all of the PROFs notes—which are now in stacks all over Washington—also had been destroyed.

MR. LIMAN: Now after you were dismissed, did Admiral Poindexter call you and say to you that he would confirm that he had given the authority?

LT. COL. NORTH: I honestly don't recall a conversation with Admiral Poindexter after I was dismissed. He—he may have called. I don't remember it.

MR. LIMAN: Did—do you recall any conversation with him in which he said, "Colonel North, don't worry. Even if you destroy all the documents, I'll stand up and say I approved it."

LT. COL. NORTH: No, I recall no such conversation.

MR. LIMAN: So that you were—once the documents were destroyed—you were out there without any kind of assurance that anyone would stand behind you, is that fair to say?

LT. COL. NORTH: That was the plan. I mean, it was planned that I would be out there. I mean, everything had gone right according to plan, right up until about 12:05 in the afternoon the next day or several days thereafter.

MR. LIMAN: And when the plan changed was when you had the IC or the criminal investigation announced?

LT. COL. NORTH: Well, I don't know where in who else's mind the plan changed, Counsel. I know that when I heard the words criminal investigation or criminal behavior or whatever the words were that were used in the press conference or shortly thereafter, I don't—it was certainly profound at that point—that my mind-set changed considerably.

MR. LIMAN: Now, you had—

LT. COL. NORTH: And I think, if you'll indulge me for a second. Over the five and a half years that I had served on the NSC staff, I had, as I hope I have testified here today, sought every possible means to do what needed to be done within the law. We had gone inextremis to find a way to live within the constraints and proscriptions of Boland. And I had sought a means in 1985 in working with various lawyers and various counsel to find a way to implement a policy that

337

started without my acquiescence or support or direction or anything else, and worked very, very hard to find legal ways to carry out the policy of the President. And there was probably not another person on the planet Earth as shocked as I was to hear that someone thought it was criminal. And I can tell you that that shock was compounded when I heard later that there was to be an independent counsel, and further compounded when I was the only name in the appointment order for that independent counsel—the only person on the planet Earth named in that appointment order, Counsel.

MR. LIMAN: Colonel, if the investigation by the independent counsel had not been instituted—if you hadn't heard the words criminal, would you still be sticking by the cover story? It's a—

MR. SULLIVAN: Objection.

MR. LIMAN: It's a—I will not press it. It's hypothetical.

MR. SULLIVAN: I know it is, Mr. Liman. I'm glad you recognize it. We don't have to get the Chair involved.

MR. LIMAN: Now, you've already testified that Casey had approved this—Mr. Casey.

LT. COL. NORTH: Which is this?

MR. LIMAN: The diversion.

LT. COL. NORTH: I had consulted very carefully on Director Casey—with Director Casey, and he, I don't know if approved is the right word—Director Casey was very enthusiastic about the whole program—

MR. LIMAN: Now—

LT. COL. NORTH: —and advocated it.

MR. LIMAN: When you met with the Attorney General on the afternoon of the 23rd of November, he asked you about the diversion, correct?

LT. COL. NORTH: He did. He asked me specifically about that memorandum.

MR. LIMAN: And is it true that he asked you who knew about the fact that proceeds from the sale of Iranian arms were being used to support the contras?

LT. COL. NORTH: I think he may well have. I, again, am not entirely clear on that afternoon. I was up till very early in the morning before it. I'd had a meeting with Mr. McFarlane on it, and I suppose he may well have. Again, I do not have detailed specific recall of that. I took no notes during that meeting.

MR. LIMAN: Do you recall that you told him that Admiral Poindexter knew, that Richard Secord knew, and that Mr. McFarlane knew?

LT. COL. NORTH: That sounds right.

MR. LIMAN: Do you recall that you did not tell the Attorney General of the United States that Director Casey knew?

LT. COL. NORTH: I don't recall that I didn't.

MR. LIMAN: Well, was it part of the plan at that stage that you would not name Director Casey?

LT. COL. NORTH: It had always been part of the plan that Director Casey would know nothing of the support to the Nicaraguan resistance.

MR. LIMAN: And, who else was it part of the plan who would not know anything about the support to the Nicaraguan resistance?

LT. COL. NORTH: Other Cabinet officers who had to testify and appear and things like that. I mean, it was a very closed circle of people who knew.

MR. LIMAN: Which other Cabinet officers?

LT. COL. NORTH: Well, I, I—the people who didn't know. I mean, it was just a matter—I've told you who I thought knew, and I've told you who, and you've seen who I sent memoranda to, and you know of the record of communications I had with various officials. I don't know who else knew. I've told you that.

MR. LIMAN: Colonel, you testified a moment ago, unless you misunderstood the questions—

MR. SULLIVAN: But counsel, I think you were missing each other there.

MR. LIMAN: Well, we'll soon see. That it was always part of the plan that Director Casey would not be, would not know. Is that, in essence, what you said?

LT. COL. NORTH: If you mean by "the plan", the fallguy plan, yes.

MR. LIMAN: And, so the fallguy plan was that even though Casey knew, you would not finger him, to use a colloquial expression?

LT. COL. NORTH: Your expression, counsel, not mine.

339

MR. LIMAN: Well, you wouldn't name him?

LT. COL. NORTH: That's correct.

MR. LIMAN: And, then the next question I asked was were there other people who knew things that you were also not supposed to name?

LT. COL. NORTH: Not that I know of. I know of no other people who actually knew. I have testified as to who I knew knew. I'm getting—confusing myself. I've testified as to who I believe knew about the plan; I've testified as to who I can actually confirm knowledge, by virtue of the memoranda that I created, the conversations we had, and the record that you see before you from the PROF system. But I had specifically talked to the Admiral, and I could well have said to the Attorney General on the 23rd, I guess it was, that Sunday, that "Oh, by the way, the President knows." But I had asked the Admiral on Friday if the President knew, and the Admiral had told me no. And so when the Attorney General asked me about the President, I told him "no."

MR. LIMAN: Well isn't a fact that what you told the Attorney General is that you didn't know whether or not he did know? Isn't that what you told McFarlane?

LT. COL. NORTH: But I think that the discussion with Mr. McFarlane was perhaps different—

MR. LIMAN: Before—no, the one in London, where he called you from London, when he asked you what the Attorney General had asked you. Let's go back, Colonel. Did you not talk to Mr. McFarlane after your conversation with the Attorney General?

LT. COL. NORTH: I believe I did. I believe I talked to both Mr. McFarlane and eventually Admiral Poindexter. I—in fact—

MR. LIMAN: Now let's talk about Mr. McFarlane—

LT. COL. NORTH: This is on Sunday afternoon after the Attorney General?

MR. LIMAN: And when you talked to Mr. McFarlane after you had met with the Attorney General, did he ask you what happened at that meeting?

LT. COL. NORTH: I suppose he did, or I volunteered it, one or the other.

MR. LIMAN: Well do you recall telling Mr. McFarlane about the fact that they had found the memorandum?

LT. COL. NORTH: Yes, I did.

MR. LIMAN: And do you remember telling him that you were asked about who knew?

LT. COL. NORTH: I don't remember that part. I remember—

MR. LIMAN: Well —

LT. COL. NORTH: —it was a profoundly difficult time because that memorandum wasn't supposed to exist.

MR. LIMAN: Now, did I understand you to say a moment ago that if Admiral Poindexter had not told you on Friday that he had not told the President you, quote "may well have told the Attorney General that the President did know"?

LT. COL. NORTH: No, I would—

MR. SULLIVAN: That's a very confusing question, Mr. Chairman—

MR. LIMAN: Well—

MR. SULLIVAN: Could you restate it, sir?

MR. LIMAN: Did you just testify a few moments ago that had Admiral Poindexter not told you on that Friday that the President was unaware of the diversion, you might well have told the Attorney General on that Sunday that the President knew? Is that what you said?

LT. COL. NORTH: Well, let me cast this the right way because I don't want to leave any false impressions. In the conversations that I had with the Admiral on Friday, all of which related to, as I recall them, my departure, the safety of the hostages and the second channel, the cleanup of the files—if that's an acceptable way of putting it—I asked the Admiral pointedly that day, "Did the President, or does the President, know about the fact that we used these monies to support the resistance?" And he told me, then, "No." I think that's the last conversation I ever had with the Admiral about that aspect of it.

Thus I, having assumed all along that those things which required presidential approval indeed had them, think I conveyed to the Attorney General on Sunday just exactly those sentiments. My recollection of it is that when he asked me, "Did the President approve these?" I told him, "I guess he didn't," or "He didn't," or what—something like that. Because that's what the Admiral had told me on Friday.

MR. LIMAN: And what you meant to say before, at least what I think you were trying to say, is that you had assumed,

341

for some nine months, that the President of the United States knew and approved of the diversion. Correct?

LT. COL. NORTH: I had assumed, from the day I took my post at the National Security Council, that those things which required the approval of the President—and I sent forward memoranda soliciting that approval, and I got the authority to proceed on various initiatives—had indeed received the approval of the President. I've testified to that.

MR. LIMAN: And it wasn't until Admiral Poindexter answered your question, that that assumption was shaken.

LT. COL. NORTH: It wasn't shaken. He simply denied that the President knew.

MR. LIMAN: Did you ask him: "Admiral Poindexter, why did you not discuss this with the President?"

LT. COL. NORTH: No.

MR. LIMAN: Why not?

LT. COL. NORTH: First of all, I'm not in the habit of questioning my superiors. If he deemed it not to be necessary to ask the President, I saluted smartly and charged up the hill. That's what lieutenant colonels are supposed to do. I have no problem with that. I don't believe that what we did, even under those circumstances, is wrong or illegal.

MR. LIMAN: And have—

LT. COL. NORTH: I've told you, I thought it was a good idea to begin with.

MR. LIMAN: And—

LT. COL. NORTH: I still think it was a good idea, counsel.

MR. LIMAN: And have you wondered why, if it was a good idea, that the President of the United States dismissed you because of it?

LT. COL. NORTH: Let me—let me just make one thing very clear, counsel. This Lieutenant Colonel is not going to challenge a decision of the Commander in Chief, for whom I still work. And I am proud to work for that Commander in Chief. And if the Commander in Chief tells this Lieutenant Colonel to go stand in the corner and sit on his head, I will do so. And if the Commander in Chief decides to dismiss me from the NSC staff, this Lieutenant Colonel will proudly salute, and say, "Thank you for the opportunity to have served," and go. And I am not going to criticize his decision, no matter how he relieves me, sir.

MR. LIMAN: Has anyone given you an explanation, Col. North, on behalf of the President, of why he did not think it was "a good idea," and dismissed you?

LT. COL. NORTH: The President of the United States saw fit to call me later the same day. and in the course of that call, which was also intensely personal, he told me words to the effect, "I just didn't know." I have no reason to disbelieve what the Commander in Chief told me, sir.

MR. LIMAN: Did you say to him, "I received approval from Admiral Poindexter and Director Casey."?

LT. COL. NORTH: I did not say those words to the Commander in Chief. I simply expressed my thanks for having been able to serve him for five and half years, and my regrets that my service had brought forth a political firestorm and difficulties, when all I sought to do was to help. And that what I may have done was to hurt him.

MR. LIMAN: Now when you were speaking to the Attorney General on the 23rd, you understood that the Attorney General was not just the chief legal officer of the United States, but he was a confidant and friend of the President, correct?

LT. COL. NORTH: Yes.

MR. LIMAN: He was an advisor of the President. (Pause while Lt. Col. North confers with his attorney.)

LT. COL. NORTH: I'm sorry, counsel. Would you please repeat the question?

MR. LIMAN: You understood that the Attorney General was an adviser of the President?

LT. COL. NORTH: Yes, I did.

MR. LIMAN: Why didn't you tell the Attorney General, an adviser to your Commander in Chief, that Director Casey knew?

LT. COL. NORTH: As I said, I don't know that I did, or I don't know that I didn't. I don't recall that conversation in any detail. It was consistent with a long pattern that Director Casey did not know about any support outside that provided by the CIA for the Nicaraguan resistance.

MR. LIMAN: Colonel North, as late as November 23, were you still prepared to conceal from the Attorney General facts relating to Director Casey?

LT. COL. NORTH: I was prepared at that point to continue

not to reveal that the diversion, as you have put it, had even occurred. You recall, I had removed those files. His people had been going through them that day. I thought that I'd gotten them all.

MR. LIMAN: Well, who were you protecting?

LT. COL. NORTH: What do you mean, who was I protecting? I was protecting the lives and the safety of the people who were engaged in the operation.

MR. LIMAN: Well, explain to us how telling the Attorney General of the United States that Director Casey approved a diversion would jeopardize lives, other than, perhaps, put him in jeopardy of this kind of investigation that you've been through?

LT. COL. NORTH: Well, I don't know, other than the fact that this investigation could indeed result in lives being put in jeopardy.Well, I mean, I don't think that a specific, you know, thought went through my mind on that issue.

MR. LIMAN: Was it just instinctive that you don't mention the name of the Director, when you're talking to the Attorney General about knowledge of support for the contras?

LT. COL. NORTH: It was instinctive, Counsel, from my earliest days of contact with the Director that his relationship and mine not be something that was publicly bandied about, and until these hearings, I don't believe that most people in Washington knew that the Director and I communed as often as we did.

MR. LIMAN: Well, how often did you commune?

LT. COL. NORTH: I would say several times a week.

MR. LIMAN: Where?

LT. COL. NORTH: Most often on the telephone, but we would meet in his office, occasionally in mine, occasionally out at the office in Langley. I can recall a couple of meetings, if not more, in his office at the Intelligence Community building across the street. I can recall meetings in his home. I recall riding in the car with him, I can recall airplane trips with him. But we met enough to be able to coordinate sufficiently and that I could seek his guidance on a number of things.

MR. LIMAN: He was a person who you could confide in?

LT. COL. NORTH: I did.

MR. LIMAN: He was a person whose advice you valued?

344

LT. COL. NORTH: Inestimably.

MR. LIMAN: Were you on a first name basis?

LT. COL. NORTH: He was with me. I called him by his first name, Mr. Director. I called him Mr. Casey to his face. I occasionally perhaps called him Bill. And I—when my father died, Counsel, there were three people in the government of the United States that expressed their condolences. One was Admiral Poindexter, one was the Vice President of the United States, and the other one was Bill Casey. And Bill Casey was, for me, a man of immense proportions, and a man whose advice I valued greatly, and a man whose concerns for this country and the future of this land were, I thought, on the right track. I may be wrong, but I don't think history will bear that out, and I took his advice to heart.

MR. LIMAN: Did you look upon him, in a way, as a boss?

LT. COL. NORTH: I've heard that said. I don't think so much as a boss, but—(pauses)—I know who my superiors are and I know the chain of command. And he wasn't a "boss" so much as he was a personal friend, and an advisor, and a person with whom I could consult and get good solid advice, and a person to whom I could turn for support.

MR. LIMAN: When you briefed him on what you were doing to keep the contras alive, did he express his approval to you?

LT. COL. NORTH: He never once, that I can recall, in any way disagreed with any of the things that I was doing. In fact, he gave me a number of ideas how they might be done better. And I don't recall him ever—I don't recall that he ever said don't do something you are doing. He often would suggest ways to do it better.

MR. LIMAN: Did he discuss the President's views with you from time to time?

LT. COL. NORTH: Not on areas bearing on this investigation.

MR. LIMAN: The President's commitment to the contras?

LT. COL. NORTH: Oh, in—in general terms. I—after all, Director Casey was the one who, in the Union League Club speech, basically formulated or laid out for the first time publicly the—what has come to be called the Reagan Doctrine.

MR. LIMAN: Did—

LT. COL. NORTH: And I think he had a very clear understanding of what the President's views were, and I think he was able to help formulate some of those in terms of a public policy position.

MR. LIMAN: Did you talk to Director Casey about the financial needs of the contras?

LT. COL. NORTH: He probably knew more about it than I did, because he was getting the raw intelligence in. But yes, we did.

MR. LIMAN: And you told Director Casey about the fact that the Ayatollah would be help paying for those needs?

LT. COL. NORTH: Yes, I did.

MR. LIMAN: That was a matter of—that had sort of a double irony, didn't it, in the sense, Colonel, that the Iranian government had been providing arms to the Sandinistas, right?

LT. COL. NORTH: You've been reading my papers, haven't you? That's right, they tried. And they also provided oil on credit. As I recall, it was about $100 million worth over several years.

MR. LIMAN: And indeed, one of the points that the President approved in the terms of reference for Mr. McFarlane to talk to the Iranian government representatives about was that they should not give this support to the Sandinistas, right?

LT. COL. NORTH: That's correct.

MR. LIMAN: And here you, a staff member of the NSC, succeeded in sort of reversing it all, getting the money for the contras, correct?

LT. COL. NORTH: We did.

MR. LIMAN: And that was something that Director Casey must have admired very much.

LT. COL. NORTH: He did. To put it mildly.

MR. LIMAN: And it was something that, as you've said, you were proud of.

LT. COL. NORTH: I didn't say I was proud of it. I thought it was—I believe I said something that it—

MR. LIMAN: A neat idea.

LT. COL. NORTH: —a neat idea.

MR. LIMAN: And did Director Casey ever tell you, "Colonel North, this is something that you must never mention to any of your colleagues at the NSC?"

LT. COL. NORTH: (Pause) I'm sorry, Counsel. Would you please—

MR. LIMAN: Did you discuss with Director Casey that this use of the proceeds was a matter that could be a political bombshell?

LT. COL. NORTH: I think we probably did at a number of points. Certainly, it—we discussed that very clearly toward the end of my tenure. Once—I think it actually came down to detailed discussions of that, once he was aware that there were outside—there was outside intelligence on it. And I'm focusing specifically on a friend of his that had approached him and told him that he, the friend, knew about the use of the funds.

MR. LIMAN: That's Furmark—

LT. COL. NORTH: Yes.

MR. LIMAN: —correct? And that was in the fall of 1986.

LT. COL. NORTH: That is correct.

MR. LIMAN: And you've testified about the fact that as a result of Furmark's statements to the director, the director asked you to clean up your files.

LT. COL. NORTH: That's correct. It was not that one singular event. I mean, things were, I think as I indicated earlier, unraveling rather quickly. We had the aircraft shot down in Honduras, investigation of Southern Air Transport which is, as far as I can determine, innocent in that transaction, General Secord's role being revealed, and then Furmark walking in, and of course that was followed by the revelations and the pamphlets in Iran and the newspaper in Syria—or Beruit.

MR. LIMAN: Colonel, in November of 1986, after the Iranian venture had been publicized initially in Lebanon and then in papers all over the world. Did you discuss the diversion with director Casey?

LT. COL. NORTH: Oh, sure.

MR. LIMAN: Now, tell us about that. Whatever you can recall.

LT. COL. NORTH: Well, I don't recall the—I mean, we had several discussions about it.

MR. LIMAN: Well, I'll take all several.

LT. COL. NORTH: My recollection is that Director Casey agreed with my assessment that the time had come for someone—had come to take the hit or the fall. He, quite frankly, did not think that I was senior enough to do that, and suggested that—I am trying to recall—but suggested that it was probably going to go up the line, or something like that.

MR. LIMAN: Did he suggest who else could take the hit?

LT. COL. NORTH: He suggested that it might be Admiral Poindexter.

MR. LIMAN: Because next up to the line from you was Admiral Poindexter, wasn't it—on this matter?

LT. COL. NORTH: Well, after Don Fortier died, that's correct. Don Fortier was the nominal deputy who had been aware, I believe, at least of some of this.

MR. LIMAN: Did you discuss blaming it on Fortier after his death.

LT. COL. NORTH: It would be hard to blame something that was going on in November on a man who died in the summer.

MR. LIMAN: No, but the original approval.

LT. COL. NORTH: No.

MR. LIMAN: So that—

LT. COL. NORTH: First of all, Don wasn't in the position to do those approval. I mean, it was just—

MR. LIMAN: So, Casey—Director Casey, as I understand it discussed with you the fact that it just might not be credible for you to take the hit, and that it might have to be Admiral Poindexter?

LT. COL. NORTH: Words to that effect.

MR. LIMAN: Did he discuss anyone else who might have to take the hit?

LT. COL. NORTH: No but he was concerned that the President not be damaged by, and I shared that belief.

MR. LIMAN: Now, this—these conversations with Director Casey took place before November 21. Correct? Before and after.

LT. COL. NORTH: I would guess so, yes. I—one has to recall that I spent the first part of December, and you now have my travel—

MR. LIMAN: November, you mean.

348

LT. COL. NORTH: I'm sorry—the first part of November in very heavy travel and so did the Director. But my recollection is that we had one conversation early in the month, perhaps during one of my layovers in Washington, and that the next conversations weren't until very much later in the month.

MR. LIMAN: Well, Colonel at the time you had that conversation in early November you had not yet been told by Admiral Poindexter that he had not told the President. Correct?

LT. COL. NORTH: I was not told that by Admiral Poindexter until the 21st.

MR. LIMAN: So that at the time you were having your converstion with Casey you were still laboring under the assumption that the President of the United States knew, correct?

LT. COL. NORTH: Yes.

MR. LIMAN: And did Director Casey tell you the President doesn't know?

LT. COL. NORTH: No.

MR. LIMAN: And when you and Director Casey were talking about the fact that someone had to take the hit, why did you understand that it was necessary for someone to take the hit?

LT. COL. NORTH: I think he and I certainly could see that we were going to have a major international and perhaps, and we obviously do, a domestic political drama on this thing, and that it would be helpful if someone were, as we originally planned, when it comes time for this thing to go down the tubes, here's the guy who gets fingered for it. And, again, none of us—at least certainly not me and no one I ever talked to—ever imagined that we had done anything criminally wrong.

MR. LIMAN: Now, and you've testified that the Director was known to you to be a lawyer?

LT. COL. NORTH: He was indeed.

MR. LIMAN: He had a reputation as a New York lawyer, a reputation of being a very, very—very, very smart lawyer.

LT. COL. NORTH: Is that a plug?

MR. LIMAN: Yes, it is.

LT. COL. NORTH: He was, indeed.

MR. LIMAN: And you—

LT. COL. NORTH: And it wasn't just his assessment of himself either. Other people—

MR. LIMAN: No, but you formed it from the relationship that you had with him, you saw how Casey's mind operated?

LT. COL. NORTH: That's correct.

MR. LIMAN: It was very quick.

LT. COL. NORTH: It sure was.

MR. LIMAN: And in these conversations that you were having with the Director, it was clear to you that he was concerned about damage to the President?

LT. COL. NORTH: I think it would be beyond comprehension, counsel, that anyone who served the President—any president, wasn't concerned about that. And that's not from a Republican or Democratic partisan perspective. That is in seeing the President as the Commander in Chief, the Chief Executive and the Head of State. And I think that it is encumbent upon all of the servants in the Executive Branch to have that kind of a concern, not so much for the man necessarily but for the institution of the Presidency. I certainly had that, and I know Director Casey had that.

MR. LIMAN: Now, on the 25th of November—let's be sure of that question—did you tell Director Casey that you were going to see the Attorney General that Sunday?

LT. COL. NORTH: I'd already him by the 25th of November.

MR. LIMAN: Yeah, that's the 25th. Did you tell him before you saw the Attorney General?

LT. COL. NORTH: I—if I may—

MR. LIMAN: Mr. Sullivan hasn't objected to your looking at it.

LT. COL. NORTH: I do not believe I talked to the Director that day about that issue.

MR. LIMAN: Did—

LT. COL. NORTH: And again, I—

MR. LIMAN: What about the prior day?

LT. COL. NORTH: No, because I didn't know I was going to see him until the 21st. My recollection—

MR. LIMAN: Let's get the dates correct on the—

LT. COL. NORTH: Okay.

MR. LIMAN: You saw the Attorney General on the 23rd?

350

LT. COL. NORTH: On Sunday the 23rd, right.

MR. LIMAN: Did—and you knew that you were going to see him on the 22nd, is that correct? The Attorney General called for an appointment—

LT. COL. NORTH: The way I remember it.

MR. LIMAN: —on the 22nd?

LT. COL. NORTH: That is correct.

MR. LIMAN: Did you speak to the Director after the Attorney General asked to see you?

LT. COL. NORTH: I do not have a recollection of doing that, no.

MR. LIMAN: Now, when you talked to the Director in October after the Furmark incident, and in November, did he ever ask you what the memoranda looked like that you had sent up the line and that you either were going to take care of, or had taken care of?

LT. COL. NORTH: I don't believe so, because I think, at least on one occasion I actually went over the memorandum with the Director.

MR. LIMAN: So he knew what it looked like? That one?

LT. COL. NORTH: Certainly.

MR. LIMAN: Now, can you recall which transaction was reflected in the memorandum that you went over with the Director?

LT. COL. NORTH: No, but I have a sense that it was probably the February one, but I don't know whey I feel that. I think it may have been the February transaction.

MR. LIMAN: The February one involved 500 Hawks and then another 500 Hawks, a total of 1000 Hawks, correct?

LT. COL. NORTH: That's correct.

MR. LIMAN: And do you recall what occasioned you to go over the memorandum with the Director?

LT. COL. NORTH: My recollection is—and it is vague because it was a long time ago, it seems—I was one, pursuing getting a CIA officer, a particular CIA officer, engaged in the initiative.

MR. LIMAN: There's only one CIA officer whose name we use with respect to this, and that's Mr. Cave, is that who you were talking about?

LT. COL. NORTH: And he is the one. And—

MR. LIMAN: Now—

LT. COL. NORTH: I'm sorry.

MR. LIMAN: No, I'd like you to complete your answer.

LT. COL. NORTH: My sense is that what Director Casey and I started talking about was getting Mr. Cave because of his experience in that country and his obvious language ability so that we had a person who is, besides myself, in the government of the United States involved in this and who knew exactly what was being said, and with whom I had absolute rapport. And he chose to make some kind of an arrangement, I'm not certain what it was, but on a contract basis or consultancy arrangement, bring Mr. Cave back to service. And it is my recollection that we then had a—I guess it was right after the February transaction, so my date's a little off—but it was at some point in that timeframe when I was trying to get Cave involved, and I showed the Director one of those memoranda.

MR. LIMAN: Colonel, I said a thousand "Hawks." I meant "TOWs", and I think that's what you understood.

LT. COL. NORTH: I did.

MR. LIMAN: All right. Colonel, was the memorandum you showed him the memorandum as it existed before you sent up the line or after it came back?

LT. COL. NORTH: It was probably before.

MR. LIMAN: Did the Director in any way caution you about not sending a memorandum that called for Presidential approval?

LT. COL. NORTH: I don't recall him ever doing that.

MR. LIMAN: Well, isn't it fair to say that given your strong sense of command, your belief in Director Casey, that if Director Casey said to you, "Do not put the President's name on a memorandum," you wouldn't have done it?

LT. COL. NORTH: Very true.

MR. LIMAN: And, you continued to put the President's name in terms of having a reference in the memoranda that Admiral Poindexter should seek approval of the President. Correct?

LT. COL. NORTH: That is certainly my recollection. If we could just go to that—

MR. LIMAN: Well, I'm going to come to it in more detail later, but if you have something—

LT. COL. NORTH: That memoranda?

MR. LIMAN: —that you want to say now, you better say it while you remember it.

LT. COL. NORTH: Unkind. Again, I would like to make the point that I did not, nor do I know that others did highlight that aspect of it in those memoranda, and if you will not that the one memoranda that still exists—memorandum that still exists, drafted at some point in April, is five pages long with a four page attachment, and there are only eight lines that refer in those many pages to that specific part of the transaction. And, what is very important is the use, and I know that that is the focus of this investigation, but that the use of the funds derived as residuals, as I call them, or you call diversions, was not viewed as the preeminent activity ongoing. The preeminent activity was to establish a relationship with Iran, and all of the other things that would derive therefrom, and that we saw, as Director Casey put it, the ultimate irony, in that as a part of this process, we could continue to support the desperately needy Nicaraguan resistance.

MR. LIMAN: All right. Colonel, you said that you didn't highlight it. It's also true you didn't conceal it in the memorandum?

LT. COL. NORTH: I don't think I concealed from my superiors anything that I did, and I think the record is very clear in the stacks of paper that you have.

MR. LIMAN: And, the record is very clear in the memorandum that has survived that you didn't conceal it?

LT. COL. NORTH: I did not.

MR. LIMAN: And, indeed, in a rather hurried inspection, Brad Reynolds spotted it pretty quickly, didn't he?

LT. COL. NORTH: I don't know how long it took him to find it. They spent many hours in my office that day, nor did they reveal it to me when they found it.

MR. LIMAN: They revealed it to you the next day, though, didn't they?

LT. COL. NORTH: Certainly did.

MR. LIMAN: All right, is the reason that Director Casey asked you after the Furmark incident to get rid of the memoranda because of that one paragraph or two that refer to diversion?

LT. COL. NORTH: I don't know that that was solely on his mind. I think what the Director was concerned about, and I'm quite sure that the Director was concerned that you have a—and, this was the mistake that I made, among

353

others, perhaps, depending on your perspective—but, the operational mistake was to cross the two operations in the person of perhaps this guy here and the others who were having to carry it out. Operationally, if you have other alternatives you don't do that, and I didn't at the time have other alternatives.

Second, I think what Director Casey saw was that there was going to be a major unraveling of the activities. Furmark was part of it. The aircraft shootdown over Nicaragua was part of it, and that was further compounded by early November, when we knew that leaflets were being handed out by another faction within the government of Iran, revealing the May trip by Mr. McFarlane and his party.

MR. LIMAN: Colonel, the Hasenfus shoot-down involved contra support, correct?

LT. COL. NORTH: True.

MR. LIMAN: And Furmark was complaining about the fact that investors hadn't gotten paid out of the proceeds of the sale. Correct?

LT. COL. NORTH: No. The problem with the Furmark revelation was that Furmark told him, as I remember it, that Ghorbanifar had already told too members of Congress that monies from the sale of weapons to Iran had been diverted to use of the contras. And those names are in the notebooks that I gave you, sir.

MR. LIMAN: Well, you gave us a lot of notebooks. And I have not seen those in the notebooks. So I'm going to ask your counsel, at a recess, to point them out to us. Do you know what the—who the—what the names are?

LT. COL. NORTH: I don't recall them now. And I sure wouldn't want to be inaccurate on that. (Laughter.)

MR. LIMAN: Now—but the Director was talking about diversion, in terms of Furmark.

LT. COL. NORTH: The concerns that the Director addressed to me, was that, "Look, you've had the shoot-down of the Hasenfus airplane. That operation's in trouble. Furmark has now come and told me that other people are very aware of the fact that the arms sales to Iran have generated funds that have gone to support the contras. And it's getting out."

MR. LIMAN: Did he—and did he say that the—this had

been called to members of Congress, who might start an investigation?

LT. COL. NORTH: I don't recall that part of it. But apparently Ghorbanifar had claimed, to Furmark, that he—that members of Congress were being made aware, or had been.

MR. LIMAN: And, you therefore were told to get rid of memoranda that reflected that?

LT. COL. NORTH: I was told to clean up the files.

MR. LIMAN: And that meant to you, to get rid of memoranda that reflected that. Right?

LT. COL. NORTH: Anything to do with the—the residuals. Or as you call it, diversion of funds.

MR. LIMAN: And that meant that you went through your files, to make sure that you found the memoranda that referred to the residuals, as you call them.

LT. COL. NORTH: Yes.

MR. LIMAN: And when you went through the files, do you recall how many you found?

LT. COL. NORTH: The specific memoranda seeking approval?

MR. LIMAN: Yes, sir.

LT. COL. NORTH: (Pause.) No, I don't. And what I probably found were dozens and dozens of memoranda relating to the residuals, and the application to the contra, among other things. And so what I'm saying is—and probably several copies of even the April one, which I thought I'd gotten all of them.

MR. LIMAN: Well, when you say that there were "dozens"—

LT. COL. NORTH: All within the five that I sought approval for. I don't—

MR. LIMAN: And so that there were copies of the five.

LT. COL. NORTH: Exactly.

MR. LIMAN: And, did you look over them, to see whose names were written on them?

LT. COL. NORTH: I think we've already been through this once, counsel—

MR. LIMAN: You said you didn't recall, and I'm asking you whether you looked.

LT. COL. NORTH: I don't even remember looking. I remember, if there was something—

MR. LIMAN: Well, you've answered it, then.

LT. COL. NORTH: Yeah.

MR. LIMAN: You've said you did not look. Is that right?

MR. SULLIVAN: Would you like to answer the question, counsel, for him?

MR. LIMAN: No, I'd like him to keep his answers to the questions. And if it's—if that's the answer, then we ought to move on. Is that the answer that you did not look?

MR. SULLIVAN: May we have the question, please, Mr. Chairman?

MR. LIMAN: Did you look, to see whose names were written on those memos?

LT. COL. NORTH: I do not recall looking to see whose names were written on the memos.

MR. LIMAN: And do you recall looking to see whether they had check marks or initials?

LT. COL. NORTH: I do not.

MR. LIMAN: Now on this day, November 25, did you find time, this is November 25 when you were dismissed to write out a list of priorities in your—your notebooks? Things that were important to you? (Long pause)

LT. COL. NORTH: Yes.

MR. LIMAN: And was that before or after the press conference?

LT. COL. NORTH: It was after. (Long pause)

MR. LIMAN: Now, when did you take these diaries out of your office, the steno pads?

LT. COL. NORTH: My recollection is that most—well, I don't know if it's most—some were already at home, some were still in the office and I think, if I remember right, all but the last one, and maybe even that too, left with me on the afternoon of the 25th.

MR. LIMAN: You testified over the last few days about the need to maintain operational security in a covert operation. Correct?

LT. COL. NORTH: That's correct.

MR. LIMAN: You testified that one of the reasons for shredding documents was to even keep them from a successor. Is that correct?

LT. COL. NORTH: A successor to my position at the NSC, yes.

MR. LIMAN: Is it fair to say—Mr. Sullivan, that's my next question. Is it fair to a—is it fair to say that a—

LT. COL. NORTH: He sometimes reads my mind too.

MR. LIMAN: Is it fair to say that the steno books that you took home contained very sensitive information?

LT. COL. NORTH: It is likely with interpretation that the steno books are sensitive, yes.

MR. LIMAN: Now, part of your interpretation is your handwriting.

LT. COL. NORTH: Well, certainly that, but I—

MR. LIMAN: But, for all—

LT. COL. NORTH: —criticizing my penmanship, I'm—

MR. LIMAN: But, there are names in those books.

LT. COL. NORTH: Yes.

MR. LIMAN: And you indeed uttered a prayer to the committee that we treat these books with sensitivity and respect their security. You did that yesterday as I recall. Correct?

LT. COL. NORTH: I did.

MR. LIMAN: Now, the home which you took these books to is a home that you've had a great deal of concern about security for. Correct?

LT. COL. NORTH: Yes.

MR. LIMAN: Can you explain to me—someone who's never been in a position such as yours—as to why you would be concerned about the security of documents locked in an NSC office, subject to all sorts of security regulations and access restrictions, you're not concerned about keeping them at home?

LT. COL. NORTH: Well again, as I said, I may have had a few of them at home. I don't really recall how many if indeed there were. I removed the rest of them on the 25th along with several hundred pages of other documents for one purpose, and that was to protect myself. Because after the press conference, my perspective changed. And it became more and more of protecting myself, and that was the reason to remove those notebooks from the NSC and to take those documents from the White House with me.

MR. LIMAN: Now when did you do your shredding before the 25th? Which was the last preceding day in which you did shredding that was out of the ordinary?

357

LT. COL. NORTH: It was entirely likely that I was shredding documents as late as the morning of the 25th.

MR. LIMAN: And the Attorney General, when you met with him on the 23rd, asked you to preserve every single document?

LT. COL. NORTH: No.

MR. LIMAN: Did you, when you returned from your meeting with the Attorney General on the 23rd, go to your office and do shredding of documents that day?

LT. COL. NORTH: I honestly don't remember, but I know I shredded documents after that fact. After the—you're talking about after the Sunday evening—

MR. LIMAN: After your meeting with the Attorney General where he confronted you with the diversion memo.

LT. COL. NORTH: I think what I did, if I remember at all accurately a time that was becoming increasingly difficult, in your words, my recollection is I went back to the White House to try and call Admiral Poindexter on the telephone. And he had, on a rare Sunday afternoon, I guess, when he could get away with his family, gone to the Redskins game. You plug New York lawyers, I plug the Redskins.

As I recall, he was not yet home, and it was probably then, if I called Mr. McFarlane, that I called him and probably from the "sit" room. And I would guess that I probably went back to my office at that point and for some time continued to clean up the files. I would also point out to the Committee that I destroyed documents that had absolutely nothing to do with either Iran or the Nicaraguan resistance that no longer would be applicable in the event that I was soon to be transferred.

MR. LIMAN: Do you recall that on Monday morning, the 24th, the shredder was full and overflowing?

LT. COL. NORTH: I don't remember that it was necessarily Monday, but I do remember that happened at some point, yes.

MR. LIMAN: Do you remember shredding documents during the lunch hour on the 22nd, when the representatives of the Attorney General's office had left for their lunch?

LT. COL. NORTH: I remember shredding documents while they were in there reading documents.

MR. LIMAN: Shredding them in their presence?

LT. COL. NORTH: Well, I mean, they were sitting in my

office, and the shredder was right outside, and I walked out and shredded documents.

MR. LIMAN: More than a few pieces of paper, right?

LT. COL. NORTH: Pardon?

MR. LIMAN: It would be more than a few pieces of paper.

LT. COL. NORTH: Well that's a pretty high speed shredder. It eats 'em pretty quick. I'm not trying to be light about it, but I mean, they were sitting in my office reading and I'd finish a document and say, "We don't need that anymore." I'd walk up and I'd go out and shred it. They could hear it, the shredder was right outside the door.

MR. LIMAN: I'm not trying to be light about it either—

LT. COL. NORTH: I'm not either.

MR. LIMAN: But they—that you would go up there and take documents that they had finished reading?

LT. COL. NORTH: No, no, no. I want to be very clear. They were sitting—I had—my office—and you've now had a diagram of this palatial "basement office" on the third floor of the Old EOB. It was up on the wall here somewhere. And the desk that I had was in the corner of my office, and then there was a table about this size, and on that table was laid out all of the Iran documents, and I was working at my desk on other things, literally cleaning up files on lots of things, and when I'd finished with a handful of documents, I'd walk up, walk past them, walk out the door. You know where the shredder was. Turn the corner. Turn on the shredder and drop them in.

MR. LIMAN: And, did anyone say to you, "Colonel, what are you doing?"

LT. COL. NORTH: No, and I didn't think anything of it either. I mean, what you've got to understand, counsel, is that I didn't think I'd done anything wrong.

MR. LIMAN: Well, I understand th—

LT. COL. NORTH: Okay, and I don't think that they necessarily thought that I had done anything wrong.

MR. LIMAN: Well—

LT. COL. NORTH: And, so an officer who's got a shredder in his office ought to be, if he's not on the telephone or reading or writing documents, and needs to get rid of them, puts them in the shredder.

MR. LIMAN: The record is that before lunch hour, Mr. Reynolds found the diversion document that he didn't—

LT. COL. NORTH: But he didn't tell me.

MR. LIMAN: I know he didn't tell you, Colonel, so if you wait for the question, you're going to get your opportunity to answer. I'm not interrupting your answers.

MR. SULLIVAN: Yet.

MR. LIMAN: Not at all. He found that document. He attached significance to that document, and what you're saying is that even after that, which occurred before lunch, you were there taking batches of documents passed these attorneys from the Department of Justice, and shredding them, and they weren't saying, "Stop. We'd like to look. What are you doing? We're concerned." None of that. Right?

LT. COL. NORTH: I'm not trying to leave the wrong impression, counsel. Okay? What I'm saying to you is, I thought, and perhaps they thought, and I'm trying to be in several people's mind at once, is that they were looking for the facts on what had transpired in September, and October, November of 1985. All right? And, what I was told they were looking for, I thought was in the files that I gave them. Let me finish.

I was also engaged in a number of other projects of national security importance. The fact that I was shredding documents, I don't think would be unusual to them. This was, after all, an office with a shredder in it. I, I'm not trying to say that these guys were just letting me willy-nilly go and shred documents. I had a shredder for that purpose. If I'd finish reading a top secret cable of intelligence value, you don't leave those things sitting around your office. You destroy them after you read them. And, that's what I was doing, Counsel.

MR. LIMAN: Were you taking single documents over to the shredder, or were you taking files over to the shredder?

LT. COL. NORTH: I was not taking files. I would go through a file. I was sitting at my desk. They were working ten feet from me, and we would go—they were working on their projects; I was working on mine.

(Laughter in audience.)

MR. LIMAN: I want to hear more about it. Go ahead. I'm not interrupting.

LT. COL. NORTH: I mean, I don't want—I don't think you ought to accuse them from incompetence because they stopped a guy from doing his job. That's why the government of the United States gave me a shredder.

MR. LIMAN: But, your job on that day was to get rid of files, wasn't it? That's what you came in for.

LT. COL. NORTH: No. That isn't what I came in for. I was working desperately, among other things I received two or three phone calls on it, to keep the hostages alive. Good grief! We'd had this stuff all over the newspapers. The Israelis were calling me every half hour, and I was working with those people. They heard me taking the phone calls.

MR. LIMAN: Colonel?

LT. COL. NORTH: I was also in the process of looking after several other action packages that I had to move across the street on totally unrelated issues.

MR. LIMAN: Colonel, was your work on the phone with the Israelis leading you to shred documents?

MR. SULLIVAN: Objection.

LT. COL. NORTH: On occasion.

MR. LIMAN: Weren't you going through your files to get rid of embarrassing documents?

LT. COL. NORTH: Embarrassing? No. Documents that would compromise the national security of the United States, documents that would put lives at risk, documents that would demonstrate a covert action and the US direction and control and relationship to it, yes. Embarrassing? No. I'm not embarrassed to be here counsel.

MR. LIMAN: Are you saying, Colonel, that it would (long pause) Are you saying, Colonel, that you thought that allowing the Attorney General of the United States, or his representatives to see documents, would jeopardize lives?

LT. COL. NORTH: No. What I—what I'm saying to you counsel, is that revelations regarding those documents would destroy lives. Many of the documents that I destroyed, that day, prior to that day, and after that day, had absolutely no relationship to the Iranian activities. They had to do with Nicaraguan resistance activities, they had to do with counter-terrorist operations. Things that were, just as this committee has, I think, a scope within which they operate, they were working for a specific Iranian associated activities. And thus, if I had a file of matters pertaining to support for the internal opposition in Nicaragua. Or people who I had contacted in Europe and with whom I had

361

worked to get weapons for the Nicaraguan resistance. And sitting there at my desk I would pull those out and look at them and say, "North, if you're not here tomorrow, this doesn't need to be found by anybody." I would take them over to the shredder and destroy them. That's what I'm saying. Beyond the pale of their inquiry.

MR. LIMAN: Colonel, those were files that you had assembled over time, correct?

LT. COL. NORTH: Five and one half years, sir.

MR. LIMAN: And those were files that had remained secure for five and a half years. Is that correct?

LT. COL. NORTH: That is correct.

MR. LIMAN: And you know whoever your successor was, who would occupy that office, would be someone who was selected by the National Security Advisor, is that correct?

LT. COL. NORTH: I did not know that the person who moved into that office would share the same responsibilities, or indeed have anything to do with the matters in which I had worked. And the documents that existed in the permanent files were all that were necessary to carry on whatever other—the activities in which I was engaged, and it was only a part of my work, counsel. In support of the Nicaraguan resistance and support of the Iranian initiative were being terminated. There was no need to retain those documents.

MR. LIMAN: Do you deny, Colonel, that one of the reasons that you were shredding documents that Saturday, was to avoid the political embarrassment of having these documents be seen by the Attorney General's staff?

LT. COL. NORTH: I do not deny that.

MR. LIMAN: I think this is a good time for a break.

CHAIRMAN INOUYE: The hearing will stand in recess for 10 minutes.

CHAIRMAN INOUYE: Mr. Liman, please procede.

MR. LIMAN: Colonel.

LT. COL. NORTH: Counsel.

MR. LIMAN: Do you remember, Colonel, that in the early morning of—between Sunday night and Monday morning, after your interview with the Attorney General, that the alarm in your office was tripped because you were there shredding.

362

LT. COL. NORTH: I don't recall the alarm being tripped but I do remember being in the office until very, very early in the morning.

MR. LIMAN: And it is exhibit 155 but if you remember —if you remember being there until early in the morning, that's enough. And you were there shredding. Am I correct?

LT. COL. NORTH: Can you take a look at the exhibit, I don't—does the exhibit say I was there shredding?

MR. LIMAN: No, the exhibit just says—gives your explanation of what happened—155.

LT. COL. NORTH: (Long pause.) What it is is a indication from the security center that the alarm in my office had gone off, and the alarm was cleared. I was there until 0450 in the morning.

MR. LIMAN: And the following morning Miss Brown told us that the shredder was full. Does that refresh you.

LT. COL. NORTH: I don't deny that. I don't remember that it was. I'm not—I—I fully and completely have testified, Counsel, that I shredded documents I believe right up until the morning of the 25th when I departed.

MR. LIMAN: Do you remember, at all, telling your secretary, at one point, that you were leaving a document that the justice department could have fun with.

LT. COL. NORTH: I do not recall that.

MR. LIMAN: Do you remember—

LT. COL. NORTH: On what day did I allegedly do this?

MR. LIMAN: The 21st

LT. COL. NORTH: I do not recall that.

MR. LIMAN: And if you don't recall it, you don't remember what the document was.

LT. COL. NORTH: I don't recall the conversation nor do I recall the thought. I'm not denying that I said it. Those were, as you indicated earlier, Counsel, difficult times. Trying to maintain a sense of humor under those circumstances is difficult at best.

MR. LIMAN: Now, do you recall—and I don't want to belabor this, believe me, but we have to get facts.

LT. COL. NORTH: I am here to give you the facts, Counsel.

MR. LIMAN: Do you recall that on that Saturday when the Justice Department representatives left for lunch that you left the room with Commander Thompson and with a group of documents that you had to shred in the West Wing because your shredder was no longer working? That ring any bell with you, sir?

LT. COL. NORTH: It does not. But, I do know that I used the shredder which was identical in the West Wing to mine on a number of occasions.

MR. LIMAN: Do you recall using it in that period?

LT. COL. NORTH: I don't, but I certainly don't deny it.

MR. LIMAN: And did you use it when your shredder was full and not operational?

LT. COL. NORTH: I may have. But again, Counsel, I'm not denying that. I may well have. If someone said that I did, it is entirely likely that I did do that.

MR. LIMAN: Did you tell Admiral Poindexter that you were going to be shredding documents other than the diversion documents which you had said you had already gotten rid of?

LT. COL. NORTH: I don't—again, I don't recall specifically saying that. But I do recall assuring them on a number of occasions that I had taken care of my files, that I had shredded things, that basically the files were cleaned up. That was the basic input.

MR. LIMAN: I want to move to another topic, Colonel.

LT. COL. NORTH: Can I—before we leave that if we may, Counsel. Again, I well recognize that there are certainly people who think it might have been something else, but the efforts to destroy those documents over the course of that period of time beginning in October, I never once believed to be anything criminal at all. I did not believe that anything I had done to that point was criminal. And I didn't think that it was anything other than preserving the integrity of activities and operations, the lives of people who were out there at stake, the various things that I had done that no longer were relevant—some of them were history and never would be done again—they simply didn't need to be exposed in any way. And one cannot be certain in the expanse of answer to your comment, that whoever came in would be chosen by a national security adviser. I'm not certain that one ought to rest with the assurance that the person that comes in to replace you shares your same values or necessarily shares the same perspective that you have on a number of things. And I'm not saying that I have an exclusive view of what is right or wrong. I believe that things I did were right, and I believe that the lives of the people with whom I worked needed to be protected. I knew that the successor that was coming in wasn't going to do that. The CIA was now back actively engaged in the support of the Nicaraguan resistance. And the names and addresses and the places and the people with whom I worked during the period of time in which the CIA was not engaged, need not be exposed by anybody. And I want you to know that that was a lot of what was going through my mind.

MR. LIMAN: Colonel, since you chose to give that answer, I'm not going to leave the subject for a moment. First, let me make a statement, that it will probably provide no comfort to you for you to understand that we're not prosecutors here, and we're not here to assess criminal responsibility. I understand that there is an independent counsel somewhere working in other offices, but you should understand that our assessment is of a different nature.

LT. COL. NORTH: Counsel, I understand that you're saying that, but I have heard members of this Committee who have said that I did wrong, that I wouldn't even need counsel, or that I wouldn't have abided by my rights under the Constitution but for the fact that I had done wrong, and I didn't believe it then, and I don't believe it now.

MR. LIMAN: Are you saying, sir, that you do not believe that it was wrong to misrepresent facts to the Congress of the United States?

LT. COL. NORTH: I have admitted that, but I didn't think it was criminal.

MR. LIMAN: I'm not talking about what was criminal, you just chose the word "wrong." Are you saying, sir, that it wasn't wrong to misrepresent facts to the Attorney General of the United States?

LT. COL. NORTH: (Confers with counsel.) I have testified as to what I believed to be right and wrong before—

MR. LIMAN: Now—

LT. COL. NORTH: —and you have had that, and it's on the record.

MR. LIMAN: Now, Colonel, you have talked about the fact that you didn't know who your successor would be, and that was one of the reasons for engaging in all of this activity in the days before you left office, correct?

LT. COL. NORTH: That is correct.

MR. LIMAN: The one thing you knew, was that people taking tours of the White House couldn't go into your office and look at the files there, right?

LT. COL. NORTH: Not without the combination to my door.

MR. LIMAN: And the other thing that you knew—(Pauses while North confers with his attorney.) And the other thing that you knew was that the President of the United States, the Commander in Chief whom you respect and revere, and I suspect love, had asked the Attorney General to do a fact finding mission, that's correct, isn't it?

LT. COL. NORTH: Actually I don't know that Admiral Poindexter, when he told me about the fact finding inquiry on the 21st, that he specified that it was the President who had asked that that be done, but I did come to know that, that is correct.

MR. LIMAN: Would it have made a difference to you in your actions if you felt that the Attorney General was proceeding on the specific instructions of the President as opposed to the Admiral?

LT. COL. NORTH: Would what have made a difference —that my actions be any different?

MR. LIMAN: Yes, sir.

MR. SULLIVAN: Objection, it's a hypothetical question—

MR. LIMAN: Would you—

MR. SULLIVAN: It's just pure speculation.

MR. LIMAN: You say that you were not sure whether the Attorney General was conducting this inquiry at the request of the President, or at the request of the Admiral. That's what I heard you say.

LT. COL. NORTH: No. What I said was, I don't know that the Admiral told me, on the 21st, that the President—at least, I don't recall knowing at the time—that the Admiral told me that this was being done at the request of the President. He may well have told me that.

MR. LIMAN: Would you have shredded less documents on the 22nd if you had been told that the Attorney General was acting at the specific request of the President, your Commander in Chief?

MR. SULLIVAN: Objection.

CHAIRMAN INOUYE: What is the basis of your objection, sir?

MR. SULLIVAN: It is pure speculation—dreamland. It has two "ifs" in it. And Mr. Liman knows better than most that—

CHAIRMAN INOUYE: May I remind—

MR. SULLIVAN: —those kinds of questions, Mr. Chairman, are wholly inappropriate, not just because of rules of evidence, not because you couldn't say it in a court, but because it's just dreamland. It's speculation. He says, "If you'd done this, and if you'd done that, and if you'd done that—what about this?" Come on, let's have, Mr. Chairman—

CHAIRMAN INOUYE: I'm certain counsel—

MR. SULLIVAN: —plain fairness, plain fairness. That's all we're asking.

CHAIRMAN INOUYE: May I speak, sir? May I speak?

MR. SULLIVAN: Yes, sir.

CHAIRMAN INOUYE: I'm certain counsel realizes that this is not a court of law.

MR. SULLIVAN: I—believe me, I know that.

CHAIRMAN INOUYE: And I'm certain you realize that the rules of evidence do not apply in this inquiry.

MR. SULLIVAN: That I know as well. I'm just asking for fairness—fairness. I know the rules don't apply. I know the Congress doesn't recognize attorney-client privilege, a husband and wife privilege, priest-penitent privilege. I know those things are all out the window—

CHAIRMAN INOUYE: We have attempted to be as fair as we can.

MR. SULLIVAN: —and we rely on just fairness, Mr. Chairman. Fairness.

CHAIRMAN INOUYE: Let the witness object, if he wishes to.

MR. SULLIVAN: Well sir, I'm not a potted plant. I'm here as the lawyer. That's my job. (Laughter.)

CHAIRMAN INOUYE: Mr. Liman, please proceed with that question.

LT. COL. NORTH: Let me answer it with a hypothetical answer.

MR. LIMAN: Colonel, you testified, when I put a question to you, that you did not recall whether the—the Admiral had told you that the President had requested the Attorney General to act. Do you recall that?

LT. COL. NORTH: I do.

MR. LIMAN: You are the person who volunteered that fact, in response to one of my questions. Do you recall that?

LT. COL. NORTH: I do.

MR. LIMAN: And my question to you was, would that have made a difference? You're the person who surfaced it.

LT. COL. NORTH: Don't get angry, Counsel. I'm going to answer your question. If the Admiral had told me that the President had asked the Attorney General to conduct a fact-finding inquiry into all of the aspects of what I had done, and that I should tell the Attorney General everything, then I would have done so. Does that answer your question, sir?

And, the Admiral did not tell me that.

MR. LIMAN: And, if the Admiral had told you that, you wouldn't have done the quantity of shredding that you did. Is that correct?

LT. COL. NORTH: We can play hypothetical games all night. If the Admiral had told me not to shred, I wouldn't have shredded.

MR. SULLIVAN: If the—

MR. LIMAN: Did you tell the Admiral that you were going to shred?

LT. COL. NORTH: Pardon.

MR. LIMAN: Did you tell the Admiral that you were going to shred?

LT. COL. NORTH: I told the Admiral that I was cleaning up my files. I told him that well before this began. I assured him on the 21st that I'd already done most of it.

MR. SULLIVAN: Mr. Chairman, may I object please. There has to be a reasonable limit to questions posed about shredding. I mean, how many hours, how many days, how many times? The Colonel has admitted shredding. I would say, conservatively, 125 times. I, please, respectfully ask, could we move on?

LT. COL. NORTH: I honestly think, and I'm not trying to be light about it, we spent more time talking about it than I spent doing it. I honestly mean that. I shredded. I was never told not to shred. I shredded because I thought it was the right thing to do. When I didn't have a shredder, I put it in the burnbag and they were burned, and when the time came that I saw the entire situation change, and I was faced with the possibility of being the victim of a criminal prosecution, I then took action to protect myself. I took my notebooks home, and I took papers home, and I kept them until I turned them over to you.

MR. LIMAN: Now, let's—

LT. COL. NORTH: And, to the White House.

MR. LIMAN: Now, let's move on to a different subject. I want to talk about Boland. You, in your statement today that you read, said that you felt like you had been caught between—in the middle of a constitutional battle between the Executive branch and Congress over foreign policy perogatives. Remember that thought?

LT. COL. NORTH: I do.

MR. LIMAN: We have up on the board the joint resolution, which is called the Boland Amendment, one of them. And, I'd like you to observe three signatures on it, sir. One of them is Thomas O'Neill, Speaker of the House. The next is Strom Thurmond, who is the President Pro Tem of the Senate, and the third signature is one that you recognize, isn't it?

LT. COL. NORTH: It certainly is, and I hope all Americans do.

MR. LIMAN: That's the President of the United States.

LT. COL. NORTH: That's right.

MR. LIMAN: So this bill here, the Boland Amendment, represented a law passed by Congress and signed by the President of the United States. Correct?

LT. COL. NORTH: That is correct.

MR. LIMAN: And—

LT. COL. NORTH: A part of a bill. That's correct.

MR. LIMAN: And you not only have sworn to uphold and defend the constitution and all of the laws, but you've risked your life to do that. That's fair to say, isn't it?

LT. COL. NORTH: Yes, sir.

MR. LIMAN: The medals on your chest, which I think all of us respect and know what they stand for, were gained in defending our way of government. Correct?

LT. COL. NORTH: Yes.

MR. LIMAN: You talked very, very eloquently, the other day, about a democratic outcome in Nicaragua. Correct?

LT. COL. NORTH: I tried to.

MR. LIMAN: And I think you believe—

REP. HYDE: (Off mike) May I ask the question of his (inaudible). May I Mr. Chairman?

CHAIRMAN INOUYE: Please.

REP. HYDE: That is not in the form in which the President signed it or Strom Thurmond or Thomas P. "Tip" O'Neill, that's a composit, I believe, part of a huge, monsterous continuing resolution with all sorts of things in it. And of course, the name of the game is give it to him in October, after the fiscal year is over, and he has to sign it. So I just kind of think there is a little over reaching here by Mr. Liman—as though the President rushed into his oval office to sign the Boland Amendment. That was part of a huge appropriation, that is absolutely indispensible to keep government going, that the President has to sign, literally with a gun to his head, because that's the way we appropriate.

We don't consider these things individually, on their merits. We wait until the 11th hour of the 11th minute of the 11th day and then we give him a huge banquet full of appropriations, and say, "Sign it or else." So, it just seems to me, Mr. Chairman, that there is a little over reaching here by Counsel and I would just like to register—incidentally I am told that was the largest continuing resolution we've ever passed to date, thirteen appropriation bills were in there—so—just a little thought that we put it in context here.

REP. FASCELL: Mr. Chairman, I am sorry to have to do this, and I am not going to make a speech, but I don't want to—certainly don't want to be part of an effort to demean the President of the United States—that he doesn't know what he is signing. And the witness is smart enough to have already said as part of the testimony, that this represents a part of the bill. So he is very much aware of what this is all about.

CHAIRMAN INOUYE: I believe that the record should show that the President did sign the bill. Please procede.

MR. LIMAN: Mr. Chairman, this blow-up was prepared by the House Committee, and as I understand it, reviewed for

370

fairness by all counsel there and accepted by us, it has been used before without objection, so far as I know.

REP. HYDE: Well, Mr. Chairman, it's not accepted by this member. That's a composite. That is not the way the amendment was signed, and it's a little fractional part of a huge bunch of appropriations, and you're pretending that the President read that and he signed it and he knew what he—I, I'm sure he knew it was in there, but I'm sure he had to take it.

(Laughter from audience.)

Well, if you're satisfied with that way of appropriating in this Jenkins Hill operation, you can be satisfied with it, but you're not kidding anybody, and I'm not referring to the Chairman. I'm referring to whoever dreamed up this composite exhibit, and I thank the chairman.

CHAIRMAN INOUYE: Thank you, sir.

MR. LIMAN: Colonel North,—

REP. DEWINE: Can I ask one additional question? I did not hear an answer from counsel if this is a composite. It looks like a composite to me, and I just want to ask if, Counsel, is that a composite?

MR. LIMAN: I believe so.

LT. COL. NORTH: It is.

MR. LIMAN: You know it's a composite?

LT. COL. NORTH: I know well that it's a composite. The President's signature is a considerable number of pages later.

SEN. HEFLIN: Mr. Chairman.

CHAIRMAN INOUYE: Senator Heflin.

SEN. HEFLIN: Mr. Chairman, in order to have fairness, I'd like to request that an enlargement of the Constitution of the way a law becomes a law be put up there?

CHAIRMAN INOUYE: I will instruct the staff—

(Laughter from the audience.)

REP. HYDE: Mr. Chairman, perhaps we can have the whole continuing resolution, of which this was a fractional part, cover the walls.

MR. LIMAN: Colonel, was the Boland Amendment the subject of some discussion at the White House?

LT. COL. NORTH: It was.

MR. LIMAN: It was not something that slipped through. Is that fair to say?

LT. COL. NORTH: The whole issue of the many different Boland proscriptions and amendments and the like were for a protracted period of time the subject of discussion.

MR. LIMAN: You participated with other members of the NSC in an effort to persuade Congress that it was wrong.

LT. COL. NORTH: Yes, we did.

MR. LIMAN: It was a matter of high priority for the President to continue support to the contras as a way of bringing pressure on the Sandinista government for what you call a democratic outcome. Is that correct?

LT. COL. NORTH: It was frequently the subject of Presidential public pronouncements, his speeches, and the President was indeed concerned that we be able to continue to provide support to the Nicaraguan resistance.

MR. LIMAN: And, you have no doubt that when the President of the United States signed the appropriations bill, he knew he was signing the Boland Amendment into law. Correct?

LT. COL. NORTH: There is no doubt that at the 11th hour of that budget action, an appropriations action, that the President was well aware that it was in it. It was also, as I recall, on the second go-round that we'd had in the continuing resolutions that year, as we often do in an effort to pass a budget, that this appeared on the President's desk, and that we were running out of time and money, not just for the Nicaraguan resistance, but for the government of the United States as well.

MR. LIMAN: And, you are well aware, sir, that while you served at the NSC that the President signed some laws which he chose to challenge in the courts on grounds of constitutionality, such as the Gramm-Rudman Bill.

LT. COL. NORTH: That's true, but I hope you're not going to engage me in the lawyerly debate—

MR. LIMAN: You can assure I will not, because I can see Mr. Sullivan's ready.

(Laughter in audience.)

LT. COL. NORTH: Sometimes I can read his mind.

MR. LIMAN: But, you understood, sir, that the President signed this, and that this was now the law of the land?

LT. COL. NORTH: Indeed.

MR. LIMAN: And, now, prior to the time that the contras

ran out of money in the spring of 1984, is it correct that the CIA was providing them with assistance?

LT. COL. NORTH: How far have we gone in admitting to that in this public hearing?

MR. LIMAN: Well, that can be answered yes or no.

MR. SULLIVAN: Objection. The problem is its been answered "yes" 15–20 times.

MR. LIMAN: Then we would have been passed this.

MR. SULLIVAN: Yes, we would have.

LT. COL. NORTH: I am still uncertain, Mr. Chairman, as to what it is that we're supposed to be confirming or denying regarding US intelligence activities. And if you tell me I can answer "yes" to that question, I will do so.

CHAIRMAN INOUYE: You may answer yes or no.

LT. COL. NORTH: Yes.

MR. LIMAN: And you then testified that you were given a task of keeping the body and soul of the contras together, correct?

LT. COL. NORTH: That is correct.

MR. LIMAN: Whose words are "the body and soul?"

LT. COL. NORTH: As they were relayed to me, they were the words of the President.

MR. LIMAN: And did you understand those words to mean to keep them together in the field as a fighting force until Congress turned the money back on?

LT. COL. NORTH: And more. To keep them together as a viable political opposition, to keep them alive in the field, to bridge the time between the time when we would have no money and the time when the Congress would vote again, to keep the effort alive because the President committed publicly to go back, in his words, "again, and again, and again" to support the Nicaraguan resistance. And I not only did that, but I went down and talked, as you now know from my notebooks, with the heads of state of Central American and other countries, with the political leadership of those other countries, in an effort to do just exactly that.

MR. LIMAN: Now, did the job—

LT. COL. NORTH: And I also believe, sir, that that action, direction to me as a member of the President's staff, was just as legal as that prescription taking away funding.

MR. LIMAN: And did you understand that that direction

373

was emanating from the President of the United States himself?

LT. COL. NORTH: I did.

MR. LIMAN: And did I read your expression correctly when you winced yesterday when someone read from the Tower Report that the President said that he didn't know that the NSC staff was helping the contras?

LT. COL. NORTH: I don't know what you read in my wince. It may have been that my back hurt.

MR. LIMAN: Well, if I were to read this to you: "The President told the Board on January 26, 1987, that he did not know that the NSC staff was engaged in helping the contras. The President" —I'm sorry, "—the Board is aware of no evidence to suggest that the President was aware of Lt. Col. North's activities." First, does it come as a surprise to you that the President did not know that the NSC staff was engaged in helping the contras?

LT. COL. NORTH: And my answer?

MR. LIMAN: Your answer, sir.

LT. COL. NORTH: It's there in the record.

MR. SULLIVAN: He's reading from the—

MR. LIMAN: I'm reading from the Tower Report.

MR. SULLIVAN: Could we see a copy, sir, to make sure it's accurate, please.

MR. LIMAN: I think I can read this correctly.

CHAIRMAN INOUYE: While we are studying the document, I'd like to advise the members of the Senate that a vote is in progress at this time.

(Pause while North examines document and consults with counsel.)

LT. COL. NORTH: Your question, sir.

MR. LIMAN: The Counsel has asked to read what the Tower Board Report says, and it's in the last paragraph on the page. "The President told the Board on January 26, 1987, that he did not know that the NSC staff was engaged in helping the contras." Take that sentence.

LT. COL. NORTH: I read it.

MR. LIMAN: Does that come as a surprise to you?

LT. COL. NORTH: Yes.

MR. LIMAN: Now, who was it who conveyed the instructions of the President that you should keep the body and the soul of the contras together?

LT. COL. NORTH: Mr. Robert C. McFarlane.

MR. LIMAN: And over the course of the period that you were at the NSC, you reported that you testified regularly to Mr. McFarlane and Mr. Poindexter, Admiral Poindexter, on what you were doing to carry out this mission. Correct?

LT. COL. NORTH: You have far more than my testimony to confirm that.

MR. LIMAN: And you also reported to Mr. Casey.

LT. COL. NORTH: That's correct. And you have more than my testimony to confirm that.

MR. LIMAN: Is it fair to say—is it fair to say, Colonel North, you were confronted with a dilemma?

LT. COL. NORTH: When?

MR. LIMAN: Well, I'll explain what it is, and you'll either confirm it or not. On the one hand, you were told to keep the contras alive including as a fighting force to run what you called a full-service covert operation.

LT. COL. NORTH: I didn't call it that.

MR. LIMAN: Well, to provide them with covert support including—covert support assisting them militarily. And on the other hand, you had the Boland Amendment there. That present a problem for you, sir?

LT. COL. NORTH: Is the question is, "Did the Boland Amendment create a problem?"

MR. LIMAN: No, did you find that you had—that you were in a conflicted position, sir?

LT. COL. NORTH: No. We sought means by which we could comply with Boland and still keep the Nicaraguan resistance in the field, politically viable, and support it diplomatically and politically throughout the world, and I think we found it.

MR. LIMAN: Did you think that you had found those means when you recommended to your superiors that they sink a ship called the *Monimbo*?

LT. COL. NORTH: I didn't ask my superiors to sink the ship. I asked my superiors for their views and recommendations on dealing with that ship.

MR. LIMAN: Did you ask your superiors to assist in providing intelligence and other assistance so that that ship could be sunk?

LT. COL. NORTH: Again, maybe we're misunderstanding each other. If I recall the event, I asked my—I proposed several alternatives for dealing with that ship. I suggested that I do certain things that the resistance, and others associated with the resistance do certain things. And if I recall correctly, the ship ended up on its side on the beach.

MR. LIMAN: Did you believe that you were complying with Boland when you made the recommendation to your superiors which included assisting in the sinking or seizure of the *Monimbo*?

LT. COL. NORTH: Indeed I did.

MR. LIMAN: Did you believe that you were complying with Boland when you took intelligence from the CIA and passed it to the contras through Robert Owen?

LT. COL. NORTH: Yes, and the intelligence that I passed myself personally. And it wasn't all from the CIA, much of it came from the Department of Defense.

MR. LIMAN: And did you understand at the time that the CIA and the Department of Defense couldn't pass that intelligence directly?

LT. COL. NORTH: Exactly.

MR. LIMAN: And you believed that it was compliance with Boland—that it was fulfilling the purposes of Boland for you to take the intelligence from the CIA or the Department of Defense and pass it to the contras. That's what you're saying?

LT. COL. NORTH: I'm not saying that it was fulfilling the purposes of Boland. I'm saying it was working around the problem that Boland would have created and trying to comply with Boland that allowed me to do that.

MR. LIMAN: Well, another word for working around, for people who've had some Latin, is circumvent. Are you saying that you thought you found a legal way of circumventing Boland or that you found a way of complying with Boland.

LT. COL. NORTH: I think we found a legal way of complying with Boland.

MR. LIMAN: Did you believe that you found a way of complying with Boland when you were recommending to your superiors that they solicit money from the current donors?

LT. COL. NORTH: I don't believe I recommended that my superiors solicit money.

MR. LIMAN: If—we will look at those memos, but you

have no recollection now of having recommended to Mr. McFarlane that he go back to the current donors, namely Country Two, to get more money in 1985?

LT. COL. NORTH: I may well have, Counsel. And if you would show me the document, I'm sure it would help to refresh my recollection.

MR. LIMAN: I certainly will. 149.

LT. COL. NORTH: Exhibit number?

MR. LIMAN: 149. (Pause) There's another one, too. (Pause)

LT. COL. NORTH: I remember the memo.

MR. LIMAN: Colonel North, if you look at your recommendation, it says that the current donors be approached to provide 15 to 20 million additional between now and June 1, 1985.

LT. COL. NORTH: It does, indeed, read that way. And I did, indeed, write the memo.

MR. LIMAN: And did you believe that you were complying with Boland when you made that recommendation?

LT. COL. NORTH: Absolutely, Counsel. I see nothing in Section 8066 of the Joint Resolution that in any way deters, prevents, stops, or prohibits me, Mr. McFarlane, or anyone else in the Executive branch from going to a current donor or a future donor and doing just exactly what's suggested there. And if it had prohibited it, I wouldn't have recommended it.

MR. LIMAN: Colonel, if you look at Exhibit 261, which is another of your memos, this one date May 1, 1985, you'll see that there it says, "Recommendation that the current donors be approached to provide the remainder of their $25 million pledge." And then Mr. McFarlane crossed out "and an additional 15 to 20 million dollars between now and June 1 1985." You wrote that, too, correct?

LT. COL. NORTH: Certainly.

MR. LIMAN: Now you said that—

LT. COL. NORTH: But again, Counsel, what I'm saying is, there is nothing in what you have so graciously put up on the wall that prohibits that action.

MR. LIMAN: Now isn't it a fact, Colonel, that you and your colleagues in the NSC spent a good deal of time formulating a legislative policy that would get permission from the Congress to solicit third countries to support for the contras? Is that correct?

377

LT. COL. NORTH: Yes.

MR. LIMAN: And do you recall that you wrote memos on that subject, reviewing the options for getting Congressional legislation?

LT. COL. NORTH: That's correct.

MR. LIMAN: And do you recall that after these memos recommending going back to the current donors were written, Congress, in December 1985, amended Boland to permit solicitation of humanitarian aid? Do you remember that, sir?

LT. COL. NORTH: If you say it was December '85, I'm sure that it must be.

MR. LIMAN: Well, you remember that the bill was passed?

LT. COL. NORTH: I do.

MR. LIMAN: And it was, I believe, in December of '85, well after this. You remember that, don't you?

LT. COL. NORTH: Yes. And

MR. LIMAN: And so, is what you are telling us, now, that this legislation that you fought to get was superfluous?

LT. COL. NORTH: No.

MR. LIMAN: Was this legislation, legislation that was intended to restrict what you already had the power to do?

LT. COL. NORTH: Not at all.

MR. LIMAN: You sought this legislation to get authorization for something that somebody in the administration thought you didn't have the power to do. Correct?

LT. COL. NORTH: Not necessarily. As I recall, the entire process of trying to restore what became $100 million worth of aid to the Nicaraguan resistance, is we took it step by step by step. As I recall, the instructions were to bite off a little at a time, and start moving back toward full support. And the next step in that was to get appropriated $27 million worth of humanitarian assitance, and the permission to get full intelligence support. And finally, we got back to full $100 million worth of military and political support.

MR. LIMAN: Colonel—

LT. COL. NORTH: Going step by step by step.

MR. LIMAN: Colonel, this—this was an additional bite, getting the permission from Congress to solicit the humanitarian aid. Correct? Using your term—bite at a time.

LT. COL. NORTH: Yes. And to have people besides the National Security Council be able to do those things.

MR. LIMAN: Well—

LT. COL. NORTH: But quite honestly, Counsel, I see nothing in either that section of the Continuing Resolution Appropriations, nor the Constitution of the United States, that in any way prohibits the President or his personal staff from interacting with foreign heads of state, as I did, as Mr. McFarlane did—or their representatives—to this end.

MR. LIMAN: Colonel, I want you to know—

LT. COL. NORTH: I think—

MR. LIMAN: —I am not trying to take away a legal position that you may have to urge in court, if the—

LT. COL. NORTH: I'm not arguing my own legal—

MR. LIMAN: —independent counsel brings a proceeding. I'm just trying to—

LT. COL. NORTH: Let me just say something about that, Counsel. If I was that concerned about that outcome, I wouldn't be here right now. The fact is, I sincerely believe that the President of the United States can send his emissaries anywhere in the world, to talk to anybody about anything.

MR. LIMAN: So—

LT. COL. NORTH: And I think the Constitution hasn't been changed since it was written in that he could do that.

MR. LIMAN: Did you recommend that the President of the United States seek legislation giving permission for the State Department to seek humanitarian aid?

LT. COL. NORTH: Yes. I was one of many—

MR. LIMAN: At the time—

LT. COL. NORTH: —who participated in that.

MR. LIMAN: And at the time you participated in that recommendation, are you telling us you believed that the— (Pause.)

MR.: Please continue.

MR. LIMAN: At the time that you participated in that recommendation, are you telling us that you believed that the President of the United States was free to solicit both lethal and humanitarian aid, by sending any emissary of his choosing?

LT. COL. NORTH: From his own staff? Any emissary that worked inside the 18 acres known as the White House complex? Absolutely no problem (emphasizes word:) whatsoever. And I see nothing inconsistent with asking for

379

legislation to support that, and still allowing us to do what we did under Boland.

MR. LIMAN: Did you or any member of your staff ever tell Congress that you were ready, were free to and were engaging in the solicitation of lethal aid at the time you asked Congress for permission to do a restricted solicitation of humanitarian aid?

LT. COL. NORTH: No, and by the way, my staff at that point in time consisted of me and the secretary, so—

MR. LIMAN: Well, did any of your colleagues, to your knowledge, tell that to Congress?

MR. LIMAN: In fact, the law changed to permit this limited solicitation in December 1985, and you have already reviewed with Mr. Nields the letters that were written in August of 1985 by Mr. McFarlane saying that you weren't engaged in solicitation, and that the NSC staff was abiding by the letter and spirit of Boland.

LT. COL. NORTH: That's correct.

MR. LIMAN: Now, is what you are telling us today that when you helped in the participation of the letter saying that we are complying with the letter and spirit of Boland, what we are saying is that Boland doesn't apply to us and so we're complying with its letter and spirit?

LT. COL. NORTH: Exactly.

MR. LIMAN: And, that is what you think is a fair reading of that letter?

LT. COL. NORTH: Well, I have not denied, Counsel. I have admitted that the letters are misleading, evasive, and wrong.

MR. LIMAN: Did you—

LT. COL. NORTH: I'm talking—if you're talking about the specific part that we are living within the letter of Boland, absolutely.

MR. LIMAN: Now—

LT. COL. NORTH: And, as you know my recommendation all along was to withhold that information.

MR. LIMAN: But your recommendation all along would have been to confront Congress on this.

LT. COL. NORTH: You got it.

MR. LIMAN: And—

LT. COL. NORTH: And, if I may, just let me answer that. I think, and I mean no criticism of my superiors or anyone else, that I think is one of the members of this panel has indicated, that we all would have been better served by that confrontation, not a confrontation of a lieutenant colonel sitting across from the panel of elected officials of the government of the United States, or even taking him to the Supreme Court in my own defense. But, the fact is there should have been that. I agree with what one of the members of this panel has said, that that should have been done, but nonetheless, it was chosen to go another way, and I believe that the way we went was legal.

MR. LIMAN: But, your Commander in Chief, the President of the United States, chose not to confront Congress on this. Correct?

LT. COL. NORTH: Correct.

MR. LIMAN: And, he chose to sell in December 1985 for a law that permitted restricted solicitation for humanitarian purposes.

LT. COL. NORTH: As one of the steps to getting back to where we are today.

MR. LIMAN: And, at the time that he was settling for that compromise, the NSC was conducting its operation as if Boland did not apply to it, and as if it could do whatever solicitation it wanted to do. Correct?

LT. COL. NORTH: Certainly.

MR. LIMAN: And, indeed, if you did not feel that that was the policy of the President of the United States, you never would have participated in the diversion of the Ayatollah's money, which was getting money from Iran. Right?

LT. COL. NORTH: That's correct.

MR. LIMAN: And you've made it very clear, and I think it's painful for you, that whatever you did here, you did because you believed that you were carrying out the policy of the administration. Fair to say?

LT. COL. NORTH: Fair to say.

MR. LIMAN: Now, you are aware it's being referred to by my friend Mr. Nields that Mr. McFarlane said that he considered that the NSC was bound by Boland. Correct?

LT. COL. NORTH: I don't want to admit—

MR. LIMAN: You're aware he testified to it. You either saw a summary or you watched him on television.

LT. COL. NORTH: But again, Counsel—

MR. SULLIVAN: Let's see the testimony, if you want to direct our attention to something, Mr. Liman.

MR. LIMAN: Fortunately, I am prepared. (Laughter.)

MR. SULLIVAN: I knew you would be.

MR. LIMAN: Can I read you something? Will you trust me to read this?

MR. SULLIVAN: If I did, I wouldn't admit it, but (laughter) surely, go ahead.

MR. LIMAN: It's for Mr. Fortier. "Mr. McFarlane, you testified yesterday morning, yesterday and the day before, about the fact that it was your opinion that the Boland Amendments, particularly the more restrictive of those amendments, applied to the National Security Council. Is that correct? Mr. McFarlane: "Yes." Question: "Is that a personal opinion of yours?" Answer: "Yes, sir" —and there is more testimony to that effect.

You are aware that that is the position he has expressed at these hearings. Correct? If you weren't before, you are now.

LT. COL. NORTH: Correct.

MR. LIMAN: And as I understand your testimony, other than in the letters that were sent to Congress in which he said that the NSC was abiding by Boland, you never heard him say that.

LT. COL. NORTH: I carried out my instructions to the letter to the very best of my ability, Mr. Liman. I have said that innumerable times over the course of the last three days.

MR. LIMAN: But, can you answer that question that (sic) did you ever hear him say Boland does not apply to the NSC?

LT. COL. NORTH: I don't recall him saying that.

MR. LIMAN: You did hear Mr. Casey say that Boland doesn't apply to the NSC.

LT. COL. NORTH: At length.

MR. LIMAN: Now, is it correct, sir, that you were put in a position in which everybody who's eager and content to have Ollie North do whatever was necessary to energize the contras—to keep them together as a fighting force, to instill democratic values in them, to open up a southern front, to promote unity, to provide them with intelligence, to provide them with advice on munitions, to help provide them with that air base in a Central American country. They were all content and eager for you to do this as long as you didn't create a record pinning it on them?

LT. COL. NORTH: You'd have to ask them.

MR. LIMAN: Well, do you remember, Oliver North, that you had a conversation once with the Chief of the Central American Task Force at the CIA right after Boland was passed? And that—and I'm going to show it to you, if you don't remember—and that you got criticized for being indiscreet in mentioning what you were doing, and you were told, "be more discreet next time," not that you shouldn't do it.

LT. COL. NORTH: I recall the event, I don't recall the time.

MR. LIMAN: It's an Exhibit here, it's—we don't have to go over it.

LT. COL. NORTH: I recall it.

MR. LIMAN: But that really was the spirit, wasn't it, of it all: don't infect other people with knowledge—

LT. COL. NORTH: "Unnecessary knowledge" is the term.

MR. LIMAN: You do it, you provide the deniable link, you take the rap, if it gets exposed. That was what this was all about, right?

LT. COL. NORTH: I have testified to that.

MR. LIMAN: And it's also fair to say that the people who chose you for this knew and appreciated your qualities?

LT. COL. NORTH: You're asking me to put myself in the minds of other people, Counsel.

MR. LIMAN: Well—

LT. COL. NORTH: I don't believe that any of those people foresaw the outcome of what has happened—

MR. LIMAN: Well—

LT. COL. NORTH: I certainly didn't. I do honestly believe that they expected that Ollie would go quietly. And Ollie intended to do so right up until the day that somebody decided to start a criminal prosecution.

MR. LIMAN: Colonel, you characterized yourself, you described yourself—(pause) You described yourself as an action-oriented person, correct?

LT. COL. NORTH: That's correct.

MR. LIMAN: You were the person, I think in your own statement, people would say, "Ollie, fix it." Right?

LT. COL. NORTH: That's correct.

MR. LIMAN: And it would get fixed, right?

LT. COL. NORTH: Usually.

383

MR. LIMAN: And you could cut through red tape, right?

LT. COL. NORTH: Didn't say that in the statement. Well, but we did.

MR. LIMAN: That's—we understand each other, I've read enough of what you've written—

LT. COL. NORTH: Mr. Liman, let me just say one thing, I think it's important for everybody to understand. I don't believe that people for whom I still have an enormous amount of respect, like Mr. McFarlane, or Admiral Poindexter, would have ever placed me in jeopardy of a criminal prosecution. I don't believe that those men —whether or not the President knew, and I don't think the President would have done that—I don't think anybody intended that Ollie North have to endure having his name be the only one appear on the appointment order for an independent counsel. I think we all saw—I certainly did —that what we were doing was within the limits of the law—

MR. LIMAN: But—

LT. COL. NORTH: —that there were great liabilities and that they were principally political, that the liabilities included the protection of the lives of other people, some of whom were at great risk, and some of whom have died. But—

MR. LIMAN: Oliver North, I hear you saying that if you weren't on the order for the appointment of an independent counsel, if there was agreement that there was no criminal liability here, people would expect you to come before Congress and say, "I did it! It's not their fault" —

LT. COL. NORTH: I did do—

MR. LIMAN: —"I was that loose cannon."

LT. COL. NORTH: I did do it. I am not, as I said in my statement, at all ashamed of any of the things that I did. I was given a mission and I tried to carry it out.

MR. LIMAN: But part of that mission was to shield the others who were giving you the orders.

LT. COL. NORTH: That is the part of any subordinate. Every centurion had a group of shields out in front of him, a hundred of 'em.

MR. LIMAN: Well, would you agree with this proposition, Colonel, that—and I think you would, because I think those medals represent—

384

LT. COL. NORTH: No, those medals represent the heroism of the young Marines that I led. That's what they represent. And I—

MR. LIMAN: You still have those values, don't you?

LT. COL. NORTH: I never called myself a hero. Those words were used by other people who describe me. I am grateful for those words, but I have never called myself such.

MR. LIMAN: Colonel—Colonel, five and a half years in the White House hasn't destroyed those values?

LT. COL. NORTH: Not at all.

MR. LIMAN: Nor has this investigation destroyed those values.

LT. COL. NORTH: Not in the least.

MR. LIMAN: And I want to talk about those values, because I think this is important for the American people. And you would agree with the proposition, wouldn't you, that in our desire to promote democracy abroad, including Nicaragua and elsewhere, we must never sacrifice our democratic values here?

LT. COL. NORTH: I couldn't agree more.

MR. LIMAN: And that part of those democratic values are that sometimes Congress is going to disagree with the Executive branch?

LT. COL. NORTH: True enough.

MR. LIMAN: And sometimes you, as a military officer, are going to disagree with what the President or the Congress decide as a matter of policy—correct?

LT. COL. NORTH: Certainly.

MR. LIMAN: And you believe very firmly in civilian control?

LT. COL. NORTH: Absolutely.

MR. LIMAN: And you do not share the view that was expressed and retacted by your secretary that sometimes you must rise above the written law?

LT. COL. NORTH: I do not believe in rising above the law at all, and I do not [think] that I have ever stated that.

MR. LIMAN: And you—

LT. COL. NORTH: I haven't—I have not.

MR. LIMAN: And when you, Colonel North, had to—in order to protect this operation and your superiors—engage in deception of Congress, in deception of other members of the Executive branch, it is particularly painful for you in view of the honor code that you subscribed to at Annapolis, isn't that so?

LT. COL. NORTH: That is correct.

MR. LIMAN: (pauses) Now, this covert operation that you found yourself in—helping to direct—in Nicaragua, for the contras, was a different type from the covert operations that you had observed in your term at the CIA—at the NSC —right?

LT. COL. NORTH: It was different in perhaps where it was being directed from. We tried to adhere to the normal procedures that one would in the conduct of a covert operation.

MR. LIMAN: Well—

LT. COL. NORTH: And indeed, counsel, that is an important reason for why protecton was important.

MR. LIMAN: Well, let's talk about that, because that's what I want to come to.

LT. COL. NORTH: Well I—

MR. LIMAN: But, but—

LT. COL. NORTH: I—what I don't want to do, is leave you with the idea that the only thing I was doing was trying to protect my superiors. That is indeed an important part in terms of plausible deniability. But part of the destruction and the deception and all the rest of what you have described was to protect those engaged in the operation.

MR. LIMAN: Col. North, when the CIA was running this operation it was running it pursuant to a finding. Isn't that so?

LT. COL. NORTH: That's correct.

MR. LIMAN: And, so that there is no misimpression, under our law, covert operations are committed. Correct?

LT. COL. NORTH: That's correct.

MR. LIMAN: And under our law, which all of us have sworn to uphold, the covert operations are regulated. Correct?

LT. COL. NORTH: Yes.

MR. LIMAN: And the law provides that the President of the United States must make a finding, must put his name on the line in committing a covert operation?

LT. COL. NORTH: Again, I'm not trying to play legal scholar. It is my understanding that there is a requirement for a finding pursuant to the CIA's conduct of a covert operation in which U.S. funds are to be expended.

MR. LIMAN: Well, did you understand, Col. North, that if the President wants to follow the law that Congress passed and that he signed on covert operations, he can sign the finding and let the CIA do it. And if he wants to do it without signing a finding, he can let the NSC do it. Is that what you're saying?

LT. COL. NORTH: That's essentially what I'm saying. I'm not—

MR. LIMAN: The fielder's choice?

LT. COL. NORTH: No. I'm saying that he—the President is not precluded by that law, nor is the NSC precluded by that law from conducting the activities that we undertook.

MR. LIMAN: Did you ever hear the President of the United States express that view?

LT. COL. NORTH: No.

MR. LIMAN: Did—this was an important matter, providing support from the contras in terms of the President's policies. Correct?

LT. COL. NORTH: The President made innumerable speeches about it. I helped write some of those speeches about it.

MR. LIMAN: Did you—

LT. COL. NORTH: There's no doubt that aid to the democratic resistance in Nicaragua was a very high priority for the President.

MR. LIMAN: Did you ever see any opinion issued by the chief legal officer of the United States, the Attorney General saying that the NSC wasn't bound by Boland and could do these things?

LT. COL. NORTH: Did I ever see a determination by the chief legal officer of the United States—

MR. LIMAN: The Attorney General.

LT. COL. NORTH: I understand who the Attorney General is, Counsel—to the effect that the NSC was not bound by Boland. Is that the question?

MR. LIMAN: Right.

LT. COL. NORTH: No, I did not. But I worked, as I indicated in my statement, directly for two national security advisers. They are at the right hand of the President. It is my understanding that the President is still charged with the responsibility for the conduct of foreign policy in this country. And I believe that what we were doing is conducting a covert operation in support of that foreign policy.

MR. LIMAN: But, the difficulty with that, Col. North, is one of those national security advisers has testified and he said he believed Boland applied, and he told that to Congress; and I'm asking you, did you ever see an opinion of the Attorney General, and you've answered no. Did anyone ever ask, to your knowledge, for an opinion from the President's counsel? Mr. Fielding and then Mr. Wallison on this?

LT. COL. NORTH: I believe, Counsel, that I sent forward a number of memoranda suggesting various legal opinions from those offices.

MR. LIMAN: Did you get any back?

LT. COL. NORTH: I don't recall them right now, but I must have generated thousands and thousands of memoranda when I was at the White House, and I don't remember whether I did specifically whether I did or not.

MR. LIMAN: Are you saying that you were looking for opinions from the Attorney General or from the White House counsel?

LT. COL. NORTH: No.

MR. LIMAN: Then, what are you saying?

LT. COL. NORTH: Well, I'm just saying that I generated many memoranda, some of which called for certain opinions from the White House counsel. I don't recall whether I got one back or not.

MR. LIMAN: You do not as you sit here today have any recollection of any legal officer giving you that opinion other than Sciaroni?

LT. COL. NORTH: Mr. Sciaroni, who is a member of the bar, gave us an opinion that indicated that it was legitimate for the National Security Council to pursue these activities.

MR. LIMAN: Did you testify yesterday that you felt that the Intelligence Oversight Board had no jurisdiction over the NSC and you didn't have to give him any facts?

LT. COL. NORTH: I did.

MR. LIMAN: But, when you had a favorable opinion from that Board, you're prepared to rely on it, and you didn't want to give him any facts, they had no jurisdiction. Is that what it amounts to?

LT. COL. NORTH: You can call it what you like.

MR. LIMAN: And, was the first time that you were aware of an executive order signed by this President requiring Presidential findings for all covert actions when it was called to your attention by Mr. Nields?

LT. COL. NORTH: You're talking about Executive Order #12333?

MR. LIMAN: Yes, sir.

LT. COL. NORTH: I was familiar with Executive Order #12333 before Mr. Nields inquired about it.

MR. LIMAN: But your belief was that just as the law signed by the President of the United States on findings didn't apply if he chose to have the NSC do it, that Executive Order #12333 didn't apply if he chose to have the NSC do it?

LT. COL. NORTH: That is correct.

MR. LIMAN: So, it comes down to the fact that because of your belief that the President is the sole authority on foreign policy, he could do whatever he wanted in that field?

LT. COL. NORTH: Would you repeat that question, please?

MR. LIMAN: Well, does it come down to the fact that from your point of view as the action officer, the staff officer, the person who had to run this covert operation, that if the President wanted it, that was enough?

LT. COL. NORTH: And was within the limits of the law, that is correct.

MR. LIMAN: As you saw it?

LT. COL. NORTH: Yes.

MR. LIMAN: And, when the former national security officer—national security adviser says, "I didn't know anything about this, and we were complying with Boland," and when the President of the United States says, "I knew nothing about the NSC staff assisting the contras," you look upon that as just another exercise in deniability. Is that the fact?

LT. COL. NORTH: You'll have to take that up with them, Counsel.

CHAIRMAN INOUYE: The past three days have clearly shown the committee the necessity to study some of the documents in closed session. The questions and answers have come very close to exposing classified information. Therefore, I will entertain a motion to go into closed session to study these classified documents.

VICE CHAIRMAN WARREN RUDMAN (R-NEW HAMPSHIRE): Mr. Chairman?

CHAIRMAN INOUYE: Mr. Rudman.

VICE CHAIRMAN RUDMAN: Mr. Chairman, pursuant to Committee Rule 2–1, I move that the hearing go into closed session because of the necessity to discuss matters which concern classified information, national security, on the confidential conduct of foreign relations.

CHAIRMAN INOUYE: Is there a second?

(The motion was seconded)

CHAIRMAN INOUYE: There is a second. However, before proceeding to a vote, is there a similar motion for the House Committee?

CHAIRMAN HAMILTON: Mr. Chairman, I will entertain a motion from Representative Cheney regarding conducting the hearing in closed session.

REP. DICK CHENEY (R-WYOMING): Mr. Chairman, in regard to the sensitive nature of the subject and material to be discussed, I move the Committee now move into executive session.

CHAIRMAN INOUYE: We have now before us House and Senate motions to close the hearings. Is there discussion from either Senate or House members before proceeding with the vote? Hearing none, the clerk of the Senate Committee will call the roll of Senators.

(The clerk called the roll and announced that the vote was 11 ayes and zero nayes.)

CHAIRMAN HAMILTON: And the question before the House is on the House motion to close the hearing and the clerk will call the roll.

(The clerk called the roll)

CHAIRMAN INOUYE: This hearing will move to room S-407 in the United States Capitol for a closed session. We will stand in recess until that time.

END OF AFTERNOON SESSION

Friday · July 10, 1987

Morning Session—9:00 A.M.

CHAIRMAN INOUYE: (Bangs the gavel.)

MR. LIMAN: Colonel, did you receive any formal training in conducting covert operations?

LT. COL. NORTH: No, sir.

MR. LIMAN: It was all on the job training?

LT. COL. NORTH: That's a good way of putting it, sir. I got a lot of guidance, of course, from Director Casey who is widely revered as an expert.

MR. LIMAN: When you were on active duty in the Marines, were you involved in any special operation, as they use that term?

LT. COL. NORTH: Un, per se, no. The military units I were (sic) with were conventional military units.

MR. LIMAN: And, you served in Vietnam during what period, sir?

LT. COL. NORTH: 1968, 1969.

MR. LIMAN: Now, when you got drawn into the Iranian venture in November, in connection with the Hawk transactions, as I understand your testimony, you had conversations with, among other people, Mr. McFarlane, Admiral Poindexter, various CIA personnel, Defense Minister Rabin of Israel, Ministry of Defense people in Israel and Department of Defense personnel.

LT. COL. NORTH: This is in November of 1985.

MR. LIMAN: Right.

LT. COL. NORTH: Yes.

MR. LIMAN: And, as the transaction was first presented to you at that time, is it fair to say it was presented as a straight arms for hostages transaction?

LT. COL. NORTH: Er—and I don't mean to give a longer than necessary answer, Counsel, but there had been a number of discussions during the summer with, as I recall, Mr. Schwimmer, Mr. Ledeen; I think eventually, Mr. Ghorbanifar, at some point during the summer or autumn.

In each of those cases, certainly every time I talk with Mr. Ledeen, he always had a vision of a broader objective. Nonetheless, by the time I became operationally engaged in November, the proposition was put forward, at least in terms of a finding, as a straight arms for hostages transaction.

MR. LIMAN: And without taking much time, your notes of the period November 20, for example, describes "120 Hawks equals five American citizens and a guarantee that no more—" and the sentence isn't completed, but "no more would be taken" and no more terrorism I assume.

LT. COL. NORTH: I do recall those kinds of things being discussed. I don't want to commit myself to the fact that it was November 20th without looking at it. But, do we have an exhibit number I can—

MR. LIMAN: Yes, there is an exhibit number. It's Exhibit 356. And are these, does this have our letters on it? (Reviewing exhibit.) It would have Q1327 on it but I can read it. It has, "Iranians hurting for cash." It goes on and says, "120 Hawks, 1) five American ships, 2) guarantee but no more." Could you just hand him this? This is a—hand him this. This will be easier. (Pause while North and Sullivan review exhibit.)

LT. COL. NORTH: Yes. And again, just to make note of the fact that as I got more engaged in this thing as time went on, I made it a definite effort working with Mr. Sporkin and others at CIA to include in a finding the broader objectives that I thought ought to be there, and I think that Mr. McFarlane shared and certainly the President.

MR. LIMAN: Colonel, when the finding was done in November, it was a finding that was straight arms for hostages and that described the state of play on the Israeli Hawk transaction—fair to say?

LT. COL. NORTH: And the previous TOW transaction.

MR. LIMAN: And the previous TOW one.

LT. COL. NORTH: Yes.

MR. LIMAN: And the point that I wanted to illicit is that

the Tower Board Report indicated that this started as a broad initiative and evolved during your period of management of it into a straight arms for hostages transaction. And is it fair to say—is it fair to say that from the time of your active involvement in November, you found that as an arms for hostage transaction and it evolved, or you attempted to evolve it into something that was broader?

LT. COL. NORTH: Well again, I was—and I'm not trying to pass the buck at all, Counsel. In the discussions I had, and the very first person to address this issue with me I believe was Mr. Ledeen, he clearly saw, envisioned the broader objectives. And even though that initial finding did not articulate that—and I think that's probably because of the compartmented nature of the preparation of that intitial finding, it's almost cyclical, that you had an intent back in June, July, August, whenever all that began—the expression of that intent, I think, is flawed in that November finding and my effort was in January to get it back on track. And that was certainly shared in the discussions I had with Director Casey, one of which was at his home in the preparation of that second finding.

MR. LIMAN: Well let's, let's just take it step by step. You went in January—in December to London with Mr. McFarlane, correct?

LT. COL. NORTH: That is correct.

MR. LIMAN: And that was—

LT. COL. NORTH: He joined me in London.

MR. LIMAN: And that was a trip that followed a meeting that Mr. McFarlane had had with the principals of the NSC?

LT. COL. NORTH: Apparently so, I was not at that meeting.

MR. LIMAN: Did he tell you about the discussion at that meeting?

LT. COL. NORTH: In general terms, yes.

MR. LIMAN: Did he tell you that the Secretary of State and Secretary of Defense and the Chief of Staff were opposed to proceeding with the Iranians?

LT. COL. NORTH: I don't recall mention of the Chief of Staff. I do recall him mentioning specifically that both Secretary Shultz and Secretary Weinberger were not enamored of the proposal. I do not recall him expressing their stringent objections.

MR. LIMAN: Did he tell you that he wanted to go to London to make his own assessment of Ghorbanifar?

LT. COL. NORTH: Yes.

MR. LIMAN: And you were with him when—when he met with Mr. Ghorbanifar in Nimrodi's apartment?

LT. COL. NORTH: I was with him when we met with Mr. Ghorbanifar, and I know the area of London, but I couldn't give you a definitive ownership of the building.

MR. LIMAN: And—

LT. COL. NORTH: Mr. Nimrodi was there.

MR. LIMAN: And is it correct that that meeting was one in which Ghorbanifar was negotiating for a certain amount of TOWs for a certain number of hostages, and it was a bargaining by—by Ghorbanifar of weapons for hostages?

LT. COL. NORTH: Well, it was that, but it was also—it was very typical of the discussions with Mr. Ghorbanifar. It was wide-ranging, rambling, very disconnected in some respects. He clearly mentioned, and I recall it because he is an effusive man, talking about the fact that there were potential openings that could be achieved, talked about terrorism, as did Mr. McFarlane in the meeting. But it was very clear that Mr. Ghorbanifar was trying to establish a price—which, as you know from my records, I found to be most unpalatable —for a number of weapons for a number of Americans.

MR. LIMAN: And did—(pauses)—Did Mr. McFarlane also find that "unpalatable" that lives were for US arms?

LT. COL. NORTH: I—again, you're asking me to—

MR. LIMAN: Did he express it?

LT. COL. NORTH: Yes.

MR. LIMAN: And in fact, did he not tell you that he was going to recommend to the President of the United States that you have nothing more to do with Ghorbanifar?

LT. COL. NORTH: My recollection is that the outcome of that meeting was that unless we could get beyond Ghorbanifar and establish direct contact with Iranians, that this was probably not going to work in the long run, that we were not going to achieve our objectives, and I share that belief, and I think I testified to that yesterday.

MR. LIMAN: Did you, when you returned from London with Mr. McFarlane, brief the President of the United States?

LT. COL. NORTH: I was in that briefing, as I recall, yes.

MR. LIMAN: And—

LT. COL. NORTH: And I probably made some contributions to it, but my recollection is that Mr. McFarlane and I went to a regular morning briefing with the President. I may be incorrect in that. It was a long time ago.

MR. LIMAN: All right. Did you also prepare a report on the meeting?

LT. COL. NORTH: I probably did. I prepared papers on almost everything.

MR. LIMAN: Did you—do you recall telling the President of the United States that if the Iranian venture was discontinued at that time, that the lives of the hostages might be taken?

LT. COL. NORTH: I recall, certainly very clearly, putting that kind of message forward. I don't necessarily recall saying it point blank to the President that morning. But I very clearly saw that as a possibility. Certainly, the Israelis did. And I think, to at least a certain extent, that was shared by the people with whom I worked at the CIA. Our concern was that having started the route, wisely or unwisely, but having started that in August and September, and having a disaster on our hands in November as a consequence of what the Iranians clearly saw as a double cross, that we had indeed increased the jeopardy to the hostages, rather than reduced it. That kind of—

MR. LIMAN: If you look at Exhibit 51, it's a memorandum of December 9, from you to Mr. McFarlane and Admiral Poindexter. It's a December 9 memo, it's headed "Next Steps." And at page three, in describing the options, it says, "Do nothing: very dangerous, since United States has, in fact, pursued earlier Presidential decision to play along with Ghorbanifar's plan. US reversal now in mid-stream could ignite Iranian fire, hostages would be our minimum losses."

Remember that, Colonel?

LT. COL. NORTH: Yes, I wrote this document, and I—but I think it's important, Counsel, to point out that I was presenting forward, as I tried to do in most cases, options that we had if we wished to pursue any intiative in getting our Americans back. And—

MR. LIMAN: Well part of your role was to point out to the President or his National Security Adviser the opportunities and the risks, correct?

LT. COL. NORTH: That's correct.

MR. LIMAN: And you were pointing out the risk of abandoning further arms sales to Iran in terms of saying that they might take out reprisals on the hostages, isn't that so?

LT. COL. NORTH: That is correct, at the least.

MR. LIMAN: Yes. And I—when you say at the least, did Ghobanifar make those threats or was that an opinion that you and some of your colleagues and the Israelis formed?

LT. COL. NORTH: I don't—I don't recall Ghorbanifar making that kind of a threat. I mean, Ghorbanifar was obviously in a—in a very difficult situation. He had made commitments on behalf of the Israelis, perhaps, or others that what they would deliver in December would be responsive to what they had asked for. And he—he had a big problem on his hands. At the same time the Israelis saw their original initiative foundering. I know that Mr. Kinky, with whom I conversed on this, both in London and before and after, expressed this kind of a view.

MR. LIMAN: Now, did—at the—at the briefing that you had with the President of the United States, did he ask Mr. McFarlane's opinion as to whether you should go forward?

LT. COL. NORTH: I don't recall that part of the discussion.

MR. LIMAN: Did you express a view as to whether you should go forward?

LT. COL. NORTH: If I did and, again, I do not recall that specifically, but if I did it was to advocate that we do something, that this whole thing not lead to the kind of outcome that is forcast right there.

MR. LIMAN: I mean, the loss, the hostages.

LT. COL. NORTH: Exactly.

MR. LIMAN: In many—

LT. COL. NORTH: —plus the potential for further reprisals. I think that's important.

MR. LIMAN: Was there any discussion about the fact that having started down the road of dealing with Iran on arms, we were now becoming hostage to that very process.

LT. COL. NORTH: I always felt that way, and I think that's articulated in this memorandum.

MR. LIMAN: And, was there any discussion of the fact that if we started selling them arms, that once we stopped, we were going to run the risk that more hostages would be taken?

LT. COL. NORTH: Yes, and—and there was frequently discussion of that aspect of—of this whole initiative. But again, and I want to make it very clear, we believed, I believed then and I still believe today, that had we been able to get to a point where we would have had a meeting with, for example, the Vice President and Rafsanjani, which was a proposal I advocated at some point along in here, by virtue of intermediate level or low-level staff contact, like I was going to do, that we could get beyond that risk, and that once you had established the dialogue that we were seeking to establish, that we could, in effect, start working an outcome to the Iran-Iraq War, which would then lead to a reduced need for this kind of thing to begin with. And, this is important, because much jocularity has been created over the fact that I gave a tour of the White House to—

MR. LIMAN: Well, I'm not joking about it, and—

LT. COL. NORTH: I know that, but I would like to say this, Counsel. One of my purposes for taking the second channel, who was also a brave young man and also a soldier in his country, through the White House was to show him the Nobel Prize that was won by Teddy Roosevelt. And, I took him into the Roosevelt Room and I showed him that prize, and I said, "This is a Nobel Peace Prize. In fact, the first one ever given to an American. And, it was given to a President who saw that it was to the advantage of our country and to world peace to sit down in Portsmouth, and have a conference with two adversaries, the Russians and the Japanese, who were fighting a war thousands of miles away from us, that had no immediate impact on America, and we solved it."

And, that's what I was talking to the young Iranian about, and that's the kind of thing that I was proposing that help us get beyond arms, as a liability, or arms for hostages.

MR. LIMAN: Colonel,

LT. COL. NORTH: Yes.

MR. LIMAN: Did you believe that when you were talking to that young man, it was the equivalent of talking to people like Cho En Lai, which Kissinger did?

LT. COL. NORTH: No.

MR. LIMAN: Did you not realize, sir, that you were dealing with a country that had very very strong feelings toward the United States—

LT. COL. NORTH: A great animus.

MR. LIMAN: —expressed by a very very powerful leader?

LT. COL. NORTH: I knew well exactly what he was and what the leadership represented. I also noted the fact that during the time that we were pursuing this initiative, there were no acts of terrorism addressed against Americans, and that the rhetoric from that very strong leader against us was reduced considerably.

MR. LIMAN: Colonel,—

(Pause while North confers with Sullivan)

MR. LIMAN: Colonel, there's a saying that "failure is an orphan." The Committee has heard testimony, and will hear testimony, that Secretary Shultz was opposed to this venture, the Secretary of Defense was opposed to it. At the meeting on December 7th, the Chief of Staff was opposed to it. Mr. McFarlane said that when he returned from London, he was opposed to it and testified under oath. Had you become the principal advocate of having this program go forward?

LT. COL. NORTH: I don't believe I was the principal advocate. Certainly Director Casey was always a supporter of it because he saw several objectives that could be achieved by it. And I would simply observe that, like some of my other activities, the opposition that I heard was far more muted while we were doing it than it ever was after it failed, or after it was exposed. And I kind of get the feeling, Counsel, that there were a lot of people who were kind of willing to let it go along, hoping against hope that it would succeed, and willing to walk away when it failed. I'm not necessarily advocating that that's the way things ought to be, but this was a high-risk venture, we had an established person to take the spear, and we had hoped we had established plausible deniability of a direct connection with the US government, and I'm not necessarily saying that that's a bad thing, that high risk operations like this, or activities like this, it's understandable that people don't complain too loudly while they're happening as long as they can be assured of protection if it goes wrong.

MR. LIMAN: Colonel, when you said there was an established person to take the spear—again, you're referring to yourself. That can be answered, I think, yes, now?

LT. COL. NORTH: Yes.

MR. LIMAN: And Mr. McFarlane testified when he was here and when he was shown this memorandum of yours that we just looked at, December 9, 1985, that he was surprised or shocked that you were still promoting this initiative when he was opposed to it. Do you recall him being opposed to it and expressing that opposition at your meeting with the President?

LT. COL. NORTH: Mr. McFarlane, I recall, expressed concern that unless we got beyond Ghorbanifar that we would not succeed. I shared that.

MR. LIMAN: Now, were you told following this meeting with the President, that the President wanted to make another try?

LT. COL. NORTH: I was told to initiate another effort.

MR. LIMAN: And who gave you those instructions?

LT. COL. NORTH: Admiral Poindexter.

MR. LIMAN: Were they given at the meeting? Did the President express a position at the meeting?

LT. COL. NORTH: I don't recall that those instructions were given at the meeting. I was simply told to pursue another initiative and I did.

MR. LIMAN: And—

LT. COL. NORTH: And I wish to point out that Director Casey was a very strong advocate of this. You have to remember at the time—

MR. LIMAN: Let's—

LT. COL. NORTH: —that we believed that Mr. Buckley was still being held, and that we had some indications that he was being tortured. And some of the things we discussed last night were possibly the subject of his torture.

MR. LIMAN: Well, wasn't it the fact that you also had information at that time that he was dead, you just didn't know?

LT. COL. NORTH: We did not know.

MR. LIMAN: And were you meeting with—did you meet with Director Casey after you returned from London?

LT. COL. NORTH: I did.

MR. LIMAN: And did you express your point of view that

the hostages would be killed or could be killed, and there could be further reprisals if you didn't go forward with the initiative?

LT. COL. NORTH: Yes, and I believe Director Casey articulated those same views, both—

MR. LIMAN: Was anyone else with you? (Pause.) It's unimportant—

LT. COL. NORTH: I don't recall, but—

MR. LIMAN: —let me move on—

LT. COL. NORTH: I think Director Casey was on record, my recollection is that there were documents he sent forward which articulated the same view. I'm quite confident that I showed him this directive, this memorandum.

MR. LIMAN: Did Director Casey tell you that he would speak to the President about it?

LT. COL. NORTH: I don't recall him ever saying that to me. You know, I—our relationship was not one that I'd say, "You know, Mr. Casey, you've got to go to the President and talk to him about this," or that he would tell me about that.

MR. LIMAN: Now, you talked yesterday about the fact that it's important for the United States to have some constancy in its foreign policy. Do you recall that?

LT. COL. NORTH: That's correct.

MR. LIMAN: You were aware at this time of Operation Staunch, correct?

LT. COL. NORTH: Yes, I was.

MR. LIMAN: And, Operation Staunch represented the official United States policy against shipping arms into Iran—

LT. COL. NORTH: —and Iraq.

MR. LIMAN: —and Iraq. Correct?

LT. COL. NORTH: That's right.

MR. LIMAN: And, we had a very strong view that we wanted to not have arms trade taking place there?

LT. COL. NORTH: That's correct.

MR. LIMAN: We weren't very successful in stopping it. That's fair to say. Correct?

LT. COL. NORTH: Not in the least.

MR. LIMAN: But, we were still making protests to our allies and friends when we were able to find out that they were shipping. Correct?

LT. COL. NORTH: Generally, yes.

MR. LIMAN: And, were you told that the Secretary of State and the Secretary of Defense had said that this would undermine the United States' credibility if, all of a sudden, we became a supplier of arms?

LT. COL. NORTH: I never heard that during the course of this activity?.

MR. LIMAN: No one brought that to your attention?

LT. COL. NORTH: Never.

MR. LIMAN: Was one of the reasons for wanting to have Israel involved, so that we could say it was Israel that was selling and Israel, everyone knows, sells arms?

LT. COL. NORTH: Well, Israel was already involved, and we were going to continue to pursue it in—

MR. LIMAN: That's not—

LT. COL. NORTH: —as part of the plausible deniability. That's correct.

MR. LIMAN: And, part of the plausible deniability—

(Pause while the witness confers with his attorney)

Did Mr. Sullivan refresh your recollection, where you want to add to the answer, because I'm not saying that in criticism. I am saying that so that if there is something that should be added to this record, it should be added.

LT. COL. NORTH: (Starts to break a smile)

MR. SULLIVAN: Next question, Mr. Liman.

MR. LIMAN: Now, did—was the point of—was the point of you, expressed to you that we have to keep Israel involved in this so that it could be blamed on them if it's exposed?

LT. COL. NORTH: I don't want to use the word "blame". I don't think I ever used it, but very clearly, because this was a covert operation, a covert activity. To the extent that we could have several layers of plausible deniability, it would serve our purposes, and as because of Staunch and the rest of it, we did not want the US government's hand, or role in this activity exposed, and thus, we were, as I said earlier, we tried to mirror the Israeli model, if you will, of—as they did.

MR. LIMAN: Your notes for January indicate a reference to the fact that you wanted them back in time for the State of the Union message. Do you recall that at all?

LT. COL. NORTH: I don't, but if you'll show me the note, I'm sure it will refresh my memory.

MR. LIMAN: Do you recall any conversations to that effect?

LT. COL. NORTH: No.

MR. LIMAN: We'll get you that note. Mr. Hakim testified under oath here that you told him that the President was exerting pressure on you to get the hostages back by—in time for the elections in November of 1986.

LT. COL. NORTH: The President of the United States never told me that, nor did any other person. I may have said that to Mr. Hakim to entice him to greater effort, but I certainly didn't hear that from the President.

MR. LIMAN: So that was your idea?

LT. COL. NORTH: Yes.

MR. LIMAN: And no one in the administration gave you that idea?

LT. COL. NORTH: No one ever. I can assure you, Counsel, that the President's concerns for the hostages outweighed his political ambitions or political concerns. They were truly humanitarian. And I don't think it would be right to leave any doubt about that. In fact, the President was willing to take great political risk in pursuing this initiative.

MR. LIMAN: Did you, when you told Hakim this, think it was right to attribute that to the President?

LT. COL. NORTH: Well, as you have in the tape recordings I made with every meeting I had with the Iranians, I said a lot of things that weren't true. And again, I'd have told them they could have free tickets to Disneyworld or a trip on the space shuttle if it would have gotten Americans home.

MR. LIMAN: Whose side did you think Hakim was on, the Iranians or ours?

LT. COL. NORTH: Oh, he's on our side.

MR. LIMAN: And did you think that he needed an inducement in order to try to get the deal done?

LT. COL. NORTH: I think exhausted men, who are working very, very hard, sometimes need all kinds of inducements.

MR. LIMAN: And the inducement that you thought would help him was to say that the President of the United States wanted them back by—

LT. COL. NORTH: Trying to put a date certain—

MR. LIMAN: —by November?

LT. COL. NORTH: —and get them out by then.

MR. LIMAN: All right. The message that I was referring

to—to in your notes is, for what it's worth on page Q1438 of Exhibit 358, and it says "try to get results by State of the Union." But you have said, as I understand it—here, let me pass it to him it's easier to read. Colonel, let your—you will spare your eyesight if you look at this—this copy here. (Long pause.)

LT. COL. NORTH: The one you—you've given me, sir, is a call from Noel Koch, 6300 and 1975. "Once we have agreement."

MR. LIMAN: If you'll keep reading down, you'll see the reference. If you look at it in a typed form.

LT. COL. NORTH: Try to get results by State of the Union? Right, which is coming up.

MR. LIMAN: Well, who originated that?

LT. COL. NORTH: Oh, I'm sure it was me. Was it made certain it was visible out there?

MR. LIMAN: Did you regard yourself as having a political objective?

LT. COL. NORTH: I have absolutely no political ambitions whatsoever, I can assure you.

MR. LIMAN: That isn't true—

LT. COL. NORTH: I'm not for anything and I'm certainly not running from anything.

MR. LIMAN: Did you regard yourself as having a political objective for the present?

LT. COL. NORTH: I think everything that is done on the National Security Council Staff ought to have some recognition that there are political concerns.

MR. LIMAN: Now, you—when the decision was made by the President to go forward, once again the NSC turned to Oliver North and said, "Get it done." Right?

LT. COL. NORTH: That's correct.

MR. LIMAN: And, you found yourself in the middle of having to write a new finding, clean up the old finding, right?

LT. COL. NORTH: In early January, or late December, somewhere along in that time frame.

MR. LIMAN: And you worked with Mr. Sporkin on that?

LT. COL. NORTH: Among others.

MR. LIMAN: And, ultimately, there was a finding signed on January 6 and then the January 17 finding, you recall that now?

LT. COL. NORTH: I do.

MR. LIMAN: And do you recall that the draft that Sporkin gave you—Judge Sporkin gave you, had as options, notify the Congress or defer notification of the Congress?

LT. COL. NORTH: Yes, I do.

MR. LIMAN: And who made the decision to not notify the Congress at that time?

LT. COL. NORTH: My recollection is that both options were presented to the National Security Adviser and I assume the President, and I would assume that the President made that decision.

They set-up a private citizen in the case of—or citizens —I think they're private citizens—Schwimmer and Nimrodi. We tried to mirror the same thing when we got engaged in it, and to separate the US government as far as possible from recognizable involvement.

MR. LIMAN: But, you not only wanted the private citizen, in our case, General Secord, but you also wanted the Israelis there so—

LT. COL. NORTH: That's right.

MR. LIMAN: Is that correct?

LT. COL. NORTH: That is correct.

MR. LIMAN: And do you recall conveying that message that Mr. Nields showed you in code to the Israelis asking them if they could live with no comment if it became exposed?

LT. COL. NORTH: I believe that was their idea, and we agreed to it. We all agreed that there would be no comment if this activity were exposed.

MR. LIMAN: Well, I'll show you the message if it's necessary, but I can tell you now that the message attributes that to Joshua. You thought when you first saw it that Joshua may have been an Israeli, but we all know that Joshua is number one, President, right?

LT. COL. NORTH: That's right.

MR. LIMAN: And now, you knew from your meetings with the President that he had deep concern for the welfare of these American citizens who were hostages.

LT. COL. NORTH: He wanted them home.

MR. LIMAN: And did you tell Mr. Cook of the Defense Department as he's testified here, that the President was, quote "driving him nuts" end of quote, to get the hostages back by Christmas?

LT. COL. NORTH: I don't recall that conversation. A lot of things have been attributed to me that I allegedly said. I don't recall saying that.

MR. LIMAN: But, were you being pressured to get them back in a hurry?

LT. COL. NORTH: It was always very clear that our objective was to get as many home as fast as possible.

MR. LIMAN: That is different from my question. Did the President of the United States ever—

LT. COL. NORTH: No.

MR. LIMAN: —make statements to that effect to you?

LT. COL. NORTH: I heard the President say—I mean the President never turned to me and said, "Ollie, I want them home by Christmas." But, the President very clearly articulated in the meetings I was in with him in the Oval Office on this issue, and the meetings that I attended with him with the hostage families—it was very clear that the President wanted as many Americans home, all of them home, as fast as possible.

MR. LIMAN: Colonel . . . Did you participate in any briefing of the President on that subject?

LT. COL. NORTH: I do not recall actually sitting down in a meeting with the President. I know that there were several meetings with the the President on that issue, and I don't recall specifically being with the President on the final formulation, no.

MR. LIMAN: And then you've been through testimony which we will not repeat about all of this scrambling to find a way within the law to do the transaction without notifying Congress, correct?

LT. COL. NORTH: That is correct.

MR. LIMAN: And all of these different strategies and versions of a transaction that Mr. Nields took you through represented an effort to find a way within the various statutes as interpreted by the Attorney General to sell the arms without the notification to Congress. That's correct?

LT. COL. NORTH: That is correct.

MR. LIMAN: And on that subject, you had the Attorney

General giving advice, correct? The Attorney General blessed the form of the transaction?

LT. COL. NORTH: It was my recollection, as I think I testified yesterday, that I actually carried the draft finding over to the Attorney General. I may be incorrect on that, but my recollection is that I met with the Attorney General and one of his deputies—I believe it was Mr. Jensen—got his approval on the finding, the procedures we were using, and the finding was subsequently signed by the President.

MR. LIMAN: And—and were you also party to any discussions in which the Secretary of Defense said that he had cleared this with his legal counsel?

LT. COL. NORTH: I don't recall talking to Secretary Weinberger directly about it. I may—I may have.

MR. LIMAN: Were you present at any meetings where the Secretary of Defense expressed his objection to the whole transaction?

LT. COL. NORTH: No.

MR. LIMAN: Were you present at any meetings at which the Secretary of State expressed his objections to the whole transaction?

LT. COL. NORTH: Not that I recall.

MR. LIMAN: Were you told of that, that they were still opposed in January? That can be answered yes (or) no, I think.

LT. COL. NORTH: Yes, I suppose I had heard that they were opposed, but I did not hear then the stringent objections that have since been indicated.

MR. LIMAN: You did draft the cover memo which is Exhibit 60 for the January 17 finding, did you not—

LT. COL. NORTH: Which exhibit is that?

MR. LIMAN: —which exists, prepared by Oliver North? It's Exhibit 60, and it's a memo from Admiral Poindexter to the President. It has the famous "President was briefed verbally from this paper, Vice President"—

LT. COL. NORTH: Where are we reading from here?

MR. LIMAN: We're reading from the third page, et cetera. That's the cover memo for the finding. You drafted that.

LT. COL. NORTH: [Aside] Page three, Counsel.

MR. SULLIVAN: What page, Mr. Liman?

MR. LIMAN: Well, page three has it—what I was just

reading in handwriting. And it says "prepared by Oliver L. North."

LT. COL. NORTH: Yes, I see it.

MR. LIMAN: And were you present when the briefing occurred, if you recall?

LT. COL. NORTH: I do not recall.

MR. LIMAN: And if you look at the first page, it says, in the last lines on the first page—four, five lines up, "Because the requirements in US law for recipients of US arms to notify the US government of transfers to third countries, I do not recommend that you agree with the specific details of the Israeli plan. However, there's another possibility. Some time ago, the Attorney William French Smith determined that, under an appropriate finding, you could authorize the CIA to sell arms to countries outside of the provisions of the law and reporting requirements for Foreign Military Sales. The objectives of the Israeli plan could be met if the CIA, using an authorized agent, as necessary, purchased arms from the Department of Defense under the Economy Act, and then transferred them to Iran directly, after receiving appropriate payment from Iran." You recall that?

LT. COL. NORTH: I do.

MR. LIMAN: And do you also recall in this memorandum to the President that you indicated that, "If all of the hostages were not released after the first 1,000 TOWs were shipped, that further transfers would cease." That's the next to the last paragraph on the page.

(Pause.)

LT. COL. NORTH: Yes, it does.

MR. LIMAN: And do you remember that it was, in fact, the stated policy of the President that he would try to get the hostages back by a initial shipment of TOWs, but if they didn't deliver them all it would stop?

LT. COL. NORTH: That was clearly the intent when this was prepared in January. That's correct.

MR. LIMAN: And did you in fact receive in the month or so preceeding the Teheran trip, instructions from Admiral Poindexter that there were to be no delivery—there was to be no delivery of arms unless those hostages was—were released first?

LT. COL. NORTH: I'm sorry, would you say that part again?

MR. LIMAN: Did you receive instructions from Admiral Poindexter before the Teheran trip that there would be no delivery of arms unless all the hostages were released?

LT. COL. NORTH: I recall that being the specific objective. And I think that was our specific objective in each of these transactions, that we would seek to limit any further transfers unless we got them all home immediately.

MR. LIMAN: And—

LT. COL. NORTH: But, I think it is important to recognize that those of us who were engaged in the endeavor, particularly myself, General Secord, Mr. Cave, recognized that there was probably going to have to be some give and take. And I think that we made every effort to achieve the primary objective, all the hostages home and then proceed with the initiative in its broader sense as we had originally defined it. But that the Iranians were unwilling throughout, not necessarily just because of Mr. Ghorbanifar, but to proceed apace so that they did not lose all of what they considered to be their leverage. I do not believe at any point that we had solid evidence, nor do we today, or did we, at the point in time when I left, anyway, that the Iranians exercised the kind of total control over the Hezbollah in Lebanon that many people imagined. In other words, they, the Iranians, were unable, not just unwilling, but unable to snap their fingers and cause all of the hostages to be released at any given moment.

MR. LIMAN: Well, Colonel, who is calling the shots on these negotiations for the United States?

LT. COL. NORTH: On the trip that I went with with Mr. McFarlane, clearly, he was the chief negotiator.

MR. LIMAN: And, on the instructions that preceeded the trip, the authorization as to how far you could go, who called the shots on that?

LT. COL. NORTH: Well, certainly, Admiral Poindexter gave the guidance.

MR. LIMAN: And, do you recall—and this is Exhibit #276—that Admiral Poindexter sent you a PROF note saying, "You may go ahead and go, but I want several points made clear to them"—meaning the Iranians—"There are not to be any parts delivered until all the hostages are free, in accordance with the plan that you laid out for me before. None of this half shipment before any are released crap. It is

408

either all or nothing. Also you may tell them that the President is getting very annoyed at their continual stalling."

And, there were other PROF messages to that effect, such as PROF message 277, which is to Mr. McFarlane, which says, which is April 21, "Here is the update on what we discussed Saturday." "Blank" is the Iranian—

LT. COL. NORTH: I'm missing you on 277, Counsel.

MR. LIMAN: I'm sorry, 279. (Pause) It says, "Here is the update we discussed on Saturday—" referring to Mr. McFarlane and Admiral Poindexter. It says, and a name is deleted for the Iranian official " ******* wants all of the Hawk parts delivered before the hostages are released. I have told Ollie that we cannot do that. The sequence has to be: 1) meeting, 2) release of hostages, 3) delivery of Hawk parts. The President is getting quite discouraged by this effort. This will be our last effort to make a deal with the Iranians." Then it says, the next step is a Frankfurt meeting with Ghorbanifar, North, Cave, and the Iranian whose name is blanked out. Do you remember that those were your instructions?

LT. COL. NORTH: That's correct.

MR. LIMAN: And is it also a fact that when you were in Teheran, the Iranians suggested that they might be able to get two hostages released if you were prepared to proceed on that basis?

LT. COL. NORTH: I recall that. But, I also recall testifying to this committee that when we arrived in Teheran, it was evident that Ghorbanifar had lied to both sides, and there were expectations on the part of the Iranians that we were unwilling to meet. And my sense is that they made an effort to compromise based on what they had told Ghorbanifar before we arrived, and Ghorbanifar had not relayed to us. And the fact is the Iranians took several steps as best we were able to determine to make those compromises given their rather difficult political situation too.

MR. LIMAN: The compromise was two hostages for the arms.

LT. COL. NORTH: For the parts.

MR. LIMAN: For the parts.

LT. COL. NORTH: Yes.

MR. LIMAN: Well, the parts were parts for missiles, right?

409

LT. COL. NORTH: Yes. Technical parts, not warheads or anything like that.

MR. LIMAN: Well, but they were parts that were necessary for those—

LT. COL. NORTH: That's very correct.

MR. LIMAN: —missiles and warheads to go and hit their targets, right?

LT. COL. NORTH: Absolutely. But, the point I'm trying to make, Counsel, is that we were misled by Ghorbanifar and so were the Iranians. And the fact is we had consistently tried to get beyond Ghorbanifar and the Israelis to establish our own direct contacts. And when we got there, there was a willingness—the Iranians expected us by what we were able to determine from them to have arrived with everything. And when we didn't have everything—in fact, they kept looking up in the skies for another airplane. And when we didn't have everything, they asked where were the other parts. Furthermore, I don't believe that the Iranians were told by Ghorbanifar that we were expecting all of the hostages to be released that day. They very clearly indicated to Mr. Cave and myself on numerous occasions both in the first and the second channel, that that was something that was probably beyond their capabilities and that if all of the hostages were released simultaneously, it would be very clear to the whole wide world, which they did not want, that the Iranians were indeed the principal holders of the hostages. One of our proposals was to take a European who had been engaged in this effort, the humanitarian effort, and have him go to Teheran and have all the hostages received there. The Iranians said, "For heaven's sakes, the last thing in the world we want is all the hostages here. This is not our doing. These are people who have a philosophical loyalty, but not necessarily control in Teheran."

MR. LIMAN: Now, Colonel, given the fact the Ghorbanifar couldn't pass a lie detector on his own name, it didn't surprise you that Ghorbanifar was acting like a broker telling each side what it wanted to hear. That wasn't a shock to you.

LT. COL. NORTH: Not at all. But the level of deception in this particular case was immense.

MR. LIMAN: Now, you also said that it was clear that the

Iranians might not have control over the hostages. Is that so?

LT. COL. NORTH: That is correct.

MR. LIMAN: Now, when the President was giving all of these instructions that we're not going to ship arms to Iran in breach of our own policy—policy staunch—unless we get the hostages back, did anyone say to the President of the United States that they don't control the hostages?

LT. COL. NORTH: I believe that there are memoranda from me—there were clear indications from the Director of Central Intelligence—that we viewed this to be, first of all, a very, very difficult undertaking. It is, after all, the only one that ever brought any Americans home. And we recognized that. And if the inference is, I exceeded my mandate, I'll dispute that with you. We very clearly tried to present to the President—certainly, I tried to present to my superiors what the facts were, as we knew them. And we modified the plan sometimes unseen and sometimes en route, and sometimes in the intervening days between meetings.

MR. LIMAN: Gen. Secord, who was over in Israel, indicated that he thought we should have grabbed the deal for the two hostages. Did you advocate that when you were in Iran?

LT. COL. NORTH: I don't know what this has to do with this.

MR. LIMAN: Did you?

LT. COL. NORTH: I did.

MR. LIMAN: And you were overruled?

LT. COL. NORTH: I was.

MR. LIMAN: You were overruled by higher authority?

LT. COL. NORTH: Mr. McFarlane was in charge of the trip.

MR. LIMAN: And Mr. McFarlane was in communication with Washington?

LT. COL. NORTH: And so was I.

MR. LIMAN: And were you told by Admiral Poindexter that, "The deal is clear—all the hostages have to be released, or no more arms?"

LT. COL. NORTH: I don't believe I communicated that directly to Admiral Poindexter. I certainly articulated my opinion to Mr. McFarlane. Mr. McFarlane made a decision, and I saluted smartly and carried it out.

MR. LIMAN: Well, didn't Mr. McFarlane have instructions from the President of the United States on what he could give and what he couldn't?

LT. COL. NORTH: Apparently so.

MR. LIMAN: Well, you knew that, didn't you?

LT. COL. NORTH: I was not present when Mr. McFarlane was briefed by the President.

MR. LIMAN: You received these instructions yourself from Admiral Poindexter?

LT. COL. NORTH: That's correct.

MR. LIMAN: And you understood that the decisions here were being made in the Oval Office?

LT. COL. NORTH: That's correct.

MR. LIMAN: And is this testimony that you're giving now criticism of the fact that the decision was made to stand firm with the Iranians?

LT. COL. NORTH: I am not criticizing the President's decision, Admiral Poindexter's decision, or Mr. McFarlane. My role as a subordinate on the NSC staff was to provide advice and input. My advice at the time was to take the two hostages and go home.

MR. LIMAN: Was the America foreign policy being driven to a great extent by concern about the welfare for these hostages?

LT. COL. NORTH: Undoubtedly it was. But I view, and I think certainly Admiral Poindexter viewed, and in all of my discussions with the Iranians and the Israelis and others, I viewed the hostages as an obstacle. The obstacle had to be overcome like a hurdle before you could proceed on down the track, to use the—a little allegory. And what I am saying to you is that if we could have gotten beyond the hostage issue, it would have been palatable publicly, internationally, and every other way, to have meetings with high-level Iranian officials, first privately, and ultimately publicly. And I viewed it all as a step-by-step process.

MR. LIMAN: Did there ever come a moment when you asked yourself, "Why doesn't the Secretary of State agree with me? Why doesn't the Secretary of Defense agree with me?"

LT. COL. NORTH: They don't have to agree with me. I was simply providing advice, and input, and recommendations, and options to my superiors. When they gave me direction, I carried them out.

MR. LIMAN: Now—

LT. COL. NORTH: I wasn't asking for the Secretary of State to agree with me.

MR. LIMAN: Now, Colonel, Mr. McFarlane testified that there was a sense of dejection after this trip, and that you told him at the tarmac in Israel, you know, not everything worked out so bad, don't feel so poorly about it, we got some money for the contras out of the proceeds. Do you remember that?

LT. COL. NORTH: I don't recall doing it specifically on the tarmac at Ben-Gurion airport, but I'm sure I said it to him at some point in that process.

MR. LIMAN: Now you testified that the concept of using the proceeds from the Iranian sale to support the contras was first suggested as you recall it, by Ghorbanifar in that, either January or February meeting?

LT. COL. NORTH: I believe it was a January meeting.

MR. LIMAN: January meeting. And at the time that he made a—the suggestion there was a profit built into the transaction?

(Pause.)

LT. COL. NORTH: I'm sorry—

MR. LIMAN: Well, let's do it this way. There were—the plan that the President had approved involved 4,000 TOWs, do you recall that?

LT. COL. NORTH: I'm trying to think if that preceded or succeeded the January meeting, sir.

MR. LIMAN: Well, the January—I will represent to you that the proposals that are described in the various memoranda, including those that went up the line, were for 4000 TOWs.

LT. COL. NORTH: Okay.

MR. LIMAN: And you knew, and the documents show this, that the Iranians were prepared to pay to the Secord organization $10,000. Whatever Ghorbanifar was going to get, $10,000 per TOW was going to the Secord organization, right?

LT. COL. NORTH: That's correct.

MR. LIMAN: And you understood at some point that the

Department of Defense was going to charge something like $3500 a TOW, right?

LT. COL. NORTH: Something like that, because the price seemed to change everytime we asked for the price.

MR. LIMAN: Well there was at one point it was $6000 a TOW. And if it was $6000 a TOW, then the gross profit on 4000 TOWs, before expenses of transportation and so forth, would be $16 million—4000 times 4000. If, you know, the price was, as it turned out to be, about $3500 a TOW, then the gross profit was over $25 million. Right?

LT. COL. NORTH: Okay, yeah.

MR. LIMAN: And so there were—there was, if this tranaction went through, going to be a considerable surplus. You understood that?

LT. COL. NORTH: Yes.

MR. LIMAN: And is it fair to say, without getting into any of the details, that the surplus was going to be used for the contras—not necessarily giving the order—for the contras. It was going to be used to pay the cost of replenishing the 500-odd Israeli TOWs and for some other covert operations of the United States and Israel.

LT. COL. NORTH: That is correct.

MR. LIMAN: And did you ever urge the Department of Defense to keep the price down so that the profits would be greater?

LT. COL. NORTH: I don't recall doing that. I recall trying to get the price accurate. We went through a dickens of a time trying to—

MR. LIMAN: But you don't recall saying "keep it down so that we'll have even more of a slush fund"?

LT. COL. NORTH: I do not recall that whatsoever.

MR. LIMAN: Now do you recall whether the idea of using profit for the contras actually first came up in a meeting that you had with Israeli supply officials in the United States, in or about December of 1985?

LT. COL. NORTH: I don't recall that. My recollection was that the first time it was specifically addressed was during a meeting with Ghorbanifar.

MR. LIMAN: Do you—

LT. COL. NORTH: It may well have come up before, but I don't recall it.

MR. LIMAN: Do you—you understood from information

you had that the Israeli group, the private group that they were using as their cutout were making profit, right?

LT. COL. NORTH: Well again, I don't want to be too specific. We knew that somebody was making profit.

MR. LIMAN: And did you not have—

LT. COL. NORTH: In fact, the first transaction may have been all profit.

MR. LIMAN: And did you not, in fact, have some suspicion that that profit was being used for some covert purposes?

LT. COL. NORTH: Yes.

MR. LIMAN: And when in December you were giving consideration to having the United States replicate the Israeli system, did you not, at that point, give consideration to the fact that you could use these funds for a covert purpose?

LT. COL. NORTH: In December?

MR. LIMAN: Yes sir.

LT. COL. NORTH: I don't believe I did. I mean, I have no recollection of that. My clearest recollection, counsel, is that the first time the issue of using residuals came up was during Mr. Nir's visit at the end of December, early January. And I recall that we met New Year's Day or the day after, whatever, in that time period. Maybe New Year's Eve. And it was his proposal at that point to use the profits by the arrangement that they envisioned, selling Israeli TOWs at a profit, replenishing them with part of that money, using part of that money for other operations, which—

MR. LIMAN: Not the contras?

LT. COL. NORTH: I do not believe that he mentioned contras at that meeting.

MR. LIMAN: Now—

LT. COL. NORTH: My recollection is we began to talk in early January about other joint US-Israeli, and in some cases, unilateral Israeli operations of a certain kind that we discussed last night.

MR. LIMAN: Colonel, was it you who raised in December of 1985 with the Israelis the idea of using residuals for the contras?

LT. COL. NORTH: I have answered the question several times now. My recollection is that the first time I addressed the issue, or the issue was addressed to me, was in January, I

415

think somewhere around the 20th, it may have been before that, at a meeting in Europe. I have absolutely no recollection. If you've got something up there that's in my notebooks that I've given you, please refresh me.

MR. LIMAN: If it were in the notebooks, I would bring it to your attention, Colonel, because I'm not trying—and I want to make this very very clear—I am not trying to trap you or to do anything like that. I just want the facts and your recollection, and you've just given it, as I understand it.

LT. COL. NORTH: That's correct, Counsel.

MR. LIMAN: Now, which isn't to say that we don't have other information, but I want your recollection, and that's all you can give.

LT. COL. NORTH: I am giving it to you.

MR. LIMAN: Right. Now, when—

MR. SULLIVAN: Excuse me, Counsel. Excuse me, Counsel. If you have other information, such as a testimony or a statement, perhaps that would refresh the Colonel's recollection.

MR. LIMAN: Well, I've asked him the question, and I gather that the statement that I just made as to whether or not you were the one who suggested, which I can represent to you is not something that I've pulled out of thin air, whether that refreshes your recollection, and your answer I gather is it just doesn't refresh your recollection.

LT. COL. NORTH: It does not. I had, as you know, a number of discussions with Israeli officials, starting in November that carried all the way on through January, when Mr. Nir was introduced to me as the principal point of contact for continuing the operation.

MR. LIMAN: Colonel?

LT. COL. NORTH: I'd kind of like to take credit for it, instead of giving it to Mr. Ghorbanifar, but my recollection is it was his idea.

MR. LIMAN: Okay, now, Colonel North, when the decision was made to use the Secord organization as the vehicle in the transaction—I won't use the word "agent" because I know that you don't like the word, has legal significance, but as the vehicle in this organization, was there any discussion about the fact that the residual would then be in the treasury of the very organization that was taking care of the contra resupply?

LT. COL. NORTH: You're talking about back in February when I engaged him?

MR. LIMAN: Well—

LT. COL. NORTH: Certainly.

MR. LIMAN: And, when you talked to Director Casey about the fact of using the residuals, was there a discussion that the Secord organization would be in control of this money, and that it was the Secord organization that had the responsibility for the resupply of the contras?

LT. COL. NORTH: By the time the February transaction occurred, which did indeed produce revenues, that was very clearly part of the objective.

MR. LIMAN: I think you testified about what you said to Casey on this, which was that, you know, you thought it was a neat idea, and that he was enthusiastic. He said it was the ultimate irony, the ultimate covert operation, words to that effect. Do you recall that testimony?

LT. COL. NORTH: I do.

MR. LIMAN: And, you said that he recognized the political risks that would accrue if this was exposed.

LT. COL. NORTH: Well, I'm not sure—when I said that, I don't think I was referring specifically to the linkage between supporting the Nicaraguan freedom fighters and the support that was being derived as a consequence of the sales. I think Director Casey throughout had a recognition of political risk.

MR. LIMAN: But was he talk—

LT. COL. NORTH: The things we talked about yesterday on Boland, on dealing straightforward with an Iranian in an effort to get the hostages back and in an effort to even open up a relationship with the Iranians. I mean, I think he saw political risk in all of these.

MR. LIMAN: Did he discuss with you the political risks of using the surplus or profits from this transaction for covert operations?

LT. COL. NORTH: Did he discuss with me the political risks of using the surpluses for covert actions?

MR. LIMAN: Yes.

LT. COL. NORTH: Specifically, I don't believe so, until well into the activity—like in October when Furmark showed up.

MR. LIMAN: Did he ever recommend to you that you

417

make sure that you get the approval through channels of the President of the United States?

LT. COL. NORTH: I recall no such discussion.

MR. LIMAN: Now you also discussed the use of the residuals or profit for the contras with Admiral Poindexter, correct?

LT. COL. NORTH: Correct.

MR. LIMAN: And that was before you put it in any memoranda?

LT. COL. NORTH: Yes. Just—and I don't recall specifically on this case, but my normal modus operandi on making a proposal such as that would be to go over and sit down with the Admiral and talk to him. And, normally, the Admiral would like to think about it. I mean, the Admiral is not a hip-shooter, as I am accused of being.

MR. LIMAN: A cautious man?

LT. COL. NORTH: I think so.

MR. LIMAN: Prudent? A man who plays by the book?

LT. COL. NORTH: My sense is that he is exactly that. Let me just make one personal observation, and maybe I've alluded to this before. You know, there's a long history of rivalry between the services. And he and I are both part of the same naval service. And, even though some of my Marine colleagues might not like to hear this, that is an admiral I would follow up any hill, anywhere. And I really mean that because I think he also saw the necessity of taking risks, and he was willing to do so himself. And he placed himself in jeopardy, and he was the kind of person who recognized the risks, weighed the benefits and made decisions.

MR. LIMAN: And he discussed the risks of using the funds for the contras with you?

LT. COL. NORTH: Yes.

MR. LIMAN: What did he say?

LT. COL. NORTH: This had better never come out. And I took steps to insure that it didn't, and they failed.

MR. LIMAN: And did he discuss that with you when you first raised it—"this had better not come out?"

LT. COL. NORTH: I don't recall that specific discussion then. We certainly had it later.

MR. LIMAN: At the time that you first briefed him on it,

did you discuss how much money could be generated for the contras, if the 4000 TOWs were sold?

LT. COL. NORTH: And I think I did. And I think I was probably always too enthusiastic in my projections. In the document that we now have shown the world, I anticipated a residual that was in excess of what was realistic.

MR. LIMAN: Do you recall how long after you first told him about this orally he got back to you?

LT. COL. NORTH: No, I don't. I guess it was a matter of weeks—days or weeks, certainly—because, by February, we did it.

MR. LIMAN: Now you testified that, in addition to the oral briefing of the Admiral that you just referred to—

LT. COL. NORTH: I got myself a little off-track. I didn't finish the story. My normal procedure would be to sit down and talk to him. He'd normally say, "Let me think about it, or prepare a memo on it." I would prepare a memo on it. On numerous occasions, I would run that memo by Director Casey before I sent it to the Admiral. And I'm confident that I did that in this case.

Director Casey would usually look at it and say, "Think about putting this here and that there. Mention such-and-so —you haven't mentioned it."

MR. LIMAN: Well, he was a good writer.

LT. COL. NORTH: He was remarkable. I'm looking forwrd to his book.

MR. LIMAN: Think he's going to cover this in it?

LT. COL. NORTH: It will be interesting to see.

MR. LIMAN: Did he tell you he was before he died?

LT. COL. NORTH: No, he didn't—not this particular thing. But I watched him write part of that book, and I'm looking forward to it.

MR. LIMAN: Colonel, when you showed him these memos which had that famous line—"Suggest you brief the President and get the President's approval," did he say, "Take that out?"

LT. COL. NORTH: No.

MR. LIMAN: Now, you testified, apart from what you've just said about how your practice was of briefing the Admiral orally first—

LT. COL. NORTH: And I don't want to leave you with the

impression that I always did it that way. But when there was a difficult issue, we would.

MR. LIMAN: That was your practice?

LT. COL. NORTH: Yes, sir.

MR. LIMAN: All right. And you testified, as I said, apart from orally briefing the Admiral—I'll get this question out before the recess. You specifically wanted, and I'm quoting you, "before proceeding on a matter of this degree of importance to have the President's approval." Do you recall that?

LT. COL. NORTH: I'm sure I said it because I certainly felt that way.

MR. LIMAN: And this was so, even though Director Casey and Admiral Poindexter were in favor of using the profits for the contras. You still wanted that President's approval, correct?

LT. COL. NORTH: Yes. But I'm—let's not attach too much significance to my proposing that because it just seemed, as I was working this issue through, that the President ought to have been aware.

MR. LIMAN: Now you worked under three different National Security Advisers, or four?

LT. COL. NORTH: Four.

MR. LIMAN: And you had substantial reponsibility under how many of them?

LT. COL. NORTH: I guess two. I worked very hard when Judge Clark was there. I'm not—

MR. LIMAN: You have direct contact with Judge Clark, too?

LT. COL. NORTH: Occasionally.

MR. LIMAN: And—

LT. COL. NORTH: Judge Clark was the one who assigned me to work with the Kissinger Commission.

MR. LIMAN: And you had, based on your experience, formed an opinion as to what issues should be elevated to the President and which ones don't—is that fair to say?

LT. COL. NORTH: I would have to be fairly inert not to have figured that out by then, yes.

MR. LIMAN: And when you wrote memos, you would sometimes have memos that indicated that you wanted just the approval of the National Security Adviser, and in other cases, you would indicate that the National Security Adviser should brief the President and get the President's approval, right?

LT. COL. NORTH: Yes. And occasionally, I was reversed on that. And you certainly have documents of mine in which National Security Advisers crossed out the line and said, "Brief the President," or, "Send the document forward," and he'd write on the bottom of it, "I've taken care of this orally," or things like that.

MR. LIMAN: Is it fair to say, Colonel, that if the National Security Adviser struck out on one, two, or three memos that related to the diversion, that you should have the President briefed or get his approval, that you wouldn't keep writing memos with that same tag line?

LT. COL. NORTH: I can assure you, counsel, that if the National Security Adviser had told me not to do any —something, anything, I wouldn't have done it.

MR. LIMAN: Now, I would like to direct your attention to the drafts of this memorandum, because actually, the memorandum that you were surprised to see that day in the Attorney General's office, exists in four different copies, and I'd like to go after that with you.

LT. COL. NORTH: Are you—are you criticising how well I did my shredding?

MR. LIMAN: Colonel, my eyesight has suffered from reading what—what you left behind. (Laughter)

LT. COL. NORTH: I deserved that one. (More laughter). Could you refer me to the Exhibit, sir.

MR. LIMAN: 283 is one and then 283A, B and C, and I'm going to put them in order for you so that— we can take a moment, I think it's important. (Long pause). Let me show you what I think was the first one. These are all drafts of the same memo. Exhibit 283C is a memorandum which I am advised that your attorney returned to the NSC, Mr. Sullivan returned to the NSC, and that, if you look at the paragraph on the first page is typed with "on September 14". Do you see the line I'm referring to?

LT. COL. NORTH: I do.

MR. LIMAN: Then, if you look at 283-B, and 283 itself, because 283-D, I believe, is just a different copy of it. They have—

LT. COL. NORTH: Which is a copy of which, now?

MR. LIMAN: Look at 283-B and 283 next.

LT. COL. NORTH: Right. Are they not the same?

MR. LIMAN: No, because if you look at 283-B, you'll see that the 14 on September 14 is crossed out, and one-three is written there, meaning September 13.

LT. COL. NORTH: Right.

MR. LIMAN: And, on 283, the 14 is crossed out, and only 3 is put in, so I believe that they are different in that respect. Or, you'll see it clearer if you look at 283-D and compare it with 283.

LT. COL. NORTH: Got it.

MR. LIMAN: Now, so the original draft appeared to have September 14 written on it. Then, the 14 was struck out, and 13 was written in, and we are told that one of those, at least, is in the writing of Colonel Earl, and then we have 283-A, in which the typist made the correction, and that was taken off, and it's typed now September 13 and that was taken off of the disk on Fawn Hall's typewriter by the FBI. So, you follow me?

LT. COL. NORTH: Okay.

MR. LIMAN: Now, first on the first version of this draft, where did you get the copy that your attorneys sent back to the NSC?

LT. COL. NORTH: Let me just make one—you say on the first version, which first version are we talking about? 283-D?

MR. LIMAN: That would be 283-C, which is the one that has September 14 typed without the correction to 13.

LT. COL. NORTH: Okay. That is one of the documents that I removed from the NSC on the 25th.

MR. LIMAN: And, do you know where you found it?

LT. COL. NORTH: In my files.

MR. LIMAN: Now, do you recall the—

LT. COL. NORTH: I want to make something also very clear, there—

MR. LIMAN: We're going to come into the removal on the 25th, Colonel—

LT. COL. NORTH: Okay.

MR. LIMAN: —so if you want to get into that subject—

LT. COL. NORTH: No, go ahead.

MR. LIMAN: —I think all you'll be doing is repeating that—

LT. COL. NORTH: Very well.

MR. LIMAN: —if you go into it now.

LT. COL. NORTH: Very well.

MR. LIMAN: And I think you want to get this over with. So do we.

MR. SULLIVAN: Excuse me, Counsel.

LT. COL. NORTH: —get the whole thing over with.

MR. SULLIVAN: This exhibit is very confusing because it does not bear the stamped numbers that we placed on the documents at the time they were returned to the NSC, so we're not sure whether in fact these are the documents.

MR. LIMAN: Well, I don't know what—

MR. SULLIVAN: And I'd like to—I have—I'd like to show you an exhibit that accompanied these documents so at least the record will be straight regarding the circumstances of their return.

MR. LIMAN: I can tell you that we were told, Mr. Sullivan, that his exhibit came from the documents that you sent back to the NSC. If you have the actual copy of the document you sent—and it is on it, it's just in the typing here, it's number 7.

LT. COL. NORTH: I'm sorry, I—

MR. LIMAN: If you look, if you look, 139, 140—(Pause while looking at exhibit.)

LT. COL. NORTH: Which one we looking at? D or C?

MR. LIMAN: It has the number, if you look, it's 283-C, which is the one you returned.

LT. COL. NORTH: Okay. (Pause while looking at exhibit.)

MR. LIMAN: You returned it on December 2.

MR. SULLIVAN: Could you show us a copy with the number stamp that our law firm placed on the records at the time they were returned? (Pause, while looking at exhibits.)

MR. LIMAN: It's been obscured by the declassification stamp. You see, we had to have them desclassified, and it's in the lower right-hand corner and I believe it has the number 139. Mr. Sullivan, I mean, do you dispute that this is the document that you returned to the NSC?

MR. SULLIVAN: Well, I'm trying to—

MR. LIMAN: You know what you returned.

MR. SULLIAN: I'm trying to determine that, Mr. Liman. Without the numbers—if I see the numbers clearly I can tell you whether it's returned because I believe the only documents in the case, there were numbers stamped by our law

423

firm, were the ones that were returned to the NSC accompanying the cover letter on the poster board dated December 2, 1986.

MR. LIMAN: Well—

MR. SULLIVAN: We number—

MR. ———: Mr. Chairman? Mr. Chairman, excuse me for interrupting here, but I'd just like to bring the attention of counsel to the fact that none of the members can see the document that Mr. Sullivan has put up on the posterboard, and I wonder if you might take that into account into your questioning?

MR. LIMAN: Okay, let me—

MR. ———: It's simply not visable from up here on the dias.

MR. LIMAN: Let me read it to you, it's a letter that Mr. Sullivan wrote on December 2, 1986 in which he said, he addressed it to the NSC, to Commander Thompson. He said: "Lt. Colonel North is herewith delivering documents to NSC. In order to insure that the documents are preserved, the pages have been number stamped 1 through 168 inclusive." The document I've just given you has a 139, 140, 141, 42 stamp. Do you want me to read the rest of it?

MR. SULLIVAN: Might as well, for the sake of a complete record.

MR. LIMAN: But to—it's Exhibit 324 in our book, and it says, "Also delivered are the WHCA Motorola Pageboy, the Motorola hand-held portable telephone, and the NSC government transportation request with its number"—which I will not read—"issued to Lieutenant Colonel North. Would you please arrange for the return of Lieutenant Colonel North's personal property which is located in his office. He is particularly interested in the prompt return of his Marine Corps uniform items, family photos, and other personal effects. Sincerely yours, Brendan Sullivan, attorney for Lieutenant Colonel Oliver L. North, copy to Brenda Rega."

And it's Exhibit—for Members and for others, press, it's Exhibit 324. And this bears a stamp number within your group. Now you got this from your office, is that established now?

MR. SULLIVAN: Well, our copies—I can see the number 1–3—

MR. LIMAN: You can see the—

MR. SULLIVAN: —written over by the stamp, so I—

MR. LIMAN: And you look at the third page and you'll see it very clearly, 1-4-1—

MR. SULLIVAN: I see 1-4. It's been cut off.

MR. LIMAN: Even on the—

MR. SULLIVAN: But I do see—

MR. LIMAN: —third page?

LT. COL. NORTH: They're all—I think the xerox has cut them all off on the right margin.

MR. SULLIVAN: —think they're all cut off. They do appear to be the number stamps that were placed on at our law firm at the time the documents were returned. If you're trying to associate the numbers with a date, particularly, or whether one was prepared before the other, I don't believe that we are able to answer that, of course. Perhaps Colonel North is able to answer from the text, but not from the numbers.

MR. LIMAN: Now—well, Colonel North, do you recall the occasion on which the September 14 was changed to September 13?

LT. COL. NORTH: No, but I can only guess it's because at some point along the line, I learned that the Israeli government had transferred 508 TOWs, not on the 14th but on the 13th, is all I can assume.

MR. LIMAN: And you try to be precise, if you learn something was wrong—

LT. COL. NORTH: To correct it.

MR. LIMAN: And here, the—you saw the corrections in handwriting, and then the last version, which has it typed, was found on your secretary's typing disk, September 13.

LT. COL. NORTH: Yes.

MR. LIMAN: And do you know where the actual typed copy of the corrected one is?

LT. COL. NORTH: I would guess it is in the bag of shredded materials.

MR. LIMAN: Confetti, as we call it.

LT. COL. NORTH: Confetti. I call it that, too.

MR. LIMAN: All right.

CHAIRMAN INOUYE: Mr. Liman, is this a good time to call a recess? May I advise members of the Senate that a vote is pending at this time. The Committee will stand in recess for ten minutes.

(Committee recess)

[The hearing resumes.]

CHAIRMAN INOUYE: Mr. Liman, please proceed.

MR. LIMAN: All right. For the record, Mr. Chairman, Exhibit 283 has attached to it a cover sheet which says, "Keep this together for me, Iran," and it has the initials of Admiral Poindexter. I believe that that cover sheet was not put on the document originally, but on November 25th or so, after the document had been found by the Attorney General and shown to various people in the White House. And so, while it is part of the exhibit as given to us by the FBI, it was not part of the original draft, as found in the office of Col. North.

CHAIRMAN INOUYE: It will be noted accordingly.

MR. LIMAN: Now, Col. North, these exhibits that we looked at—the 283 and so on—said that, in the recommendation form, tht "the President approved the structure depicted above under current situation," and the "terms of reference at Tab A." You recall that?

LT. COL. NORTH: Which one are we looking at? A, B—

MR. LIMAN: Well, you can look. They all have the same paragraph—that "the President approved the structure depicted above under current situation" —

LT. COL. NORTH: Right.

MR. LIMAN: And that "terms of reference at Tab A."

LT. COL. NORTH: Yes.

MR. LIMAN: And, as I understood your testimony earlier, that the transaction is described in this exhibit in its various corrected forms changed prior to Teheran. Am I correct that—the structure of it—

LT. COL. NORTH: Yes. This particular transaction was never concluded.

MR. LIMAN: In that form?

LT. COL. NORTH: That's right.

MR. LIMAN: And, as the structure was changed you would do other memoranda summarizing the strucutre in the same form as this one?

LT. COL. NORTH: Yes.

MR. LIMAN: And is it a fact, sir, that the terms of reference were, in fact, approved by the President, either this or the ones that you attached to later memos?

LT. COL. NORTH: And I do not know if it's this particular

426

version of the terms of reference, but we did have a memo very similar to this that we carried with this to Teheran that had been, I was told, approved by the President.

MR. LIMAN: And the terms of reference were transmitted to Admiral Poindexter for the President in—

LT. COL. NORTH: Memoranda similar to this.

MR. LIMAN: —in memoranda similar to this one?

LT. COL. NORTH: That is correct.

MR. LIMAN: Now, you've testified—and we don't have to belabor it, but since the originals of these memoranda that referred in one paragrah or so to the use of proceeds have been destroyed, you have no way of recalling which boxes were checked. That's correct?

LT. COL. NORTH: I do not. I do not recall.

MR. LIMAN: But you did do a series of memos after this on other aspects of the Iran initiative which you passed up to Admiral Poindexter for Presidential approval? Do you recall that?

LT. COL. NORTH: I'm not sure I understand the question.

MR. LIMAN: Well, look at Exhibit—I'd like you to look and I think—have we put—we're going to put in front of you, just out of the Exhibit Book so you don't have to wander through them all, Exhibits 296, 297, 302, 303. You see those documents?

LT. COL. NORTH: Okay.

MR. LIMAN: 296 was a memorandum that you sent to John Poindexter and it said "Next steps on American hostages" and it describes the release of Father Jenco and the shipment of the balance of the Hawk parts. I'm—I'm not sure you were able to hear the question—

LT. COL. NORTH: Please,

MR. LIMAN: I said this memorandum of July 29, 1986, describes the release of Father Jenco and the shipment of the remaining Hawk parts that were owed to the Iranians. And if you look at your last paragraph, it has a recommendation, recommendation that you brief the President regarding our conclusions on the Jenco release as indicated above and obtain his approval for having the 240 Hawk missile parts shipped from Israel to Iran as soon as possible, followed by a meeting with the Iranians in Europe. You see that?

LT. COL. NORTH: Yes.

MR. LIMAN: And there—there's a check under approved JP?

LT. COL. NORTH: Yes.

MR. LIMAN: And a date—

LT. COL. NORTH: Right.

MR. LIMAN: And then it says, "President approved with JP's signature."

LT. COL. NORTH: Yes.

MR. LIMAN: Now, this is a document that referred to the shipment of the Hawk parts that had been paid for in May, correct? The balance of the Hawk parts.

LT. COL. NORTH: Let me just think, now, where we are, the chronology of events. I believe that the Hawk parts were indeed paid for in May.

MR. LIMAN: And because the hostages weren't released and that mission aborted, you did not ship the rest of the Hawk parts.

LT. COL. NORTH: That is correct.

MR. LIMAN: And then after Father Jenco was released, you delivered the balance, or some of the balance, of the parts, correct?

LT. COL. NORTH: I believe that's correct, yeah.

MR. LIMAN: And, are you—even—and this—there was no money that was going to flow from that shipment of the Hawk parts because they had already been paid for, correct? You remember that.

LT. COL. NORTH: I believe they had been, yeah.

MR. LIMAN: And this memorandum, therefore, doesn't discuss the use of proceeds.

LT. COL. NORTH: I don't—I can't talk and—

MR. LIMAN: Well, I can tell, I will represent that to you.

LT. COL. NORTH: I mean, do you know what was under the black stuff?

MR. LIMAN: Yes I do—

LT. COL. NORTH: Okay—

MR. LIMAN: And it doesn't—

LT. COL. NORTH: Okay.

MR. LIMAN: It was sensitive classified material that I think you would appreciate should have been blacked out.

LT. COL. NORTH: No, I understand. I—I just did not recall what was underneath, in fact, I was a little curious that—

428

MR. LIMAN: And—and it has the approval, JP, and it indicates the President approved?

LT. COL. NORTH: It does.

MR. LIMAN: And this memorandum was preserved, and it's a System IV document, you notice?

LT. COL. NORTH: I, I do, but I don't want to attach any particular significance. There were other documents that were preserved that I didn't know were preserved.

MR. LIMAN: Now, another one that was preserved is Exhibit #297, which is a memorandum dated June 27, or rather July—there's a cover—there's a first sheet which says June 27, but then there's a memorandum of July 26, which asks their permission for you to travel to Frankfurt and do other things, in connection with the Jenco release. Do you see that memo?

LT. COL. NORTH: I do. I'm not quite sure I understand what that—this is an unusual format for me to be sending something to forward, in that normally the first thing underneath this sheet, right here, would have been this sheet right here.

MR. LIMAN: It would have been the second sheet?

LT. COL. NORTH: Yes.

MR. LIMAN: But, the way in which we got papers from the NSC, which is the way we've kept them together, had this attached, and that may have just been in the way they did their production to us, but if you look at your July 26 memo, you again said that recommendations that you initial and forward, your memo to President at Tab One, and you prepared a memo for Admiral Poindexter for the President.

LT. COL. NORTH: Yeah, let me—if I can, just one second, Counsel, I believe that the memo that is right beneath the cover sheet. This is a standard NSC cover sheet.

MR. LIMAN: Right.

LT. COL. NORTH: I believe that this memo right here is probably a KL-43—I'm trying to figure out what it is, but it looks to me like a KL-43 message back to my office, that was then typed and probably put in an envelope and sent to, or given to Admiral Poindexter. I, I'm guessing.

MR. LIMAN: Well, however the file you people—

LT. COL. NORTH: But, what I'm saying—

MR. LIMAN: —handled it, if you look at the actual

System IV document, which is a memo from you to Admiral Poindexter enclosing a memo from Admiral Poindexter to the President outlining certain aspects of the Jenco release, and again you asked that he forward it to the President, and you have a note that indicates from Admiral Poindexter that he brief the President on the secure phone and the President approved.

LT. COL. NORTH: I, I do not see the note that the President approved.

MR. LIMAN: Well, do you not see on the page of the 26th July—the first sheet—July 26th, 1986—

LT. COL. NORTH: Right, okay.

MR. LIMAN: —a note, "7/26/86"—

LT. COL. NORTH: I see it.

MR. LIMAN: —"briefed President on secure phone, President approved"?

LT. COL. NORTH: Understood. I was looking too far. I'm sorry.

MR. LIMAN: And then, if we look at Exhibit 302, which is a September 8th, 1986 from you to Admiral Poindexter, again, it says, has a recommendation to Admiral Poindexter that "you use the attached papers in discussing our next steps with the President." Do you see that?

LT. COL. NORTH: Yes, I do.

MR. LIMAN: And that also has an approved mark by the Admiral, or by someone.

LT. COL. NORTH: I do not know that that's necessarily the Admiral. There is a check mark in the box. But, as you have seen, the Admiral put his initials.

MR. LIMAN: Do you know anyone who was just forging his check marks?

LT. COL. NORTH: No, I don't know if anyone—

MR. SULLIVAN: You know, Counsel, I don't know whether you can forge check marks.

MR. LIMAN: Well, do you know anyone who was putting check marks for Admiral Poindexter without his authority?

LT. COL. NORTH: I do not.

MR. LIMAN: Do you have any reason to believe that Admiral Poindexter didn't put the check mark on this document that was delivered to us by the NSC?

LT. COL. NORTH: Counsel, I have no idea who put the

check mark. It is a memorandum from me to Admiral Poindexter. There is a check mark in the approved box. As I just indicated to you, in almost every other document I got from the Admiral, there was a "JP."

MR. LIMAN: Again, you have recommendations. One is that he discuss something with Director Casey relating to Mr. Nir and the Iran initiative.

LT. COL. NORTH: Yes.

MR. LIMAN: And the second is that you brief the President on the initiative outlined on Tab 3.

LT. COL. NORTH: "Initiatives," plural.

MR. LIMAN: "Initiatives," I'm sorry.

LT. COL. NORTH: I believe these are the ones we talked about last night.

MR. LIMAN: And there, again, there is "approved, J, done," correct?

LT. COL. NORTH: Yes—"JP."

MR. LIMAN: "JP." And these initiatives, were these initiatives that were going to be funded out of the residuals?

LT. COL. NORTH: Yes.

MR. LIMAN: And then we have Exhibit 311. And that's another next-steps memo from Ollie North to Poindexter, right—to Admiral Poindexter?

LT. COL. NORTH: Yes.

MR. LIMAN: And here, again, you were asking for travel authorization. You were asking for him to have the President inscribe the famous Bible and do a letter to Prime Minister Peres?

LT. COL. NORTH: That's correct.

MR. LIMAN: And it's fair to say that the Admiral indicated his initials where he approved?

LT. COL. NORTH: That's correct.

MR. LIMAN: And on one of them where it says that you "tell Director Casey to prepare an appropriate intelligence package," there is no notation of approval or disapproval?

LT. COL. NORTH: That's correct. There was also a notation on the fourth point for talking points for use by COP with Nir.

MR. LIMAN: And that says "JPC?"

LT. COL. NORTH: Right.

MR. LIMAN: So it was not unusual for you, when you were

dealing with the Iran initiative, to get back memoranda from Admiral Poindexter indicating that he had accepted the recommendation and had briefed the President?

LT. COL. NORTH: That's correct. But it was also not unusual to have initiatives that were not sent back —memoranda on initiatives that were not sent back, and I tried to make that clear yesterday.

MR. LIMAN: Now, as you sit here today are you in a position to say that every single one of the five memoranda that you sent to Admiral Poindexter referring to the use of the residuals was not sent back?

LT. COL. NORTH: No, sir. I did not say that yesterday, and I do not say it today. I also told you that I—

MR. LIMAN: Is it fair to say—

LT. COL. NORTH: —admitted an effort to destroy all of those.

MR. LIMAN: Now, is it also correct—

LT. COL. NORTH: And, I also indicated the reason why I had destroyed those.

MR. LIMAN: Now, Colonel, did you also participate in a number of briefings of the President on the Iran initiative?

LT. COL. NORTH: I'm sure that I did. I wouldn't care to characterize how many it was, but I met with the President a little bit more often than some people say, less than others.

MR. LIMAN: Well, how many times would you approximate that you met with him in 1986 to discuss the Iran initiative?

LT. COL. NORTH: Well, at least three.

MR. LIMAN: And, is it fair to say that at none of those meetings was there any discussion of the use of the proceeds for the contras?

LT. COL. NORTH: I do not recall ever discussing with the President the use of the residuals to support the Nicaraguan freedom fighters.

MR. LIMAN: Now, at the meetings that you had with the President, was Mr. Don Regan present?

LT. COL. NORTH: There was always someone else present. I wouldn't say that Mr. Regan was necessarily always there, but certainly there was always someone else there.

MR. LIMAN: And, in addition to the meetings that you had with the President on the Iran initiative, did you also have meetings with the President and others, because

432

you've said that someone was always there, on contra support?

LT. COL. NORTH: Sure. I mean we had national security planning group meetings on that issue.

MR. LIMAN: And, did you in addition to those meetings have meetings with him and the national security adviser to talk about the status of the contras?

LT. COL. NORTH: Yes, but, you know, it was not unusual, particularly when Mr. McFarlane was national security adviser to have that be the subject of a morning briefing, 9:30.

MR. LIMAN: And, that would be the 9:30 briefings?

LT. COL. NORTH: That's correct.

MR. LIMAN: And, would you be asked to do the briefing?

LT. COL. NORTH: Occasionally.

MR. LIMAN: And, do you recall what topics you discussed?

LT. COL. NORTH: It would usually be the hot issue of the day, inevitably it would focus at some point on the need for additional Congressional funding.

MR. LIMAN: Would it discuss what the financial condition of the contras was?

LT. COL. NORTH: As the memorada that I sent forward did.

MR. LIMAN: Now, do you recall that at the time that you were involved in the Iran initiative and the Tehran visit that the contras were running out of money?

LT. COL. NORTH: Yes.

MR. LIMAN: And, there are a whole series of exhibits which were in Mr. Nields' exhibit book but which he did not go over, but I think I can point them out to you and then move on to the question. Exhibit #3, #4,—it's the first book. Exhibit #3 was a KL-43 message on April 21, 1986 to you from Mr. Secord indicating that they were running out of money. Said, "Current obligations over next few weeks nearly wipe us out except for CD."

LT. COL. NORTH: Right.

MR. LIMAN: Incidentally, did you know what the CD was for?

LT. COL. NORTH: It was a, as I understood it, a $2 million dollar allocation set aside for insurance of aircraft that were not ours. They were the property of another government.

MR. LIMAN: Now, and who told you that?

LT. COL. NORTH: I'm quite confident it was General Secord. It could also mean—and I don't know the value of that particular CD—but as I testified last night, I had frequently told General Secord to set aside monies for other activities, and I think it's important you note when, in my discussion with Mr. Nir, going all the way back to January, Mr. Nir indicated the desire to use the residuals for other activities, and as I testified last night, I often did not reveal to General Secord or any others, aside from my superiors when I was apprising them of the planned Israeli operations, that those monies were specifically for those purposes. I also indicated that I tasked General Secord frequently to provide on short notice other support for other operations.

MR. LIMAN: Now, if you look at—

LT. COL. NORTH: And, thus, the bottom line of all this is I don't recall at this point, here two years later or a year later, what the specific CD reference.

MR. LIMAN: Now, if you look at Exhibit 4 which is an April 21, 1986 memorandum, (inaudible) it's a PROF note, actually, to McFarlane. And I can read to you from the second paragraph that says, "There is great despair that we may fail in this effort," referring to the contra support, "and the resistance account is darn near broke. Any thoughts where we can put our hands on a quick $3 to $5 million, Gaston is willing to go back to his friends, who have given $2 million so far in the hopes that we can bridge things again." And in fact, as you understood it, the resistance was darn near broke at that point.

LT. COL. NORTH: That is correct.

MR. LIMAN: Is that correct? And when you indicated that Gaston was willing to go back to his friends, that's Gaston Sigur,—

LT. COL. NORTH: That's correct.

MR. LIMAN: And does that refresh you as to whether you knew who those friends were at that point?

LT. COL. NORTH: Those were the friends that I had already met with.

MR. LIMAN: And does it refresh you that you knew that they had already given $2 million?

LT. COL. NORTH: Certainly.

MR. LIMAN: Now, on Exhibit 5, which was a note from you, again, a PROF note, again you talked about the—the —to say that the weekend's trip to Central America is the most depressing venture in four years of working the Central American issue. And you've described your anxiety that Congress won't act in time. And that really did reflect your point of view at that time.

LT. COL. NORTH: Certainly did.

MR. LIMAN: And was that really the—the—did it not only reflect your point of view, but was that a state of anxiety that existed in the White House at that time?

LT. COL. NORTH: Oh, I think it was not only in the White House, it reflected the sense of the Central American leaders with whom I visited; it reflected the sense of the Nicaraguan resistance. I'd like to just point out that one of the sentences in there is that all hospitalization for wounded in action will cease at the end of this week. Troops returning to Nicaragua this week will carry only, I can't read how many because it's not xeroxed well, blank rounds of ammunition, instead of the 500 they had been carrying. No new radio batteries are available, so there's no way to pass commands or intelligence.

MR. LIMAN: (very faintly) Do you know this to be true?

LT. COL. NORTH: That is exactly what I was seeing when I was on the ground.

MR. LIMAN: And, do you recall discussing with the President of the United States, that dire condition?

LT. COL. NORTH: I don't recall specifically discussing it with the President.

MR. LIMAN: Now do you recall that there was an NSPG meeting that was going to take place on May 16, 1986?

LT. COL. NORTH: I don't specifically recall that.

MR. LIMAN: Well, if you look at—at the Exhibit 8, is that a memorandum that you prepared for Admiral Poindexter for this meeting?

LT. COL. NORTH: I helped. As I see in this memorandum,—

MR. LIMAN: You helped—you—

LT. COL. NORTH: —it was prepared by myself and another staff officer.

MR. LIMAN: And do you recall, sir, that the subject of this

435

meeting was the dire condition that the contras were facing in terms of funding?

LT. COL. NORTH: Yes, yes.

MR. LIMAN: And you actually attended the meeting, am I correct?

LT. COL. NORTH: I do not remember whether I actually attended that meeting or not. I guess I did, since my name is on the attendance list.

MR. LIMAN: Do you recall attending a meeting at which it was suggested that, pursuant to the authorization that Congress has granted for humanitarian solicitation, that the Secretary of State would try to come up with a list of countries to solicit? And I can show you your Exhibit 343 which is in the classified book. Do you recall attending that meeting? Do you see yourself listed as the last name there—the most junior person there?

LT. COL. NORTH: That was frequently the case, Counsel.

MR. LIMAN: Do you see yourself listed?

LT. COL. NORTH: I do.

MR. LIMAN: And, if you look over those, does it refresh your recollection that the discussion there was how to get money for the contras, including going back to Congress, going to third countries?

(The witness perused the document.)

MR. LIMAN: In fact, if you look at page seven, you'll see a reference to statements by Secretary of State Shultz. Does that refresh your recollection at all, Colonel?

LT. COL. NORTH: Somewhat. I must confess not to have a vivid recollection of this meeting, but I obviously was there, and this was obviously the subject of discussion. I'm not trying to be evasive. I just don't remember.

MR. LIMAN: Do you recall that the meeting ended with a suggestion that a list of countries who might be approached would be prepared and submitted to the President?

LT. COL. NORTH: I do not remember that, but I'm not saying that it didn't happen at the meeting.

MR. LIMAN: Now, do you recall that, following that meeting, you wrote a PROF note to Admiral Poindexter which appears at Exhibit 10? This is not in the classified.

(The witness perused the document.)

MR. LIMAN: Is that PROF note that you wrote?

LT. COL. NORTH: I have a note—

436

MR. LIMAN: "From Oliver"—

LT. COL. NORTH: You're talking about the bottom note?

MR. LIMAN: It's the note—

LT. COL. NORTH: "This is further"—

MR. LIMAN: Second page, "Note from Oliver North, subject—Iran and terrorism." And then, if you look at the third paragraph—or so, third or fourth—

LT. COL. NORTH: Yes.

MR. LIMAN: It reads, "You should be aware that the resistance support organization"—that's Lake?

LT. COL. NORTH: I don't see it.

MR. LIMAN: Are you looking at Exhibit 10?

LT. COL. NORTH: Yes.

MR. LIMAN: Do you see a sentence that begins, "You should be aware?"

LT. COL. NORTH: I see it, yes.

MR. LIMAN: "You should be aware that the resistance support organization now has more than $6 million available for immediate disbursement."

LT. COL. NORTH: Yes.

MR. LIMAN: And, in fact, that was $6 million that was generated from the deposits for the arms sales. That's correct, isn't it?

LT. COL. NORTH: I believe it is, yes.

MR. LIMAN: And then it says, "This reduces the need to go to third countries for help."

LT. COL. NORTH: That's what it says.

MR. LIMAN: Now does that refresh your recollection that, earlier that day, there was a discussion the President at the NSPG meeting that you participated in about going to third countries for help?

LT. COL. NORTH: Again, my recollection of the meeting with the President is not altogether clear. Very obviously, I wrote this note, and it does refer back to that reference that you have made.

MR. LIMAN: Now, did you ever discuss with Admiral Poindexter the subject of this note, namely, that the need for the Secretary of State and the President to get involved in third country solicitation had been relieved to a little extent by the $6 million dollars that you now had available?

LT. COL. NORTH: Oh, I think the issue is not so much the need. The issue was—and certainly it was my

437

understanding—is you needed a lot more than $6 or even $10 million from Brunei. You needed a lot of money.

MR. LIMAN: But, this was good news. Wasn't it?

LT. COL. NORTH: Well, I would guess so, yes.

MR. LIMAN: That's what you were conveying.

LT. COL. NORTH: Yes.

MR. LIMAN: Did you ever discuss with Admiral Poindexter that this was good news that ought to be brought to the attention of the President of the United States or the Secretary of State?

LT. COL. NORTH: I did not. I was no need to. I still believed that we ought to have gone to others and go back to others that have already given because the need was much greater than six million.

MR. LIMAN: Well, this said—

LT. COL. NORTH: The need, and you know—and—

MR. LIMAN: Didn't you say, "This reduces the need." Those are your words?

LT. COL. NORTH: Well, perhaps, the immediacy of the need. Those are not—I'm not going to back away from the words that I wrote at the time. The point that I'm trying to make is, just like the one I tried to make yesterday when we were talking about Boland, is there was always a need to get more money, to get the CIA back involved, and this note says that.

MR. LIMAN: What occasion—

LT. COL. NORTH: No, I didn't want to be able—to be out there doing these things, Counsel. What I was trying to do is to get a full program reestablished by the government of the United States, and we were trying to bridge it, until that happened.

MR. LIMAN: Colonel, what occasioned you to write to Admiral Poindexter saying that this reduces the need?

LT. COL. NORTH: Well, I think probably that it was important he understand that Secretary Shultz didn't need to go out that afternoon and go ask for additional help, but as we all know, Secretary Shultz eventually did.

MR. LIMAN: Now, let's go on here, because you do in this note, and you've already testified to it, you plead for the legislation to get the CIA back into it.

LT. COL. NORTH: Yes.

MR. LIMAN: And, you say, "The more money there is," and see if you can follow me. It's the next paragraph.

LT. COL. NORTH: Why don't we read the whole thing, because I think that is the most important, Counsel.

MR. LIMAN: Well, I would like to read this, and then we can come back and read anything that you feel that I haven't done in context, but—

LT. COL. NORTH: Well, but I think that the entire context of the note is important.

MR. LIMAN: I am asking the questions now, and I would like to read these and ask you about them.

LT. COL. NORTH: I will answer your questions, Counsel.

MR. LIMAN: "The more money there is, and we will have a cons—"

MR. SULLIVAN: Where are you reading, Counsel? Where are you reading?

MR. LIMAN: It's the paragraph, that same paragraph but it has a break, and it be—where the break is, there's a "to arrange." Do you see that?

MR. SULLIVAN: Is this the bottom paragraph on the page?

MR. LIMAN: It's the bottom paragraph, though it's not broken into paragraphs.

LT. COL. NORTH: "Unless we do this, we will run increasing risks of trying to manage this program from here with the attendant physical and political liabilities." Is that what you're talking about?

MR. LIMAN: Yes. And, then it says, "I am not complaining, and you know that I love the work, but we have to lift some of this onto the CIA, so that I can get more than 2, 3 hours of sleep at night. The more money there is, and we will have a considerable amount in a few more days." And, let's stop there. That was also going to be more money from the Iranian deposits—"We will have a considerable amount in a few more days. The more visible the program becomes (airplanes, pilots, weapons, deliveries, et cetera), the more inquisitive will become people like Kerry, Barnes, Hawkins, et al." Those are members of Congress?

LT. COL. NORTH: They are.

MR. LIMAN: "While I care not a whit what they may say about me, it could well become a political embarrassment for the President and you."

439

LT. COL. NORTH: I think that's been borne out.

MR. LIMAN: And what was the "political embarrassment" that you were focusing then?

LT. COL. NORTH: We have it before us, Counsel.

MR. LIMAN: It would come out that you were generating the funds for the contras and doing what you described to assist the support operation?

LT. COL. NORTH: Yes.

MR. LIMAN: And you then come up with the proposal, "Much of this risk can be avoided simply by covering it with an authorized CIA program undertaken with the $15 million." You say that Shultz doesn't seem to understand that, right?

LT. COL. NORTH: That's what I said.

MR. LIMAN: Then you say, "I have no idea what Don Regan does or does not know of my private United States operation, but the President obviously knows why he has been meeting with several select people to thank them for their support," right?

LT. COL. NORTH: That's what it says.

MR. LIMAN: And those were people who you had put the scheduling request in for?

LT. COL. NORTH: Again, my recollection is that I did relatively few of those, that that procedure was eventually taken over by others.

MR. LIMAN: And, incidentally, I don't want to get into a semantic argument about solicitation or not solicitation. The slides that you have identified for us are part of a program that you would show, is that correct?

LT. COL. NORTH: It was described earlier by this committee as a one-two punch.

MR. LIMAN: Right, and that was what it was?

LT. COL. NORTH: I disagree with that characterization, Counsel. I think that it denigrates the intelligence of the people with whom I was speaking and their willingness to contribute to a cause that was important to the national security of the United States.

MR. LIMAN: Well, do you deny that what you were doing was that you were pointing out to them what you believed the national security of the United States required in terms of support for the contras and then telling them that you could not ask them for money. That that had to be done across the street?

LT. COL. NORTH: I would stop my presentation where—at the point where somebody—where I would say that they had to go to somebody else. I don't think I ever told anybody else to go to Mr. Channell or Mr. Miller or anyone else. I would simply indicate to them that I could not and would not solicit money. And I don't believe the committee has any evidence to the effect that I did.

MR. LIMAN: Well, do you deny that you told them that they—if they were disposed to give, they should see Channell?

LT. COL. NORTH: My recollection, Counsel, is that I stopped at the point that I just told you. I'd spoken to thousands of people. Perhaps even tens of thousands of people, about the needs of the Nicaraguan freedom fighters, and I did not solicit from them a penny.

MR. LIMAN: You just prepared them for the pitch that would be made by Channell?

LT. COL. NORTH: Call it what you will, Counsel, I was explaining exactly what the situation was in Central America and how it would affect the National security of the United States of America. And if good Americans were motivated to give money to the Nicaraguan freedom fighters as a consequence, all I can say is, "Thank God." Because without that help they could well have died in the fields of Nicaragua, under the helicopter gun ships provided by the Soviet Union.

MR. LIMAN: Well, Colonel, do you think its an unfair characterization that you were trying to encourage them to give.

MR. SULLIVAN: Sir, it's the Committee's job to draw its own conclusions. Don't have him characterize anything. Just ask him the question and he'll give you the answer.

MR. LIMAN: I'm asking him what his motive was.

MR. SULLIVAN: He's answered it several times, Mr. Chairman. And Mr. Chairman—He's answered the question several times. The Committee members will draw their own conclusions about this.

MR. LIMAN: I—I will withdraw that—that question—

MR. SULLIVAN: Thank you—

441

MR. LIMAN: —I think we can draw our own conclusions.

LT. COL. NORTH: Counsel, I would be willing to give that briefing to this Committee if you'd indulge me and you can draw your conclusions from that and I will it verbatim, the way I gave it tens of thousands of Americans. Some who were disposed towards the resistance and some who were desparately opposed to it.

MR. LIMAN: Did you give munitions lists?

LT. COL. NORTH: Oh, I'm sure that I did. I gave the cost of various munitions, the cost of various aircraft, the cost of blowpipe missiles as they were provided to me.

MR. LIMAN: Did you give costs of advertising?

LT. COL. NORTH: I don't know that I did. I wasn't quite as familiar with advertising as I was with weapon systems.

MR. LIMAN: Did you ever tell the President of the United States that the only thing the people were being asked to do was to contribute for advertising?

LT. COL. NORTH: I do not recall ever telling the President that.

MR. LIMAN: When you testified that one reason that Mr. Casey was excited about the plan for use of the residuals was that he wanted to have a funded organization that he could pull off the shelf to do other operations. Is that what in essence his view was?

LT. COL. NORTH: Are you talking about my alleged solicitation now?

MR. LIMAN: No, now we're back to the use of the residuals.

LT. COL. NORTH: I'm sorry, Counsel. Would you please repeat the question?

MR. LIMAN: Do you remember giving testimony and it was not clear to me at least about the fact that Director Casey wanted something that he could pull off the shelf and that that's why he was excited about the fact that—

LT. COL. NORTH: Yes.

MR. LIMAN: —you were now able to generate some surpluses that could be used.

LT. COL. NORTH: That is correct.

MR. LIMAN: Well, why don't you give us a description of what he said, or as you understood it, what he meant about pulling something off the shelf.

LT. COL. NORTH: Director Casey had in mind, as I

understood it, an overseas entity that was capable of conducting operations or activities of assistance to the US foreign policy goals that was a "stand alone," it was—

MR. LIMAN: Self-finance?

LT. COL. NORTH: —self-financing, independent of appropriated monies and capable of conducting activities similar to the ones that we had conducted here. There were other countries that were suggested that might be the beneficiaries of that kind of support—other activities to include counterterrorism.

MR. LIMAN: Now, did I understand you to say, and if I'm wrong just tell me, that the chart that you had drawn by Hakim, which is Exhibit 328, was a chart to reflect that concept?

LT. COL. NORTH: I don't recall asking Mr. Hakim for that chart. I think—my recollection, (clears throat) excuse me, if my recollection is correct, that chart was something that I had asked General Secord for.

MR. LIMAN: But, was it intended to reflect the concept as described by Director Casey?

LT. COL. NORTH: Yes.

MR. LIMAN: Now, Director Casey was in charge of the CIA and had at his disposal an operations directorate, correct?

LT. COL. NORTH: Certainly.

MR. LIMAN: And, as I understand your testimony, Director Casey was proposing to you that a CIA outside of the CIA be created, fair?

LT. COL. NORTH: No.

MR. LIMAN: Well, wasn't this an organization that would be able to do covert policy to advance US foreign policy interests?

LT. COL. NORTH: Well, not necessarily all covert. The Director was interested in the ability to go an existing—as he put it—off-the-shelf, self-sustaining, stand-alone entity that could perform certain activities on behalf of the United States. And, as I tried to describe to the Committee last night in the executive session, several of those activities were discussed with both Director Casey and with Admiral Poindexter. Some of those were to be conducted jointly by other friendly intelligence services, but they needed money.

MR. LIMAN: Colonel?

LT. COL. NORTH: Yes, Counsel?

MR. LIMAN: You understood that the CIA is funded by the United States government, correct?

LT. COL. NORTH: That is correct.

MR. LIMAN: You understood that the United States government put certain limitations on what the CIA could do, correct?

LT. COL. NORTH: That is correct.

MR. LIMAN: And I ask you today, after all you've gone through, are you not shocked that the Director of Central Intelligence is proposing to you the creation of an organization to do these kinds of things outside of his own organization?

LT. COL. NORTH: Counsel, I can tell you that I am not shocked. I don't see that it was necessarily inconsistent with the laws, regulations, statutes and all that obtain. I don't see that it would necessarily be unconstitutional. I don't see see that it would necessarily be in any way a violation of anything that I know of. And if, indeed, the Director had chosen to use one of these entities out there to support an operation in the Middle East or South America or Africa, and an appropriate finding were done and the activities were authorized by the Commander-in-Chief, the head of state, in his capacity to do, what would be wrong—

You know, maybe I'm overly naive, but I don't see what would be wrong with that.

MR. LIMAN: Well, maybe you are. But did the Director ever tell you that he contemplated that this private organization would operate pursuant to presidential findings?

LT. COL. NORTH: We never got that far.

MR. LIMAN: Did the Director ever tell you that this private organization would be subject to oversight, pursuant to the laws of the United States by Congress?

LT. COL. NORTH: Again, the discussion didn't get that far. Let me just give one example to you, if I may. When we ended up needing a ship: to perform a certain task, there was nowhere to get on on short notice, and so this organization produced it practically overnight.

MR. LIMAN: But, is it a fact—

LT. COL. NORTH: And, that was because the Director said, "We can't find one anywhere else. Get a ship." And, we got a ship.

MR. LIMAN: And, that was a ship to be used for a covert operation. Correct?

LT. COL. NORTH: As I defined them to you last night, there were several that were to be done with that ship.

MR. LIMAN: But, that ship was to be used for a covert operation?

LT. COL. NORTH: That is correct.

MR. LIMAN: And, is it a fact, sir, that it was purchased out of the funds that were generated by the Iranian arms sale.

LT. COL. NORTH: It didn't cost the taxpayers of the United States a cent.

MR. LIMAN: But, was it generated out of the proceeds of the Iranian arms sale?

LT. COL. NORTH: I cannot tell you exactly what the source of those funds were other than it was not taxpayers' money.

MR. LIMAN: Well—

LT. COL. NORTH: And, you and I both know there were many sources for the funds that went into those accounts.

MR. LIMAN: Those accounts were the enterprise accounts.

LT. COL. NORTH: I never referred to them as the enterprise. I refer to them—

MR. LIMAN: I refer to the Lake Accounts.

LT. COL. NORTH: —by several—the Lake Account was the money in—

MR. LIMAN: Project Democracy.

LT. COL. NORTH: Thank you.

MR. LIMAN: You used terms like that. Now,—

LT. COL. NORTH: I don't have a problem with using the term called "Project Democracy."

MR. LIMAN: Well, let's talk about that because part of democracy here, was that there was a law that said that the President of the United States should authorize covert operations. Right?

MR. SULLIVAN: Point of order, Mr. Chairman.

CHAIRMAN INOUYE: Ordered.

REP. MCCOLLUM: I think that Mr. Liman, if I might make a point of order. I think Mr. Liman is out of line in asking questions that prejudge opinion of this committee. He is phrasing his questions to make an argument to slant it as though the entire committee thinks that this is a horrible thing. He doesn't speak for everybody. I don't know that it is or it isn't, but I thought that Mr. Liman was supposed to be getting facts out today, not expressing views, not expressing shock, not expressing the idea that of his own opinion, or this committee. And, I just am greatly concerned that this is not the appropriate—if one of us wants to do it, maybe that's our role, but I didn't think counsel should be doing it, Mr. Chairman.

CHAIRMAN INOUYE: Your point of order has been noted and the record will show that you disagree with the method by which Mr. Liman is questioning. Please proceed.

MR. LIMAN: Colonel, you worked on the Presidential finding on the Iran venture?

LT. COL. NORTH: I worked on a number of Presidential findings.

MR. LIMAN: Was there a provision in that Presidential finding signed by Ronald Reagan for the purchase of this ship?

LT. COL. NORTH: No, but there was nothing that prohibited the purchase of the ship by the private commercial companies that were supporting that activity.

MR. LIMAN: And,—

LT. COL. NORTH: And the ship was there to serve the foreign policy goals of the United States. The fact that we were—the whole operation was terminated before it could do so was unfortunate in my humble opinion.

MR. LIMAN: Was the President of the United States told about the fact that that ship had been purchased?

LT. COL. NORTH: I do not know.

MR. LIMAN: The Congress wasn't told. Correct?

LT. COL. NORTH: They certainly know now.

MR. LIMAN: They weren't told at the time.

LT. COL. NORTH: I don't believe they were, sir.

MR. LIMAN: So that, as far as your own personal knowledge was concerned, the people who approved the purchase of this ship in this covert operation were you, the Director of Central Intelligence and Admiral Poindexter.

LT. COL. NORTH: And, Richard Secord who was managing the private commercial operation.

MR. LIMAN: Did Richard Secord do it at the request of you?

LT. COL. NORTH: He did.

MR. LIMAN: Did you feel that you needed the approval of Admiral Poindexter to do it?

LT. COL. NORTH: I believe I sought that approval.

MR. LIMAN: Did you seek that approval with a memo that went up the line in the same form as the ones we've been talking about?

LT. COL. NORTH: What do you mean by "the same form"? We've seen several different forms here this morning, Counsel.

MR. LIMAN: Well, the forms say, "Recommend that you brief the President"—

LT. COL. NORTH: I don't know that it did or not.

MR. LIMAN: And, you also got the approval of the Director of Central Intelligence.

LT. COL. NORTH: I got the request from the Director of Central Intelligence. It didn't—the idea did not originate with me. When we found ourselves without the capability, unbelievable though that may seem, to put a radio broadcast ship out at sea or off a hostile nation, and we couldn't find a ship in the entire CIA inventory or the United States Navy that was able to do it, the Director of Central Intelligence came to me, and within, I think, 72 hours we had a ship.

MR. LIMAN: Don't you think that's a decision that the President of the United States should make?

LT. COL. NORTH: If the Director of Central Intelligence asked me to produce a ship, and I did so, I think that is good and sufficient.

MR. LIMAN: Now, if you look at the PROF note from Admiral Poindexter on this ship. 515? Do you remember that Admiral Poindexter—I'll get you the number, but—

LT. COL. NORTH: Please do.

MR. LIMAN: One-ninety-one.

LT. COL. NORTH: One-ninety-one?

MR. LIMAN: One-ninety-one.You remember, Admiral Poindexter—

(Pause to look for exhibit.)

MR. SULLIVAN: Do you know what book that's in, Counsel?

MR. LIMAN: Do you remember Admiral Poindexter sending you this PROF note?

LT. COL. NORTH: Now that you show it to me, I do.

MR. LIMAN: Let's read it. It's dated 5/15/86. "In a memo from Ken"—who's Ken?

447

LT. COL. NORTH: Mr. DeGraffenreid, who was the director of—the intelligence director—the special assistant to the President.

MR. LIMAN: "In a memo from Ken to me today, he talks about your offering a Danish ship under your control to CIA for broadcasting into"—and then it's blanked out. That's a hostile country, right?

LT. COL. NORTH: Yes.

MR. LIMAN: And then Admiral Poindexter says to you, "I am afraid you are letting your operational role become too public. From now on, I don't want you to talk to anyone else, including Casey, except me, about any of your operational roles. In fact, you need to quietly generate a cover story that I have insisted that you stop." Remember that?

LT. COL. NORTH: I do.

MR. LIMAN: So he wanted you to continue, but to have a cover story that you stopped. Right?

LT. COL. NORTH: And the last line is, "Be cautious."

MR. LIMAN: "Be cautious." And—

LT. COL. NORTH: That note was sent to me at 9:21 at night, while the Admiral was still at work.

MR. LIMAN: And you talked about the fact that—

LT. COL. NORTH: I can tell you exactly why that note—

MR. LIMAN: I will give you the second—that opportunity in a second. You talked about the fact that Director Casey described the Iran initiative, with the residuals being generated, as the—and these are your words—"the ultimate covert operation"?

LT. COL. NORTH: Yes.

MR. LIMAN: Would you agree that this here is the ultimate covert operation, even one that you're not to talk to the Director of Central Intelligence about?

LT. COL. NORTH: The problem that was generated—that generated this note was that Director Casey had told someone on his staff that they could go to me for the ship. When I was out of town or out of the office, a call was placed to Mr. DeGraffenreid's office instead of mine because he was the normal point of contact for the CIA, and that's what generated this note. It was not my indescretion in that case, it was Director Casey's. Unfortunately.

MR. LIMAN: So—

LT. COL. NORTH: Unfortunately.

MR. LIMAN: So this business of covert operations reached a point where not only Congress was regarded as too indiscrete to be told, but that even the Director of Central Intelligence made that list. I have no further questions this morning. Mr. Chairman.

REP. CHENEY: Mr. Chairman.

CHAIRMAN INOUYE: Mr. Cheney.

REP. CHENEY: Mr. Chairman, I would like to inquire as to the plans for this afternoon. We've now had 21 hours of questioning and no member of the committee has yet had the opportunity to ask any questions of the witness. Our original intent was to finish by this evening. Obviously, we aren't going to make that now. But, without in any way casting any aspersions on Mr. Liman, he's had a full day to ask questions and I wonder how soon we can expect him to finish his examination of the witness?

CHAIRMAN INOUYE: Mr. Liman.

MR. LIMAN: I believe that I can finish it in no more than an hour and I'm going to try to do it in a half-hour.

REP. CHENEY: Well Mr. Chairman, I would hope we can hold to that deadline. I do think we need to move on and I do think that the original purpose of this exercise was to allow members to question. And I think the procedures we've adopted badly need to be addressed and I hope we'd take that into consideration in connection with our next witness. Thank you.

REP. COURTER: Mr. Chairman.

CHAIRMAN INOUYE: Mr. Cheney, I'm certain you realize that this matter is presently under consideration.

REP. COURTER: Mr. Chairman.

CHAIRMAN INOUYE: Mr. Courter.

REP. COURTER: I thank the Chair. Mr. Chairman, Mr. Liman, in his examination of the witness has implied that the speech that Colonel North gave was a solicitation for funds or that during the speech he solicited funds. The Colonel indicated that it wasn't so and asked permission to give that briefing to this committee so we could form our own opinion. Since it is a relevant point made so by the questions of Mr. Liman, I ask the Chair that the witness be given permission to give that briefing to this Congress or to this committee so we, with the slides—so we can form our own conclusions as to whether he solicited money. I ask the Chair.

CHAIRMAN INOUYE: I will discuss this matter with the Co-Chairman, Mr. Hamilton. May I ask how long—

REP. COURTER: Will we have a ruling on that—

CHAIRMAN INOUYE: May I ask—

REP. COURTER: —this afternoon, Mr. Chairman?

CHAIRMAN INOUYE: —the Colonel a question, sir? How long will this briefing take, because we're trying to cut down our consideration of you as a witness?

LT. COL. NORTH: I believe it can be done in 20 minutes, sir.

CHAIRMAN INOUYE: We will make every effort to have that briefing as soon as the slides are available.

REP. COURTER: Thank you, Mr. Chairman.

CHAIRMAN INOUYE: If there are no further questions at this juncture, we'll stand in recess until 2:00 P.M. this afternoon.

END OF MORNING SESSION

Afternoon Session—2:00 P.M.

CHAIRMAN INOUYE: The hearing will please come to order.

REP. COURTER: Mr. Chairman, I wanted to thank you for your favorable ruling on the request, and I think it was a reasonable request, in light of the implication and the innuendo in the questions, and it's my understanding that the briefing material and the slides are here at hand. The question I have now is when will Col. North be given the opportunity to present that briefing?

CHAIRMAN INOUYE: This matter was considered during the lunch hour, and I would like to report and recommend the following: We do have the slides. We're now in the process of getting an appropriate slide projector. However, we have a few problems. One, some of the slides are still classified. As the Colonel knows, we have some aerial photographs involved. Secondly, in order to give the panel of senators and congressmen the full flavor and the full aura

450

of what happened during the presentation, we're now in the process of inviting Mr. Channell and Mr. Miller, because they're all part of the operation. And, when that is available, we will get a room, but not at this time.

SEN. COHEN: Mr. Chairman.

CHAIRMAN INOUYE: This is still under consideration.

SEN. COHEN: Mr. Chairman.

CHAIRMAN INOUYE: Mr. Cohen.

SEN. COHEN: Mr. Chairman, shortly before we broke for lunch, there was an indication that perhaps our counsel should cut short his questioning of Col. North. I wanted to point out just for the record that no member of the Senate interrupted House counsel during their questioning of Col. North; not one member ever interrupted either Mr. Nields or Mr. Van Cleve. Number two, there were no time limits imposed upon House counsel. It took two and a half days, and I reject the notion that somehow because the members don't like either Mr. Liman's tone or style, that he should be forced to cut short his questioning. Point number three, is Oliver North has demonstrated he's not only a brave military officer, but he's also a superb witness. And, I think he's had a lot tougher things thrown at him during his lifetime than questions by Arthur Liman, and I think he's fully capable of handling those questions without the able assistance of members of Congress.

And, the final point I'd like to make is, perhaps, the most serious revelation to have taken place during the course of these proceedings is that of a planned, proposed by or conceived by high-ranking officials to create a contingency fund for the intended purpose of carrying out other covert operations at sometime in the future, with or without Presidential findings, with or without notice to Congress, remains to be heard from; but if members of Congress are not disturbed about that revelation, then I think the American people should be, and if it takes more time to discuss this in depth and other related issues, I am perfectly happy to yield whatever time I have allocated to me so that Mr. Liman might continue. But I strongly object to the notion raised by House members of trying to impose a gag rule upon Mr. Liman.

REP. COURTER: Mr. Chairman—

CHAIRMAN INOUYE: Mr. Courter.

REP. COURTER (R-NJ): Would the gentleman yield?

SEN. COHEN: I would yield.

REP. COURTER: I'm not sure which House members the gentleman from Maine is referring to. I specifically recall that during the morning recess, it was a United States Senator that expressed publicly and on television his irritation with the fact that all counsels—not Senate counsel —but all counsels were taking four days, not having any limitation on their time, while members were permitted four, five, or ten minutes.

SEN. COHEN: Not once did that Senator interrupt any member, any counsel, or any member of the House. The Senate has not objected or interrupted during the course of these proceedings while Mr. Nields and others were questioning.

REP. MCCOLLUM (R-FL): If the gentleman would yield to me, I would like, since there's a point of privilege, I am the one who did the interrupting intially. Mr. Cheney didn't. His point on length of time came at the end of the proceedings. And I didn't interrupt because I thought that Mr. Liman was taking too much time, although I think counsel—maybe Mr. Nields was the one taking too much time, as Senator Boren said on television earlier this morning. The point that I was interrupting for was because I don't think that Mr. Liman or Mr. Nields, as our counsel, should be advocating or slanting questions to advocate a bias or a position or a slant of opinion. Their job, I thought, in my opinion, whether it's Senate counsel or House counsel, is to bring out facts, not to give positions, not to slant biases. And I think that Mr. Liman has been going through a whole pattern of biased questions today. He has done some of that in the past, but it's been particularly egregious this morning. And I didn't think it was fair to let it continue without making the point that it does not represent this member's views. It may represent yours, Senator Cohen, but it doesn't represent mine.

SEN. SARBANES (D-MD): Mr. Chairman?

CHAIRMAN INOUYE: Mr. Sarbanes?

SEN. SARBANES: Mr. Chairman, I totally reject the characterization that Mr. McCollum has put on Arthur Liman's questioning. I think it's clearly been within proper bounds. I think it's been very professional. It has certainly been well within the parameters of the charge to this Committee. It was Mr. McCollum who, in response to the testimony of Mr. Cooper before this Committee, said, speaking about Colonel North, Mr. McFarlane and Admiral Poindexter, and I quote him now, with respect to their conversations with the Attorney General, this is Mr. McCollum now speaking about Colonel North and the other two gentlemen, "I think that that in itself may well be a crime. If it is not a crime, it is certainly one of the highest acts of insubordination and one of the most treacherous things that has ever occurred to a president it seems to me in our history." Now, I'm quite prepared to talk about fairness. I haven't accused anyone in this matter of criminal conduct. I recognize that that's being examined in a different form. And I think the witnesses that come before us come here in order to help us to get at the truth and the what happened—or what needs to do in terms of the—what we need to do in terms of the nation's policy. But, I think Counsel's questioning has been reasonable and tough, but it's been within proper parameters. And it certainly doesn't behoove it seems to me my distinguished friend. In light of his comments at that earlier hearing encompassing this witness to raise this kind of objection at this point.

REP. MCCOLLUM: (Inaudible) a point on that—

SEN. SARBANES: Certainly.

REP. MCCOLLUM: —a matter of personal privilege?

SEN. SARBANES: Certainly.

REP. MCCOLLUM: I certainly did criticize those the other day when I examined Mr. Cooper whom I thought then and I still do think now misled the Attorney General. The facts are beginning to come out and I think it's a prerogative of members of this committee to make points and to bring out things of that nature. To the degree to which they're brought out, it was the members role to do that. To the degree to which Mr. Liman is acting, it seems to me that's not his role. We had many discussions in the House side. Maybe the senators didn't have it. But, we did about the role of Counsel at the inception of these hearings. And that role was to be impartial, to bring out the facts, to lay the predicates, to leave the comments and the judgments and the opinions to the members. It's my judgment Colonel North explained a good deal of what I was concerned

453

about. He hasn't completely satisfied me, but he's explained a lot of it. And I think that those answers were not available when I questioned Mr. Cooper. It does not bear on my point today. My point today is that the Counsel does not have any business slanting questions in a biased fashion that look to me like he's trying to add inference on inference to come to conclusions that would lead in a certain path to persuade the public in a way you couldn't even do in a court of law. He's acting like a prosecutor. Not a prosecutor of Colonel North's so much as a prosecutor of the President, a prosecutor of the Administration, instead of a fact finder. And I thought our role here was to find the facts and then the members make the judgments.

SEN. SARBANES: Mr. Chairman, let me just conclude this by making this observation. I think it's Arthur Liman's responsibility to press hard for answers particularly —particularly in light of the fact that members such as Mr. McCollum have stated about this matter involving Colonel North—"It is certainly one of the highest acts of insubordination, one of the most treacherous things that has ever occurred to a president it seems to me in our history." And I submit that those kinds of statements from Mr. McCollum, it's a responsibility of Counsel and of the members of this committee to press the witnesses very hard to find out the truth in this matter.

REP. HYDE: Mr. Chairman.

CHAIRMAN INOUYE: Mr. Hyde.

REP. HYDE: I may have a little different perspective, but if I may trespass on the time of the committee to explain to my friend from Maine. Occasionally, one interrupts when the iron is hot. Those of you that passed your bar exams the first time have heard of the phrase, "sleeping on your right." And when an issue is brought up, the interruption is not to foreclose the questioning, but simply to deal with that issue while it is current. And secondly, this member has no quarrel whatsoever with Mr. Liman's questioning nor Mr. Nields' questioning. I think they're doing a superb job and I'm delighted with the results and I would wish that Mr. Liman would go on and on. I thank you. (Laughs)

CHAIRMAN INOUYE: When we recessed at noon, Mr. Liman was considering a very important aspect of the investigation—the creation and the maintenance of a secret

454

government within our government. The business before us is very serious. I've said this on several occasions. We may have reason to laugh and chuckle, but what has brought out to date gives me little cause to laugh.

Mr. Liman, proceed sir.

MR. LIMAN: Colonel, did there come a time when the pricing of the arms to Iran, which were yielding the profits, began to cause a problem?

LT. COL. NORTH: I'm not quite certain, Counsel, whether it was the pricing or simply the person we were arranging it through. But there was some difficulty with that, yes.

MR. LIMAN: In fact, did there come a time when you were advised that Mr. Ghorbanifar was saying that the Iranian government had concluded that it had been substantially overcharged?

LT. COL. NORTH: Yes, that is correct.

MR. LIMAN: And he reported that the Iranian government had gotten hold of some microfiche of Defense Department prices?

LT. COL. NORTH: In fact, to be more explicit, the Iranian government was apparently still on the mailing list for those microfiches.

(Laughter)

MR. LIMAN: And he said that looking at those microfiches and what Ghorbanifar had charged, there was a 600 percent mark-up, or something like that?

LT. COL. NORTH: I'm not sure of the percentage that he alluded to, but he did indicate that they had been over-charged.

MR. LIMAN: And when you first got deeply involved in December, January, one of the problems you had encountered then was that the Iranians were claiming that they had been cheated by Nimrodi at all, right?

LT. COL. NORTH: The cheating in that case was the delivery of a system that did not fulfill their expectations and what they had been told that it would do.

MR. LIMAN: And now—

LT. COL. NORTH: It was not, as I understood it, an issue of price, but more of capability.

MR. LIMAN: And now you were faced with accusations from the first channel that they were being cheated by our pricing, right?

455

LT. COL. NORTH: That was what he told us, but it turns out that it was not so much an internal Iranian problem, I don't think, so much as it was his personal problem.

MR. LIMAN: Now, did you have a conversation with Director Casey about the fact that the Iranians had failed to pay the financiers of the transaction?

LT. COL. NORTH: We had several. But the one that is, of course, most easily recollected is the one that I had with Director Casey after Mr. Furmark had approached him.

MR. LIMAN: And did you consider, with various of your colleagues in the government, ways of dealing with the problem that you now had?

LT. COL. NORTH: Yes, along with discussions with the Israelis as to how to deal with that problem.

MR. LIMAN: Now, was one of the things that you considered increasing the charges to the second channel so as to generate money to pay the first channel?

LT. COL. NORTH: That was considered.

MR. LIMAN: And indeed, are you aware it's reflected in your notes?

LT. COL. NORTH: I couldn't guess at this point, Counsel.

MR. LIMAN: It's Exhibit 353 and it's—it bears our date stamp Q2559. (Brief pause while North looks for documents.) And if you look at the top—

LT. COL. NORTH: The highlighted—

MR. LIMAN: Yes, the highlighted portions. There are some portions there which I think you can appreciate we should not read because it refers to the second channel. "The best way to recoup funds to pay off Furmark at all is to overcharge on subsequent deliveries." And then the next highlighted mixed shipment will have to be higher, $10,000 each," and then it says, "or we cannot"—and then I don't think the word is finished.

LT. COL. NORTH: I believe that is a discussion with Mr. Nir. Those are notes taken, I think—I don't have the preceding pages, but looking at what does follow and what is on—is the page behind that, Counsel, 353, the preceding page?

MR. LIMAN: It's the preceding one and it appears to be a conversation with Mr. Nir. It was the only name that appears—

LT. COL. NORTH: Yes, I have been looking at this. I

456

recollect that this is most likely one of many conversations I had with Mr. Nir about this problem. I would also point out that throughout this entire endeavor, Mr. Nir insisted that we keep the prices up, whether, as we assumed, that was because the Israelis did not want us underbidding what they were normally doing or whether that was simply to generate more revenues. I do not know.

MR. LIMAN: Well, in any event, did you discuss with Mr. Casey that you had to find some way of dealing with the claims of the first channel and their financiers? Is that fair to say?

LT. COL. NORTH: Yes, although I must tell you that there were many who advocated—not many, but some—there weren't many who knew about this, but within the group of people who knew about it, there were some of us who advocated letting Mr. Ghorbanifar deal with it himself. It was a problem that he had created. I would point out that although we had certainly run the charges up, Mr. Ghorbanifar had almost doubled it on top of that. And so many of the problems that were created were of his own design.

MR. LIMAN: Well, is it a fact that the problem that you were concerned about was his threat or the threat of his financiers to make this public?

LT. COL. NORTH: Well, yes, absolutely.

MR. LIMAN: And so an operation that had been kept quiet from Congress was now in danger of being blown by people who said they hadn't been paid?

LT. COL. NORTH: Well again, I don't want to leave anyone with the misapprehension that it was simply a matter of keeping it secret from Congress. As I have testified for nearly four days, this was an operation that was to be kept secret across the board. And it wasn't simply a matter of keeping it from the Congress.

MR. LIMAN: When you say—

LT. COL. NORTH: It was a covert operation for all of the reasons that I have described the need for secrecy in covert operations.

MR. LIMAN: Well when you say "secret across the board" would you agree with me that at the very least, the following people knew about our involvement, one, Mr. Ghorbanifar?

LT. COL. NORTH: Certainly, he started it.

MR. LIMAN: The Israelis?

LT. COL. NORTH: Some in the Israeli government.

MR. LIMAN: The Iranian government officials in the first channel?

LT. COL. NORTH: Yes.

MR. LIMAN: The Iranian government officials in the second channel?

LT. COL. NORTH: That's correct.

MR. LIMAN: So that you were willing—now, when I say "you" I'm not talking just about you, obviously—

LT. COL. NORTH: Those of us engaged in the activity, I understand.

MR. LIMAN: Yes, those who were engaged in the activity were willing to take the risk on trusting them with secrecy, but concluded that it was not possible or prudent to reveal it to the leadership of Congress? That's what it comes down to?

LT. COL. NORTH: Counsel, you're asking me to second-guess the decision not to have advised the Congress in the initiation of this activity on the finding of six- or seventeen January. I'm not going to second-guess that decision. I would point out that in the previous administration just prior to this one, there was a similar effort to rescue hostages, and to my knowledge, the Congress was not briefed on that one. And there were Iranians, and Israelis, and foreign government officials, and officials throughout our government who were apprised of that activity, and because of the risk to life of American citizens, to include the hostages, the Congress was not briefed.

MR. LIMAN: Was the leadership briefed?

LT. COL. NORTH: I don't know. I was told that it was not. But I was not here.

MR. LIMAN: All right. Colonel, the—on this operation, was there any discussion that took place that you are privy to, between the beginning of January and the time that this first appeared in that Lebanese newspaper about whether the time had come to tell the intelligence committees?

LT. COL. NORTH: I was not privy to any conversation to that end, Counsel.

MR. LIMAN: Now, you were involved in a—in providing the bank account number to Elliott Abrams for the Brunei solicitation, right?

LT. COL. NORTH: I was.

MR. LIMAN: All right. And I—the fact that the number was transposed was just an error that you never noticed?

LT. COL. NORTH: Had I noticed it, it wouldn't have been transposed.

MR. LIMAN: Now, (pause)—

LT. COL. NORTH: Again, Counsel, I have not seen that card. I would point out that my secretary—and as I indicated yesterday, I believe was not only given the gift of beauty by the good Lord, but she had brains, I think the Committee had the chance to see that—she made very few errors, and I don't know that she made the error on that card or someone else did, or that that was precisely the card that was carried to give to the representatives of the Brunei government. I would not have given intentionally a wrong number to Mr. Abrams, you can be sure.

MR. LIMAN: Now, did you ask Mr. Abrams not to tell the CIA about the bank account—

LT. COL. NORTH: No. As I recall—

MR. LIMAN: —number that you gave them?

LT. COL. NORTH: As I recall, he asked me not to tell the CIA.

MR. LIMAN: So that there was a request and an agreement that the CIA wouldn't be told about that?

LT. COL. NORTH: Yes.

MR. LIMAN: Did you understand that the money from Brunei had been solicited for humanitarian purposes pursuant to the authorization of Congress?

LT. COL. NORTH: I'm not—I quite honestly don't think I focused on that. I knew that there was an authorization for the State Department to proceed, and solicit monies from other governments, and I honestly don't know that it was specifically for one purpose or ano—I don't recall knowing at the time, or focusing on the time, that it was for one specific purpose or another. What I did assure Mr. Abrams is that those monies would indeed be set aside for whatever purposes he deemed appropriate.

MR. LIMAN: Did he tell you what purposes he deemed appropriate?

LT. COL. NORTH: Well, he deemed—I deemed that the purpose was to support the Nicaraguan democratic resistance.

459

MR. LIMAN: And, that would have included, if they needed it, lethal support, not just rations?

LT. COL. NORTH: Well, I, I was fully willing to live within whatever constraints he wished to impose upon that account.

MR. LIMAN: Did he impose any constraints?

LT. COL. NORTH: Well, we never got any money.

MR. LIMAN: Well, but you thought you were getting money when you gave him the number.

LT. COL. NORTH: True. And we looked for it assiduously until the day I was—literally, the day I was leaving the NSC.

MR. LIMAN: Colonel, did he when he asked you for the account, say anything to you about the fact that this is supposed to be used for the purpose for which it was solicited: Humanitarian aid?

LT. COL. NORTH: He may well have, Counsel. I'm in—and, I—well, I guess my problem is I think folks may be trying to make things appear more sinister than they already were, if they were indeed at all, and the point I'm trying to make is that if Mr. Abrams asked me to do that, I would have done it, and I'm not saying he did and I'm not saying he didn't. Those monies were to be allocated for the purposes that the Department of State solicited them for. It was never an intention on my part to allocate them to some other purpose.

MR. LIMAN: Well, are you saying that those funds, as opposed to the other money in the Lake Account, would be disbursed at the direction of Mr. Abrams?

LT. COL. NORTH: Precisely.

MR. LIMAN: Now, did you give instructions to Mr. Hakim or Mr.—to General Secord that of the ten million, seven million was to set aside and three million was to be available for other purposes?

LT. COL. NORTH: I do not recall those instructions, but it was not infrequent that we would hope to have some operating revenue, for example, to support airlift—which, certainly, some can argue was a lethal activity. And yet we funded airlift out of the $27 million in humanitarian assistance. And I do believe that I talked to Mr. Abrams about the need for additional aircraft and supporting—continued support for the airlift operations in Central America.

MR. LIMAN: Did the airlift include the drops of lethal supplies behind enemy lines?

LT. COL. NORTH: It is my distinct recollection, Counsel, that we came to the committees to use a portion of the $27 million appropriated by the Congress under what came to be called the Nicaraguan Humanitarian Assistance Office for the purpose of one, communications eqiupment, number two, mixed loads. Mixed loads meant you took beans and Band-Aids and boots and bullets. And we got authorization to do that from the Congress.

MR. LIMAN: Now did you—in connection with this money, do you have any recollection of giving instructions on allocations?

LT. COL. NORTH: Not specifically, no. I'm not saying that I didn't.

MR. LIMAN: Did you participate in the briefing of the Congressional committees on this subject?

LT. COL. NORTH: On the Nicaraguan Humanitarian Assistance Office?

MR. LIMAN: Yes.

LT. COL. NORTH: Yes, I believe I did.

MR. LIMAN: And when you briefed them, did you tell them? Is this what you're saying—that you told them that some of the $27 million was to be used to carry bullets?

LT. COL. NORTH: No. As I recall—and I may be recalling incorrectly. We came back to the Congress after the appropriations of the $27 million and sought and obtained permission to provide intelligence and communications support and to deliver mixed loads. I may be imagining that. I've been accused of having fantasies, but I—that's a fairly distinct recollection on my part.

MR. LIMAN: But in fact you know that the law was changed to permit intelligence information and military or—and advice?

LT. COL. NORTH: You recall the law, subsequently, was changed to provide $100 million in assistance.

MR. LIMAN: But even before that.

LT. COL. NORTH: That's correct. And that's what I am referring to, Counsel.

MR. LIMAN: On the Brunei money, was there ever any discussion that some of that money was going to be used to repay the financiers of the first channel?

461

LT. COL. NORTH: Never.

MR. LIMAN: That was never contemplated?

LT. COL. NORTH: It was never a contemplation in my mind.

MR. LIMAN: And never—

LT. COL. NORTH: And I never heard it mentioned to me. I didn't mention it to anyone else.

MR. LIMAN: And never discussed?

LT. COL. NORTH: Never, sir.

MR. LIMAN: Now were you involved in the decision to seek the second channel?

LT. COL. NORTH: Yes.

MR. LIMAN: And you got approval on that from Admiral Poindexter?

LT. COL. NORTH: I did.

MR. LIMAN: And you were involved in the various negotiations with that channel?

LT. COL. NORTH: I'm not sure how many there were before I got involved, but the initial contact was made, I think, by General Secord in a European country. He evaluated it, reported back, and if my recollection serves me right we then had a meeting here in the United States.

MR. LIMAN: And you understood that Mr. Hakim was the person who helped locate that channel?

LT. COL. NORTH: Yes.

MR. LIMAN: And did Hakim tell you that a two million-dollar reserve had been set aside in order to make payoffs for the second channel?

LT. COL. NORTH: As we—we discussed last night and I think even during the day yesterday, Mr. Hakim made it clear that there was a necessity to compensate those engaged in the activity. I did not press the issue. I know well the meaning of the term "bakshish," and I know it is a long established tradition in that part of the world. I did not—I do not recall discussing a specific amount, but I—it was very clear to me that that was part of the activity.

MR. LIMAN: Now, was Mr. Hakim presented to the Iranians as the President's interpreter?

LT. COL. NORTH: Not for the second channel; he was for the first.

MR. LIMAN: For the first channel?

LT. COL. NORTH: That's correct.

462

MR. LIMAN: Were there some people in the second channel who were also present at meetings with the first channel?

LT. COL. NORTH: Well, I was.

MR. LIMAN: No, I mean on the Iranian side.

LT. COL. NORTH: Initially, I don't believe so, but then eventually—

MR. LIMAN: Ultimately?

LT. COL. NORTH: —as we established contact with —directly with government officials, yes.

MR. LIMAN: Was General Secord presented as an official representative of the United States government or as a businessman? How was he presented to the second channel?

LT. COL. NORTH: I don't recall. I know that in the first channel—I may be mixing them up now—he had an alias identity, and I don't recall his specific title within that. But he did have an alias identity, and we had, as you know, alias documentation.

MR. LIMAN: When you were present at the negotiations, who headed the American negotiating team?

LT. COL. NORTH: We're talking first or second channel?

MR. LIMAN: Second.

LT. COL. NORTH: I guess I did.

MR. LIMAN: Did you present to the second channel the so-called "Seven-point Plan?"

LT. COL. NORTH: I guess, if that's what you're calling it. I suppose I wrote seven or six or eight or whatever number of points on a piece of paper. I didn't refer to it at the time, I don't think, as the "Seven-point Plan."

MR. LIMAN: Can you look at Exhibit 308?

(Pause)

MR. LIMAN: Is that your writing on the—

LT. COL. NORTH: That is my writing.

MR. LIMAN: And it's headed, "United States proposal?"

LT. COL. NORTH: That's what it says.

MR. LIMAN: Now is that a proposal that you presented to the second channel?

LT. COL. NORTH: I'm sure it was. I don't recall whether this was done at the meeting in Washington or the meeting in Europe, but I'm sure that that is one of many proposals, all of which I had tape recorded by the Central Intelligence or by myself with Central Intelligence Agency equipment so that there would never, ever be any doubt as to what I was saying or obligating or committing to.

MR. LIMAN: Now Colonel, before you made your proposals to them, did you get authority from anyone as to what you would, as you just said, commit to, present to them?

LT. COL. NORTH: In general terms, yes. And as you can see, one of them were "all American hostages released" right up at the top.

MR. LIMAN: Do you recall having a discussion on this subject in Germany?

LT. COL. NORTH: Well as I said, I thought maybe this was what I presented in either one of the meetings in the United States, in Germany, in Geneva, Paris—

MR. LIMAN: I think this has been—

LT. COL. NORTH: —any of the other places that we met.

MR. LIMAN: This has been identified and was produced by Mr. Hakim as being presented in Germany.

LT. COL. NORTH: Was there a date on this? And I could check my travel schedule—

MR. LIMAN: There wasn't—

LT. COL. NORTH: —but I—

MR. LIMAN: There wasn't. You may have—

LT. COL. NORTH: I don't think that the location is all that important.

MR. LIMAN: Now did you have any conversations with State Department representatives before you made the various proposals that you were making during these negotiations?

LT. COL. NORTH: No.

MR. LIMAN: Now you've already testified that in these negotiations, it was necessary for you to make representations that weren't accurate—

LT. COL. NORTH: No, they were blatantly false.

MR. LIMAN: Among other things that you would describe as blatantly false, were the statements that the head of state of Iraq had to go, that the President of the United States regarded him in an unfavorable way—

LT. COL. NORTH: Sure, and others—

MR. LIMAN: —including an expletive.

LT. COL. NORTH: —lots of others, all on tape.

MR. LIMAN: And did you discuss with your superiors, in particular, Mr. Casey or Admiral Poindexter, before you went into the negotiations, that you would be saying to an official of the Iranian government that the United States supported the removal of the head of state of Iraq, that the United States would give some assistance on the Dawaa prisoners, et cetera?

LT. COL. NORTH: I did not discuss those specifics, no. Many of these were ideas that came up in the course of the earlier parts of the negotiations as seemingly important to those with whom I was dealing, and we were trying to appear responsive. There was no effort whatsoever to deceive anybody in our government from that, that I was reporting to. I had with me one of Director Casey's finest officers. I had with me CIA communications intelligence support. I had with me CIA personnel who were recording these meetings through surreptitious means. And I made no bones about the fact that these were available to my superiors.

MR. LIMAN: Well—

LT. COL. NORTH: If anybody had any doubt as to what I was saying, they could have stopped me, and they didn't.

MR. LIMAN: Colonel, I can say for the record that we do have recordings—

LT. COL. NORTH: Thank you.

MR. LIMAN: —and they do reflect those statements. Now—

LT. COL. NORTH: I guess my only question then is, Counsel, if you have the tapes, and I think I am the one that pointed out—

MR. LIMAN: Or the transcripts, I should say.

LT. COL. NORTH: —the existence of those tapes—the transcripts—I see no reason to have a memory quiz with a man who's been through five and a half years trying to recall a specific meeting in a certain place.

MR. LIMAN: This isn't a memory quiz. You're making a statement about the removal of a head of state, about the United States committing to defend Iran, those are things you remember without looking at the tapes, right?

LT. COL. NORTH: Yes, and let me just make one observation about the United States committing to defend Iran. That is not the way it was portrayed. The specific statement, reinforced by me after General Secord said it, dealt with the fact that we had built a US central command for that

465

specific purpose. And it wasn't something that was a deep, dark secret. The fact is, that's why it exists. That's why the Congress spent literally billions of dollars building that command. It is in every defense journal and foreign affairs journal in the country.

MR. LIMAN: And it was because of that that you felt comfortable in stating that the United States would defend Iran?

LT. COL. NORTH: The United States would contend that the Soviets should not occupy Iran. And the fact is, whether we had or had not gotten Iranian support, we were not about to relinquish control of Iran to the Soviet Union, and that is why the Senators in the back row voted for a US central command, and the United States armed forces organized one. That is no deep, dark secret—not even to the Iranians.

MR. LIMAN: Colonel, before you made those statements, you've already said you didn't talk to Admiral Poindexter about it.

LT. COL. NORTH: About that specific point, nor these specific points, in the midst of a negotiation that went on over several days, no.

MR. LIMAN: Did you also talk about the fact that there were two million homeless people in Iran?

LT. COL. NORTH: Which also happens to be a fact.

MR. LIMAN: And did you talk about the fact that the United States would supply aid, like a Marshall Plan, for them?

LT. COL. NORTH: I talked about the fact that they ought to get beyond the issue of trading weapons for a few live bodies, and that what our initiative was all about was reopening with Iran, and that the President of the United States shared those concerns. The fact that I exaggerated my connection with the President of the United States in order to further this initiative, I have already admitted to. The fact is, we in this country have always expressed concern for those kinds of matters. And the fact is, if we could have gotten beyond where we are and established a relationship with Iran, I am confident that we would be doing something for the missions of homeless in Iran and the hundreds of partial paraplegics and those that need prosthetic limbs on both sides of that war.

MR. LIMAN: Did you say words to that effect that you've just expressed with this conviction here?

LT. COL. NORTH: Yes, and they're on the tape.

MR. LIMAN: Now, Colonel, you have talked about the fact that you found yourself very much involved in the management of a covert operation. Did you now find youself very much involved in a diplomatic assignment?

LT. COL. NORTH: My whole purpose—as is also on the tape and is also in the memoranda that I sent forward to my superiors—my whole purpose was to find a way of establishing contact so that a senior US official—and the names of those officials are in the memoranda that I sent to my superiors—could eventually have a meeting with senior Iranian officials; that it would be feasible, politically, for both sides to be able to do that. And the names of those officials are in the memoranda that I sent forward—the suggestion that the Vice President or the Secretary of State meet with senior Iranians for the purposes of ending that horrible conflict, which happens to be the largest war on the planet earth right now, would be to the best interests of our country and both of theirs.

MR. LIMAN: Did you have any discussion with Admiral Poindexter as to whether the State Department should be consulted about whether this was the way to achieve the objective that you talked about?

LT. COL. NORTH: I don't recall that specific discussion. But I think you'll find those general ideas in the terms of reference that were approved by the State Department.

MR. LIMAN: Is it a fact that the Secretary of State was not told that a mission was going to be going to Teheran?

LT. COL. NORTH: I have no idea.

MR. LIMAN: Do you recall, and you can look at Exhibit #193—

MR. SULLIVAN: What book is that?

MR. LIMAN: —that—the question, it's—well, I have them all in two books. I don't know how they were broken up in the exhibits you were given, but it's #193. Do you recall that you suggested before the Teheran mission to Admiral Poindexter that there be a meeting with Secretary Shultz and Secretary Weinberger, and that he rejected that?

LT. COL. NORTH: I recall suggesting those kinds of things on occasion.

MR. LIMAN: Do you reca—

LT. COL. NORTH: I, this is—that particular suggestion, that's fine.

MR. LIMAN: Do you recall your suggestions being rejected?

LT. COL. NORTH: On occasion.

MR. LIMAN: Is it a fact that they were cut out?

LT. COL. NORTH: I don't know. It was not my responsibility to walk up to Secretaries of State and Defense and apprise them of things. It was my responsibility to carry out the lawful orders of my superiors, and, as I have indicated for the last three and a half days, I tried to do so, sir.

MR. LIMAN: And, did there come a time when Albert Hakim told you that he had negotiated a 9-point plan?

LT. COL. NORTH: Again, I don't recall it being referred to specifically that way, but I've heard it since.

MR. LIMAN: Did he communicate to you points, whether he called them "nine points" or something else, that he had gotten agreement from the Iranians on?

LT. COL. NORTH: I believe he may have.

MR. LIMAN: Did you then seek approval from your superior on those nine points?

LT. COL. NORTH: If it was something that I judged ought to proceed, and it did proceed, I obviously sought that kind of approval.

MR. LIMAN: If you would look at Exibit #310, which is the translation that we have of the document that he provided to us, and that he said he had cleared with you, and that you had cleared with Admiral Poindexter, see if you recognize it?

LT. COL. NORTH: It starts out with "the Library of Congress"?

MR. LIMAN: They're the ones who did the translation for us.

LT. COL. NORTH: Well, obviously, if I had a copy of this, I would have gotten it from him in English, since I don't read Farsi—

MR. LIMAN: Well, you don't—

LT. COL. NORTH: —or Mr. Cave would have done the translation. But I'm not unfamiliar with this general proposal—

MR. LIMAN: Do you know whether you shredded the one you got from him?

LT. COL. NORTH: I may have.

MR. LIMAN: And you're not unfamiliar with this? With these points?

LT. COL. NORTH: Those points look familiar, yes.

MR. LIMAN: Did you communicate to him approval of these points?

LT. COL. NORTH: Well I—if we proceeded in this direction, and I would guess maybe we did, then I did seek approval, yes.

MR. LIMAN: And did you include in the approval that you sought the item about his presenting a plan for the release of the—

LT. COL. NORTH: Dawaa?

MR. LIMAN: —the Dawaa.

LT. COL. NORTH: Yes.

MR. LIMAN: And at the time—and did you get that approval?

LT. COL. NORTH: Yes.

MR. LIMAN: And at the time that you got that approval, did the NSC have an official position against the United States asking for that?

LT. COL. NORTH: That plan did not involve the United States asking for that. The plan that we presented to the Iranians, which we probably ought to take up in Executive Session, if you want the details, did not involve the United States, and that's an important thing to understand. I knew well what our position was on the Dawaa, I had written it with the concurrence of the Department of State. Of course that was always one of the demands of the Hezbollah the Americans hostage, because one or two or maybe even three of the members of the Dawaa are related to family members of the Hezbollah.

MR. LIMAN: Colonel, I don't want to get into matters that ought to be on Executive Session—

LT. COL. NORTH: Oh, I—

MR. LIMAN: —but this question to you—

LT. COL. NORTH: Let us leave it at this, that it did not involve in any way the sacrifice of our position or the compromise of our position on the Dawaa.

469

MR. LIMAN: Did—do you—

LT. COL. NORTH: It was a straight forward proposal to the Iranians as to how they could solve the problem.

MR. LIMAN: Do you—you draw a distinction between Hakim and the United States government, is that fair to say?

LT. COL. NORTH: Absolutely.

MR. LIMAN: Do you think that the Iranians who were dealing with him drew that distinction?

LT. COL. NORTH: I don't know. You're asking me to put myself into the minds of the Iranians.

MR. LIMAN: Well you were there when he was being presented, when he was presented originally as the President's interpreter—

LT. COL. NORTH: Again, I don't recall as I presented him that way at the second channel. I'm not too sure what role he was playing in that case, but I did present him that way in the first meetings. I did so in the presence of two CIA officers, one of them relatively senior. I did so with the concurrence of the Director of Central Intelligence and the National Security Advisor. And the reason for that is the Central Intelligence Agency could not or would not provide a translator for that session, which I think we've gone over that one.

MR. LIMAN: What you're saying is that these were not decisions of Lt. Col. North, they were decisions that were fully authorized?

LT. COL. NORTH: That's correct.

MR. LIMAN: I wasn't questioning the fact that you had authority from Mr. Poindexter or Casey or that you had made tape recordings of it, we have the tape recordings.

LT. COL. NORTH: I understand, Counsel. I just didn't want anybody to be left with a misapprehension. After all of the paper that you now have gone nearly blind on, and I wore my fingers to the bone typing—or my secretary did—or typed myself on my PROFs, that I left anybody uninformed who needed to be informed in the conduct of these operations.

MR. LIMAN: And you—where you talked about "needed to be informed," your universe was the NSC, not the State Department, not—

LT. COL. NORTH: My universe was the National Security Council on the President's personal staff.

MR. LIMAN: And it was up to the President or the National Security Advisor to determine whether negotiations with Iran should involve the State Department or whether you should be the one left to handle them.

LT. COL. NORTH: That's correct.

MR. LIMAN: And they charged you with that.

LT. COL. NORTH: I carried it out to the very best of my abilities, Counsel.

MR. LIMAN: Now, you said, and I'm coming to the end now—you said in yesterday's session and before when you were talking about the reasons why it was important not to disclose to Congress the support that was being given for the contras by the NSC, that you and the others were put in the position of balancing lives for lies. Remember that?

LT. COL. NORTH: I remember that.

MR. LIMAN: I'd like to just pursue that with you for a moment. Is it a fact that before the Boland period that Congress had publicly appropriated money for the CIA to support the contras?

LT. COL. NORTH: Even under some of the Boland proscriptions, yes.

MR. LIMAN: It is a fact that even during the Boland period, the President had publicly proclaimed his support for the contras.

LT. COL. NORTH: That is correct.

MR. LIMAN: And it is a fact that the President had publicly said that he was going to seek more money from Congress when they cut it out.

LT. COL. NORTH: My recollection he said, he would go back again and again and again and he did so.

MR. LIMAN: And it is a fact that Congress publicly appropriated the 27 million dollars for humanitarian aid for the contras.

LT. COL. NORTH: And they gave us several waivers on the application of that.

MR. LIMAN: And then Congress publicly authorized the exchange of intelligence information to assist the contras. Right?

LT. COL. NORTH: Correct.

MR. LIMAN: And Congress then for fiscal 1987 publicly appropriated a hundred million dollars for the contras for both lethal and non-lethal support.

LT. COL. NORTH: Thank God.

MR. LIMAN: It's a fact that even during the Boland period, you wanted all of the Central American countries to know that notwithstanding Boland that the United States was not abandoning the contras and the President would go back again and again to get money for them. Right?

LT. COL. NORTH: Correct.

MR. LIMAN: And you also wanted to make sure that the Sandinistas knew that the contras weren't through, right?

LT. COL. NORTH: On one occasion, I told them myself.

MR. LIMAN: And so, can you then just explain how you thought lives would have been endangered? And when I say "you," I'm talking not just about me but Mr. McFarlane, if you know who wrote the letters, and Admiral Poindexter —how you thought lives would be endangered when Congress said, "Are you giving support to the contras," by saying, "We sure are, notwithstanding Boland?"

LT. COL. NORTH: Quite simply that the exposure of the operation would have caused it to be terminated.

MR. LIMAN: And it would have caused it to be terminated by Congress?

LT. COL. NORTH: By the very exposure of it, by the very fact that the Sandinistas would then know, for example, the origin of the supplies, the schedules of the flights, the place where things were landing. It put such enormous, enormous pressure on the local governments that they were unable to support it.

MR. LIMAN: Colonel, you've missed—

LT. COL. NORTH: I have not missed it at all. I'm talking about the political debate that would have occurred here in this country and the relevations piece by piece by piece, just like we have on this activity.

MR. LIMAN: So that it was the political debate and the possibility that, if our covert policy became known, that it might be—I'm sorry. So it was the risk of political debate and the possibility that, if it became known that we had continued support of the contras, that it would be blocked—

LT. COL. NORTH: No.

MR. LIMAN: —that caused this—

LT. COL. NORTH: No. You're misunderstanding what I said. What I was saying was that the revelations of the actual details of this activity—some of which, thankfully, have still not been exposed—would have cost the lives of those with whom I was working; would have jeopardized the governments which had assisted; would have jeopardized the lives of the Americans who, in some cases, were flying flights over Nicaragua; would have put at great risk those inside Nicaragua and in Eastern Europe and in Europe and in other places where people were working hard to keep them alive. And some of those details have still not been exposed. Yet, because of things like these hearings, there will be governments who will be less willing to assist our country in the conduct of operations, even with findings and Congressional approval and the rest of it. That's what I'm talking about, Counsel.

MR. LIMAN: Colonel, you said that the disclosure of details could cause people to be less willing to support, or could even cause risks. Would the disclosure that we were supporting the contras and that we were not abiding by the letter and the spirit of Boland have done that?

LT. COL. NORTH: No, I don't believe so, Counsel. It was not an issue of whether or not we were abiding by the spirit and letter of Boland. We did that. We lived within the constraints of Boland, which limited the use of appropriated funds. What we were concerned about—and we talked about some of this last night. The very fact that, when there was a briefing held and lives were, indeed, placed at risk —because people weren't quiet about it—and we talked about a couple of incidents last night, one of which I was closely associated with. And the fact is I have said consistently through my appearance here before these committees that there must be a better way. It is not easy for honorable men with whom I served, or myself, to sit in the White House or anywhere else in Washington and to have to weigh the differences between lives and lies. These were men who had high purposes. These were men with whom I worked on a daily basis, who suffered great anxiety and internal discontent over what they were forced to do.

The fact is, there must be a better way.

MR. LIMAN: Who forced them?

473

LT. COL. NORTH: And, I have suggested one of those better ways. I suggested an earlier way, and that was to divulge nothing. I make no excuses for those letters or my presentation before Chairman Hamilton's committee assembled in the Sit. Room. I have told you why I did it.

MR. LIMAN: I'm not asking you that. Who forced them?

LT. COL. NORTH: I think the relationship that exists between Executive and the Congress on these issues has given us the consequence of what happened in these events.

MR. LIMAN: So, that it is Congress' fault, in your view, that you had to send letters that misrepresented what the NSC was doing on Boland?

LT. COL. NORTH: I make no debate with the Chairman, with Chairman Inouye's comment that there are many many leaks from the other side of Pennsylvania. But, I would point out to you, sir, that for over two years, this operation was indeed covert. It did not become a matter of public exposure and damage to this country until the very end, and I would say to you, sir, that if a way could be found to work with the Congress, the way I worked with the people who I had to work with, then we could indeed solve that problem.

MR. LIMAN: Colonel, wasn't the problem that the Congress had decided that it did not want the contras supported, and so you couldn't work with the Congress?

LT. COL. NORTH: Counsel, if the Congress had decided that nobody in the United States of America should render any support whatsoever to the Nicaraguan democratic resistance, then it should have passed a law saying that. The law that was passed, a part of an appropriations bill, didn't prohibit what we did.

MR. LIMAN: And, is it Congress' fault because of the way it worded the law that the letter said, "We are abiding by the letter and spirit of Boland"? Yes or no?

LT. COL. NORTH: I have told you that that was not correct, and I have told you what I proposed to do.

MR. LIMAN: Is it Congress' fault?

LT. COL. NORTH: I say it is the fault of the Congress for not being able to understand what the problem was, and indeed the fault of those of us who prepared those letters for sending them away that we did. And, I have accepted my responsibility for my role in that, sir.

474

MR. LIMAN: Is it Congress' fault for the various representations that were made to the Attorney General that were
wrong?

LT. COL. NORTH: I'm not sure—I'm not at this point sure
what you're referring to.

MR. LIMAN: The ones on the Hawks and so forth. Is that
Congress' fault?

LT. COL. NORTH: I think we've already been over that.

MR. LIMAN: I just want to know whether your view, as
you sit here, is that it was Congress' fault? (Pause) I have no
further questions, Mr. Chairman. If it needs consultation
with counsel to answer whether it's Congress' fault to
represent things that are wrong to the Attorney General—

LT. COL. NORTH: Counsel, let me—

MR. LIMAN: —I have no further questions.

LT. COL. NORTH: —let me answer the question if I may,
Mr. Chairman.

CHAIRMAN INOUYE: Please do.

LT. COL. NORTH: My answer to the question is quite
simple, and I've answered it before. I think there's fault to
go on both sides. I've said that repeatedly throughout my
testimony. And I have accepted the responsibility for my
role in it.

CHAIRMAN INOUYE: The hearing will stand in recess for
ten minutes.

(Committee recess)

CHAIRMAN INOUYE: The hearing will please come to
order. The chair recognizes Chairman Hamilton.

CHAIRMAN HAMILTON: I recognize Mr. Jenkins to begin
one hour of questioning.

REP. JENKINS: Thank you, Mr. Chairman.
Colonel North, I know you have been for a long, long
time, and—and I will try to keep my questions very, very
short. Maybe I will not use the entire time. Let me say in the
beginning that with an issue like this I'm sure there will be
many repetitive questions, and I want to apologize in
advance because I know you will have answered some of
them, but I want to get the picture in my mind so that I fully
understand as best I can from your testimony as to what
actually occurred. Before I ask you a question, as one
Democrat as you probably know, I have always supported
contra aid.

LT. COL. NORTH: Yes, sir. And I am sure that they are grateful for that. I am.

REP. JENKINS: I wanted to—as I know that you all —already knew that. Nevertheless, there are many areas in this entire episode that greatly disturb me.

LT. COL. NORTH: I understand that, sir.

REP. JENKINS: And I'm going to pick right up where—on the same subject matter really that you've answered many, many questions because I want to know in my own mind what really occurred.

In the enterprise that—Secord, I believe, calls it an enterprise. I want to go back for you to explain once again how Secord and Hakim were first brought into the picture.

LT. COL. NORTH: My recollection, Congressman Jenkins, is that in the early days of 1984, when we saw the money running out, we had a number of discussions within the administration as to what the alternatives were, and my recollection is that the first person to suggest General Secord was Director Casey as a person who could, acting outside of the government of the United States, provide assistance, relying on his abilities that he had demonstrated while on active duty, his experience with covert operations, and his connections throughout the world, having come from a Pentagon job where he had that kind of a background where he had contacts with senior officials in other governments. We all knew that the Nicaraguan resistance could not survive without the support of others. And, in fact, if I may just digress for a moment, that is a very important part of all this—is that the Nicaraguan democratic resistance could not support, if it only had our support—just the support of the United States—if we were the only ones backing them, they would not survive.

Such was the case with the Sandinistas when they came to power. It took more than just the support of the Soviet Union, the Cubans, to help the power seize power in 1979. Thus, the initiation was that the NSC, first of all, would pick up responsibilities increasingly as the CIA was basically phased out. It wasn't quite as abrupt—not as the final cut-off in October of 1984, I believe it was.

REP. JENKINS: Who gave you at that point—or gave the NSC the direction to contact Gen. Secord? Did that come from Casey, or did that come from someone else?

LT. COL. NORTH: The person who suggested Gen. Secord to me—and I then took the name to Mr. McFarlane—was Director Casey.

REP. JENKINS: And did you at that time already know Gen. Secord?

LT. COL. NORTH: I had met Gen. Secord in 1981, shortly after I arrived on the NSC staff. He was at that point, I believe—I don't want to get his title wrong, but I think his title was Deputy Assistant Secretary of Defense for International Security Affairs. I may have the title wrong. It was a long time ago.

REP. JENKINS: Let me ask you about him. At that time, did you know that there had been some question at one time or another about a security clearance for Gen. Secord?

LT. COL. NORTH: No, I did not, sir.

REP. JENKINS: All right.

LT. COL. NORTH: And I think that issue arose later, and I—quite honestly, I didn't even know about that aspect of it because my contact with him was essentially broken after our work together—and my mind was very peripheral, compared to his, on the Saudi Arabian air defense enhancement program.

REP. JENKINS: All right. At any rate, you made contact with him, and it was [he] that brought in Mr. Albert Hakim?

LT. COL. NORTH: Yes, sir.

REP. JENKINS: Again, I went to Gen. Secord. As I recall, it might have been in the spring or summer of '84, basically seeking someone who can give the kind of advice and logistic support, and the kind of activity support to the resistance that we perceived they needed because the CIA was, as I indicated, being pulled away, and of course with the most stringent of the Boland strictures in October, basically cut off very abruptly at that point. And by then General Secord had been engaged—

REP. JENKINS: All right.

LT. COL. NORTH: —and of course, by then money had already started to flow to the Nicaragua resistance from outside sources.

REP. JENKINS: And those outside sources, through Calero, primarily?

LT. COL. NORTH: The one I am aware of, and there may well have been others that I'm not aware of—

477

REP. JENKINS: Right.

LT. COL. NORTH: But the one I was aware of started in the spring or summer of '84. Mr. McFarlane came to me, asked me for my recommendations. I went to Director Casey and asked for his advice.

REP. JENKINS: Well let me ask you at that point, did you always go to Director Casey for directions in this type of activity?

LT. COL. NORTH: Well, I—I, in answering that question earlier, I take a little bit of contention with the word "direction", and I don't want either of my previous superiors to think that I was working for Director Casey. I know who I worked for—

REP. JENKINS: You worked for McFarlane and Poindexter.

LT. COL. NORTH: And prior to that, Judge Clark, and before that Dr. Allen. But I did have a lot of advice from Director Casey—

REP. JENKINS: All right. And—

LT. COL. NORTH: —which I valued, Congressman Jenkins.

REP. JENKINS: Yes, I understand. Then Secord and Hakim commenced the arms purchases for the contras—

LT. COL. NORTH: Yes, sir, you—well, I think we got off a little bit. But after I gave—after I conferred with Director Casey, I then, with his advice, recommended to Mr. Calero the establishment of an off-shore bank account. And he then gave me that account number. I gave that account number to Mr. McFarlane, and shortly thereafter money started to flow. And I can't say for certain even today that there's a direct connection, but I certainly assume there was, and it flowed to that account. And then General Secord began providing the kind of support which is now so evident. At that point in time I had never even heard of Mr. Hakim, and it wasn't until some time later that I met him.

REP. JENKINS: All right. But at any rate, Mr. Hakim and General Secord were in this, as I understand it, as a profit-making business?

LT. COL. NORTH: Oh, again, my understanding was, and I—the word "profit" may have come up, but the two criteria that Director Casey and I talked about—three criteria actually—and that I communicated with General

Secord on, was that these had to be stand-alone, off-shore, commercial ventures. That they ought to be, ultimately, revenue producers; that they would generate their own revenue and be self-sustaining. And that those engaged in these commerical ventures, were certainly deserving of fair just reasonable compensation.

REP. JENKINS: Which you never did define—

LT. COL. NORTH: I did not, sir.

REP. JENKINS: —and it was never defined to you?

LT. COL. NORTH: No, sir.

REP. JENKINS: And at that time, Mr. McFarlane and later, Mr. Poindexter understood that. Is that correct?

LT. COL. NORTH: I certainly believed they did, sir.

REP. JENKINS: All right. And as a matter of fact, at some point in the initial stages, Mr. Hakim and General Secord decided to eliminate the Canadian arms dealer and give that portion of the profits to Mr. Clines. Is that correct?

LT. COL. NORTH: Again, I'll have to say apparently so because I'm not—those were the kinds of details within the operation in which I do not involve myself. I didn't see any necessity for that. It was—I'm not even sure that I was aware of that at the time.

REP. JENKINS: You left that entirely to General Secord.

LT. COL. NORTH: Exactly.

REP. JENKINS: And did he have a superior in the government?

LT. COL. NORTH: No. He was not a part of—by then he had retired from the United States Air Force and was a businessman outside the government. In fact, when I approached him, he did not jump at this chance. I think that should be noted for the record—that he thought about it for some time. I, at one point, importuned Director Casey to see if he could encourage it along. And it was not for several days or even weeks that he came back and agreed that he would do it.

REP. JENKINS: And then later you decided with the approval of your superiors to bring General Secord and Mr. Hakim into the Iranian deal.

LT. COL. NORTH: That was in November of 1985.

REP. JENKINS: It was. I want to—I don't want to repeat everything. But I want to know had you ever met Hakim up until that November?

479

LT. COL. NORTH: I may have, but I do not recall meeting him at this point. I don't recall having met him until February of 1986.

REP. JENKINS: The first time you had a meeting.

LT. COL. NORTH: I believe that's correct, sir.

REP. JENKINS: And at that time that you met him in February, what was the occasion?

LT. COL. NORTH: We were in desperate need of a translator.

REP. JENKINS: All right.

LT. COL. NORTH: As I have indicated earlier, there was no translator available within the CIA at that point that could provide those kinds of services. I did not speak Farsi. The Iranians with whom we were talking obviously spoke Farsi but not English. I did not want—

REP. JENKINS: So it was at that point—

LT. COL. NORTH: I did not want to have to rely on the translations being provided by Mr. Ghorbanifar. And when I mentioned this to General Secord, my recollection is that he said, "Well, I will get Albert Hakim," who perhaps by then I knew the name. But, in any event, Mr. Hakim came and served as translator for those meetings.

REP. JENKINS: All right. And that was the meeting that you have testified to where the seven points were first discussed with the first channel?

LT. COL. NORTH: No, sir, I—

REP. JENKINS: Or was that later?

LT. COL. NORTH: My recollection is that the seven points issue came up with the second channel—

REP. JENKINS: All right.

LT. COL. NORTH: —somewhat later.

REP. JENKINS: Now at the time that you asked for Mr. Hakim at the suggestion of General Secord and met with the first channel, was, in fact, Mr. Hakim the only person on our side—you were handling the trip—that spoke Farsi?

LT. COL. NORTH: Yes, he was—well, General Secord speaks some Farsi. He served in Iran, and he does speak some. I hope I'm not insulting him, but I don't think he speaks it as well as Mr. Hakim.

REP. JENKINS: So the only representatives that we had when we made contact with channel one that spoke Farsi were two people outside the government?

LT. COL. NORTH: That is correct.

REP. JENKINS: And you later learned, I'm sure, that Mr. Hakim was obviously into the enterprise—as he has testified to this Committee—entirely for the money?

LT. COL. NORTH: I'm not too sure how he testified to the Committee, Congressman Jenkins. But—and I'm not here to impugn anyone else or to defend anyone else. My understanding throughout was that the people who were engaged on our side, in both this activity and the support for the Nicaraguan resistance, were in it for reasons that served our national security interests. I had made it clear to General Secord, as I indicated a few moments ago, that fair, just, reasonable compensation was deserved, that these were commercial entities, and I don't recall at any point Mr. Hakim saying to me, or to others in my presence, that I am in this only for the money. I do recall Mr. Hakim saying that he cared deeply about the fact that his native country, where he was born and raised and lived, was essentially a state of seige or no relations at best with his adopted country. And like many people who are victims of totalitarian regimes in Eastern Europe or Cuba or Nicaragua, who have fled to this country and become Americans, my sense was he had the same kind of aspirations that many Eastern Europeans have—Poles, Lithuanians—

REP. JENKINS: I understand that he had some mental heart-felt interests as he was born in Iran and he's an American citizen—

LT. COL. NORTH: Yes, sir.

REP. JENKINS: —now, I believe, living in Europe. Nevertheless, he has testified—

LT. COL. NORTH: Actually, I don't believe he does live in Europe. I think he lives in California.

REP. JENKINS: All right. He always maintained a home, I think, according to his testimony, in Europe. He has testified to this Committee already, and he stated—testified to the Committee that he not only informed you—and of course, General Secord knew—but that he also informed the Iranians—in channel two now, where he—he did most of the negotiating—that his interest was financial interest.

LT. COL. NORTH: Well, he certainly did indicate that he had a financial interest.

REP. JENKINS: Yes.

481

LT. COL. NORTH: And—and I believe I even surrendered to the Committee notes of mine that indicated discussion that he and I had at some point about his view of where he hoped a new relationship with Iran would lead, and as a businessman—and as I understood it at the time, a very successful businessman—he saw, not just for himself but for American enterprise as well, enormous opportunities in a restoration of—of a positive relationship—

REP. JENKINS: Certainly, he—he testified to that also, and he also testified that his interest—one of his primary interests was to open up the channel, channel two, get stable relations back, because with 15 billion dollars in trad—

LT. COL. NORTH: I remember the number—he mentioned that to me, and I think that—that is in my notes.

REP. JENKINS: Did he hope to get 2 percent of it?

LT. COL. NORTH: I don't remember the 2 percent; I remember the 15 billion.

REP. JENKINS: No. And he was very much interested from a financial standpoint in making this succeed is the question I'm asking, isn't that correct?

LT. COL. NORTH: He did express that to me, yes.

REP. JENKINS: Alright. Now, you commenced at the second channel, as you have told Mr. Liman, and the 7-point plan has been introduced. You were unable, together with our other representatives at the second channel to consumate an agreement at that time, is that correct?

LT. COL. NORTH: That is correct.

REP. JENKINS: Now, as I understand his testimony, at that point you told Mr. Hakim that you were leaving, coming back to Washington, and he had 6 hours if he could change their minds. Is that basically correct?

LT. COL. NORTH: Well, if I recall correctly, and I may not be accurate in this, but I think what happened is that I had arrived in Europe for a meeting with the second channel. During the time in which I was transiting to Europe, the aircraft with Mr. Hasenfus aboard and in which Captain Cooper and Captain Sawyer were killed had been shot down over Nicaragua, and when I got there, I was informed of that as soon as I established secure communications back with my office. And there was a desparate need for me to turn around and come right back.

REP. JENKINS: So you had to leave?

LT. COL. NORTH: That's right.

REP. JENKINS: And General Secord left, as he has testified to this Committee?

LT. COL. NORTH: I believe he did. I think he was working on the same problem.

REP. JENKINS: And Hakim at that point was left as the only US negotiator for the agreement that was ultimately agreed upon by the Iranians in the US, is that correct?

LT. COL. NORTH: That is my recollection, yes, sir.

REP. JENKINS: Mr. Hakim testified that he had to wait after he had gotten the agreement with Iran, which he added these two very controversial sections in there—as you have previously testified to. And he waited to see whether or not the US accepted those. He sent you a message—Gen. Secord did, didn't he—with the nine points?

LT. COL. NORTH: Again, I am fuzzy on that. But eventually I got the nine points.

REP. JENKINS: And your superior approved those, and you sent the message back to Gen. Secord and Hakim?

LT. COL. NORTH: I believe that's the way it went.

REP. JENKINS: That we had agreed to the nine-point agreement?

LT. COL. NORTH: Again, I would like to refresh myself on the nine-point agreement before I come up to the that.

REP. JENKINS: Well, I will give you the exhibit number. It is 310. But while your counsel is getting that, if I could just—so that you can refresh your memory. You signaled that we had accepted that agreement, based upon the approval of Secord?

LT. COL. NORTH: Yes, I did.

REP. JENKINS: Yes, sir. Later, did you stop to think at all—and I know that you sought approval from your superior—that the only person negotiating for the United States of America with Iran that ultimately attained the agreement was a private citizen who had a substantial financial interest in the outcome of those negotiations?

LT. COL. NORTH: I don't believe that I communicated that to Admiral Poindexter, no, sir.

REP. JENKINS: And that never concerned Admiral Poindexter or yourself?

LT. COL. NORTH: Well, it may well be, Congressman Jenkins, that I was most injudicious. I've certainly

483

—difficult though it has been and painful though some of it has been—told the Committee things that I have done. I quite honestly considered that to be motivation to make it succeed in that he had interests that went beyond just his next promotion or going back and getting an accolade from his boss, that in fact it offered a greater chance for ultimate success.

REP. JENKINS: The fact that he had a financial interest?

LT. COL. NORTH: The fact that he saw long-term the potential for financial interest.

REP. JENKINS: All right, sir. All right, now let me ask you at this point, I know that—(pause) I know that you have just testified today that you told many falsehoods to the Iranians, as you indicated, would have told them anything in order to get the hostages out at that time.

LT. COL. NORTH: I may have overstated it when I said "anything," but practically anything—

REP. JENKINS: Yes, I understand. But what is disturbing me about that part is that it was my understanding that we were attempting to open up a new understanding and initiative with Iran, why would we start that off with a lot of falsehoods that would later, obviously come back to haunt us very quickly?

LT. COL. NORTH: Well I quite honestly don't think that any of these would necessarily have lead to that kind of confrontation. I think that these things were, if you'll excuse the expression, fuzzy enough, with the exception of the issues on return of Americans, that if you could have just gotten beyond my level and up the Secretary of State level, or as one of my proposals went forward, even as late as mid-November after everything was blowing up, a meeting with the Vice President and a high-level Iranian official in a Mideastern state, that we could have gotten beyond the issue of hostages and arms and quickly toward the kind of thing that would have yielded a solution to the war—

REP. JENKINS: Yes.

LT. COL. NORTH: —between Iran and Iraq—

REP. JENKINS: Colonel North—

LT. COL. NORTH: I think that's—well, Congressman Jenkins, at that level, I mean my counterpart on the Iranian side, although young, was of more senior level than I, and—

REP. JENKINS: So you didn't think that any falsehood that

484

you told at that time in order to get them to accept the agreement would bother relations and future—

LT. COL. NORTH: I didn't think it would jeopardize the next step, is what I am saying, and I was judicious at least in that, Congressman Jenkins, that I didn't believe that the things I was saying would result in an increase of jeopardy for the next level of meeting that we were hoping for.

REP. JENKINS: Well it—I must say that disturbs me somewhat, but I'm assuming that in your discussions with Admiral Secord—Admiral Poindexter, that he had authorized you to make any type of statement that you might desire at that particular meeting?

LT. COL. NORTH: No.

REP. JENKINS: He didn't?

LT. COL. NORTH: Admiral Poindexter gave me certain basic perimeters, and I tried to follow those in the midst of very difficult and sometimes very protracted negotiations.

REP. JENKINS: Okay.

LT. COL. NORTH: And I tried to keep him apprised when I was overseas through difficult communications methods. But nonetheless, I tried to live within the boundries that had been established for me and yet still make progress on a very difficult issue.

REP. JENKINS: And you felt that you had the perimeters at that time to make statements, excessive statements or some outright misrepresenations to the Iranians because it was in our interest to try to get the hostages back at that particular time.

LT. COL. NORTH: And foster the hope of a further meeting with senior-level officials.

REP. JENKINS: I see. Now, let me follow up the private sector just a bit and get away from—from that particular meeting. While I've supported contra aid by the United States government, I'm—I'm deeply concerned about this type of set-up that some people call a "government within a government," and I want to pursue that so that I understand it.

LT. COL. NORTH: I—if I may, Congressman Jenkins, I take issue with that description.

REP. JENKINS: I understand, and—and maybe I will too. That's the reason I want to ask you some questions about it. Now, as I understand, this continuing fund that would be

485

funded from the profits or the residuals, as you refer to them, of the sales to Iran, as well as some of the gifts from at least one of the countries that went into the account, that would go into an off-budget account that would not have anything to do with the United States government.

LT. COL. NORTH: It did not.

REP. JENKINS: But the projects that would be financed by that would all be directed by the United States government?

LT. COL. NORTH: Yes.

REP. JENKINS: And it would be directed by people within the National Security Council?

LT. COL. NORTH: Well, I'm—I'm not too sure how other people viewed my continued tenure at any one point in my time at the White House, but Director Casey clearly saw the need for something, as he put it, "that you could pull off the shelf and use" that was, as I indicated earlier, self-sustaining and was there.

REP. JENKINS: Well, I'm not so awfully concerned at this point what Colonel North would do, but I'm worried about the next person that has control over this account. Now, if I understand what you have testified to, that has been approved by your superiors, the Vice President did not know that any of the funds from this account were being used for the contras.

LT. COL. NORTH: If he did, I didn't tell him, sir.

REP. JENKINS: All right. So far as you know—I believe he's made the statement he did not know.

LT. COL. NORTH: As far as I know, he did not know.

REP. JENKINS: And while you assumed that the President knew—is that correct?

LT. COL. NORTH: I did.

REP. JENKINS: You know that he has stated that he did not know.

LT. COL. NORTH: That's correct.

REP. JENKINS: And of course, neither the United States Senate nor the House of Representatives knew nor their committees because, as you have testified, they were misrepresented—I'll be charitable—in their statements. Is that correct?

LT. COL. NORTH: I did misrepresent that, yes.

REP. JENKINS: So what concerns me from your testimony —and I'm not saying it's your policy—

LT. COL. NORTH: I'm willing to take—

REP. JENKINS: —because you're simply—

LT. COL. NORTH: —responsibility, sir.

REP. JENKINS: You're simply following orders.

LT. COL. NORTH: I don't think that's an excuse for doing something against the law.

REP. JENKINS: Well let me make the statement, and ask you if it's correct. Not a single official elected by the people of the United States of America had any knowledge about the use of that fund. Is that correct, or is it incorrect?

LT. COL. NORTH: Let me, let me go—that is current knowledge, Congressman Jenkins, and that goes back to what I said a few moments ago. It was my view then, and it continues to be my view now, that we were not breaking the law, that what we were doing was within the law. That I had assumed that the President of the United States, who is after all the senior elected official in this land, was aware of it.

The fact is, I believe that the President ought to be able to carry out his foreign policy. And if one goes back to 1984 when this activity began—and I don't see a great deal of difference between what we were doing, in terms of the actual arrangement, between what we did in 1985 with the sale of Hawk missiles, or TOW missiles, excuse me, or the earlier contributions made by other countries to these activities—that they are within the bounds of the executive.

REP. JENKINS: I understand that. And I understand where you were because you assumed that the President knew.

LT. COL. NORTH: I did.

REP. JENKINS: And I understand your position. But I hope you understand what I am disturbed about.

LT. COL. NORTH: I do.

REP. JENKINS: That there is not a single official elected by the people of this great nation that had any knowledge of that. Isn't that correct?

LT. COL. NORTH: That is correct, Congressman Jenkins, and I have suggested a solution to that.

What I said earlier, in fact just before the break in response to Mr. Liman, having made the assumption that

487

the President was aware, certainly through my chain of command indicated that we should proceed—

REP. JENKINS: I understand.

LT. COL. NORTH: And what I said that this whole thing represented to me was an indication of a broader problem. And as early as 1985, well maybe it was June of '86, I had given a speech before the American Bar Association in which I had proposed a solution for being able to consult discreetly with members of Congress to get the kinds of appropriations to carry out these activities.

I think that there was fault to be found on both sides.

REP. JENKINS: Oh, I understand that, and would agree with you fully. And there ought to be bi-partisanship in foreign policy, and I've always tried to follow that as you well know.

LT. COL. NORTH: Your votes for the Nicaraguan resistance were difficult for you and the party, and I understand that.

REP. JENKINS: All right, now—but I believe that the United States government ought to do it. I don't believe—

LT. COL. NORTH: I do, too, sir.

REP. JENKINS: —that any profiteers ought to be doing it secretly. You see, that's what disturbs me.

LT. COL. NORTH: I understand. But I, again, I want to say, Congressman Jenkins, that I never, from the earliest days of this activity, envisioned that I was in this to make anyone rich.

REP. JENKINS: Oh, I understand your position.

LT. COL. NORTH: And I am not certain at this point that that's the intention of any of those engaged in it. And as I said the other day, if someone were to ask me to arbitrate —and I'm sure that they won't. But since we had hypothetical questions, this is another hypothetical answer. If I were asked to arbitrate as to what should be done with the remaining funds that are in accounts or wherever, once those bills were paid and the liens were covered and the expenses that had accrued were taken care of, I think every single penny that's left ought to go to the Nicaraguan resistance.

REP. JENKINS: Well we asked—

LT. COL. NORTH: And save the taxpayers a couple of dollars.

REP. JENKINS: We asked Mr. Hakim about that, who has control over it, and he would not agree to that.

LT. COL. NORTH: Give me ten minutes with Mr. Hakim. (Laughter in room)

REP. JENKINS: You think—you think if you have ten minutes, that you can get Mr. Hakim to turn over that $8 million?

LT. COL. NORTH: If I could meet with anybody without a bunch of lawyers around, I reckon I could, sir. (Laughs)

REP. JENKINS: Well, let me ask you about that. Really, you are a very articulate person and persuasive. And looking back on this, do you think that sometimes you may have persuaded your superior to take certain action, even when Cabinet members were opposed? Simply because of your eloquence, and very sincere beliefs.

LT. COL. NORTH: I have no doubt about that.

REP. JENKINS: Many times—

LT. COL. NORTH: I have indicated that I accept responsibility.

REP. JENKINS: Yes, I understand that. That's not a bad trait. It's a good trait, that you were able to persuade people, isn't that correct?

LT. COL. NORTH: The good Lord gives us all certain gifts.

REP. JENKINS: And you certainly have a good one there that you should be very grateful for. You persuaded Poindexter to continue this, even against Shultz and Weinberger's position, didn't you?

LT. COL. NORTH: I don't know that it was only me. But I—it certainly resulted in that, yes, sir.

REP. JENKINS: And on many other occasions, you were the principal voice, I am assuming, within the National Security Council as far as persuading the administration to take a certain position? Do you think that you played the most important role?

LT. COL. NORTH: Congressman Jenkins, on some issues, I was probably the only voice, and that's not to say that's necessarily good or bad. But that all of the men that I worked for, for whom I still have enormous regard—

REP. JENKINS: Sure.

LT. COL. NORTH: —were judicious men of great intellect and patriotism. And to go back to one of our earlier

489

comments, none of this—particularly when it came to drafting letters that were not accurate, were misleading —none of that came easy to any of us.

REP. JENKINS: I'm not—as I indicated to you, I'm not so concerned what you would do with this permanent fund, but I'm concerned about the future Ollies that may have the jurisdiction over the fund, or the people who follow Mr. Poindexter under any administration. Based upon what you have said, I mean if they'd decided to—I'm not talking about you, but whoever had control of this fund—if they wanted to give the money to the Sandinistas they could have.

LT. COL. NORTH: They better look out for me if they did.

REP. JENKINS: Well, I'm not talking about with you being there. I'm talking about your successor. This was going to be an ongoing fund—

LT. COL. NORTH: That was the intention.

REP. JENKINS: —was it not?

LT. COL. NORTH: It was. Again, I can't say for sure when we started talking with the Israelis about the kinds of activities I described to you last night what the time frame would have been. Most of those were relatively short-term operations as I described them to you.

REP. JENKINS: Well, the exhibit—well I hope I've—well, part of this has been repetitious. I wanted you to see the concern that I have with this type of operation. I don't know where you see any dangers in that type of operation or not.

LT. COL. NORTH: I share some of your concerns, but I also share a belief that there were responsible people within the executive who were competent to undertake those kinds of activities. And given the lack of alternative, again, I still see it to be within the law.

REP. JENKINS: Do you think that we ought to have within the law that type of fund set-up that has maybe no supervision whatsoever by any elected group?

LT. COL. NORTH: No, I did not say that I thought we ought to do that, (inaudible).

REP. JENKINS: As long as the President knows I'm assuming.

LT. COL. NORTH: That's first of all, correct, and second of all, I don't necessarily think we ought to have to be in that kind of a predicament. My sense is that it would be far better to be able to consult discreetly with those committees that make the authorizations and appropriations for intelligence activities, to have a clear understanding between the executive and the Congress that revelations regarding those activities are totally unacceptable to our national security interests, and that those monies ought justifiably to come from this body. After all, it is the Congress that appropriates. So I share your desired outcome completely.

REP. JENKINS: Oh, it's not that. I just could not ever support any type of private foreign policy under that type of description is my concern.

LT. COL. NORTH: I understand what you're saying, sir. And that's why I took issue with the description of a government within a government. It was not nearly so broad, although it was described by Director Casey as a full-service covert operation—

REP. JENKINS: But, if it's not—this private money coming in as you have indicated.

LT. COL. NORTH: It was.

REP. JENKINS: But, the direction as to how it is spent is coming right from the government, our government.

LT. COL. NORTH: It was.

REP. JENKINS: And by future administrations, if the fund remained permanent.

LT. COL. NORTH: I've given the solution for how to take care of that, sir.

REP. JENKINS: Well, I understand that and we may have to look at it. Let me go into another area for a moment. As you probably know, I've had great difficulty, also, with the practice of either soliciting funds from third countries or foreign policy actions which may or may not be—which are not supported by the Congress. I'm not going to get into the argument as to whether or not the Boland Amendment —different definitions.

LT. COL. NORTH: I understand, but if I may, part of the understanding that I had with Director Casey was a parallel, in which there is as we all know, at least the Intelligence committees know, a covert operation, approved by the Congress, in which contributions are provided by other governments.

REP. JENKINS: Oh, I understand that, and the initial contributions from country number two.

LT. COL. NORTH: You got me again, here.

REP. JENKINS: —was really sought by the Secretary of State I believe, by some higher official. You were not instrumental in that, if I understand it correctly.

LT. COL. NORTH: I was instrumental in that I established —I had Mr. Calero establish an account. I passed that account note card to Mr. McFarlane. It was number two, sir.

REP. JENKINS: Now, I still don't know you—the difficulties that I have which have been well publicized is that I think that when we place ourselves in such a position of seeking donations from third countries that may have no direct interest in Nicaragua, that we compromise ourselves and place them in a compromising situation. You understand the difficulties with that approach.

LT. COL. NORTH: I understand what you're saying, Congressman Jenkins. And if I may, I'm not sure that I entirely agree with you. And the reason I say that is because, as I indicated in my testimony, I didn't have to use a great deal of convincing to encourage or however one wants to put it, have other people make contributions. Almost without an exception, there were others who saw it to be in their interests to support the cause of the Nicaraguan resistance. It was mind-boggling how—how very clearly they saw the consequences of a communist take-over and consolidation in Nicaragua. And the inevitable expansion of communism in Central America is creating vulnerabilities to them even though they were tens of thousands of miles from here. And thus, if one uses the parallel of the support provided by another country for an authorized covert operation, that is now, unfortunately known, I don't think that we incurred any liabilities by asking them to—to assist us in that activity. And they have done so. And, honestly, I don't think that we have incurred liabilities by asking others to help us with the cause of democracy in Central America.

REP. JENKINS: Well, I noted that you made a similar response, and I might say that I had some concern with what you said. It was a good speech, but a good response, as far as your position, but you indicated that many members of the Congress hear these other nations were giving, and the Congress of the United States would not do what they were doing for the cause of democracy.

LT. COL. NORTH: You did.

REP. JENKINS: Yes, I know I did, but I've picked up this list, and I know there is differences of opinion on this panel, but I respect their views, even though they may be opposite of my views. And, I looked at this list of nations, and I do not see a single democracy on the list, except the first one, who gave us no financial help; and, is it—I think it's unfair to the panel, do you not, or to the Congress, to say that nations that are not even democracies themselves have more interest in democracy in Nicaragua than the Congress of the United States?

LT. COL. NORTH: Mr. Jenkins, I, I did not make the accusation in that form. What I said was that those countries demonstrated an awareness of the consequences of a communist takeover in Central America that made them want to contribute to a democratic outcome in Nicaragua. The fact is that if we were to have been proscribed from doing that kind of activity and the Congress sought to proscribe the executive from their doing that, then it should have passed a law that forbade it, and there should have been the ultimate constitutional confrontation.

REP. JENKINS: I want to ask you then, and I apologize if you did not make that type of a statement. I understood that you were being critical of the Congress as compared to foreign countries who love democracy, maybe more than members—

LT. COL. NORTH: No, I was being critical of the Congress. I will leave it at that, sir.

REP. JENKINS: All right, sir. It just struck me as ironic that none of these were democratic countries. Let me move into the negotiations. Let me move into a bit further in your testimony as to how these countries were willing to give. As I look at the nine countries on the list, we received contributions only from—financial contributions from Number Two and Number Three, and one that has been identified as Brunei, which was never used.

LT. COL. NORTH: Never found or it would have been, sir.

REP. JENKINS: (Laughs) It was placed in the wrong account.

LT. COL. NORTH: Unfortunately.

REP. JENKINS: You made contact with Country Number

Five. I assume that they did not make contact with us, wanting to give?

LT. COL. NORTH: I don't recall the exact arrangement of who contacted whom. But there were discussions and there was assistance provided.

REP. JENKINS: Well, the question is, as I look down the list, did any of these countries voluntarily come to us and want to donate?

LT. COL. NORTH: Well, yes, one that was turned down —Number Six. It was through an intermediary, not directly.

REP. JENKINS: Yes, sir.

LT. COL. NORTH: I'm not too sure how the approach with Three started. I believe it was through a person who has already testified.

REP. JENKINS: Gen. Singlaub?

LT. COL. NORTH: Exactly.

REP. JENKINS: And it took a year or so before they contributed. And you met with them one time, did you not?

LT. COL. NORTH: I did. Perhaps I misunderstood, Congressman Jenkins. You said none of those ten countries are democracies, or none of those who gave were democracies?

REP. JENKINS: Did you see another there besides Number One who did not give?

LT. COL. NORTH: Number One, and Number One did make a contribution, but it wasn't necessarily money, although some money was used. Number Seven is certainly a democracy, and they provided—

REP. JENKINS: They didn't give any money.

LT. COL. NORTH: No, they provided services.

REP. JENKINS: Yes, sir. Did any of these countries voluntarily come to us to give, is my question?

LT. COL. NORTH: I can't say that they did, no.

REP. JENKINS: So that they were not exactly beating our door down to make contributions.

LT. COL. NORTH: Just to clarify—if you're talking about giving being financial only, that's correct. But if you're talking about looking for ways to support the democratic outcome in Nicaragua, that's not correct. And various countries made various proposals as to how they could help, and we took them up on most of them—particularly in Central America.

REP. JENKINS: Well, I was simply looking at the ledger of the money that came in, and I did not see any there that they came. In your meeting with the delegate of Country Number Three, that eventually gave us—that did contribute—

LT. COL. NORTH: Yes.

REP. JENKINS: —a total of $2 million?

LT. COL. NORTH: I believe so, yes.

REP. JENKINS: At that particular time, what did you discuss with that representative that was set up for you—the appointment was set up by the State Department, as I understand it?

LT. COL. NORTH: Actually, it was prior to his arrival at the State Department. He was still working on the National Security Council staff at the time. And I discussed—well, he said that various overtures had been made to him by various parties, and that there was interest back in his capital, but that he wanted to be sure that that was something that we would, indeed, want done. And I confirmed that. I told him that we would be very grateful, as, indeed, we were. No quid pro quo was suggested; none was offered; and the contributions were made.

REP. JENKINS: Well, as you probably know from previous hearings, at that particular time there was a very important trade bill that affected—

LT. COL. NORTH: I do understand that.

REP. JENKINS: —that affected that country.

LT. COL. NORTH: I do understand that.

REP. JENKINS: And that it had been passed by the Congress, but not dealt with at this particular time, vetoed or signed, by the President and that the contribution came after the bill had passed the Congress, adversely affecting Country Number Three, and it was subsequently vetoed. There was no discussion about trade issues or any issue?

LT. COL. NORTH: Never.

REP. JENKINS: Because that's outside of your jurisdiction anyway, and you would not have discussed that, would you?

LT. COL. NORTH: I dealt intensely on trade issues which were political-military issues in Central America. That issue was never ever raised, discussed in any way, Congressman Jenkins. I want—I want it to be very clear in the record that

495

neither he nor I discussed it, and I, because it was a part of the world in which I did not have political-military policy activity, was totally unaware that that was an issue. Totally.

REP. JENKINS: Totally unaware that it was even an issue—

LT. COL. NORTH: Yes.

REP. JENKINS: —on the Hill, is that correct?

LT. COL. NORTH: That is correct.

REP. JENKINS: I—I'm not saying that you had any because I understand—

LT. COL. NORTH: I understand.

REP. JENKINS: —that's outside of your sphere of discussion. I just don't know what else.

LT. COL. NORTH: Yeah, and I feel the same about Dr. Sigur. I just can't imagine that Dr. Sigur, in any way, used that meeting or the fact of this meeting to influence that activity at the White House whatsoever.

REP. JENKINS: But you would have no reason to know either, I assume—

LT. COL. NORTH: No.

REP. JENKINS: —if that ever crossed the minds of the officials from Country Number Three.

LT. COL. NORTH: I have tried hard not to read other people's minds, sir.

REP. JENKINS: You don't think that that would ever enter into their—

LT. COL. NORTH: I don't know.

REP. JENKINS: —considerations?

LT. COL. NORTH: I do not know. They did not mention to me, sir.

REP. JENKINS: I understand. Do you know whether or not any other official, Mr. Poindexter or Mr. McFarlane or anyone else, ever discussed this subject?

LT. COL. NORTH: The subject was never ever raised with me. I never even heard of it until these hearings, sir.

REP. JENKINS: All right, sir. I want to very quickly, for what little time I have left, go into another area. (Pause) Mr. O'Boyle has testified that in the course of a meeting with you, following a fund-raising solicitation with Mr. Channell —not with you, but Mr. Channell. You indicated a plan for US involvement in Nicaragua that was extremely, in his words, "very, very secret" and that you indicated that should not be revealed to anyone else. Did that conversation ever take place?

LT. COL. NORTH: I do not recall the specific conversation with Mr. O'Boyle or conversations because it appears that I met more than once with Mr. O'Boyle by my recollection. I cannot imagine that I used the word "secret." I probably used the word "sensitive." It was probably in response —and that question was asked by others, and the question would be asked, "Look, is there any end to this? How can this possibly come to a conclusion? I hear on the one hand that there's no way for the Nicaraguan resistance to ever militarily win a victory over the Sandinistas given the preponderance of numbers and force on their side." And I described to him a plan which had been discussed with the Nicaraguan resistance. It was not summarily dismissed as—as others may have indicated and, in fact, was designed to preclude US military ground combat operations.

I want this committee—or these committees to be abundantly clear that I personally, in every policy paper I wrote for the President and for my superiors and for coordination with the other departments and agencies with whom we were in contact at the NSC vociferously advocated solving the problem of democracy in Nicaragua without the use of US military force. And that's very, very important.

REP. JENKINS: I understand that.

LT. COL. NORTH: But, but Congressman, I think people have left the wrong impression. This man saw too many Marines die to in any way advocate using US military force in Central America unless it was the last source—

REP. JENKINS: Well there's no disagreement on that issue. The point I'm asking was, did you discuss any, in his words "very, very secret involvement."

LT. COL. NORTH: My words would be, "look this is a sensitive issue."

REP. JENKINS: It's not classified?

LT. COL. NORTH: This is—it is not classified. It was discussed with the resistance.

REP. JENKINS: All right, that's all I want. Okay. That's the only, that's the answer that I was—if it was not classified. He is one of the people who later contributed the hundred-and-something thousand?

LT. COL. NORTH: I was told that he did, and I was never

present when any check was ever handed to Mr. Miller or Mr. Channell.

REP. JENKINS: Oh, I understand that. You've already testified to that. I'm just curious about the security aspect. Let me ask you about one other thing in security that since I'm not on the Intelligence Committee—are the—is the software for the KL-43 machines, are they—is that classified?

LT. COL. NORTH: I'm told, I was told many months ago, that the machines, once the zeroize key was pushed on it, that the machine is as unclassified as this microphone.

REP. JENKINS: The software is not classified?

LT. COL. NORTH: No, it's the internal hardware of the machine. Once it—once the zeroize button was pushed, removing the encryption, that the machine was completely unclassified.

REP. JENKINS: I may not clearly understand, but I understand there is software also. Is that classified?

LT. COL. NORTH: As I understand software, sir, it is the program that is put into the machine. Type in—

REP. JENKINS: That is classified, is it not?

LT. COL. NORTH: The tapes that were used to enter the encryption tapes were classified. That's correct.

REP. JENKINS: Yes, sir. Now, Mr. Hakim had a machine with software?

LT. COL. NORTH: I know that Gen. Secord did, and Mr. Hakim may have had one too.

REP. JENKINS: Did either of those have security clearance?

LT. COL. NORTH: Gen. Secord certainly did. I don't know—

REP. JENKINS: Gen. Secord had security clearance?

LT. COL. NORTH: Well, I, I said that perhaps too—I was under the belief that Gen. Secord had a security clearance for the entire time that he was engaged with us.

REP. JENKINS: I believe he's testified that he did not have—

LT. COL. NORTH: If that's the case, I misunderstood.

REP. JENKINS: Who provided those machines, and the software to those people?

LT. COL. NORTH: I did.

REP. JENKINS: At the direction of Adm. Poindexter?

LT. COL. NORTH: I—when—you say the direction of Adm. Poindexter?

REP. JENKINS: Well, at the approval.

LT. COL. NORTH: I'm sure that I told him I was using these machines. I provided one back to his office so that I could communicate with him. And I'm sure that I told him at some point who had them.

REP. JENKINS: And there were about seven or eight that were given out with software including the airplane company down in Florida?

LT. COL. NORTH: We passed out cassettes every month. Cassettes expire—

REP. JENKINS: Well, the only question I'm asking, did anyone check to see whether any of these people had security clearance?

LT. COL. NORTH: I was led to believe that the airplane did have the security clearances—

REP. JENKINS: And who—

LT. COL. NORTH: —they do classified government work. And that the people who had it, with the possible exception of Mr. Hakim, had security clearances.

REP. JENKINS: And that was—who led you to believe that?

LT. COL. NORTH: Oh, I guess the people with whom I was working.

REP. JENKINS: Poindexter? Casey?

LT. COL. NORTH: No, no. Admiral Poindexter never told me that so-and-so down in Florida or Central America had a security clearance. But I made an assumption, perhaps erroneously, that those people who had the machines were empowered or authorized to have them.

REP. JENKINS: Just basic on all the facts, you assumed—

LT. COL. NORTH: Yes.

REP. JENKINS: —that they had security clearances, isn't that correct?

LT. COL. NORTH: Yes.

CHAIRMAN HAMILTON: Mr. Jenkins, your time has expired.

REP. JENKINS: Thank you, Mr. Chairman. And Colonel North, thank you for your testimony before this panel. I know that it's been a long a grueling week, and I appreciate your testimony very much.

499

LT. COL. NORTH: Thank you, Mr. Jenkins.

CHAIRMAN HAMILTON: The Chair recognizes Mr. Cheney for one hour.

REP. HENRY HYDE (R-IL): Mr. Cheney, would you yield to me for one minute?

REP. RICHARD CHENEY (R-WY): This is always dangerous, but certainly, Mr. Hyde, I'll be happy to. (Laughter.)

REP. HYDE: It's a high-risk operation! Just referring to the list of countries that my dear friend from Georgia mentioned that there were no democracies on there, I don't wish to quarrel with him, I see three full democracies, a couple of half democracies. But a little bicentennial note for my friend, it was Louis XVI's France which made our revolution possible and democracy in this country, and he was so undemocratic that a guy named Robespierre took care of him in a few years. So sometimes democracy can get helped from strange sources. And I thank you.

REP. JENKINS: If the gentleman will yield just for one half second?

REP. CHENEY: I certainly will yield to the gentleman from Georgia.

REP. JENKINS: I certainly looked at the list of countries and hoped that I specified the countries that gave. The only ones that I saw other than Number One, that was in fact a full democracy—as a matter of fact one, I think, is communist—(laughter) but the rest were not—

REP. HYDE: (Off-mike)—democracy, and a couple of them—one of them is making a great move towards democracy! (Laughter.) Thank you.

REP. CHENEY: Mr. Chairman, I think I should reclaim my time. (Laughter.)

REP. HYDE: We yield back!

REP. CHENEY: Thank you. Colonel North—

LT. COL. NORTH: Mr. Cheney.

REP. CHENEY: I know it's been a long difficult week. Let me say at the outset that I've been tremendously impressed by the way you've handled yourself in front of the Committee. And I know I speak for a great many people who've been watching the proceedings because the Congress has been absolutely buried in the favorable public reaction to your testimony in phone calls and telegrams. And I know I speak for a great many people when I say I, for one, believe

500

you've been very direct and very candid and very forthright with the Committee, and as a member of the Committee, I certainly appreciate that.

LT. COL. NORTH: Thank you, sir.

REP. CHENEY: Let me—I've got several things I'd like to touch upon, but there—a key point for me through these proceedings is to try to place the events of the Iran arms transaction and the support network for the contras within a broader context so that we understand the way that some of these decisions were made, and why the President and his key advisers made the decisions they made.

I don't think, for example, that it makes sense to focus on the contra operation without talking about Central America, and we did that yesterday. I don't think it makes sense, or that it's possible to understand these events without understanding the impact of numerous changes in Congressional policy. And I think with respect to the Iranian arms transaction, at least it's my theory, that it doesn't make sense to try to understand that without focusing specifically upon the role of the hostages and the impact that they had upon the thinking of the President and of those people around him, as he wrestled with the difficult responsibilities that he obviously had to weigh in deciding to undertake these actions. Can you briefly describe for the Committee your role and responsibilities in connection with the hostage families? I believe you served as a sort of a liaison person part of the time you were at the NSC for the hostage families.

LT. COL. NORTH: My specific role was that of the NSC staff officer responsible for policy and activity, coordinating government activity on terrorism and hostages fell within that, since it's through terrorist acts that they were taken. We made enormous efforts in our government to locate and to recover our hostages through a variety of means. That inevitably led to contacts with the families, which were necessary by the fact that the families of most of these men had lived in the region for years.

I believe Rev. Weir was in Lebanon or the Middle East for 30 some odd years. They, of course, had sources of information that our government didn't have by virtue of the tenure that they had, and it became necessary, even if one didn't think that meeting with the families was going to have a good policy impact, because it is a devastating experience to meet with a wife or the daughter or the mother or the son of a hostage repeatedly and see the anguish in their face, and know in your heart that your government can't, try as it would, can't do anything about it.

It was—I think I tried to give an accolade to a young man by the name of John Adams yesterday at the State Department, who is within the consular service, or at least he was, and whose job was to be the US government's principle point of contact. The anguish that that man has gone through with these hostage families, there's almost a kin to their own. For that reason, and seeing that, and knowing how I felt, having met with the families, both in groups and individually a number of times, I did not want the President to meet—in fact, we had set up a program by which the Vice President would meet with the families, not that the Vice President is more callous, but that the ultimate decisions on things to be done would have to be the President's. Nonetheless, it was taken as a decision that the President would meet with them.

I don't mean this in any way to be critical of our political process in the White House. I think that places an unfair burden on the heart of our President. And, the President felt deeply about it, as I did. And, I am willing to admit that that may have colored my decision or my recommendations or even his. I know that those of us, like John Adams who met with the families frequently, saw that anguish as something that we wanted to solve. On top of that, we had Director Casey who, as I indicated last night, had a very, very good reason for wanting one of his own back. And in spite of taskforces and increased intelligence and enormous diplomatic activities, nothing succeeded until we came to this initiative. All of which I am telling you is now history, but it can nonetheless affect presidential decisions in the future—not just this President, but others.

The longer term solution is to create circumstances where hostage-taking is not a viable alternative, or groups that believe in that find that it is not in their interest. Now there are a number of ways of doing that. We can leave our hostages that are now taken forever and show that we just don't care about hostages. You and I know that not to be true. You can take action against the hostage-takers until they feel that the price is too high. The Soviets did that and got their people back almost instantly. Or you can try to influence the environment of support for the hostage-takers, and that's what we tried to do.

In other words, the environment of support philosophically, religiously, financially for the Hezbollah in Iran—in Lebanon—came from Iran. And we sought to exert influence over the terrorists by going to their backers. We also had broader goals and objectives that I tried to articulate in the findings that I worked on. And I think that if we were able to get to the point where that we were able to establish a high-level dialogue, well above my pay grade, that we would have been able to achieve the kind of outcome that we were seeking. But we all knew that we couldn't establish that dialogue unless we got beyond the obstacle of the hostages. And so one begat the other problem, and that course of action, which started in September of 1985, was still at play as late as November of 1986.

And though people can criticize the President for not choosing to notify the Congress at any one point in time, pursuant to a finding that he had signed, I also had in my files the Hostage Act. The Hostage Act goes all the way back to the early 1800s. And I believe I had sent that forward to my superiors, saying, look, here is the authority to do whatever is necessary. That's basically the words that are in the Hostage Act—to recover American hostages. And after you have them back, tell the Congress what you've done and how you did it. In this day and age, we Americans are increasingly at risk with terrorism and they are. We ought to think very carefully about proscribing presidential authority to do those kinds of things. We ought to think very carefully before we start to stricture statutes and regulations and requirements that would bind him in such a way that he cannot act and that we could not retrieve or recover our people safely. I do not believe we have seen the last of it. No matter what the outcome of those who are now held in the Lebanon, it is very likely that we will see more no matter how callous we pretend to be, Americans are not, and the rest of the world knows that. And I would say, sir, that perhaps what we ought to do is offer an exception to the requirements for findings and perhaps add on to the Hostage Act so that the president is allowed to take such actions

503

as necessary and carry them on for as long as necessary to recover our people.

REP. CHENEY: To follow-up on that, Colonel, I believe, and I'm not certain what the source of this information is—it may be press stories—that at one key point, one important decision was made I believe in the summer of 1985 by the President after he'd been to Arlington National Cemetery to lay a wreath on the tomb of the young sailor, Dean Stethem, who was killed—brutally murdered by the hijackers who took TWA 847. Do you remember that incident?

LT. COL. NORTH: I remember it well, sir.

REP. CHENEY: Could you tell us about it?

LT. COL. NORTH: There were several events that the President was deeply moved by and the murder of Robert Stethem was one of them. The murder of the Marines in El Salvador by terrorists and two American citizens along with them was another. The murder of Leon Klinghoffer—all of those affected I think all Americans and certainly the President. And that trip to Arlington was perhaps one of the most difficult that I saw the President have to make. And this is a president who had to—who would have gone to meet the bodies of those killed in Beirut, some of whom were my fellow Marines. Much has been made of, "How callous could North be, to deal with the very people who killed his fellow Marines?" The fact is we were trying to keep more Marines from being killed, and more Robert Stethems from being killed, and more Marines in El Salvador and Al Schoffelbergers in places like El Salvador from being killed. And I believe that our policy needs to be broad enough to be able to take action, perhaps even astringent as that taken by the Soviets in Lebanon that allowed their people to come home, as well as actions similar to the ones perhaps that I took and that are in so much debate, or actions like we took with the Achille Lauro, to be able to allow the terrorist to come to the conclusion that it's not wise to mess around with America citizens. And I think the President was deeply moved.

REP. CHEYNEY: Do you recall anything he might have said at the time—any specific words? Did he ever discuss his feelings with you or in meetings you attended?

LT. COL. NORTH: I don't recall them sir.

REP. CHEYNEY: Let's move on for a moment to the question of Mr. Buckley. I know we discussed some of this in executive session last night, and clearly, I don't want you to get into an area that is classified and needs to remain classified, by any means. But it's generally known that Mr. Buckley occupied a very sensitive post, and I wonder if you might talk briefly about that situation. He was our CIA station chief in Beirut.

LT. COL. NORTH: He was. And he was an expert on terrorism. And he was also involved in another program of enormous—before he went, when he was back here at the headquarters—a program of extraordinary sensitivity.

REP. CHEYNEY: And what happened to him in Beirut?

LT. COL. NORTH: Mr. Buckley was—from indications that we have—and it's been assembled over some period of time, and I'm not sure what the current analysis was. But when I left the government—I haven't left the government yet. When I left the Administration, the analysis we had was that Mr. Buckley was healthy when he was taken. He was beaten severely. He was probably tortured considerably. A tortured confession of some four hundred pages was extracted from him, the contents of which may well have been passed to the Soviets. Mr. Buckley probably died of the complications of pulmonary edemia—and that is that he'd been kicked so brutally in his kidneys that his lungs filled up with fluid, and he basically suffocated.

REP. CHEYNEY: And that obviously was known to Director Casey, was it? I assume reports on that were provided to the President during the period of time that Mr. Buckley was still a captive?

LT. COL. NORTH: Yes. We have never recovered the body of Mr. Buckley, as you know, sir.

REP. CHEYNEY: Right. How was that information presented to the President?

LT. COL. NORTH: There were CIA reports that came down with the PDB, the President's Daily Brief and the like. They were contained in reports that I sent up to the President.

REP. CHEYNEY: Was it the kind of issue he asked about from time to time in the course of the morning briefings?

LT. COL. NORTH: It's my recollection that the President frequently asked about the status of the hostages—not only to me but to my superiors in briefings. The President

505

certainly wanted to meet with all of those hostages who had been released. He met with the TWA 847 hostages when we got them free and went aboard the airplane, as I recall. He met with the three hostages that we were able to get out through our effort, and I made a plea to the American media when David Jacobsen came home, asking for their consideration that free revelations not complicate the release of others.

REP. CHENEY: Were special efforts made to recover Mr. Buckley?

LT. COL. NORTH: Yes, there were.

REP. CHENEY: I would assume, partly on the basis that he was literally one of our own, and a man in service to the Nation, that there were special feelings on the part of Director Casey for Mr. Buckley as well.

LT. COL. NORTH: It is my understanding that there is not only a professional relationship between Mr. Buckley and Mr. Casey but a personal one. And that Director Casey felt very strongly about William Buckley. He, to the very end, Director Casey was anxious to get the body of Bill Buckley home, and certainly the tortured confession.

REP. CHENEY: Would it be fair to say that the situation the hostages and especially Mr. Buckley had an impact at least, upon the policy decisions we've been talking about here, in connection with the opening to Iran the decision to ship weapons to the Ayatollah?

LT. COL. NORTH: I believe it did.

REP. CHENEY: There is a piece that appeared in one of the London newspapers which I happened to pull out today that I've brought with me that—that is headlined that the kidnapped and video-taped torture of William Buckley, the CIA's head of station in Beirut, shocked his superiors in Washington and led the Reagan Administration to reverse its policy on negotiating for hostages and selling arms to Iran. Is that too strong a statement or do you think it has some truth to it?

LT. COL. NORTH: One of the most difficult things that I experienced in this rather lengthy ordeal, and I'm sure it was the same for both Mr. McFarlane and Admiral Poindexter and the President, was to see the pictures that we were able to obtain, the video tapes, particularly of Bill Buckley as he died, over time. To see him slowly but surely being wasted away. And we were able to obtain through Intelligence sources those kinds of pictures with the assistance of a European who worked with us in this activity. And it was awful, to say the least.

REP. CHENEY: You mentioned a proposal at one point that you were involved in and we've had testimony on it from other witnesses as well, to try to remove the President a step from having to consider the intense emotional burden, or carry the burden, if you will, with respect to dealing with the hostage families on a regular basis. Did anything ever come of that?

LT. COL. NORTH: No. The decision was taken to have the President meet with those families.

REP. CHENEY: Who made that decision?

LT. COL. NORTH: I don't know, sir.

REP. CHENEY: Do you know if the plan ever went to the President for his consideration?

LT. COL. NORTH: I do not. I don't recall. I certainly proposed that he not. And that may well not have ever been realistic anyway. The President is a man with deep human emotion, in my experience. The call he made to me was a deeply personal one, and I think heartfelt, and I was grateful for it. And I saw him interact the same way with other people for five and a half years.

REP. CHENEY: Would it be fair to say, then, by way of conclusion on the hostages, that it's a little bit easier to understand why the President made the decisions he did with respect to the operations you ran in an effort to recover the hostages. And that the policy, which has obviously been widely criticized in some quarters, appears in a somewhat different light when we understand the depth of concern on the part of the President over the fate of a handful of American citizens in the brutal torture and subsequent death of Mr. Buckley, a man who obviously gave his life in the clandestine service of the nation.

LT. COL. NORTH: I could agree entirely with that, sir.

REP. CHENEY: Thank you, Colonel. I'd like to move on to a couple of other areas of not so sensitive a nature and not so emotional a nature and focus a little bit, if we can, upon the question of how the NSC operated. One of the comments that's made with respect to the Tower Commission, or in the Tower Commission Report, has to do with the notion that somehow the NSC became operational instead of advisory to the President. As I look at your record on the NSC, you were involved in a great many operational activities, planning the Grenada operation, the Libyan raid, running the operation—or certainly having a significant hand in the operation that captured the hijackers of the Achille Lauro. Was that a—were—were you ever conscious or ever involved in debates within the NSC or with your superiors about the wisdom of running those kinds of operations out of the NSC? And let me say at the outset I don't approach it with any preconceived notion of what the right way is necessarily to do it, but it's—it's not unusual for there to be a debate within the administration as to who's going to have responsibility for these kinds of programs and whether it ought to reside in the White House or in some other location in government.

LT. COL. NORTH: Congressman Cheney, I—I—I've read the Tower Report, and as I'm sure most, if not all, that are here have. My sense is that legislating how the President's staff would work would be most unwise, and I'm not even sure to be constitutional. My sense is that the NSC was at times operationally engaged and successful, and you just cited a number of successes. And success has a thousand fathers, and failure is an orphan.

And all of those activities that you cited as successes were not just operations of the NSC. They may have all engaged the same few handful of people at the NSC, but they also engaged the attention and efforts, incredible efforts, of other people at the Department of State, and the—and the CIA, and the Department of Defense. We could not have done Achille Lauro without a personal relationship between an NSC staff member and an Israeli intelligence official, nor could it have been done without a personal relationship between an NSC staff member and the National Security Adviser or between the National Security Adviser and a very high level Pentagon official, Admiral Art Moreau. And at one point in time, we all had phones up to each ear—one phone with information in, another phone with information out. It was probably the best example of coordination that could exist. And for those, we were given accolades. And as I described it yesterday, one of the real heroes was Major General Carl Steiner who was at the far end of the other phones, and those pilots off the carriers, flew the F-14s. And it all worked like clockwork, and everybody smelled good when it was done.

And then you end up with one that goes really wrong. And if you think about it, the one that went really wrong exposed another one that had been going pretty good. People might disagree with it. People might have great policy differences as to how it was handled and great policy differences as to whether or not it complied with Boland, but it had worked. And on balance, I'm not real sure that it is absolutely necessary to change a great many things except the process by which we can accord the Congress its Constitutional role in being apprised of activities as they're happening.

But when you think about it, there are some who would have said that before I talk to that Israeli intelligence official, or before we committed those aircraft or those personnel under General Steiner, we should have had a Congressional consultation. If we had had to do that, we'd still be looking for the terrorists that killed Leon Klinghoffer. And so what I'm saying is there has got to be a judicious balance, and I am certainly not the man to have to choose it. I believe it's got to come about as a consequence of a dialogue between the leadership of the Congress and the chief executive.

I don't believe that there ought to be such rigorous proscriptions that when it becomes necessary, like it did on the night of the 14th of April, 1986, that we cannot take actions without the possibility that those actions would be revealed afore and risk the lives of Americans. I think those things eventually have to be resolved, and they ought to be resolved soon, because as I have said, this is a nation at risk in a dangerous world. And it's not going to be easier, and I don't think it's going to be more difficult because of the things that Ollie North or John Poindexter or Bud McFarlane did. I think it's necessary that the administration and the Congress come to an accord as to what will be told, and when, and how, and to whom, and have absolute confidence that if it's done, it won't be revealed before hand. And if the decision is taken not to do it, that won't be bandied about town, because those are things that create an even more dangerous world.

REP. CHENEY: A point I'd like to touch on briefly if I can, Colonel.

There is a long tradition in the presidency, of presidents and their staffs becoming frustrated with the bureaucratic organizations they're required to deal with—to increasingly pull difficult decisions or problems into the White House to be managed because there's often times no sense urgency at state or at defense or any of the other departments that have to be worked with.

And I have seen, obviously we've seen other administrations operate in this fashion. It's a well-established practice. But one wonders if there aren't problems that we encounter in departments and agencies that automatically lead presidents, sooner or later, to move in the direction of deciding that the only way to get anything done, to cut through the red tape, to be able to move aggressively, is to have it done, in effect, inside the boundary of the White House.

I notice one point in one of your PROF messages you've got a comment that, "it's amazing that Dick Secord can do in five minutes what the CIA can't get done in two days."

To what extent did that kind of thinking led to the decisions that your unit should exist and that you should be assigned the duties you were assigned?

LT. COL. NORTH: I think there was a major—that was a major factor in much of it. There is enormous frustration with the ability to cut through red tape, as I believe it was counsel indicated. I must confess to being guilty of wanting to cut through red tape, being impatient.

There are certainly times for patience and prudence, and there are certainly times when one has to cut through the tape. And I think the hope is that one can find that there are good and prudent men who are judicious in the application of their understanding of the law, and understanding of what was right. And I think we had that.

But I'm not sure that the great political debates of this land will resolve that, that friction that exists even within the executive. And I'm not sure that you'll find a president who is unwilling to wait so long that he doesn't draw things in closer to himself. And in fact, it goes all the way back to the foundation of the Republic, where the president himself sends out his own agents to negotiate the Jay Treaty.

And by the way, I would point out to someone who made

an observation the other day—I didn't get that thing from my lawyers. I wrote it up a year before I met them. And the fact is there will always be times when a president wants to send out his own agents. And he should not be proscribed from doing so, and he should be able to do so, unless we're about to change the Constitution.

REP. CHENEY: In your discussions, and your testimony obviously, one of the themes that comes through repeatedly is your relationship with various officials of the Israeli government, Israeli intelligence services, Israeli citizens working apparently as emissaries or on behalf of their government. Would you call those back-channel comunications between the President or the President's representatives in the Israeli government?

LT. COL. NORTH: Back-channel has a connotation to it that I'm not sure is necessarily—

REP. CHENEY: I don't mean it in a negative sense at all. I'm questioning whether, whether or not, for example, the Secretary of State would be unhappy if he were to discover that the NSC staff were communicating with another country without his knowing about it?

LT. COL. NORTH: I, I'm not trying to characterize the Secretary's opinion of me, but my sense is he is very unhappy.

REP. CHENEY: When he finds out about it?

LT. COL. NORTH: When he found out about it.

REP. CHENEY: Yes. Did—can you relate that to us? Express his dissatisfaction to you.

LT. COL. NORTH: I'd rather not.

REP. CHENEY: (Laughs) Can we let the record show that your activities in that regard though did generate a certain amount of friction between yourself and key members of the President's Cabinet, or at least in this case the Secretary of State?

LT. COL. NORTH: Apparently so.

REP. CHENEY: Apparently so? All right. Good enough. I'd like to move on. I'll try to end before I use my entire hour so we can get out of here on a Friday night, but I—as you know, I've been a strong supporter of the contra program. You and I worked on it some prior to all of these developments, and we're actively engaged right not in an effort to persuade Congress to renew assistance for the Nicaraguan

511

democratic resistance, and that vote's gonna come up this fall. And, I must admit to a certain ambivalence when I think about the operation you ran because, on the one hand, I'm delighted that the resistance survived, and I am persuaded based in large part on your testimony as well as information that comes to me through my service on the Intelligence Committee, that the resistance might well not have survived, at least certainly not survived as well as it did during the period the Boland Amendment was in effect if it had not been for your actions.

On the other hand, I am persuaded that one of the most difficult assignments any President has isn't so much deciding what our foreign policy ought to be. That's oftentimes simple, compared to the larger task of building domestic political support to be able to sustain that policy, and it would seem our history is rife with examples, whether it's Woodrow Wilson and the League of Nations or FDR in the period before World War II, or Lyndon Johnson in Vietnam, of situations in which Presidents have tried to pursue a policy, and ultimately have been defeated, or found themselves in circumstances where they were unable to build the level of public support required.

Many of us think that one of the most useful contributions this administration may be able to make before the President leaves office is to institutionalize the so-called Reagan Doctrine, the notion that the United States be prepared to intervene to support anti-communist insurgents in key parts of the world when it's in our interest to do so: Nicaragua, Angola and Afghanistan. But, we've had problems in that regard, obviously, in Nicaragua, with the off-again on-again nature of congressional support, and a lot of that goes right back to our inability, so far, to be able to persuade the American people that what's at stake in Central America merits the kind of commitment that we've talked about.

And, I'm concerned, or at least I raise the possibility, going back to my comment of a moment ago about my ambivalent attitude towards your support operation. I'm concern about the possibility that the controversy surrounding your activities in connection with supporting the resistance may generate the kind of political opposition that will make it difficult, if not impossible for us, to be able to renew that assistance later on this year. And what I wonder and would ask you to comment on is whether or not those kinds of considerations between, on the one hand, the need to build public support for the program, and, on the other, the need to run a covert operation to keep the resistance alive, were ever discussed within the administration.

Did you ever participate in meetings where administration officials expressed concern about that point? Was there ever a feeling that somehow the covert operation could conceivably generate long-term support for the contras?

LT. COL. NORTH: Yes, it did. I think I answered that question in part earlier. Director Casey was always concerned about that, and I shared that concern. Nonetheless, I felt—and I'm sure it was felt by others, or we wouldn't have pursued it—that, although that risk was very high, the risk of having the resistance annihilated while we waited for the Congress to restore appropriated assistance was even greater. And that in pursuing the activities we did, we at least ensured that the resistance would still be viable, because there was absolute confidence that eventually we would get back to where we knew we ought to be—and that was with an authorized, government-sponsored program of support for the resistance.

My own personal sense is that I would have the greatest burden of all on my soul if what I have done or what I have failed to do, as a consequence of supporting the resistance from 1984 to the resumption of US assistance in 1986 resulted in a cut-off at this point. And I would beg you, gentlemen, all—that the cause of the Nicaraguan resistance is our own. And that regardless of whether you judge me to be right or wrong, that what we have done is we have decided, once again, with $100 million to support a cause that is just. We have decided to again support an army in the field, and a political outcome of democracy in Nicaragua. And that if, as a result of what you deem me to have done wrong, you decide to stop that again, that will be compounding a tragedy.

I am not trying to make a speech, Congressman Cheney. I'm making an appeal. Hang whatever you want around the neck of Ollie North—and I have a few millstones that I have laid before you, and I have tried to do so fully and honestly, as difficult as some of that may be. And it has been difficult. But for the love of God and the love of this nation, don't hang around Ollie North's neck the cut-off of funds to the Nicaraguan resistance again. This country cannot stand that, not just because of Nicaragua, but because of all the other nations in the world who look at us and measure by what we do now in Nicaragua the measure of our whole commitment to their cause—to things like NATO, to things like our commitment to peace and democracy elsewhere in the world. How far would we have gotten with the efforts of Dr. Sigur in Korea, just weeks ago, if they didn't really believe that we really wanted democracy. And how long will the people all around the rest of the world who rely on us, abide by us, and stand with us if we—if they don't believe that we want democracy enough just a few hundred miles from our own borders.

REP. CHENEY: Thank you very much, Colonel. Mr. Chairman, I believe I have about fifteen minutes left, to the great relief of the Committee. It's not my intention to use that time, but I would respectfully request that I be allowed to reserve the time in the event some questions arise between now and the end of Colonel North's testimony.

CHAIRMAN INOUYE: According to my clock, you have 20 minutes left. Without objection, 20 minutes will be reserved for Congressman Cheney.

REP. CHENEY: And by way of closing, Mr. Chairman, let me again simply thank the witness. Colonel North has been, I think, the most effective and impressive witness certainly this Committee has heard, and I know I speak for a great many Americans when I thank him for his years of devoted service to the nation, both in the United States Marine Corps and as a member of the NSC staffs. Thank you very much, Colonel.

LT. COL. NORTH: Thank you, sir.

CHAIRMAN INOUYE: The Joint Committee will stand in recess until 9:00 A.M. Monday morning in this room. However, before doing that, the following Exhibits will be entered into the record and made part of the record: OLN-1, 2, and including 4, 6–8, 10–35, 40–73, 76–78, 80–81, 83–93, 95–96, 98–155, 158–179, 181–214, 251–333(c). And the following classified Exhibits which, if not declassified prior to publication, will be included in the

514

classified annex: OLN-5, 9, 36–39, 74, 75, 79, 82, 94, 97, 156, 157, 180, 334–360, 500, 501.

And when we resume our hearings, on Monday morning at 9:00 A.M., July 13th, our witness will be Colonel Oliver North and Senator Mitchell will conduct the investigation and questioning.

END OF AFTERNOON SESSION

Monday · July 13, 1987

Morning Session—9:05 A.M.

CHAIRMAN INOUYE: The chair recognizes Senator Mitchell.

SEN. MITCHELL: Good morning, Colonel North.

LT. COL. NORTH: Good morning, Senator.

SEN. MITCHELL: Good morning, Mr. Sullivan.

MR. SULLIVAN: Good morning, sir.

SEN. MITCHELL: Colonel, this should be the last day of your appearance, and I'm sure you're relieved of that.

LT. COL. NORTH: I am, sir.

SEN. MITCHELL: All right. The questions last week were mostly about the facts. They're important, but it's also important to consider some of the broader policy and legal issues. One of the purposes of the committee is to consider the relevant laws, see how they worked or didn't work in this case, and recommend changes in those laws if appropriate. Another is to try to find out how and why these important policy decisions were made and whether we ought to change the manner in which decisions are made, and I'd like to try to do that, at least to some extent, this morning and—so perhaps, out of all of this, we could all learn something.

Now, you said last week that you've obeyed the law. You haven't claimed, and I understand you don't now claim, that you are in any way above or exempt the requirements of the law, is that correct?

LT. COL. NORTH: That is correct, sir.

SEN. MITCHELL: And you agree, don't you, that every American, whatever his or her position, must obey the law?

LT. COL. NORTH: I do.

SEN. MITCHELL: And that's true even if a person doesn't agree with a particular law?

LT. COL. NORTH: Yes, sir.

SEN. MITCHELL: Now, if the law is properly enacted and is constitutional but that law is [in] conflict with the President's policy, domestic or foreign, which is controlling, the law or the President's policy?

LT. COL. NORTH: Well—(pause)—well, certainly, as I have indicated in my earlier testimony, the law is the law, and as you have also indicated in my testimony, I do not believe that any of us are above the law, and certainly in this case, while I am not a lawyer and—and do not profess to be able to play the various issues, pro and con, I continue to believe that the President's policy was within the law, that what we did was constitutional in its essence, that the President's decisions to continue to support the Nicaraguan democratic opposition in the way that they were carried out from 1984 through my departure in 1986 fully fit within the strictures of the particular statutory constraints that were contained in Boland.

And so I don't see, Senator, that—that there is a distance at all between what was passed and what we did. Certainly there are folks who can argue the constitutionality of Boland, as to whether or not the Congress has the authority to tell a president that he can or cannot ask a head of state or send his agents, in this case myself, out to talk to foreign leaders. It is my understanding of the Constitution and the laws that there is no separation between what we did and the Boland constraints—

SEN. MITCHELL: And—and—and—

LT. COL. NORTH: —in my going out to talk with foreign heads of state or foreign leaders or to arrange for non-US government monies to be used that met the rigorous constraints imposed by Boland.

SEN. MITCHELL: Right, then I—and I, of course, have not suggested that. I've only asked and I believe you've agreed that if a properly constituted law has been enacted and it's constitutional, that even though it conflicts with the President's policy, the President—(long pause)—I've only asked that, and I think it's rather an unremarkable question that, when a law of the United States is properly enacted and is

517

constitutional, even though it conflicts with a President's policy, the President, all members of the Executive branch and indeed all Americans must obey that law.

LT. COL. NORTH: I—I have no debate with that, whatsoever, Senator, but what I—what I would not want to leave the record lacking on is the fact that I think there are many people who debate whether or not the issue of—of Boland, as it's interpreted by a number of different people —complying—

SEN. MITCHELL: I—I'm not debating that—I'm not debating that and I—and I think the record is very clear of your view on that, sir.

Now, as I said, one of the purposes of this Committee is to find out how and why these important policy decisions were made. And I speak now, particularly, with respect to the sale of arms to Iran. And so I'd like to ask you a few questions about that. You've testified that the Iranians with whom you dealt in both what have been called the first and the second channels, included officials of the government of Iran. Am I correct in that?

LT. COL. NORTH: Yes.

SEN. MITCHELL: Now, you and the other persons meeting with the President on this matter were aware, weren't you, that the President had been highly critical of the Iranian government in a widely reported speech in July of 1985, just a month before the first shipment of arms from Israel to Iran which the President agreed to, the President described Iran as an outlaw state run by the strangest collection of misfits, loony tunes and squalid criminals since the advent of the Third Reich. To your recollection, during the meetings you attended with the President with others, did anyone in your presence specifically point out to him that his representatives were dealing with officials of that same government of Iran, point out that statement to him, and point out the at least apparent inconsistency in the two and the problems that might cause for him?

LT. COL. NORTH: That particular issue was not addressed in the meetings that I attended with the President on this matter, but what I think is important is that we clearly attempted to establish contact and, ultimately, the objective of a strategic dialogue with pragmatic or moderate or less unreasonable elements of the Iranian government and even if we could have, people who were willing to bring about a cessation of terrorism, a more pro-Western view of the world, an end to Shiite-sponsored revolutionary fundamentalism, and, ultimately, secure the relationship between the United States and Iran to the point where we could bring about an end to the Iran/Iraq War. The characterization of the Iranian government I don't take any issue with, but the fact is that there are people in their government of differing political philosophies who see the long-term benefit to their country as well as to the rest of the world in achieving the kinds of things that we set out to ultimately achieve.

SEN. MITCHELL: Well, the—

LT. COL. NORTH: The problem that is created is matching one set of words with another set of policy goals that were not publicly stated.

SEN. MITCHELL: Yeah.

LT. COL. NORTH: And yet I see nothing inconsistent with the fact that the characterization of the Iranian government as the President made it vividly clear does not in any way prevent trying to establish contact with a more reasonable channel within it.

SEN. MITCHELL: Right. Well, in fact the President's publicly stated policy at that time was not to provide arms to Iran and to work actively to keep other nations from doing so. As you'll recall, in 1984 the Secretary of State had branded Iran a country which has repeatedly provided support for acts of international terrorism. And by his action, he placed Iran on a list of countries to which American arms could not be shipped. And the President's publicly stated policy on terrorism was that there would be no negotiation, no payments, no ransom of any kind, to obtain the release of terrorists (sic). In fact, I think in about that same time as he made the speech on Iran the President said, and I quote, "America will never make concessions to terrorists. To do so would only invite more terrorism. Once we head down that path there will be no end to it."

Now my question is, am I correct that every person dealing directly with the President on this matter was a member of the Executive branch and therefore subordinate to and totally dependent upon the President?

LT. COL. NORTH: When you say "this matter" you're referring to the Iran intitiative?

SEN. MITCHELL: The Iran—the advising him on the issue of the sale of arms to Iran.

LT. COL. NORTH: To my knowledge that's correct. I do not know of any others that specfically talked to the President regarding our Iran initiative. But in the records I turned over to the Committee and in some of the documents that were removed from my office and provided by the White House to this Committee, it is very clear that there were a number of other initiatives ongoing; some by members of Congress, both houses, both sides of the aisle, who had an interest in some kind of dialogue with the Iranian government for the purposes that were identical to the ones that we pursued, perhaps more vigorously than some would agree. But nonetheless, there were a number of other initiatives undertaken by private Americans, by senators, by congressmen, to get to a faction within Iran that would be more moderate.

I would also take issue, Senator, with one of your comments. To my knowledge we have never said nor should we say that we will not negotiate. We have a policy of no concessions. We have a policy that is very clear, and I still do not to this day believe that we made concessions to terrorists. We were dealing again, in hopes of establishing a dialogue—a strategic dialogue—with elements within Iran that could bring about a more pro-American, pro-Western, anti-terrorist philosophy within that country.

SEN. MITCHELL: Well, I—and I understand and appreciate your point of view, as I'm sure you understand and appreciate that there are others who would characterize these events different from you do, but the point is, that every person advising the President was his subordinate, and when the finding authorizing the sale of arms to Iran was signed by the President, it specifically directed that no one in the Congress be notified of the covert action—you recall that—

LT. COL. NORTH: —I do.—

SEN. MITCHELL: —your testimony to that effect. And you said, that the reason for that was concern over leaks, and the problem that because it might be leaked, it would jeopardize the action. And you've, in the course of the last several days, expressed very forcefully that point of view. I raise that, because there's another point of view on that

520

same issue that hasn't been expressed, and I'd like to do that now, because I think we ought to have the benefit of all points of view on this—as we consider what we should do about this law, which is so very difficult.

Now—now, in our democracy, public policy is made in public. It's the product of open, competitive debate. There are two reasons for that. The first is, that the American people have a right to know what their government is doing and why. And the second is our belief that if all points of view are heard, especially opposing points of view, the person making the decision is more likely to make the right decision—the decision that's in the national interest. Open debate is one of democracy's greatest strengths. Its absence is one of the great weaknesses of totalitarian societies, and I believe it's one of the reasons why freedom is going to win the worldwide struggle in which we're now engaged.

Now, when covert action is necessary, as it is from time to time, obviously, there can't be an open debate. And that's a real loss, especially to the decision maker who's deprived of the full range of opinion on an important issue. So, the law tries to compensate for that—at least to some extent —it requires the President to notify just eight of the top congressional leaders—four from each party—he either can notify the Intelligence Committees, or at his option he may choose to notify just eight of the top congressional leaders, four from each party.

Now, the reason for that law, at least one reason, is to give the president the benefit of different points of view. Each of the congressional leaders is elected independently of the president, is therefore not subordinate to and dependent upon him, and more likely to give the president the frank advice that any president needs in making these very difficult decisions.

Now, of course, the concern which you expressed about leaks is a real one. There have been leaks by members of Congress, and I believe every member of this Committee joins me in dismay when a member of Congress leaks sensitive information. But, let's be clear. The fact that a few members of Congress leak doesn't mean that all members of Congress leak, just as the fact that some members of the Administration leak cannot be fairly said to mean that all members of the Administration leak.

521

Now obviously, not just in these matters, but in life generally, every time you tell one person a secret, you increase the odds that the secret won't be kept. And so, there has to be a judgment. How much benefit does the president get from the advice of independently elected congressional leaders against how much the risk of leak increases by their knowledge?

Now, let's apply that to the facts of this case. Many people in the Executive branch of our government knew. Private American citizens, some without security clearances, knew. Some Israelis knew—some of them government officials, some private citizens. Some Iranian officials knew. Some Canadians knew. At least one Saudi Arabian knew. And Mr. Ghorbanifar, an Iranian citizen who you said is an Israeli agent, and who you and others have described as a liar and a cheat—he knew. In those circumstances, how much would the risk of exposure been increased by telling eight of the highest elected officials in the United States Congress? And against that, how much did the President lose when he was deprived of the independent advice of those eight officials? Every person will make his or her own judgment on those questions. I just want to say that for myself, I am convinced that if the President had told these independent public officials of his intention to sell arms to Iran to swap arms for hostages, to pursue a private policy that directly contradicted his public policy, at least some of them—maybe Lee Hamilton, or Dick Chaney, or Bob Dole, or Bob Michel —some of them would have said before the fact, what the American people have said after the fact, "Mr. President, we respect and admire your concern for the hostages, but it is a mistake to sell arms to Iran. It is a mistake to swap arms for hostages, for you and for the country. Don't do it." Perhaps then the President would have chosen another course. We'll never know, but I thought it important that at least that point of view be expressed. A point of view which has not been expressed so far with respect to that provision of the law, which I believe to be an important one.

Now, that whole area of covert operation is one which this committee will have to explore in detail. And I would like to get into that and ask you some questions about that. Now, you made a strong statement in favor of covert action.

522

General Secord made a similar statement when he was here. Let me assure you, there is no dispute on the need for some covert action. I know of no member of this committee who favors prohibiting all covert action. We all recognize that there are going to be circumstances in which the United States simply must conduct covert actions in the national interest. But the problem is that covert actions, by their very nature, conflict, in some respect, with democratic values. You've said that covert actions require secrecy and deception. Our democratic process places a high value on the very opposite characteristics of openness and truth. So the real question, and the much more difficult question, is how to conduct covert operations in an open, democratic society in a lawful manner in which public officials are accountable for their acts. And so my first question is, do you believe that the President has unrestricted power to conduct covert action?

LT. COL. NORTH: Within the limits of the constitutional authority to prosecute the foreign policy of the United States, the President has a very wide mandate to carry out activities secretly or publicly, as he chooses.

SEN. MITCHELL: Well—

LT. COL. NORTH: I do not believe that the things that we did in pursuing the two principal covert actions we've discussed and some of the subsidiary activities that were pursued as a consequence of the revenues generated were in any way prohibited. And the fact is that the president, since the founding of the Republic, has always held that he could send his agents, he could discuss things and negotiate with foreign leaders, and to do so within the framework of the constitutional authority as the head of state and the commander-in-chief has widely been held to be within his presidential purview.

There are certainly those who can debate whether or not a certain period of time is appropriate for notification, given the constraints of Hughes-Ryan and the National Security Act, and I am certainly not going to sit here and debate them with you. My sense is that we are going to agree to disagree at the end of this hearing on how wide and perhaps even how deep the presidential authorities go.

SEN. MITCHELL: Well, let's look at the current law, which I

think we can agree isn't working very well. And you said last week there must be a better way. If there is one, it's part of our job to find it.

LT. COL. NORTH: When I was saying that there must be a better way, Senator, I was talking—I hope I was responding to a question on notification and seeking the advice of Congress.

SEN. MITCHELL: Well, I want to get to the law. And first, the law requires that the President personally make a finding that the action is important to the national security of the United States and authorize it before the covert action can occur. Do you agree with that provision of the law, that the President—

LT. COL. NORTH: That is my understanding of the statutes pertaining to covert action—

SEN. MITCHELL: Right. Do you agree—

LT. COL. NORTH: Let me, if I may, just continue—

SEN. MITCHELL: Oh—all right.

LT. COL. NORTH: It is my understanding again—and I don't have the statute in front of me—but that it also applies to the fact that the President need do so when he is going to use appropriated monies for the pursuit of one of those covert actions. And, again, I do not have the statute before me, and I'm not sure that it pays to have a professional lawyer and experienced jurist debating with lieutenant colonel infantry officers on this issue.

SEN. MITCHELL: Well, it's an important issue and I— you've been involved in covert actions. You held a high position in the government, and—

LT. COL. NORTH: I would even debate that part of it with you, Senator.

SEN. MITCHELL: Oh, all right. Do you agree that no covert action should occur unless the President first finds that it's necessary and specifically authorizes it?

LT. COL. NORTH: Well, again, I want to go back to what I just said a moment ago. It was—and I'm leading with my recollection unrefreshed, but the law provides that the President does or makes a finding in the case of covert actions which will expend taxpayers' monies.

SEN. MITCHELL: Is it your—you've said that twice now. Is it your contention that the President could authorize and

524

conduct covert actions with unappropriated funds? Is that the point you're trying to make?

LT. COL. NORTH: Yes.

SEN. MITCHELL: And in such event, to whom would the President be accountable?

LT. COL. NORTH: To the American people—

SEN. MITCHELL: Well—

LT. COL. NORTH: —that elected him, Senator—

SEN. MITCHELL: Since he couldn't—

LT. COL. NORTH: —and that's one of the issues that came up the other day that no elected official knew A, B or C, and my point is that the President is the highest official in the land—

SEN. MITCHELL: Indeed, he is.

LT. COL. NORTH: —answerable to the American people and ultimately under the Constitution answerable to the people through a variety of means. Reelection; they can vote him out of office. They chose not to do so.

SEN. MITCHELL: But of course, if, by definition, covert action is secret and he doesn't tell them about it, there's no way the American people can know about it to be able to vote him out of office on that basis, is there?

LT. COL. NORTH: But, in fact, that—that's the issue I tried to raise in the letter that I wrote well before I ever met—met counsel. When I was talking about the Jay treaties, it was not that President Washington in any way was not cooperative with the Congress; he simply refused to lay before the Congress all of what had gone on in the—in the negotiation of those treaties. That was debated again in the 1930s in the US versus Curtis Wright Export Corporation, and the Supreme Court held again that it was within the purview of the Present—President of the United States to conduct secret activities and to—and to conduct negotiations to further the foreign policy goals of the United States.

SEN. MITCHELL: If I may just say, Colonel, the Curtis Wright case said no such thing. It involved public matters that were the subject of the law in a prosecution. You said this isn't the appropriate forum to be debating constitutional law, and I agree with you. I just think the record should reflect that the Curtis Wright was on a completely different factual situation, and—and there is no such statement in the Curtis Wright case—

MR. SULLIVAN: Excuse me, Senator.

SEN. MITCHELL: But—but—and—and I disagree with you.

MR. SULLIVAN: I think it's a little unfair to have a debate with—

SEN. MITCHELL: I just said that there's no point in debating it.

MR. SULLIVAN: —Colonel North over the law.

SEN. MITCHELL: Yeah.

MR. SULLIVAN: I think the key—

SEN. MITCHELL: Let me get to this specific covert action.

MR. SULLIVAN: —if I—if I could suggest, sir, if you ask him what he did, what the facts were, and what his understanding was at the time, rather than get into a general debate about the—what the law is, it might be more helpful to the committee.

SEN. MITCHELL: Colonel, you testified earlier about the contra resupply effort and your role in it. You said, and I quote you, "This was a covert operation, run by the US government." You said, "We were conducting a covert operation." And you testified that Director Casey described it as a "full-service covert operation." Now, under the law, for any agency of government, other than the Central Intelligence Agency, to conduct a covert operation, three things must occur. First is that the President must specifically designate that agency to conduct covert operations. The second is that the President must make a finding authorizing this particular covert operation and finding it in the national interest.

Now, in this respect, I'll start with these two. You've already testified that the President did not make a finding authorizing a contra resupply covert operation. Is that correct?

LT. COL. NORTH: I have seen no finding.

SEN. MITCHELL: Right. Did the President specifically designate the National Security Council to conduct covert operations?

LT. COL. NORTH: I have no specific knowledge of that, as I have testified. I have told you what I know about the decision process that obtained in that case.

SEN. MITCHELL: And the third thing that the law requires

526

is that Congress be notified, and, as you've testified, that did not occur. So my question—

LT. COL. NORTH: Senator, if I may—not to interrupt, and respectfully so—but the law, as I understand it, requires that the President notify the Congress in a timely manner.

SEN. MITCHELL: Right.

LT. COL. NORTH: That has not been—been noted. And second of all, it is in regards to operations involving the use of appropriated funds. And I think those are important omissions that have not been entered in the record.

SEN. MITCHELL: So, all right, then let me go back to the first two then. Since the law and President Reagan's written instructions required that before the National Security Council could conduct a covert operation, the President had to specifically designate the National Security Council for that purpose. And second—

(Pause while North confers with his counsel)

SEN. MITCHELL: And secondly, since the law requires that before any covert action could be conducted, the President must specifically authorize it. Since you've testified that you conducted a covert operation, and since you've further testified that the President neither designated the National Security Council to conduct covert operations nor did he make a finding authorizing this covert operation, what was the legal basis for your activities with respect to this covert operation?

LT. COL. NORTH: To go back once again to Curtis Wright, because I do believe it does speak to the issue of what the President can or cannot do with his own staff, and I believe it does talk to the issue of conducting secret diplomacy. The fact is, the President can do what he wants with his own staff. The National Security Council staff is not included within the constraints that are depicted in either the executive order or the NSDD as an intelligence agency. And thus, in neither case does the law provide that the President had to do what you are saying he had to do.

SEN. MITCHELL: You're referring to NSDD 159?

LT. COL. NORTH: Yes, right. This is the first page of an order signed and approved by President Reagan. And the first sentence of paragraph number two reads: "In accordance with Executive Order 12333, the Central Intelligence

527

Agency shall conduct covert actions unless the President specifically designates another agency of the government."

SEN. MITCHELL: Now that is not limited to other intelligence agencies. I think a fair reading of that can only mean that no agency of government can conduct a covert action other than the Central Intelligence Agency, unless the President specifically designates that agency for that purpose.

You have testified that as a member of the National Security Council staff, you conducted a covert operation. And my question is, did the President specifically designate the National Security Council staff for that purpose?

LT. COL. NORTH: Again, I think we're going to end up agreeing to disagree, Senator. I think what I have said consistently is that I believed that the President has the authority to do what he wants with his own staff; that I was a member of his staff, that Mr. McFarlane was, and that Admiral Poindexter was, and that in pursuing the President's foreign policy goals of support for the Nicaraguan resistance, he was fully within his rights to send us off to talk to foreign heads of state, to seek the assistance of those foreign heads of state, to use other than US government monies, and to do so without a finding. I would also point out again that that language, right here in paragraph two of the NSDD extract that you have, is taken directly from the Exeutive Order.

SEN. MITCHELL: That's right.

LT. COL. NORTH: An Executive Order signed by the President. This NSDD was signed by the President. If the President chooses to waive his own Executive Orders, or chooses to waive the provisions of his own NSDDs, which do not have the force of law, it is fully within his rights to do so.

SEN. MITCHELL: But the President told the Tower Board, and I quote: "The President told the Board on January 26, 1987 that he did not know that the NSC staff was engaged in helping the contras." And therefore, the President could not have waived the provisions of the orders as you've described, and could not have so designated the NSC if, as he said, he did not know that the NSC staff was engaged in helping the contras, could he?

LT. COL. NORTH: You're asking me to speak for the

President. What he said to the Tower Board—and I have not talked with the Tower Board, nor was I there when he did. The fact is, as I have testified for four straight days—and I think there's no one on this Committee that would debate it—[I] kept my superiors fully apprised of just exactly what I was doing. They were and I was a member of the President's staff. The President has since said, I believe publicly, that he was aware of what was being done, and that in fact it was at least partially his idea. There is no doubt that the President wanted the policy of support for the Nicaraguan resistance pursued and I did so to the very best of my abilities.

SEN. MITCHELL: Well, I think you were right, we will agree to disagree and so I take it your position is that your understanding of the President's general knowledge of what you were doing represented your standpoint, a specific designation by the President, of the NSC to conduct such activities. And with respect to a finding, I gather its your position that no finding was necessary in any event.

LT. COL. NORTH: That is, sir.

SEN. MITCHELL: All right. Thank you. I—I would just—I would just note again that there is another point of view that should be expressed which is that—that the law and President Reagan's own orders, as specifically set forth, the means by which covert actions would be approved and conducted. It represents an attempt to balance the difficult and conflicting interests of conducting covert operations in a democracy. And I think that the only way covert actions can be conducted in a manner consistent with democracy is if those laws and orders are followed. And—and—and I—I simply think it's—it's obvious in this case that there is at least a question about that. So, we'll just have to disagree—

LT. COL. NORTH: If—if I may just respond to that briefly, sir—

SEN. MITCHELL: Go—go right ahead, Colonel, yes.

LT. COL. NORTH: As I have also testified, I—I came here to tell you what I did and what others told me to do or allowed me to do, or however one wants to characterize it.

SEN. MITCHELL: Right.

LT. COL. NORTH: Not so much to take positions on this or that aspect of the law because I am not a lawyer. I think what's also important is that we believed, certainly I believed, that what we were doing was consistent within that, the constraints of the various statutes and laws. And lastly, I have told the Committee that as early as June of 1986, I, not the Tower Commission, proposed in a public speech to the American Bar Association, that there were indeed problems and recognizably so in the conduct of covert operations in a democracy.

And I—if nothing else, we can agree on the fact that there is a need for an appropriate—of conferring with the Congress. And I suggested, as one means of doing that, the formation of a very discreet intell—joint intelligence committee with a very small and professional staff that would allow those types of advise and consult conferences to occur between the Executive and the Legislative branches.

SEN. MITCHELL: I'd like to turn now to another area of your testimony, and that's the plan that you described: for you to take the blame for this matter. You said Mr. Casey called it "the fall guy plan." Over what period of time did your discussions with Mr. Casey occur about this plan? That is, as best you can recall, when did it first come up, and when did you last discuss it with him?

LT. COL. NORTH: My sense of the discussions with the Director on that aspect of it—it probably began in the early spring of 1984. It was a time in which the money for the resistance was running out, and as members of the intelligence committees know, appeals had been made to the intelligence committees for the release of certain monies that could be applied to the program. It was seen that was not to be forthcoming. And I—at that point in time when alternatives were discussed and we eventually decided to pursue availing ourselves of offers from foreign governments, it was seen that there would need to be someone who could, as I put it so bluntly, take the fall. My sense is that that occurred off and on, periodically, as we discussed various initiatives, over the course of time between early '84 until the end of my tenure right up at the last days before I departed the NSC in November of 1986.

SEN. MITCHELL: Now, you testified that the purpose of the plan was to limit the political embarrassment that might result. Are you shaking your head no?

LT. COL. NORTH: No, I mean, it was not only to limit the political embarrassment.

SEN. MITCHELL: That was in part—

LT. COL. NORTH: In part—

SEN. MITCHELL: —it was a purpose, all right—from a disclosure of these events. And my question is that, when you said that, did you mean either the sale of arms to Iran, or the use of proceeds from the sale to the contras, or the contra resupply effort, or all of them?

LT. COL. NORTH: All of them.

SEN. MITCHELL: All of them.

LT. COL. NORTH: In fact, one must recall that it goes back to the spring of '84 before there was any Iran initiative, and the discussion was you needed to have the plausible deniability which ought to be a part of any covert operation.

SEN. MITCHELL: Right. Now, did you ever discuss this subject with anyone else either in or out of Mr. Casey's presence?

LT. COL. NORTH: Well, I discussed it with Admiral Poindexter and Mr. McFarlane. And I don't recall whether Director Casey was there for all, or any, of those discussions necessarily. But I certainly did talk to both of them about it.

SEN. MITCHELL: Do you know, of your knowledge, whether Mr. Casey discussed it with anyone other than Mr. McFarlane and Mr. Poindexter?

LT. COL. NORTH: I don't.

SEN. MITCHELL: All right. So to your knowledge, at least, the only four people were aware of the plan (sic), and who participated in the discussions about it were you, Mr. Casey, Mr. Poindexter and Mr. McFarlane. Is that correct?

LT. COL. NORTH: Well, I have also been asked questions about, did I say it to such and so, or another witness, or whatever, and I—I suppose that I did—

SEN. MITCHELL: —Something like that?

LT. COL. NORTH: Yes.

SEN. MITCHELL: Yes, I was going to ask you about that later—I'll ask you about that now. In a recent magazine article, you're quoted as telling friends, beginning in 1984, that "the day will come, when I have to resign in disgrace from the administration, and take the heat for the President." Did you ever say that, or something like that to anyone?

LT. COL. NORTH: First of all, I'd like to make sure that you understand, Senator, I haven't read a magazine article or

531

anything else about myself in some time, except as other people bring it to my attention. And second of all, I've seen my words mischaracterized, misquoted, and described to other people for so long, that I wouldn't want to indicate that I actually agreed with anything—

SEN. MITCHELL: —Well, we've—

LT. COL. NORTH: —But I'm sure that I said something like that—

SEN. MITCHELL: —Something like that to people—

LT. COL. NORTH: —at various points in time.

SEN. MITCHELL: All right.

LT. COL. NORTH: I certainly said it to the Committee.

SEN. MITCHELL: Now, did the suggestion, that you be the fall guy, originate with you or with Mr. Casey?

LT. COL. NORTH: My guess is, it was probably Director Casey— I mean, we—I've tried to describe the relationship I had with the Director, and at some points it was that of a teacher, or a philosophical mentor. And in some cases it was that of a experienced hand in intelligence matters, or, in some cases, just getting the job done. And I would guess that Director Casey was the one who pointed out that there would come a time when there would need to be, if these activities were exposed, somebody to stand up and take the heat for it—or those kinds of words.

SEN. MITCHELL: So, your recollection is that it was Mr. Casey who was responsible?

LT. COL. NORTH: I'm not sure that Director Casey ever said, "and it's got to be you, Ollie;" it was probably Ollie saying, "Well, when that happens, it'll be me."

SEN. MITCHELL: And you also said, though, that at one point, Mr. Casey said that you might be too junior a person, to be the fall guy, that there wouldn't be plausible deniability then, and he—

LT. COL. NORTH: —Well, I think—

SEN. MITCHELL: —Excuse me, may I finish the question? And he suggested that Admiral Poindexter, might have to be a fall guy. Do you recall that testimony?

LT. COL. NORTH: I'm not sure—I recall that kind of thing happening right toward the end—I mean that wasn't at some point during the earlier phases of this activity—I think it was after the revelations in the McFarlane trip, and the press queries about it here in this country. And at some point, probably after the first week of November, talking with Director Casey, or in that time frame, Director Casey indicating that, you know, "You're not big enough, buddy, you're going to—it's probably going to go higher."

SEN. MITCHELL: And my question is, did you, or anyone else, ever tell Admiral Poindexter that he was under consideration, as the fall guy? (Laughter)

LT. COL. NORTH: (laughs) I don't recall a specific conversation, Senator, that I said, "boss, it's now you, not me." I do recall, again, right toward the end, discussing with Admiral Poindexter the fact that it was more likely that both of us would leave.

SEN. MITCHELL: So, did anything ever become of that suggestion, or was that—

LT. COL. NORTH: —We both left, sir.

SEN. MITCHELL: Both left, so, it may turn out that Mr. Casey was more correct than he realized at the time?

LT. COL. NORTH: He was right about a lot of things, Senator.

SEN. MITCHELL: During your discussions with Mr. Casey, Mr. McFarlane and Mr. Poindexter about the plan, did a question ever arise among you as to whether what was being proposed was legal?

LT. COL. NORTH: In which case? Across the board? On all activities?

SEN. MITCHELL: No. On the plan—the "fall guy" plan, limiting it to that.

LT. COL. NORTH: Oh no. I don't think it was—first of all, we operated from the premise that everything we did do was legal, and therefore, the fact that there would be somebody who took the blame as it were was not inconsistent I don't think with any of the rest of what we said.

SEN. MITCHELL: So, your answer is, "No, there was no discussion or consideration about the legalities."

LT. COL. NORTH: I do not recall any discussion about the legality of some guy standing up and saying, "I did it all and I'm gone."

SEN. MITCHELL: Right. Yes.

LT. COL. NORTH: I don't recall any—

SEN. MITCHELL: Did a question ever arise as to whether what was being proposed was appropriate since it necessarily involved false statements by high public officials?

LT. COL. NORTH: No. In fact, I'm not sure that they are false. I think you have before you the culprit who did all these things and has come here and testified to that.

SEN. MITCHELL: Well, of course, you didn't intend that there would be such an investigation and such testimony.

LT. COL. NORTH: I surely hope that there wouldn't have been, Senator.

SEN. MITCHELL: Yes. Right. In fact, you said that neither you nor anyone else anticipated the possibility of a criminal investigation and that—but for the criminal investigation, you were prepared to go through with the plan, resign in disgrace, and take the heat for the President.

LT. COL. NORTH: That's correct.

SEN. MITCHELL: But you said that because of the criminal investigation, you changed your mind and decided to protect yourself.

LT. COL. NORTH: Exactly.

SEN. MITCHELL: Now, after you changed your mind, did you tell Mr. Casey that you had done so?

LT. COL. NORTH: I had no discussions with Director Casey on the day that my mind changed and that was the 25th of November. I never talked to him again unfortunately.

SEN. MITCHELL: And after you changed your mind, did you tell Admiral Poindexter or Mr. McFarlane that you changed your mind and that because of this pending criminal aspect, you no longer intended to be the "fall guy" in the "fall guy" plan?

LT. COL. NORTH: They probably learned it when I appeared here, sir.

SEN. MITCHELL: Probably not a happy day for Admiral Poindexter listening to your testimony last week.

LT. COL. NORTH: I don't want to characterize how the Admiral feels. I have not talked to the Admiral in months.

SEN. MITCHELL: All right. And that—really, you've answered my questions and it was, as I understand your earlier testimony, that there simply wasn't any discussion about whether it was legal or appropriate. You assumed the legality of your actions.

LT. COL. NORTH: Again, I want to emphasize the fact that it wasn't so much for any political motive on the part of any of the participants so much as it was an effort to protect the detailed knowledge of what had transpired and protect the covert operations themselves. And, again, none of us to my recollection ever discussed a legal propriety aspect to the whole thing.

SEN. MITCHELL: But then, however, Congress had resumed aid to the contras and the covert action was no longer necessary, was it? Indeed, it had been terminated —what would be the need to protect that action by making up a false story about it?

LT. COL. NORTH: Well, I'm not too sure how the false story aspect really obtains in this case, Senator—

SEN. MITCHELL: Well, to—

LT. COL. NORTH: —to have this guy stand up and say, "I did it" and have the finger pointed at him and let him go protects the people with whom I worked in Central America and elsewhere, protects the lives and safety of people inside Nicaragua, protects the people in Europe who worked with us on these activities, protects the lives of people who worked in Lebanon with us, the lives of the people inside Iran who worked with us, the lives of the American hostages. I mean, if one could prevent those things from coming out—

SEN. MITCHELL: Well, my question—

LT. COL. NORTH: —it ultimately would be well served.

SEN. MITCHELL: My question was limited to the contra resupply effort, which of course was only indirectly related to the hostage situation. But I want to—my time is nearly up and I want to make some closing observations because you have, as I indicated, expressed several points of view with respect to which there are other points of view, and I think they ought to be expressed. And I'd like to do that now. You've talked here often and eloquently about the need for a democratic outcome in Nicaragua. There's no disagreement on that. There is disagreement over how best to achieve that objective. Many Americans agreed with the President's policy. Many do not. Many patriotic Americans, strongly anti-Communist, believe there's a better way to contain the Sandinistas, to bring about a democratic outcome in Nicaragua and to bring peace to Central America. And many patriotic Americans are concerned that in the pursuit of democracy abroad we not compromise it in any way here at home. You and others have urged consistency in our policies. You've said repeatedly that if we are not

535

consistent our allies and other nations will question our reliability. That's a real concern. But if it's bad to change policies, it's worse to have two different policies at the same time; one public policy and an opposite policy in private. It's difficult to conceive of a greater inconsistency than that. It's hard to imagine anything that would give our allies more cause to consider us unreliable, than that we say one thing in public and secretly do the opposite. And that's exactly what was done when arms were sold to Iran, and arms were swapped for hostages.

Now, you've talked a lot about patriotism and the love of our country. Most nations derive from a single tribe, a single race. They practice a single religion. Common racial, ethnic, religious heritages are the glue of nationhood for many.

The United States is different. We have all races, all religions. We have a limited common heritage. The glue of nationhood for us is the American ideal of individual liberty and equal justice. The rule of law is critical in our society. It's the great equalizer, because in America everybody is equal before the law.

We must never allow the end to justify the means, where the law is concerned, however important and noble an objective. And surely, democracy abroad is important, and is noble. It cannot be achieved at the expense of the rule of law in our country.

And our diversity is very broad. You talked about your background, and it was really very compelling; and is obviously one of the reasons why the American people are attracted to you. Let me tell you a story from my background.

Before I entered the Senate, I had the great honor of serving as a federal judge. In that position I had great power. The one I most enjoyed exercising was the power to make people American citizens. From time to time I presided at what we call "naturalization" ceremonies. They're citizenship ceremonies.

These are people who came from all over the world, risked their lives, sometimes left their families and their fortunes behind, to come here. They'd gone through the required procedures, and I, in the final act, administered to them the oath of allegiance to the United States, and I made them American citizens. To this moment, to this moment, it was the most exciting thing I've ever done in my life. Ceremonies were always moving for me because my mother was an immigrant, my father, the orphan son of immigrants. Neither of them had any education, and they worked at very menial tasks in our society. But, because of the openness of America, because of "Equal Justice Under Law" in America, I sit here today, a United States Senator. And, after every one of these ceremonies, I made it a point to speak to these new Americans. I asked them why they came, how they came, and their stories, each of them, were inspiring.

I think you would be interested and moved by them, given the views you've expressed on this country. And, when I asked them why they came, they said several things, mostly two: The first is, they said, "We came because, here in America, everybody has a chance, opportunity." And, they also said, over and over again, particularly people from totalitarian societies who came here because here in America, you can criticize the government without looking over your shoulder. "Freedom to disagree with the government."

Now, you've addressed several pleas to this Committee, very eloquently, none more eloquent than last Friday, when in response to a question by Representative Cheney, you asked that Congress not cut off aid to the contras "For the love of God and for the love of country." I now address a plea to you. Of all the qualities which the American people find compelling about you, none is more impressing than your obvious deep devotion to this country. Please remember that others share that devotion, and recognize that it is possible for an American to disagree with you on aid to the contras and still love God and still love this country just as much as you do.

Although he's regularly asked to do so, God does not take sides in American politics, and in America disagreement with the policies of the government is not evidence of lack of patriotism. I want to repeat that. IN AMERICA, DISAGREEMENT WITH THE POLICIES OF THE GOVERNMENT IS NOT EVIDENCE OF LACK OF PATRIOTISM. Indeed, it's the very fact that Americans can criticize their government openly and without fear of reprisal that is the essence of our freedom and that will keep us free.

Now, I have one final plea. Debate this issue forcefully and vigorously, as you have and as you surely will, but please do it in a way that respects the patriotism and the motives of those who disagree with you, as you would have them respect yours.

Thank you very much, Colonel. Mr. Chairman, I have no further questions.

CHAIRMAN INOUYE: The session will stand in recess for ten minutes. . . .

SEN. TRIBLE: (Network interruption)—support Ronald Reagan, and I believe in the contra cause. I should note that there's been absolutely no evidence of wrongdoing on the part of the President, and I, like you, believe that the essence of the American experience is the pursuit of freedom at home and around the world. That's why we must oppose the Marxist tyranny in Nicaragua, and that's why we must help young Nicaraguans fight for their freedom as well.

Now, the last week has not been an easy one for any of us. It's been a time of probing questions and honest answers on your part, and you've done well. You've captured the imagination of the American people, and you've done that, I think, because you told the truth, fully and candidly, because you're a man who was obviously doing his duty as he saw it, because you were acting with the knowledge and authority of your superiors. And you've also demonstrated an amazing ability to get results in a city so often tied in knots. I know it's been a difficult time for your family.

But I believe these hearings are necessary. Anyone who values truth, the Constitution, the rule of law, must be troubled by what we've heard over the last 10 weeks, but when public policy is taken private, when government attempts to operate outside of established channels, there are no checks and balances, there's no accounting or oversight, and there's a consequence. People—good people and policy get into big trouble. And that's what we've seen.

President Kennedy used to tell a story that I believe captures the spirit of these hearings. In June of 1780, there was a total eclipse of the sun. At noon it was as dark as at midnight, and in those days, as you know, people attributed this kind of happening to the day of judgment, to the Coming of the Lord. The Connecticut Legislature was meeting in Hartford, and the members were thrown into chaos and there were motions to adjourn. The Speaker of the House, Colonel Davenport, silenced those motions with his gavel, and he spoke these words. He said, "Gentlemen, I don't know if the world's coming to an end or not. If it's not, there's no reason to adjourn, but if it is, I want the Lord to come and see me doing my duty. So therefore, I will entertain a motion that candles be brought into this chamber so we may enlighten this hall of democracy."

Our duty is to light a candle so the American people can see and judge what has gone on. It's not an easy job or a happy one, but it is one that must be done. That obvious problem when public policy goes private is that the distinction between the public good and private ends is often blurred. Private citizens may be motivated by profit and pursue interests that are inconsistent with the goals of the United States. Now, Colonel North, it's clear to me and it's clear to the American people that you're motivated by ideals, by love of country and not pursuit of profit. You've spoken eloquently and powerfully about that before us. But I'm not sure the same thing can be said about everyone involved in your activities. So what I'd like to do with your help is to ask some questions about the financial aspects of the enterprise directed by Mr. Hakim and Mr. Secord. Last Wednesday you testified that you understood Hakim and Secord would be compensated and I quote, "at a just, fair and reasonable compensation." Is that correct?

LT. COL. NORTH: I'll take your word, Senator, that that's what I said when I said it. But that's certainly what I felt and what we had talked to.

SEN. TRIBLE: Now the evidence from Mr. Hakim himself, from his records, establishes that he and Secord amassed over $8.1 million in bank accounts. Did you know those huge sums of money were being socked away?

LT. COL. NORTH: Senator, my recollection is that what I testified to is that I did not know the magnitude of the funds that were remaining in whatever accounts. I didn't know the names or numbers of any but one, and that was the Lake account which I also provided, for example, to the State Department for use by Brunei, and I provided it to representatives of another country for the monies that they were providing to support the resistance. I think I also testified to the effect that I had asked on a number of occasions to General Secord who, after all, was the man that I engaged in this activity at the suggestion of Director Casey and with the approval of my superiors, that I had asked on a number of occasions that General Secord set funds aside for other activities. I testified in Executive Session as to what some of those other activities were. And I have not gone back to say that if I had added up all of those other activities it would have come out to be $20 million that I had asked him to set aside—I don't know what the final tally would be. The important thing is that I did not know that there was that sum remaining. I do not know the purposes for which that sum was set aside. I did not know the accounts or the names or numbers on any of those, and I certainly never considered that a penny of that was mine. And, I have also testified that were I to be the adjudicator of where that money went, after all the bills were paid and all the liabilities were covered, I would sent that money, evey nickel of it, to the Nicaraguan resistance, which was, indeed, the original purpose for setting up all of those non-US government entities.

SEN. TRIBLE: Now, last week when you testified about this huge sum of money, you used the word "shocked" —that you were "indeed shocked." Is that a fair characterization?

LT. COL. NORTH: I was. And, I would again point out, I believe it was under questioning by counsel, I did not know until these hearings began that there was any such sum set aside, but again, I have not communicated with these people for yea these many months. I do not know the purposes for which they had established these accounts or even that the accounts existed.

SEN. TRIBLE: I absolutely believe that, Mr. North. Absolutely, Col. North. Now, let me ask another question. These monies came from several sources. They came from the sale of arms to Iran, and they also came from solicitations from countries and individuals. Is that correct?

LT. COL. NORTH: That's my understanding, yes.

SEN. TRIBLE: Now, is it true then that neither Mr. Hakim or Mr. Secord contributed any capital to this enterprise?

LT. COL. NORTH: I do not know.

SEN. TRIBLE: There's no question in your mind, is it, that the money was to be used for governmental purposes?

540

LT. COL. NORTH: I, I'm gonna beg to differ with that particular description of it.

SEN. TRIBLE: Please.

LT. COL. NORTH: I have said that, when we go all the way back to 1984 when this activity was initiated, that the purpose was for these outside non-US government entities to assist in prosecuting the foreign policy goals of the United States, it was never intended that anybody get rich. It was never intended that anybody do anything with the money other than support those foreign policy goals. Unfortunately, there seems to be an idea that developed as a consequence of my testimony that there was a government within the government, or that there was a CIA within the CIA, or that somehow these monies belonged to the US government. I don't view it that way. I am certainly not a financial expert or a legal authority on those kinds of activities. I saw those foreign entities, those—the network of companies and the like that were set up as being there to support the prosecution of foreign policy goals. It was never envisioned, in my mind, that this would be hidden from the President. I know that there is some debate—apparently raised while I was away this weekend, thankfully, blissfully, unaware of the media coverage, but now apprised of it —that somehow we were going to use these for things the President wouldn't know about. I will tell you that it was always my understanding that it was a short-term project. Not something that was going to go on ad infinitum. And that, partially, is a question that was raised by Representative Jenkins last week. It was a fix for a short-term problem. And I described to you in Executive Session some of the activities that were to be supported by these non-US government monies.

SEN. TRIBLE: I thank you. All my question contemplated was that these monies were to be used to advance the foreign policy goals of the United States?

LT. COL. NORTH: Yes.

SEN. TRIBLE: Thank you. Now, you've talked about some other initiatives that were contemplated. It is my understanding that they were contemplated but not undertaken. Is that true?

LT. COL. NORTH: We actually, as I told this—the committees in Executive Session, we actually started on a number of them. For example, the purchase of the ship was undertaken to pursue a particular activity. So monies were, indeed, expended on that, and the ship was used for a number of different purposes as I indicated the other night. There were also monies set aside, at least to my understanding, monies were set aside for the purchase of a particular weapon system, which—

SEN. TRIBLE: Those monies were not expended, however?

LT. COL. NORTH: I do not believe they were, but I cannot speak with certainty on that.

SEN. TRIBLE: I understand. Now, let's move to a discussion of prices, commissions, and accountability. Did you or General Secord establish the prices for the arms sold to the contras?

LT. COL. NORTH: I established no prices whatsoever. And, as I think I testified and certainly as is well known, it was a very competitive marketplace, if you will, to which the Nicaraguan resistance could turn. The only thing that I did was to intervene at the direction—at the direction—at the suggestion of Director Casey that two particular arms purveyors not be used until the agency was able to determine: one, the source of funding for one of them—I believed I talked to that in Executive Session, and whether or not a certain European who had provided arms was indeed involved in reverse-technology transfer to the East bloc. He asked me to intervene, to keep arms from being purchased from those two individuals, and I did so. I established no prices; I established no levels; I established no amounts, of any kind.

SEN. TRIBLE: And I am not suggesting you did. In fact, the answer to the question is, General Secord did that.

LT. COL. NORTH: Again, I don't know whether General Secord did that. I viewed those transactions as being taking place between General Secord and those with whom he was dealing. I do know that toward the end of the activity in establishing the southern front, that munitions were provided without cost.

SEN. TRIBLE: So—

LT. COL. NORTH: —The stuff that was flown down and air-dropped to the southern front, for example.

SEN. TRIBLE: Well, Albert Hakim has testified before us that it was Secord.

LT. COL. NORTH: I'm not here to—I don't know the substance of his testimony.

SEN. TRIBLE: So, is it fair to say then, Colonel North, that it was Hakim or Secord or someone else, who had the responsibility of determining what was fair and just compensation?

LT. COL. NORTH: Yes.

SEN. TRIBLE: Now, did Mr. Secord or Mr. Hakim ever sit down with you and give you an accounting of their profits?

LT. COL. NORTH: No.

SEN. TRIBLE: Did they ever sit down with the contra leaders, and give them an accounting of their activities?

LT. COL. NORTH: I do not know.

SEN. TRIBLE: So, what you're telling us then, is there really was no financial oversight by you or by anyone else in the United States government?

LT. COL. NORTH: I have given to the committees the records that I maintained—or those that remain anyway —and you also had from my files, a number of KL-43 messages, which refer in gross terms, to funds remaining in various overseas entities. That is about the level that I had specific knowledge on. I did not do an accounting. I didn't hire an accounting firm to do it—I mean, we didn't bring in the GAO, and I'm not trying to be lighthearted about it, it was simply a matter of—things were moving very, very quickly—

SEN. TRIBLE: —Absolutely.—

LT. COL. NORTH: —and that kind of accounting was not done.

SEN. TRIBLE: Obviously, you were a busy man, and you were relying on them to handle these matters. Isn't that correct?

LT. COL. NORTH: That is correct.

SEN. TRIBLE: Now, let me ask you this. Under established channels, when covert operations are undertaken by the CIA or by CIA operatives, isn't there strict financial oversight and accountability?

LT. COL. NORTH: Generally, yes. And I'm not intimately familiar with the comptrollers office at Langley, but it's well enough known, that they do a rigorous accounting of the expenditures of funds in the conduct of a covert operation. I would point out, however, Senator, and I think it's impor-

543

tant that there is still a debate, ongoing, within the Congress and the GAO, and the State Department, over the accounting of $27 million in Nicaraguan humanitarian assistance funds. It has been widely reported in various media accounts, that I was somehow engaged in siphoning money off from those activities. Those reports are untrue. It is a difficult thing to do, and even under the best of circumstances, trying to account for monies like the $27 million, is a difficult task, and I am confident that at the end of all of the review of the $27 million in Nicaraguan humanitarian assistance monies, there will still be people who debate whether or not an accurate or sufficient accounting has been done.

SEN. TRIBLE: Is it fair to say, Col. North, that under normal and established procedures, when covert operations are undertaken by the government, there is always a strict accounting of those activities? And that here, there was not?

LT. COL. NORTH: Given my knowledge, I think that's a fair statement.

SEN. TRIBLE: All right. So now, let's move on and talk for a moment about the relationship between Mr. Hakim and Mr. Secord. Now Col. North, I know you've known Gen. Secord for many years, and you have great respect for him.

LT. COL. NORTH: I'm sorry, Senator?

SEN. TRIBLE: No problem. I know that you've known Gen. Secord for many years, and you have great respect for him. But isn't it true, you really didn't know much about Albert Hakim, and you still don't know much at all about the business relationship between Secord and Hakim?

LT. COL. NORTH: I first met Mr. Hakim, I believe, in February of 1984. I came to recognize that this was a man who certainly wanted to assist the US government, and a restoration of a relationship with his native land. Excuse me—correction. I first met him in February of '86, not '84. I don't know the nature of the financial relationship with Gen. Secord, or business relationship that he's had. And I did not necessarily consider that to be a prerequisite of using him as an interpreter for one of our meetings, or a series of meetings which occurred in Europe; nor did I see it inconsistent that he would be engaged, after I found out about it, in establishing the European entities—and foreign entitites, not all in Europe, but some in Latin America —that supported this initiative.

SEN. TRIBLE: Now, Mr. Secord, in his testimony before us, said the money, the residuals in the accounts, belonged to the enterprise, and that the enterprise was owned by Mr. Hakim. Did you know that?

LT. COL. NORTH: No. But again, what I knew was that a series, a network if you will, of overseas entities had been established to carry out these activities. To the extent practicable, different overseas companies would carry out discreet activities, to avoid the crossover of knowledge between various operations.

And thus, one of the companies would carry out the purchase of land in a Central American country for the purpose of building an airstrip. They would fund for that airstrip, they would conduct the construction and the like; whereas another company would be engaged in, for example, the delivery of munitions. And that network, as I understood it, was basically laid out for these activities by Gen. Secord. And now, obviously, with the assistance of Mr. Hakim. But I did not know the details of that relationship, no.

SEN. TRIBLE: Well, I guess the point that I want to make here is that the money was controlled not by Mr. Secord, a man you knew and trust, but rather by Mr. Hakim, a man that you have admitted you hardly knew. That must come as a surprise.

LT. COL. NORTH: Well, it does. And that's one of the reasons why I said I was shocked at the magnitude of the money remaining in the various accounts. I am not entirely sure that we're all speaking from the same sheet of music. And that's—somewhat tongue-in-cheek the other day—

SEN. TRIBLE: Uh-huh. It's a problem for all of us.

LT. COL. NORTH: —But that has been somewhat serious, that when Mr. Hakim describes profit, and I am talking about what Director Casey referred as "self-sustaining entities." I'm not too sure that those are inconsistent. I look forward to the day when I could actually sit down and talk about where those remaining monies go with the people, whoever they are, that control them.

SEN. TRIBLE: I wish you could spend 10 minutes with Mr. Hakim. I think you could be a great help to the committee.

545

Now, let's talk about the future of these enterprises. Did you and Bill Casey or Admiral Poindexter establish plans for the future in the event that Bill Casey left the CIA or became disabled or died?

LT. COL. NORTH: No.

SEN. TRIBLE: What about your reassignment in the Marine Corps? Were there contingency plans for that?

LT. COL. NORTH: Well, I—I think one of the things that Director Casey was looking to was not something that was going to be sustaining out through the 1990s in these activities, that he was talking about the use of outside entities to support limited foreign policy goals of the government. I described some of those activities to the committees the other evening in the Executive Session. It was not the kind of thing that—that—I don't think—Director Casey had in mind for outliving even his tenure as director of Central Intelligence. Although, as I indicated in my testimony, we never got to that point.

We were never able to—to establish the longer term where is it all going from here. I regarded this as a—as an imaginative solution to some short-term problems. A number of the initiatives that were undertaken, that I briefed the committees on the other night, assumed that these were immediate short-term—once you conducted that activity, you could actually put the company back on the shelf or do away with it, and that's how I saw it being pursued. It was not a matter, as Representative Jenkins and I discussed, I don't think, as a matter of what happens after Bill Casey goes and Ollie North goes who the successor is that would carry those activities out.

SEN. TRIBLE: Well, but that really is an important question, is it not? Marine colonels are reassigned. Directors of the CIA die. Mr. Secord could have suffered a disability or a loss of life. Who really was going to control this operation in the future? Was there any plan in place?

LT. COL. NORTH: We never got to the point where a plan such as that was—was developed.

SEN. TRIBLE: What was going to happen when the Reagan Administration came to an end?

LT. COL. NORTH: Well, I think we all looked to the fact that these operations would simply shut down. I mean, this

546

was not something that would go in per—prep—perpetuity. I got that one out.

SEN. TRIBLE: You weren't going to turn it over to the Democrats then?

LT. COL. NORTH: You said that, Senator; I—

SEN. TRIBLE: That's right, and I did with a smile on my face and that does not deserve an answer, Colonel North.

Now, let's move to another area, if we might. Albert Hakim volunteered in his testimony that he was trying to pass money to you and your family. Earlier, a lawyer named David Lewis called the Committee and volunteered that William Zucker had asked him to find a way to get money to your wife, Betsy. Now at first we didn't follow that up because it was absolutely inconsistent with our image of you. But then, Hakim, a man who says that he loves you, testified that he asked Zucker to try to pass money to you and nothing came of those efforts. And we know that you were not in this for profit, and you've spoken very powerfully and convincingly about that. But my question is this. Doesn't it appear that Mr. Hakim and Zucker were trying to compromise you or set you up to gain influence or leverage?

LT. COL. NORTH: Senator, I did not hear that testimony. And I guess my concern is that this Committee not have any reservations whatsoever. I was unaware of any activities beyond what I described.

SEN. TRIBLE: Absolutely understand that.

LT. COL. NORTH: Number two: Even if that attempt was known to me, and as I described them the other night, there were other attempts at those things, doesn't mean that it works. I don't know the motivation of Mr. Hakim or his lawyer in trying to pursue various initiatives. I do know that having reviewed certain testimony before this Committee, that an indication of calls being made or arrangements being made to meet with my wife after the one meeting that I described to you, and the one telephone call in June, are patently untrue. And thus, the characterization of motivations by Mr. Lewis or others, or events by Mr. Lewis and others, are, to my knowledge and that of my wife, totally untrue. Now, I cannot speak to the motivations of those other people who've described other events.

SEN. TRIBLE: And I appreciate your reluctance to do so.

And the record certainly demonstrates that you acted most appropriately under this situation. However, I ask you those questions because I really can conceive of no other reason for those initiatives. If they were really trying to help you, they would have gone to you directly it seems to me. And they surely would not have volunteered this information as they did. But I thank you for your answer there. We'll just have to sit back and judge as best we can as the pieces of the puzzle come together.

Now, let's talk about profits. There's been testimony that Mr. Hakim and Secord were reaping large profits by marking up the arms being sold to the contras. For example, Albert Hakim has testified before us that during August of 1986, Mr. Secord agreed to a suggestion of Tom Klein's that they maximize the profits from the last sale of arms to the contras. Were you aware of that?

LT. COL. NORTH: No.

SEN. TRIBLE: Now, Hakim has testified from his records that a profit of $861,000 was made on that $2.1 million transaction. Now that's a markup of about 41 percent. Were you aware that that kind of profit was being made?

LT. COL. NORTH: No, I was not.

SEN. TRIBLE: Do you believe that kind of profit is fair or just?

LT. COL. NORTH: Again, I would have to sit down and go over these issues with General Secord, who was my principal contact, and Mr. Hakim. I don't know what their expenses were. I don't know what the activities were that they planned for the use of those monies. But I certainly did not know that there was anything of that magnitude in that transaction.

SEN. TRIBLE: Were you aware that the $861,000 profit was divided equally between Hakim, Secord and Klein?

LT. COL. NORTH: No. As I have testified throughout, I was unaware of the fact that these accounts even existed.

SEN. TRIBLE: Isn't it true that their taking of such outlandish profits is absolutely inconsistent with your goal of helping the contras keep their body and soul together?

LT. COL. NORTH: There's no doubt that if it was done for personal gain, as I indicated in my testimony, that I never set out in any of this activity to make anybody rich. I don't know what was envisioned by those transactions. I did not know of them when they occurred, and I did not know the magnitude of any of the use of those in terms of compensation. The only thing that I specified right out at the very beginning is that it was understood that fair, just and reasonable compensation would be derived by those people involved in the activities. That included the pilots who put themselves at risk and those involved and taken out of their normal discourse of day-to-day events, day-to-day business would in some way be compensated. That was the sole level of my understanding on it.

SEN. TRIBLE: I have no question about your motives here, Colonel North. But it seems very clear to me that this kind of profit—$861,000 from the $2.1 million transaction —cannot be categorized by anyone as fair or just or appropriate. You don't disagree with that?

LT. COL. NORTH: I didn't try to characterize it, Senator.

SEN. TRIBLE: I understand. Now, was anyone in the government of the United States aware of these kinds of profit margins?

LT. COL. NORTH: To my knowledge, no one else was aware of the details of those activities at all.

SEN. TRIBLE: So you would be the only person, and you were not aware?

LT. COL. NORTH: I was not. And I do not know of others who may have been.

SEN. TRIBLE: Now let's move it beyond that and talk about the investment of these funds for private purposes. The testimony also reveals that Mr. Secord and Hakim invested huge sums of your residuals in private business ventures. For example, did they inform you that they had invested $150,000 in Tri-American Arms?

LT. COL. NORTH: I don't think I ever heard of Tri-American Arms until these hearings started.

SEN. TRIBLE: So the answer's no?

LT. COL. NORTH: No.

SEN. TRIBLE: Albert Hakim also testified that another $100,000 of residuals were invested in Washington timberland from which they expected to make millions—his words—and that the residuals were also used as collateral for the purchase price of $1.5 million. Did you know about that?

LT. COL. NORTH: No.

SEN. TRIBLE: Is that an appropriate use of these funds, in your judgment?

LT. COL. NORTH: Again, I don't even know that those are those funds. What I am saying to you, Senator, is that I was totally unaware of these transactions.

SEN. TRIBLE: I understand, and I'm not suggesting you knew about it, the record is very clear. I'm representing to you that the record establishes that that's how the money was used, and I'm asking you, Colonel, is that an appropriate use of those funds?

LT. COL. NORTH: I do not believe that this—these funds, any of them, should be or should have been used to make anybody rich. You're asking me to make judgments on certain transactions, the source of which I have absolutely no knowledge, and I don't think it would be fair for me to characterize anybody's decisions based on lack of that kind of knowledge. What I am saying, and I will repeat it again, I did not engage in this to make anybody—not myself, not General Secord, not Mr. Hakim, or any of their other people, rich in the process, no one.

SEN. TRIBLE: The problem is here they were getting rich, and they were investing huge sums of these monies to advance their own self-interest: the record establishes that, and that's the point of this line of questioning. Certainly these kinds of private investments have no governmental purpose, do they?

LT. COL. NORTH: None that I know of.

SEN. TRIBLE: All right, sir, thank you. Now let's move to another area, Colonel North, and that's one that's of importance to both of us, and that is the democratic resistance in Nicaragua, their fortunes, their hopes, and their future. Is it fair to say that you were doing everything humanly possible to help the contras, the democratic resistance, in their fight for freedom?

LT. COL. NORTH: Senator, without going overboard on the statement, I don't think that there's anyone else in the United States of America that worked as hard as I did to ensure: a) a democratic outcome, and b) the survival of the Nicaraguan resistance from 1984 to 1986.

SEN. TRIBLE: Colonel, there's no question about it. Now, this is a peasant army, is it not?

LT. COL. NORTH: It is indeed a peasant army, but it also

includes people of the middle class, and even the intelligencia, if you will, of Nicaragua. But it is predominantly a campesino army.

SEN. TRIBLE: Colonel, I visited those camps, as you have. I remember walking down the long line of these young Nicaraguans, looking in their faces and every once in a while stopping and asking, "What is your name? Where are you from? Why are you here?" You know the answers were different, and yet the theme was the same. They said, "Well I've left because my family farm was taken away by the Sandinistas." Or they'll say, "My church was closed," or "My priest sent away." Or, "My brother was taken by the Sandinistas and made to serve in the army." And then he said simply, "The Sandinistas haven't given us the freedom they promised."

These are young men who are laying their lives on the line for freedom. And you care about them, I care about them, a lot of people care about them.

I read with special interest one of your PROF notes. It's Exhibit #5, where I think far more eloquently than I, you laid out their needs, and your concerns about their plight. Would you reach for Exhibit #5, and would you read that for me, please.

I have a copy of it here, if it might—if you would accept my representation that that's Exhibit #5, and it is your PROF note, Col. North. I think you will—would you just read it from the start to the finish for me, please? And tell us the date that you wrote that, and perhaps to whom it went, if you can decipher that as well?

LT. COL. NORTH: This appears to be a note from myself to Don Fortier, with copy on to Admiral Poindexter, I believe. The subject is Special Meeting on Central America.

"Will"—that's Wilma Hall, mother of my secretary—"Please pass to Don."—Don Fortier was at the time the principal deputy assistant to the President for national security affairs, who has since died.

"This weekend's trip to Honduras and El Salvador was the most depressing venture in my four years of working the Central American issue. There is great anxiety that the Congress will not act in time to stave

551

off a major defeat for the resistance. This sense exists in the governments of Honduras and El Salvador, but most alarmingly is now evident in the resistance itself. The lack of a viable source of resupply has not only affected combat operations; it is now beginning to affect the political viability of the Unified Nicaraguan Opposition leadership as well.

"Colonel Bermudez in front of the southern front commanders, El Negro and Chamorro, questioned the need for UNO and the drain of scarce resources to support the Atlantic and southern fronts. While he committed to send six to eight thousand troops in in the next few days, he openly admitted in front of ******** that they would have to come back out in 15 to 20 days if there is no resupply.

"As you know, their most pressing need is for anti-aircraft, but the other things are now running short as well. The entire force is back to one meal per day and no more boots, uniforms, packs, ponchos, or weapons are available for the new recruits. New trainees will be turned away, effective today. All hospitalization for wounded in action will cease at the end of the week.

"Troops returning to Nicaragua this week will carry only 70 to 100 rounds of ammunition, instead of the 500 that they had been carrying. No new radio batteries are available, so there is no way to pass commands or intelligence.

"The picture is, in short, very dismal, unless a new source of bridge funding can be identified. While we should not raise specific sources with ******* at all, we need to explore this problem urgently, or there won't be a force to help when the Congress finally acts.

"Warm regards—North"

SEN. TRIBLE: Col. North, on the very day you wrote that note of despair, there was over $4.8 million dollars in the accounts controlled by Mr. Hakim and Mr. Secord. You couldn't have known that, could you?

LT. COL. NORTH: I did not, but as I testified earlier, Senator, I do not know to this day whether or not those funds were set aside for the other activities that I briefed this committee on.

SEN. TRIBLE: How many boots could have been purchased, Colonel? How many lives could have been saved, if just a portion of those monies had been sent to the Nicaraguan resistance?

LT. COL. NORTH: [text missing]—from where they are purchased. Ammunition, as you know from the charts and information you have, varies in cost. The aviation resupply costs considerably. Certainly the more money that was available to the resistance, the better their fortunes would be. There is no doubt about that.

SEN. TRIBLE: Certainly, throughout all this time, a matter of the very highest priority in your mind was helping the contras stay alive to fight their battle.

LT. COL. NORTH: It was.

SEN. TRIBLE: Chairman, I have no more questions for Colonel North. I want to thank you, Colonel, for your testimony. I do believe you testified truthfully and you certainly have helped us put the pieces of this puzzle together. But I would, Mr. Chairman, like to make one personal observation. In the activities of Mr. Hakim and Secord we have seen private interest riding roughshod over public motives. A cause compromised as individuals reaped enormous profits. And in my judgment, the trust of Colonel North betrayed. All this demonstrates to me the sheer folly of conducting the people's business without checks and balances. I thank you, Mr. Chairman, and I'd like to reserve the balance of my time.

CHAIRMAN INOUYE: Thank you very much, Senator Trible. Mr. Hamilton?

CHAIRMAN HAMILTON: We are serving under the 15-minute rule, now. The Chair recognizes the Vice-Chairman of the House Select Committee, Mr. Fascell. (Audio interruption.)

REP. FASCELL: It has been, now, about six months or more before you first appeared before the foreign affairs committee of the House of Representatives, and it is stated that at that time that no one wanted to tell the story more than you did. And we gave you the opportunity then to take advantage of your constitutional rights, which you have every right to do, and in my judgment you should have done. Now, the Congress has provided you this opportunity in the last several days. Your testimony has been remarkable. You, as a colonel in the White House, were largely instrumental in implementing the President's policy. You were exercising executive authority, clearly. You conducted a major covert operation. Ordinarily it would have probably kept the operations division of the CIA pretty busy. You planned and directed major military operations.

Can I get you gentlemen in front of me to move one way and the other way, so the witness can see me, and I can see the witness? Thank you very much.

As I was saying, you planned and directed major military operations, and acquitted yourself in a fashion that would do justice to the Joint Chiefs of Staff. You arranged for the sale of lethal weapons out of the Department of Defense, a matter which is normally undertaken by a whole Division of International Security in the Department of Defense. You conducted secret, sensitive, important diplomatic negotiations, which under normal circumstances would have used up a pretty big chunk of the State Department. Millions of dollars were raised to support and implement the President's policies. Arms were sold. Funds were received from government. Many patriotic private citizens in the United States and elsewhere provided funds. And so, there had to be an effort, some way, to keep track of these millions of dollars, and make sure that in some way they went to serve the President's policy.

In addition to that, there was an enormous effort undertaken, in which you played a very important part, to influence the American people in support of the President's policy, to lobby the Congress, to make sure the votes were there for contra aid. And in the process, Colonel, you probably produced and disposed of more government paper than anybody I ever heard of in my life. And as a matter of fact, I think you ought to be in the Guinness Book of World Records on that score. And I don't say any of this disparagingly.

Now, all of this was done without the slightest knowledge on the part of the Congress. And we wouldn't have known, even today, based on your preference, which as I recall your testimony, because this was a covert operation and should be done that way. And that you were doing everything that

554

was legal in carrying out the President's policy. But if it hadn't been for three events, two of which you had absolutely no control over—one of them was the Hasenfus plane was shot down in the resupply operation. And that was a sad blow, tragedy.

And Casey said, "Well, son," or words to that effect, "you know, this thing's beginning to unravel. We'd better start cleaning things up." And he was so right. And then someone, probably our adversaries, because they had charge of the information, decided to leak a story about the McFarlane trip, and it came out in a Lebanese periodical. And then the unraveling gathered up a lot of steam because every media in the world was then focused on what happened.

The third event was, in my judgment, a very unusual event, Colonel—I was probably as surprised as you were —and that was to hear the Attorney General of the United States get on television and say for the first time, "Well, folks, got to tell you that 30 million dollars"—I believe he said; don't hold me to the exact amount, but it was a lot of money, residuals, funds, whatever—"were diverted or—or used for the contras." Otherwise, nobody would have known about that. And I wondered at the time why that was done. I just couldn't believe it myself.

As a matter of fact, I made a statement at that time, Colonel; I said that it is inconceivable to me that an operation of this magnitude and sensitivity, involving many countries, millions of dollars, very sensitive operations on behalf of the United States, could be laid in the lap of a colonel operating out of phone booth in the White House or that, in some magic way, he got hold of some bad torpedo juice and just started running crazy and running the government on his own. Anybody'd believe that would believe in the tooth fairy. But that's not even a good analogy. The tooth fairy is not bad. I just didn't believe that, and testimony up to this point has strengthened my belief even more.

Now, having all of this and applauding your sterling character and patriotism, which millions of people around the country have done, and properly so, because you've been a very direct, sincere believer and you carried out your orders—you did it in a fashion which people understand, okay? But I keep asking myself, "How come I don't feel good?" And it's not because of anything you've said; it's got nothing to do with your testimony, except in laying out the mosaic of this gigantic jigsaw puzzle, which under ordinary circumstances would—might have taken which were to go to the direct support of the Nicaraguan resistance—

REP. FASCELL: Should go to the off-shore accounts?

LT. COL. NORTH: Should go to the off-shore account. And then, to other activities.

REP. FASCELL: All right. Let's see. I have a couple of others here. Do you recall, just off the top of your head, the last direction you gave Gomez and Miller with regard to the transfer out of the Cayman Island account?

LT. COL. NORTH: I do not recall the last one, sir.

REP. FASCELL: Did you ever ask Roy Godson, who was as I understand it, a special consultant to the NSC, to help the private fundraising efforts in support of the Central American activities?

LT. COL. NORTH: For two specific purposes, both of them nonmilitary, both of which, we ought not to, I don't think, raise in here.

REP. FASCELL: Right, but the point is, you did ask him to do something—

LT. COL. NORTH: He did. I did, and he did.

REP. FASCELL: Did you ever have—do you recall a meeting at the White House with Roy Godson, Terry Sleese and Bud McFarlane?

LT. COL. NORTH: Yes, sir.

REP. FASCELL: And—

LT. COL. NORTH: I don't recall the specific details of the meeting, but—

REP. FASCELL: Yes. They—but it was, in general, about your activities in Central America?

LT. COL. NORTH: It was. But those were nonmilitary, I would point out.

REP. FASCELL: By nonmilitary, you mean it was a different operation, other than the Nicaraguan contras?

LT. COL. NORTH: It was in support of the Nicaraguan resistance. It was nonmilitary—

REP. FASCELL: But it was nonmilitary—

LT. COL. NORTH: —activity in support of—

REP. FASCELL: I got you. Did you, did you authorize Gomez and Miller to deduct about $20,000 for their expenses?

LT. COL. NORTH: I never got into those kinds of details with them. We did discuss that they would derive fair, just, and reasonable compensation for their services. We never talked about specific amounts.

REP. FASCELL: Were you ever—were you aware of the fact that John Donahue contributed $100,000?

LT. COL. NORTH: The name does not ring a bell, Congressman.

REP. FASCELL: It doesn't ring a bell with you?

LT. COL. NORTH: No, sir.

REP. FASCELL: Do you recall any connection with regard to a disbursement to the Heritage Foundation?

LT. COL. NORTH: It's the first I've—I—this is the first I can recall hearing about it.

REP. FASCELL: And therefore, you wouldn't know anything about an award by the Heritage Foundation to a Miller-Gomez operation?

LT. COL. NORTH: I do not recall knowing anything about that. No, sir.

REP. FASCELL: Do you recall John Hertle? Do you know a man named John Hertle?

LT. COL. NORTH: Yes, sir. I do.

REP. FASCELL: Did you meet with him and discuss the Central American effort?

LT. COL. NORTH: Yes, we did.

REP. FASCELL: Do you know whether or not he ever contributed any money?

LT. COL. NORTH: I don't believe he, personally, did. But he did arrange for me to meet with others who, I believe, did so.

REP. FASCELL: Do you recall their names, by any chance?

LT. COL. NORTH: I do not. You're hitting me pretty quick, Mr. Chairman, but I—

REP. FASCELL: Well, I know—but we don't have that information, either.

LT. COL. NORTH: I understand.

REP. FASCELL: We don't have it. So that's—I thought you might. It's pretty tough to remember stuff over a period of five years—I recognize that. Well, let's get to—

LT. COL. NORTH: If I could make—just make one more point on Mr. Hertle—

REP. FASCELL: Certainly.

LT. COL. NORTH: It is my recollection that the meetings he did arrange for me in Philadelphia, I believe—and there may have been another one or two down here—were all, again, for nonmilitary purposes. There were specific activities, I think we have agreed not to raise publicly here—

REP. FASCELL: Right.

LT. COL. NORTH: —that were supported through this.

REP. FASCELL: In other words, it was for the effort, the total effort—

LT. COL. NORTH: Yes, sir.

REP. FASCELL: —but non-military in nature?

LT. COL. NORTH: That's right.

REP. FASCELL: Now, did you authorize Rich Miller, or anyone else for that matter, to draft letters for your signature which were sent to individuals who were helpful?

LT. COL. NORTH: Yes, I did.

REP. FASCELL: And were those letters actually drafted by Rich Miller, and did you authorize him to sign it, or did you sign it?

LT. COL. NORTH: No, I believe I signed out several hundred letters to people who had supported the resistance.

REP. FASCELL: Thank you very much, Colonel, you've been extremely helpful.

LT. COL. NORTH: Thank you, Mr. Chairman.

CHAIRMAN INOUYE: Senator Hatch.

SEN. ORRIN HATCH (R-UT): Thank you, Mr. Chairman. Colonel North, for the past four days, really the fifth day now, I've listened to your testimony. You've sat there at the witness table armed only with that potted plant there at your side, or should I say non-potted plant, I think that would be more accurate. And in some respects from where I sit, you have shed new light on matters that have come before this Committee. You've admitted error, you've accepted some blame, you've provided some helpful explanations of what was going on and why they occurred in the first place. And from what you've said, your motives and your intentions were, it seems to me, from your perspective were always good for our country; were always well-intentioned in the best interests of our country, and I think that's important.

You've helped take this affair, it seems to me, away from the media, some of whom I think have for months tried to make of it something it was not. Now having said that, Colonel North—and I didn't say all of them, I said some of them—now having said that—and they can judge themselves whether they fit in one or the other category, but I think the American people know—now having said that, I don't want to give the impression that I believe that there weren't some mistakes made here, there were.

And I think that trading arms for hostages is wrong, and to the extent that the Iran initiative become strictly an arms for hostages deal, which it was not, but nevertheless has been portrayed by certain people in the media to be, I think that was wrong. I also don't feel that misleading or lying to Congress can ever be condoned; you need to know that. As a general proposition, Colonel North, would you agree, however, that we've got to come up with a workable system where the Executive branch does not feel that it has to mislead the Congress? Do you agree with that?

LT. COL. NORTH: I do.

SEN. HATCH: Okay. What about drug smuggling? There've been a lot of allegations thrown around that the contra resupply operation was involved in cocaine trafficking. A news program over the weekend suggested that Rob Owen, who testified earlier, was involved in drug smuggling. Now is there any truth to that? Can you shed any light for us on that subject?

LT. COL. NORTH: Absolutely false. Mr. Owen is the last person—perhaps right beside me—that would ever be engaged in those kinds of activities. And when Mr. Owen found any information pertaining to the possibility of involvement in drugs, he told me and I would tell the appropriate federal authorities. And there were several of such instances. Absolutely false, Senator.

SEN. HATCH: I believe that. I take exception with something you said in your opening statement, Colonel North. You stressed several times that this Committee's final conclusion would be apt to put the blame on the Executive branch and not be willing—we would not be willing to share some of that blame ourselves. In that regard, Colonel North, I think you are pre-judging us. In my view, thanks in part to your testimony over the past number of days, we may yet stand a chance of understanding the broader foreign policy objectives of the Iran initiative.

I'd like to read something from the infamous diversion memo, which I might add says very little about diversion. It's interesting to me that the foreign policy goals in that memorandum don't get much attention, while the eight lines relating to the diversion have been, it seems to me—they've been dwelled on incessantly. Now, in that memorandum you make the following statement, quote, "The US side made an effort to refocus Iranian attention on the threat posed by the Soviet Union and the need to establish a longer term relationship between our two countries based on more than arms transactions." It was emphasized that the hostage issue was a quote, "hurdle," unquote, "which must be crossed before this improved relationship could prosper," unquote. Now, does that statement accurately reflect the objectives of the arms transaction?

LT. COL. NORTH: It does and I wrote them, sir.

SEN. HATCH: You bet you did. And there hasn't been much said about that. And in a PROF note you sent to Admiral Poindexter dated September 17th, 1986, a half-year later, you wrote that your talks with the Iranians were going well and that quote, "they and we want to move quickly beyond the, quote, 'obstacle,' unquote, of the hostages . . . sincerely believe that we can be instrumental in bringing about an end to the Iran/Iraq war," unquote. Now, Colonel North, if you had achieved that objective alone, the Iran initiative probably would have been considered a great success, would it not have?

LT. COL. NORTH: I'm sure it would have, Senator.

SEN. HATCH: That was quite an initiative. That was quite a desire, right?

LT. COL. NORTH: Yes, it was.

SEN. HATCH: Colonel North, hopefully these hearings can educate the American public of the broad foreign policy goals that were associated with the Iran initiative as stated in your diversion memorandum. In addition to the ones I just referred to was the protection of the northern tier states

560

such as Pakistan, Afghanistan, India—was that part of what you were trying to do?

LT. COL. NORTH: It was.

SEN. HATCH: And keep them supporting the freedom fighters in Afghanistan?

LT. COL. NORTH: Yes, sir. You bet.

SEN. HATCH: And was the protection of the southern tier states such as Israel, Kuwait, Saudi Arabia, Jordan, Egypt —was that part of your goals?

LT. COL. NORTH: It was.

SEN. HATCH: An important part, wasn't it?

LT. COL. NORTH: We thought so.

SEN. HATCH: It could have been disastrous. It still could be disastrous, couldn't it?

LT. COL. NORTH: There's great potential for that, sir.

SEN. HATCH: The part of those goals to wean Iran away from its support of terrorism.

LT. COL. NORTH: It was.

SEN. HATCH: By opening up a second channel to moderates who believed that it was not in Iran's best long-term interest to continue to foster and support terrorism?

LT. COL. NORTH: Yes, and for 18 months it worked, sir.

SEN. HATCH: Was the delivery to the United States of captured Russian military equipment a significant part of this plan and one of the goals?

LT. COL. NORTH: Yes, sir.

SEN. HATCH: Was the lessening of Iranian reliance on the Soviet Union as an arms supplier one of the goals?

LT. COL. NORTH: The Soviet bloc. That's correct, sir.

SEN. HATCH: Was the elimination of the Iranian support for the Sandinistas one of your goals?

LT. COL. NORTH: It was. And we clearly told them that.

SEN. HATCH: And finally, if we could have gotten the hostages out, which unfortunately appears, of course, in the end to have consumed all of these broader foreign policy goals, that still would have been an excellent result, wouldn't it?

LT. COL. NORTH: Yes, sir.

SEN. HATCH: And you would have been really happy about that.

LT. COL. NORTH: I would not have been alone.

561

SEN. HATCH: In the end, you were mainly concerned about that because you were afraid they were going to be killed, isn't that right?

LT. COL. NORTH: Yes, sir.

SEN. HATCH: In fact, there are memoranda that you have brought forth that are part of these stack of documents that are taller than you—

LT. COL. NORTH: Yes, sir.

SEN. HATCH: —that have indicated that, that you were terribly afraid that they might be murdered or killed?

LT. COL. NORTH: Yes, sir.

SEN. HATCH: That's one of the reasons you were so frenetic, isn't it, that you were flying all over the world, running back and forth, working 18–20 hours a day? Isn't that right?

LT. COL. NORTH: We did a lot of travel, Senator.

SEN. HATCH: And you weren't the only one concerned either, were you?

LT. COL. NORTH: No, sir. I don't believe so.

SEN. HATCH: In your view, would these hearings be beneficial if they result in a better understanding by Congress and the American people and the media that sometimes covert operations are necessary and that, if they are to be given a chance to succeed, they have to be kept secret? Would that be a good result of these hearings?

LT. COL. NORTH: It certainly would, Senator.

SEN. HATCH: And do you think these hearings may achieve some success, and I might—I must admit that I may be on a moonshot with this one—do you think these hearings might achieve some success if they result in Congress recognizing that the President needs to be given some latitude to carry out his foreign policy objectives without 535 members of Congress, mini-Secretary of States, second-guessing everything the President's trying to do?

LT. COL. NORTH: Yes, sir.

SEN. HATCH: You believe that, don't you?

LT. COL. NORTH: I do.

SEN. HATCH: I believe that too. I think Congress has been interfering far too much in a reasonable foreign policy, although Congress certainly has a role. You agree with that too, don't you?

LT. COL. NORTH: There is a role, and that is the appropriation of monies to carry out that policy, sir.

SEN. HATCH: Well, and we can look at the policy and determine whether we think it's good or bad, but it shouldn't be a constant micro-managing of the policy, should it?

LT. COL. NORTH: Not at all.

SEN. HATCH: Okay. Do you feel that it would be a good thing if we finally learned the lesson that the leader of the free world—and if we say we're going to—that we're the leader of the free world, and if we—if we say we're going to help a neighbor, such as the freedom fighters in Nicaragua, that we better dig in for the long haul, rather than cutting and running every other year? Do you think that's a good thing?

LT. COL. NORTH: Yes, sir.

SEN. HATCH: Maybe these hearings can get that across too. Do you think?

LT. COL. NORTH: I hope so.

SEN. HATCH: Because that's what you had to face, wasn't it, at the White House? Every time you thought you had things on track, Congress would come up with some other theory or some other different approach, isn't that right?

LT. COL. NORTH: It seemed like an annual affair, sir.

SEN. HATCH: And it not only contradicted what you were trying to do, but it sent different messages to the rest of the world. Is that right?

LT. COL. NORTH: That is correct, sir.

SEN. HATCH: And weren't you afraid that the United States might be considered an unreliable partner in world affairs because of what we were doing up here in the Congress?

LT. COL. NORTH: Yes, sir.

SEN. HATCH: In fact, we are considered an unreliable partner in part by some nations of this world. Is that correct?

LT. COL. NORTH: By many.

SEN. HATCH: And it's precisely because of some of these things. Is that right?

LT. COL. NORTH: Yes, sir.

SEN. HATCH: Now, do you think it would be a good thing

if, as a result of these hearings, we start to provide consistent support to the contras so that they effectively—as the effectively seek to bring about a democratic resolution to the situation in Nicaragua and to ensure that we won't ever have to send our American boys down there, and girls, to fight in that troubled region that's so close to our own borders? Do you think that'd be a good result of these hearings?

LT. COL. NORTH: Yes, sir. It would.

SEN. HATCH: I do too. Now, if we don't support the Nicaraguan democratic resistance and ignore the communist threat that exists right now in Central America, what, in your opinion—what, in your opinion do you think, might happen in the next 20 years in this hemisphere and maybe throughout the world?

LT COL. NORTH: It won't take 20 years, Senator. It will take a whole lot less. The consolidation of the communist regime in Managua will result in the spread of that revolution as they themselves have advocated. You will see democracy perish in the rest of Central America, a flood of refugees crossing the American borders, and potentially, the construction of a Berlin-type wall across along the Rio Grande to keep people out. This country took over a million illegal refugees last year. Just last week we authorized 200,000 Nicaraguans to stay in this country. And that's just the tip of the iceberg. And they are—

SEN. HATCH: They are all going to want to come here, aren't they, if we don't do what's right now.

LT. COL. NORTH: You're talking about something in the neighborhood of 10 million refugees, the potential for drawing down on NATO support in order to defend our own southern border. And ultimately, with the consolidation of communism in Central America, the commitment of American troups, the very thing we sought to prevent.

SEN. HATCH: Well, I don't think we've heard too much about that. I'm glad to hear you articulate some of those things. Do you feel that these hearings may be important if they cause us to finally stand behind the Reagan Doctrine, and give assistance to the freedom fighters in Angola, Cambodia, Afghanistan and elsewhere where people are, really, committed to pushing out the communist aggressors who want to take away their farms and their businesses and, of course, their freedoms.

LT. COL. NORTH: That would be a magnificent outcome, Senator.

SEN. HATCH: If we could. Do you think it would be a good thing if, as a result of these hearings, both ends of Pennsylvania Avenue begin to understand just how counterproductive leaks can be? And how they jeopardize lives and national security? Is that right?

LT. COL. NORTH: It would be, sir.

SEN. HATCH: In fact, one of the points you've made here, one of the reasons that you said you lied, is because you were worried about lives; you were worried about sources and methods and assets and ambassadors and representatives of other nations, and our own people as well. Isn't that part of the problem?

LT. COL. NORTH: Yes, sir.

SEN. HATCH: It is a pretty tough choice, sometimes, between telling the truth if it means the death of some of our most important assets in the world, or if it means the disruption of some of our most important policies in the world. I have to admit that it is a tough choice. I'm not sure that I am Solomonic enough to have made the choice one way or the other. But I still think it is wrong to not tell the truth to Congress. But I understand why you feel the way you did. Do you think it would be a good thing if the next time the Senate Intelligence Committee does a 150-page secret report—such as it did in this very affair, last December, and was voted by the members of the committee not to release—that it not be leaked to the press, and just one segment of the press rather than the whole press? Do you think we ought to—do you think that would be a good thing if we get that across?

LT. COL. NORTH: It would indeed, Senator.

SEN. HATCH: I like that, sir. Do you think it would be a good thing that if as a result of these hearings, if we considered—if we reconsidered the staging of these kinds of public media shows where we disclose in great detail to our international friends and our enemies, our documents, our methods, our secret plans and the details of our own national security?

565

LT. COL. NORTH: I have testified to that end, Senator.

SEN. HATCH: This is what's happening here to a degree.

LT. COL. NORTH: Yes, sir.

SEN. HATCH: And I have to say to you, I think these hearings are very important in spite of that, but I think that's something we have to be concerned about and I agree with you. In that regard, would you agree that if we must ever have these kinds of hearings at all they should not be turned into forums where persons, especially those under investigation by the Independent Counsel are prematurely judged and accused of criminal conduct.

LT. COL. NORTH: It would have been nice, sir.

SEN. HATCH: I saw a lot of premature judging in—in the—the process—in this process, and I kind of resented it then, and I still resent it today. Along these lines a scholar once wrote, "How individuals who have been pilloried by Congressional investigating committees can be guaranteed a fair trial before an unprejudiced jury is hard to see unless the jury be illiterate." Would you agree with that?

LT. COL. NORTH: At the very least, sir.

SEN. HATCH: And would you also agree with another statement by the same author when he states, "If the investigative power of Congress is unlimited, the separation of powers and systems of checks and balances must break down." Is that correct?

LT. COL. NORTH: That was the position I've taken throughout, sir.

SEN. HATCH: Well, these statements were written, by the way, by one Arthur Lawrence Liman in the thesis entitled "Limited Government and Unlimited Investigation." This was in partial fulfillment—I—I know that he's going to appreciate my comments and—before I get through. (Laughter)

LT. COL. NORTH: I thought I had written them, sir.

SEN. HATCH: Well, let me tell you, they were true then and they're true today. It was in partial fulfillment of the requirements for the Bachelor's Degree at the Harvard University, April 2, 1954, shortly after the McCarthy Hearings. And I happ—and I'm personally happy to say that regardless of what others have done here, Arthur Liman has, for the most part, conducted himself in accordance with what he wrote 33 years ago.

Now, let me just say this to you, and Mr. Chairman, I'll finish with these remarks. I've been a little tough on our committee, but I do respect these people up here and I have terrific respect for every member of this—of this panel, and for the attorneys. But I also have a great deal of respect for you. It isn't easy to sit there five days and go through what you've gone through and admit what you've had to admit and express some of the mistakes that have been made. Let me just say this, based upon what I've seen and heard in these hearings, there are mistakes here. To the extent that this was a purely an arms transfer for hostages, I have to disagree with that if that's all that it was. But I think your answers have shown that it's more.

I don't think the NSC should ever operate covert operations. I just don't think they should. And frankly, I don't think we should have had a diversion of funds here, even though I have to confess, I kind of think it's a neat idea, too, to take monies from the Ayatollah and send them over to the freedom fighters in Nicaragua. What a nice use of those funds, except you have to be—I don't think it was right. I think it points out the difficulties—(laughter) it points out the difficulties of the private—it's still a neat idea, I got to admit (chuckle), and I don't care who laughs. And I think you were right, at least, well motivated in your desires to help them. Because we weren't helping them like we should up here. We weren't supporting this policy in our own hemisphere. Fourthly, I think this—these hearings point up the difficulties with privatization of our foreign policy.

I'm not saying you should never do it, but they point up the difficulties of privatization, and last but not least—and let me end with this—I think these hearings should not let the Congress escape. By gosh, I think if there's anything that ought to come out of these hearings, it ought to be that we beat our breasts and act very sanctimonious and act like we just would never have made any of these mistakes when we've never had really the responsibility of day-to-day carrying them out. Now mistakes were made here. I think good people can acknowledge that, and we can all agree, whether we supported the policies or didn't, mistakes have been made. But, by gosh, we don't have to beat our country into submission or people like you just because mistakes have been made. I want you to know that it's hard for us to believe it up here, but Congress makes mistakes too. And it's been making mistakes for most of this Iran/contra and most of the contra affair that we've had and going on in this hemisphere. Now, whether you believe in supporting the contras, we ought to come up with a consistent policy of support and non-support in the Congress. Everybody knows that America stands in a matter of integrity for certain things. Now I'll just be honest with you. Based on what I've heard thus far, with your admission of mistakes, with your admission that some of the things you did you feel are wrong in retrospect—and it's always easier to do these things in retrospect—I don't want you prosecuted. I don't. I don't think many people in America do. And I think there's going to be one lot of hell raised if you are. Now that doesn't mean they won't. It doesn't mean that sticklers in the Mall won't pursue the last pound of flesh. But I tell you—I don't want you prosecuted. Now there may be something in the remaining part of this testimony or these hearings that might change my attitude, but as of right now I don't want that to happen. And I don't think many people who've watched this, whether they believe in what you did or didn't, want that to happen. And I just want to personally tell you I think you've conducted yourself very well here. Now, I want to tell you I appreciate having the benefit of your testimony. Thank you, Mr. Chairman.

LT. COL. NORTH: Thank you, Senator.

CHAIRMAN INOUYE: Mr. Broomfield is recognized.

REP. BROOMFIELD: Thank you, Mr. Chairman. First of all, I want to say at the outset that comments made by Senator Orrin Hatch follow my thinking very closely. But actually, Colonel North, I'm particularly pleased to finally see you before this Committee. For many months I have been urging to do everything we possibly can to give you this opportunity to get your story across, and you certainly have done it and I want to congratulate you on your very impressive handling of the questions that have been directed to you. And I also want to pay tribute to Mr. Sullivan for his excellent handling of some of the difficult questions that you've had to answer. First of all, I've been around quite a few years and I can share the frustrations that you must have had at least the last five years in dealing with a lot of subjects but particularly the one in Central America with

568

the contras. I think we here in Congress are just as much on trial as the administration. I really believe that because for some reason foreign policy seems to have fallen apart. There's a lack of trust both on the part of the administration and on Congress. We've got members that think they should be entitled to all information of what's going on. I think there's areas though that when you're getting into these high-risk areas—I think we've got to have trust among the leadership of Congress and the administration. I can't help but recall when I first came here and that was back in the Eisenhower times, and I remember Sam Rayburn talking about how they went about getting approval for the atom bomb, and this was back in 1942, and what they did then, they called in the leadership of both parties and they agreed that they would put certain amount of money in the defense budget, and this would be used for research and development for the atom bomb. And, no one gave away that information, and by 1945 the bomb was developed and obviously was used during President Truman's time, during the bombing of Hiroshima.

And, I can recall just recently, in the last few years, even with the Reagan administration, and you were there, it was on the question of the bombing of Libya. What did the adminstration do? Well, they called the senior members of Congress to come to the White House before that bombing attack took place. The President was there. The Vice President, all the top cabinet people, Bill Casey was there. And they went over the plans. It was about 3:00 in the afternoon, and we knew at 7:00 that the bombing would take place, and, of course, we were watching our watches as the debate was going on, knowing that the time was getting closer. Of course, one good thing about it, the administration, the President and the rest of them, kept us there.

In other words, they didn't let us get out in the street and let the information out, but nevertheless, the point that I'm getting at—it was that consultation that I think was extremely important, and I think that's where the administration had made the most serious and grevious error in this whole thing, is the fact that we don't have the consultation between Congress and the administration.

Now, I have to say that I agree with some of the members who said they wouldn't support an arms sales to Iran just for the sake of release of the hostages. I think it was a dangerous mission, but I have to say this, that I think had the administration been more forthright, I think things would probably had worked out better. What I'm getting at, that I think in these areas of very high risk, and I certainly agree with Senator Hatch that we shouldn't be carrying on covert activities in the NSC. I think that's another mistake that was made. I think if we don't stick to the normal channels, either through the CIA or State Department, we run into the problem of accountability. But, what I would really like to see—I'd like to see us get back, that when we have these areas where we might call it "supersensitive covert activities," at least the very senior members of Congress on both the House and Senate, would be consulted before such action would take place.

So, you bring Congress in as a full partner in these decisions. That's the area that probably troubles me the most about this entire investigation and what has transpired. Of course, I think there has been mistakes made, and I think it's regrettable, and I agree with Senator Hatch, I don't want to see you go to jail, because I think you're a great patriotic American and I'm proud of what you've tried to do. And this has been a very difficult time.

I would like to ask you, however, a few questions with respect to the Sandinista problem. What are the diplomatic efforts, if any, that the United States could pursue to get the Sandinistas to honor the promise they made, clear back in 1979 to the Organization of American States, to bring democracy and freedom to Nicaragua?

LT. COL. NORTH: Well, you're asking me to take over the role of the Secretary of State, Congressman Broomfield, and I don't want to be accused of exceeding my mandate again. My sense is that the administration has indeed taken a number of steps to offer a diplomatic opening. The Sandinistas have consistently said that what they want is a bilateral treaty or arrangement with the United States, and then they could go about doing what they wanted with their neighbors. We have consistently taken the position that there should be no such bilateral relationship or arrangement, that in fact, Nicaragua's argument is with its own people, and with its neighbors. And if we're going to

570

support the neighbors and the people of Nicaragua in achieving the democratic outcome that we believe we have to have in that part of the world, and their neighbors know that they have to have it too.

REP. BROOMFIELD: We've heard in great deal about it, and I think many of us would agree, that this off-again, on-again policy toward the situation in aid to the contras, have caused great problems. But as you know, this last year, of course, we got $100 million; $70 million for lethal and $30 million for humanitarian aid. But I'm fearful that we got another program coming up very shortly in a few months, and I think the feeling generally right now is that we might go back to what we did before, and that's a cutoff. And this is what disturbed you probably the most, isn't it?

LT. COL. NORTH: It is. And I think that that outcome would be disastrous for this country. I have no doubt—with what Senator Mitchell said, that that is an issue open to political debate, and that good and loyal Americans do disagree. And certainly that does not impugn their patriotism, to have an opinion different than mine. But the fact is that the American people have not been given all of the information on what's going on. It is a very difficult thing to get out the straight story on the Nicaraguan resistance, and the true perversion of the revolution, undertaken by the Sandinistas. Their propaganda machine is very, very effective. And in fact it is difficult to get the straight story out, on either the repression of the Sandinistas, the threat that they pose to their neighbors, or the realities about the Nicaraguan resistance.

And I must tell you that from a personal perspective, I feel a great deal of empathy for the Nicaraguan resistance soldier, the men and women who are the resistance. I came back from a war that we fought in Vietnam to a public that did not understand, in my humble opinion, they had been lied to. The American public did not know what we suffered, what we endured, or what we tried to achieve. And I think the same thing prevails for the Nicaraguan resistance today. They have been maligned, they have been—great mistruths have been told about them, and the Sandinistas have been glorified as land reformers, and labor leaders, and the like. It isn't true, and those facts ought to come out.

571

I can have a great deal of empathy for those soliders in the Nicaraguan resistance who today find themselves cast as misfits, and mercenaries, and in fact, what they are is Nicaraguans who want nothing more than the same kind of liberties that we hold dear in this country, and are fighting for them with an on-again, off-again policy of support from the United States.

And I would tell you, sir, that if we cut them off again, it will have disastrous effect not only for them but for our foreign policy across the board because our ambivalence and lack of will will be evident not only to our adversaries but to our friends.

REP. BROOMFIELD: On the basis that Congress does continue to provide some aid to the contras, will the contras only be able to keep the Sandinistas' regime in Nicaragua from spreading communism into neighbor countries, or will they actually have a chance of bringing about a democratic government in Nicaragua? I think that's a key question a lot of people are asking.

LT. COL. NORTH: I—there is no doubt that a combination of diplomatic, political, economic and military pressure can bring about the kind of democratic outcome this President has advocated since he came into office. And those kinds of things are necessary, and they are necessary in combination; it is not one, or two, but all of those measures that will achieve that kind of any outcome.

REP. BROOMFIELD: I wonder if you could tell us the genesis of this whole question of the diversion, how that came up? How did it—we ever get involved in it? What was the very beginning, in your estimation?

LT. COL. NORTH: Well, I don't call it a diversion—

REP. BROOMFIELD: Well—

LT. COL. NORTH: —I call it use of the residuals or the results of the transactions with the Iranians. The very first mention of use of residuals came from an Israeli official who was meeting with me in early January. The original express purpose was to pay for the replacement of TOW missiles that the Israelis had sent in August/September of 1985, and for the purpose of supporting other operations. The actual proposal to have funds generated by the sale of munitions to Iran, and use funds from that sale to support the Nicaraguan resistance, came in a meeting with Manucher Ghorbanifar in Europe at the end of January 1986.

REP. BROOMFIELD: Why was it necessary, though, to get into other areas of covert activity outside of the normal channels of where the President has to submit a finding, and so forth? Why was that necessary? And you indicated, I think this morning, that it was only a short-term operation. Why was it even a short-term? I mean, what brought that about?

LT. COL. NORTH: Well there was no other source of monies for those activities.

REP. BROOMFIELD: Was it the fact that Congress continued to refuse to supply adequate funding for the CIA operations?

LT. COL. NORTH: Exactly. I mean, Congress had cut off all use of US monies. In fact, before the rigid proscriptions of Boland in October of 1984, the CIA had long before run out of money to support the resistance.

REP. BROOMFIELD: Colonel, based on your experience at the National Security Council, what is your evaluation of the State [Department], in formulating and implementing US foreign policy?

LT. COL. NORTH: There are good and decent men who work hard every single day, to look after the national security of the United States at the State Department, Congressman Broomfield. And you and I know that. And I don't think, given my current status as a lieutenant colonel in the United States Marine Corps, it would be fair for me to go beyond that.

REP. BROOMFIELD: Well, I just want to conclude by saying that I'm very pleased and honored to have you before this Committee. I think you've done so much for our country. I think the American people probably have a better understanding of the problems that this administration has had to face with in the last five and a half years, to have any kind of a consistent foreign policy.

And I think it's been extremely regrettable that we've not had what I call a bipartisan foreign policy. I really, frankly, don't know how we're going to get back on track. But I think it's extremely important that we try to work toward those goals. And I would think that one of the—there are several things that probably this panel will be recommending. And one of them, I hope that we can make sure that in the future, that we don't have any covert activities that at least some of the members, particularly the leadership of Congress, is not informed on. I think it's very important not to work outside of our normal government agencies.

I want to thank the Chairman very much.

CHAIRMAN INOUYE: Thank you very much. Senator Sarbanes.

SEN. PAUL SARBANES (D-MD): Thank you very much, Mr. Chairman. Col. North, first I want to touch very briefly on a subject you've brought up. And I'm—I just want to satisfy my curiosity about it. You mentioned, I think, on some two or three occasions, that one of the things you were working towards in the Iranian initiative was to have a meeting of the Vice President with a very high-ranking Iranian official. Do I recall your testimony correct, in that regard?

LT. COL. NORTH: I did. I believe I also advocated, in another document, that the Secretary of State should meet with a high-ranking Iranian official.

SEN. SARBANES: But here, I think, two or three times, you mention the Vice President. My question is, did you have any reason for thinking the Vice President would be agreeable to such a meeting?

LT. COL. NORTH: No, but I had reason to believe that the Vice President would be a good person to do that. And that was based on my experience with the Vice President in 1983 in El Salvador. And if I may, to answer the question in somewhat more specificity. In December of 1983, I went with the Vice President to El Salvador to address the issue of human rights, democracy, and support for the Salvadoran army in its war against the communist guerrillas in El Salvador. And during that meeting—there were several meetings in San Salvador, one with provisional President Magania, another one with the Defense Minister, Vidas Casanova, and the President. And then, a following meeting with 31 of the field commanders of the Salvadoran army.

And you will recall, Senator Sarbanes, this was a time of great difficulty. And the death squads in Salvador were active, and the United States government, both in the

574

Congress and the executive, was opposed to those activities as being polarizing and destructive of the democratic process that we were trying to further, and that President Magania was committed to. And in that meeting, the Vice President of the United States sat down with a number of men who were violently opposed to our policy, and they were armed men. And his Secret Service detail objected to the meeting, vociferously so, tried to prevent it. And the Vice President himself demanded that the meeting proceed and sat down in a room full of people, many of whom were very, very much opposed to our opposition to the human rights program that we were advocating, the judicial reform programs that we were pushing, and to the democratization process. And the Vice President sat there with those people and told them what must be done in order for the United States to continue its program of security assistance. It is, in my humble opinion, one of the bravest things I've seen for anybody. Certainly, the Vice President of the United States was a man with the kind of courage it took to have that meeting and, I felt, would be the kind of person who would be appropriate for a meeting of high risk with an Iranian official of commensurate rank.

SEN. SARBANES: Well, let me—let me just come back to the question.

LT. COL. NORTH: That was the question.

SEN. SARBANES: Did you—did you discuss the possibility of such a meeting with the Vice President at any point?

LT. COL. NORTH: I do not recall specifically addressing it with him, no. I do recall putting it in memoranda that I sent forward to my superiors.

SEN. SARBANES: And did you discuss it with staff or counselors to the Vice President, the possibility of the Vice President having a meeting with a high-ranking Iranian official as part of this initiative that you were undertaking to make?

LT. COL. NORTH: I want to—I want to just clarify that. I may well have addressed that issue with the Vice President. There was a meeting that was established with the Vice President and an Israeli official during a trip to the Mideast, and I may have briefed the Vice President—I do not recall, Senator—on that proposal.

SEN. SARBANES: Do you recall when that was, approximately?

LT. COL. NORTH: I believe it was in mid-1986. I don't recall—

SEN. SARBANES: All right.

LT. COL. NORTH: —the specific date, but it was in conjunction with a trip the Vice President [was] making. I then was in communication with the Vice President's chief of staff while he was over there, and I believe that the Vice President was given a briefing in general terms about—by the Israeli official, and indeed that issue may have come up. I just don't recall.

SEN. SARBANES: All right. Now—

LT. COL. NORTH: I wouldn't—I—by the way, Senator, I would not have objected at all to—to—to making that suggestion because I felt that the Vice President was as—as I indicated earlier, a man of courage—

SEN. SARBANES: No, no. I—no, I understand your position.

LT. COL. NORTH: —to carry that—

SEN. SARBANES: I understand your position—

LT. COL. NORTH: —proposal forward.

SEN. SARBANES: —and—and the basis for—for—for your making it. I was just interested to what extent the Vice President was involved in this initiative and cognizant of it. Now, let me turn—

LT. COL. NORTH: I have no specific recall of—of the—

SEN. SARBANES: Let me turn now to Exhibit Number 326. If—if counsel—if Mr. Sullivan could provide that to you, I want to ask just a couple of questions about it.—(Long pause as North looks for Exhibit 326.)—

SEN. SARBANES: And the reason I want to focus on it, Colonel, is because it seems to me that one of the questions we have to face in this hearing is how our policy is to be made. We may differ, agree or differ on the substance of what the policy should be, but we need to be clear on how we're going to arrive at that policy, particularly if people hold sharply differing views about what policy should be.

Now, this is a memo. General Singlaub testified to this memo when he was before the committee, and what it does is it sets up a—(long pause)—it sets up a scheme whereby the United States would provide credits and high technology to, say, Country A. Country A would provide advance military weaponry to Country B, and Country B would then provide Soviet-made arms, which apparently are what are used in these around the world on both sides in these battles, to a trading company; and then the trading company could then put the arms out, I take it, anywhere it chose, and it mentions here, as examples, Afghanistan, Angola, Nicaragua, Cambodia, but there could have been others as well, I take it. Are you familiar with this memo?

LT. COL. NORTH: I believe that this may be a copy of a memo that General Se—did you say Secord or Singlaub, sir?

SEN. SARBANES: Singlaub.

LT. COL. NORTH: Okay. That General Singlaub had provided to me. I don't honestly recall when that was.

SEN. SARBANES: Now, he said he discussed it with Director Casey. Were you aware of that?

LT. COL. NORTH: No. I don't believe I was.

SEN. SARBANES: Well, now, this scheme is in many respects comparable to the arrangements that you had worked out with General Secord and Mr. Hakim, although it eliminates the 3-way play amongst the nations, but it nevertheless allows in the end for support to go to these various efforts, and if you'd turn to the third page of the memo, the one headed "Results" —what the results would be of this arrangement. It says:

"The United States then has at its disposal a large and continuous supply of Soviet technology and weapons to channel to freedom fighters worldwide mandating neither the consent or awareness of the Department of State or Congress."

Now, I take it in a sense this is another example of a covert operation capacity that you could take off the shelf that Director Casey made reference to. Do you perceive it the same way? I mean, it's a comparable way—it's an alternative way of accomplishing that purpose.

LT. COL. NORTH: I've just two observations, sir. This is not my document. People sent me many, many documents, and I would not wish to be held responsible for the mail I receive. I have enough trouble accepting responsibility for the mail I sent, and I do not recall that General Singlaub ever discussed this. I do not recall ever discussing this with Director Casey. And while this—in fact, I don't even know that this was indeed found in my office, but I'm sure that there were many, many things that were found in my office that I did not originate nor did I endorse just by virtue of the fact that people sent them to me.

SEN. SARBANES: Well, Colonel, let me say that the Committee—just for the record—the Committee did find this memorandum in your safe.

LT. COL. NORTH: I understand. I'm not denying that. I'm simply saying that it is not a document that I originated, that I solicited, that I encouraged, or that I believe I ever talked to the Director about.

SEN. SARBANES: All right, just for the record, let me just note that General Singlaub stated that he believed that it had been discussed with you—this particular memo. In any event, what this memo outlines is really something comparable to what the Director—I take it you said as early as 1983—Director Casey said to you he wanted to develop an off-the-shelf covert activity capacity, is that correct? As far back as 1983?

LT. COL. NORTH: It is my recollection that was 1984, early 1984.

SEN. SARBANES: And this was the Secord/Hakim operation whereby you'd be able to direct activities—well, let me ask you this question. When you purchased the Aria, purchased the radios for the Carribean countries, under oath of the DEA agents, all of which have been publicly stated on the record—I'm not going to get to the other activities that we're engaged that were discussed in closed session—on whose authority were those things done?

LT. COL. NORTH: Well, the authority of the superiors—my superiors, to whom I sent the memoranda asking for permission to do them.

SEN. SARBANES: And who would that be?

LT. COL. NORTH: Well, as you have seen from the memoranda that I sent forward and cases where I'd in my humble opinion deemed it appropriate that the President be apprised and his authority solicited, I believed I had those authorities. In other cases, I'm not at all certain that it requires the President to make those kinds of decisions.

SEN. SARBANES: Well, now you, you—

LT. COL. NORTH: In every case, I sent memoranda up the line, talked to Director Casey about it and carried out what we all believed to be lawful activities, undertaken by foreign entities in pursuit of the national security goals of the country.

SEN. SARBANES: Oh, I'm not trying to get you in the box about legal or illegal activities. I'm just trying to find out where the authorities were coming from. In effect, to take the operation off the shelf and to do these activities. I mean, clearly, there was no congressional oversight over this because it was kept totally hidden from the Congress, and, in other words, if you decided to ask Hakim and Secord to do something, somewhere in the world with this private network—

LT. COL. NORTH: Just for the record, General Secord was the person I asked.

SEN. SARBANES: Secord? All right.

LT. COL. NORTH: That's correct.

SEN. SARBANES: From whom would you have to get the green light in order to make the request or the direction, I take it, to Secord to move ahead?

LT. COL. NORTH: Well, as I have testified, Senator, I talked to Director Casey and I talked to, before he departed, Admiral—er, General—gracious, they just promoted him—Mr. McFarlane. I talked to Admiral Poindexter, or, and I wrote memoranda to that effect, which you have in stacks.

SEN. SARBANES: Well, Colonel, let me—I just want to close here because my time is almost up. First of all, let me say to you that we appreciate your appearance before the Committee. I want you to know I don't think there's any member of the Committee who not have been touched by your very heartfelt statement about the pressures that were, that you were feeling that were applied and posed upon your family. And I think your concern for their security and your very moving statement in that regard is a matter that touched all of us, and it's regrettable that that problem

579

could not have been addressed in some other way, and that it led to it being dealt with as it was and the difficulties that flowed from that, and the statement you made about the whole letters exchange being a mistake, but we understand the motivation that was behind that.

I want to make this observation. You know, we put up in the Capitol and in other places quotes from our respected leaders to draw lessons and morals from. There's one in the Capitol of the United States quoting Justice Brandeis, and it says, "The greatest dangers to liberty lurk in insidious encroachments, by men of zeal, well meaning, but without understanding." And I think the understanding that Justice Brandeis was talking about, is that in a democracy, reasonable people can differ on the substance of policy. In fact, that's the essence of democracy. And the thing we fault in the totalitarian regimes, which we are opposed, is the fact that they don't permit those differences and establish a system for resolving them peacefully.

It's part of our system that you have a respect and tolerance for the views of others, no matter how deeply your own policy views may be held, and that a civility ought to exist between us. Others may equally hold strong policy views. In fact, they may even agree with your goals, but disagree with the methods or tactics by which you hope to achieve them. Many of the goals about which you have spoken before this Committee, I think are goals that are subscribed to by members of the Committee, and by the American people. Some members agreed with the tactics you wanted to use, others disagreed with it.

In countries where they don't have a process for resolving those sharp differences, they resort to violence. Here we have a constitutional system that established procedures for resolving those differences and we make our policy through an interaction between the Congress and the President. If one loses in that process, the constitutional system guarantees you the right to come back and to seek to make your policy views prevail. We protect people's right to do that. We recognize they may feel deeply, and they may not prevail as the process works. The other side may prevail. But we guarantee their right to come back. But if we have a system where policymakers are seeking to implement their views regardless of the decisions that have been made constitutionally, then we're undermining the integrity of the political process.

That's the concern about these private networks, that go outside of the established way of reaching a decision. Decisions that are very controversial, in which there are very sharp differences. But once we start going down the path of people saying, we're not going to respect that decision that has been made through the constituted channels, we're going to go outside of it, shrouded in secrecy, then, I think, we're facing very deep difficulties. And that's why I simply close by making the point that the depth of one's conviction, and the well-meaning aspect to it, is not enough, in and of itself, that view has to prevail. Now, you've been very persuasive. You've been persuasive in the past as you've dealt with—with the Congress and with others. But the essence of our constitutional system, the thing that makes it respected throughout the world, that commands the allegiance and the support of the American people, is that it gives us a process by which we can resolve these sharply held differences amongst ourselves. And we have to maintain that process. The substantive goal does not justify compromising the means we have put into place. Thank you, Mr. Chairman.

CHAIRMAN INOUYE: The joint hearing will stand in recess until—

REP. CHENEY: Mr. Chairman, Mr. Chairman—

CHAIRMAN INOUYE: Mr. Cheney?

REP. CHENEY: Yes, I would like to take this opportunity, before we adjourn for noon, to express a concern that I have about statements that were made yesterday on the Sunday talk shows that have become headlines overnight. And I refer specifically to the *New York Times,* which talks about a Poindexter memo said to describe informing Reagan, "Diversion of Iran funds in no way asserts Admiral told of plan to use profits for non-contra projects." The *Washington Post,* "No way Reagan told of covert initiative—Poindexter gave briefing on arms profits," or the *Washington Times,* which states, "Committee holds a smoking gun, Chairman reveals."

Mr. Chairman, I've read that memo very carefully this morning and I don't find any reference in there at all to the notion of generating profits from selling arms to Iran, nor do I find any reference to the use of those profits in the memo that allegedly went to the President. I would suggest that the President could have read it from cover to cover and not have had any knowledge of an alleged diversion. And I bring this up, Mr. Chairman, not because I like to dispute the distinguished chairman of the Senate Select Committe, but because I think the significance of these hearings and what it means for all of us and for the reputation of the President of the United States is such that we need to be very, very cautious before we make statements that, in the opinion of this member, Mr. Chairman, aren't justified or supported by the evidence. Thank you.

CHAIRMAN INOUYE: For those who watched "Face the Nation," I'm certain they would have gotten my message that there was this document that indicated, according to our witness, that the Admiral had briefed the President. At least the notation said so. The witness also testified that the covert initiatives set forth in this document were to be financed from the residuals, or the profits, or whatever you call it, of the sale of arms to Iran.

I did not say that the President was briefed. I said, "We will have to ask the Admiral." First, did he or did he not put his initial on this document saying that "I approve the recommendation of Col. North." Second, when he put the word "done," did that mean that the President was briefed? If so, what did you say to the President? Did you tell the President that these initiatives were to be financed? That's why I said that the Admiral, when he sits before us, will have to respond to these questions.

This was put out clearly, yesterday, to make it very clear to the administration that they'll have to answer this. I did not want to suddenly thrust this in their faces. They have now time to come up with a response. I thought I was playing it rather fair with the administration. But it is up to the Admiral, now, to tell us. First, did he brief the President? If so, what did he tell the President?

SEN. MCCLURE: Mr. Chairman—

CHAIRMAN INOUYE: Yes, sir?

SEN. MCCLURE: Mr. Chairman, just that I may understand exactly what this exchange means, I too was disturbed

582

by the headlines that I saw, because I think the implication of the headline and the article was, the President had been briefed with respect to the use of residuals in covert operations, which implies that he knew of the existence of residuals. If I understand you correctly to say now, it's the linkage between the covert operations and the use of residuals that might have been carried forward into that briefing. Do I understand you correctly?

CHAIRMAN INOUYE: Well, I made it—I thought I made it very clear, that we would have to ask the Admiral: "Did you brief the President? If so, what did you tell him?"

SEN. MCCLURE: Well, I think—the reason I asked that question, to follow on Congressman Cheney's question, was that I have read that memorandum very carefully. And there is absolutely no reference to the use of funds in that memorandum.

CHAIRMAN INOUYE: The Senator is absolutely correct.

SEN. MCCLURE: So that before there was any implication that the President was briefed with respect to them, you would have to assume that the President was given information which was not contained in the memorandum.

CHAIRMAN INOUYE: We will have to wait until the Admiral comes before us to find out.

SEN. MCCLURE: So any inference made that the memorandum has within its bounds the information is a false inference, is that correct?

CHAIRMAN INOUYE: We will have to wait until the Admiral comes before us. Senator Rudman?

SEN. RUDMAN: Mr. Chairman, I want to prolong this very briefly. None of us are totally accountable for how things are written or what headlines are written. I think the Congressman from Wyoming and the Senator from Idaho make valid points. I sat next to the Chairman during that entire interview and if anyone wants to read the transcript of the interview, I turned to the Chairman as well as to the host and said, "Of course, the point is what did Admiral Poindexter brief the President about?" The record will show the Chairman agreed with that.

The headline was unfortunate because the document does not disclose that. The Chairman's statement, I think, is accurate. I think some implications were drawn that were not. I thought my comment was important for the very concerns raised here. The Chairman agreed with those. And I would hope that everyone would understand that no member of this Committee, especially the Chairman whom I have appeared with on countless programs, has ever intentionally mischaracterized anything that came before this Committee.

CHAIRMAN INOUYE: I thank you very much. And we will stand in recess until 2:00 P.M.

END OF MORNING SESSION

Afternoon Session—2:05 P.M.

CHAIRMAN INOUYE: The hearing will please come to order.

I hope that this afternoon we will be able to complete the questioning of the witness before us, Colonel North. According to our arrangement and statistics, we have approximately 5 and a half hours remaining in questioning. That is if all of us discipline ourselves and limit our discourses and questions to 15 minutes. I hope we can do that. However, I believe I should observe that, during much of the hearings we've had, at about 4:35–5:30 in the afternoon, members and witnesses tend to get a bit testy. I hope that we will able (sic) to control ourselves, conduct questioning in gentlemanly manner, and close this segment of the interrogation and investigation in a way that we can all be proud of. Please keep in mind that our nation is watching us.

So with that, Chairman Hamilton.

CHAIRMAN HAMILTON: The chair recognizes the distinguished Majority Leader from the House, Mr. Foley.

REP. FOLEY: Thank you, Mr. Chairman.

Good afternoon, Colonel North. Colonel, you've testified, I believe, that from 1981 until your dismissal on November 24th by President Reagan as a staff officer of the National Security Council you did not undertake any activities, except on the express authority or approval of your superiors?

LT. COL. NORTH: That's correct, sir.

REP. FOLEY: Directing your attention to the period of

1984 to 1986, at that time it was either Mr. McFarlane or Vice Admiral Poindexter that was the National Security Adviser. Is that correct?

LT. COL. NORTH: That is correct.

REP. FOLEY: And in all major actitivites that you undertook, is it fair to say that Mr. McFarlane or Vice Admiral Poindexter was your superior?

LT. COL. NORTH: Yes, sir.

REP. FOLEY: And other than that, your superior as a National Security officer would have been the President himself. Is that correct?

LT. COL. NORTH: Well, that is correct, but I happen to believe strongly in the chain of command, and I reported to my superiors. When Don Fortier was alive and was my immediate superior, I reported through him or directly, as instructed, to either Mr. McFarlane or Admiral Poindexter.

REP. FOLEY: So there was a chain of command, but it was, in fairness, a limited one between you and the President?

LT. COL. NORTH: Yes, sir. That's correct.

REP. FOLEY: You received, as you've testified, information from Mr. McFarlane that the President wanted you to keep the contras together, body and soul, as a viable fighting force. Is that true? Is that a correct—my

LT. COL. NORTH: I think that it is—

REP. FOLEY: I believe that my characterization was that the President had clearly stated that that was an objective as a part of a process of bringing out a democratic outcome in Nicaragua. But when you—

LT. COL. NORTH: And Mr. McFarlane tasked me to be the person who was the principle action officer, if you will, in that regard, sir.

REP. FOLEY: Did you understand that that was an instruction which was being passed on directly from the President, or Mr. McFarlane's decision as to who should be the operations officer for that—

LT. COL. NORTH: I clearly understood that to be what the President's desires were, sir.

REP. FOLEY: That he had singled you out, through Mr. McFarlane, for that—

LT. COL. NORTH: No, I don't necessarily mean to infer

that the President said, "Look Bud, I want Ollie to do this and nobody else." I clearly understood that Mr. McFarlane wanted me to be the person who was the point of contact.

REP. FOLEY: When did Mr. McFarlane give you that instruction? Do you recall?

LT. COL. NORTH: No, but my sense would be that it was coming off the conclusion of the National Bipartisan Commission on Central America which had begun in 1983 and by the time that concluded, I, having been the National Security Council's staff representative to that effort, clearly had established—perhaps for the designs of others, I do not know, but—sufficient contacts with the resistance and with the governments in the region who were being helpful to the resistance.

REP. FOLEY: How were these special implementations of this policy conveyed to you. Did Mr. McFarlane task you specifically to do these things—to provide for financial assistance, to provide for military delivery of weapons and—

LT. COL. NORTH: I would guess that the very first requirement was to go down and establish discrete contact with the resistance. and I did so at a period in time when the CIA was still the authorized entity of US government to provide that kind of contact. I was introduced to the leadership of the resistance by the CIA and there came a time when the CIA began to wean itself away as a consequence of reduced funding availability. And by the time the Boland proscriptions of October, the most rigorous of them that we've now come to call, the "Boland Restrictions," came to effect, I was the person left to contact. Mr. McFarlane was the person who turned to me to establish the initial resistance account offshore to which money was sent by a foreign government.

REP. FOLEY: Did—he specifically directed you to do that?

LT. COL. NORTH: Yes, sir.

REP. FOLEY: And that was the so called "Lake Resources account?"

LT. COL. NORTH: No, sir. That was in 1984, I asked the—one of the resistance leaders to establish an offshore account to which money could be provided by a foreign government.

586

REP. FOLEY: Did you specifically direct the establishment of the Lake Resources account?

LT. COL. NORTH: I don't recall saying that, I want it called Lake Resources. As a consequence of the discussions I had with Director Casey, with the concurrence of Mr. McFarlane, the offshore entities, as part of the overseas, non-US government activities were established by General Secord. I don't recall that anybody in the US government mandated that it be called Lake Resources or anything like that.

REP. FOLEY: You've testified from time to time about your relations with Mr. Casey, Director of the Central Intelligence Agency, as a friend and a teacher and so on. Did you ever consider him—yourself, under his direction, as Director of the CIA?

LT. COL. NORTH: No, sir. I did not.

REP. FOLEY: You were never under the authority of, or under the direction of the Central Intelligence Agency—

LT. COL. NORTH: —No, sir.—

REP. FOLEY: —or any of its officers, or the Director?

LT. COL. NORTH: No, sir.

REP. FOLEY: But sometimes you took discussions with Mr. Casey to Mr. McFarlane and recommended policies to him, that had been suggested out of your conversations with Mr. Casey?

LT. COL. NORTH: I did, and with Admiral Poindexter.

REP. FOLEY: And you were always—did you always await their approval before you undertook such actions?

LT. COL. NORTH: It's certainly my recollection that I did. Yes, sir.

REP. FOLEY: Sometimes however, you acted on the basis of not receiving the disapproval, isn't that correct?

LT. COL. NORTH: With the expression that we used, Congressman Foley, was, unless otherwise directed, I will proceed as follows, and I did so.

REP. FOLEY: And there were whatever time lapses you considered to be appropriate before proceeding. Is that correct?

LT. COL. NORTH: Yes, sir.

REP. FOLEY: In any of these activities that we've discussed, the establishment of the accounts, or the solicitations, the development of the resupply activities, providing of arms to the contras, did you ever have any direct confirmation from the President that it was his intention that you carry out these activities?

LT. COL. NORTH: I did not.

REP. FOLEY: So, as far as you knew, the responsibility for discussing these matters with the President and obtaining his authority, was on the shoulders of Mr. McFarlane and Vice Admiral Poindexter. Is that correct?

LT. COL. NORTH: Yes, sir.

REP. FOLEY: And you believed that they had indeed obtained that authority and—for those issues that would have required a Presidential decision?

LT. COL. NORTH: Yes, sir.

REP. FOLEY: The—you testified that Colonel Dutton gave you a photograph album of the resupply effort. Is that correct?

LT. COL. NORTH: Col. Dutton gave me a photo album that contained photographs of the efforts being made to resupply particularly the southern front but also the northern front, and to a certain extent the Atlantic front, and those photos contained—or the album contained photographs, as I recall, taken at several different locations in Central America.

REP. FOLEY: Illustrating the resupply effort?

LT. COL. NORTH: Yes, sir.

REP. FOLEY: And, you told Col. Dutton that you would take it to the top boss, meaning the President?

LT. COL. NORTH: I told him that after he had shown me the photograph album, I told him that I thought that was something that the President ought to see because I believed then, as I believe now, that the President should see the heroism of the young men that we were assisting in this effort.

REP. FOLEY: Do you know, in fact, whether the President ever saw the album or not?

LT. COL. NORTH: I do not know.

REP. FOLEY: You sent it up the line, so to speak, and as far as you know, the President may have seen it or may not, you don't know?

LT. COL. NORTH: I do not know, sir.

REP. FOLEY: Did Admiral Poindexter say anything to you when you gave him the photo album?

LT. COL. NORTH: I don't recall that he did. I probably just

sent it over with a normal package, probably in an envelope—

REP. FOLEY: Do you know whether Admiral Poindexter ever got it? Did you ever discuss it with him?

LT. COL. NORTH: As I recall, it was relatively close to the end of my tenure, and we were very engaged with the Iranian initiative at that time. I don't remember talking to him about it again.

REP. FOLEY: Did the President ever talk to you about the admiral?

LT. COL. NORTH: No, sir.

REP. FOLEY: So, you don't recall any conversation with either Admiral Poindexter or the President about the album?

LT. COL. NORTH: I do not.

REP. FOLEY: But, you told Col. Dutton, while he wouldn't receive a medal for his work, but one day the President would shake his hand and thank him?

LT. COL. NORTH: I told Col. Dutton that I deeply believed, first of all, that he certainly wouldn't receive any medals, but at some point in the future, all going well, the President would receive these people that had worked so hard and so long to support the Nicaraguan resistance. I believe that that's something that could have been arranged, had it been successful.

REP. FOLEY: You assumed that the President knew about the resupply?

LT. COL. NORTH: I'm sorry—?

REP. FOLEY: You assumed the President knew about the resupply then?

LT. COL. NORTH: Well, otherwise I wouldn't have made that kind of a suggestion.

REP. FOLEY: Right. Let me ask you about another matter. You had some contact with David Walker?

LT. COL. NORTH: I did.

REP. FOLEY: Who is David Walker?

LT. COL. NORTH: David Walker is a British subject who runs a business in the Channel Islands.

REP. FOLEY: He's a security specialist?

LT. COL. NORTH: I'm sorry—?

REP. FOLEY: He's an international securities or international specialist in insurgency and military matters?

589

LT. COL. NORTH: The firm that he represents or runs specializes in a number of activities like security assistance and the like, but I'm not—

REP. FOLEY: Did you ever engage him?

LT. COL. NORTH: —entirely certain that we really want to go too far in this discussion in a public session.

REP. FOLEY: The—Mr. Chairman, I believe that there has been a discussion of this matter within the testimony of General Singlaub, who testified as I recall that there was a contact between Colonel North and Mr. Walker for the purpose of carrying on certain activities, covert activities specifically described by him in a general way in Central America. I'll be guided by the Chairman's instruction on this.

LT. COL. NORTH: Well, Mr. Foley, I have no knowledge whatsoever that I can recall about a direct contact between Mr. Walker and General Singlaub. And while I would feel comfortable in discussing this issue in an Executive Session—

REP. FOLEY: No, my question, Colonel—

LT. COL. NORTH: —I don't feel particularly comfortable discussing it in open session. I think there are equities that belong to other governments that are at stake here.

CHAIRMAN INOUYE: May I suggest to my distinguished colleague to set this aside temporarily, and we will check this out with the proper authorities?

REP. FOLEY: I'll do so, Mr. Chairman. The—Mr. McFarlane testified that he told you not to solicit, encourage, or otherwise broker financial contributions to the contras from foreign countries. You testified last week I believe, that you could not recall such an instruction—

LT. COL. NORTH: I don't want to characterize Mr. McFarlane's testimony. When I was asked the question: "Had I been instructed accordingly," I said no. My testimony stands, sir.

REP. FOLEY: So that it's possible that there is a disagreement here between you and Mr. McFarlane, but you—your relationships with Mr. McFarlane were always on a professional basis, you admire him as the National Security Adviser and—

LT. COL. NORTH: I do.

REP. FOLEY: —there's no reason for you to be otherwise

at odds with his testimony except on a fair basis of disagreement. Is that correct?

LT. COL. NORTH: Mr. Foley, I have said numerous times in my testimony that I am not here to impugn the testimony of others, nor do I wish to characterize the testimony of others. I simply will tell you that I do not recall ever being instructed by Mr. McFarlane to the directions that you have just indicated.

REP. FOLEY: Colonel North, you've testified that there was above you the National Security Adviser, and then in effect the President, except for perhaps one other deputy at one time. And that while you were never authorized directly by the President to carry out these activities that you've testified about over these last days, did you always believe that the President knew and approved? Would it trouble you if testimony or information develops that the President did in fact not know about critical National Security Council actions that you assumed to be authorized?

LT. COL. NORTH: Congressman Foley, that question has indeed been asked before and yes, my testimony is on the record. I don't think it's fair to be asked what troubles me and what doesn't. And, as I've already indicated in some respects these hearings trouble me. And, therefore, I have testified as to the facts as I know them and I mean no disrespect whatsoever, sir, but I think my presentation of the facts as they were known to me should stand as it is.

REP. FOLEY: Well, you're familiar with the chain of command as an officer. If you found in the chain of command that it wasn't clear who authorized an order, or how it was generated from higher authority, you'd recognize that as a problem in the chain of command, wouldn't you?

MR. SULLIVAN: Excuse me, sir, that's a hypothetical question. You're just asking him to speculate on what would occur if certain facts were in existence. He's testified to the facts. He's demonstrated—

REP. FOLEY: What I'm asking, Counsel, is if—

MR. SULLIVAN: —no uncertainty about his chain of command. The record is filled with documents which show that he reported to his superiors. And I don't think your question's a fair one, sir.

REP. FOLEY: Well, let me put it this way, Counsel. We are trying to discover what Colonel North's advice is with respect to matters that he had an intimate knowledge about. We're trying to discover what went wrong in our national security planning. The Committee's purpose here is not to bring this important witness before us except to learn how we can correct the mistakes and deficiencies of the past. And he's an able officer who's been at the heart of these decisions and actions. And I think it is fair to ask him if he believes in the chain of command, whether or not we have a possible problem in the National Security Council staffing and operation, if it appears, as it already—I would suggest to you, Counsel—has appeared from the President's own statements that he denies authorizing activities which this officer believed were authorized.

MR. SULLIVAN: Well, sir, I understand what your purpose is. My suggestion is that hypothetical questions are not the way to approach it. The witness is here to provide you the facts. He's given you the facts. You have to draw those conclusions. That's your job.

REP. FOLEY: Well, in other words, I think, Mr. Chairman, we have a suggestion here that while we can take advice from Colonel North in response to questions about what our policy should be in Central America on legal questions of the constitutionality of certain acts and a variety of other things, through the counsel's objections, we're not going to get his answers about what he thinks is an appropriate line of command for national security staff? And it seems to me that that's a little—

MR. SULLIVAN: Sir, we can talk all day about this, Mr. Foley. I'm just asking that you not ask hypothetical questions, as you did, in the form you asked it—

REP. FOLEY: All right—

MR. SULLIVAN: Why don't you try asking another question?

REP. FOLEY: I'll ask this question. You didn't, at any time, receive—

CHAIRMAN INOUYE: Before proceeding—before proceeding, I'd like to advise my distinguished colleague that I've just been told by the Committee counsel that the White House has declassified the David Walker material. So if you wish to use that, proceed, sir.

REP. FOLEY: David Walker is an international arms and security specialist, and is a British subject. Is that right?

LT. COL. NORTH: That is my understanding, yes sir.

REP. FOLEY: Did you authorize, or have any discussions with him regarding activities inside Nicaragua?

LT. COL. NORTH: I did.

REP. FOLEY: Did you authorize him to perform military actions in Nicaragua?

LT. COL. NORTH: I did.

REP. FOLEY: What were those actions?

LT. COL. NORTH: David Walker was involved—his organization, as I understand it—in support of the Nicaraguan resistance, with internal operations in Managua and elsewhere, in an effort to improve the perception that the Nicaraguan resistance could operate anywhere that it so desired.

REP. FOLEY: It involved so-called policies of intimidation, is that what we're talking about?

LT. COL. NORTH: No. Those were other activities—

REP. FOLEY: Other activities—

LT. COL. NORTH: —that we talked about.

REP. FOLEY: We're talking about military actions, attacks on military aircraft, of the—

LT. COL. NORTH: Yes, sir.

REP. FOLEY: —Sandinista government?

LT. COL. NORTH: Yes.

REP. FOLEY: Did you directly authorize that?

LT. COL. NORTH: I don't directly—I didn't directly authorize anything. I encouraged Mr. Walker to be in touch with the people who could benefit from that—

REP. FOLEY: Did you report—

LT. COL. NORTH: —the expertise that he had.

REP. FOLEY: Did you report that recommendation to Admiral Poindexter?

LT. COL. NORTH: I did.

REP. FOLEY: Did he approve of it?

LT. COL. NORTH: I reported what I thought was a good idea for certain expertise that the Nicaraguan resistance did not have, as a consequence of insufficient training, insufficient operational capability—

REP. FOLEY: Did he ever tell you he approved that?

LT. COL. NORTH: He never told me not to.

REP. FOLEY: He didn't tell you he disapproved?

LT. COL. NORTH: That's correct.

REP. FOLEY: Do you know if the President was ever informed of this?

LT. COL. NORTH: I do not know, sir.

REP. FOLEY: Col. North, do you believe that the President knew of the diversion of funds, or the residuals as you call them, from the Iranian arms sales to the President—to the—to the contras? You testified that you assumed that that was true, but you were told it was not true by Vice Admiral Poindexter and the President. Is that right?

LT. COL. NORTH: That is correct, sir.

REP. FOLEY: And yet, at the time you were doing it, you thought it was authorized?

LT. COL. NORTH: I did.

REP. FOLEY: And it apparently was not authorized?

LT. COL. NORTH: The President of the United States told me so himself. The National Security Adviser told me so himself. I have no reason to disbelieve either one of them, sir.

REP. FOLEY: Do you think it is appropriate and proper to carry on an activity if the President does not authorize that activity and that's a major national security undertaking?

LT. COL. NORTH: Congressman Foley, I have, going on five days now, testified to the effect that I believed that the President was aware. I fully reported my activities, sought approval from my superiors. I believe that there are certain circumstances in which my superiors could authorize activities, and they did so.

REP. FOLEY: Do you believe that Vice Admiral Poindexter as your superior, or Mr. McFarlane when he was the National Security Council Adviser as your superior, has the right to make these decisions in the absence of presidential authority?

LT. COL. NORTH: Mr. Foley, I have consistently told you that I assumed that when it was appropriate, they sought the authorities that I had recommended, and that they had obtained them. And therefore, I proceeded.

REP. FOLEY: Mr. Chairman, I'll conclude my time here. Because the counsel's advice to his client discourages his giving us advice, we are left with the decision to make, and the American people are left with the decision to make, as to whether or not critical decisions of national security policy of this country involving far-reaching impacts on our foreign policy and defense policy, can be properly undertaken in the National Security Council by a lieutenant colonel acting in response to the orders of or the acquiescence of Mr. McFarlane or Vice Admiral Poindexter and in the absence of presidential authority. In a few days, Vice Admiral Poindexter will be sitting in that seat and we'll have to ask this question to him. But, I think we're left with a disturbing problem that while every single matter of advice as being given by this officer on foreign policy, on national security policy, on his reactions to legal matters —what he knows most about—the internal activities of the National Security Council and his role with respect to his superiors, he will not on the advice of counsel give us his evaluation of whether there is not a deep deflect and flaw in that policy apparatus if in fact the President did not know and these policies were carried on by his subordinates without his authority.

LT. COL. NORTH: Mr. Chairman, may I respond?

CHAIRMAN INOUYE: Please do.

LT. COL. NORTH: Mr. Foley, what I deeply believe is that it is up to the executive, and in this case, the President of the United States himself, to make whatever changes he deems appropriate in the functioning of his staff. I do not believe then—I did not believe then and I do not believe now that it is within the purview of the Legislative branch of our government to mandate those kinds of changes, that if the President sees fit to make changes in the order of his—of his staff, the structure of his staff, the activities of his staff, then it is within his purview to do so.

REP. FOLEY: I would remind you, Colonel, that the National Security Council itself and the staff that served it was created by law, by statute, not just by the President, but by the Congress.

Thank you, Mr. Chairman.

CHAIRMAN INOUYE: All right. Thank you very much.

Senator Cohen.

SEN. COHEN: Thank you, Mr. Chairman.

SEN. COHEN: Colonel North?

LT. COL. NORTH: Sir.

SEN. COHEN: Colonel North, there—there are a number of items that have been left a bit unresolved in my mind. I'd like to touch upon them quickly if I could. Mr. Felix

Rodriguez, also known as Max Gomez, testified before the Committee at one point you and he were together and looked up at a television screen and you said, "You see those guys up there?"—Meaning members of Congress —"They're out to get me, but they're not going to get me because"—words to the effect—"the old man loves me." I was wondering who the old man was.

LT. COL. NORTH: I have absolutely no recall whatsoever of that conversation, Senator.

SEN. COHEN: Second question would be—

LT. COL. NORTH: I don't believe it ever happened.

SEN. COHEN: All right. The second question: Senator Mitchell mentioned the *Washingtonian* Magazine, which is a fairly lengthy piece, and I think you indicated you don't have the time and did not read that article.

LT. COL. NORTH: I read the captions on one photograph that were so erroneous as to be unbelievable, and that's where I stopped.

SEN. COHEN: I just wanted to clarify that. At—at one point in the article itself it indicated that you had stated that you had had direct access to the President on at least one occasion without logging in consistant with the recording keeping. That's false?

LT. COL. NORTH: I never made any surreptitious visits to the President, sir.

SEN. COHEN: And also *Time* Magazine, again, many of us have been victimized by having anonymous sources quoted, and I'd like to just get your reaction for the record. But according to *Time* last week, it said that someone who was associated with you on one occasion you held up a copy of the Boland law and said, "This is the—the law I'm violating and I could go to jail." And I think from your testimony yesterday or the day before, you said that's false.

LT. COL. NORTH: It's hogwash, sir.

SEN. COHEN: Did you ever have occasion to call the President of Costa Rica to threaten to cut off foreign assistance in the event that he held a press conference revealing the airstrip in Costa Rica?

LT. COL. NORTH: I did not make the call. The PROFs note to which you refer was specifically cast the way it was to protect the two party—the other two parties engaged.

SEN. COHEN: So you never made the call yourself?

LT. COL. NORTH: I did not.

SEN. COHEN: I think you indicated earlier today, in the past three or four days, that you were prepared to take the hit, so to speak, from the time it started to come unraveled, I think, on November 21st, when the—the activity started in your office in terms of the increased shredding. And you prepared to take the fall in terms of any political damage, but that once on November 25th, I believe that's Tuesday, the Attorney General announced that a independent counsel was going to be appointed and target—target you, that you changed your mind at that point; you no longer were going to be the fall guy for the administration. Now, at that time—

LT. COL. NORTH: Can I clarify—

SEN. COHEN: Is that correct?

LT. COL. NORTH: Well, I—first of all, the—the concept of a person—a person who would be held responsible and take the political spear, if you will—

SEN. COHEN: Right—that's right.

LT. COL. NORTH: —began way back in 1984. On November 25 of 1986 I recognized for the very first time that someone really did consider this—all of what I had done or at least the Iranian activities in which I had been engaged, to be some kind of a criminal act. And I, at that point, my perspective changed considerably.

SEN. COHEN: Your mind—your mind set I think you used the phrase, changed considerably, as it should. Now after that disclosure, you went back to your office on that day and met your secretary at the office and I think you were with your prior attorney, Mr. Green, is that correct?

LT. COL. NORTH: That is correct.

SEN. COHEN: And certain documents were taken out of the office at that point.

LT. COL. NORTH: Alright, I want to clarify the record on that. I had already, after the press conference, I removed documents from the White House, some of which I have just given to the Committee in the last few days, and I subsequently removed documents later on in the evening when I returned to the White House.

SEN. COHEN: Oh, you mean those documents that were taken out at that time, that's been testified to by Ms. Hall, those documents.

LT. COL. NORTH: You talking about the—later in the evening.

SEN. COHEN: The ones that were taken out in their clothing.

LT. COL. NORTH: Yes.

SEN. COHEN: And perhaps I might just get the advice of counsel on this. Could you tell me what documents they were? What were the documents that were taken out or smuggled out that afternoon? And maybe counsel could advise me or the Committee in terms of whether he would be able to respond to that.

MR. SULLIVAN: No, sir. I'm not in a position of answering that kind of factual question.

SEN. COHEN: Well, I asked only to find out whether or not that information or those documents have been returned to the committee or to the NSC, I believe there is some indication that documents were, in fact, returned at a subsequent time. And I was inquiring as to whether those were the documents returned?

MR. SULLIVAN: My letter of December 2, 1986 indicates that documents were returned at that time. The documents which you have that bear the law firm's number stamp in the bottom right hand portion of the documents—of the documents that were returned.

SEN. COHEN: Could I inquire as to whether those documents were for the purpose of either protecting the initiative or protecting yourself in terms of showing that you had higher authority at that point?

LT. COL. NORTH: The original intent of gathering those documents was to destroy them. When I heard the announcement at noon, I removed some of those 168 pages of documents and the remainder of them are the ones Miss Hall removed from the office later that evening. And they were all returned to the White House.

SEN. COHEN: Col. North, as I at least understand this case, and I've been listening to evidence since last November and December, I come away with a picture that—that you were charged among many other things, that you had to do with running two essential railroads, as I've described it. Number one, you were charged with getting arms to Iranians to further relations with the Iranians and hopefully to get our hostages out. And the second railroad that you were in charge of, is keeping the heart and soul alive, getting money and/or munitions to the contras. And as it turned out, you've had quite heroic undertakings being engineer, conductor, perhaps even the fireman on both of those railroads. But at some point in time, namely between December and January, those two railroads that were running parallel, started to merge. And they merged in the beginning of January of 1986 when you were approached by—I believe Mr. Nir, who suggested that perhaps you could combine the two efforts and accomplish the killing of two or three birds with one stone, and then Mr. Ghorbanifar elaborated specifically with reference to giving aid to the contras.

And I think you indicated that you thought it was a neat idea—some members of the Committee do as well—that Bill Casey was enthusiastic, that Admiral Poindexter approved, and that you operated on the assumption that the President himself approved. I think that's clear from the evidence. And I must say, that that notion has some rather surface appeal, the notion of twisting the tail of the Ayatollah, in that fashion. But it seemed to me, there were some other considerations, and I was wondering if they were taken into account.

You indicated that the Iranians at that time, were very distrustful of—about everybody. I think you characterized them as being unsophisticated, they were angry at being scammed—I think is your word—by the Israelis back in November of '85. They were sort of on the ragged edge of rationality. They could kill the hostages at any time, just by giving the word to their Lebanese captors. But in spite of this, we agreed to a program, whereby we inflated the cost of those munitions 300 or 400 percent. And then we're going to use that residual margin for the contras and other special programs. And the Iranians find out at some point that they were being gouged, and they complained rather bitterly about it, and then we were left with the only alternative, of coming up with some phony price lists, rather than try to reduce the price.

And it occurs to me, that—didn't this run the very risk, at the time when the Iranians were so sensitive about being gouged, and taken advantage of, and lied to by a host of people—at that very time, that we would risk the lives of the hostages that you were very passionately concerned about, as evident from the record—by combining these two covert programs in that fashion?

LT. COL. NORTH: It did, and we discussed that at length, Director Casey and I. And I recall at least one occasion where the Admiral and I discussed it. The fact is, that we knew that the Iranians would pay even more than we were charging from intelligence that we had gathered. We knew that during the first channel, for example, that Mr. Ghorbanifar had a little frolic and diversion of his own going on in which he had pocketed at least some for himself, if not for others, a considerable sum. And that even the prices we charged, he further inflated. And so, we judged that risk to be minimum, given that they would basically pay whatever they could to get these items or weapons from the source that—whatever source they could.

SEN. COHEN: I'd like to clear up one other item. The money that was generated by the sales of the weapons to the Iranians, they were to be used for the contras and other special purposes. And I think you've indicated very clearly that you had general control over the disposition of those funds. In other words, you could tell Mr. Secord, General Secord, Albert Hakim, so much roughly so much for this program and so much for another—that you had the residual authority at least to control those funds. Did you indicate that yesterday?

LT. COL. NORTH: Well, I don't like to use the word control because I never felt that I actually controlled a nickel of the funds. I did talk not to Mr. Hakim but to General Secord about the fact that "Look, we need some money for this." General Secord would frequently point out to me, "You've got to stop coming up with these unforeseen contingency requirements if we're going to run this—keep the Nicaraguan resistance alive, continue the Iranian initiative and still do these other things that you've come up with on very short notice."

SEN. COHEN: But there's no doubt in your mind that had you directed that amount of money, a certain amount that had to go to the contras, he would have agreed with that?

LT. COL. NORTH: Well, again, I don't think it's right to say directed. There were frequently times when General Secord would point out that my expectations were unreasonably high and that I should be more considerate of the fact that there were other expenses engaged in this effort.

SEN. COHEN: There's another point that was made this morning I'd like to at least offer a couple of observations about. And that is, there are many covert actions that are carried out by this administration, past administrations we would believe, future administrations as well. And you would agree, would you not, Colonel, that they are all life-threatening, life-endangered situations?

LT. COL. NORTH: Yes.

SEN. COHEN: And to my knowledge—and I've served on the Intelligence Committee for going on six years now—I can think of only one or two occasions in which the Administration has not notified the Congress about those covert operations, and you would agree with that statement, would you not?

LT. COL. NORTH: Yes, I would.

SEN. COHEN: For the most part, as a general rule, and I've found maybe with one or two exceptions, notice has been given even when lives were at stake in those particular operations, correct?

LT. COL. NORTH: That's correct.

SEN. COHEN: And there were larger sums of money in those particular covert operations even than what we're dealing with with the contras and certainly the sales of weapons to the Iranians?

LT. COL. NORTH: Absolutely.

SEN. COHEN: So the notion that somehow when lives are at stake Congress cannot and has not been trusted is not the correct perception.

LT. COL. NORTH: I did not try to leave that—

SEN. COHEN: No—

LT. COL. NORTH: —perception, Senator.

SEN. COHEN: Well, I wanted to make it clear because I think that we have to analyze or at least ask ourselves why was this case so different. Why in all the other cases that we were aware of with the possible exception of one or two cases would the administration, knowing that lives were at stake, nonetheless comply with the law and notify in a timely fashion, but not here? And I'll offer just a couple of observations myself. And number one is that this case was different because there was a law on the books that prohibited the sale of weapons to those countries who sponsor or support terrorism, and, of course, Iran was listed, if not at the top then very near the top of that particular list. Secondly, I think, what distinguished this covert action from all of the others is that the administration was deeply divided within itself, that we had the Secretary of State who was fundamentally opposed, if we can believe his statements, and I believe he's going to have an opportunity to testify to this; Secretary Weinberger was opposed; Bud McFarlane, when he came back from London December of 1985, was opposed to going forward; John McMahon, the deputy director, was opposed to going forward.

So we had some rather deep division within the administration itself, and I think it's fair to say under those circumstances, the last thing the administration wanted at that time was to risk coming to Congress to start a debate about the wisdom over a program which was being rather heatedly debated within itself, but I don't think that the American people should be left with the perception that either the administration doesn't notify Congress, does not trust Congress when lives are at stake, because I think the record is rather clear that they have had a long history of trusting us with very serious covert operations, and those secrets have, in fact, been maintained.

Another question that's been raised is why do we have these hearings. I've been reading many articles and watching many programs about whether or not these hearings should have been conducted in the first place, but even in the *New York Times* an article appeared on Sunday. A very gifted writer thought that perhaps they should be conducted, if at all, in secret, and I'd like to say, Col. North, that I think that that would have been a mistake. I think that you have done an enormous amount of good for yourself as well as for the Committee and for the country, and I think, had these hearings not been public, the millions of people who are now watching, here and across the globe, would not have had the opportunity to hear your statement about why you did what you did, under what circumstances you conducted yourself, and the rationale that moved you, and I think that has been of enormous benefit to you and I would suggest to the Committee and to the country.

I'm also familiar with another Elliott. You were asked

about an Elliott the other day. There's another one that I'm familiar with who said that there should be a sudden illumination, that we had the experience but missed the meaning, and I think I'd like to comment just about having the experience and not missing the meaning, because long after the sheer force of your personality has faded from this room, and that may be a very long time indeed, and long after these cameras that are here today are clicked off, I think the American people are going to be left to deal with the policy implications of what has occurred and what's been said in this room.

Number one, and this is somewhat disturbing to me, but we'll have to resolve this as a committee or committees in the Congress and in the country,—we'll have to determine whether any administration can avoid complying with an established law by "going black," as it's been said, or taking it covert. And, then once having decided to take a program covert, whether notice can be withheld by a President in his sole discretion until such time as he decides, or she decides that the action is completed, which could be days, it could be weeks, it could be months, or in this case even, possibly, years. Number two, we're going to have to decide whether, even in covert actions, deception should be practiced upon Congress by deletion, or official documents reduced to confetti, while false statements are given to public officials. I think the answer is quite clear on that. Number three, whether those in the Executive branch may authorize the covert sale of US assets, inflate the prices to be paid, and then fund programs that were either not known or authorized by Congress, and in fact, maybe even rejected by Congress. Number four, whether it is appropriate to use private entrepreneurs to carry out covert objectives without specific and very rigid guidelines to make sure that profit motives don't contradict or corrode the public purpose.

Number five, whether it is a tolerable practice to authorize a covert solicitation of foreign countries to pay for programs either not authorized by Congress or rejected by Congress. And here, I should point out, the record is rather clear that once the discussion started about going to certain countries to solicit funds, it was made clear that certain countries should be stricken from the list because the price would be too high. And secondly, when Elliott Abrams went

603

to a representative from the country of Brunei, he also indicated one of the first questions asked by that representative was, "What's in it for us?" So I think we have to keep that in mind.

Final point would be, whether Congress should adopt policies that deal as severely with members of Congress who reveal our nation's secrets as they would with those who would lie about them. And that, I think, calls for a resounding yes by members of this committee and this Congress. We must deal as severely with ourselves as we would with those who would lie to cover up any covert activity.

And finally, I want to just recall the words of General Singlaub. I know that he is somebody that you admire. He has appeared before this Committee. I think we're all satisfied at his dedication and patriotism, and he retired from the Army because he was upset. He was upset because President Carter had declared a unilateral withdrawal of troops in South Korea. Now, a number of us were also upset about it. I recall that Senator Nunn, myself and several others who went to South Korea—we met with our troops, we met with the leadership of South Korea, we came back, we went to the White House, we sat down with President Carter and we pleaded with him not to carry forward that plan to unilaterally withdraw troops from South Korea. And, in some small measure, perhaps we were successful because he withdrew that plan.

But General Singlaub didn't have that option. He was faced with the prospect of having criticized the Commander and Chief and he couldn't do that and remain in uniform, so he resigned. After his retirement he said the following: he said, "This administration doesn't want to hear anything that is contrary to decisions they've already made." He said, "That's a bad thing. It's the first symptom of a totalitarian regime when you start rejecting any legitimate criticism, any advice from the loyal opposition."

Well, if General Singlaub is right then we have to ask what it means to reject not the voice of the loyal opposition but the voice of the majority in Congress and the country. Because I think that has been cleared by—on the part of a number of us. A democracy demands not only that the rights of the minority be protected, but that the rules of the majority be respected. And that's true even if you and I believe the majority is wrong. We have to respect the rule of law until we can change the law itself. Because otherwise, the rule of law will be reduced to the law of rule. And I think that is one of the central lessons of this hearing, and I thank you very much for your testimony.

CHAIRMAN HAMILTON: The Chair recognizes Mr. Hyde.

REP. HENRY HYDE (R-IL): Thank you, Mr. Chairman. Colonel North, I would like to direct your attention to an exhibit on the wall here, one that you had seen before from that other vantage point, it's the first one. It's entitled Public Law 98–473, October 12, 1984, it's the Boland Amendment, one of the five versions that was in effect then. And at the bottom of that exhibit is the signature of Thomas P. O'Neill, Speaker of the House; Strom Thurmond, President Pro Tempore of the Senate; and the President of the United States, Ronald Reagan. Do you see that up there?

LT. COL. NORTH: I do, sir.

REP. HYDE: Now that was presented to you the other day to make a point, and the point was that the President signed the Boland Amendment, that it is the law, and the President signed it. And of course, if the President signs it, why who are we not to observe it, because it's a law?

Now I was taken aback when I saw that because the purpose, it seemed to me, was to convey the impression that the President was sitting at his desk and someone put the Boland Amendment in front of him and he said, "My god, give me my pen, I want to sign the Boland Amendment!" (Laughter.) Because that's a phony, that's a fabrication, that's contrived. The Boland Amendment is a couple of pages in this (holds up documents)—this is the way it appeared to the President. It was brought to him 14 days—12 days after the fiscal year was over, the operations of government would have to close down if he didn't sign this; there were military appropriations, Social Security money, the Department of Interior, the Navy would have to bring the ships back to the dock and say to the sailors, "Hitchhike home, we have no money." (Laughter.) We have no money, so we have to sign, Mr. President, you've got to sign this.

So what the staff did—and I might suggest if I tried this in a municipal court in Chicago, phonying up an exhibit to make a point that was half true—I'd be held in contempt.

But of course, we're in a hurry and we got to get there quickly, so we contrived and fabricated that to show the President signed it. Now I stipulate it is the law; the President did sign this (holding up documents)—and, by the way, here's his signature, it's the back page—

LT. COL. NORTH: I saw one.

REP. HYDE: —the back page, yeah. (Laughter.) And the President had to sign it because that's the way we legislate around here. The only thing we're here for largely is to spend the taxpayers' money; collect it and spend it. And do you know how we do it? At midnight after the fiscal year is over when there's no time to debate or to understand, and we pass this massive glob of legislation, where I challenge anybody in the building to know what's in all of it.

I'm sure the Chairman of the Armed Services knows what's in his chapter, and the Judiciary knows what's in his chapter. But nobody, not even the staff, understands what's in here. And we—we vote for it because we've got to be responsible. But I don't think we needed that shortcut. It seemed to me it was a little deceptive. And I just want to, for my—for myself, nobody else—apologize, that this Committee, you know, used a little deception on you.

I won't ask that this be put in the record, Mr. Chairman —(Laughter). That—that would be overreaching, so I won't do that.

Now, there's another exhibit up there, Col. North. It's called—well, I call it the Hostage Rescue Act. It's right over there. And it's been the law since 1868. And under that—by the way, it isn't just an old, musty law in the parchments in the archives. This law was cited by President Carter, January 19th, 1981, when he was trying to get hostages out. And incidentally, promised to send $150 million worth of armaments, aircraft spare parts, if we could get our hostages out.

So—weapons for hostages is not unique with this administration. But in any event, he cited that law. And it seems to me correctly that under that law, if you assume that the Hezbollah is under the influence of Iran—and obviously, you did, you did and the NSC did—because you were dealing with Iran to free the hostages.

But under that law, it seems to me you don't need findings, you don't need LOAs. You don't need anything

606

except the President's determination to get the hostages out. Now, the one thing he can't do is make war. And he does have to report to Congress, as soon as practicable. But I assume that was when the hostages were released.

But in any event, since we are so punctilious on the law, I think—we keep missing that, so much. And I just keep bringing it back, to call your attention to it.

Now, we've heard that a free nation cannot operate in a shroud of secrecy. That is one of the great testaments that we've learned from these hearings. A little bicentennial note again, because I'm kind of into the bicentennial—our Constitution was fashioned in secrecy. It was shrouded in secrecy. Nobody was permitted to the debates. And the Bill of Rights was born in secrecy.

That's one of the problems. We don't really have many notes. We've got Madison's notes, which are incomplete, about what really went on in the Constitutional Convention. And the greatest triumph in diplomacy since I've served in Congress was Camp David—was Jimmy Carter bringing Menachem Begin and Anwar Sadat together, putting them in a room, locking the door—secrecy, secrecy.

So, secrecy has its uses. I'm told that the Senate met in secret, its first ten years. Maybe it was the first six. I'm trying to research it. But somehow or other, they met in secret—a plan that I wouldn't recommend today.

Now, you've been accused of shredding the Constitution. And that's serious—

LT. COL. NORTH: I don't believe that was one of the documents that I shredded. (Laughter.)

REP. HYDE: Well, I would say—I'm sure you didn't shred that as a document. But symbolically, I have heard many a media person, and some legislators say you shredded the Constitution. Now, you know, the Preamble to the Constitution is an important part of that. And I heard my friend from Florida, Mr. Fascell, talk about "we the people, in order to form a more perfect union." Those are powerful words. And as you go on down there, it says "to provide for the common defense." Then it says, "to secure the blessings of liberty for ourselves and our posterity."

Now, if anybody thinks that a new Soviet client state on the land bridge between Texas and the Panama Canal is a threat to our national security interests, it would seem to me that he would take very seriously the presence of the Sandinistas and what they're doing down there.

And again, it would seem to me that if that conviction possesses you as it does me I might add, that one has at least some ambiguity about the Constitution and violating it or shredding it when you take steps to keep the contras—and by the way, I don't mind the term "contras" —I know that's a matter of some dispute. It depends what you're against. "Contra tyrannis," as Jeanne Kirkpatrick has said, is a noble phrase—against tyranny. And so, I refer to them as the contras. But, I don't think you have shredded the Constitution at all. I think you have paid attention to an obligation to provide for the common defense and to secure the blessings of liberty for ourselves and our posterity.

Now, I want these hearings to be comprehensive. Not just picking on a few Administration people who have been implementing a foreign policy gone awry, I want to really find out what happened and who's to blame. Now, there are enough prosecuting attorneys here to make the points that they have well made. And I don't disagree with all of them, but it seems to me there's more to be accomplished here in these hearings. And I take as my text something Robert McFarlane said, and I quote, "The policymakers who created conditions like this, must bear some of the moral responsibility for the failures that follow." And that seems to me very important.

Senator Mitchell, a dear friend of mine, and someone whom I've known—I've come to know and admire, said, quote, "You don't claim you were above the law, do you?" I remember that and you said, "No." Now, that's a distinctly American notion about no man is above the law, and no man is beneath it. But, it seems to me the idea is a little more nuanced than simply to make that statement. For example, we, in Congress—now, we have a way of dealing with laws we don't like. Now, I've been accused of "Why do I—why do people elect me here if I think we're a bunch of poltroons and dolts and things like that?" I love this place. I love this place and I love the people who are here. And in trying to make it better, I make the distinction between the institution and trying to improve it. So, when I criticize the Congress, please understand it's out of a sense of a feeling of love and not contempt. Now, if we don't like a law, Colonel, and you guys ought to learn this at the NSC and then the administration, you just exempt yourself. You see, we exempt ourselves from OSHA, the Occupational Safety and Health Act. We exempt ourselves from the Ethics in Government Act; no special prosecutors are going after us. We have our own committee of our own brethren that'll take care of that. So we—we—we are exempt from equal opportunity, equal employment opportunity; none of that because we're political people. The Budget Act; waive it. Pass it, kid the people, and waive it. Every time something comes up that's in excess of the budget, pay no attention to it. The Public Law 95435, which was passed some years go, says that we can't spend any more money than we take in. That is as ignored as the 10th Amendment to the Constitution. And some day I hope the legal scholars on this Committee will find time to do a paper on the 10th Amendment and why it is atrophied and ignored.

Now, if we can't ignore the law or exempt ourselves from it, we play games with the process. Do you know how we got our pay raise? Now, the senators voted no. Terrific. And by the way, thank God we got the pay raise. I'm happy. I need the money, and I earn the money. But you know what we did in the House? We waited, under the guidance of the stage director over there, the Speaker, until 30 days had elapsed, until it was vested, it could not be unvested and then we got a vote on it. We waited until it was locked in, and then we voted. And we could all tell our constituents "I didn't vote for that pay raise." That's the way we—we do things. So—so there's much to be learned from watching us.

Now, let me—and they don't watch us close enough. Let me—let me put my own views on record, Colonel North. I think lying to Congress, I think arms for hostages, arms to Iran, I think operating the contra support operation out of the White House was wrong, and I think the failure to confer with Congress was wrong. And we're paying a fearful price for that.

But having said that, I think a few more points need to be made. Now why was this different? Why didn't you—why did you have to lie to Congress? Why was this different from other covert actions? Well, you know, it's very simple when you have a covert action that everybody agrees with, isn't that correct? When you get a controversial one, then you have a whole different problem, is that not so?

LT. COL. NORTH: It is.

REP. HYDE: In other words, when you have a liberal Democratic Congress—God bless them all, the people elected them and that's democracy and all that good stuff —and you have a conservative Republican President, you've got a recipe for gridlock, don't you? You have—you have a controversial program that cannot get the consensus that's necessary, and so it's—it's a recipe for gridlock. Nothing will happen. And those are the problems that we have to deal with here in our Central American policy. Now, the consequences, Colonel North, of what happened has damaged the administration, hopefully not terminally but seriously damaged it. Our policy in Central America has been damaged. We have embarrassed 10 countries, at least 10 countries, who helped to keep the Nicaraguan resistance alive while Congress played Hamlet over what to do, to support or not to support.

And I think of little Brunei, the one country we're permitted to mention. Brunei is a—Brunei is an enclave on the northwest corner of the island of Borneo, with less people in it than Shreveport, Louisiana, and yet it contributed $10 million to protect our interest in Central America when Congress was unable to do so. And Brunei doesn't want anything from us. Nothing. They don't need anything from us. But we have embarrassed them, and we embarrass ourselves when we do that. The end doesn't justify the means. We have heard that sermonized often, and it's a useful ethical statement, I suppose. But I'll tell you, that phrase—the end doesn't justify the means—doesn't seem to me to establish the moral context for every tough decision someone in government has to make. The incident of August 6, 1945, at Hiroshima where President Truman decided to drop a nuclear weapon, killed 150,000 people, but the purpose was to save perhaps a million people for the invasion of Japan, the classic high school ethics question, ten people on a raft that's going to sink unless you throw one over, nobody wants to jump over, what do you do, what do you do. Well, the end doesn't justify the means doesn't help you there, does it? So the moral choices that you have to face as to keeping faith with people who have relied on you and who are out there with their lives in the mountains of Nicaragua or obeying one of the five versions of a very ambiguous law that is attached to a military appropriation is a very tough moral choice. But it isn't simple, and many times you end up with having to take the lesser evil. And I think that ought to be realized by people who are so quick to condemn and to give you the phrase "the end doesn't justify the means." I ran across a fascinating article the other day written—and I, believe me, this is beautiful—it's written by Tom Braden. Now, Tom Braden was in the CIA years ago, and he wrote an article that's in the May 20, 1967, *Saturday Evening Post,* "I'm Glad the CIA Is Immoral." Now, the way he says, "Back in the early '50s when the Cold War was really hot, the idea that Congress would have approved many of our projects was about as likely as the John Birch Society's approving Medicare." That's interesting, that doing things without Congress' assent back in those days, but here's the most interesting thing he says, and I think this is quite true and worth remembering. He said, "The choice between innocence and power involves the most difficult of decisions. But when an adversary attacks with his weapons disguised as good works, to choose innocence is to choose defeat. So long as the Soviet Union attacks deviously, we shall need weapons to fight back, and the government locked in the power struggle cannot acknowledge all the programs it must carry out to cope with its enemy." Now, there's so much that I would like to go over with you. My time is up and it's a shame because we get—counsel got two days each and we get 15 minutes. But let me give you a quotation that you might carry with you, and I quote: "A strict observance of the written laws is doubtless one of the high duties of a good citizen, but it is not the highest. The laws of necessity, of self-preservation, of saving country when in danger are of higher obligation." And that same person said quote: "On great occasions, every good officer must be ready to risk himself in going behind the strict line of law, when the public preservation requires it." Now the person who said those things had a little bit to do with the founding of this country. We have a monument to him called the Jefferson Memorial. So, I think it's worth understanding that.

And let me close by just saying, that you, Colonel North,

are a reproach, to many of us you are a dangerous person, and the reason you are, is you personify the old morality, loyalty, fidelity, honor, and worst of all, obedience. Obedience is so—is so out of step with today's spirit of the age—zeitgeist—obedience is just the opposite of what defines the modern man, which is rebellion. And so, the notion of betraying freedom fighters bothers you, whether they're at the Bay of Pigs, or whether we're taking off from the roof of the embassy at Saigon on April 25th, 1975, or whether leaving them to fend for themselves in the mountains of Nicaragua. So, you've got a few more mountains to climb, Colonel North, but remember, everybody remembers Billy Mitchell and nobody remembers who his prosecutors were. Thank you, Mr. Chairman.

CHAIRMAN INOUYE: Not wishing to be accused of muzzling my dear friend, I did not interrupt. I wish to advise the House members that a vote is now in progress. Senator Heflin.

SENATOR HOWELL HEFLIN (D-AL): Colonel North, one of the purposes of these hearings is to get the facts, and in my judgment there are still some missing facts. And I want to try to spend my time exploring some of those missing facts, if they be missing.

You have testified and told us of the dire need of the contras after the humanitarian aid of $27 million had ended, which it ended on March 31st, 1986. And thereafter, made a trip to Central America, and I quote from Exhibit Four, which is a PROF note from Colonel North to Colonel McFarlane, "and also, not a good weekend, went to Central America to try and reassure our friends, both governments and resistance, that we would get funding through Congress," meaning by that I assume, that you hoped to be able to get some military aid at a later time, and there was optimism as of that time, that it could be coming. Then you state, "In the four years that I've been working on this effort, it is the most depressing session to date. There's great despair that we may fail in this effort, and the resistance support account is darn near broke."

Then on the 22nd, in Exhibit #4, which, as I understand is to Mr. Fortier, you again in a PROF note, state that "the entire force is back to one meal per day." No more boots, uniforms, packs, ponchos or weapons are available—

LT. COL. NORTH: I'm lost.

SEN. HEFLIN: —for the new recruits.

LT. COL. NORTH: Senator, I'm lost on your exhibit, if you would, sir.

SEN. HEFLIN: I believe this is Exhibit #5.

LT. COL. NORTH: Right.

SEN. HEFLIN: My purpose is—is to show that as of that time, you not only stated that there was dire needs but wrote contemporaneous PROF notes to emphasize the great need. You go on into this and say that "all new trainees will be turned away, effective today. All hospitalization for WIAs" —which I understand is "wounded in action" —"will cease at the end of the week. Troops returning to Nicaragua this week will carry only 70 to 100 rounds of ammo, instead of the 500 they have been carrying. No new radio batteries are available, so there is no way to pass commands or intelligence. The picture is, in short, very dismal unless a new source of bridge funding can be identified."

And, then in another exhibit, Exhibit #8, which has already been mentioned, which is a memorandum that you helped prepare along with Mr. Burkhardt, that went to Admiral Poindexter, and then was to be used with a meeting with a national security planning group, you state there in the beginning, "The resistance itself is increasingly desperate as available supplies are depleted, as of May 1, no further medical supplies or clothing are available. By mid-June the outside support the resistance has received will be consumed, and no further significant support appears readily available."

Now, in that memo, it was for the purpose of bringing to the National Security Planning Group various options, including the options of trying to convince Congress that you might take $15 million from the appropriation to DOD, and give it to the CIA for humanitarian assistance to the resistance group, and on page two it states that "an immediate reprogram of $15 million from the DOD to CIA for humanitarian assistance to the DRF, these funds would reduce our subsequent request from 100 million to 85 million. This action would require approval in the House Senate Intelligence Committee, Armed Service Committees and Defense Appropriations Subcommittees. We can make

613

a good case that this humanitarian assistance—" and then in parentheses: "($5 million per month) through August of 1986, is essential to maintain the option of DRF pressure" and so on.

Now reading all of that, and at the time, and your statement, is it fair and accurate to state that after the humanitarian aid of $27 million ran out, that the contras were in dire circumstances as to the need for food, clothing, medical supplies, arms, amunitions, and all other necessities to carry on a resistance movement?

LT. COL. NORTH: That is the facts and they're those facts as I knew them, as supported by intelligence that we were receiving, and as reviewed by my colleagues.

SEN. HEFLIN: Now did Mr. Elliott Abrams go with you on this trip that you mention in Exhibit 4 to Central America in mid-April 1986?

LT. COL. NORTH: I don't recall, sir.

SEN. HEFLIN: You don't recall. Well, anyway, Mr. Abrams testified about the contra needs at this time, for bridge money until the $100 million in military and humanitarian aid could be authorized. And he mentioned that it would take something like $3 million a month. Now you mention in this Exhibit 8 that I've just read that $5 million a month. Well, do you agree that from $3-to-5 million a month was needed for humanitarian assistance and we can, I suppose, and military during this period of time, from the time that the humanitarian aid terminated March 30th, until the $100 million was appropriated and was available?

LT. COL. NORTH: Yes. And furthermore, the war had been prosecuted at a rate of about 1.25 to 1.5 million a month in the intervening years. The fact is that for the resistance to continue to accept the new recruits that were volunteering —and these were people who were not enticed in any way except to know that there was a place where they could go to take up arms against the communists in Managua, these people were walking into the base camps by the dozens, and otherwise would have to be turned away. And so the estimate was you would need between 3 and 5 million dollars a month to allow the resistance to continue to grow at its natural rate, to train them, field them, equip them, send them back into combat.

SEN. HEFLIN: Now how much would it take to keep them as they were at the status quo?

LT. COL. NORTH: I guess you could live at about, you know, one to one-and-half million [dollars] a month. The fact is, Senator, I think it's important that the government of the United States, when it finally came back and provided the kind of support that we'd been talking about, put up $100 million for a year's worth of help.

SEN. HEFLIN: All right. So, well, that's true, in that that was on October the 16th, 1986, when it was approved. And I would assume that military and humanitarian aid after that, after that was signed by the President, became available shortly thereafter, something like November 1.

LT. COL. NORTH: But, Senator, something else that's important—and I believe you have testimony separately —is that even though that was signed into law in November, it was after I had left the NSC, and in January, before the first supplies actually arrived on scene.

SEN. HEFLIN: All right. So well, then, I'm trying to get the period of time that we were looking at, if it was—at that time, it would have been from about April 1 until after you left in November, which would have been close to eight months, that you really had a situation therein of dire consequences, and there was this—there was a great need for some type of financial assistance to help them in their movement.

LT. COL. NORTH: Yes. With the completion of the expenditures of the principal overseas backers, which was well running out by this point in time—

SEN. HEFLIN: Was it?

LT. COL. NORTH: —was a serious concern.

SEN. HEFLIN: If they needed, then, say $5 million times eight months, that's $40 million; or $3 million times eight months, $24 million. Or say, we get down to $1 million. They would have been in need—the basics thing of at least $8 million during that period of time.

LT. COL. NORTH: That's right.

SEN. HEFLIN: All right. So now—

LT. COL. NORTH: Senator, there is just—and I'm not trying to interrupt your train of thought here. But it's also important to know that shortly after I wrote this memorandum on May 16th, both Houses voted to approve the $100 million. And I believe it was both during June and maybe July, but by the end—certainly, mid-July, both Houses had, indeed, voted to approve the $100 million. And yet, we were still desperate to get those bills conferenced, and sent to the President for his signature.

SEN. HEFLIN: All right. So now, on May the 16th, 1986, which is Exhibit 10, I believe, of your—of your exhibits, you make a note on the second page. "You should be—" this is a PROF note from you to, I believe, Admiral Poindexter—"You should be made aware that the resistance support organization, now has more than $6 million available for immediate disbursement—" some other things there. Now, at that time, when you made that on May 16th—

LT. COL. NORTH: I'm lost on the note here, sir.

SEN. HEFLIN: Well, it's on the second page, in the paragraph—it's down—I reckon it's really the—

LT. COL. NORTH: I got it.

SEN. HEFLIN: He should be made aware that resistance support organization now has more than 6 million available for immediate dispersal. Now, did you—where—is that 6 million—in your judgment, at the time you made that, was that to come from the Hakim-Secord enterprises, Lake, or where?

LT. COL. NORTH: I believe, and I'm—I'm trying to recall without a whole lot to remind me here, but I believe that this would reflect the transaction that came to be known as the Hawk parts shipment, in which there was money placed in what has come to be called the Lake Resources account and therefore available at that point in time. Now, I—as I've also testified, I was accused frequently by General Secord—and I did not talk to Mr. Hakim about these issues, but I certainly did talk to General Secord of being overly ambitious in prognostications as to how much was available for certain activities. But I believe that the reason I put this in this particular note is I had just been informed that the deposit had been made.

SEN. HEFLIN: Well, according to the financial records of the Secord-Hakim various groups and organizations, that's true that just about that time was when that deposit—as of that date, there was something like over a 11 million dollars balance in it. But you do—that was to come from the

Hakim-Secord group, that money of 6 million. That's what I'm—

LT. COL. NORTH: Yeah, yeah, I see what you're saying. Yes, my sense that, if I can recall the time frame right, is that 6 million would have been derived as part of the Ayatollah's money that had been placed in the account to pay for the parts that we were due to ship in May. This is just prior to the trip to Teheran by Mr. McFarlane.

SEN. HEFLIN: Well, now, we have run from that—well, from April 1 on until after you leave. Of the records of the Hakim-Secord companies, their records—and auditors have—have gone through from that period forward, and we can find no expenditure for humanitarian aid whatsoever coming from the Hakim-Secord group. There was 632 thousand dollars for arms, and the rest of their expenditures —and they expended something like 3 million, three and a half million, I reckon, altogether—are in relationship with transportation-related expenses. In other words, there was no humanitarian aid, no military aid for arms or ammunition from the 1st of April on, and that their expenditures were in connection with aircraft, transportation-related expenditures. Now, during this same—I'll ask you this: did you—were you led to believe that they were supplying humanitarian and military aid in addition to transportation-related aid to the contra movement at that time?

LT. COL. NORTH: I'm not quite sure I understand the question. I—I understood, and I—I believe it to be accurate, that not only was Lake Resources, but the other off-shore accounts, the ones that have been identified as Mr. Miller's, were indeed sending monies, that General Secord's organization was providing boots, clothing, uniform items, packs, parachutes, and the aircraft support to deliver that, and that they were also flying ammunition and the military supplies necessary to support them.

SEN. HEFLIN: Well, at the same time, the auditors' review of the accounts of the Calero accounts from April until the period that you left the government, would reflect that he received very little money, and very little American influence donated money. In particular, after July of 1985—I believe it was a meeting in Miami about that time—but that the records of the Calero accounts from April 1 to after you left would reflect that the donations that he received during this time would have amounted to approximately a million dollars, including the donations from Channell and Miller and their companies.

Now, according to those accounts, it would have indicated that from Hakim and Secord, for humanitarian and military ammunition, that there would have been a total during this period of around 1.632 million dollars. There was 632 [thousand dollars] that was paid for arms. Now, granted that they could have made money by on exchange rates and it could have had some credit for buying arms on credit, or some humanitarian aid needs on credit, but it would appear that during this time that from either Calero, Hakim and Secord, Miller and Channell that there was inadequate money for the contras to have existed on. Now, that gets down to this: Do you know whether or not there could have been another source of money which could have been used to support the contras from April 1 until the time that you left the government?

LT. COL. NORTH: There are none that I know of positively, Senator. We did have reports of other countries having been approached directly by the resistance leadership, and other foreign donors, as well as perhaps other Americans who donated directly and simply gave it to Mr. Calero or one of the other resistance leaders, or made deposits directly to their accounts, but, again, I was—I am not familiar with the facts on that, but we certainly had some indication that they were receiveing other reports. Some of those reports caused us to look very carefully at the possibility of drug running. We found absolutely no evidence during my tenure at the NSC that any of the resistance leaders were themselves or their subordinates involved in drug-running. The only one case that we actually had some information on, I reported in the executive session as to who those people were. And, that was not any of the main resistance organizations.

SEN. HEFLIN: I see my time is up.

CHAIRMAN INOUYE: Thank you very much. The hearing will take a short recess. Ten minutes. . . .

CHAIRMAN INOUYE: The hearing will please come to order. Chairman Hamilton.

CHAIRMAN HAMILTON: Mr. Rodino.

REP. RODINO: Thank you very much, Mr. Chairman. Good afternoon, Colonel North.

LT. COL. NORTH: Good afternoon, sir.

REP. RODINO: Colonel North I have some questions. They're pertinent to this inquiry and I believe they're important for us to have responses to if you can respond, if you do have recollection or you do know. When you met with the Attorney General and Deputy Attorney General Jenson on January 6, 1986, regarding the January 1986 finding, to your knowledge, was this the first time the Attorney General knew of the Iranian initiative?

LT. COL. NORTH: My—well to my specific knowledge, yes. I had, as I believe I testified earlier, Mr. Rodino, we had worked on an earlier version of the finding which I believe was transmitted to the White House by Director Casey at the end of November, somewhere around the 25th or 26th of November 1985. I had worked with Mr. Sporkin of the office of General Counsel, at the CIA, on it and it was my understanding, perhaps faulty, that it was in the process of working on that finding that the Attorney General had come across or found or made note of an earlier determination by then Attorney General French Smith, to the effect that arms sales can be conducted in accord with a presidential finding.

And further that the retroactive or ratification language that was included in the November finding had been run by the Attorney General. And since, in my experience, other findings were cleared by the Attorney General's office, this one had been too. And thus when the finding was signed by the President, that finding had been, by my reckoning, at that point in time cleared by the Attorney General. I do not recall specifically addressing that prior finding with the Attorney General and Mr. Jenson when I met with them in January. My principal focus in the January finding was to include within it the language of the broader objectives as I have earlier testified.

REP. RODINO: How did that meeting come about, the January 6th meeting?

LT. COL. NORTH: My recollection, Mr. Rodino, is that it derived from an earlier meeting in December, which I was led to believe all of the cabinet officers were—I think it was around December 6th or 7th. I was in Europe, or at least had gone to Europe, to meet with the Israelis and the

Iranian intermediary, Ghorbanifar. I believe there was a meeting held, either in the Oval Office or in the residence, with the President—and I was led to believe the Attorney General was at that—at which there was a full review of what had transpired up to that point.

Coming back from the rather unsuccessful trip, with—at which Mr. McFarlane met with Mr. Ghorbanifar, the next thing that really transpired was Mr. Nir showing up on the scene, with an emphatic proposal that this should continue. The initiative was worth the risk. And the new finding, if you will, the January 6th and then I—maybe it was the 7th. But anyway, there was a version of the 6th or 7th that was then handwritten in. Words had been left out of it. The President then signed another version, I think on the 16th or the 17th.

And it's my recollection that I personally carried that over to coordinate with the Attorney General, because that was our standard practice, that the Attorney General look at the findings and make sure that they were within the law. And my recollection is that I hand-carried it to meet with both—to meet, principally, with the Attorney General. And as I recall, Mr. Jensen was present at that meeting.

REP. RODINO: Did you brief the Attorney General on the initiative?

LT. COL. NORTH: Well—yes. My recollection is that I covered with him, and again, I've—it's not a very specific recall—that I probably had the finding, itself, and probably my draft cover memorandum, which I would have prepared for Admiral Poindexter's signature and transmission to the President.

REP. RODINO: And when—

LT. COL. NORTH: I don't recall that specifically, but that would have been the normal practice, sir.

REP. RODINO: And when the Attorney General read the January finding, was he surprised to learn of the Iran initiative?

LT. COL. NORTH: I do not recall any expression of surprise, no. It's—

REP. RODINO: The reason I asked that question, Colonel, is because we know that it was the stated presidential policy at that time, to the contrary. And that had been stated, I think, in December of 1985.

620

LT. COL. NORTH: Well, I understand that, sir. But, my recollection is that I was at least told that the Attorney General had been part of the larger Cabinet group that met with the President back in December.

REP. RODINO: But the Attorney General himself didn't ask any questions or make any comments regarding it?

LT. COL. NORTH: I'm sure that there were questions asked, but again, I do not recall the essence of the conversation.

REP. RODINO: Do Lowell Jensen ask any questions or make any comments?

LT. COL. NORTH: Again, I'm sure that he did, which was normal under those circumstances to have queries made about it, but I do not recall the substance of the conversation, sir.

REP. RODINO: Col. North, you've testified here that you had no recollection of meeting with the Attorney General on Friday, November 21st, 1986, just after he met with the President and just before he began his weekend inquiry. Now, Robert Earl, who was on your staff at the NSC, has testified, and we have a deposition and if you want to, we'll refer you to the pages of that deposition. On page 63 and 66, he said that you spoke with him, Earl, in your office after meeting that day with the Attorney General, and I want to read you what Col. Earl's testimonty to the committee on this point is.

LT. COL. NORTH: Could we look at that, sir? The exhibit? (Pause)

LT. COL. NORTH: Would you refer the dates again, sir?

REP. RODINO: The date was, concerning a meeting with the Attorney General on Friday, November 21st, just after he met with the President and just before he began his weekend, and Robert Earl is supposed to have made this statement concerning you and what had been said, after a meeting that day with the Attorney General. And, as you will note, Col. North, Col. Earl testifies that you told him that you'd met with the Attorney General on November 21st, and according to Col. Earl, at that meeting you asked Mr. Meese if you had 24 or 48 hours, and the Attorney General responded that he did not know whether you could have that much time. And it was later that day that you walked in and shredded documents. Does that refresh your recollection, that deposition with Col. Earl's testimony.

MR. SULLIVAN: Excuse me, Congressman, if I might. You said that we were being given pages 63 and 66. We have only pages 65 and 66. Moreover, it appears that we need the earlier pages in order to understand the context here. Obviously, for example, the very first question on the pages you just gave, indicate that there were earlier related questions.

REP. RODINO: The pertinent testimony occurs on page 65, which you have and which is stated, and he says he had asked—he had said to the Attorney General, or asked the Attorney General, "Can I have—or will I have 24 or 48 hours." He didn't see both; he said one or the other. I can't recall whether he said 24 or 48, but he asked for that. And he told me that the Attorney General has something like —like that he didn't know whether he could have that much time. Something like that. Again, I am not quoting; that's his deposition. You have that page.

LT. COL. NORTH: I—I do have the page, and I—I believe I testified about this earlier. My—I do not specifically recall a meeting with the Attorney General on the 21st. I do recall discussions with the Attorney General's office and maybe the Attorney General himself on the issue of an investigation that was ongoing regarding Southern Air Transport and our concerns that pursuing that investigation was going to create a liability for a potential hostage release. I indicated to the Attorney General that Southern Air Transport was being investigated by, I think it was, the FBI and perhaps Customs and maybe even others regarding its support for the Nicaraguan resistance as a consequence of the Hasenfus aircraft shootdown. And they were also engaged, as we all now know, in supporting the Iranian initiative. And our concern was that further exposures on the Iranian initiative would jeopardize both the hostages and the second channel, and we, right up until the end, were hopeful of another hostage release. I don't recall specifically what that conversation refers to—

REP. RODINO: You don't recall—

LT. COL. NORTH: —but I do remember asking for more time from the Attorney General before turning in the Justice Department or FBI or whatever investigations were ongoing with regards Southern Air Transport back on again.

REP. RODINO: What I'm trying to get at, Colonel, is to be

able to determine whether or not what Colonel Earl told us at that time that you were requesting is 24 or 48 hours is a fact or whether it's not a fact, and he told that to us, to this Committee.

LT. COL. NORTH: Well—

MR. SULLIVAN: I direct your attention to page 66, where he says he's not positive about it, sir.

REP. RODINO: Well, he may not be positive about it, but he did say that that's what he recalled.

LT. COL. NORTH: Well, I—I—I can assure the—the congressman of this: that if this discussion, which Colonel Earl refers to, and I, you know, took place—I'm certainly not saying that it did not—that it is probably referring to Southern Air Transport, and it is certainly not referring to "do I have more time to shred documents" because I—I—I'm not—I want to answer that very clearly. I never addressed the Attorney General or anyone else whether or not I had enough to time to shred—

REP. RODINO: In other words, you did not ask for 24 or 48 hours more?

LT. COL. NORTH: For me, no sir. For Southern Air Transport, I certainly asked for more time.

REP. RODINO: Let's move on to something else, Colonel. We've heard testimony that during the interview with the Attorney General on November 23, 1986, after you were confronted with a copy of the diversion memo, you asked if they found a cover memo. Do you recall that?

LT. COL. NORTH: I recall that that has been raised several times here in this—

REP. RODINO: Was there a cover memo, Colonel?

LT. COL. NORTH: I honestly don't recall, Congressman Rodino. It was not uncommon for me to put cover memoranda on my memos, and you've certainly seen many of those in which I did. There were also occasions when I did not. And it was not a question asked in subterfuge of the Attorney General, it was simply a straightforward, bald question by a person who was surprised that the document still existed. And I don't mean that lighthearted, I mean very seriously it was an honest, straightforward question. I just did not remember.

REP. RODINO: Well, the reason that I ask Colonel, is because reference was made to the fact that you did refer to a cover memo, and I wondered why you would refer to it if such a cover memo did not exist?

LT. COL. NORTH: Well again, I was inquiring was there a cover memo with this document? They had found a document that I truly did not believe existed anymore, and they had put it before me in that "Q" and "A" session that they had, and I asked the question, was there a cover memo with this, because obviously it is an incomplete memorandum.

REP. RODINO: Well let me ask this, Colonel, since you've been very honest and truthful with the Committee in telling us that you shredded a number of documents, did you shred any cover memo, any of the five documents that have been referred to and testified to?

LT. COL. NORTH: I do not recall specifically shredding that cover memo or any other. I shredded many, many memoranda in that period of time from early October through the time of my departure.

REP. RODINO: Colonel North, Mr. McFarlane has testified that on November 23rd, 1986 on Sunday morning before your interview with Attorney General Meese, you told Mr. McFarlane that there was a memo describing the diversion that may cause a problem. Is that a fact?

LT. COL. NORTH: I don't recall that part of the conversation. What I do recall assuring him, as I had assured others, to include Admiral Poindexter, that the documents pertaining to the use of residuals to support the Nicaraguan resistance had been taken care of. I assured him of that fact, and I assured Admiral Poindexter, and in both cases I was wrong.

REP. RODINO: Did anyone tell you on Saturday afternoon, Saturday night, or Sunday morning, or at any time before your interview with Mr. Meese, that the diversion memo had been found by attorneys from the Justice Department?

LT. COL. NORTH: No, sir, they did not.

REP. RODINO: No one did?

LT. COL. NORTH: In fact, they didn't tell me until well into the interview with Mr. Meese.

REP. RODINO: Colonel, you have phone logs which indicate that on November 24th, 1986, at 11:15, you spoke to Brad Reynolds, the Assistant Attorney General, for 15 minutes. Could you tell us if you recall what he did say? And I refer you to your own phone log which describes that you had a conversation for 15 minutes at 11:45.

LT. COL. NORTH: Could I see that? That may help refresh my memory, sir. (Pause while reviewing phone log.) I—

REP. RODINO: I'd just like to know, Colonel, if you recall from your—the fact that your phone logs state 15 minutes, that you recall just what your conversation might have been—what he said to you?

LT. COL. NORTH: I do not recall a conversation with Mr. Reynolds at any time after I left the Attorney General's office on the day before the 23rd. I think—first of all, that is, as I recognize it, my secretary's writing. And what my sense of looking that—at what's on this piece of paper—this means is that Tom Green is the one who called, that he had talked to Brad Reynolds, that perhaps the call came in at 11:45, and that perhaps he was seeing or talked to Reynolds for 15 minutes. I have no recall of the conversation with Mr. Reynolds—

REP. RODINO: In other words, your—

LT. COL. NORTH: —after Sunday the 23rd, sir.

REP. RODINO: In other words, though that log has Brad Reynolds, you did not talk with Brad Reynolds?

LT. COL. NORTH: No, sir. I—I'm not denying that I talked to him. I probably talked to a lot of people that day. My point is, sir, that my recollection is I did not talk to Mr. Reynolds, but I did talk at some length with Mr. Green. And I note that Mr. Green's name is above that and he was at that point in time my counsel.

REP. RODINO: Let's—let's ask you whether or not the Attorney General ever suggested that you get an attorney? And if he did, when and why?

LT. COL. NORTH: I do not recall the Attorney General suggesting that. I do recall Director Casey suggesting that several times. And my sense of the first time he recommended that was shortly after the Hasenfus airplane went down and he talked to Mr. Furmark. And he specifically told me at that point in time there was very much likely to be a civil suit and I would be named in it. And he suggested at that point in time that I get counsel. There was also a suggestion at some point later on that same month that there might be an inquiry by the Attorney General's office. I believe that reflect as I testimony earlier—in my testimony earlier that there had been a request for an independent

625

counsel, but that had been turned down by the Attorney General's office. And that independent counsel action pertained to my role in supporting the Nicaraguan Resistance.

REP. RODINO: You do know, Colonel North, that Richard Miller, Michael Ledeen, and Robert McFarlane, all testified that you told them, that you had been advised to get an attorney.

LT. COL. NORTH: Yes, sir. As I've just testified and as I testified earlier, Director Casey suggested that to me in early October and then several times thereafter. But, my understanding of why he was recommending I seek counsel, pertained to—

REP. RODINO: —I know, but I'm asking, did the Attorney General advise you.

LT. COL. NORTH: I do not—sir, the Attorney General, to my recollection, never once recommended that I seek legal advice, ever.

REP. RODINO: Did you tell anyone from the Department of Justice—from November 21st to November 24th, that is Friday through Monday—that you had consulted with an attorney?

LT. COL. NORTH: I don't recall telling anyone in the Department of Justice that, although Mr. Green did tell me that he was going to talk to some people at the Department of Justice. It may have been Mr. Reynolds that he was going to talk to. Our effort at that time, was to insure that the hostages and the second channel could indeed have time to get out. And that indeed may be what Colonel Earl is referring to in the conversation. It may have been the Southern Air Transport, it may have been the hostages and the second channel, as we were taking every effort to insure that those people who needed to get out of Iran, could, and that the hostages, if we were going to get any more out, could indeed be rescued.

REP. RODINO: Colonel North, when Admiral Poindexter told you that the President did not know, that was a result of your having asked him whether or not the President knew?

LT. COL. NORTH: Yes, sir. My recall on that is, that on the 21st, the Attorney General had told him—I mean this is the way it was conveyed to me—that he was going to conduct a factfinding inquiry into the activities that had occured in

1985, specifically the August-September and then November transfers of Israeli equipment to Iran. And that as a consequence of that, during our discussion of that inquiry, in which the Admiral told me to lay out everything, I told him that I had destroyed the references to the use of residuals to support the Nicaraguan resistance. And I specifically asked him, as I remember it, "By the way, does the President know about this," since it's my recollection that he had said the President had asked the Attorney General to look into this. And, he at that point said, "No, the President does not know about it."

REP. RODINO: Did Admiral Poindexter tell you that he had talked with the President, learned that he didn't know?

LT. COL. NORTH: No. As I remember, it was a very brief conversation, and I think, basically, just the way I described it to you as I remember.

REP. RODINO: Did you ask him whether or not the five memos which you had sent forward requesting that the President be advised had been sent forward [with the] President's knowledge?

LT. COL. NORTH: No, because I wa—had already—what precipitated this conversation was my assurance to him that those memoranda no longer existed.

REP. RODINO: Was this a surprise to you?

LT. COL. NORTH: I think so, yes, but by that point in time, I was one, exhausted, and number two, I suppose nothing much surprises you after that point.

REP. RODINO: Did this, Col. North, at this point then send a flash through your mind that now you were the fall guy, that this was what was being said to you?

LT. COL. NORTH: No. Not all, because in that same conversation I told the Admiral again that I thought I ought to go right away, that I ought to leave now in an effort to diffuse this thing. Director Casey had, by that point, suggested to me that it was probably going to take someone above my pay grade, as he put it, or above my level at the NSC, or within the administration to take this on the nose, as it were, and I thought that we at least ought to make an effort to diffuse it at the lowest level possible before it worked its way up. I don't believe I related to the Admiral what Director Casey had told me about him.

REP. RODINO: Colonel, moving on—

MR. SULLIVAN: Excuse me, Congressman. I don't mean to be offensive, but I noted that you started at 3:45, and the red light is on. It's been 25 minutes. Unless we adhere to the time, we'll never get out of here.

CHAIRMAN INOUYE: As I indicated to you in our telephone conversation, there are certain members here who have received special allotments from others who are not present.

MR. SULLIVAN: Well, that'd be perfectly all right, Mr. Chairman. Perhaps you could tell it to begin with.

CHAIRMAN INOUYE: That explains, so that's why we have this extra time.

MR. SULLIVAN: How much time is the Congressman designated?

CHAIRMAN INOUYE: Proceed.

MR. SULLIVAN: Excuse me, sir. You told me that some people were going to get an extra five minutes, and I perfectly well understand that. Can you please inform us on—

CHAIRMAN INOUYE: The determination of time, I'm certain you will agree, is up to me as Chair, and I try to be very fair.

MR. SULLIVAN: Well, it is, sir, but the red light is on, and I took that as a clue that the time is finished. Now, we're not going to get out of here unless we adhere to some regulations about time, and I respectfully request that we try to limit the amount of time.

CHAIRMAN INOUYE: Who's next? Senator Boren?

SEN. BOREN: Thank you very much, Mr. Chairman.

Colonel North, as I've sat here day by day, I've had a question in my own mind that I'm sure is running through your mind over the last several days, and that is, "Will anything good come from these hearings?" The reason I've asked myself that question is the same reason that you've raised some questions about it. We end up after all these hearings, with the country more divided than ever, more fragmented in terms of what this country ought to be doing, more polarized. We end up having simply diverted time and attention away from serious economic problems. And being from a state like Oklahoma, I understand the economic challenges that we're facing. We end up with a lot of pain for a lot of families, and a lot of people around this town. And we haven't learned anything from it, in terms of something that will benefit the country and the future. Then I think we'd all have to say that it hasn't served a useful purpose.

So I think we all have a real determination, here. I'm sure it's a determination you feel, having gone through this painful process, that we try to learn some lessons from all of this, that will help the country in the future, so we won't have these kinds of confrontations again in future years. We won't have concerns about the rest of the world watching us have this kind of confrontation, concern about allied countries having sensitive information being divulged about them. So, we won't go down this same path again.

So every day I try to ask myself, "Have we learned something that we can apply to help this country in the future?" And I'm sure you hope that through these proceedings, the American people have learned about the situation in Central America. As a supporter of the contras, I hope that they have learned, also, about the strategic importance of that region, and why we cannot afford to create a power vacuum in that region that will be filled by communist forces and those hostile to our country.

And I would hope we would have also learned a broader lesson. I had to ask myself, "How is it that a person like Col. North has ended up sitting before this congressional committee with this kind of inquiry, being watched by the world?" Because you projected yourself as a person that cares about this country, has deep love for this country. You've convinced me of that. You've clearly convinced the American people of that. I'm not surprised by that. I'd heard about you before—from people, for example—when you came to defend a young Oklahoma Marine who'd been falsely accused of wrongdoing during the Vietnamese conflict. So I don't think people that know your record are surprised about that affection that you have for this country.

So I had to ask, "How has it come to this?" And I have to believe that your appearance in these proceedings is really a reflection of something that's gone wrong in this country over the past two decades, perhaps. And that is, we lost sight of something that we used to always believe in, in this country. It was called a bipartisan approach to foreign policy. We had an old saying, "We might fight among

629

ourselves about domestic politics, but politics stop at the water's edge." When we spoke to the rest of the world, we spoke with a united voice. And the congressional leaders, and the presidents, would get together and work toward that end.

I guess the greatest example we've had in modern times was the kind of cooperation that we have between President Eisenhower, Republican President, and Sam Rayburn, the Democratic Speaker of the House. And they worked together, not because there were some rules or regulations that required it, but because they each understood the importance of it. We don't have a Cabinet form of government here, or a Parliamentary system. In a Parliamentary system there is no division of powers. The Executive branch and the Legislative branch are really melded together. Members of the Cabinet are also members of Parliament.

And so you don't have the split that can develop in the kind of system that we have under our Constitution where you have the President and his Commander-in-Chief, but you also have the Congress. And they're empowered to declare war and they're empowered to appropriate the funds that are necessary for the carrying out of foreign policy. And I'm convinced that Mr. Rayburn and President Eisenhower worked so well together, because they both understood that. They understood the history of our government, they understood our form of government, they knew that where the powers were divided, you're going to have a united front to the rest of the world, you had to work harder than ever. You had to make a special effort to get together and to speak together with one voice.

When people talk to me, my constituents talk to me, they say, "You know, we don't understand, aren't you all working for the same people? Aren't the people in the White House, the people in the Congress, all trying to work for the American people? When are you people going to stop being Democrats and Republicans or members of Congress and members of the Executive branch and get together and work together as Americans for the same country? Then we'll have continuity in foreign policy. We won't have a stop and start policy." And we're going to have to do that. The President can start a policy but he can't continue a policy. Not unless the Congress is going to support it and appropriate money. So, if we're going to speak with one voice, it seems to me critically important that we get back to that old-fashioned concept of bipartisan foreign policy because each has a role to play.

And Eisenhower and Rayburn, when they met together, they met each other halfway, it takes two. The President has to understand the role of Congress, he has to be willing to meet the Congress halfway; Congress has to understand the role of the President; have to realize you can't have 535 Commanders-in-Chiefs, that you have to have continuity of policy. But I think that the fact that you're here, that we're in these circumstances, that we're having to have these kinds of hearings is a reflection, basically, of the breakdown of that concept of partnership, constructive partnership, all of us working together as Americans to try to serve this country. Partnership between Democrats and Republicans, Executive branch, and the Legislative branch. And it's going to take both.

Doesn't mean the President always gets his way; doesn't mean the Congress always gets its way, means they're going to have to have a meeting in the middle. Then come out as Eisenhower and Rayburn did and announce an American policy to the rest of the world. We're trying to do that. And I want to report that to you and the Intelligence Committees. I happen to believe very strongly that we have to have covert operations sometimes. We have to be able to operate in secret. We have to be able to keep those secrets. And I think you've expressed appropriate concern as a witness, that those secrets must be kept. We have instituted new procedures in the Intelligence Committee to make sure that those secrets are kept; we lock up the documents, we don't let them out of the room, we don't even let members take their notes out anymore. Senator Cohen and I have gone to the leadership in the Senate, both Democratic and Republican, and received a commitment that if a single member of our Committee leaks classified information, their resignation as member of that Committee will be demanded.

And of course there are procedures in place for the President, under current law, if the President does not want to tell the entire Intelligence Committees of the both the House and the Senate, as you know, the President can notify only eight people: the Speaker of the House, the

Majority Leader of the Senate, the Minority leaders of both Houses, and the Chairman and Vice Chairman of the two committees. And we're working very, very hard to re-establish the kind of mutual trust that is going to be necessary for us to be able to start policies and sustain policies, and speak to the rest of the world with a unified voice.

So I want to make it clear that I don't disagree with you that we have to have covert actions, secret actions. Secrecy must be maintained, but we must also have accountability. We need to have accountability to make sure that the money is spent appropriately as was intended. In this case, you've said you, as one person you couldn't possibly keep up with all the funds for example, in this operation. If we'd been able to do this through regular channels, through the CIA, with the proper accountability, we would know where all the money is and how it was spent. We have to have accountability also to make sure that the President signed off on it, that the objectives are being properly carried out. And so we're working very, very hard. We've been in conversations with Mr. Carlucci and others at the White House between the Intelligence Committees, in the last several days, to try to come up with a positive new approach.

So we have to have covert actions, but we have to have accountability. And we also have to have a sharing of information between at least the leaders of the Congress, and the White House, if we're going to rebuild this kind of bipartisan unified approach.

Now I would just like to ask you, as we consider how we conduct foreign policy, especially covert operations that have to be kept secret, how do we do that while preserving the democratic values and institutions that we hold so dear? And do you think that we're on the right track in the way we're trying to develop this relationship of absolute candor and absolute trust between the Executive branch and the Intelligence Committees of both the House and Senate?

LT. COL. NORTH: Well, as you've described them, Senator Boren, I agree with the noble objectives, and I think I have testified thereto during my five-and-half days here before you. I continue to be concerned at the size of the committees. I think that the larger the group of people involved, the larger the staffs, the more likely it is that we'll end up with a compromise and that certainly, while the provisions of the law allow only the Big 8 to be notified, it would be, by my opinion, appropriate that—we've got experience in working with the Congress and the Executive branch of a joint committee, and— and you know the one I'm referring to, a very small, very professional staff and a small committee that worked very closely with the administration on carrying out policy on nuclear matters. And my sense is that that is an idea whose time has come. There is no doubt that we can do it better, and there is no doubt that there must be the ability to confer and to—and to obtain the monies that are necessary to conduct these activities.

SEN. BOREN: Well, I—I agree largely with what you've said. I'm not sure I agree with a joint committee for this reason, that because of the appropriations process and other responsibilities my fear is that committee might not have sufficient influence with the committees of the two Houses to keep other committees in both Houses from again invading the jurisdiction. And we might end up inadvertantly with more committees, several committees, again asserting jurisdiction. But I think the important thing is we're— we're compartmentalizing our staffs so that not even all the members of the staff know about these various operations. They only have a—have a knowledge of one or two operations on a need-to-know basis. I think the important thing, though, is, if we're going to have this bipartisan approach and this partnership in the future, wouldn't you agree we have to concentrate on this method of consultation and the rebuilding of mutual trust between the two branches of government?

LT. COL. NORTH: I couldn't agree more, Senator.

SEN. BOREN: Now, one other item has disturbed me as I—I've listened, and this perhaps grows out of my experience as a former governor. Occasionally, people would call me on the phone when I was governor, and they'd say, "Governor, we're getting ready to do something because we were told you wanted it done, but I just wanted to clear it with you because it didn't sound quite right or we wanted to make sure." And sometimes those things that were getting ready to be done by someone in the bureaucracy were not things I wanted done at all. Somebody had simply come to those people and said we want—the governor wants this done. I didn't even know about it.

Now, as I've—as I've listened to you and you've indicated that the President told you on the phone he did not know about the diversion, and you've said—and I believe you—that you sincerely believe that this was an approved policy to use the residuals, that the President had approved this policy. Now, if those indeed are the facts, do you have any suggestions for us as to what we could do because I think this is an area we need to think about. We've talked frankly with the White House about making sure that in the future significant orders are put in writing so the people who have to carry them out will either hear it directly from the President, one on one, or that they will be placed in writing so that people out in the bureaucracy won't be able to go around saying the President wants this done and have people carry it out without the President knowing.

Here, the President's been damaged by this situation. There's a political crisis that's developed over it, and how do we protect future presidents from having that situation develop where people might be going around carrying out things, thinking in all sincerity that the President wanted it done, when in fact the President might not have known?

LT. COL. NORTH: Well, I think, while we may have agreed on the last point, we will agree to disagree on this one, because I think that those are clearly matters for the executive to resolve within the executive, and although, certainly, the National Security Council itself was created by the National Security Act of 1947, the National Security Council staff was not. There was an executive secretary appointed by that act, and the staff has grown to meet the needs of various presidents and will continue to do so.

SEN. BOREN: No, I don't think we do disagree. I—

LT. COL. NORTH: But—

SEN. BOREN: —think we agree on whether the President setting up his own standards about how to do that, but how would you do it?

LT. COL. NORTH: Well, again, I—certainly, I will never be president, and I, as I indicated before, I am not running for anything and not running from anything, and I want to make that clear again. But, my sense is that if we required

634

that the President reduce every word to writing, that every single authority ever sought by the President had to be reduced to some kind of official format, we would never have been able to succeed in things like Achille Lauro, because the timing on that was so—

SEN. BOREN: Oh, wait, no, no I—

LT. COL. NORTH: —that it wouldn't have been done otherwise.

SEN. BOREN: No, I certainly agree with that. I think the President has to be able to turn to someone immediately and give an order. We don't want to tie his hands from being able to do that, and have it carried out. But, on something like this that went on for a long, relatively long period of time, how could we change the procedures to make sure that an Oliver North, let us say, or someone else in the future, who is carrying out a policy in good faith, that he thinks is the policy of the President, or the order of the President, can really know for sure that it's the policy of the President and the order of the President.

LT. COL. NORTH: Well, again, I think it goes back to your original proposal, that there must be the kind of sense of trust that exists between the executive and the legislative that those things are, indeed, conferred by appropriate agents of the executive to discuss those things with the Congress.

SEN. BOREN: No. The joint oversight process, both executive and legislative, then would make sure that it was being carried out appropriately.

LT. COL. NORTH: I think so.

SEN. BOREN: Let me turn to the CIA briefly, and as you know I have institutional responsibility there, and there are some questions that I would like to ask in that regard, and I might say, Mr. Chairman, that Senator Trible has indicated to me that he would yield me five additional minutes of his reserve time to carry forward with this line of questioning.

I've had a theory, and I shared with you briefly in executive session, for some time. Mr. Casey, as an individual, was willing to get involved in things and take risks, but he had a great love for the Central Intelligence Agency. He was determined to make sure that that institution not involve itself in anything that might place it in jeopardy, and that he went to great lengths to try to insulate the CIA as an institution, from doing anything that might be improper or questionable as far as the law was concerned. In fact, Mr. Gates, in testifying before the Senate Intelligence Committee, indicated during our hearings that on October 9th, 1986, he had lunch at the CIA with you and with Director Casey. So it was Mr. Gates, yourself, and Director Casey. And that at that lunch, Mr. Gates asked you whether the CIA was involved in your private supply operation, and private fundraising operation for the contras, during any period of time in which that was banned by law. And he indicated that you answered that the CIA was completely clean, speaking about it as an institution, and that you had worked very hard to keep it that way.

LT. COL. NORTH: That's correct, sir.

SEN. BOREN: Now, was that under orders, or direction from Director Casey, that he wanted to keep the CIA as an institution totally insulated and apart from this operation?

LT. COL. NORTH: Yes, yes. And there was no contact that I had with any CIA officer that Director Casey was unaware of.

SEN. BOREN: Now, did anyone at the CIA assist in obtaining money for the contras from any third countries?

LT. COL. NORTH: Not to my knowledge, sir.

SEN. BOREN: Did any of the CIA officials ever send you names of countries, or make any suggestions to you about countries to contact?

LT. COL. NORTH: Other than in the discussions with a restricted inter-agency group, chaired by the State Department, after the law was passed authorizing State Department contact—other than that, no sir.

SEN. BOREN: Did Mr. George ever make any comments? Or was that after this time? About possible third country—

LT. COL. NORTH: As I indicated earlier, the Director of Operations and I had a number of discussions that dealt along the periphery of these things. And I have turned over to you my notes on those.

SEN. BOREN: Did—did you ever tell anyone in the CIA, other than Director Casey, about the residuals being the sources of funding for any of the contra operations?

LT. COL. NORTH: Not specifically, or directly, no. But as I indicated in my earlier testimony, there are no doubt people who had suspicions relatively early on, even before Mr. Furmark's approach. That's as a consequence of the intelligence that we talked about the other night.

SEN. BOREN: Yes. But you did not explicitly inform—

LT. COL. NORTH: I explicitly—

SEN. BOREN: —any other individual at the CIA?

LT. COL. NORTH: I explicitly tried to deceive a number of people at the CIA as to the actual source of those.

SEN. BOREN: So—

LT. COL. NORTH: I do not recall specifically addressing those matters to anybody.

SEN. BOREN: So my view, that Director Casey intentionally set up Mr. Gates, for example, to be the deputy in charge of day-to-day operations of the agency, and to keep him more or less insulated from this other operation, you would say is an accurate description of the way Director Casey was trying to operate?

LT. COL. NORTH: I would.

SEN. BOREN: Now, there was a period of time in which it would have been unlawful for the CIA to have provided intelligence directly to the contras. And Rob Owen testified that you were giving intelligence information to the contras during this period of time.

LT. COL. NORTH: I was.

SEN. BOREN: And where did that information come from?

LT. COL. NORTH: Both from the CIA and the Department of Defense.

SEN. BOREN: Well now, did you tell anyone at the CIA—and of course it would be perfectly lawful for the CIA to give you intelligence, as a member of the National Security staff.

LT. COL. NORTH: That's why we did it that way.

SEN. BOREN: But if they had known that you were—they gave it to you knowing that you were simply going to hand it on to the contras, then that would have been illegal during that period of time.

LT. COL. NORTH: Again, I'm not trying to—

SEN. BOREN: —Well, let me rephrase it. In fact, Mr. Casey, I believe—Colonel North, if I could rephrase the question, maybe counsel's advice would not be relevant. Mr. Casey, as I understand it, told you that he would hope that you would do it that way, so as you would not put the Agency in the position of having given it to you, knowing that it was being sent?

LT. COL. NORTH: That is correct, but as I have indicated in my earlier testimony, I had numerous discussions with people at CIA and the Department of Defense—particularly Admiral Moreau, which certainly could lead one to the conclusion that there were other people who were aware of what I was doing.

SEN. BOREN: Who were the people at the CIA that had conversations with you, that were of a nature, that would have given them knowledge, that you were involved with the resupply and that you were passing intelligence on to the contras at that time? If you could tell us by title, rather than by name.

LT. COL. NORTH: Well, as I—again, those conversations are recorded in the notebooks that I provided to this Committee.

SEN. BOREN: Was the Director of Operations, Deputy Director for Operations, one?

LT. COL. NORTH: He and I had conversations that are recorded therein.

SEN. BOREN: The—were there any—all of those that are recorded in the notebooks are the ones—that's the list, as far as you know in terms of those that you know?

LT. COL. NORTH: No, as I indicated earlier and in our discussion the other night in closed testimony, there were discussions with the Central American Task Force Chief.

SEN. BOREN: Chief.

LT. COL. NORTH: There were discussions with the Station Chief in—two Station Chiefs or there deputies in two different Central American countries.

SEN. BOREN: Did anyone at headquarters, in regard to that—those conversations with the Chiefs of—Chief of Mission for the CIA in two Central American countries, did anyone at headquarters authorize you to make those direct contacts that you made with those individuals?

LT. COL. NORTH: Director Casey.

SEN. BOREN: But no one else?

LT. COL. NORTH: No, sir.

SEN. BOREN: No one else.

CHAIRMAN HAMILTON: Thank you very much.

SEN. BOREN: Thank you.

CHAIRMAN HAMILTON: Congressman Brooks.

REP. JACK BROOKS (D-TX): Thank you, Mr. Chairman. And Colonel North, I want to thank you for your testimony before these Committees. As you know, I didn't vote to grant you immunity from prosecution, because of the general principal. I think government officials should be fully accountable for their actions. You've stated numerous times during the past few days, that you didn't think you'd broken any laws and you may not have. In any case, you felt so strongly—if you felt so strongly that you hadn't, I had a little difficulty understanding your reluctance to testify without immunity—

LT. COL. NORTH: —Very simple—

REP. BROOKS: —But nevertheless—

MR. SULLIVAN: —Mr. Chairman—

REP. BROOKS: —you did—Counsel, did you have a answer to a question? Nevertheless—

MR. SULLIVAN: You know, I'm so shocked at your statement with regard to the Fifth Amendment that I interrupted before you were through. And I'll apologize.

REP. BROOKS: All right.

MR. SULLIVAN: You may—

REP. BROOKS: That's a new first—

MR. SULLIVAN: —go ahead.

REP. BROOKS: —for you.

MR. SULLIVAN: Well, I interrupt when I find things so appalling, Congressman.

REP. BROOKS: Yes.

MR. SULLIVAN: Do you know anything about the Fifth Amendment and its purpose?

REP. BROOKS: I said, and I would say again, I had a little difficulty understanding why the Colonel, if he thought he had broken no laws whatsoever, was reluctant, it seemed, in their discussions with the counsel for the Committee and with you about immunity. And I didn't vote for it. And if you don't like that, I'm sorry.

MR. SULLIVAN: I don't care whether you—

REP. BROOKS: Not very sorry.

MR. SULLIVAN: —voted for immunity. We prefer not to be up here—

REP. BROOKS: Thank you.

MR. SULLIVAN: —at all. But don't ask any questions about the Fifth Amendment.

REP. BROOKS: Mr. Chairman, I've had quite enough listening to Mr. Sullivan. He's a distinguished criminal lawyer. But you know, we didn't hire him as our lawyer, and I don't need him to advise me.

CHAIRMAN INOUYE: I believe this exchange has just convinced the Chair, as I feared, that about this time, we all get testy. (Laughter.) And that being the case, not desiring to present to the people of the United States a distorted picture of what is happening here, I will recommend to my colleagues that after listening to the questioning by Senator Rudman, we recess until tomorrow morning.

MR. SULLIVAN: Your honor, may I propose—

REP. BROOKS: At any rate, Colonel, you did play a central role in the events that we're charged with investigating. And we're not here to prosecute anyone for accepting gratuities or diverting public funds, destroying government documents, lying to Congress or any other conduct. We are here to determine only what did happen and the serious impact these activities may have had on the conduct of American foreign policy and, indeed, on our national security.

And I want to tell you that I believe your testimony has been quite revealing. And the most revealing thing to me has been that you confirmed that you were not acting alone. And you put it, I believe, that you were not a lone wolf. And lieutenant colonels in the Marine Corps simply don't have that kind of authority. I was one. You've testified very persuasively that you had lots of help. And I thought you did.

The Defense Department helped, provided the missiles and the Hawk parts, modified the TOWs to meet the specs. The Department of Justice helped, provided DEA agents and held off the FBI. The Department of State helped. Ambassadors were used to facilitate the movement of weapons, construction of clandestine airstrips. And despite what Assistant Secretary Abrams said about not knowing nothing about nothing, he had to be authorized to tell the truth, you recall. It was very clear that you testified that he didn't have to ask—he already knew everything you were doing in Central America. The CIA helped, you testified. You talked to Director Casey several times a week, worked closely with him. The CIA bought the missiles from the DOD and sold them to Iran. CIA operatives assisted in setting up and running the air supply into Nicaragua. And of course you were not the only one at the National Security Council involved. You testified that everything you did, all of the machination, the operations, the phone calls, the traveling, was supported by your superiors Mr. McFarlane, Admiral Poindexter. Your secretary, Miss Hall, even testified that your travel was authorized by someone higher than you. And you've testified repeatedly that you thought you even had the help of the President of the United States.

Now, Colonel North, you've added a great deal to our knowledge about the involvement of a large number of people in these events. Most of these activities could have been carried out by these same people in the normal course of their duties. They would have had to comply with certain accountability provisions like written findings, as provided by the President's own National Security Decision Directive 159; a reporting to the House and Senate Select Committees on Intelligence, as required by the Intelligence Oversight Act; a reporting to the Foreign Affairs Committee, as required by the Foreign Military Sales Act; and I guess they would have had to deposit the proceeds in the US Treasury since those missiles were paid for with taxpayers' money.

Now instead, this elaborate scheme was to carry out these activities was worked out by the government within a government. And it's a rather interesting variation of "now you see it, now you don't." The US government was acting as a party, when needed, and it was a private citizen when it came to reporting to Congress or counting the profits. And I believe, Colonel, you testified that Director Casey really wanted a more or less off-the-shelf independent, stand-alone, self-sustaining operation for covert activities. Is that—was that your understanding of what he requested?

LT. COL. NORTH: Yes.

REP. BROOKS: Now according to the statute which created the National Security Council, and I want to read a part of it so people know what it said, it said, "The function of the Council shall be to advise the President with respect to the integration of domestic, foreign, and military policies relating to the national security, so as to enable the military

641

services and other departments and agencies of the government to cooperate more effectively in matters involving the national security." That's what it's about.

Now, Colonel, the National Security Council was never intended to be an operating agency of the federal government, was it?

LT. COL. NORTH: Operating agency of the federal government—

REP. BROOKS: Operating agency as—

LT. COL. NORTH: It is the President's staff.

REP. BROOKS: I don't follow you. As the President's staff?

LT. COL. NORTH: The National Security Council staff is a staff of the President of the United States.

REP. BROOKS: And it was authorized as—and the function for authorized, as I just read from the statute, to advise the President.

LT. COL. NORTH: You have just read the provision for the National Security Council, which consists of the President, the Vice President, the Secretaries of State and Defense, with two statutory advisors—

REP. BROOKS: Correct.

LT. COL. NORTH: —the Joint Chiefs of Staff and the Director of Central Intelligence.

REP. BROOKS: And you think the staff was not bound by the functions of the commission, of the council?

LT. COL. NORTH: I don't believe it was.

REP. BROOKS: Well, notwithstanding your insistence on that, someone must have been pretty nervous because there was a lot of altering and shredding and removal, destruction of official documents. Now, Colonel, are familiar with the Presidential Records Act of 1978?

LT. COL. NORTH: No, sir.

REP. BROOKS: Well, I'll tell you, then. That act was passed in an effort to prevent White House documents from being shredded or burned in fireplaces or removed from history in other creative ways as we have seen in the Watergate case a decade and a half ago. And it provided that documents generated by the President and his staff are the property of the United States government and are not to be disposed of unless certain requirements are met. And that law was intended to prevent the very thing that you did—with the support of Admiral Poindexter, I concede—but certainly the loss of the documents that you shredded has altered our understanding of our nation's history, if not the course of history itself. And I would ask you, would you retrieve those documents from the shredder today if you could?

LT. COL. NORTH: (Long pause.) Congressman Brooks, I have testified to the facts as to what I have done, to those who told me to do what I did, to those with whom I was involved throughout. I have answered every question about those facts that I possibly could in the last 5 and a half days. I have now been told we're going to extend it further. And I don't think it's appropriate now, nor is it at any point in this, for to me to answer hypothetical questions about things that can never be.

REP. BROOKS: Colonel North, in your work at the NSC, were you not assigned at one time to work on plans for the continuity of government in the event of a major disaster?

MR. SULLIVAN: Mr. Chairman?(Gavel sounds.)

CHAIRMAN INOUYE: I believe the question touches upon a highly sensitive and classified area. So may I request that you not touch upon that, sir?

REP. BROOKS: I was particularly concerned, Mr. Chairman, because I read in Miami papers and several others that there had been a plan developed by that same agency, a contingency plan in the event of emergency that would suspend the American Constitution, and I was deeply concerned about it and wondered if that was the area in which he had worked. I believe that it was, but I wanted—

CHAIRMAN INOUYE: May I most respectfully request that that matter not be touched upon at this stage? If we wish to get into this, I'm certain arrangements can be made for an Executive Session.

REP. BROOKS: Well, we'll do that in another forum, I believe, but, this week—

MR. SULLIVAN: Well I must say, the inferences from that statement are ridiculous.

REP. BROOKS: Mr. Chairman—

CHAIRMAN INOUYE: We'll decide whether it's ridiculous or not.

REP. BROOKS: That's right, Mr.—

CHAIRMAN INOUYE: Mr. Brooks—

REP. BROOKS: This week, Mr. Chairman, we are celebrating the not ridiculous bicentennial of the Constitution with an historic session of the Congress in Philadelphia on Thursday, and I look forward to going down there. It should serve as an occasion to remind all of us that Article I of the Constitution provides for a bicameral US Congress, gives it great power to set the policies of this nation, domestic and foreign, including the decision of when to conduct wars.

President Reagan said on April 27 of 1983 in an address to the House and Senate that the Congress shares both the power and the responsibility of our foreign policy. Then again, on December the 6th of 1986, in a radio address from Camp David on the Iran-Contra situation, President Reagan said, what he said was "We live in a country that requires we operate within rules and laws. All of us. Just cause and deep concern and noble ends can never be reasons enough to justify improper actions or excessive means." End quote from the President's statement of 1986.

That lofty principal appears to have gotten caught in somebody's shredder. Instead of operating within rules and law, we have been supplying lethal weapons to terrorist nations; trading arms for hostages; involving the US government in military activities in direct contravention of the law; diverting public funds into private pockets and secret unofficial activities; selling access to the President for thousands of dollars; dispensing cash and foreign money orders out of a White House safe; accepting gifts and falsifying papers to cover it up; altering and shredding National Security documents; lying to the Congress. Now I believe that the American people understand that democracy cannot survive that kind of abuse. And I yield back the balance of my time.

CHAIRMAN INOUYE: The Chair is pleased to recognize the Vice-Chairman of the Senate Select Committee, Senator Rudman.

SEN. RUDMAN: Chairman, thank you very much, and Mr. Chairman, although I understand the Chairman's comment, as one who can be testy at any time of the day, I would like to see if maybe we could demonstrate that even though the hour is late, that we all could maintain civility. I have some, I think, important questions to ask the Colonel,

644

and I would hope, Mr. Chairman, that we might be able to complete this evening for a whole variety of reasons, and I think if we all try hard to stay with them, and our time, and prove that the Chairman occasionally can be wrong, that the Inouye post-4:30 testiness rule does not prevail, maybe we could get through the afternoon.

MR. SULLIVAN: I'll do my best.

SEN. RUDMAN: Thank you, Counsel. Colonel North, I'm going to try to ask you some questions which I think your counsel prefers, those which require declarative answers. I will just say parenthetically at the beginning of what I have to say and ask that it's kind of the world turned upside down that a subordinate takes responsibility for superiors. In the Army I served in, and the Marine Corps you served in with distinction, and in government generally, superiors are supposed to take resonsibility for subordinates.

And, I must say, the statements out of the White House when this all broke, pyramided by the fact that you were, to use any other word, "reassigned," "fired"—what you want —and your superior was allowed to gracefully resign, gave a clear message, aided and abetted by soft stories about you and what you did, that have proved ultimately in my view false, but in fact were designed to make you the scapegoat, whether you liked it or not, and evidently it wasn't until you came here a week ago today and testified for the first time that some folks must have finally found out a phrase that you will understand, Colonel: "Somebody didn't get the word."

I want to talk to you about Director Casey's legal opinion, and I want to start out by saying that I have concluded at the end of your testimony but actually before you came here, in reviewing literally hundreds and thousands of documents, that you indeed were authorized to do what you did in terms of the policies. I'm not going to talk about the collateral issues of shredding and statements to the Congress and other personal matters, but the basic things that you did; not only is your testimony candid and believable, but it's true and it's supported and it's corroborated, and it will be corroborated by the other witnesses.

You relied on others for their view. You testified, and I have the transcript. I don't want to go through it, but you essentially testified that Director Casey told you that the NSC was not covered by Boland. Am I correct?

LT. COL. NORTH: That is correct, sir.

VICE CHAIRMAN RUDMAN: He also told you that the Defense Department, the CIA, the State Department were covered, but the NSC was not. Whether he was right or not, that is what this respected lawyer and the head of the CIA told you.

LT. COL. NORTH: Yes, sir.

VICE CHAIRMAN RUDMAN: The thing that disturbs me, Colonel, and again, I am not being critical of you, but I want to lay this all out, is that you were employed by DOD. Your superiors knew it. Admiral Poindexter knew it. I checked to make sure I was correct—and you correct me if I'm wrong, but since the day that you were assigned to the NSC you have been compensated as a Marine from the Marine Corps. Am I correct?

LT. COL. NORTH: As a major and then a lieutenant colonel, sir.

SEN. RUDMAN: That is correct, Colonel. Now, as a matter of fact, Mr. Sciaroni in his opinion said, "although the NSC is not subject to the Boland Amendment prohibitions, nevertheless Lieutenant Colonel North might be as he evidently is on a non-reimbursed detail Marine Corps." He went on to say, "If it was reimbursed by the NSC, then it might change." But the fact was it was never reimbursed by the NSC. Am I correct?

LT. COL. NORTH: I don't know that it was and I don't know that it wasn't. I assume it was not.

SEN. RUDMAN: I will represent to you that it was not. So your superiors took some liberties with the law because it is my understanding from talking to our staff and from what we know that no one ever said to you—either Poindexter, Casey, McFarlane or anyone else—"Colonel, if you want to continue this activity, either you resign from the Marine Corps or we do something else," because you were prohibited by Boland and yet they ordered to do what you did. Is that correct?

LT. COL. NORTH: No, sir, that is not correct because it did not occur to any of us that my salary—whether I would be paid as a lieutenant colonel in the ADAC, whether I was being paid as a lieutenant colonel in the NSC was covered

646

by that particular proviso. And in fact, Director Casey, I think, accurately pointed out that this was to avoid using appropriated monies of the CIA—of anybody, to pay off the cost of doing business in Nicaragua, or doing the business of the democratic resistance. And it never—it never in my wildest dreams occurred to me that my salary would be subject to that kind of a proviso.

SEN. RUDMAN: Well, let me just say, Colonel, that Casey might have been right about some things—there are many who think he was wrong about that—but that's not your problem. No one at the White House ever told you that you were prohibited. Am I correct?

LT. COL. NORTH: That is correct.

SEN. RUDMAN: And Admiral Poindexter knew who was paying you. Correct?

LT. COL. NORTH: Yes.

SEN. RUDMAN: Thank you. I want to turn to your speech making and your fund raising. You made an oblique reference to it and I want to—have a couple of questions about that. Colonel North, there is not one shred of evidence before this committee that you ever personally asked anyone to donate money to the contras.

LT. COL. NORTH: Thank you, sir.

SEN. RUDMAN: And no one has ever said that, at least, this Senator hasn't said that, privately or publicly. As a matter of fact, each speech that you gave, you were authorized to give it, is my understanding.

LT. COL. NORTH: That is correct.

SEN. RUDMAN: So we're not talking about the speeches. I want to characterize Mrs. Garwood's testimony to you because in no way was I using the pejorative phrase. I was saying it probably more in awe. Mrs. Garwood told us that you sat in the Hay-Adams, and Spitz Channell and you went over all of the needs of the contras and you left. What happened after that you probably only know from public testimony. She also testified that you met her in Houston, that you told her about the needs of the contras and said specifically, quote, "I am not asking you for money. I am not supposed to," and continued to lay out the need and left. Thereafter, the evidence is clear, that Mr. Channell asked for money and received it. I assume that you knew that Mr. Channell was engaged in fund raising. You may not have known the details of his representation, but you certainly knew he was a fund raiser. He was an individual American; he had a right to do that.

LT. COL. NORTH: I did.

SEN. RUDMAN: Well, Colonel North, the point I was making that day, I'll make again to you today; in fact, I'll even amend it. Watching you testify here for five days and knowing the fervor with which you speak, I will amend it by to say that the one-two punch wasn't necessary—only the one punch. You made a strong case and it was only natural that people gave funds. Do you want to deny that was —I won't use the word scheme, but it was certainly part of an effort to raise money for the contras. That's my question.

LT. COL. NORTH: Quite clearly it was.

SEN. RUDMAN: Thank you. I only have two other points. I want to talk about the Dawaa prisoners in Kuwait. I've read your testimony very carefully and, as I understand that testimony, Mr. Hakim made his nine-point representation; part of it was for a method to get these prisoners released, but not by the United States. In a way that the United States would not be accountable. And that you, in fact, according to your sworn testimony, Mr. Liman said: "And did you include, in the approval that you sought, the item about presenting a plan for the release of the Dawaa?" Colonel North: "Yes." Mr. Liman: "Did you get the approval?" "Yes." Is that accurate so far?

LT. COL. NORTH: Yes.

SEN. RUDMAN: Here is the problem I have with all of this. Let's agree—and some of it's classified; we won't talk about it—that the effort would be done by someone else. That the United States would not have its fingerprints in anyway on these people.

LT. COL. NORTH: Absolutely correct.

SEN. RUDMAN: The thing that troubles me, Colonel, and you might explain if you—if you could briefly, these people—and you understand this better than anyone —they're not unlike the people that killed Natasha Simpson or Robert Steedham, Leon Klinghoffer; they're not unlike Abul Nadil (sic), who you thought might be threatening your family. How in the world could the United States, either directly, tangentially, or any other way—not your policy, NSC policy—well, ask Poindexter—how could we possibly be advocating in some way that they be released?

LT. COL. NORTH: I don't believe that what I was talking about was an advocacy for release. It is a simple fact of reality that there will come a time when those seventeen will be released. It is not unusual in that part of the world to see those kinds of transactions work. We have seen it with our friends, with our allies, and, quite simply, we have seen it with our adversaries. There will come a time when those people will walk free.

SEN. RUDMAN: I hope not, Colonel North.

LT. COL. NORTH: I—I am simply making a bald statement of fact. We have seen it happen countless times. We have seen Americans who have been convicted of the most heinous crimes possible turned loose to our free and American cities.

SEN. RUDMAN: Well, Colonel North, you will [hear] testimony next week or the week after that you'll find interesting, that when the President of the United States, after you had left your present assignment, learned of some efforts tangentially to talk about the Dawaa prisoners, but to use your term, he would have gone ballistic. To use my term, he went hyper-orbit, out of sight. This was a stated policy of the President, and I would only make the observation. And you had authority for what you did. And others will speak to it, Colonel North, but it seems to me, if we are to learn anything around here, we are not to talk about people like that, who are scum, in return for anything.

LT. COL. NORTH: I could not—I could not agree more, Senator, but the fact is, if those people were going to come to be released anyway—and I—I believe they will because history is a precedent in that particular part of the world, and with those kinds of groups—then there ought to be some benefit derived from that for us, not just for the two parties transacting that kind of a release. And it will happen as sure as I am sitting here.

SEN. RUDMAN: Colonel North, finally, everyone else has had something to say to you. I have something to take —take some difference of opinion with you on, and it's in your statement that you delivered here last Thursday morning. You said about the Congress, "I suggest to you that it's the Congress which must accept the blame on the Nicaraguan freedom-fighting matter. Plain and simple, you are to blame because of the fickle, vacillating, unpredictable on-again, off-again policy towards the resistance." You're entitled to your view, but I—I want to share some of my views with you.

It's interesting that national polling data over the course of the last three years have shown that—in the latest Harris poll in June—74 to 22 people in this country oppose aid to the contras.

In April of '86 was an astounding poll—which I think totally refutes your idea that the American people somehow don't understand what's going on—that indicated that 56 percent of the American people were aware of the threat which Nicaragua poses to its Latin American neighbors —that 50 percent of those polled believe it's in the long-term interest of the United States to eliminate communism from Latin America—so far, so good. And then, 62 percent of the same polling group say, "No aid to the contras."

And I can tell you myself, Colonel North, from campaigning in New Hampshire, a fairly conservative state, in the fall of last year, as one who has, with reluctance on occasion, but in the final analyis found there was no other solution, voted for that aid to the contras. The people in this country just don't think that's a very good idea. And that is why this Congress has been fickle and vacillating.

Now, you may suggest that some of us voted anyway, even though it's against what our constituents believe. But, I want to point out to you, Colonel North, that the Constitution starts with the words, "We the people." There is no way you can carry out a consistent policy if we the people disagree with it, because this Congress represents the people.

The President of the United States—the greatest communicator probably we've seen in the White House in years —has tried for eight years and failed. You have tried and I think probably failed in that—we'll see what the polls show in two or three weeks. And this relatively obscure senator from New Hampshire has tried with no success at all.

You know, Colonel North, I go back to Korea in 1951. We won and then we lost, and we're in a position to win again. And Harry Truman and Dwight Eisenhower, who succeeded and recognized that although it was a crime to leave the North Korean people to the subjugation of North Korea, we walked away. We could have won that war at that point. We could have liberated the North, and many of us who were there wanted to. But, the people didn't. They'd had enough of a killing—550,000 casualties. Lyndon Johnson wrecked his presidency on the shoals of Vietnam.

I guess the last thing I want to say to you, Colonel, is that the American people have the constitutional right to be wrong. And what Ronald Reagan thinks or what Oliver North thinks or what I think or what anybody else thinks, makes not a whit, if the American people say, "Enough." And that's why this Congress has been fickle and has vacillated—that is correct. But not because the people here necessarily believe differently than you do. But there comes a point that the views of the American people have to be heard.

Finally, Colonel, I want to thank you for your testimony. You have been an extraordinarily helpful witness. You have filled in many details that are necessary, and we appreciate that very much.

Thank you.

CHAIRMAN INOUYE: The hearing will stand in recess for ten minutes.

(Recess)

CHAIRMAN INOUYE: I wish to announce that after conferring with a majority of the members of the panel —bipartisan membership—I have concluded that in the best interest of the hearing, the witness, and the members of the panel, we should stand in recess until nine o'clock tomorrow morning. However, before doing so, I'd like to place the following Exhibits in the record: OLN 215 to 220, 222 to 230, 232 to 233, 235 to 237, 240 to 242; and the following are classified Exhibits and will be placed in the classified annex unless declassified prior to publication: 221, 231, 234, 238, and 239.

Following the Colonel's testimony tomorrow morning, which will be in this hearing room, the Committees will hear again from Mr. Robert C. McFarlane, former National Security Advisor to the President of the United States. Mr. McFarlane requested an opportunity to return for further testimony in the light of certain statements made by Colonel North. We decided to grant this request for the sake of a complete record and as a matter of fairness to Mr. McFarlane, who testified at a time, when neither he nor the Committees had any knowledge of what Colonel North would say. After Mr. McFarlane's testimony, the Committees will receive testimony from Mr. James Radzimsky, the former Security Officer for System Four Documents at the White House. After that, the Committees will receive testimony from Admiral John Poindexter.

The hearing will stand in recess until nine o'clock tomorrow morning. (Chairman Inouye bangs the gavel.)

END OF AFTERNOON SESSION

Tuesday · July 14, 1987

Morning Session—9:00 A.M.

CHAIRMAN INOUYE: The hearing will please come to order. I would like to assure the witness and Mr. Sullivan that we will finish this morning.

Chairman Hamilton.

CHAIRMAN HAMILTON: The chair recognizes Mr. Courter.

REP. COURTER (R-NJ): Thank you very much, Mr. Chairman.

A good morning, Colonel North.

LT. COL. NORTH: Good morning, Congressman Courter.

REP. COURTER: Mr. Chairman, before I ask a question, I was the individual a few days ago that asked if Colonel North could give the briefing that he had given to so many groups before this committee, and it's my understanding that the chair's answer was yes. Late yesterday, I discovered, or at least I heard, that that briefing would be permitted, but it would not be permitted in this room; it would be permitted elsewhere, in another room. And of course, it bothers me because I know that this room is very well equipped technologically. And I remember the chairman's words in the beginning of this hearing when he said we believe that sunlight is the best disinfectant. I believe that, and I believe that, if the question can be put here, the answer can be placed here as well. The chair said that the full story should be presented to the public expeditiously and fairly, and it seems to me that nothing is presented to the public if we move to a different room under different circumstances, different exposure, and in different surrounding. It was said that we must clear the air and let the facts of this unfortunate and sad affair emerge; I would argue that that's true. We should let them all emerge, that what is accused in the sunlight should be able to be answered in the sunlight and not the twilight.

And Mr. Hamilton said, and I agree, that these hearings will be devoted to finding out what was done during the period that the Boland Amendment was in effect to supply the contras, by whom has it been done, at whose direction, what funds were used, and who raised them. It seems to me that the charge by Mr. Liman that the briefing by Colonel North was a solicitation for funds, that he asked for those funds—and it seems to me that if the charge can be made here in this room, the response can be made here in this room. I understand the briefing is not secret, it's not classified, it's not code word. It would be ironic in my mind, as well as tragic, to tell the American people that this committee, which is dedicated to presenting all the evidence, has now decided, if that in fact is the final decision, to cover up part of the evidence, to engage in a little shredding of its own.

And Mr. Chairman, I know that everybody in this committee has endeavored to be bipartisan, and we have. I'm just going to mention the fact that, if the decision is made by the chairs that we move to a different room for the briefing of Mr. North, that I put that question to a recorded vote.

There was a statement yesterday by—towards the end of the day—

CHAIRMAN INOUYE: If I may respond?

REP. COURTER: Absolutely.

CHAIRMAN INOUYE: Do you want to take a vote at this time?

REP. COURTER: Not on my time. If the light goes off, I'd be happy to.

CHAIRMAN INOUYE: Please proceed.

REP. COURTER: Thank you. It was indicated by someone late in the day that what we should do is take a public opinion poll to determine what our foreign policy should be, and I would like to say that I disagree with that. I think, indeed, the opinion of the President is important, the Congress is important, and the American people is very important. But I would say that if what we did was stick our fingers in our mouths and hold it up to the political winds each time we cast a vote, sometimes those votes would be the wrong ones.

I'm wondering whether the Voting Rights Act of 1964 would have been passed if that's what we did, or the Panama Canal Treaty would have been passed if that's what we did, if important foreign aid appropriations bills would have been passed if that's what we did. What I am suggesting here, of course, is that this Congress and this President from time to time has to assert some leadership, and show, as well, some courage.

I was talking about this to a friend of mine yesterday who sits on this panel, and he said that if Jesus Christ had taken a poll, he wouldn't have gone to Jerusalem. I was reading last night—in fact, late into the evening—a book that probably everybody in this room at one time read—at least, we picked up. And the book is called *Profiles in Courage,* by John Kennedy, and Kennedy wrote:

> "In the days ahead, only the very courageous will be able to take the hard and unpopular decisions necessary for our survival in the struggle with the powerful enemy, and enemy with leaders who need give little thought to the popularity of their cause, pay little tribute to the public opinion they themselves manipulate, and who may force without fear of retaliation at the polls their citizens to sacrifice present laughter for future glory."

And I would hope and I pray and I really respect and expect that this Committee and this Congress in the future will show sometimes less profile and more courage.

Into an area that I would also like to get into, it's the area of leaks. Lt. Col. North has indicated that one of the main reasons that he was not totally candid with the Congress is because he deeply felt that what he said to the Congress would not be kept by the Congress.

It was indicated by the Chair—who has, by the way, acted—both of them—in remarkable bipartisan way and they've shown splendid leadership here, and none of my comments today should be interpreted as criticizing them. But it was indicated by the Chair on the Senate side,

Senator Inouye, that he had received a communication from Gen. Odom. And Gen. Odom said that, in fact, no leaks had come from this panel, or this joint panel. And I would like to set the record straight there, if I can, and I would suggest that the full letter of Gen. Odom be placed in the record, because I don't have time to read the whole thing, and I'd like to read just part of it.

He did indicate that, as follows, to a letter from Gen. Odom to the Chair: I did not say that there have been no leaks by the Committees. I simply do not know whether or not this is true. I've been told that there have been some leaks on non-signal intelligence material. I do not, however, [feel] that you have accurately conveyed in your public references to me what I actually said about these leaks. It's my feeling and my judgment that this Congress and this Committee has leaked important information. And I think, therefore, sometimes the reluctance of people like Col. Oliver North to tell us what they know is understandable.

CHAIRMAN INOUYE: (off-mike)—because my name has been mentioned, and I'll give you extra time.

This is a letter from Gen. Odom. He says, "Dear Mr. Chairman, I want to express my gratitude for the painstaking care taken by your Committee to protect the uniquely sensitive material provided to you by this agency. I particularly appreciated your staff's excellent cooperation in agreeing to view our material here at Fort Meade, and not to reproduce these documents for storage elsewhere, as well as their sensitivity in handling our communications security equipment during early sessions of the hearings."

Please proceed, sir.

REP. COURTER: Now going on, I notice, also, that sometimes leaks would deter the willingness of people like yourself, Lieutenant Colonel, from notifying the Congress on things. And I indicated that I was sensitive to that concern because I believe that [at] this body, as well as across Pennsylvania Avenue, leaks occur. But it is quite remarkable that sometimes policy changes can be affected by the mere threat of leaks. And what I'd like to do is just mention an article that was written in *The New Republic* by Britt Hume. And it indicated on Page 20 that Biden—I think we all know who that refers to—it says he twice threatened to go public [with] covert actions, plans by the

Reagan Administration, that were hare-brained; and thereby halted them. So it's not only the leaking of classified information that causes the problem. It is obvious that we've reached the stage here where individual members of the Senate and the House of Representatives have threatened to go public, thereby frustrating covert activities.

And I'd like now to ask Lt. Col. North a question, if I may. Now you indicated in your testimony that now spans six days and will go on to the seventh day, that you were concerned about leaks. It was indicated to you that no leaks had occurred here. And I would like to ask you whether you can give us any statements that would indicate to us that you were correct, that some leaks with regard to covert activities did take place in the past, and I'd like you to be as specific as you could. What I have in reference—probably you may know—has to do with the *Achille Lauro* affair as well as the raid on Libya. If you could address those two situations, I'd appreciate it, Colonel North.

LT. COL. NORTH: There were relevations immediately after the *Achille Lauro* capture of the terrorists that very seriously compromised our intelligence activities which allowed us to conduct the activity itself. The operation could not have been done without the availability of certain intelligence, and the statements made by a number of members of Congress thereafter seriously jeopardized that effort and compromised those intelligence-gathering means. And I don't think we need to speak in further detail about that, but that is precisely the kind of thing we're talking about. In the case of the Libya raid, there was a detailed briefing provided at the White House in the Old Executive Office Building which was hosted by the President. Members of the Cabinet were there that were part of the National Security Council and the National Security Planning Group. The President several times in the course of that briefing on what we were planning to do that evening noted the sensitivity and the fact that the lives of Americans were at risk. Nonetheless, when the briefing concluded at about five or five-thirty, two members of Congress proceeded immediately to waiting microphones and noted that the President was going to make a heretofore unannounced address to the nation on Libya. I would tell you that the volume of fire over the Libyan capital was immense that

657

evening. Two American airmen died as a consequence of that anti-aircraft fire, as best we can determine. And I will also tell you that in my military experience nobody keeps that volume of ammunition sitting around in their guns; they need a half hour or an hour to break it out, get it ready. And any one of the magazine photographs that you look at shows—or the gun camera films themselves, show an enormous volume of fire that would indicate that while we may have had tactical surprise, strategic surprise was probably sacrificed by the comments made about the fact that the President was going to address the nation that evening on the issue of Libya. If I were Muammar Qaddafi hearing those words, and there's no doubt that he did—this very session is being broadcast all over the world, as you all know. The words that I am saying are instantly available in Moscow; the same thing happens on all of our network news. Those kinds of things alert our adversaries.

REP. COURTER: Thank you, Colonel North. Colonel North, some days ago you were asked a question with regard to the need of Presidential concern about leaks, the right of the President to withhold, temporarily, information from the Congress of the United States, and you had before you a decision, Curtis Wright. And it was a decision of the United States Supreme Court, and what I would like to do is to give you an—You were asked at that particular time about it, you were about to read parts of that decision and unfortunately were not permitted to read the parts of the decision that you wanted to. And if you have it before you today—I don't know if you do—I have a copy here—

LT. COL. NORTH: Yes, sir, I have it.

REP. COURTER: —but if you do, I'd like to provide you the opportunity to read that which you did not have the opportunity a few days ago.

SEN. GEORGE MITCHELL (D-ME): Mr. Chairman?

CHAIRMAN HAMILTON: Yes, Senator Mitchell.

SEN. MITCHELL: May I be recognized? I merely wanted to make one correction—

CHAIRMAN HAMILTON: I don't believe the mike is on.

SEN. MITCHELL: Oh, I—well, the note says it's on all the time! But—(Laughter.) You mean I've been keeping quiet—

MR. _____: At the wrong time, it's on.

SEN. MITCHELL: —I've been keeping quiet all these weeks and I didn't have to do so? (Laughter.) I merely want to correct what I'm sure—certain was an inadvertant statement by Representative Courter. The reference is made during my questioning. I did not ask Colonel North about the Curtis Wright case; he raised it on his own and I then commented on it, and we didn't get into it. I'm sure the Congressman did not mean to state otherwise, and I believe the Colonel will recall that himself.

LT. COL. NORTH: Precisely.

SEN. MITCHELL: Right. I'd like to thank—

REP. COURTER: I thank the Senator—

SEN. MITCHELL: Thank you, Mr. Chairman.

REP. COURTER: —if the Colonel could proceed.

LT. COL. NORTH: My intention was to simply read an extract from the opinion of the Court and then a quote contained in that opinion from an earlier president, and it's relatively brief. "He"—and this refers to the President —"has his confidential sources of information. He has his agents in the form of diplomatic, consular and other officials. Secrecy and respect of information gathered by them may be highly necessary, and the premature disclosure of it productive of harmful results." Indeed, so clearly is this true that the first president refused to accede the request to lay before the House of Representatives the instructions, correspondence and documents relating to the negotiation of the Jay Treaty, a refusal the wisdom of which was recognized by the House itself and has never since been doubted.

In his reply to the request, President Washington said, quote, "The nature of foreign negotiations requires caution, and their success must often depend on secrecy. And even when brought to a conclusion, a full disclosure of all of the measures, demands or eventual concessions which may have been proposed or contemplated would be extremely impolitic, for this might have a pernicious influence on future negotiations or produce immediate inconveniences, perhaps danger and mischief, in relation to other powers. The necessity of such caution and secrecy was one cogent reason for vesting the power of making treaties, etc., with the President."

That is a quote from President Washington contained within the opinion of the court in US *vs.* Curtis Wright. And my purpose for trying to raise that as early as 1985 was that the President does indeed have, as has long been respected by the courts and by the Congress itself, the authority to withhold certain information from the Congress in the area of foreign policy.

REP. COURTER: I thank you. Mr. Chairman, I see that my red light is on—

CHAIRMAN INOUYE: Please proceed for an additional two minutes, sir.

REP. COURTER: I thank the Chair very much. Col. North, before you came to testify, others, of course, testified about your activities, about accounts. Travelers checks were listed on the board to your left. And as you know, there was—or you may not know there was a great deal of snickering and laughter about that, about snow tires, about food. You answered those questions, and I think probably everybody on the panel appreciates those answers. And I believe those answers, and I think most people on the panel do as well. Obviously the laughter has now stopped. The jokes have now ended. People are treating your testimony with a great deal of seriousness. That is absolutely the way it should be. It was suggested a few days before you came here that you were engaged in plans to become rich—we know that's not the case now—and that you had taken money that wasn't yours, that we know that's not the case now. Albert Hakim testified, I think quite remarkably, about an incident where you were in Iran, and you were given the opportunity to walk away with an $8,000 rug. Do you recall that incident?

LT. COL. NORTH: It was in, I believe, Meinz, Germany that that event occurred, but it was an Iranian who offered the rug, yes, sir.

REP. COURTER: When did that event occur, and what happened there, very quickly?

LT. COL. NORTH: My recollection is it occurred in one of the meetings during the summer or autumn of 1986. The Iranian intermediary of the second channel brought the rug with him to the meeting, a beautiful Persian carpet, and offered it to me, and suggested that it was an appropriate gift from a person who cared deeply about reopening a

660

relationship with his country. And I simply told him that that was something I couldn't do, couldn't accept it. He offered me a handful of pistachio nuts, which are something grown a lot of in Iran, and I took them—and I ate them.

(Laughter.)

REP. COURTER: Did you eat them all?

LT. COL. NORTH: I did, sir. And they were good nuts.

(Laughter.)

REP. COURTER: Mr. Chairman, again, I appreciate the extra time. I see that my time is up. It is pretty obvious—I think it's appropriate for me at the present time to make my motion. So, Mr. Chairman, I move that Col. North be given the opportunity to give his presentation here, as the question was raised here in this room with Americans watching. I ask for a roll-call vote on that, Mr. Chairman.

REPRESENTATIVE DANTE B. FASCELL (D-FL): I got an amendment, Mr. Chairman.

CHAIRMAN INOUYE: Will you state your amendment?

REP. FASCELL: Let's have Spitz Channell and (inaudible) and all the rest tell us the other side of the story.

CHAIRMAN INOUYE: Before we—

REP. COURTER: I'd be delighted to agree with that. I'd like just five minutes to cross-examine each one of them.

CHAIRMAN INOUYE: Before we proceed, I would like to advise the panel that, pursuant to your desires, we have made arrangements to have the special viewing of the slides in Room S-358—385—in this building at seven-thirty this evening—485, seven-thirty this evening. We have not discussed this, but since this matter has been brought up, I think it should be made public. I'm certain this morning's session will go until about one o'clock. And it will take two hours to clear this place. Many people have thought that we've been taking long lunch hours. But some of the members of this panel are well aware why we take two-hour lunch breaks—and that is to sweep this room. I'm certain you realize what I mean by "sweeping this room." Therefore, we will resume again at three o'clock.

We've already advised Mr. McFarlane, Mr. Radzimsky that they'll be testifying. I would presume that they will go until about six, six-thirty. And therefore I have scheduled it for seven-thirty. After we've cleared this place, the crews that are here now would have to clear out and move off to the House. It takes a little while. If you want to meet in this room, we can set it up for ten o'clock this evening.

REP. COURTER: Mr. Chairman, is that a question?

CHAIRMAN INOUYE: Do you want to meet here at ten o'clock this evening?

REP. COURTER: No, I see no reason why we can't have that briefing now.

SEN. HATCH: Mr. Chairman—

REP. COURTER: —that briefing is part of the testimony—

SEN. HATCH: Mr. Chairman—

REP. COURTER: —this room can be set up for that type of a briefing.

CHAIRMAN INOUYE: I should also point out that what is in the slides, as I indicated in my opening statement, refers to the question whether we're for or against the contras. That is not the issue before us. That issue will be before another panel. We are here to discuss policy processes; I'm certain my distinguished friend is well aware of that. Senator Hatch?

SEN. HATCH: Mr. Chairman, Mr. Chairman, I don't see any reason why we can't have it right here in full purview. Testimony has been that these slides and this presentation has been shown to thousands of people. And I think it ought to be shown to the American people right here as part of this morning's thing. The slide show, it seems to me, should be presented because it is relevant. It seems to me it's relevant to these proceedings. Much has been made here of the so-called one-two punch. It is a fair comment under those circumstances, but now it ought to be explained and the other side ought to be given a chance. And earlier in these proceedings as part of a panel of three witnesses to give testimony that seems to be designed to make the point that Colonel North was part of a process to raise money. That same point was raised again by Mr. Liman, and that's properly so. I'm finding no fault with that in his direct questioning of Colonel North. So I think the subject is not only relevant, it's crucial to the understanding of this. And I think it's crucial to the American people. And if Colonel North, as I would expect him to do, makes a good case for the contras, so be it. I mean, there are lots of things that we've had to put up with in here before he ever had a chance

662

to explain himself. And now he's had a chance and people don't seem to—I'm not saying on the panel—but people don't seem to like that, except the American people. The American people like it. They like what they've heard in many respects. Now I think we ought to see the presentation. We ought to see it in this room. We ought to see it this morning. He ought to be given an opportunity to express it rightly or wrongly. There may be people as a result of that expression and seeing that will disagree with Colonel North. There may be many people who would agree with him. And I really don't see why there's a necessity for a vote. For the life of me, I think it's just something that needs to be done.

REP. CHENEY: Would the gentleman yield? Would the gentleman yield?

SEN. HATCH: I'd be happy to, yes.

REP. CHENEY: Mr. Chairman, I believe at the end of my questioning the other day I reserved 20 minutes, and I would be happy to devote my remaining 20 minutes to Colonel North's presentation of his briefing.

SEN. HATCH: I think that's fair. I think that's the only fair thing to do. There are lots of implications here that he did something wrong in presenting the contra side as he did, in spite of the—and—and because of the private fund-raising. Maybe that will be the final conclusion, but maybe it won't, too. And the only way I'm going to know is if Colonel North has an opportunity to express himself and to show what he did and to do it basically the way he did it to thousands of people, as I recall his testimony. I think it's unfair if we don't do that, and I think it's unfair to the American people if we don't do it right here.

CHAIRMAN INOUYE: Senator Rudman?

SEN. RUDMAN: Mr. Chairman, since evidently something I said several weeks ago precipitated all of this, I—I think it might be well to refresh everyone's recollection. I believe the Senator from Utah was taking a telephone call in the anteroom at a part of my examination of the Colonel.

I think the Colonel's answered the question forthrightly. Let me just remind people of yesterday's testimony. I asked the Colonel—first, I stipulated he had never raised money, had never asked for money, had never gone out and said, "I want money." In fact, quite the contrary; in fact, Senator

Hatch, you might be interested to know that I amended my one-two punch to say that I only thought that the one punch was necessary, judging the Colonel's fervor.

Secondly, in response to a question about the Garwood incidents, the Colonel was very direct in his answer to me, and I think we all heard it. It needs no repeating. And that was not a question that had any legal significance. It was to describe broadly what happened.

Now, as my friend from Utah and my friend from New Jersey—now, I—I'm with them on—on voting —supporting the contras, although many disagree with that. But quite frankly, let's face it; what's going on here is an attempt to further that cause in this hearing. And in some ways I think that that would be a good idea, but in other ways we have managed to get through to the last two weeks of these hearings to discuss the important policy issues. I'm sure Mr. Sullivan would like to take his client out of here. I'm sure that Mr. Sullivan has a lot of potted plants in his office he'd like to water this noon.

And, you know, I'm—I'm going to—I'm going to vote against this because I want this Committee to stick to its business. The Colonel answered the question precisely. The original reason for asking him to show that was to prove that he didn't raise money. We've stipulated he didn't raise money. The Colonel, in response to my question, said, "Thank you, sir." And I said, "That's fine." We all know the facts.

SEN. HATCH: Will the Senator yield?

SEN. RUDMAN: So let's—let's not turn this into something it isn't, or let's admit what we're doing.

SEN. HATCH: Would the Senator—

SEN. MCCLURE: Would the Senator yield?

SEN. HATCH: Would the Senator yield to me?

SEN. MCCLURE: Senator, yield.

SEN. HATCH: Mr. Chairman, Mr. Chairman.

CHAIRMAN INOUYE: I believe you wish to—you wish to—

SEN. RUDMAN: I'm all done.

SEN. HATCH: Would the Senator yield for just one question from me and one comment about his remarks? If I could just say this, I find no fault with any—anything that's been done, except that for a good percentage of these hearings we had a lot of people who were prejudging this witness based upon charts and—and—and security fences and a lot of other things, and I think he came in and explained those. The purpose of my request here in support of the request of the distinguished Congressman from New Jersey is not to prove the battle for the contra case. That is not the purpose. Now if that happens, I will be very pleased, I might as well say that, because I believe in the contra cause. I believe in what's happening, what you believe, Lieutenant Colonel North. I believe that you were fighting for correct principles and for this hemisphere and against what really is a deleterious force and all of that.

But he hasn't had a chance—now I agree also with Senator Rudman. He has stipulated some of the things that he has said, and I admire him for it. And I respect him for it. And he has corrected some of his statements. But there still is an impression left here that you were a loose cannon running around doing something deleterious to our country, when in fact you were telling people of what was happening.

And there's an implication here that because Channell and Miller have pled guilty to what—regardless of what they pled guilty to, the fact that they pled guilty, that you may have had some connection with them. And frankly, I think that's got to be cleared up. I think it ought to be cleared up publicly. You ought to be able to give this presentation.

The slides are not—are something I think the American people ought to see at this time. And I'd like to do it this morning, rather than 7:30 tonight in some small room or at 10:00 tonight in here with nobody in attendance.

MR. _____: Mr. Chairman—

CHAIRMAN INOUYE: May I say something before I call a recess so that the two panels can discuss this matter separately. To have a slide show in this room, it will necessitate the darkening of this room. TV lights are such that the slide show cannot be seen by anyone. Therefore, the slide show will not be seen by the people of the United States. The reason we do not wish to darken this room at this stage, unless we clear out everyone in this room, is security. And it will take at least 45 minutes to set it up.

I have promised Mr. Sullivan, I've promised the Colonel that we will quit this morning. At the rate we're going, I'm sorry Mr. Sullivan, you'll have to wait until 3:00 to water your potted plants. But do you wish to have a vote now?

(Chorus of voices: "Mr. Chairman")

REP. COURTER: Mr. Chairman, if I may respond—I thank the Chair for recognizing me. Number one, it's my understanding that this is a request that's been around for a long period of time, and I believe what you say, but I find that those people in charge of the technological aspects of this room should be able to create a situation such that slides can be shown on television. I've had hearings for nine and a half years or nine years as a member of the House, and many of those slide programs are picked up on TV. I just find it remarkable that for—somehow it can't be done here, when it's been done nine years in a row in the House of Representatives.

Number two, it's my understanding that if there is a technological problem, which I believe could have been surmounted, then Mr. Cheney has yielded twenty minutes, and it can go on, irrespective of the clarity of the slide program. It seems to me that, even if I fail the motion, Mr. Cheney is prepared, stands in the wings prepared to yield twenty minutes to Col. North for that purpose. So I would say that I'd like to have the vote. If I fail that vote, it's my understanding that Congressman Cheney will yield his time to Col. North, and Col. North should be given the opportunity immediately to proceed with his briefing.

SEN. MCCLURE: Mr. Chairman, will the gentleman yield?

CHAIRMAN INOUYE: I would like to advise the panel that the yielding of time must be for a purpose that will be approved by the panel or by the chair.

REP. COURTER: Well, I don't know what he's going to say, so I don't know whether it's going to be—

SEN. MCCLURE: I would still ask the gentleman to yield.

CHAIRMAN INOUYE: Senator McClure?

REP. COURTER: I have to get prior approval from the chair as to what I'm going to say? I don't quite understand. Will the gentleman yield? I've asked the gentleman to yield. If the chair will let me yield, I'll use permission to have the gentleman yield to me.

CHAIRMAN INOUYE: I was advising Mr. Courter that one may yield his time to another panel member. But the purpose of that yielding must be subject to the approval of this panel, to wit, the chairman.

REP. COURTER: I would ask the Chair's permission.

SEN. MCCLURE (R-FL): Mr. Chairman?

REP. COURTER: Mr. Chairman, I'd like—

CHAIRMAN INOUYE: Senator McClure? I'm recognizing the Senator. He's been waiting a long time now. And after that, I'll recognize you, sir.

SEN. MCCLURE: Mr. Chairman, I know that it's almost impossible to separate the subject matters in this kind of a discussion or the question that the panel will now address as to whether or not the time to have Col. North make the presentation. But, Mr. Chairman, there was the implication raised at earlier stages of this proceeding that Col. North was involved in an activity proscribed by the Boland Amendment in raising funds for the contras. Now that implication he didn't raise—was not an implication raised by him in his testimony. It was an implication raised through the means of other witnesses' testimony and comments by members of this panel that, indeed, there was in effect a conspiracy to evade Boland by the device of having Col. North make the pitch and someone else come in and make the solicitation. And Senator Rudman made reference to it again today, that he had described that as the old one-two punch.

I don't think it is possible for us, under those circumstances, to deny the opportunity for this panel to see what that really was—not for the content alone, although certainly it does have content. But, because it has a fair relationship and a bearing upon the question that was raised in this Committee, that somehow Col. North's activities were erroneous under the statutes that were in effect at that time. I understand that those who are opposed to contra aid, and I am not one of those, I am in support of aid to the contras, and I am in support of what the Colonel has done. But I don't, I don't and will not vote on this matter because I'm in favor of contra aid, but because I'm in favor of fairness to Colonel North and the others who were involved in this process.

SEN. RUDMAN: Would my friend yield for one moment?

SEN. MCCLURE: I'd be happy to.

SEN. RUDMAN: Just so the record is clear, the description of Colonel North's activities—you can read the record —was not his slide presentations, his speeches to the ABA, which were authorized, his other speeches which were authorized. My remarks and other remarks of this panel were directed to two meetings with Mrs. Garwood at the Hay-Adams Hotel, with Mrs. Garwood in Houston, Texas; the Colonel and I discussed that yesterday, I think we had a meeting of the minds on that issue, so that is not what the description was. I think we all understand that the Colonel had every right to give those speeches, those slide presentations, because he testified yesterday they were authorized by his superiors, and we know that to be true—

SEN. MCCLURE: Well, I would—

SEN. RUDMAN: We are talking about two isolated incidents, so let's not confuse the issue.

SEN. MCCLURE: I am not at all confused about what the issue is, Senator Rudman, although you may attempt to do that. The fact of the matter is that there were questions raised about the activity and the presentations made by Colonel North. And this presentation is essential to that, in my judgment.

As I started to say a moment ago, this panel certainly has the right to make the determination as to whether or not he will be heard, he will be permitted to make that presentation, which I think is essential from his standpoint and essential from my view as to whether or not the story has been fully and fairly told. Now if the panel votes not to do so, I recognize that the majority rules, and I will certainly abide by the wishes of the majority, as though I had any other choice. (Laughter.)

CHAIRMAN INOUYE: Mr. McCollum.

SEN. MCCLURE: But I would certainly—I do want the panel to understand why I will vote in favor of the motion that the Senate—that the gentleman from New Jersey has made.

CHAIRMAN INOUYE: Mr. McCollum.

REP. MCCOLLUM (R-IA): Thank you very much, Mr. Chairman. I think the issue on the vote as to what time of day we have this presentation is the essence of the question of what is fair to Colonel North and what is fair in the sense of what the American public views it. We've had a lot of discussions, not in this panel so much, but in the media and amongst the public over the last few days of Colonel North's testimony about whether we've been fair to him or not.

I don't impugn the motives of anyone on the Committee or the leadership, but the impression is out there among many people in the public that this Committee has not been fair. And it seems to me that if we're going to relegate this slide presentation to 7:30 tonight, the night of the All-Star baseball game on television, if we're going to put him in the back burner like that so that he cannot have an opportunity to give this presentation that we, I think, all have now agreed he should be allowed to give so the American public can see it. And I agree with Congressman Courter technically, whether we could shine it here with the lights in the right way for the TV media or not, they certainly can put these slides on, and duplicates could quickly be made to give them. They can put them on television if they want. If we're going to shun him and his opportunity away like that, we're going to be unfair to him and, in addition to that, I have not been a party to it and I'm sure better wisdom, perhaps, than mine prevail, but we are bringing forward, this afternoon presumably, or shortly after Colonel North leaves, Mr. McFarlane, for a period of testimony presumably in rebuttal to what Colonel North's going to say or has already said. And it seems to me that that also will tend to be an appearance of unfairness unless we parade—give Colonel North an opportunity to parade back up here again and rebut whatever Mr. McFarlane says. So, in the context of all of this I think it's important for the integrity of this process that we allow the presentation of these slides at a reasonable hour during the testimony of Colonel North during the daytime and not put it somewhere back against the All-Star game tonight or in some dark corner in some abyss where the American public will never actually see or appreciate the delivery, the style, the nature of the presentation and always wonder about it. Thank you, Mr. Chairman.

REP. DEWINE (R-OH): Mr. Chairman?

CHAIRMAN INOUYE: Mr. DeWine.

REP. DEWINE: Thank you very much, Mr. Chairman. Mr. Chairman, the issue is not aid to the contras. This is being offered because really it's the best evidence of what Colonel North's intent was. It is the best evidence of what actually happened. There have been allegations, maybe not on this Committee, but there have been allegations that there was something wrong with what Colonel North was doing, that he was directly involved in solicitation. The best evidence of whether he was or was not is the actual presentation itself, the presentation that he—it is my understanding —gave to over a hundred groups, only a few of those actually had to do with fund raising. But that's the best evidence. I would also add, Mr. Chairman, the intense interest of the American people in this presentation. I was home in Ohio for the weekend for two days, and I can't tell you how many people came up to me not only expressing interest in these hearings but who specifically said, "I want to hear that presentation." I even had a call yesterday back to my office and someone said, "I want the Congressman to yield his 15 minutes of time. If you can't get it any other way, have DeWine yield that 15 minutes of time." So there is an interest in this, and I think I agree with Bill McCollum. We have an obligation to put this on in the normal sequence of events and not pick a time at night when the All-Star game is going on or we're going up against Jeopardy or something else. It ought to be in the normal procedure, and I think it's unfair not to have it in the normal procedure. Thank you.

CHAIRMAN INOUYE: Senator Cohen.

SEN. COHEN (R-ME): Mr. Chairman, I just—

CHAIRMAN INOUYE: But before you proceed, I would like to advise the panel that a vote is in progress, and I believe we just have about three minutes to report to the Senate. So please proceed, sir.

SEN. COHEN: I have about a 30-second question, Mr. Chairman. Is it the presentation or the circumstances under which the presentation was given and the particular time that's in question? If it's the presentation per se, then we should have the slide show alone. But if it's the circumstances under which the presentation was given, it seems to me that we would have to consider calling the "second punch," as Senator Rudman has talked about, and that would be under what circumstances follow the presentation, what was the relationship. So, I am perfectly prepared to have a presentation, but I think it has to be placed within the context under which it was given, that's to present a fair picture of what took place in those given times.

MR. ——: Would the Senator yield for the moment?

CHAIRMAN INOUYE: I am certain you recall my statement, at the time this matter was brought up, that in order to provide the appropriate fora and the flavor of that moment, we would have to call in Mr. Channell and Mr. Miller, and arrangements have been made to call upon Mr. Channell and Mr. Miller and Mrs. Garwood—I believe it is—so that we will have a full picture—

SEN. SARBANES: Would the Senator yield on that point?

CHAIRMAN INOUYE: Yes, sir.

SEN. SARBANES: Mr. Chairman, I just make this observation, that even if you bring Channell and Miller and Mrs. Garwood to make a presentation now, today, that doesn't establish for the Committee what the presentation was that was made then—

CHAIRMAN INOUYE: —Obviously.—

SEN. SARBANES: —yesterday. In other words, the issue, if there is an issue, and I'm not sure there is, because I think Senator Rudman has effectively addressed that question, but if there is an issue, the issue is the nature of the presentation that was made then, and putting together a presentation now doesn't answer that question.

VICE CHAIRMAN RUDMAN: Mr. Chairman.

CHAIRMAN INOUYE: Mr. Rudman.

SEN. RUDMAN: Mr. Chairman, I just want to make an observation, if we're talking about fairness—and I think I know how this vote might go. I don't particularly want to see Colonel North sitting here, describing circumstances with Mr. Spitz Channell sitting next to him or in the same room with him—a man who's already been indicted, and pled guilty to an event—I don't think that's fair to this witness, and so, if the only way we're going to settle this thing, is to have it that way, then I think we ought to think long and hard, talking about fairness, that—associate the Colonel with a man that's already been found guilty. Thank you, Mr. Chairman.

SEN. HATCH: Mr. Chairman, I'll just take 30 seconds. That's fine with me. I think it's time that we get this out publicly, and just plain, give the Lieutenant Colonel a chance to explain what he did; that's what's important. I don't care what the others did, I'll be listening with great interest, what they did, but I want to know what he did. And to be honest with you, I think he ought to have that opportunity to tell the American people, and I think the technological problems can be resolved, as Mr. Courter says, and it should be done.

REP. COURTER: Mr. Chairman, I—

CHAIRMAN INOUYE: —Give us time to cool our soles and to cast our vote. We'll stand in recess for 10 minutes. (bangs the gavel)

(Recess)

CHAIRMAN INOUYE: The hearing will please come to order. Contrary to belief held by many Americans, this panel has tried its best to be fair. On the matter before us, to wit, the showing of the slides, I have tried my best to advise one and all that because of security considerations the lights in this room cannot be turned off. Accordingly, the slides will not be seen either by members of the panel and, more importantly, by the people of the United States. However, I believe we have worked out something that might serve the purpose intended by Mr. Courter. We have no desire to keep any information away from the people of the United States. It was our intention to do so, and, as a result, a special room had been set aside, a special screen had been acquired, a special projector was acquired. But apparently under the arrangement we may not see the show. Chairman Hamilton?

CHAIRMAN HAMILTON: Thank you very much, Mr. Chairman. Members will recall that Congressman Cheney had 20 minutes reserved on his time. So the chair recognizes Congressman Cheney at this time for 20 minutes for the purpose of asking questions. Congressman Cheney.

REP. CHENEY (R-WY): Thank you, Mr. Chairman. Mr. Chairman, I think on behalf of many of us—Mr. Courter and Senator McClure and others who spoke to this issue —we feel very, very strongly that given the line of questioning developed by counsel for the Committee, it's only fair that Colonel North have the opportunity to present that information that was a part of his briefing with respect to the question of what kind of efforts he made in providing information to American citizens or ultimately cooperated in and supported fundraising efforts for the contras. I think

672

the key thing for us, Mr. Chairman, is that the permanent record of these proceedings show what in fact was in that presentation and that the American people have access to that information. And I would concur in the Chairman's statement that it is impossible from a technical standpoint this morning to present the slides in this setting in a manner that would make them available to the public. So I'm going to make the following request, Mr. Chairman. First of all, I ask unanimous consent that the slides that are part of Colonel North's briefing be made a permanent part of the printed record of these proceedings.

CHAIRMAN INOUYE: Before responding to that, I have a question. How many slides involved, Colonel, because I've been told that slides are selected for different purposes?

LT. COL. NORTH: The briefing in its current format—and there were many different formats for it, of course, and we tried to update it—has 57 slides, Senator.

CHAIRMAN INOUYE: And is there a written text that accompanies the slide show?

LT. COL. NORTH: No, sir.

CHAIRMAN INOUYE: Are there notes that you refer to?

LT. COL. NORTH: No, I would—in the format that I gave it in many times, sometimes even up here on the Hill, I would simply put the slides up on the screen and describe the—the slides. And of course the—the contents of the entire briefing demonstrated the Soviet threat in this hemisphere and how the resistance was—

CHAIRMAN INOUYE: Fine, sir.

LT. COL. NORTH: —responding to it.

CHAIRMAN INOUYE: Then we are submitting 57, is that correct, Mr. Cheney?

REP. CHENEY: Yes, Mr. Chairman, that's correct.

CHAIRMAN INOUYE: Without objection, 57 slides will be made part of the permanent record.

REP. CHENEY: And secondly, Mr. Chairman, if I might, I ask unanimous consent that the material in the slides be produced in printed form and made available to the press and the public by that means.

CHAIRMAN INOUYE: So ordered. So ordered.

SEN. HATCH: Can we have that done today? Is it possible for that to be—

CHAIRMAN INOUYE: We will expedite the matter, sir.

SEN. HATCH: Thank you, sir.

REP. HYDE (R-IL): Will the gentleman from—

REP. CHENEY: Thank you, Mr. Chairman.

REP. HYDE: Will the gentleman from Wyoming yield for a question?

REP. CHENEY: I'll be happy to yield to the gentleman from Illinois, Mr. Hyde.

REP. HYDE: Will there be captions on these slides? They will be meaningless if they're just reproduced as—as pictures, unless we know what they portray. So somebody had best compose captions for them or, as I say, I don't think they'll be too helpful.

REP. CHENEY: I would be happy to ask our staff to work with Colonel North and take the slides and put them out on in an appropriate fashion in four colors if the gentleman from Illinois so desires.

CHAIRMAN INOUYE: We'll do whatever we can to accommodate you, sir.

REP. CHENEY: Colonel North, in the time remaining to me, I would like to ask you to give us a general description of your briefing, if you will. I'm especially interested in putting on the public record as part of these hearings information about the nature and the extent of the Soviet threat in Central America and Nicaragua.

LT. COL. NORTH: All right, sir. Perhaps the best way to do that is to simply go through the presentation as it—as it exists, and I will try to quickly go through the slides and indicate what I would have said had the slides been up on the screen.

The first slide simply demonstrates the geography and why this part of the world seems to be of so much interest to the Soviets. The first slide shows the effect of Soviet penetration in this hemisphere in the form of a consolidated communist regime in Cuba and the threat that poses to our sea lines of communication, both to Europe and through the Panama Canal, and the threat it poses to 55 percent of our oil supplies coming up from Latin America.

The second slide is a photograph of Andrei Gromyko, then the Foreign Minister of the Soviet Union, and a quote from Mr. Gromyko to the effect that he said in Moscow in 1983, "The region is boiling like a cauldron. Cuba and Nicaragua are living examples for the countries in that part of the world," talking about their intentions. A second quote from Marshal Ogorkov, then the head of the Soviet Armed Forces, in Moscow, when he was talking to Maurice Bishop, then the head of Grenada, in which he said—a note taken by Bishop and his people in visiting Moscow in March of '83—"The Marshal said"—forgive me (pauses) —"The Marshal said that over two decades ago, there was only Cuba in Latin America. Today there are Nicaragua, Grenada, and a serious battle is going on in El Salvador." A 1983 pronouncement by Marshal Ogorkov.

There is then a summary of Soviet policy in the region, based on Soviet literature, and summarized, that their goal is to create such turmoil in the Caribbean Basin that the United States must divert attention and military resources from areas critical to the Soviets. A follow-on slide depicts the fact that the Soviets are out-spending us in our own hemisphere on a ratio of about five to one, and that's a 1985's figures—1984's figures. They have since gotten worse.

A photograph showing the Soviet warships deployed in the Caribbean, what used to be referred to as an American lake. Sixteen miles off the coast of Louisiana, the Kiev battle group deployed for a refueling and replenishment exercise.

A photograph of the Soviet submarines provided to Cuba. And the text that would have gone with it will describe the fact that Adolph Hitler was able to shut down 44 percent of the shipping from the United States during the opening days of World War II from submarines based 4000 miles away, and these submarines are based less than 200 miles away in Cuba.

A photograph of a US Navy F-4 escorting a Soviet Bear-F strategic reconnaissance aircraft, 13 miles off the coast of the Virginia cape. And then a photograph taken by a US reconnaissance platform, of the Soviet military facility at San Antonio de los Baños in Cuba. It is that facility which allows the Soviets to recover their reconnaissance aircraft which fly down the east coast of the United States. And, until they complete their base in Nicaragua, they aren't able to do so in reconnoitering the west coast of the United States. Then a photograph of the Soviet signals intelligence site at Lourdes, Cuba, by which the Soviets—not the

675

Cubans, but the Soviets—intercept our communications, particularly our telephone and satellite communications on which we rely for almost all of our military and diplomatic correspondence via telephone and telex. A photograph showing the militarization of the Cuban children—a sixth-grade class out for their firing exercises. Then a photograph showing a map showing where Cuban forces, as the mercenary army of the Soviet Union, are deployed—3000 in Nicaragua, 400 in the Congo, 35,000 in Angola, 700 in Mozambique, 5000-plus in Ethiopia and 500 in Yemen. That chart would have been updated, had I still been in my current employ, to show the 1500 now in South Yemen. And the fact is that the Soviets are, indeed, using the Cubans as a mercenary army throughout the world.

To point out that the Soviets weren't satisfied simply with having Cuba, that the militarization of the island of Grenada was first observed by US reconnaissance platforms in the extension and expansion of an airfield at Point Salinas, far in excess of that required for normal commercial operations first cued us to the fact that something was seriously wrong on the island of Grenada. And, of course, in October of 1983, the next slide shows some of the Cuban economic aid going to the small island nation of Grenada, some of the packing crates from the warehouses full of weapons, stamped with "Cuban economic office," and full of munitions.

The next slide shows a Chinese rocket launcher, probably made in the 1950s, probably captured in Vietnam, shipped to Grenada, and the shipping documents for that document —"weapon captured in El Salvador," the shipping documents found in Grenada showing that Grenada was being used as a location to support Soviet designs for subversion and revolution in this hemisphere. Then a photograph of the five secret military agreements found in Grenada after the US rescue operation. Military agreements for the Soviet Union, Bulgaria, North Korea, Cuba and Hungary. Somehow, we were unable to get those things before the American people in such a way as that they understand what was really happening in this hemisphere. It has not only happened in Cuba, it is now happening in Nicaragua.

The next slide shows simply a map of Nicaragua, describing the fact that this country of about the size of Iowa, or

Michigan, a country with about 3 million in population, the only country in Central America with a—or Latin America —with a decreasing population. And why that population is decreasing is because of the internal repression perpetrated on the people of Nicaragua. It shows the growth of the active duty forces in the Sandinista military machine, an enormous military buildup supported by the Soviet Union.

The next slide—next series of slides—show some of the military equipment, on which I have already been questioned, but it shows the T-55 tanks, now numbering over 150; the PT-76 tanks and the armored personnel carriers numbering over 300. The buildup taken from reconnaissance platforms at Sandino airfield, turned from a civilian air facility under Somoza into one of the most sophisticated military facilities in Central America.

This is the armored storage area at El Tempesque, built along the Cuban model. The special airfields built by the Soviets to support their—and the Cubans—to support the Sandinista military operations along the nothern tier of that country. The construction of another armored storage area inside Nicaragua. The construction of a major port facility along the Pacific coast in order to handle the off-load of Soviet military supplies being delivered along the Pacific Coast at Corinto, two shots of that. A photograph of the Soviet-Bulgarian-Cuban construction being conducted at Punta Juete along the Atlantic coast. For the first time, the Soviets will have the ability not only to deliver, they can do it pier-side, and the construction of an El Bluefields, which the Soviets the are supporting.

An aerial reconnaissance platform photograph of Punta Juete, the largest airfield south of the Rio Grande, bigger than Andrews Air Force Base, which is capable of launching and receiving any aircraft in the Soviet inventory to include the reconnaissance aircraft shown in the earlier slides, allowing them to reconnoiter the west coast of the United States, or even, if they wish, to recover Backfire bombers at such a location.

The next slide shows some of the supplies delivered to the Sandinistas during the period of Soviet support which began not in 1982, but in 1979. The first of them shows one of the MI-8HIP helicopters, delivered originally as agricultural support equipment, it shows some of the unique agricultural support uniforms, and of course the party emblem next to the agricultural rocket-launcher on the side of the aircraft.

The next photograph is the Soviet HIND Helicopter, the most sophisticated assault platform in the world today, it has been delivered by the dozens to the Sandinistas. Assembled by Soviet technicians and test flown by them, it is flown by Cuban and Nicaraguan pilots against the resistance, and to intimidate their neighbors. There is also a photograph of a Soviet AN-30 reconnaissance aircraft flown by Soviets in this hemisphere, not Cubans, not Nicaraguans, marked neatly with aeroflowed markings on the side, photographed surreptitiously from an aircraft landing at Sandino Airport. Some quotes from the Ortega brothers, and then the folks down in Nicaragua in which somehow we have been unable to explain to the American people what their real intent was in bringing out this revolution. And I think the quotes are important because it really does depict what they've been saying all along. In 1981, when Humberto Ortega, the defense minister, interestingly enough a mere image of what is going on in Cuba. The minister of defense in Cuba is the brother of Fidel Castro. The minister of defense in Nicaragua is the brother of El Presidente Daniel Ortega. Umberto has said, "Marxism-Leninism is the scientific doctrine that guides our revolution. Our doctrine is Marxism-Leninism." And he said that in August of 1981. And what he is saying is every other word is that communism is what they want. And this was being said at a time when we somehow couldn't explain to the American people effectively that these people really were communists and they were all along. Bayardo Arce: "Any investment project in our country belongs to the state. The bourgeousie no longer exists. It's subsists." 1984. The great political thinker, the Che Guevara, in many respects of the current revolution in Nicaragua, Tomas Borge, the Minister of Interior. He doesn't run the national parks. He runs the secret police: "You cannot be a true revolutionary in Latin America without being a Marxist-Leninist," said in Havana in 1984. And then two photographs of Mr. Ortega and some of his associates, one with Fidel Castro, and then with some of his other brothers in arms, in this case the leader of Libya, Muammar Qaddafi, shown with Tomas

Borge and the Minister of Foreign Affairs, Miguel D'Escoto, along with Mr. Qaddafi on the deck of a Korean gunboat. And then a series of photographs which showed the attempt to subvert their neighbors. In one case, a lighted automobile I described the other day which crashed into a bridge abutment, an automobile accident in Honduras, and then the photograph showing what was inside that automobile to include the counterfeit money, the arms, the ammunition, the Soviet-bloc radios, the code sheets, all of the things of subversion for subverting their neighbors. Then there are two photographs showing the arms captured after the M-19 assault on the Supreme Court in which the entire Supreme Court of Columbia was murdered. All the records of the drug running that was perpetuated and supported by the M-19 guerilla faction. All of the weapons in those photographs originated in Nicaragua. Then a photograph that starts a series on what has happened to the people of Nicaragua; a photograph of one of the 11 new political prisons inside Nicaragua; a photograph of one of the victims, with his arms and face terribly burned from having been trussed, bound, thrown into his Pentecostal church and set afire while he was alive, and he managed to push himself out of the church.

A photograph from a Nicaraguan school book, printed in East Germany or Cuba, showing how young Nicaraguan children learn to count by counting grenades and AK-47s. And of course, the textbooks talk about anti-imperialism and anti-Americanism. A photograph of some remarkable quantity—quality—showing an entire town which fled in their Sunday best across the border, simply to go to church on Sunday, wearing everything that they had because they could never go back home. A series of photographs showing the dislocation of the Miskito Indians, 25,000 to 30,000 of which have been driven from tribal homelands across the border into Costa Rica and Honduras, bringing with them their entire culture, left alone for hundreds of years. These people no longer can go home.

Then some photographs showing the Nicaraguan resistance. It shows the young men and women who have taken up arms because they've been denied any other recourse in their own country. It shows the 57-year-old coffee farmer who I described earlier, who came home and found his entire family murdered by the Sandinistas because they gave water to a passing contra patrol. A series of photographs showing how the resistance looks as a consequence of the assistance I am accused and admit to having delivered. A photograph showing the leadership of the FDN, and in that photograph of 16 men, 11 of them are former Sandinistas.

A photograph of a resistance unit crossing into Nicaragua; another one of a patrol deep inside Nicaragua. A photograph of a wounded resistance soldier who benefited from the support that we provided during the cutoff, and then a photograph of what it looked like before that help arrived. A photograph of the emergency aid station intensive care unit, which is nothing more than a field tent without even mosquito netting. A photograph of the plastic maps that they were forced to draw their own battle plans and patrol routes on because we couldn't even give them that. And then finally a photograph showing the grave of a resistance fighter. And the conclusion of the briefing is, gentlemen, that we've got to offer them something more than the chance to die for their own country and the freedoms that we believe in. Thank you, sir.

REP. CHENEY: Thank you, Col. North. I yield back the balance of my time, Mr. Chairman.

CHAIRMAN INOUYE: The Chair recognizes Senator McClure.

SEN. MCCLURE (R-FL): Thank you, Mr. Chairman. And thank you, Colonel North. And I—Mr. Chairman, before commencing my questioning, thank you for the accommodation that was reached in order to allow Colonel North to make the presentation that he has.

And I think, without asking the Committee to enter into the stipulation which Senator Rudman offered earlier on behalf of himself, he stipulated that indeed this presentation, followed, as it was in other settings, by contacts of other people, did not, in and of itself, constitute a solicitation of funds. And I think Senator Rudman's words were that he would stipulate that those activities were not, that you did not, and you had not, been involved in raising funds in these activities.

I say that because I realize that every member of the two Committees that are here will make their own judgments about that fact, and so will the American public. But I do want to at least follow Senator Rudman's suggestion to the extent of—to the extent that I can by my remarks, indicate that I, too, think the record is very, very clear that you were very, very careful that you did not personally solicit money.

LT. COL. NORTH: That is correct, sir.

SEN. MCCLURE: You've testified to that, and while some say, "Well, you went right up to the line; that indicates you tried to get over it," while others are saying, "You went up to the line and you carefully followed the law that was in effect at that time."

LT. COL. NORTH: I did, sir.

SEN. MCCLURE: Colonel North, I want to go back in just a few minutes and kind of reconstruct where we are on the basis of your testimony and what it is this Committee is really—these Committees are really about. Our charge is to find out, indeed, what was US policy in Iran? What was US policy as reflected by the evolution of our policy with respect to Iran? And what does that mean with respect to the evolution of that policy? What were the influences? How did it come about? What were we really about? And secondly, the point that we began in these hearings, what was this contra network and how did the two get mixed together?

I don't want to put words in your mouth, but I do want to get the background laid very quickly, and I will ask you if, indeed, you agree or disagree with my summary. And I hope, indeed, if you disagree, you'll state it briefly. And if you agree, just state that.

If I understand your testimony to this point, the United States was approached by representatives, first from Israel and then from Iran, suggesting that we open a dialogue with elements inside Iran looking towards the time when there would be a different regime and a different relationship between the United States and that new regime in Iran, am I correct?

LT. COL. NORTH: Yes, and to assist in furthering that change of regime.

SEN. MCCLURE: And I—I would submit from my own standpoint that any administration that was given any hint that that was possible and did not pursue that opportunity would be derelict, not because we like Khomeini, because obviously we do not. We're not seeking to deal with Khomeini; we're seeking to find a way to deal with a different government in Iran than the one that exists there now, recognizing the importance of that country geostrategically and also economically because of the importance of oil to the world's economy. Am I correct?

LT. COL. NORTH: Yes, sir.

SEN. MCCLURE: That from that initiative the—the representatives of this country and of Israel began exploring ways in which that might be accomplished. And in that process we ran into some rather strange bedfellows, people like Mr. Ghorbanifar, who made suggestions in spite of the fact that we didn't really have any reason to trust him. But nevertheless, he made suggestions about the means by which we could accomplish the end of making contact with those elements in Iran. And among those suggestions was: "You've got to prove you're really serious. Who is this guy, Colonel North, or who—whoever else the representatives might have been of the United States? Were you really speaking for the President of the United States? Show you're serious. Show you really speak for the United States." And that gave birth to the notion of proving bona fides by supplying arms. Is that correct?

LT. COL. NORTH: That is my understanding of how it initiated, because I was not there at the conception, if you will, sir.

SEN. MCCLURE: Colonel North, this isn't a summary because you haven't yet testified to this fact, but isn't it a fact that Israel was already involved in arms trades with Soviet Union—with Iran, involving—involving not only arms which they produced themselves inside Israel, but also arms which had been supplied by the United States to Israel?

LT. COL. NORTH: Apparently so. Yes, sir.

SEN. MCCLURE: So that this was not an unprecedented or a new idea so far as the relationships between Israel and Iran were concerned?

LT. COL. NORTH: We do not believe it was.

SEN. MCCLURE: That following that time we—it was suggested, and I think again suggested to us be representatives of Israel—that Iran could prove their bona fides with us by putting pressure upon the Lebanese captors of US hostages, to put pressure upon them to release hostages as an evidence to the fact that they indeed had clout within their own government?

LT. COL. NORTH: Yes.

SEN. MCCLURE: And that led to what has been described as the arms-for-hostages transaction?

LT. COL. NORTH: That's correct.

SEN. MCCLURE: Rightly or wrongly, that's the way it evolved?

LT. COL. NORTH: It did.

SEN. MCCLURE: It was also suggested to us that, if you really want to get any kind of a new relationship with Iran, you've got to solve the question of hostages first because no responsible American government can deal with the government in Iran so long as Iran has the key, or can put pressure upon those who do have the key, that locks up our hostages.

LT. COL. NORTH: Exactly.

SEN. MCCLURE: So it wasn't hostage-generated from the beginning, but hostages were both a means of proving bona fides and also as removing a roadblock to the evolution of that kind of a new relationship with a new element inside Iran.

LT. COL. NORTH: Correct.

SEN. MCCLURE: Following that then came the escalating demands and the difficulties that came along with those escalating demands in the arms transactions with Iran and the pressures that would result in the release of hostages. And there were a whole series of those difficulties.

LT. COL. NORTH: There certainly were, sir.

SEN. MCCLURE: Now I have been intrigued—and I asked earlier witnesses about this—I have been intrigued by the fact that Israel, who is so competent in so many ways, screwed up that arms transaction so badly. Did it ever—

LT. COL. NORTH: You're talking of the November one?

SEN. MCCLURE: Yes. And they had had successful arms transactions for a long while. But suddenly in November, at about the time the United States was about to withdraw from the whole initiative, they suddenly have a stranded arms shipment stranded in Portugal because they didn't have the right kind of clearances, because they're trying to fly shipments in aircraft with Israeli markings, whole host of different kinds of problems, all of which should have been very familiar to them. Is that correct?

LT. COL. NORTH: Yes, and I have tried not to hypothesize, although many have, as to why that happened.

SEN. MCCLURE: Well, did it cross your mind at the time that that's odd that this group of people, who are so very, very competent in so many different ways and have carried on these arms trade—this arms trade for a period of years, suddenly finds themselves in grave difficulty on a shipment and have to ask us for help at the very time that we're about to withdraw from the entire initiative?

LT. COL. NORTH: It did, sir.

SEN. MCCLURE: But nevertheless, we did, at some time about then, begin to have further overtures from Israeli agents—and I think you have testified that Ghorbanifar was an Israeli agent?

LT. COL. NORTH: At least that's how he was seen by our intelligence service.

SEN. MCCLURE: So you believed at the time—

LT. COL. NORTH: Right.

SEN. MCCLURE: —of the contacts that he was an Israel agent.

LT. COL. NORTH: I believe then and I believe now.

SEN. MCCLURE: That indeed, they wished this to go forward and they were trying to find a way to persuade us to go forward.

LT. COL. NORTH: Yes.

SEN. MCCLURE: And as a matter of fact, you had meetings with Mr. Nir, I believe, during the—at the end of December or early January, and nothing was said about the diversion of the funds or the use of the funds derived from arms sales, with respect to contras, he was talking about the use of proceeds for other covert activity?

LT. COL. NORTH: That is correct.

SEN. MCCLURE: And the US government at that time, both yourself and others, were still saying, "no."

LT. COL. NORTH: That's correct.

SEN. MCCLURE: I think Mr. McFarlane had made a trip to London and he came away and said, "It's done, it's finished, this is a bad deal, let's don't go any further with that." That had occurred before your meeting with Mr. Nir?

LT. COL. NORTH: I don't recall the meeting quite as emphatically as that, but certainly Mr. McFarlane expressed reservations about continuing on, if all we could get was Mr. Ghorbanifar as an intermediary.

SEN. MCCLURE: And that went on through December and into January, and then sometime later, you had this meeting that you have referred to, "somewhere in Europe, probably" with Mr. Ghorbanifar in the bathroom, when he suggested to you, "Hey, wouldn't it be a great idea to use the Ayatollah's money to support the contras?

LT. COL. NORTH: That's correct, sir.

SEN. MCCLURE: And that struck a spark with you?

LT. COL. NORTH: It did, indeed.

SEN. MCCLURE: He found the right sales pitch?

LT. COL. NORTH: One-two punch.

SEN. MCCLURE: Yes. With one guy?

LT. COL. NORTH: Yes, sir.

SEN. MCCLURE: The—but nevertheless, that was the genesis of the connection between Iran and the contras?

LT. COL. NORTH: Yes, sir. It was.

SEN. MCCLURE: In spite of the fact that some people will point to an earlier time, when you had called upon General Secord and Lake Resources, to help expedite the shipment in December?

LT. COL. NORTH: And that was the sole purpose in calling upon him back in November.

SEN. MCCLURE: In November?

LT. COL. NORTH: Yes, sir.

SEN. MCCLURE: But it has nothing to do with a Iran-contra connection at that time?

LT. COL. NORTH: It did not.

SEN. MCCLURE: One of the things that is—that I can't help but turn over in my own mind, that the United States policy was and is, a neutrality—if that's the right word —between our policy towards Iran and our policy towards Iraq—

LT. COL. NORTH: That was our publicly stated policy, but members of the Intelligence Committee already know that we were not entirely neutral in that activity.

SEN. MCCLURE: And the—that stated policy was not the same as Israel's stated policy?

LT. COL. NORTH: No, it was not.

685

SEN. MCCLURE: Part of our stated policy was also to bring about an end to the war?

LT. COL. NORTH: It is, and—was and it is.

SEN. MCCLURE: And that's not Israel's stated policy?

LT. COL. NORTH: I'm not entirely sure, Senator, that I could clearly state what their public policy is. But, clearly, they were not as interested in ending the war as we were.

SEN. MCCLURE: As a matter of fact, from an Israeli standpoint, the continuation of the war that keeps Iraq occupied—

LT. COL. NORTH: Is to their benefit.

SEN. MCCLURE: —is to their benefit?

LT. COL. NORTH: That's correct.

SEN. MCCLURE: And Iraq is a greater threat to them than Iran, simply because Iraq has been involved in armed conflict with Israel in the past.

LT. COL. NORTH: Precisely.

SEN. MCCLURE: And is close to their borders.

LT. COL. NORTH: Yes, sir.

SEN. MCCLURE: And has the largest active tank force in the Middle East.

LT. COL. NORTH: That's correct.

SEN. MCCLURE: And, if there's one thing that the Israelis have to be concerned about, it's not air superiority. It is ground warfare. It's ground warfare in the personage, in the use of armored vehicles, is that correct?

LT. COL. NORTH: Yes, sir.

SEN. MCCLURE: I think the war between Iran and Iraq indicates that just masses of manpower, as Iran has used, are not necessarily going to dominate a war in which the other side has adequate armor.

LT. COL. NORTH: That's correct.

SEN. MCCLURE: And so, Israel's concern with Iraq has to be based upon their willingness to use arms against Israel, their past history of doing so, their current capability of doing so, if the war between Iran and Iraq were to end.

LT. COL. NORTH: Yes, sir.

SEN. MCCLURE: And it is also a fact, is it not, that the one weapon that the Israelis urged us to provide to Iran was the TOW?

LT. COL. NORTH: Well, they were also engaged with the Hawks.

686

SEN. MCCLURE: But the Hawks was as a result of the request by the Iranians?

LT. COL. NORTH: As best we can determine, yes, sir.

SEN. MCCLURE: And the TOWs were the suggestion that we received from Israel?

LT. COL. NORTH: Yes, sir. It was.

SEN. MCCLURE: And TOWs are an anti-tank weapon?

LT. COL. NORTH: And a darn good one.

SEN. MCCLURE: And that would also coincide extremely well with the concerns that Israel has with the Iraqi armor?

LT. COL. NORTH: Yes, sir.

SEN. MCCLURE: So that, if we could provide Iran with enough TOW weapons to destroy Iraqi tanks, that's perfectly consistent with Israeli policy and Israeli concerns?

LT. COL. NORTH: Yes, sir.

SEN. MCCLURE: From the standpoint of the success or failure of a policy, the failure of this policy would be extremely damaging to the United States. You discussed that. If the cover got blown and the public began to discuss what it was we were trying to do in Iran, that would be damaging?

LT. COL. NORTH: Yes, sir—and I believe it has been.

SEN. MCCLURE: However, if the cover got blown, and we were talking about the connection and contra policy, it would be extremely damaging?

LT. COL. NORTH: Yes, sir.

SEN. MCCLURE: As has proven to be the case. But you discussed that. You recognized there was a tremendous downside, a tremendous risk in failure?

LT. COL. NORTH: Yes, sir.

SEN. MCCLURE: But despite that, the opportunities for success or the opportunities to move the US interests on those several different fronts outweighed the hazards of failure in your minds or in the minds of those who were making policy?

LT. COL. NORTH: Yes, sir.

SEN. MCCLURE: Now, to the Israelis, a failure of this policy would not be nearly so damaging, would it?

LT. COL. NORTH: It does not appear to have been.

SEN. MCCLURE: Well, wouldn't that be apparent at that time?

LT. COL. NORTH: Yes.

SEN. MCCLURE: We'll try it. If it works, fine. If it fails, so what? More or less, the risks of failure on the Israeli scale of cost-benefit was far less important to them than it was apparent would be to us.

LT. COL. NORTH: I could agree to that.

SEN. MCCLURE: I go through that because not because I have any disrespect for the Israelis, but I do wonder why it was that US policymakers walked in step with Israeli policy and didn't respond to what were apparent inducements being offered by them at a time when the risks to them were much less than the risks to us.

LT. COL. NORTH: Well, you're asking me a question that I think we all weighed. And we simply estimated that the long-term benefit to us was worth the risk. The necessities. And having weighed all of those, we decided to proceed.

SEN. MCCLURE: Well, I see my time is about expired and I don't have time to detail all of the contacts that were made by various people from Israel to the United States. Mr. Schwimmer, who has been identified a number of times—I understand, a man with dual citizenship—a citizen of the United States as well as a citizen of Israel—

LT. COL. NORTH: I was unaware of that until this time, sir.

SEN. MCCLURE: —has also been in the past a registered foreign agent for the Israeli government, although he's sometimes portrayed as being nothing but an arms merchant or private citizen in Israel. Mr. Ledeen is a US citizen, but he shows in the early contacts and in the persuasions that were attempted to keep us involved in this process, is that not correct?

LT. COL. NORTH: Again, I think, as I testified, Mr. Ledeen was, indeed, interested in the long-term benefit to the United States by pursuing this.

SEN. MCCLURE: Mr. Chairman, I'll not abuse your time. But I wanted to just close with this statement on another subject, because I don't want to overemphasize it, but I do want to state it. I agree with Sen. Cohen that we should not overstate the magnitude of security leaks, that there are an awful lot of contacts between the administration and the Congress in which security is maintained—sensitive, important, with-lives-at-risk kinds of operations in which the Congress has fully shared information and continues to fully share information with no damage to the security of the people that are involved or of the policy itself.

But having said that, I think it is equally important that we not overlook the impact of the apparent insecurity on the part of the Congress with respect to the administration deciding to withhold information from the Congress in a matter of this kind. And I'm not going to go through a listing of all of the security leaks that have occurred and the impact that they have had upon the security of the United States. But I would like to just at least call attention for those who want a broader look at it to an article which appeared in *Readers Digest,* entitled, "Congress is Crippling the CIA," by Rowland Evans and Robert Novak in the November issue of the *Readers Digest.* Now I can't give you the—I can't tell you whether that article is accurate or inaccurate. I will not either agree with all of the statements that are made or disagree, but there has been a lot of comment, there have been comments during the process of this hearing, any number of news reports that attribute information to members of the Congress and to members of this Committee. And it suggested that it's wrong for us to suggest that there is a danger in selective leaking of information. There is, whether it's done by the Congress or whether it's done downtown, and it's done at both ends of the street.

LT. COL. NORTH: I agree.

SEN. MCCLURE: By people who seek to gain an advantage in the public dialogue over questioned—not questionable —questioned public policies. And so people do indulge themselves in various kinds of comments, of leaks, of speculation. And I rather suspect, without knowing it, but I rather suspect that some of those unattributed sources are simply a cover by a journalist who desires to write a story and give it credibility by saying they have a source when indeed they don't have one at all. And that makes it look like the leaks are greater than they really are. And finally, as to whether it's wrong to withhold information from the American public, I wonder how many journalists are willing to tell us what their sources are.

Mr. Chairman, finally, if you were held captive, if you were suddenly picked up as a hostage, and they were to indulge you in that good old American custom of one phone call, would you call the Congress, or the FBI, or Colonel North? Thank you, Mr. Chairman.

CHAIRMAN INOUYE: Senator Cohen, do you seek recognition?

SEN. COHEN (R-ME): I do for one question, Mr. Chairman. Senator McClure raised the issue, and I'd like to direct this to Colonel North if I could. Senator McClure raised the issue as to whether or not the Israelis intentionally aborted the transfer of Hawk spare parts in November of 1985 in order to draw the United States into an Iranian web. And I'd like to ask you, Colonel North, is there any information that the Committee or the Intelligence Committees in the House and the Senate have not received that would indicate that at that time, in November of 1985, we were actually considering pulling out of this relationship that we had established with the Israelis in August of 1985? I am not aware of a single shred of evidence that that was the case.

LT. COL. NORTH: No, and I want to make sure that I responded correctly to Senator McClure. There were always misgivings, as you have seen in the documents that I sent forward to my superiors, about proceeding with the initiative. The question I thought I was responding to was, had we considered how badly and why the November initiative was so badly fouled up. And I have, indeed, asked myself that a number of times.

The conclusion I came to at the time, and that furthered us in the January findings, was the fact that there was extraordinary incompetence on the part of those engaged, first of all, in the offering of something that the Iranians really didn't want, and second of all, in the procedures they used to make the deliveries.

Why it was that that happened I think can possibly be explained by the people engaged in it. But there were always misgivings throughout all of this, and I think the documents I sent forward show that.

SEN. COHEN: But we had no intention of withdrawing from that plan and working with the Israelis at that time in November. The discontent, as the records will reflect before the Intelligence Committees, did not really set in until we started—Bud McFarlane went to meet with Mr. Ghorbanifar, we knew the Secretary of State was opposed to the transaction to begin with. But I'm not aware of any evidence that we were contemplating withdrawing this relationship with the Israelis in November of 1985. And I think the implication that this may have been an Israeli plot to draw us into this spider's web, I think is not correct.

SEN. MCCLURE: Mr. Chairman, if I may respond, since it was with respect to a question that I had asked. I don't think I indicated or intended to indicate that we were attempting to withdraw from a relationship with Israel. I think what I intended to imply, and I—to state, and I think there is evidence that supports it, is that we were—we had about given up on the initiative with respect to Iran.

LT. COL. NORTH: I'm not entirely sure of that, Senator McClure. And again, my operational involvement began in November. And I cannot speak with certainty about how Mr. McFarlane or those that had approved the September —the August-September and then the November shipment —actually felt about it at the time. And I don't mean to mischaracterize how they felt about it, because my sense is there were misgivings, there was concern about proceeding, but that they didn't necessarily feel like, "Well, this is the last chance," coming up to November.

CHAIRMAN INOUYE: Chairman Hamilton.

CHAIRMAN HAMILTON: Mr. Stokes is recognized.

REP. STOKES (D-OH): Thank you, Mr. Chairman. Colonel North, for the past several days I've heard statements that suggest to me that there is confusion about why these hearings are being held and specifically why you are here. On the day that the House adopted the resolution creating the House committee, January 7th, 1987, this matter was very intelligently and articulately addressed in a speech on the floor by Congressman Dick Cheney, the ranking Minority member of the House Committee. I want to read a couple of excerpts from his speech on the floor.

Firstly he said, and I quote him, "I would like to remind my colleagues, especially on this side of the aisle, that we're not here today because of a plot by anyone in the Congress to create problems for the administration or for our party. No one in the Congress decided to sell arms to Iran. No one in the Congress decided to enter into negotiations with the release of hostages. No one in the Congress was involved, to the best of our knowledge, in the alleged diversion of funds to the contras. We're here today because problems developed in the administration."

He then went on to say the President is the one who removed two senior officials NSF (sic) staff, called for the appointment of a special prosecutor, and urged us to create select committees to deal with this matter on Capitol Hill. Then I quote him again, where referring to the committee being created, Mr. Cheney said this, "To give it a mandate so that it can, in fact, do what our President said that he wanted to have done, which is to get to the bottom of the matter as quickly as possible, to thoroughly investigate the allegations that have been made, and to produce for the American people a report, and for this Congress, that will us make judgments, decisions, and determinations about whether any additional action is required with respect to legislation governing the conduct of US foreign policy or covert operations." He closed by saying it is a "very important charter." Close quotes.

I agree with Mr. Cheney. That is a very important charter. It brings you here today. With that induct —introduction, I'd like to begin my questions.

Colonel, you have, on several occasions, made reference to the term "plausible deniability" with reference to covert operations. I really do not want anyone to think that that concept, as you describe it, has any real validity today. In fact, yesterday afternoon you used the term in these hearings: "plausible deniability." (Text missing here.)

LT. COL. NORTH: It is my understanding, and I do not want to speak with absolute definity on it, you have seen the documents that I have provided to the Committee—or that were provided to the Committee from my files—it is my understanding that he was paid by the Nicaraguan resistance or by General Secord.

REP. STOKES: Did you have to arrange any type of approval in conjunction with his work there?

LT. COL. NORTH: I am quite certain that I sought the approval of my superiors—I don't recall the specific event, but when Mr. Walker's advice and counsel was sought on those kinds of activities, I'm sure that I informed my superiors.

REP. STOKES: And by your superiors, to whom do you refer?

LT. COL. NORTH: I'm talking specifically of—and I do not recall when Mr. Walker was first engaged to provide assistance, if it was 1984, it would have been Mr. McFarlane, and if it was 1985, it would have been Admiral Poindexter. I would simply have advised him that he was being brought in as a person to provide that kind of assistance.

REP. STOKES: Did you seek approval—

LT. COL. NORTH: —And when I say he, I'm not so much referring to he personally as [to] his organization—people that he would hire, et cetera.

REP. STOKES: Did you seek approval beyond either Mr. McFarlane or Mr. Poindexter?

LT. COL. NORTH: No, as I have testified throughout, those were the people to whom I reported. I'm sure that I gave indication to Director Casey that this had been done. Other than that, no different than I have testified, sir.

REP. STOKES: Was there any discussion with your superiors about the possibility that this action might violate the Boland Amendment?

LT. COL. NORTH: No, I don't recall any such discussions, and furthermore, I don't recall any specific planning on my part for that specific activity, prior to its—you know, the event.

REP. STOKES: Colonel, your full service covert operation sounds to me a great deal like what is known as the CIA's Reserve for Contingencies fund. You're aware of that fund, aren't you?

LT. COL. NORTH: I am, sir.

REP. STOKES: And you know that that's a fund that we appropriate; it's authorized under the Intelligence Committee of the House and the Senate, and it's a fund where the President can spend from that fund, and not have to account to the Congress for his expenditures. Is that correct?

LT. COL. NORTH: I am not quite certain of the last part of it. I believe that those funds all have to be identified—my understanding, Mr. Chairman, was that when the Agency expended those funds, they had to then—and they have to today—report to your Committee, and to Senator Boren's committee, how those funds are being expended. That was my understanding, anyway.

REP. STOKES: Yes, but they don't have to come to us to seek approval of it, that's what I'm saying. Once we appropriate that funding for them.

LT. COL. NORTH: But, it was also my understanding that in the case of the Boland proscriptions, going all the way back to 1984 when we sought the release of reserve funds to continue support during the summer of '84, that that release was forbidden.

REP. STOKES: All right. Let me tell you what I think the difference is between the CIA's Reserve for Contingencies and your operation. Their contingency fund requires the approval of the President, requires review by the NSC, and notification to Congress. Your covert operation was different. Your operation had no Presidential approval; it had no finding. All the covert operations that I know of had findings. Your covert operation had no financial accountability. That is not true of any covert action that I am aware of run by the CIA. Your covert operation generated and spent funds for projects that were not the subject of appropriation requests. And, finally, your covert operation was not subject to oversight by the Congress, by the statutory members of the National Security Council, and, according to your account, by the President.

So wasn't the basic difference between your cover operation and the Reserve for Contingencies, yours was outside the framework of government, and the reserve—with all of its flexibility—was within the framework of government?

LT. COL. NORTH: I guess my problem in answering that, Mr. Chairman, is that, having testified for five-and-a-half days as to what I did and how it was done and the way it was all conducted, I'm sure that you're going to draw conclusions like the one you've just drawn. I find myself in a difficult spot trying to summarize five-and-a-half days of testimony. There is no doubt about what you say, if those are the regulations pertaining to the Reserve for Contingencies. I have tried to describe to you the authorities I sought to conduct the activities I did. If that's outside the US government, in your view, I'm sure that's the conclusion that will obtain. In the case of the activities that we conducted, I sought, and thought I had, the approval to do what we did, using non–US government entities to carry them out.

REP. STOKES: Colonel, at the beginning of your testimony, you told us that you came to tell the truth—the good, the bad, and the ugly. And I want to commend you for keeping your word. I think it has been good; I think it has been bad; and I think it has been ugly. I suppose that what has been most disturbing to me about your testimony is the ugly part. In fact, it has been more than ugly. It has been chilling, and, in fact, frightening. I'm not talking just about your part in this, but the entire scenario—about government officials who plotted and conspired, who set up a straw man, a fall guy. Officials who lied, misrepresented and deceived. Officials who planned to superimpose upon our government a layer outside of our government, shrouded in secrecy and only accountable to the conspirators.

I could go on and on, but we both know the testimony, and it is ugly. In my opinion it is a prescription for anarchy in a democratic society.

In the course of your testimony I thought often about the honor code at the US Naval Academy. For 19, now almost 20 years, I have appointed young men to that Academy. I've always taken great pride in those appointees, knowing that they would be imbued with the highest standard of honor, duty and responsibility toward their government. The Academy catalog speaks of the honor concept of being more than an administrative device, that it fosters the development of lasting and moral principals, it becomes part and parcel of the professionalism expected of graduates as commissioned officers.

But more than that, I think of the young students all over America sitting in civic and government courses. You've said many times that you worry about the damage these hearings are creating for the United States around the world. I worry, Colonel, about the damage to the children of America, the future leaders of America. I worry about how we tell them that the ugly things you've told us about in our government is not the way American government is conducted. That is not our democracy's finest hour.

And then lastly, Colonel, I was touched yesterday by the eloquence of Senator Mitchell who spoke so poignantly about the rule of law and what our Constitution means to immigrants. He spoke eloquently of how all Americans are equal under our law. Senator Mitchell's words meant a great deal to another class of Americans, blacks and minorities, because, unlike immigrants, they have not always enjoyed full privileges of justice and equality under the Constitution which we now celebrate in its 200th year. If any class of Americans understand and appreciate the rule of law, the judicial process and constitutional law, it is those who've had to use that process to come from a status of nonpersons in American law to a status of equality under the law. We had to abide by the slow and arduous process of abiding by law until we could change the law through the judicial process.

In fact, Colonel, as I sit here this morning looking at you in your uniform, I cannot help but remember that I wore the uniform of this country in World War II in a segregated army. I wore it as proudly as you do, even though our government required black and white soldiers in the same army to live, sleep, eat, and travel separate and apart, while fighting and dying for our country. But because of the rule of law, today's servicemen in America suffer no such indignity.

Similar to Senator Mitchell's humble beginnings, my mother, a widow, raised two boys. She had an eighth-grade education. She was a domestic worker who scrubbed floors. One son became the first black mayor of a major American city. The other sits today as Chairman of a House Intelligence Committee. Only in America, Colonel North. Only in America. And while I admire your love for America, I hope too that you will never forget that others too love America just as much as you do and that others too will die for America, just as quick as you will.

Thank you, Mr. Chairman.

CHAIRMAN INOUYE: I thank you very much.

The chair is pleased to recognize the gentleman from Georgia, Senator Nunn.

SEN. NUNN (D-GA): Thank you very much, Mr. Chairman.

Colonel North, it may have been covered during these proceedings and I may have missed it, but I have never heard the answer to a question that I think is rather important before we get testimony from Admiral Poindexter. And that is, was—to the best of your knowledge, was Admiral Poindexter aware that Director Casey of the CIA knew about the—what we've called diversion, what you've called residual funds for the contras?

LT. COL. NORTH: I—

SEN. NUNN: In other words, did—we—we know that Admiral Poindexter knew.

LT. COL. NORTH: Yes, sir.

SEN. NUNN: We know that Director Casey knew by your testimony.

A question I have, did Admiral Poindexter, was he aware that Director Casey knew about the residual funds?

LT. COL. NORTH: I believe that he did know that I had—he being Admiral Poindexter—knew that I had talked at length with Director Casey about it, although I don't recall the specific discussion with the Admiral.

SEN. NUNN: You think that he knew but you're not, you don't recall a specific discussion?

LT. COL. NORTH: No, sir, I do not.

SEN. NUNN: But your—

LT. COL. NORTH: I'm—

SEN. NUNN: But your general impression, your best recollection is—

LT. COL. NORTH: Yes, sir—

SEN. NUNN: —that he would have known.

LT. COL. NORTH: Yes, sir. But I would have told him that I had told, talked to Director Casey at length about it.

SEN. NUNN: And, of course, Director Casey knew that Admiral Poindexter knew—

LT. COL. NORTH: Yes, sir.

SEN. NUNN: Is that correct?

LT. COL. NORTH: He did.

SEN. NUNN: Colonel, there's an article that just came to my attention, this morning as a matter of fact, in the *Los Angeles Times* dated July the 11th, 1987. And just so you and your counsel can take a look at it, I'm going to quote one paragraph in here. I'll send it to you and let you take a look at it. It's a rather short article and it says, the caption is, "Robertson Says North Told Him of Iran Hostage Talks." Going down to a paragraph which I have circled and labeled "1." Quoting from the article—and this a quote of Reverend Robertson, "'We just happened to bump into each other,' Robertson said about his encounter with North on September 13, 1985, 'at a private air terminal in Washington. He just happened to say "I'm going to Iran to meet some of the leadership to try to negotiate the release of some of our hostages."'" My question, Colonel North, did you, do you recall that conversation with Reverend Robertson?

LT. COL. NORTH: I do not, sir. I would also note that it goes on and it said that North asked the Reverend Robertson to pray for me. I've done that often and am grateful for the prayers of many. I do not recall that conversation. I also note that if it was September 13th, 1985, it is well before we had made those plans. I don't believe that we actually addressed plans to go to Teheran until February of '86. So—

SEN. NUNN: So you wouldn't have been going to Teheran at that time?

LT. COL. NORTH: Sir, I only went once and that was in May of '86, and my recollection is that those plans were laid down actually for two trips in February of 1986 during our first meetings face to face with the Iranian government officials.

SEN. NUNN: So really this is an erroneous article, and Reverend Robertson's memory is not correct on this point?

LT. COL. NORTH: Well, I'm not even sure that that's a quote from Reverend Robertson.

SEN. NUNN: Well, if it is—and I don't know either—but I'm just judging. If it is an accurate quote, it's in error?

LT. COL. NORTH: It is in error, sir.

SEN. NUNN: Thank you. Colonel North, I think the thing that has impressed these Committee members, most of them, many of them, and the American people more than anything else by your 5 and a half days of testimony is the unequivocal statement that you made at the beginning, and you've backed it up throughout your testimony, where you state, "I never carried out a single act, not one, Mr. Nields, in which I did not have the authority from my superiors. I haven't been, in the 23 years that I've been in the uniformed service of the United States—I haven't, in the 23 years that I've been in the uniformed service of the United States of America, ever violated an order. Not one." End quote. That was a very impressive statement, and you backed it up in your testimony.

My problem at this stage is how we reconcile some of this

with some of the previous testimony. And I would like to give you an opportunity to do that, because I think if there's one thing that most people agree with in this country, is that people at the lower end of the overall chain of command should not take the blame for problems that originate in orders that were carried out in good faith from those above them.

We're going to hear from Mr. McFarlane this afternoon, and I want to go over just briefly with you a few of the things that appear to me, at least on the face, [to] be contradictions between your testimony and his previous testimony.

Mr. McFarlane testified he had no knowledge of your activities with the private group raising funds for the contras. Specifically, quoting from his testimony, Mr. Liman asked him, "Were you involved at all in the activities of the Channell group to obtain monies from [sic] the contras?" Mr. McFarlane replied, "No, I wasn't." Mr. Liman went on, "Did you know that Colonel North was involved with them?" Mr. McFarlane answered, "No, I didn't."

Now could I ask you, Colonel North, if Mr. McFarlane is correct on that point or was he in error?

LT. COL. NORTH: (Pause) Senator Nunn, I have, over five and a half days, in some very difficult testimony, testified as to what I did and the authorities that I had to do it, as I understood them. One of the most difficult positions that a person can be in is to be in a situation where they are forced to contradict the testimony of anyone. I believe that within the volumes, as Mr. Liman has described them, of documents that were taken from my office, is ample evidence that I sought approval from my superiors, that I kept them fully informed, and that I did nothing without permission. And I want that made very clear. I did not come here to impugn the testimony of others. I did not come here to contradict others. But I have told you honestly and straightforwardly what I did. Some of it has been very, very unpleasant for me, as I'm sure you know, and very difficult.

SEN. NUNN: Did you get authority from Mr. McFarlane for the activities and fundraising?

LT. COL. NORTH: There was never a speech that I made or a presentation that I made that I didn't get approval to actually conduct.

SEN. NUNN: Let me go on. Mr. McFarlane testified that he did not know that you went to Florida in July of 1985 on a government plane to meet with Calero, Bermudez and Secord concerning the airlift. The specific testimony—Mr. Liman says, "Were you aware, sir, that Col. North was holding that meeting or attending that meeting?" Mr. McFarlane: "No, I wasn't."

Do you remember getting authority from Mr. McFarlane on that, or informing him of that?

LT. COL. NORTH: Yes, sir, I do.

SEN. NUNN: So that statement is in error?

LT. COL. NORTH: Are you talking 1985?

SEN. NUNN: July of '85.

LT. COL. NORTH: Yes, sir.

SEN. NUNN: So you had authority on that?

LT. COL. NORTH: Yes, sir.

SEN. NUNN: Mr. McFarlane testified also that he did not know that you had asked Gen. Secord to undertake the airlift effort. Quoting from that testimony, Mr. Liman said, "Did he ever tell you that he was turning to Gen. Secord to undertake that mission?" Mr. McFarlane: "No, he didn't."

And do you recall letting Mr. McFarlane know what you were doing in that regard?

LT. COL. NORTH: Yes, sir.

SEN. NUNN: So that's in error?

LT. COL. NORTH: Those are your conclusions.

MR. SULLIVAN: I think it's unfair to ask about—

SEN. NUNN: I'll withdraw the last question.

MR. SULLIVAN: Thank you.

SEN. NUNN: Mr. McFarlane testified that he did not know that you had instructed Ambassador Tambs to open up the southern front. Did you inform Mr. McFarlane that you were asking Ambassador Tambs to open up the southern front?

LT. COL. NORTH: Yes, sir.

SEN. NUNN: So you had specific authority from Mr. McFarlane in respect to the airlift and Gen. Secord's participation therein?

LT. COL. NORTH: Everything that I have testified to, Sen. Nunn, is exactly the way it happened—everything.

SEN. NUNN: One other point I wanted to ask along this line—is it clear in your mind that you never received

700

instructions from Mr. McFarlane in regard to soliciting contributions? I believe that he testified very clearly—I won't read all of it—that he did give instructions to his staff in the NSC not to in any way solicit contributions for the contras?

LT. COL. NORTH: And I never solicited contributions.

SEN. NUNN: I understand that. But the question really is, you made that very clear. Did you get those instructions from him? Do you remember receiving those instructions?

LT. COL. NORTH: I may have been told to separate myself from dollar operations, or however one calls it. But I was very much of the understanding that I personally would not sit and solicit. Every single activity that I conducted, as I described them to this committee, I conducted with the authority of my superiors. And to this day, Sen. Nunn, I do not believe any of them to be illegal. I didn't then; I don't now.

SEN. NUNN: I understand that completely. Turning to another subject, and this gets to testimony you gave, I believe, last Wednesday. You expressed grave reservations, and this goes to the time frame at the end of '85, 1985 or early 1986, quoting you, page 33 of your testimony, grave reservations about the state of the negotiations at that point with the Iranians, so forth, relating to the overall initiative.

You stated, quote: "In that meeting I expressed our grave reservations as to how the structure, which at that point in time focused on several thousand TOWs, would result in what we wanted. And what we wanted were laid out very clearly in the January findings," end of quote. Do you recall that?

LT. COL. NORTH: Yes. The meeting I am referring to, I believe, and I'd have to look at the testimony, but certainly my recollection is the meeting I was referring to was a meeting with the Iranians, probably Mr. Ghorbanifar.

SEN. NUNN: Right, that's correct.

LT. COL. NORTH: And that was probably the January 20th or 17th or 30th or whatever that meeting was at the end of January—

SEN. NUNN: Of '86?

LT. COL. NORTH: Yes, sir.

SEN. NUNN: Of '86. Was Mr. Nir at that meeting, Mr. Nir at that meeting?

LT. COL. NORTH: Yes, he was.

SEN. NUNN: Now when you say you had grave reservations at that time, Colonel North, about the plan and whether it would achieve the findings, which findings were you—did you have reservations about the likelihood of achievement at that stage?

LT. COL. NORTH: The January 6th or 17th finding.

SEN. NUNN: Was that where we set—the President set forth his goals of, I believe you described it as a strategic breakthrough in relations with Iran as one goal, and the Iran-Iraq war as another goal, and get the hostages back as a third goal?

LT. COL. NORTH: I—if you're not asking me to quote directly from a finding I don't have in front of me, yes, and to rescue American hostages, I believe was also—

SEN. NUNN: Yeah, I listed that as the third goal.

LT. COL. NORTH: Yes, sir.

SEN. NUNN: Now, you were having reservations at that time—

CHAIRMAN INOUYE: Mr. Nunn, there is a vote pending in the House of Representatives and members of the House will have to leave. Please proceed.

SEN. NUNN: Thank you, Mr. Chairman. At that time you had reservations about the likelihood of achieving those three goals, is that what you're saying here in this quote?

LT. COL. NORTH: Well, the concern I had was that we weren't getting to meet with the Iranian officials that we sought to meet face-to-face with. And I was instructed to express those concerns, and I did so.

SEN. NUNN: Well, you stated here you had grave reservations as to how this would result in achieving what you were trying to achieve in the January finding. So you were concerned that the way it was going you weren't going to be able to achieve those goals, so it wasn't really going the way you had hoped, is that right?

LT. COL. NORTH: That's correct.

SEN. NUNN: Now then you testified at that same meeting, Mr. Ghorbanifar, quote, "took me into the bathroom and suggested several incentives to make the February transaction work. And the attractive incentive for me was the one he made that residuals could flow to support the Nicaraguan resistance," end quote. Do you recall that testimony?

702

LT. COL. NORTH: Yes, sir.

SEN. NUNN: You mentioned several incentives. Do you recall any of the other incentives besides the—

LT. COL. NORTH: I recall one specifically.

SEN. NUNN: We've gotten that one, is that right?

LT. COL. NORTH: No, in addition. And that was Mr. Ghorbanifar offered me a million dollars if we could make this prosper.

SEN. NUNN: To you personally?

LT. COL. NORTH: Yes, sir.

SEN. NUNN: So he offered a bribe to you right there on the spot?

LT. COL. NORTH: Yes, sir.

SEN. NUNN: And tell us what you said in response to that.

LT. COL. NORTH: It's out of the question.

SEN. NUNN: You told him you would not accept any financial favors at that point?

LT. COL. NORTH: Could not, would not, and that if those kinds of discussions pursued, that he would be out of the picture very quickly. And it was then that he came up with what I considered to be a far better idea.

SEN. NUNN: So he—were there any other incentives besides those—the two that we now know about?

LT. COL. NORTH: He talked in terms of other operations that his people, whoever they were, could provide in terms of support for the United States.

SEN. NUNN: All right. When you came back after that meeting, at that stage he had—he'd put something on the table that was of real interest to you.

LT. COL. NORTH: Not the million dollars.

SEN. NUNN: Not the million dollars. I got—I got that very clearly. When you came back, did you report to your superiors about the million-dollar bribe offer?

LT. COL. NORTH: No, we knew what Ghorbanifar was, and everybody involved in it knew what bakshish is. And it was expected.

SEN. NUNN: Did you tell anyone else?

LT. COL. NORTH: Actually it wasn't expected; it was un—it was not unexpected.

SEN. NUNN: Did you tell General Secord or anyone of—of that conversation?

LT. COL. NORTH: I don't believe General Secord was with

me at that meeting. I think I may have described it to one of the CIA officers. I honestly don't remember.

SEN. NUNN: All right. But you didn't report it to any of your superiors when you came back?

LT. COL. NORTH: I may have. I don't recall, sir.

SEN. NUNN: Now, the real point I want to get to is, when you came back, obviously your perspective had changed somewhat. You did not—you were not very optimistic at that stage about achieving those original findings, goals, but you'd become more optimistic and more enthused because of the new incentive of being able to create a residual.

LT. COL. NORTH: And—well, I want to go back just one moment to clear up the record if there's confusion. The original proposal for the creation of residuals came from Mr. Nir, and that was to conduct other operations and to replenish the Israeli TOWs that had been shipped the year before.

SEN. NUNN: Correct. Right. I think you—

LT. COL. NORTH: In January—later in January, at the meeting in—and I—I can find out—I think it's—it was either London or Frankfurt, I'm sure—when Mr. Ghorbanifar suggested his incentives, he also coupled that with a promise of a meeting in February with Iranian officials. And so for those two reasons, the promise of a—of a meeting with Iranian officials and the attractiveness of what I saw as the use of residuals to support the resistance, I came back and advocated that we pursue—pursue the initiative.

SEN. NUNN: Well, at that point, did you make it plain to Admiral Poindexter, who I believe was in charge of—he was your superior—

LT. COL. NORTH: Yes, sir.

SEN. NUNN: —at that time. Did you make it plain to him that one of the main reasons you were more enthused at this stage was based on the residual possibility?

LT. COL. NORTH: Yes, I'm—I'm sure that I told him, look, the meeting in—in London has resulted in two things, if not several other arrangements that were logistically improved in terms of how you do things, but those two principle factors. I'm confident that—

SEN. NUNN: Could you repeat—

LT. COL. NORTH: —or we wouldn't have proceeded.

SEN. NUNN: Could you repeat those, just for clarity, here?

LT. COL. NORTH: The two factors?

SEN. NUNN: Yes.

LT. COL. NORTH: One, the use of residuals to support the Nicaraguan resistance, and number two, the promise of a meeting—direct face-to-face meeting—with Iranian officials, which indeed took place—

SEN. NUNN: You're not clear that you told Admiral Poindexter that. Did you tell him orally or in writing or both? Or do you recall?

LT. COL. NORTH: I do not recall, but I am confident—

SEN. NUNN: There's no doubt you told him about both of those—that stage?

LT. COL. NORTH: There's no doubt in my mind.

SEN. NUNN: All right. Wouldn't you think at that stage, Colonel North, that Admiral Poindexter had an acute obligation to share that with the President of the United States?

LT. COL. NORTH: Well, as I have—it's kind of like the other question you asked me, Senator. I have testified, again, as to what I knew and what I assumed others knew and what others told me to do. You're asking me to put myself in Admiral Poindexter's mind—

SEN. NUNN: Well, let me rephrase that question then.

(Unidentified): Excuse me—

SEN. NUNN: May I rephrase the question, counsel?

(Unidentified): I don't know whether you saw the red light, sir—

SEN. NUNN: I did, and I have a secret signal up here with the Chairman. He gave me two more minutes.

(Unidentified): Okay.

SEN. NUNN: We had it worked out. Thank you for helping us. Colonel North, did you expect—it seems to me that was a very important kind of new dimension to the original finding, both of those two things. I think they were very important. You probably told Admiral Poindexter. Didn't you expect that the President of the United States would be informed about those two new incentives?

LT. COL. NORTH: Yes. Again, as I said, I had expectations throughout my tenure that when it was appropriate that my superior solicit and obtained the President's permission that they had done so. And I proceeded throughout my tenure that way.

SEN. NUNN: Well, I think that was an appropriate assumption because it seems to me it was enormously important since the original finding that the principal operation officer out there had become less optimistic about the original goals of that January finding and the principal operations officer had become more enthusiastic because of two new incentives seems to me that there was an imperative obligation on Admiral Poindexter to convey that to the President of the United States. That's all, Colonel North. Thank you for your patience. I want to thank your wife also for her patience during this proceeding. I know she's been there the whole time and she has been very loyal to you, and I'm sure that you are enormously grateful for that.

LT. COL. NORTH: Amen.

SEN. NUNN: We thank you.

CHAIRMAN INOUYE: I wish to announce that we have remaining Congressmen McCollum, Boland, DeWine and the Chairman of the House Select Committee, Mr. Hamilton. Also Mr. Trible has 20 minutes remaining, and I intend to say a few words also. As all of you recall, before we began the questioning of our witness I announced that, once we complete the first round, those wishing to question for the second time may do so. I've been asked by two members —one in the House and the Senate—to be given an opportunity to propound a few questions. Accordingly, according to that, it would appear that we have approximately two hours remaining. Therefore, instead of torturing ourselves, I will be calling a recess until two P.M. this afternoon.

(The hearing recesses until 2 P.M.)

END MORNING SESSION

Afternoon Session —2:00 P.M.

CHAIRMAN HAMILTON: The hearing will please come to order. The chair recognizes Mr. McCollum.

REP. MCCOLLUM (R-FL): Mr. Chairman. Colonel North,

706

you have very eloquently described for us in some detail on more than one occasion during these five and half, now stretching into six, days the difficulties that this country is going to encounter if in fact the Sandinista government remains unchecked and the contras are not supported. I think you've made it abundantly clear in both your own presentation and in answers to questions that were raised this morning regarding some of the slides you had with you that if indeed the contras are not able to put a check on the Sandinistas, they're going to continue to assist revolutionaries of the communist persuasion in the neighboring democracies, they're going to continue to spread that communism and ultimately your concern is—I think you very eloquently expressed the other day is that—someday, some place, somewhere the United States young men and women in our armed forces are going to die to stop that spread of communism, and that indeed if we were to proceed to support the contras as you've suggested, maybe, just maybe that would not be necessary for our national security. I have a series of unclassified State Department cables that I want to put in the record. They deal with Radio Venceremos, and I'd like to do that to augment some of the things you've said. Could you tell us just for the record what Radio Venceremos is?

LT. COL. NORTH: Radio Venceremos is the voice of the FLN guerillas in El Salvador. It has been broadcasting from Managua since at least the early '80s. It provides the propaganda, the command and control and the instructional capacity for the FLN. It has also been noted that Radio Venceremos uses Soviet-bloc retransmitters to appear to be broadcasting from inside El Salvador. But in point of fact the programming, the direction, the specific content of all of it probably originates in Cuba, certainly it comes out of Nicaragua.

REP. MCCOLLUM: Colonel North, we talked a lot this morning about the ugly. I'm going to read you something that I really think is ugly that came out of Radio Venceremos. It's from one of these cables. The cable is dated January 29, 1986. The text of that is quoting from Radio Venceremos's broadcast of earlier that date. "The US Space Shuttle Challenger exploded on Tuesday morning one minute and twenty seconds after it had taken off from Cape

707

Canaveral, Florida. And the seven astronauts on board the space shuttle were killed. The US failure in the space shuttle project marked by the Challenger's accident represents an overwhelming blow to so-called Star Wars. The United States wanted to use outer space for military purposes through this program. Reagan has announced that all the flights to outer space have been suspended. In addition, two members of the Challenger's crew worked as pilots in the Vietnam War. In other words, they were two killers who sowed napalm in the martyrized Vietnamese land. Given that the Challenger's ostentatious failure represents an overwhelming blow to the US government's plans to extend the war in outer space, and given that two war criminals have died aboard the Challenger, we share the happiness felt by those who reject and condemn the US imperialism's war-mongering policy."

To me, Colonel North, that's ugly.

LT. COL. NORTH: Yes, it is.

REP. MCCOLLUM: And to me that represents the nature of the threat that we have to deal with that unfortunately too many Americans don't fully realize.

Mr. Chairman, I would like at this time to ask unanimous consent to enter into the record these 7 unclassified State Department cables dealing with Radio Venceremos.

CHAIRMAN INOUYE: Without objection, so ordered.

REP. MCCOLLUM: Colonel North, we also have had quite a bit of discussion about what we can do to be constructive. I'm glad to—frankly to see—after all these days and these hearings to finally get some of our colleagues on this panel and—with your help and your prodding—to think about not just asking you facts, but trying to come up with some things we can do to—to bridge that gap, to get that trust back in, that mutual trust in the intelligence area and in our sensitive matter areas, that—that you have pointed to very much in the last few days as a critical problem.

In the process of this, there has been some discussion of a manner or procedure that exists presently for the President, for the administration, to notify a small group of 8 of the House leadership and the Senate leadership and the chairmen of the two Intelligence committees whenever they want to talk about something that's really sensitive without calling the whole committee in. What bothers me about that a little bit is that I know in the past that some of the committee chairmen occasionally have refused to hear some of those briefings. I chatted with Senator Boren. I wish he were here at this moment. He's not. But I chatted with him because I sit beside him quite a bit. And I know that he's made a point since he's been chairman—I'm sure that Chairman Stokes is probably making the same point—to hear those briefings.

But it's my understanding there's no law that compels them to do that, and if they do not hear those briefings, if they do not accept the offer of the administration to brief them on these sensitive matters, oftentimes those policies either aren't carried out or the briefings are stopped at the other side because there's a feeling that that's unfair. I'm sure you'd agree with me that we'd all be better off if every time the administration asked for a briefing to be given, asked that it be received by the chairmen of the Intelligence Committees of these bodies, that they acquiesced and agreed and listened, even if they didn't agree with what they heard. Would you not agree that ought to be done?

LT. COL. NORTH: I would agree, sir.

REP. MCCOLLUM: I'd like to move on to one other thing. Speaking of being constructive, we have a situation now where the Soviet Union as I perceive it, and I've read quite about this, has a fairly simple and flexibile and indeed a massive special operations program. The United States has a special operations program, obviously, and it's pretty big but its decentralized. Some of my colleagues on this Committee urged Senator Nunn, Senator Cohen, members in the House like Mr. Daniels that we establish in the Department of Defense an Assistant Secretary of Defense for special operations in low-intensity conflict. And that law passed. That became law. We signed into law. Months have gone by now, and we still do not have a person appointed as that Assistant Secretary of Defense. We still do not have that plan being implemented by the Department of Defense. Would it not improve the situation as you see it in dealing with things like the Iranian hostage situation and the situations you faced in so many occasions in Central America with this low-intensity conflict to have a more orderly process not only established on the books but in reality over at the Department of Defense?

LT. COL. NORTH: Congressman McCollum, eight months ago I'd have been more than pleased to answer that question. I am now a lieutenant colonel assigned to the United States Marine Corps, and I don't want to start sounding like I'm critical of current activities. I would just as soon stick to my answers on subjects.

REP. MCCOLLUM: Well, let me ask you this question. Eight months ago and before that—

LT. COL. NORTH: Yes—

REP. MCCOLLUM: Were you not, you were supportive of this, weren't you?

LT. COL. NORTH: Yes sir, I was.

REP. MCCOLLUM: And I have in front of me a special study that was done entitled "The United States and Soviet Special Operations." It's a study by the Congressional Research Service of the Library of Congress prepared at the request of the Special Operations Panel of the Readiness Subcommittee of the Committee of Armed Forces of the House of Representatives dated this April, April 28. I think it lays it out. I think every American ought to read this study, and I would like to ask unanimous consent, Mr. Chairman, to place this study into the record.

CHAIRMAN INOUYE: No objection. So ordered.

REP. MCCOLLUM: Thank you. You told us yesterday about an occasion in Central America where you were with the Vice President, and he was presented with a situation where there was some armed men that were there, and he wanted to meet with them—I think maybe his Secret Service were a little dubious about it—but he insisted on meeting with them. And you told us that that was one of the most courageous things you'd seen anybody do, especially a Vice President, and you related some of the things that went on there. But I think you dropped that one a little like Paul Harvey on his newscast. I'd like to hear the rest of the story. What happened? What came of that meeting? That was about something going on down there, you told us. And I'm sure you didn't realize it, but you didn't quite finish that story. You didn't tell us what the product of that meeting was. Could you go back over that briefly and do that?

LT. COL. NORTH: The Vice President's trip in December of 1983 came at the midpoint, if you will, or near the midpoint, of our efforts to bring about the support for a full democratization in El Salvador. You'll recall that President Magaña had accepted the two year provisional presidency. We had been working very closely with President Magaña to have national elections. There was, as many will recall, a great deal of polarity which existed in El Salvador. There were death squads that were active. Some of those were as a consequence of opposition from both extremes in the political spectrum. The Congress had imposed certain constraints on our ability to provide security assistance and even economic aid to El Salvador under those conditions and it was decided that the Vice President would stop in El Salvador and return from the inaugural of the President of Argentina, and he did so.

The specific purpose for that meeting was to insist that the human rights reforms, the judicial reform, the cleaning up of the death squads which we had been working on assiduously indeed did occur, and that the elections which were promised for later on in the spring did indeed occur. The consequence of that was probably the most popular turnout for an election that's ever occurred in a free country. It's easy to get turnouts for the elections in the Soviet Union, where everybody votes for the party official that's nominated. But in El Salvador, the people of El Salvador turned out for an election in which they were threatened by the guerrillas that if they voted they would die.

The fact that those elections occurred, that the human rights reforms we had been pushing for and that many members of the Congress had been pushing for and that the judicial reform which we had been working on so hard and that the death squad activity which we had been trying to get stopped, all of that happened as a result of those initiatives and the capstone of those initiatives was the Vice President's trip. When we arrived in El Salvador, the Vice President made it clear that he wanted to meet with the military leadership as well as the civilian leadership and he did so. And the event I described was an afternoon meeting, well after the Vice President was due to leave the country and against the advice of his Secret Service detail and others with the party, he, Ambassador Motley and his Chief of Staff, Admiral Dan Murphy, and I, met with those 30 —actually 32—military leaders, some of whom were very,

711

very much opposed to our policy. And as I indicated, many of them were armed. His Secret Service detail was very, very concerned about that. The Vice President's points that he made in that meeting, which, I think, kind of like the Jay Treaty, need not be repeated here in public, because they were the communications approved by the President of the United States, transmitted to another head of state, but they were very forcefully delivered in a very straightforward manner, making it clear that we could not and we would not continue to support the process in El Salvador, if they would not take the steps we had indicated.

REP. MCCOLLUM: And they took them and they had the elections and that's why, in part, in large measure, we have some form of democracy in Central America today.

LT. COL. NORTH: As a matter of fact, Mr. McCollum, if I can just say one thing, one of the sad facts of lack of education of the American people is that many people in this country still don't know that El Salvador is a democracy today. It isn't ruled by a military junta. Neither is Honduras. Neither is Costa Rica. And neither is Guatemala. And those things have occured since Ronald Reagan has been President, and they've occured because of an insistance on democracy. The only country in Latin—in Central America today that isn't a democracy is Nicaragua.

REP. MCCOLLUM: Let me change the subject. I hate to do it, but my time is restricted. I think your point is well made, and you answered the question very much as I had anticipated.

With regard to an incident that occured in the White House in the waning days of your being there, I'd like to see if I can refresh your recollection and clear up something that appears to be completely contradictory testimony that was given in private by Colonel Earl in his deposition and something you said with regard to the Saturday, the 22nd of November. I think it's important to give you the opportunity because it is completely in contrast.

The other day, you testified, if I recall correctly, that when the Attorney General's men, Mr. Reynolds and others, were in the office spaces of yours in the White House on Saturday, the 22nd of November of last year, that you did, indeed, continue the process of shredding, that there was some of that going on routinely or whatever while they were there. And you were asked a number of questions about it, and like a lot of other folks, I don't know if it's accurate or it's not accurate. My recollection's often not right. Maybe you're going to, as you've done a number of times, say, "I remember that very distinctly, and that's right."

But Colonel Earl, in his testimony—we can give you a copy of that; if somebody'd like to take it down to the desk, I'd appreciate it—on pages 79 to 80 or 81 has testified that he saw you about noon that day and—and came up on the situation, and you told him that the shredder had been broken the night before. And he said he tried and worked with that shredder, and that, indeed, it was broken, and that, as a consequence of that and the fact it wasn't fixed all day that day, he went to the Situation Room and all the shredding, as to his knowledge, that was done that day was done in the Situation Room.

There's been—as you know, the Justice Department officials have said in the open—not in the hearing, but out in the press—that they don't remember the shredding that day. I'm just wondering if this refreshes your recollection at all if, indeed, perhaps you were mistaken about the—the date in which—where the shredding was going on or the timing of it that day.

LT. COL. NORTH: My recollection is that the shredder was not broken, that the shredder had jammed with an overload of documents in the—in the teeth of the gears or whatever, that it had been reset. We needed to reset it again, as I recall, on Monday. But I do recall specifically taking documents that I was working on, some of which were current intelligence and the like, and shredding them. My recollection is that I did it in my own office, and I—I—again, I attach no spec—specific relevance to that. Some of those documents that I shredded had absolutely nothing to do with the issues before these Committees.

REP. MCCOLLUM: Well, Colonel Earl's recollection could have been faulty too, and sometimes we just never can resolve all things in these hearings. But I wanted to bring it up because I didn't want you, later after the fact, to have that—without having an opportunity.

LT. COL. NORTH: Thank you.

REP. MCCOLLUM: I want to straighten out a couple of other things if I can too just for clarification for what we anticipate to be future testimony. You testified that you wrote some 5 different memoranda referring to the use of the proceeds from the Iran arms sale for other covert operations, the contras. And I'm going to call them, for the sake of anything else, the diversion memos, which I think that's what generally we've said. You said it's—you call it something else. Whatever, we're going to call that.

LT. COL. NORTH: I don't believe the word "diversion" appeared in any of my memos.

REP. MCCOLLUM: No, they didn't, but you don't mind my referring to them—if you want something else, I'll do it. But anyway, for the public record, to your knowledge, were any of these memorandas (sic) written in connection with a November 1985 Hawk shipment?

LT. COL. NORTH: I do not believe so, sir.

REP. MCCOLLUM: Were any of them written in 1985?

LT. COL. NORTH: No. It is my recollection that they were all written after January—and again, I—my—the date is uncertain, but the meeting I had in Europe with Mr. Nir and Mr. Ghorbanifar, and the first transaction that we actually conducted after that meeting, was in February —and so my recollection is, that the first memorandum that would have addressed that, would have defined the parameters in which that February transaction would have taken place. I don't believe that we planned another one between the January 20th meeting—or whatever it was—and what I remember as a February 10th or 15th meeting in Frankfurt with the Iranian intermediary.

REP. MCCOLLUM: To your knowledge, Colonel, were any of the five diversion memo documents logged into the NSC Systems Four, record keeping system?

LT. COL. NORTH: I don't believe so. We talked a little bit about that in the Executive Session. My recollection is that, by this point in time, those kinds of sensitive documents were all what I referred to as "non-logged." They were not entered into the system.

REP. MCCOLLUM: I'd like to know if it's not true that the record keeping procedures at the NSC, generally require that a copy or an original of a document be logged into the Systems Four system, be maintained in the main files and kept in the NSC Intelligence Directory?

LT. COL. NORTH: All Systems Four documents had to be

logged there, and as I indicated, the April memorandum which we now have, was not one of those System Four documents.

REP. MCCOLLUM: So, since you don't think one got logged in, I suppose the answer to any questions I ask about whether you personally ever attempted to alter a document of this nature, in the Systems Four machine, or know of anybody who did, or took it out, or whatever, would be "no."

LT. COL. NORTH: Oh, I certainly altered documents that were in the System Four system, but none of these.

REP. MCCOLLUM: But not a diversion memo?

LT. COL. NORTH: That's correct.

REP. MCCOLLUM: None of these memos, themselves. Colonel North, my time is up, but I would like to make one comment in respect. We've been here together quite awhile, and I've heard speechifying by members up here, and admissions of this, and accusations of that. I think that you've done a great deal of service for us, by being here, to say the least. And I know the country feels that way. I don't know whether you're going to go down in history as a hero or not. I don't know what the fate of all of the discussions we're having here will be. I know there were some mistakes made you've admitted to. There are some things I'm sure, you and I would disagree about, with regard to some of the policies, though many of them, I agree more with you, than some of my colleagues do.

I do know, that Douglas MacArthur was, and is to this day, considered a hero. And yet, he was fired by President Truman. So, I would say that you don't have to be perfect to be a hero. And one thing is for certain, Colonel Oliver North, you've served your country admirably. You have been a dedicated, patriotic soldier, and there's no question you've gone above and beyond—on many occasions—the call of duty. For that, I personally, and I know the country is grateful, and will remember forever, regardless of anything else. Thank you very much.

LT. COL. NORTH: Thank you, sir.

CHAIRMAN HAMILTON: The Chair recognizes Mr. Boland.

REP. EDWARD BOLAND (D-MA): Colonel North, I finally made it.

I know you'd be disappointed if I didn't talk a little bit

about the Boland Amendments, which from—(laughter) —which from October 1st of 1984 until October 18th of 1986 prohibited the provision of military assistance to the contras. The amendments are much aligned (sic). It has been called so many different things during the course of these hearings. But I sort of like it best when it is described simply as it was: the law. And I know that you wouldn't quarrel with that description, because you have spent a great deal of time in describing how you were complying with the particular law or series of laws. And so I would like to ask you a few questions about your activities in compliance with the laws known as the Boland Amendments.

And I noted yesterday that Senator Rudman asked you about an activity wherein you supplied maps and documents to Robert Owen to be carried to the contras in a planned operation to destroy Sandinista military equipment. You responded to that. And also, he indicated that you indicated to the chief of the Central American Task Force that he was aware of the Secord supply operation. And you testified to that. You also—

LT. COL. NORTH: Mr. Chairman, if I may just—

REP. BOLAND: Yes—

LT. COL. NORTH: I'm not sure that I ever told the Central American Task Force chief that it was General Secord. I did tell him about the facts of that resupply operation.

REP. BOLAND: Okay. Now you testified that you kept your superiors advised of your actions. Did Mr. McFarlane know that Robert Owen was taking, at your request, militarily significant material to the contras?

LT. COL. NORTH: I do not know that I ever told Mr. McFarlane or Admiral Poindexter that it was Robert Owen who was serving in that capacity. I did apprise my superiors of intelligence that I was having passed to the resistance.

REP. BOLAND: In July of 1985, Louis Tambs became the ambassador to Costa Rica. He has testified that before he left for that post, you instructed him to open a military front inside southern Nicaragua. From whom had you received the instructions you gave to Ambassador Tambs?

LT. COL. NORTH: As I believe I testified at the time this first came up, Mr. Chairman, I did not refer to that specifically as an instruction. I don't believe I said to the ambassador, "You are hereby instructed." I certainly did encourage him in every way possible to support an open, active southern front, both politically and militarily. That had been widely discussed by the restricted inter-agency group. The need for that was very obvious. The documents that I have turned over and those of others, and those documents that were provided to the Committee, clearly indicate that—

REP. BOLAND: But let me ask you this, Colonel. Whether or not—all right. Go ahead.

LT. COL. NORTH: It is my recollection that I discussed this actively with Mr. McFarlane and that he gave the go-ahead for opening those kinds of activities in the south.

REP. BOLAND: And was there anyone in the Department of State from whom you had permission to so instruct a United States ambassador?

LT. COL. NORTH: No, sir.

REP. BOLAND: Ambassador Tambs also testified that later in the summer of 1985, he received instructions from you to approach the government of Costa Rica about constructing an airfield in that country for the benefit of the contras. Who directed you to give those instructions to Ambassador Tambs?

LT. COL. NORTH: My recollection is that that also had been widely discussed within the restricted inter-agency group, that I had certainly made it clear that we needed to have that kind of an activity in the south, and I apprised my superiors of the need for that construction. I don't recall specifying the location, but I even provided photographs at some points of the airfield.

REP. BOLAND: So in effect you really were the originator of that suggestion, is that correct?

LT. COL. NORTH: No, actually I think the originator was probably General Secord who knew more about the requirements for those kinds of abort bases in order to support the resupply operation.

REP. BOLAND: All right, was there anyone in the State Department that had approved this kind of instruction being given to Ambassador Tambs?

LT. COL. NORTH: Again, I do not recall ever addressing the issue specifically as a request for approval from the State

Department. But I certainly apprised them of the fact that the airfield was under construction, as a process—as part of that process within the restricted inter-agency group.

REP. BOLAND: The senior CIA official in Central America has testified that during the time when military assistance to the contras was prohibited by US law, he was active, at your request, in assisting the Secord lethal resupply operation. Another had testified that the assistance of this official was crucial to the success of the Secord operation. Who in the CIA authorized you to bring this individual into the resupply network?

LT. COL. NORTH: Director Casey.

REP. BOLAND: Who else in the agency did you know to be aware of his activities besides Director Casey?

LT. COL. NORTH: Well, you've asked me—who was I actually firmly aware? I'm sure that the Central American Task Force Chief was aware. I can't say that with absolute certainty, Mr. Boland, but it is—I'm pretty sure that he did by virtue of the discussions I had over the course of time. It is likely that the—as I answered Mr. Boren yesterday, that the operations director knew. But I can't state that with certainty.

REP. BOLAND: Colonel, in my judgment the law was clear. It authorized the provision of certain types of intelligence information to the contras. It did not authorize CIA officials to coordinate the aerial supply or resupply of the arms to the contra units in the field. And as you might agree, the supply of fighting units in the field is a military operation, and CIA participation in that type of operation was not authorized by law. That's correct, isn't it?

LT. COL. NORTH: I am not certain of that, Mr. Boland. In fact, it was my understanding that at the time these things were being done that we—

REP. BOLAND: Well, wasn't the CIA barred from getting into any military operations under the amendment?

LT. COL. NORTH: It certainly was barred from expending funds for those purposes—no doubt about it.

REP. BOLAND: And what was your understanding of the level of knowledge of CIA official Duane Clarridge in the Secord contra supply operation?

LT. COL. NORTH: My sense is that he had a general knowledge of the activities that—

REP. BOLAND: Did Clarridge assist the Secord operation in any way, and, if so, in what way?

LT. COL. NORTH: I would say that his assistance was principally one of advising me on procedures. I don't believe he ever talked directly to any of those people involved, and I don't believe he talked to any of the field officers involved. I'm not certain of that. But I don't believe he did. But he certainly—and I talked a good bit. I used his expertise.

REP. BOLAND: Are you aware of any efforts by Mr. Clarridge to provide the contras with weapons between June of 1984 and October of 1986?

LT. COL. NORTH: I'm talking off the top of my head now, Mr. Boland, but I don't know of any circumstances in which he was involved in those time periods with weapons.

REP. BOLAND: Now you've testified in great detail about Director Casey's knowledge of and interest in your activities on behalf of the contras. What degree of control did he exert over these activities? You testified that on one occasion, in connection with another activity, Mr. Casey told you to get a ship, and you got a ship.

Was there ever a time when Director Casey told you to do something that you didn't do it?

LT. COL. NORTH: I didn't get a lawyer soon enough.

REP. BOLAND: Now, when you "communed," as you put it, with Director Casey, did you give him details of the Secord contra resupply operation, the amount of weapons being delivered, the money available and expended, the number of aircraft and personnel involved, and so forth?

LT. COL. NORTH: Well, there were times when we did have detailed discussions. I don't recollect ever having specific knowledge of how much was left in any one account, as I have already testified. And I think my testimony ought to stand on those other things that the Director and I talked about in detail.

REP. BOLAND: And whether or not you had an alternate point of contact on the resupply operation in the event that you couldn't reach Mr. Casey—because Mr. Casey used to travel a lot, was there someone else in the CIA you contacted when you were not—when it was not possible to meet with or talk with Casey?

LT. COL. NORTH: Well, in my testimony and in the records

that I turned over to the Committee and those that were provided by the White House, it is very clear that I was in direct contact with the station chief in a Central American country.

REP. BOLAND: You know, you're many things, you're many great things, but there's one thing you really do great and that's keep magnificent memos—beautiful penmanship, no cross-out, you know exactly what you're doing all of the time. You write it down in perfect English in perfect language.

Now the documents that you supplied to this Committee indicate clearly that you are an inveterate notetaker. How about Mr. Casey? Did he take notes when you met with him?

LT. COL. NORTH: No, on a number of occasions, I walked into the Director's office or for meetings with the Director and he would tell me to, "Put away the notebook," if I couldn't remember it, I didn't belong in the business.

REP. BOLAND: Several witnesses who have testified and made references to the assistance provided to the Secord contra arms resupply effort by Colonel James Steele, the then Military Assistance Group Commander in Country Seven. Who in the Department of Defense had authorized Colonel Steele's participation in this operation?

LT. COL. NORTH: I don't know, sir.

REP. BOLAND: Did you ever report to anyone in the Defense Department about the help Colonel Steele was providing to the Secord resupply effort?

LT. COL. NORTH: I'm trying to recall when Colonel Steele arrived in the country to which he was assigned. It is entirely possible that Admiral Moreau and I talked about it. It is possible that I talked about it with General Gorman or his replacement, but I don't recall those specific conversations.

REP. BOLAND: Was Colonel Steele subject to the command of General Paul Gorman when General Gorman was the commander with the Southern Command?

LT. COL. NORTH: Well, that is the point of my earlier statement—I don't recall when he arrived down there, sir.

REP. BOLAND: Well, I can understand. You've testified here, this is the sixth day and you've had a million questions thrown at you and I don't expect you can remember everything. Now you have testified that you had been advised that the National Security Council was not covered by the Boland Amendment. It won't surprise you to learn, I suppose, that I believe that that advice was wrong. I mean, I don't think we're going to debate the coverage of NSC here with you. I only want to know this: The CIA was covered by the Boland Amendment, so was the DOD, and also the State Department, because everyone knows the State Department has an intelligence capability. Why do you believe you had the ability to direct employees of those agencies to do things which the law said they couldn't do?

LT. COL. NORTH: Congressman Boland, I will take issue again with the word "direct." I certainly solicited from them help. If I didn't solicit money, I sought help, and I did seek a lot of that and they provided it. My understanding of the Boland proscription was that funds could not be expended for those purposes and I don't know that any of those people engaged ever expended a nickel on behalf of the programs that I sought their help for.

REP. BOLAND: Incidentally, the Boland Amendments in effect from October 1984 until October 1986 spoke about funds available to the CIA, DOD or any other agency or entity of the United States involved in intelligence activities. Would it surprise you to learn that Congress chose those particular words because it understood that the CIA, for example, operates proprietaries, and those proprietaries might have funds available to them. And thus the CIA, which did not appropriate it, but the funds would be available to the CIA even though not appropriated, but which Congress still wanted to include within the Boland proscriptions. You've described the residuals in the Iran arms sales transactions as intended to support Director Casey's off-the-shelf covert operations entity. Weren't the residuals, therefore, funds available to the CIA?

LT. COL. NORTH: No sir. The CIA never had, except for those monies transferred to the CIA from those entities to pay for weapons purchased under the Economy Act from the DOD, the CIA never had available to it a nickel.

REP. BOLAND: Colonel North, I never met you. I never saw you, never met you until last Tuesday, and I'm sure you never saw me—

LT. COL. NORTH: That's not correct, sir. Congressman

Boland, I briefed you on the special project at the direction of William Clark—

REP. BOLAND: Well, I don't recall—

LT. COL. NORTH: —when he was National Security Adviser. You were part of the Intelligence Committee.

REP. BOLAND: Anyway, ever since this investigation started I have not given any interviews with respect to you, have never indicated what my position would be on this Committee, never indicated at all what my opinion was of you and your testimony. I think that was something which should be left for the final report of this Committee. But I do want to make an observation, and you don't have to respond. I share your belief that this nation needs effective and aggressive intelligence agencies and that covert operations must at times be employed in intelligence activities. For seven and one half years, I chaired the House Intelligence Committee, a committee created in large part as a result of the history of failures and abuses in intelligence described by the Rockefeller Commission, the Church Committee and the Pike Committee. When the House Committee was established, relations between the Congress and the intelligence community, particularly the CIA, were at very low ebb. And there were serious questions about the Agency's future. Had that situation been allowed to continue, our nation's security would have been imperiled. Fortunately, the House Committee and the Senate counterpart were able to not only increase the resources available for intelligence collection and analysis, but through properly conducted oversight to significantly improve the degree of trust within Congress and between Congress and the intelligence agencies on intelligence activities. That trust, I fear, has been one of the casualties of the Iran-Contra affair. When I chaired the Intelligence Committee, we reviewed a number of covert operations. Our role was primarily consultative, although we did have the ability to recommend to the House that covert operations, as defined by a presidential finding, which we thought to be inadvisable, not be funded—and we made some suggestions at the time. That recommendation was rarely made, but its potential was a reflection of the concern expressed by George Mason, a delegate in the Virginia delegation of the Constitutional Convention 200 years ago—"that the purse and the sword

722

must never be in the same hands." And I believe the Iran-Contra affair demonstrates the dangers in ignoring Mason's warnings.

Covert activities can furnish and support foreign policy, but they cannot be foreign policy. When covert activities become subsitutes for a foreign policy developed in a manner consistent with the dictates of our Constituion, they endanger, rather than promote our security. These hearings are, in part, about the lessons to be learned from the Iran-Contra affair. For me, one of the chief lessons learned thus far has been the wisdom of an observation made by Sir William Stevenson, who was a great friend, incidentally, of Wild Bill Donovan, who was a great friend of Bill Casey and who was the great chief of the British intelligence in World War II. And he said, "Among the increasingly intricate arsenals across the world, intelligence is an essential weapon, perhaps the most important. But it is, being secret, the most dangerous. Safeguards to prevent its abuse must be devised, revised and rigidly applied. But, as in all enterprise, the character and wisdom of those to whom it is entrusted would be decisive. In the integrity of that guardianship lies the hope of free people to endure and to prevail."

Thank you, Col. North, and I want to express my appreciation to the manner in which you have testified here today. I can understand the ordeal it's been for you and your family, and all your friends. Thank you very much.

CHAIRMAN HAMILTON: The Chair recognizes Mr. DeWine.

REP. MICHAEL DEWINE (R-OH): Thank you very much, Mr. Chairman.

REP. HYDE: Mr. DeWine, would you yield to me just for a second?

REP. DEWINE: Yes, I would.

REP. HYDE: At the break, [would] you lean over to Mr. Boland and tell him that George Mason never signed the Constitution. He refused to.

REP. DEWINE: I'm not in the habit of giving Mr. Boland advice, Henry. But you can. You can.

Colonel, when I was a young boy growing up in Ohio, one of my jobs was to load boxcars with bags of seed. And that was kind of a hot job, at least this time of year. And in the winter, it was kind of a cold job. But there was an old boy who worked with me. Actually, I worked with him because he'd been there longer than I ever was. And he had a saying. We'd work all day loading that boxcar. And when we got to that last bag, he always would look down at the bag and then look up at me and then say, "Mike, that's the bag we've been looking for." Colonel, I think probably I'm the Congressman you've been looking for because I'm the last one down here on the end, and we're just about done. And I think the Chairman's got a few questions—both of them probably do. But I'm the last one on the panel. So the end is in sight, and we appreciate your six days of testimony. We appreciate the fact that you've hung in there and borne with us.

Let me, if I could, ask you a question about—to ask you a question about something you said at the beginning in your opening—well, in your opening statement that was delivered two days into it, but it was your opening statement. You stated that in your opinion, the—this Committee had not really been totally fair. That it had been selective in the testimony that it had brought forward. Let me quote, if I could, from the transcript. Quote, "You put the testimony which you think is helpful to your goals up before the people and leave others out."

Now I'd like to give a couple examples to you and ask you if this is the type thing that you're talking about. On May 20th, over a month ago, when this Committee put right up there on the wall a chart that listed all the travelers checks that you had written to Parklane Hosiery and some food store out in northern Virginia and a few other places, knowing full well that it would be a month or two before you'd have a chance to come in here and refute that or make any comment about it at all, is that the type thing that you mean by unfairness?

LT. COL. NORTH: Yes sir, it is; and further, that none of the other thousands of travelers checks, which were available and cashed by the very people that I described having turned them over to, were displayed; only those ones that I had signed.

REP. DEWINE: All right. Let me give you another example. When General Secord was on the stand, and he was confronted on cross examination by a statement that had been made by Robert Dutton in a deposition, and it seemed

724

to contradict what Secord said about the willingness to give some of the assets over to the CIA, or all the assets of the enterprise over to the CIA, I went back—actually, Ken Buck of our staff went back at noon and looked it up and found that that was really taken out of context, that when you read the whole deposition, just one page later, actually, what you found is that there wasn't a contradiction at all. Is that the type of taking things out of context that maybe you're talking about?

LT. COL. NORTH: Yes, and I don't want to take too much of your time—

REP. DEWINE: Because I don't have much time.

LT. COL. NORTH: —but let me make one thing very clear about the—whose idea it was to cause those assets to be sold to the CIA. That idea was Director William J. Casey's. And I caused it to be put back into the proposals.

REP. DEWINE: I'm glad you clarified that for us. Let me give you another example. When the *New York Times* published, on June 18th, 1987, and I quote, the following: "According to congressional investigators," end of quote, and then that article went on to state that Glenn Robinette had told our Committee in closed, executive session, deposition, of a direct link, that there was a direct link between General Secord and Edwin Wilson. That was the story that ran. Yet when he came in, Robinette came in to testify, he didn't say that at all. In fact, he said just the opposite. Is that the type of problem you have seen with this Committee?

LT. COL. NORTH: Certainly would seem that way, sir.

REP. DEWINE: Let me give you another example. There were three donors who were brought in here to testify. We put on this panel, the panel had three donors. One had been shown a munitions list, one had been told that if he gave enough, he could meet with the President, if he hit a certain level. And one, who spoke with Director Casey and then, after that, he gave directly into the Lake Resources account.

There was a clear implication at that time that all the private donors approached by Spitz Channell had been given munitions lists, all had been told they could see the President, and all donors had given to the Lake Resources account. It wasn't said, but that was the implication.

Would it surprise you to know that this Committee interviewed many, many, many people, the staff did. And those were the only three, each one, that could testify about that particular thing. Again it wasn't false, but it was just a little bit misleading, gave the wrong impression. Is that the type thing you're talking about?

LT. COL. NORTH: Yes sir.

REP. DEWINE: Let me give you another example. Brett Sciaroni came in here. He's the man who did the legal opinion about the Boland Amendment. He wasn't—oh, he was asked a little bit about his legal opinion, the quality of the opinion, what it looked like, to defend it. But the majority of the attack on him wasn't on that. It was an attack on him. It was, "Let's try Mr. Sciaroni. Let's see if he passed the bar the first time. Let's get into all of these things."

Does that seem to you to maybe be missing the point of what this whole Committee should be dealing with, which is—one of things, a policy question; another is a legal question, about the Boland Amendment. We all have difference of opinions. We're, I hope, good friends on this Committee. But we have difference of opinion. Is that the type thing you're talking about?

LT. COL. NORTH: Yes sir.

REP. DEWINE: And finally, and I could go on and on, but my time is very limited, would it surprise you to know—I don't imagine it would—but the fact that I went back and counted and prior to yesterday afternoon—now it changed yesterday afternoon—but prior to yesterday afternoon, by my calculations, going through the transcript, on 24 different times, your very able lawyer had made an objection. For some reason on 24 straight times, your able attorney had been overruled. Now does that surprise you?

LT. COL. NORTH: Nothing surprises anymore, Congressman.

REP. DEWINE: I don't think, and I want to be fair, I don't know—I want to put this in its historic perspective, I'm not criticizing our Chairmen. I think they're both good Chairmen. I'm really not. Now let me explain that to you.

CHAIRMAN INOUYE: Will the Representative yield—

REP. DEWINE: If I could finish, and I think—I will yield, if you want me to now, or if I could finish, Mr. Chairman, I think—

CHAIRMAN INOUYE: —on a point of personal privilege?

REP. DEWINE: Certainly, but I would—it won't cut down on my time, will it, Mr. Chairman?

CHAIRMAN INOUYE: I'll give you time. If you, at any time, felt that the ruling of the Chair was unfair, you know very well that the rules would have provided you to speak up. On each ruling that this Chair made, not a single member of the panel objected to my ruling and, as far as I am concerned, my rulings were correct. Please proceed.

REP. DEWINE: (To the Chair.) Well, I made a mistake and I'm sorry. I'm sorry that I didn't object at that time.

(To Lt. Col. North) Let me put it in a historical perspective, if I could, and as I started to say, I'm not blaming either one of the able Chairmen. I'm really not. The problem is a more organic or a more basic problem and I think it's something that's been with us for many, many years and I think it is something that Arthur Liman—I don't see him—but Arthur Liman, when he was a young undergraduate or maybe a graduate student, I don't know, in the early fifties and we had just come off—or the country had just come off of the Army McCarthy hearings and he saw some of the abuses. And he wrote and indicated that maybe some changes needed to be made.

I think some changes need to be made and I think that's one thing that maybe people on both sides of the aisle will be able to deal with after these hearings are over. We need some firm rules. We need some rules which guarantee fairness and guarantee that we can get at the truth. Now I don't propose to turn this into a court of law. Lord forbid. We don't need to do that. We have other functions. We have a function of debating policy and we've all done that we disagree but I don't know that the Congress could have more able people than the Chairman and Jack Brooks—I look over there, I look all around about debating policy. That's proper here. This is not a court of law.

But when we get to the question of fact, away from policy into fact, which is another one of our responsibilities, it seems to me that some of the rules that are used in court, not all of them, but some of them that have come down through the ages, literally, and that we have evolved, that have evolved and that we have used in our court and we have tested them, some of those should be used. Basic hearsay. We've had hearsay and double hearsay and triple

727

hearsay, and the reason we have had it is because there are not any rules that say that we shouldn't have it. That's a problem and it's a problem when we ask witnesses and I've probably been guilty of it, too.

But we ask witnesses to speculate about what someone else was thinking about. What did that person think? What was their motive, and we all know that's not probative, that's not accurate. That's not the way we tell what the truth is. These rules didn't just come down, handed to us from someone else, and they just didn't evolve in order to protect defendants or to straitjacket a court. They came down because they deal with two things. One: It's a good way to tell the truth. It's the best way. And two, it's fundamentally fair—it's fundamentally fair that one person should not be examined, based upon that hearsay. And so maybe if something—I think a lot of good things are going to come out of these hearings, but maybe that's one that the liberals, the conservatives, the Republicans and Democrats can all agree on, and maybe we can work—work in that area. Let me move on if I could. I've got some—some areas that I would like to clean up at least in my mind, Lieutenant (sic), that—that are not clear.

Let me start with—with Bud McFarlane. He's going to be following you apparently as a witness on the stand. I want to get into the question about the NSC and about the application of the Boland Amendment to the NSC. Now, when Mr. McFarlane—you've already expressed your opinion about that, that it does not apply—Boland does not apply to the NSC. Mr. McFarlane previously testified and told this Committee that, in his opinion, it did. And in in fact, he even went on to say—talking about my—my chairman, the chairman of our Foreign Committee, that if Dante Fascell tells you to do something, by golly, you better not do it. I—I understand that. I respect that. But I want to know, did he ever tell you that? Did he ever tell you, if the chairman of the Foreign Affairs Committee says don't do something, then, by golly, you shouldn't be doing it?

LT. COL. NORTH: I never heard that, sir.

REP. DEWINE: Did he ever call a staff meeting and he sat down and said, "Look, in my opinion, Boland applies to the NSC"?

LT. COL. NORTH: I never heard that.

728

REP. DEWINE: Did he ever send you a memo that you can recall or a memo to the rest of the staff that said that?

LT. COL. NORTH: No. There are memoranda that I—that I received back from both Mr. McFarlane and Admiral Poindexter telling me not to do certain things, and when they told me that, I didn't do them.

REP. DEWINE: But you don't recall that?

LT. COL. NORTH: No, sir. And I want to make it very clear again. Every single thing that I did that required a decision I sought approval for, and if I didn't get approval, I didn't do it.

REP. DEWINE: All right. Let me move on to Elliott Abrams. And again, I'm trying to clean up the record in—in the sense that these are things that I don't understand or I think there's blanks in the record. I may be wrong about that, but if you'll just bear with me.

You've testified that you believe Assistant Secretary of State Elliott Abrams was aware of your activities, and I want to ask you some specific questions if—if I could. Did you ever tell Elliott Abrams about your—I was going to say instructions to Ambassador Tambs to open up a southern front, but you've already told us you really didn't give him instructions in that area. But did you ever have a discussion about the southern front, the opening up of that with Elliott Abrams, that you can recall?

LT. COL. NORTH: As I have testified, the opening of southern front was viewed as an absolute political and military necessity by everybody on the restricted interagency group, and there's no doubt that I had told members of the group that an airfield was being built by the private benefactor organization or whatever—Project Democracy, whatever euphemism I used at the time.

REP. DEWINE: All right.

LT. COL. NORTH: And that it was being done with the assistance of people at the embassy. I do not recall whether I specified that it was Ambassador Tambs.

REP. DEWINE: Okay. Do you recall—and I don't want to quibble with you here, and I appreciate your recollection —do you recall any specific coversation with Elliott Abrams about that? I—I appreciate what you've said, but I'd like to know that, a specific—

LT. COL. NORTH: I do not recall a specific conversation.

There is no doubt that that subject came up at some length and there was, after all, a conference call among Ambassador Tambs, Mr. Abrams and myself one evening when the exposure of that airfield became an issue.

REP. DEWINE: When it became an issue? Do you ever recall any conversation with Elliott Abrams about any other aspect of that prior to that date, prior to when it became an issue? About the resupply—

LT. COL. NORTH: No, but I would point out again, when I called him or he called me, or however it worked, neither of us were surprised.

REP. DEWINE: Neither was surprised?

LT. COL. NORTH: Well, in other words, when that issue of exposure of a secret airfield in that country came to be an issue, it was no great surprise to him or to the ambassador, or to anyone. I mean, we knew that we did not want it exposed, we did not want to jeopardize the previous administration in that company—in that country that had helped us build it, nor jeopardize the personnel that were engaged in it.

REP. DEWINE: Colonel, I want to thank you very much for your testimony, I appreciate your time. I appreciate also your very distinguished service, record of service to this country. It is appreciated by all of us and seems to really have touched a chord with the American people.

As I stated before, I think that in the past this Committee maybe has been a little unfair with you, particularly putting that chart up there, and you didn't have a chance to respond to it. That bothers me. But I think that in the last six days you have been given an opportunity, an opportunity to talk about your involvement and frankly, you have used that forum very ably, as ably as I have ever seen a witness in front of the United States Congress.

The only thing, parting comment that I would make, is that I am a little troubled as you leave. And I am troubled by the fact that we—the suspicion that we may revert to our old pattern on this Committee again—we seem to have started where opportunity is going to be given for witnesses to come back. Bud McFarlane is going to come back—and I don't object to that. But he's going to be coming back and apparently try to to contradict some of the things that you have said, and I just wonder how far we take this. Are we going to allow every witness who wants to come back for the second and third time to come back? Are we going to turn this into a debating club where we go back and forth?

And I guess that I'm bothered by what may happen in the future, that maybe some memos will be brought forward, or witnesses will be brought forward that we have not seen, who will directly attack you or who may make a comment about you, about the facts and then you will—a new fact, and then you will not have the opportunity to respond to that. I suspect however, that there are some members of the Committee that don't want to see you come back here. You have used this as a platform, the opportunity to be a, I think, a very effective witness, particularly when you have talked about some of the areas in Central America, the threat that the United States faces down there, what is going on in regard to Iran. You have been a very eloquent and, I think, very effective witness and I appreciate your time. Thank you very much.

REP. COURTER: Will the gentleman yield?

REP. DEWINE: I'd be glad to yield.

REP. COURTER: The gentleman just has a few seconds. I thank the gentleman for yielding and I would just like to say that I, in each and every occasion did not feel that the rulings of the Chair were correct. But I, as well as probably Congressman DeWine, did not object at that time because of our respect for the Chair, and particularly because of our respect and high esteem for the individuals that are the Chairs, and I think that silence indicates that and nothing else. Thank you.

REP. DEWINE: Well, I would concur on that. I'll take my time back and agree with the gentleman. There should not be misinterpreted lack of respect. I have had more opportunity to work with Chairman Hamilton than I have with Senator Inouye simply because we've worked longer on these committees. And I have a great deal of respect for both of them. I don't think that either of them has ever done anything that they did not think was absolutely correct. I have disagreed with them. I will disagree, I'm sure, in the future about a lot of things. But the one nice thing about serving on this Committee, I think from a personal point of view, has been the opportunity to get to know a lot of my colleagues a lot better. Ed Boland and I see each other in

731

the gym every morning, but we've had a chance to work a little closer on this Committee. (Laughter) He opens the gym. Thank you very much, Mr. Chairman.

CHAIRMAN INOUYE: I thank you very much. I'm certain Chairman Hamilton joins me in thanking you for your respect, sir. When we began the questioning of Colonel North, I announced that after we were completed with the round of questions, it will be open again for those who may be desirous of asking additional questions. I've been advised that two members of the panel wish to be recognized. First, Senator Boren.

SEN. BOREN: Thank you very much, Mr. Chairman. Colonel North, during the discussion earlier and under questioning from Congressman Brooks, the question of the so-called Marshall Law Plan had come up. We had some discussion about this in the Executive Session. And, of course, we cannot here go into detail as to any emergency plans for continuation of government that we might have in this country in the event of nuclear attack, and I'm not asking that we go into that. I have had discussion with White House counsel over the last two days about this matter because great concern has been voiced by the American people since some of the stories appeared in the news media to the effect that there was a plan to have Marshall law to suspend the Constitution in the event of civil dissent, civil disorder. And the White House counsel's office has indicated it would be appropriate as long as we do not get into a general discussion of emergency plans dealing with nuclear attack to put a couple of questions to you about this as long as I refer to matter that's been printed in the media and is in the public domain. So I would like to do that. Staff would hand you a copy of an article in the *Miami Herald* that appeared on Sunday, June the 5th, 1987, and was carried in several other newspapers in the country on the wire. And I ask this because it has caused grave concern in the country. And I admit it caused great concern to me when I read these reports. Let me just quote one paragraph that is there marked. It says, "Lieutenant Colonel Oliver North, for example, helped draw up a controversial plan to suspend the Constitution in the event of national crisis such as nuclear war, violent and widespread internal dissent, or national opposition to a US military invasion abroad. And I

732

would ask you, did you participate in or advocate any such plan to suspend the Constitution, in the event of national crisis, such as nuclear war, violent and widespread internal dissent, or national opposition to a US military invasion abroad?

LT. COL. NORTH: Absolutely not.

SEN. BOREN: To your knowledge, has the government of the United States adopted any such plan, or does it have in place—in being, any such plan?

LT. COL. NORTH: No, sir. None.

SEN. BOREN: Well, I felt it important to ask those questions of you. Let me say, the Intelligence Committees will be in the process of being briefed. We've had periodic briefings on our Emergency Plans, in terms of nuclear attack, in the past. We intend to have additional briefings on the status of these plans, and that would be the appropriate place for those briefings to take place. But I felt it very important that we put that—put those questions to you, and put them into the public record, in light of the concern that had been expressed to me about it.

LT. COL. NORTH: I thank you, Senator Boren.

SEN. BOREN: Thank you, Mr. Chairman.

CHAIRMAN HAMILTON: Thank you. Mr. Rodino.

REP. PETER RODINO (D-NJ): Thank you very much, Mr. Chairman. I'd hoped that it would not be necessary for me to come back today, but I had assumed yesterday, when the Chairman decided that I was not to continue, that I had five extra minutes allotted to me by Mr. Aspin. But nonetheless, not to take any further time, Colonel North, I have just a few questions, and I'm sure that you can answer them, probably, either yes or no. They're very simple questions. These Committees have heard evidence that DEA agents worked with you in your efforts to locate and free the hostages held in Lebanon. My question, did you brief the Attorney General on that activity?

LT. COL. NORTH: It is my recollection that I did personally brief the Attorney General. I don't recall the specific meeting. In my—the records I turned over to the Committee, there is reference to that briefing, and I believe, in the documents that the Committee was provided by the White House.

REP. RODINO: Has it identified a date, Colonel?

LT. COL. NORTH: I do not recall that, but we did discuss that, I believe in, perhaps it was Executive Session—but my recollection is, that I personally briefed the Attorney General, on it.

REP. RODINO: Thank you. Did you tell the Attorney General that private funds were going to be used to bribe foreign officials and others, to locate and free the hostages?

LT. COL. NORTH: That is my recollection, sir.

REP. RODINO: Did the Attorney General ever tell you, that it would not be proper for you to use government funds to bribe foreign officials and others, but that it would be acceptable to use private money for that purpose?

LT. COL. NORTH: Let me just clarify one point in this. My first answer, "Who told me what," my recollection is that Director Casey and the Director of Operations at CIA had both indicated that US government monies could not be used for those purposes and I don't recall specifying—or asking the Attorney General whether or not it was appropriate to use US monies. It may well have been that the DEA officers themselves made it known that those monies—US government monies couldn't be used for those purposes.

I also want to specify, it was not, when you say, "bribing foreign officials," I'm not entirely certain that they were foreign officials.

REP. RODINO: Foreigners.

LT. COL. NORTH: Foreigners, yes, sir. But, in any event, I came to understand, by virtue of my discussions, certainly with Director Casey, I think with the Director of Operations at Langley, possibly with officers in the FBI with whom I worked on counterterrorism, that we couldn't use US government monies for those purposes and that we would use outside monies.

REP. RODINO: But the Attorney General, as you recollect, did not advise you?

LT. COL. NORTH: I do not believe the Attorney General recommended one way or the other on that, sir.

REP. RODINO: My last question on this subject. Did you tell the Attorney General that expenses for the DEA agents were paid for from private sources, such as Albert Hakim, Richard Miller and Adolfo Calero?

LT. COL. NORTH: I honestly don't recall the full nature of that discussion. I do know that in a memorandum that I did for Admiral Poindexter on this that I did specify where the source of funds was coming from and I believe I probably told the Attorney General that. But I do not recall the conversation and the specificity.

REP. RODINO: One final question, Colonel. In your response to Mr. Nields the other day with reference to a question concerning a meeting on November the 21st, you made some reference to the Attorney General and let me read you the statement: "And so that is, early on November 21st"—these are your words before this Committee—

LT. COL. NORTH: Which year are we talking about, sir?

REP. RODINO: We're talking about a statement that you made the other day before this Committee with reference to the meeting of November the 21st of 1986.

LT. COL. NORTH: Okay.

REP. RODINO: And your answer to Mr. Nields, "And so that is early on November 21st, because I believed the decision was—the decision to make an inquiry, to have the Attorney General"—and then you added, and this is what I'm confused about, "For Mr. Meese, in his role as a friend of the President, conduct a fact-finding excursion on what happened in September and November in 1985, I assured the Admiral"—you were talking about, "Don't worry, it is all taken care of." My question: When you refer to Mr. Meese as a "friend of the President," why do you use that term?

LT. COL. NORTH: Well, I'm not sure what—exactly what I meant in those terms. What I clearly intended to say was that no one told me then—it was not until four days later, on the 25th—that there was any criminal investigation or criminal concern in this whole issue. And my recollection is that the Admiral told me that morning, or that day at some point, that there was going to be a fact-finding inquiry conducted by Mr. Meese, not in his role as chief law enforcement officer or as attorney general, but because he was close to the President; he was a person the President relied upon to be able to get to the bottom of all of this.

REP. RODINO: In other words, your answer, then, is that Admiral Poindexter said to you that Mr. Meese would be coming to conduct an inquiry, but he would be coming as a friend of the President.

LT. COL. NORTH: Again, I'm making the characterization.

735

I don't believe Admiral Poindexter said, "He's coming as the friend of the President." My recollection of the discussion—

REP. RODINO: He just used those terms—

LT. COL. NORTH: I understand, but I'm saying that was my characterization, not the Admiral's characterization. Does that answer the question? I mean, what I'm saying to you, Mr. Rodino, is that I characterized it after the fact as that kind of an inquiry. At the point in time—I would guess, and I don't recall—

REP. RODINO: Was there any reason why you wanted to characterize—

LT. COL. NORTH: Yes, I wanted to make it very clear that I had absolutely no inkling of criminal investigations, criminal inquiry, criminal behavior, anything criminal until the 25th of November, 1986. I mean, when the Admiral told me that, it was—in fact, I don't even think he said the Attorney General was coming; it was, "The Attorney General is going to send some people over," or, "Mr. Meese is going to send some of his people over," one of those kinds of things. But the characterization I gave it in my discussion with Mr. Nields was my characterization, not the Admiral's.

REP. RODINO: You assumed that he would be coming as a friend to make a friendly inquiry?

LT. COL. NORTH: What I'm saying is I assumed he was coming not as a criminal investigator. No mention was made to me when the officers arrived in my office on Saturday morning, the 22nd, nobody said we're going to conduct a criminal inquiry into your behavior, North, or the documents that you've got. It was simply described to me as a "fact-finding inquiry"—I think those were the three words that were used—and I had—as I indicated to you earlier on Friday, I started laying out the documents. And the characterization I gave Mr. Nields is one that I—the spin that put on it and as I have described it to you here in the Committee.

REP. RODINO: Thank you, Colonel North.

Thank you, Mr. Chairman.

CHAIRMAN INOUYE: Senator Sarbanes.

SEN. SARBANES: Mr. Chairman, because of the assertions which will appear on the printed record questioning the fairness of this Committee, I think it's important to place on the printed record a demonstration of Committee fairness, which I think has been very visible and obvious to all of us as we have sat through this hearing and to those who have watched it, and that is that Colonel North's counsel has had unlimited scope throughout these proceedings to defer his responses to questions while they engaged in consultation and counsel. And that has happened frequently and often, and I simply underscore it to place it on the printed record because, although it is very visible, unless a statement is made about it, it will not appear in the printed record reflecting, I think, a very significant measure of fairness extended to the colonel and his testimony before this committee.

CHAIRMAN INOUYE: Representative Hyde.

REP. HYDE: Thank you very much, Mr. Chairman. Since a very brief second round has been permitted, I—I just wanted to avail myself of that window of vulnerability.

I—I just want to say to Colonel North, we have heard a great deal and—and a lot of it quite learned conversation and talk about the Constitution. And there have been some serious allegations made about your conduct with reference to the Constitution, and I just want to say to you, Colonel, that part of that fundamental document of our country contains some words about bill of attainder. Now, bills of attainder are legislative findings of guilt. And it may comfort you to know, and I'm sure you already know it, that the Constitution forbad bills of attainder. So I just thought that little bicentennial note might help.

And as long as we're talking about fundamental documents of this country, our birthday certificate, the Declaration of Independence, has some comments that might refer to an earlier comment by the distinguished junior senator from Maine, who said God does not pick sides on political questions. And I am happy to agree with that, but the Declaration does say, in Jefferson's magnificent words, that "we are all endowed by our Creator with certain inalienable rights, among which are life, liberty, and the pursuit of happiness." Now, if Jefferson was right, and I fervently believe he was, I would suggest that God doesn't pick sides on political questions, but wherever God is, and I believe he's everywhere, including Nicaragua, I just bet he's on the side of liberty and human dignity.

And so with those words, I thank you very much for your or—enduring your ordeal so well today. Thank you.

CHAIRMAN INOUYE: Any further questions? Senator Rudman?

VICE-CHAIRMAN RUDMAN: Mr. Chairman,—(interrupted by network voice-over)—Vice Chairman of the Committee not to address any comments or questions to Col. North, but because something has occurred in the last 48 hours or the last 72 hours that is—sure is a small minority of the American people. And yet, it has been so disturbing to me that I wanted to say what I'm going to say, probably over the Chairman's objections. And I'm sure Col. North will agree with every word that I say. I am sure of that.

We received some calls in the Committee and our offices over the last 72 hours of ugly ethnic slurs against our Chairman, and other kinds of calls that were extraordinarily insulting to the members of this Committee. Col. North has been respectful of this Committee; I think this Committee has been respectful of Col. North. There seems to be vision out there, not shared by this witness or his counsel or by most Americans, about this Committee that I want to set straight. Represented on this panel are sixteen members who served in the service, eight who served in combat, a number with great distinction—with medals for valor and heroism from Guadacanal to the Lingayen Gulf. The Chairman was recommended for the Congressional Medal of Honor for assaulting two German machine gun nests in northern Italy, and then failing on the third one which was destroying his company, when he lost his arm which he left on that battlefield in Italy. He holds the nation's second highest award—the Distinguished Service Cross. He is one of the greatest men I ever have known, and the country ought to know the kind of leadership the Senate Chairman exerts—and for all Americans to condemn the kind of ethnic slurs that have no place in America.

Thank you, Mr. Chairman.

LT. COL. NORTH: I fully agree, Mr. Rudman.

CHAIRMAN INOUYE: I thank you very much. Col. North, we're just about finished. Do you have any final statement to make sir.

LT. COL. NORTH: A very brief one, sir.

CHAIRMAN INOUYE: Please proceed.

738

LT. COL. NORTH: I would simply like to thank the American people who have responded with their good wishes, their support, their prayers through what has been for me and my family a long and difficult ordeal. I thank them for that, and I salute them. That is my statement, sir.

CHAIRMAN INOUYE: Thank you very much. And now it is my privilege and great honor to recognize the chairman of the House Select Committee, Congressman Hamilton.

CHAIRMAN HAMILTON: Mr. Chairman, may I express to you my personal appreciation for the manner in which you have presided over these Committees these last several days. You've had some rather difficult moments. I think you have been firm and fair, and you have kept these proceedings moving along, and all of us are most grateful to you.

Now Colonel North, let me join with others in expressing my appreciation to you for your testimony. And as the Chairman has indicated, I will use my time just to give you some of my impressions.

I recognize that a President and those carrying out his policies sometimes face agonizing choices, and you've had more than your share of them. I've never for a moment over the years that I have known you, doubted your good intentions to free hostages, to seek democracy in Nicaragua, to fight communism, and to advance the best interests of the nation. And for many in this country, I think the pursuit of such worthy objectives is enough in itself, or in themselves, and exonerate you and any others from all mistakes.

Yet what strikes me is that despite your very good intentions, you were a participant in actions which catapulted a President into the most serious crisis of his presidency, drove the Congress of the United States to launch an unprecedented investigation, and I think probably damaged the cause, or the causes that you sought to promote. It is not my task, and it is not the task of these Committees to judge you. As others have said, we're here to learn what went wrong, what caused the mistakes, and what we can do to correct them. And the appropriate standard for these Committees is whether we understand the facts better because of your testimony and I think we do, and we're grateful to you.

In your opening statement you said that these hearings have caused serious damage to our national interests. But I wonder whether the damage has been caused by these hearings or by the acts which prompted these hearings. I wonder whether you would have the Congress do nothing after it has been lied to and misled and ignored? Would we in the Congress then be true to our Constitutional responsibilities? Is it better under our system to ignore misdeeds or to investigate them behind closed doors, as some have suggested? Or is it better to bring them into the open and try to learn from them? I submit that we are truer to our Constitution if we choose the later course.

These Committees of course, build on the work of other committees, and I think that work is part of our Constitutional system of checks and balances. There are many parts of your testimony that I agree with. I agree with you that these Committees must be careful not to cripple the President. I agree with you that our government needs the capability to carry out covert actions. During my six years on the Intelligence Commitee, over 90 percent of the covert actions that were recommended to us by the President were supported and approved. And only the large-scale paramilitary operations, which really could not be kept secret, were challenged. I agree with you, when you said in your opening statement, that you're caught in a struggle between the Congress and the President over the direction of American foreign policy, and that most certainly is not your fault. And I agree with you, that the Congress, who's record in all of this—is certainly not unblemished—also must be accountable for its actions.

Now let me tell you what bothers me. I want to talk about two things, first policy, and then, process. Chairman Inouye has correctly said, that the business of these Select Committees is not policy, and I agree with him, but you made such an eloquent and impassioned statement about policy, that I wanted to comment. I am very troubled by your defense of secret arms sales to Iran. There's no disagreement about the strategic importance of Iran or the desirability of an opening to Iran. My concern is with the means employed to achieve those objectives.

The President has acknowledged that his policy, as implemented, was an arms for hostage policy. And selling arms to Iran in secret, was, to put it simply, bad policy. The policy contradicted and undermined long-held, often articulated, widely supported public policies in the United States. It repudiated US policy to make no concessions to terrorists, to remain in the Gulf war, and to stop arms sales to Iran. We sold arms to a nation officially designated by our government, as a terrorist state. This secret policy of selling arms to Iran damaged US credibility.

A great power cannot base its policy on an untruth without a loss of credibility. Friendly governments were deceived about what we were doing. You spoke about the credibility of US policy in Central America, and you were right about that, but in the Middle East, mutual trust with some friends was damaged, even shattered. The policy of arms for hostages sent a clear message to the States of the Persian Gulf, and that message was, that the United States is helping Iran in its war effort, and making an accommodation with the Iranian revolution, and Iran's neighbors should do the same.

The policy provided the Soviets an opportunity they have now grasped, with which we are struggling to deal. The policy achieved none of the goals it sought. The Ayatollah got his arms, more Americans are held hostage today than when this policy began, subversion of US interests throughout the region by Iran continues. Moderates in Iran, if any there were, did not come forward.

And to those—today, those moderates are showing fidelity to the Iranian revolution by leading the charge against the United States in the Persian Gulf. In brief, the policy of selling arms to Iran, in my view at least, simply cannot be defended as in the interests of the United States. There were and there are other means to achieve that opening which should have been used.

Now let me comment on process as well, first with regard to covert actions. You and I agree that covert actions pose very special problems for a democracy. It is, as you said, a dangerous world, and we must be able to conduct covert actions, as every member of this panel has said. But it is contrary to all that we know about democracy to have no checks and balances on them.

We've established a lawful procedure to handle covert actions. It's not perfect by any means, but it works reasonably well. In this instance, those procedures were ignored. There was no presidential finding in one case, and a retroactive finding in another. The Intelligence Committees of the Congress were not informed, and they were lied to.

Foreign policies were created and carried out by a tiny circle of persons, apparently without the involvement of even some of the highest officials of our government. The administration tried to do secretly what the Congress sought to prevent it from doing. The administration did secretly what it claimed to all the world it was not doing. Covert action should always be used to supplement, not to contradict, our foreign policy. It should be consistent with our public policies. It should not be used to impose a foreign policy on the American people which they do not support.

Mr. McFarlane was right. He told these Committees it was clearly unwise to rely on covert action as the core of our policy. And as you noted in your testimony, and I agree with you, it would have been a better course to continue to seek contra funding through open debate. You have spoken with compelling eloquence about the Reagan Doctrine. And laudable as that doctrine may be, it will not succeed unless it has the support of the Congress and the American people.

Secondly, with regard to process, let me talk about accountability. What I find lacking about the events as you have described them is accountability. Who was responsible for these policies, for beginning them, for controlling them, for terminating them? You have said that you assumed you were acting on the authority of the President. I don't doubt your word, sir. But we have no evidence of his approval.

The President says he did not know that the National Security Council staff was helping the contras. You thought he knew. And you engaged in such activities with extraordinary energy. You do not recall what happened to the five documents on the diversion of funds to the contras. Those documents radically changed American policy. They are probably, I would think, the most important documents you have written. Yet you don't recall whether they were returned to you, and you don't recall whether they were destroyed, as I recall your testimony. There's no accountability for an $8 million account earned from the sale of US government property. There is no accountability for a quarter of a million dollars available to you.

You say you never took a penny. I believe you. But we

742

have no records to support or to contradict what you say. Indeed, most of the important records concerning these events have been destroyed. Your testimony points up confusion throughout the foreign policy making process. You've testified that Director Casey sought to create an on-the-shelf, self-sustaining, stand-alone entity to carry out covert actions—apparently without the knowledge of other high officials in government. You've testified there was an unclear commitment to Israel concerning replenishment of missiles to Iran. You've testified that it's never been US policy not to negotiate with terrorists. Yet the President has said the opposite—that we will never negotiate with terrorist. You have testified that a lot of people were willing to go along with what we were doing, hoping against hope that it would succeed and willing to walk away when it failed. Now my guess is, that's a pretty accurate description of what happened. But it's not the way to run a government.

Secret operations should pass a sufficient test of accountability. And these secret operations did not pass that test. There was a lack of accountability for funds and for policy, and responsibility rests with the President. If he did not know of your highly significant activities done in his name, then he should have, and we'll obviously have to ask Admiral Poindexter some questions.

Now the next point with regard to process relates to your attitude toward the Congress. As you would expect, I'm bothered by your comments about the Congress. You show very little appreciation for its role in the foreign policy process. You acknowledge that you were "erroneous, misleading, evasive and wrong" in your testimony to the Congress. I appreciate, sir, that honesty can be hard in the conduct of government. But I am impressed that policy was driven by a series of lies—lies to the Iranians, lies to the Central Intelligence Agency, lies to the Attorney General, lies to our friends and allies, lies to the Congress, and lies to the Ameican people. So often during these hearings—not just during your testimony, but others as well, I have been reminded of President Thomas Jefferson's statement. "The whole art of government consists in the art of being honest."

Your experience has been in the Executive branch, and mine has been in the Congress. Inevitably our perspectives will differ. Nonetheless, if I may say so, you have an extraordinarily expansive view of presidential power. You would give the President free rein in foreign affairs.

You said on the first day of your testimony, and I quote, "I didn't want to show Congress a single word on this whole thing," end of quote. I do not see how your attitude can be reconciled with the Constitution of the United States. I often find in the Executive branch, in this administration as well as in others, a view that the Congress is not a partner, but an adversary. The Constitution grants foreign policy making powers to both the President and the Congress and our foreign policy cannot succeed unless they work together.

You blame the Congress as if the restrictions it approved were the cause of mistakes by the administration, yet congressional restrictions in the case of Nicaragua, if the polls are accurate, reflected the majority of the American people. In any case, I think you and I would agree that there is insufficient consensus on policy in Nicaragua. Public opinion is deeply divided.

And the task of leadership, it seems to me, is to build public support for policy. If that burden of leadership is not met, secret policies cannot succeed over the long term. The fourth point, with regard to process, relates to means and ends. As I understand your testimony, you did what you did because those were your orders and because you believed it was for a good cause. I cannot agree that the end has justified these means, that the threat in Central America was so great that we had to do something, even if it meant disregarding Constitutional processes, deceiving the Congress and the American people.

The means employed were a profound threat to the democratic process. A democratic government, as I understand it, is not a solution, but it's a way of seeking solutions. It's not a government devoted to a particular objective, but a form of government which specifies means and methods of achieving objectives. Methods and means are what this country are all about. We subvert our democratic process to bring about a desired end, no matter how strongly we may believe in that end. We've weakened our country and we have not strengthened it.

A few do not know what is better for Americans than

744

Americans know themselves. If I understand our government correctly, no small group of people, no matter how important, no matter how well-intentioned they may be, should be trusted to determine policy. As President Madison said, "Trust should be placed not in a few, but in a number of hands."

Let me conclude. Your opening statement made the analogy to a baseball game. You said the playing field here was uneven and the Congress would declare itself the winner. I understand your sentiments, but may I suggest that we are not engaged in a game with winners and losers. That approach, if I may say so, is self-serving and ultimately self-defeating. We all lost. The interests of the United States have been damaged by what happened.

This country cannot be run effectively and major foreign policy—major foreign policies are formulated by only a few and are made and carried out in secret and when public officials lie to other nations and to each other. One purpose of these hearings is to change that. The self-cleansing process, the Tower Commission and these joint hearings and the report which will follow, are all part, we hope, of a process to reinvigorate and restore our system of government.

I don't have any doubt at all, Colonel North, that you are a patriot. There are many patriots, fortunately, and many forms of patriotism. For you, perhaps patriotism rested in the conduct of deeds, some requiring great personal courage, to free hostages and fight communism. And those of us who pursue public service with less risk to our physical well-being admire such courage.

But there's another form of patriotism, which is unique to democracy. It resides in those who have a deep respect for the rule of law and faith in America's democratic traditions. To uphold our Constitution requires not the exceptional efforts of the few, but the confidence and the trust and the work of the many.

Democracy has its frustrations. You've experienced some of them, but we, you and I, know of no better system of government. And when that democratic process is subverted, we risk all that we cherish. I thank you, sir, for your testimony, and I wish you and I wish your family well.

Thank you, Mr. Chairman.

Thank you very much.

Colonel North, Mr. Sullivan, I think we're now at the end of a long 6 days. The questions I have cannot be answered because some of those who could have answered these questions are not here with us. And furthermore, I'm certain you'll agree with me that we've had enough questions here.

I'd like to, first, before proceeding with my statement, because of the call of fairness, clarify the record. Much has been said about fairness to the witness, fairness to the President, fairness to the government. In response to the question of two of my fellow panel members relating to the bombing of Libya, you said, for example today, "When the briefing conducted by the President concluded at about 5:00 or 5:30, two members of Congress"—and you met two members of the Senate—"proceeded immediately to waiting microphones and noted that the President was going to make a heretofore unannounced address to the nation on Libya. I will tell you the volume of fire over the Libyan capital was immense that evening. Two American airman died as a consequence of that anti-aircraft fire. As best as we can determine, they alerted our adversaries."

When the response was made a few days ago, I checked with the senior officials of the Senate and looked into the record. First, when the briefing was concluded, these two members did not stop at the bank of microphones near the White House. They immediately left and returned to the Senate. There they were confronted by members of the press. One leader responded, "No comment," the other said, "you should ask the President the question. He might have something to say tonight at nine."

The eighteen US F-111s, left Britain on Monday, April the 14th, at 12:13 P.M. The briefing began at 4 o'clock, and the bombs fell at seven. However, a week before the bombing, CBS Evening News had this to say: "Top US officials acknowledge that detailed military contingency plans for retaliation already exist. Said one source, they involve five targets in Libya."

On the same day, *The Wall Street Journal* had this to say: "US officials are putting out the word that they are laying the groundwork for possible retaliatory actions against Libya for its suspected involvement in the bombing of the

West Berlin discotheque." Then the next day, Tuesday, April 8, *The Wall Street Journal* again—"Reagan and his advisers are united in wanting to respond militarily against Qaddafi, but haven't agreed on a time or place to strike back, a senior administration official said."

On the same day, CBS Evening News—"Forty-eight hours after the bombing in West Berlin, the Reagan Administration had reached a consensus for military retaliation against Libya." On Wednesday, April the 9th, CBS Evening News—"According to a highly placed source President Reagan has approved another possible military strike against Libya. The White House denied rumors today that a military response was already on the way, but a well-placed intelligence source said that a military response has been approved."

That same evening, ABC World News Tonight—"The understanding now is that a strike against Libya is in the works. If it comes to that, seldom will US military action have been so widely and publicly advertised in advance." Thursday April the 10th, NBC Today Show—"Administration officials say that intense planning is under way for retaliation against Libya,"

On the same day in *The New York Times*—"An administration offical said that Libyan military sites are the prime options under consideration for retaliation, and that among the key possibilities are Libyan air bases near the coast. The official said that coastal electronic listening posts, including early warning radar sites as well as units that pick up airplane and ship traffic, are also key targets." And as we know, they were the targets.

On Friday, April the 11th, NBC Today Show—"The goal is to strike as many targets as possible as close to the coast to reduce the danger to American aircraft." Saturday, April the 12th, *New York Times*—"Administration officials speculated that the Walter strip placed in abeyance, at least for the moment, a retaliatory strike against Libya. But officials declined to rule out a raid even in the next 48 hours."

Associated Press—"The *British Mail* on Sunday said Mrs. Thatcher had, quote, "Cleared the way for President Reagan to use British bases to launch a massive new air attack on Libya."

Another AP: "Italian Premier Bettino Craxi told reporters Saturday, April 12 in Milan, 'I don't believe there will be a military intervention there before Monday.'" (Laughter.)

Same evening, NBC Nightly News: "By Monday, the diplomatic lobbying tool will be complete, and Administration sources indicate that means a strike could come as early as Tuesday."

The Washington Post: "After consulting conservative Prime Minister Jacques Chirac by telephone, Mitterrand decided to reject the US request for overflight rights, and the French refusal was communicated to Washington the following morning, Saturday April 12."

And the day before the bombing, NBC Nightly News: "Administration officials say the President is moving towards a decision about whether to make a retaliatory strike against Libya and White House officials confirmed the President will have a special National Security meeting tomorrow to evaluate the situation. Today the President conferred with Vice President Bush and Secretary of State Shultz, both of whom are believed to favor a military strike. Noticeably absent from the Camp David meeting was Defense Secretary Weinberger, who is believed to oppose such action."

I think it is grossly unfair that two American lives were lost because one leader said, "No comment" and the other said, "I believe you should ask the President. He may have something to say tonight at 9:00."

From the beginning of the history of mankind, organized societies, whether they be tribes or clans or nations, have nurtured and created heroes, because heroes are necessary, they serve as a cement to unite people, to bring unity in that nation. It provides glory to their history, it provides legends. We have many heroes. This hearing is being held in Washington, the city of heroes, the city of monuments. We have hundreds of monuments in this city. In the Capitol in Statuary Hall, each state has honored two of their heroes or heroines. The State of Hawaii honors King Kamehameha, the warrior king, and Father Damien, who is soon to become a saint.

And if you step on the west steps of the mall, and look down the majestic mall, you will see the monument of George Washington, very majestic. I remember as a child, long before I heard of the revolutionary war, that one day

George Washington was confronted by his father, who asked "Who cut the cherry tree?" And little George answered, "Father, I cannot lie, I cut the cherry tree." It was an important lesson to all little children, and I believe it still is a very important lesson.

Then if you go further down you'll see the Lincoln Memorial where we honor a great President for the courage he demonstrated in upholding the brotherhood of men. It wasn't easy during those days. Then you have Arlington, a sacred place. Men you served with and men I served with used that as their final resting place, all heroes. Then you have Lee's mansion. This was the home of the great gentleman from Virginia. We honor him today for his great demonstration of loyalty and patriotism. And as we get back to the Lincoln Memorial nearby, we see this new and exciting monument—one to your fellow combat men, the Vietnam Memorial.

I believe during the past week we have participated in creating and developing very likely a new American hero. Like you, who has as one has felt the burning sting of bullet and shrapnel, and heard the unforgettable and frightening sounds of incoming shells, I salute you, sir, as a fellow combat man. And the rows of ribbons that you have on your chest will forever remind us of your courageous service and your willingness—your patriotic willingness to risk your life and your limb. I'm certain the life and the burdens of a hero will be difficult and heavy. And so, with all sincerity, I wish you well as you begin your journey into a new life. However, as an interested observer and as one who has participated in the making of this new American hero, I've found certain aspects of your testimony to be most troubling. Chairman Hamilton has most eloquently discussed them—because, as a result of your very gallant presence and your articulate statements, your life, I'm certain, will be emulated by many, many young Americans. I'm certain we will all of us receive an abundance of requests from young citizens throughout the land for entrance into the privileged ranks of cadets of the military services. These young citizens having been imbued with the passion of patriotism will do so. And to these young men and women, I wish to address a few words.

In 1964, when Col. North was a cadet, he took an oath of

office, like all hundreds throughout the service academies. And he also said that he will abide with the regulations which set forth the cadet honor concept. The first honor concept—first, because it's so important, over and above all others, is a very simple one: a member of the brigade does not lie, cheat, or steal. And in this regulation of 1964, the word "lie" was defined as follows, quote: "A deliberate oral or written untruth, it may be an oral statement which is known to be false or a simple response to a question in which the answer is known to be false." End of quote. The words, "mislead" or "deceive," were defined as follows: "A deliberate misrepresentation of a true situation by being untruthful or withholding or subtly wording information in such a way, as to leave an erroneous or false impression of the known true situation."

And when the Colonel put on his uniform and the bars of a second lieutenant, he was well aware that he was subject to the Uniform Code of Military Justice. It's a special code of laws that apply to our men and women in uniform. It's a code that has been applicable to the conduct and activities of Colonel North throughout his military career, and even at this moment. And that code makes it abundantly clear, that orders of a superior officer must be obeyed by subordinate members—but it is lawful orders.

The Uniform Code makes it abundantly clear that it must be the lawful orders of a superior officer. In fact, it says, members of the military have an obligation to disobey unlawful orders. This principle was considered so important, that we—we, the government of the United States, proposed that it be internationally applied, in the Nuremberg trials. And so, in the Nuremberg trials, we said that the fact that the defendant—

MR. SULLIVAN: —Mr. Chairman. May I please register an objection.—

CHAIRMAN INOUYE: —May I continue my statement.—

MR. SULLIVAN: —I find this offensive! I find you engaging in a personal attack on Colonel North, and you're far removed from the issues of this case. To make reference to the Nuremberg trials, I find personally and professionally distasteful, and I can no longer sit here and listen to this.

CHAIRMAN INOUYE: You will have to sit there, if you want to listen.

MR. SULLIVAN: Mr. Chairman, please don't conclude these hearings on this unfair note. I have strong objections to many things in the hearings, and you up there speak about listening to the American people. Why don't you listen to the American people and what they've said as a result—(Chairman Inouye bangs the gavel)—of the last week. There are 20,000 telegrams in our room outside the corridor here that came in this morning. The American people—

CHAIRMAN INOUYE: I'm sure that there are.

MR. SULLIVAN: The American people have spoken and please stop this personal attack against Colonel North.

CHAIRMAN INOUYE: I have sat here, listened to the Colonel without interrupting. I hope you will accord me the courtesy of saying my piece.

MR. SULLIVAN: Sir, you may give speeches on the issues, it seems to me. You may ask questions, but you may not attack him personally. This has gone too far, in my opinion, with all due respect.

CHAIRMAN INOUYE: I'm not attacking him personally.

MR. SULLIVAN: That's the way I hear it, sir.

CHAIRMAN INOUYE: Colonel North, I'm certain it must have been painful for you, as you stated, to testify that you lied to senior officials of our government, that you lied and misled our Congress. And believe me, it was painful for all of us to sit here and listen to that testimony. It was painful. It was equally painful to learn from your testimony that you lied and misled because of what you believed to be a just cause—supporters of Nicaragua freedom fighters, the contras.

You have eloquently articulated your opposition to Marxism and communism and I believe that all of us—I'm certain that all of us on this panel are equally opposed to Marxism and communism. But should we, in the defense of democracy, adopt and embrace one of the most important tenets of communism and Marxism—the ends justify the means?

This is not one of the commandments of democracy. Our government is not a government of men. It is still a government of laws. And finally, to those thousands upon thousands of citizens who have called, sent telegrams, written letters, I wish to thank all of you most sincerely and

751

commend you for your demonstrated interest in the well-being of our government, of our freedoms and our democracy. Your support or opposition of what is happening in this room is important—important because it dramatically demonstrates the strength of this democracy.

We Americans are confident in our strength to openly and without fear put into action one of the important teachings of our greatest Founding Fathers, Thomas Jefferson, who spoke of the right to dissent, the right to criticize the leaders of this government and he said, "The spirit of resistance to government is so valuable on certain occasions that I wish it to be always kept alive. It will often be exercised when wrong, but better so, than not be exercised at all."

Unlike communism, in a democracy such as ours, we are not afraid to wash our dirty linen in public. We're not afraid to let the world know that we do have failures and we do have shortcomings. I think all of us should recall the open invitation that we send to the press of the world to view the spaceflights, to record our successes and record our failures. We permit all to film and record our spaceflights. We don't, after the fact, let the world know only of our successes. And I think we should recall that we did not prohibit any member of the world press to film and record one of the bloodiest chapters of our domestic history, the demonstration and riots in the civil rights period. This was not easy to let the world know that we had police dogs and police officers with whips and clubs denying fellow citizens their rights. But I've always felt that, as long as we daily reaffirm our belief in and support of our Constitution and the great principles of freedom that was long ago enunciated by our Founding Fathers, we'll continue to prevail and flourish.

I'd like to make one make more closing remark. Throughout the past 10 days, many of my colleagues on this panel, in opening their questions to the colonel, prefaced their remarks by saying, "Colonel, I'm certain you know that I voted for aid to the contras." Ladies and gentlemen and Colonel North, I voted against aid to the contras. I did so not as a communist. I did so not as an agent of the KGB. I did so upon information that I gathered as a member of the bipartisan commission on Central America, based upon information that I gathered as chairman of the Foreign Operations Committee, based upon information that I gathered as a senior member of the Defense subcommittee, and based upon information that I gathered as chairman and member of the Senate Intelligence Committee.

I voted against aid to the contras. It wasn't easy to vote against your Commander-in-Chief. It's not easy to stand before my colleagues and find yourself in disagreement, but that is the nature of democracy. I did so because I was firmly convinced that to follow the path or the course that was laid down by the Reagan proposal was—would certainly and inevitably lead to a point where young men and women of the United States would have to be sent into the conflict. And, Colonel, I am certain, having experienced warfare, that is not what we want our young people to go through again. You have lost many friends, and their names now are engraved on the black marble. I have lost many friends who are buried throughout this land.

I know that the path of democ—diplomacy is frustrating —at times angering. But I would think that we should give it a chance, if it means that, with some patience, we could save even one life. So that is why I wish my colleagues to know that I voted against aid to the Nicaraguan freedom fighters.

This has been a long day. I know that all of us are desirous of a rest. Col. North, with all sincerity, I thank you for your assistance these past six days. You have been most cordial, and your presence should make your fellow officers very proud of the way you have presented yourself. And to your lady, I wish her the best. She has sat there throughout these days with patience and grace. You have a fine lady.

The panel will stand in recess for ten minutes.

(The hearing recessed.)